Francis Galton

# Vacation Tourists and Notes of Travel

in 1860, 1861, 1862-3

Francis Galton

**Vacation Tourists and Notes of Travel**
*in 1860, 1861, 1862-3*

ISBN/EAN: 9783337291891

Printed in Europe, USA, Canada, Australia, Japan

Cover: Foto ©Andreas Hilbeck / pixelio.de

More available books at **www.hansebooks.com**

# VACATION TOURISTS

### AND

### NOTES OF TRAVEL

### IN

### 1861.

# VACATION TOURISTS

### AND

## NOTES OF TRAVEL

## IN 1861

EDITED BY

### FRANCIS GALTON,

AUTHOR OF "THE ART OF TRAVEL," ETC.

*WITH TEN MAPS TO ILLUSTRATE THE ROUTES.*

Cambridge

MACMILLAN AND CO.

AND 23, HENRIETTA STREET, COVENT GARDEN

London

1862

# PREFACE.

LAST Easter, when the volume of "Vacation Tourists in 1860" was published, I mentioned in its preface that it would probably be followed by others in future years, and that the work would grow into a periodical publication, if the favour, with which the earlier volumes were received, permitted such a result.

Hitherto that favour has been amply bestowed. The principle upon which "Vacation Tourists" was designed, and, I may add, the character of the articles it contained, drew forth an almost unanimous verdict of approval, while the good opinion of the critics was practically endorsed by the book-buying public.

I now feel no doubt whatever, that the want had a real existence, which this publication was intended to satisfy —namely, means of collecting, in substantial volumes, a selection of tours and travels which, while containing too little incident to admit of expansion into independent books, were in other respects well worthy of publication.

Maps to illustrate the Routes of the several travellers have been given to every paper in the present volume, excepting Mr. Grove's, which, from its nature, did not require this kind of illustration.   It is hoped that this will enhance the interest and value of this year's publication.

FRANCIS GALTON.

42, Rutland Gate,
*Easter*, 1862.

# CONTENTS.

# LIST OF MAPS.

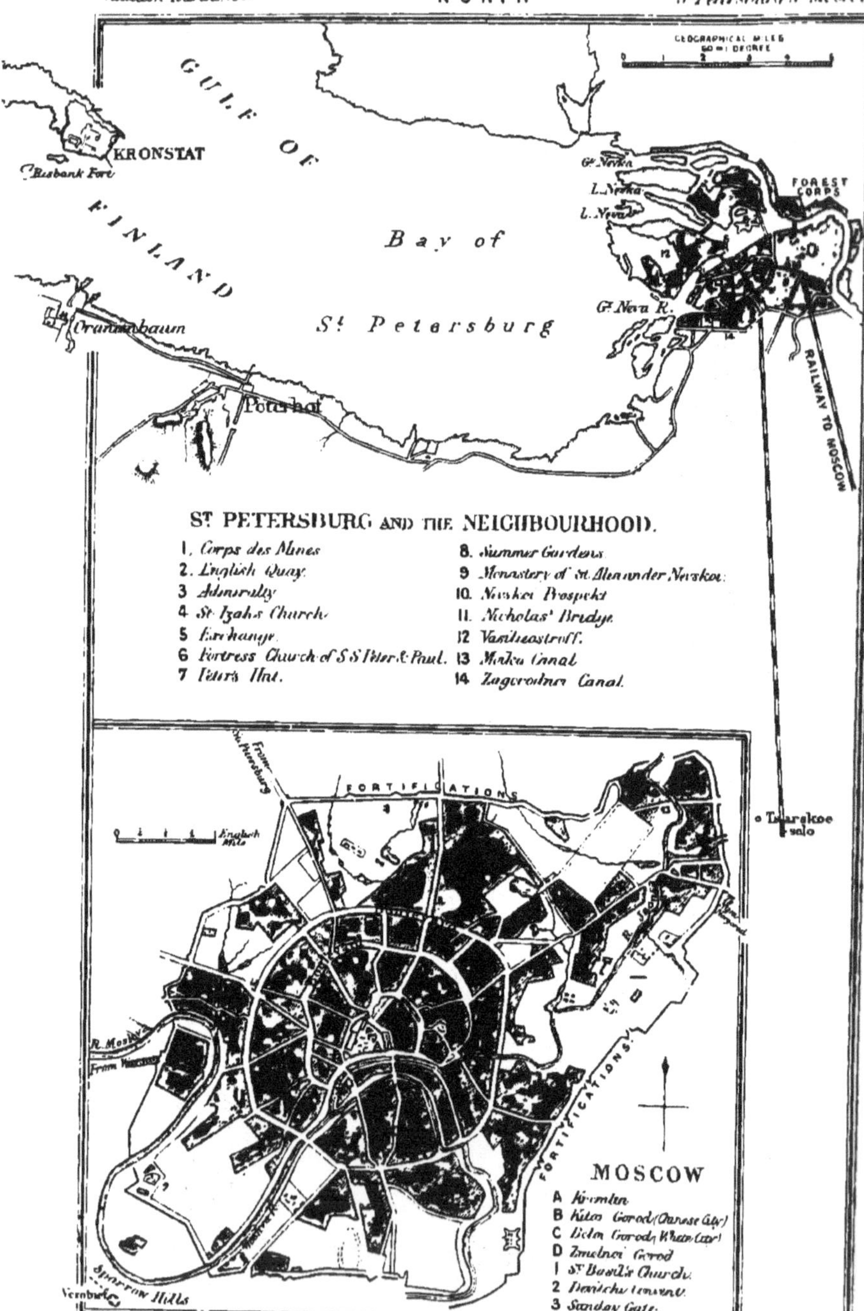

Vacation Tourists. 1861
NORTH
St Petersburg & Moscow
GEOGRAPHICAL MILES
60 = 1 DEGREE
GULF OF
FINLAND
KRONSTAT
C. Risbank Fort
Oranienbaum
Bay of
St Petersburg
Peterhof
Gt Nevka
L. Nevka
L. Neva
Gt Neva R.
FOREST CORPS
RAILWAY TO MOSCOW
ST PETERSBURG AND THE NEIGHBOURHOOD.
1. Corps des Mines
2. English Quay.
3. Admiralty
4. St Izah's Church.
5. Exchange
6. Fortress Church of S.S Peter & Paul.
7. Peter's Hut.
8. Summer Gardens.
9. Monastery of St Alexander Nevskoi.
10. Nevskoi Prospekt.
11. Nicholas' Bridge.
12. Vasileostroff.
13. Moika Canal.
14. Zagorodnoi Canal.
FORTIFICATIONS
From St Petersburg
English Miles
R. Moskva
From Warsaw
Sparrow Hills
Vorobief
Tsarskoe salo
FORTIFICATIONS.
MOSCOW
A Kremlin
B Kitai Gorod (Chinese City)
C Beloi Gorod (White City)
D Zmelnoi Gorod
1 St Basil's Church.
2 Danilov Convent.
3 Sunday Gate.

# VACATION TOURISTS, &c. IN 1861.

## 1. *ST. PETERSBURG AND MOSCOW:*

## BY THE REV. ARCHIBALD WEIR, B.C.L. M.A.

AT four o'clock on the fourth morning after our leaving
Hull, I awoke, and found my cabin window facing a large,
grey building, which, with its gabled roofs, its spire, and its
turrets, looked half like a cathedral, half like an Oxford
college. It was the " Castle of Elsinore." I hastened on deck,
and was rather disappointed to find that the captain had gone
ashore without me. But it was all for the best. There was
a drizzling rain ; the hour was too early for seeing the town,
and, moreover, the best view of " Helsingör og Kronborg " (as
the Danes call the town and palace), is decidedly from the
sea. By the way of being quite classical, " Horatio " (not
" friend to Hamlet," but a small Danish boat) steams out of
the harbour. We also steam away, having provided ourselves
with food and a pilot. The coast, thickly studded with
pleasant-looking houses, surrounded by gardens, and fields,
and abundant trees, refreshes the eye, which for three days
has looked upon nothing more like home than the low, barren
sandbanks of Jutland. Now the spires of Copenhagen are
quickly growing upon us, and in a few minutes we are alongside of the Danish capital. " There it was that Nelson
punished you," says a passenger to one of the crew, who is a
Dane. " Yes ; a shameful business it was. The English had
not declared war," is the answer. " Ah ! but how was it that

B

you were so well prepared ? " is the retort ; to which no reply is vouchsafed. The passage through the Sound was most charming, the sea smooth as a mill-pond, the sky clear as a mirror. Craft of all rigs and nations crowd the channel. The little Danish vessels, with their red sails, contrast prettily with the white canvass of the larger ships. After passing through " The Grounds," the coast of Denmark grows fainter on our starboard side, and the coast of Sweden more interesting on our port-side. With the help of a pair of glasses, one can very clearly make out the picturesque succession of villages, woods, meadows, with church towers here and there, and the back-ground of hills gently waving in the distance. The island of Bornholm now comes into sight, and we know that we are half-way to Kronstadt. We are also fairly in the Baltic.

Between the voyages out and home I have had the opportunity of seeing the Baltic under very different aspects. In fair, sunny weather, nothing can exceed the pleasure of cruising in this sea. The interest never flags. Now a line of coast, now some island, claims attention. There is always something to talk of, something to ask about. But the very reasons why the Baltic is so pleasant in calm weather, make its navigation very dangerous in rough. The frequent sighting of land gives much interest when the sea is smooth, and the wind fair, but also much anxiety when all is stormy and adverse. On our passage out we see a ship stranded on Gottland, with her mizen gone ; we also make out the hull of a steamer, wrecked off Dago. These tell us that there is another side to this bright picture ; and on our passage home, as we toss, and roll, and beat up against a head-wind, and through a heavy sea, we catch a glimpse of what that side is. " Rain fit to spit your eyes out, and wind fit to blow you out of the water,"—to repeat the vigorous expressions of our captain—such was the last night I spent in the Baltic.

As we draw towards the end of our voyage, conversation turns upon Sir Charles Napier and the Baltic fleet. A man in the crew, who served in that expedition, is glad to get you to listen to his bitter complainings that men ashore should have the power to control the action of men at sea. He is more disposed to lay the blame of that fruitless demonstration at the door of the House of Commons than on the shoulders of "Charlie," although he thinks the admiral was not quite such a fire-eater as he had been. We are shown the spot where the officers of the English fleet used to land and play cricket on the dominion of the Tsar of all the Russias, whose subjects, in that particular locality, thought it much more profitable to turn a penny by accommodating their enemies, than by patriotically turning their backs upon them. A hill, commanding a good prospect of the Gulf of Finland, is also pointed out to us as a favourite place for Russian pic-nic parties at that time, on account of the fine view of the British fleet which it commanded.

We are at Kronstadt. As our ship draws too much water to let her pass the bar at the mouth of the Neva, we and our luggage have to be transferred to a small steamer, to be taken up to St. Petersburg. This process gives us time to enjoy the greatest pleasure the traveller knows, namely, feasting his eyes upon novel scenes. Imperial gun-boats, swift, clean-made little craft, dart in and out among the vessels in the harbour, frequently sounding their warning whistle, manned by officers and men looking very neat in their dark uniforms and white caps. But the common Russian boat-man is the most picturesque object. Whether paddling about Kronstadt harbour, or ferrying people across the Neva for five kopeks (equal 1¾$d$.), he is the same in all respects. Flat features, fair hair, sunburnt face; these are his looks: a pink-striped shirt hanging outside a pair of very loose, light-blue trowsers, and tied round the waist; this is all his clothing. A piece of string round his neck suspends a cross, which is worn from baptism to death.

If we had come to Russia resolved to find fault with everything Russian, as some persons, who have recorded their "journeys due north," seem to have done, we had a fine opportunity given us at the outset of indulging our humour.

For the skipper of the "Mercury" (the name of our little steamer,) was in a state in which he preferred kissing a large dog to taking the command of the vessel. But such accidents will happen in the best regulated countries.

I had read and heard so much about the approach to St. Petersburg, that I was anxious to compare the picture I had formed in my mind with the reality. The result was disappointing. The atmosphere was not favourable, I believe. It certainly did not throw a veil of enchantment over the plain fact that we were drawing near to a city built on a swamp, the outskirts of which, like all other outskirts, had the usual irregular, unfinished, and mean appearance. The truth is, in order to enjoy the first sight of a magnificent city, as St. Petersburg is, resting on the banks of a noble river, as who can say the Neva is not, you ought to keep down below until the steamer has passed the beginnings of the town, and be called up about opposite the *Corps des Mines ;* then will burst upon your view such a sight as no other in the world can rival. I have looked up the river from this point by sun-light and by moon-light, and my admiration has increased at every view.

It would be absurd, in a general way, to notice the formalities of the custom-house. But books and travellers had filled me with such fearful anticipations of the Russian *douane,* that I think it right to say how agreeably they were disappointed. The search to which my luggage was subjected was of the most superficial kind. The things were handled gently, and whatever was taken out was replaced with care. Some delay occurred, but this arose from the extraordinary amount of packages which some of the passengers had with them. Perfect civility, too, marked all the proceedings. I had heard enough of the venality of Russian officials, and I was reminded of it by a great, ugly, soldier-looking fellow coming behind me once or twice, and nudging my elbow, and stealthily holding out his hand for a bribe, in return for which I have no doubt he would have promised no end of quick and easy scrutiny. But this was no more a

proof of the rottenness of the system, than the protracted
attentions of a railway porter would argue the corruptibility
of the directors.   And here a word about the censorship of
the press.   I had been told that all books, without exception,
were detained for inspection by the censor ; I found, however,
that mine and my friend's were allowed to pass without
hesitation.   If they had been stopped, we should have probably but just recovered them in time to take them home
again.   The fact is, the censorship is exercised with a good
deal of irregularity, and it varies as to stringency in different
parts of the empire.   It is considered to be more rigorous at
Moscow than at St. Petersburg.   I saw several cases of expur-
gation in the newspapers at the former place.   Here is a
specimen ; it was erased from *Galignani* for 8th June last :—

" *Cracow, 6th.*—The *Czar* states that the Pope has addressed an autograph
letter to the Emperor of Russia, in which his Holiness refuses to accede to the
request of the Czar to publish a pontifical brief against the Polish movement.
On the contrary, he menaces the Emperor with the vengeance of Heaven, if he
persists in persecuting the Roman Catholic Church, and shedding the blood of
unarmed men.   The *Czar* adds that, in consequence of this letter, Count de
Kisseleff will be recalled from Rome."

I should observe that, while at Moscow they *rub* out, at
St. Petersburg they *blot* out, the offending passages.   If only
advertisements cover that part of the other side of the sheet
on which the censured words occur, the scissors lighten the
labours of the expunger at the expense of the advertiser.   I
was told by a man living in the interior, that the *Athenæum*
and the *Revue des Deux Mondes* often do not reach him till two
months after the proper time, and then sometimes with whole
pages torn out, especially from the *Revue*, in articles bearing
upon religious questions.   Heresy is more jealously watched
than sedition.

Clear of the custom-house, we fall among the isvostchiks—
*alias* droshky-drivers, habited all alike in blue cloth, cassock-
shaped, coats—veritable " Noah's-arks " for length ; wearing,
as do all men of the moujik class, unlimited beards, and
having their hair very neatly and straightly parted down

the middle. They all talk at once, loud and fast; and as they speak, a tongue unknown to us, their talk sounds very loud and fast indeed. But their talk is nothing to their driving for fastness, and their language nothing to their vehicles for bewilderment. No one can deny that the Russians are good drivers; but they are very reckless ones. If furious driving were punishable in Russia, every isvostchik and every private coachman would be charged with the offence before he had gone a hundred yards. Their style of driving has an eager, excited air about it. They take a rein in each hand, stretching their arms out, and holding them wide apart, and leaning the body slightly forward, as a jockey does when he is working his horse up to the winning-post. Their whips which are very short, are sparingly used; a shout and a shake of the reins being generally enough to send the horse flying. The reins are very long, and sometimes knotted at the end, so as to serve as a whip. Considering at what a headlong pace the droshkies tear through the streets, and whirl round the corners, it is surprising that there are not more accidents. I only saw one up-set while I was in Russia, and in that case the driver was drunk, and only upset himself. But it requires one to be on the look out to avoid coming to grief. Through the close shaving of a driver, it was only by swerving aside that I escaped, by a hair's breadth, having my shoulder run into by the shaft of another droshky. At another time I was all but thrown out, in consequence of the driver crossing a gutter at a very sharp angle, and at a very great pace. Rarely is equilibrium so tempted!

Droshkies and their drivers, as well as the driving, are worth notice. The former are quite a national institution. From the Tsar to the serf, the droshky is the favourite conveyance. A man may keep any number and any variety of carriages he likes, but the droshky must be one. And no wonder. For one person they are very handy, neat turn-outs; the horses are generally in good condition; (a Russian merchant's ambition is to have a fat wife, a fat horse, and a fat coachman); the harness is very light, and when, as is often the case, studded over with silver, has a very elegant appearance. Moreover, those ugly appendages, blinkers, are not known in Russia. Droshkies are capable of great speed, and easily managed. Their size suits the build of horses, commonly used, low and short in the draught. One fault only is to be found with them—the leg accommodation is scanty. I speak of the modern droshky, in which one sits as in a common chaise. The old-fashioned type, across which one sits astride, has well-nigh disappeared from St. Petersburg. A good many are to be seen at Moscow; but they are the shabbiest on the streets, and will soon die out there. At St. Petersburg a tariff restrains the extortioning of the isvostchiks. It is true they never take the fare without a grumble; but the fare is small enough, sevenpence the *course*. If they take you beyond the range, or with luggage, they make good use of their freedom from rule. But at Moscow things are different There is no tariff there, and consequently one must bargain before one hires, or pay any penalty the driver chooses to levy. There is also a marked difference in the manner of the Moscow isvostchiks. Such abusive, cunning, impudent fellows I never saw. Their eyes twinkle with roguery and insolence.

No doubt every one who has ridden in a droshky associates it with insufferable jolting. But the blame is to be laid upon the roads, not upon the carriages. Over a smooth surface, such as the wood pavement in the Nevsky Prospekt, or the beautiful roads at Peterhoff or Tsarskoe-Selo, nothing can be more easy and pleasant than the swift motion of a droshky. But no springs in the world could ever soften the frightful joltings occasioned by the bad roads which mostly prevail. I thought nothing could be worse than the streets of St. Petersburg, till I got to Moscow, where, to the vileness of the pavement is added the hilliness of the ground. It is perfect dislocation to be driven down the hills there. Out of self-defence you gather up your scraps of Russ and cry, "Not so fast!" But to go slower is only to protract the torture. With proper irony are the Moscow droshkies called "bone-setters." The intense frost, and the consequent enormous expansion when it breaks up, baffle all attempts at paving in Russia. Every experiment has been tried, but to no purpose. In St. Petersburg the evil is increased by the swampy nature of the ground. The immense blocks of granite, which form its magnificent quays, and line the Neva and the canals, are tilted up and displaced in every direction by this cause. One would think there had been an earthquake.

My arrival at the door of the Misses Benson's Hotel, so well known and so highly esteemed by English travellers in Russia, induces my first payment in Russian money. The state of the currency may be understood by the fact that all the while I was in the country the highest coin that passed through my hands was a twenty-kopek piece, value seven-pence. A silver rouble (3s.) was not to be seen in St. Petersburg. At Moscow I bought a couple at a premium of five-pence each. Gold there is none; and silver is so scarce that, notwithstanding the assurance, which is printed in three sizes of type on the back of the notes, that cash will be given for paper at the Government bank, the answer is " no assets." The rate of exchange averages about 3s. to the rouble. It has been as high as 3s. 3d. Sir A. Alison would seem to be doubly wrong when he says (vol. ix. 349, ninth edition), "the nominal pay of the soldier—nearly a rouble (or about 1s.) a day—is not inconsiderable." The copper is plentiful and burdensome enough. It is very unpleasant to receive in change *rouleaux* of thirty kopeks, or ten five-kopek pieces. But its cumbersomeness is nothing to what it has been. In 1792 a five-kopek piece weighed $1\frac{1}{2}$ oz., now it weighs 1 oz. In 1840 a two-kopek piece weighed scarcely a grain less than a three-kopek piece now. The one rouble notes, which have the most wear, are often reduced to tatters. One sometimes receives them carefully folded in paper, looking more like a leaf that has lain a long time on the ground in autumn.

To describe a city is the province of guide books; to relate his impressions and experiences may be allowed to the ordinary traveller. My first walk in St. Petersburg was at the time of twilight; and I think it was a most favourable time for the purpose. Twilight in the northern latitudes means much more than we understand by the word. It is all the summer night they have. Unlike what we call twilight, which is only day shading into night, the northern twilight has a permanence about it which gives to every thing a very singular and beautiful appearance. It is not the interval between light and darkness, but between light and light. You do not feel that it is growing dark, but rather that it will grow no darker; and this gives you time to look around and observe at leisure. Twilight magnifies; it also deceives. In St. Petersburg there is full scope for its producing these effects. For St. Petersburg is a great, and yet not a great, city. In population and the number of dwellings it is comparatively small; in area it is superlatively large. In short, it is a small city built on a grand scale. In a narrow, confined town the thickly blending shadows of the crowded buildings make all dark below when the sky is only half-dark above. But in St. Petersburg the spaces are much too broad for the shadows to deepen the actual gloom. Never shall I lose the impression of vastness and solitude which my first walk gave me. We seemed to be crossing a desert when approaching, from the river-side, the church of S. Izak. A strange sense of loneliness also presses upon one walking through the great streets and across the broad plains, with no sound to catch the ear but the occasional responsive clapping of the watchmen's rattles, and one's own foot-fall.

But here is another view. It is mid-day, and we take the opportunity of a cooling shower to make the toilsome ascent to the top of the dome of S. Izak's. We are guided by an old soldier, whose hand one is obliged to hold in order to be led through the perfectly dark passages. When we come to climbing the ladder which carries us up inside the dome, the heat is fearful. It feels as though the gold plates on the outside were all molten. But the summit is gained, and the reward is rich. The sun has broken through the cloud, the sky is undimmed by smoke, the city lies out-spread around you. Look northwards and you see the beautiful, tranquil Neva, with its many mouths, flowing towards the gulf. Just below you the Great Neva, bordered by splendid quays and faced by palace-like buildings: further off the Little Neva, the Great Nevka, the Little Nevka, intersecting the land in their course, and forming the "islands" so much resorted to in the evening by the citizens for the cool retreat of parks and woods, which they afford from the dust and heat of the city. The chief part of the town lies on the left bank of the river, but a considerable portion also stands upon the Vassilieostroff, or William Island, embraced by the Great and Little Nevas. Look around you, and you see the many-coloured roofs of the houses; the spires and domes, gold and silver, of the churches and public edifices; making the whole seem like an illuminated page in an ancient missal. "This alone is worth the voyage"—so I said, and so I now think.

Did I say that the scene just left was like an illuminated page in an ancient missal? Nay, it ought rather to be likened to a modern fac-simile "printed in gold and colours." It is all new. One hundred and sixty years ago and it was a dreary, tangled swamp; not one stone on another; not a creature dwelling on it but the water-fowl. Other cities trace back their history into the cloudy past when all that can be said is, "*aut Cæsar, aut diabolus.*" A hundred ancient relics dispute the honour of being the most ancient. But if you ask for the oldest building in St. Petersburg, a walk along the quay and across the Troitskoi Bridge will bring you to it. It is the hut of Peter the Great, date 1703. Here we learn how St. Petersburg is unique among cities. All others read you chapters in history; this alone a chapter in biography. From Peter's hut we pass to Peter's grave. In the church of SS. Peter and Paul, commonly called the Fortress Church, lie the remains of the great Emperor. All the Tsars before him rest in the Cathedral of the Archangel Michael, at Moscow; all after him in this church. As though the bodies of the Emperors were the Palladium of Russia, they are laid in the strongest place in the city; they will be the last booty to fall into the hands of an enemy. The beautiful gilded spire of this church is seen glistening in the sun far and wide, and rivals, for its slender elegance, the spire of the Admiralty. But the spire is all the beauty it has to boast of. Whitewash outside, dazzle and glitter of gold inside, there is nothing to call for a word of admiration. As one enters one expects to see something that would betoken it as the burial-place of all the sovereigns of Russia, since Russia has been great. There is nothing of the kind. In front of the " ikonostast," or screen, are arranged, in rows, dark oblong blocks, looking like the beds in a barrack or a hospital, for size and shape. These are the tombs of the Tsars. They are covered with dark green cloth, and all that distinguishes one from another is the initial letter and number of the sovereign, designed in yellow braid on the top. There is something very striking in this unostentatious sepulture of the emperors in a country where the Emperor is supreme—where the peasant far away in the interior thinks of him as a high and half-divine being, and calls him, " earthly god." But this sinking of the individual in the office is generally observable. The coinage bears no effigy of the Tsar upon it, only the two-headed eagle, and sometimes (not always) the initial and number.

The remarkably earnest manner with which an aged military officer was performing his devotions in the chapel at Peter's hut when we were there, calls for a few words respecting the prominence given to religion in Russia. In his " *Lectures on Heroes*," Carlyle observes, " Condemnable idolatry is *insincere* idolatry." If this dictum be true there is very little condemnable idolatry in Russia. It is impossible to believe that the men and women who surround you in the streets of a Russian city, crossing themselves and bowing, now to this picture, now to that church, are insincere. It is impossible to believe that a religion can have got so fast hold of the habits and actions of a people, without also having grasped their faith. I speak only of what I saw, and give merely the impression which the sight would make upon the most ordinary lay observer. You cannot stir in Russia without meeting with something to remind you of religion. Every room in a Russian house has its ikon in the corner ; every apartment, every place with a roof on it, one might almost say.   In the ante-chambers of the Exchange large pictures, or images (*ikon* means image, but it is always either a flat surface, or in relief, never detached) are hung up, with lamps suspended in front of them ; and before these the merchants, as they come on and go off 'Change, reverently perform their devotions.   In the public offices, in the palaces, in the museums, in the railway stations, in the ship cabins, in the shops, in the tea rooms—everywhere is to be found an ikon, and everywhere the ikon is respected. So that one should never enter beneath any roof in Russia, no matter what the place may be, without taking one's hat off ; for there is sure to be an image somewhere, and to remain covered is to be disrespectful to it, and consequently to offend the Russians.   I observed in an English merchant's office the usual picture ; and on inquiry I was told that it was needful to set one up out of respect to the religious feelings of their Russian connexion.   When dining with an English gentleman at his *dacha* (or country box), at Peterhoff, I noticed that every room had its ikon ; and he told me that his landlord, who was a member of the Russian Church, had been occupying the house before him, and had left the pictures in their places, and it would be an affront to his religion to remove them. No false shame restrains the Russians from their devotions. Sidney Smith would have had no reason to preach to them from the text, " Oh that *men* would praise the Lord ! "   The men are the devotees in the Greek Church.   They are the majority in all congregations.   They are as assiduous and frequent in their devotional acts as the women.   Military officers come into churches and kiss the ikons, and prostrate themselves, and set up candles before them as often as the peasant.   Your droshky-driver will uncover and cross himself three or four times as he passes a church.   When starting on a journey, and on arriving, by land or by water, men and women cross themselves.   And the crossing is not done in the slight care- less way one sees in Romish countries, but is performed in a most deliberate and emphatic manner, by touching the brow,

the right shoulder, the left, and the breast, and is generally
accompanied with a bow.*  A very elegant structure at the
north end of the Nicholas Bridge encloses a sacred picture
of St Andrew, and one is often turned out of one's path
by a man performing his devotions before it, and this in
the most public thoroughfare in St. Petersburg.  It is true
one sees things that make one think that the letter and
the spirit of religion have parted company; *e. g.* the little
dingy ikon sometimes looks out from the corner of an imperial room, the walls of which are hung with French pictures
of a very doubtful character.  But this much is certain, that
religion has an immense hold on the Russian mind, whatever
its influence may be on Russian morals.  And that this hold
is not confined to a mere mechanical observance of certain
ceremonies and gestures, but extends to something like a
recognition of doctrine, even by the most ignorant, may be
gathered from a simple but significant fact which was told
me at Moscow.  The common people, when helping themselves to a third glass of tea, or, in fact, when about to do anything a third time, are wont to say, carelessly, "One, two,
three; God loves the Trinity."

A place so modern as St. Petersburg cannot be expected to be
rich in associations.  The man of history finds little to interest
him; and this is true of Russia generally.  The horse-tail
standards taken from the Tartars, which adorn, or disfigure, so
many of the churches, point to struggles, bloody enough,
doubtless, but barely of sufficient importance to invite research.
In fact, the age of St. Petersburg measures the length of the
history of Russia; the ancient Moscow and Kieff represent
the obscure annals of Muscovy.  And this the Russians themselves admit.  A professor of history, whom I met at Moscow,
felt bound to make some apology for the scantiness of his

---

* You can tell whether a man is one of the orthodox, or a "raskolik"
(schismatic), by the way he holds his fingers in crossing himself.  If the former,
he presses the tips of the thumb and first two fingers together to signify the
Trinity in Unity; if the latter, he holds the thumb stretched apart, and the
first two fingers extended close together, to signify the two natures in Christ.
This distinction is observed by the very lowest classes.

national records ; and a colonel of artillery, in whose company I happened to visit the Romanoff Palace, shrugged his shoulders, as he turned over the leaves of an old volume of Russian history there, and said, "Russian history is very meagre and very obscure ;" and he seemed to think that what passed for it must be taken *cum grano.* But the man of letters finds still less to interest him. Russian literature is yet in its infancy, though promising a vigorous future. The author whose works have had the deepest and widest influence on the national mind, is the fabulist Kriloff. I was anxious to see what sort of a tribute the Russians had paid to him, and so lost no time in finding out his statue, which was put up in the Summer Gardens in 1855. As a work of art it is highly creditable. The poet is represented sitting, reading a book. The pedestal is adorned with very clever groupings of animals in high relief, the *personæ* of his admirable fables. Kriloff died November 9th (21st), 1844, aged seventy-six, having been born at Moscow in 1768. His fables have been widely circulated beyond his own country. A beautiful illustrated edition was published in Paris, in 1825, under the direction of Count Orloff. Metrical versions from divers pens in French and Italian accompanied the original text, and a French introduction by M. Lemontez, and an Italian preface by M. Salfi, were prefixed. An Italian translation by A. Cesari was also brought out at Genoa, in 1828. A little brochure, entitled, " *Kryloff, ou le La Fontaine Russe, sa Vie et ses Fables: par A. Bougeault,*" appeared at Paris, in 1852, containing translations of a few select fables. But nothing has been done, that I am aware of, to make Kriloff known to English readers, beyond a prose version of one or two pieces, introduced as specimens by Mr. Sutherland Edwards into his excellent book, "The Russians at Home." The following English rendering of one of his fables may give some idea of his mode of satirizing social and political evils.

### "BREAM.

"In the pleasure grounds of a baron there was a pond, in which throve and gambolled a number of bream. Life passed very happily with these fish, till, one day, the baron ordered his men to turn in fifty pike. A friend of his, who heard him give the order, exclaimed, 'Now, then! what have you given such an order as this for? What good do you expect to come of it? You will soon have not a bream left in your pond. But perhaps you don't know the nature of the pike?' 'My good Sir,' replied the Baron with a smile, 'you waste your words; I am quite aware of all you say. But let me in return ask you what makes you think that I am fond of bream?'"—Book viii., fab. 20.

His fables number 197 in all, and are arranged in nine books.

Around the base of the statue, and in other parts of the gardens, were seated wet-nurses, with their little charges, and arrayed in all the finery for which they are remarkable. The wet-nurse is quite an institution in Russia, as well it might be, when we look at the gigantic foundling hospitals, where infants are taken in by scores a day, and a wet-nurse has to be provided for each. These women, I was told, are very particular about their dress. When hired, they always expect their employer to deck them out in national costume of the gayest colours. And certainly the specimens I saw verified this statement. One had on a light-blue *serafan*, or gown, bordered with gold lace, and a bright-coloured kerchief bound round her head. (The women of the lower orders never wear bonnets, but bright-coloured kerchiefs folded across the head, and tied under the chin.) Another had on a much-tinselled head-dress, in shape like a Glengarry cap; I believe it is called a *pavoinik*.

But for the isvostchiks and the moujiks (peasants), one might walk about the streets of St. Petersburg and hardly know that one was in Russia. If, however, you want to see something national, turn out of the Nevskoï through the Gostinnoï Dvor, to the second-hand market, and you will find yourself in the midst of genuine Russian sights and sounds. Here is a perfect labyrinth of booths, or shops. The keepers of these shops step into your path, repeating the list of their wares, with many profound bows, and adding a hissing sound to the end of each word, which is, in fact, the first letter of *soodar*, "Sir." Here the Wardour Street, Rag-Fair, and Thieves' Alley of St. Petersburg are all combined in one vast bazaar. As you look along the rows of shops, you fancy that wondrous bargains are to be made in them.   All sorts of rarities you hope to pick up for " next-to-nothing," on the supposition that the sellers are not aware of the value of their goods. But experience soon undeceives you.   The tradespeople in the Nevskoï know that their fine shops and high prices would not stand long  against the  competition of these brokers ; so they send persons round the markets to buy up the bargains you had  hoped to secure, or to give to the dealers a hint of what their goods ought to fetch.   One article, however, may be got cheap here, namely, literature. English books, in good condition, can often be met with for a song.   Second-hand ikons and Scripture prints are exposed for sale in abundance.   One of the prints which I bought was a complex tableau of the history of Jonah, representing the prophet thrown óverboard, in a blue coat, and brought up by the whale in a yellow one.   My friend, who had done the dealing for me, said, " You will see that picture in a church at Moscow."   " Impossible ! " thought I ; but when I got to the Holy City, and was viewing the Cathedral of the Assumption, I discovered on the wall of a corridor the original of my picture, life-size, the drawing exactly the same, the colouring just as absurd.   And this is no exception. All the old church-pictures are of a like character.   Wonderful defiance to perspective, proportion, outline, and shading, is done in the paintings which cover the walls and roofs of Russian churches.   A Pre-Raphaelite would revel in them. Look up, and you see the black face of a saint, some yards long, staring  down upon you from the roof, with a nimbus as big as a cart-wheel, and eyes like tea-saucers.   At one shop in the market I was invited to drink a glass of tea, of which a huge *samovar*, or tea-urn, was kept always ready for customers.   These shops have no dwellings attached, and at night they are closed, and sealed up.   A seal is greatly respected by the Russians, and will secure property better than the most cunning Chubb or Bramah.   This brings Scriptural allusions to one's mind.   The cases of gems and other valuables in the museums are all sealed as well as locked. A man will hesitate to break a seal, who would at once pick a lock.

We spent a very pleasant and interesting day at Kronstadt, where we met with a hearty and kind reception from the English chaplain. Englishmen heard and read so much about this island during the war, that they came to know it quite well ; and maps had made them as familiar with its bearings, as if they had visited it. The distance is about two hours by steamer from St. Petersburg. The road from the pier to the town was as bad as it could be. The regular way was blocked up for repairs, and we had to take our course along the shore of sand, fish-bones, and shells, for a short distance, and then through a broken hedge, plunging on the other side of it into great deeps of dust. I was glad to find what comfortable and spacious quarters were appropriated to the English chaplaincy. The chapel is a really church-like building, standing alone, and having a very respectable spire at the west end. Close to it is the chaplain's house, a large and commodious dwelling, surrounded by an excellent garden, and having all sorts of offices attached. A wall incloses the whole, so that within his own domain the minister may well fancy himself in a snug, country living in England. The windows of the principal rooms look upon the green slopes of the ramparts, over which come the sea breezes from the west, keeping the rooms cool in the summer, when the thermometer stands at 22 Reau. (81 Fahr.) in the shade. Altogether it is the pleasantest spot in the island.

The chief things to be seen at Kronstadt are the forts. We took a boat and went to one, called the Rysbank Fort It stands out some distance in the gulf, and we had a dancing voyage in our little craft to get to it. We were taken over the works by a lieutenant of artillery. They are far from finished ; and this was all the better for our seeing the actual construction. It was the time of day when the Russian workman takes his siesta, two hours from noon being set apart for dining and napping. As we went about the fort, we had to be careful lest we should stumble over them, as they lay stretched in all directions. The Russian labourer lies down for his mid-day snooze just where he happens to be working. I have seen a man rolled up like a dog at the bottom of a deep hole in the Nevskoï Prospekt, where some repairs were being done to the drains. Indeed, Moujik will make his bed anywhere. In an hotel, you find him lying about the passages, or at his master's door.

The masonry of this fort is quite colossal, and is put together in the most beautiful and perfect manner. All that stone walls can do to resist ordnance, these ought to do. One gallery of guns is mounted. They are of various calibres, but all heavy metal. The complement, I understood, would be 112. Other forts are also being built; and are the fruits of the alarm which the Russians really felt when the Baltic fleet stood off Kronstadt.

On our return to the town we went to see the docks of Peter the Great. Few monarchs have laid so good a claim to the epithet as he. His broad vigorous mind could comprehend the wants of ages beyond his own. His conceptions were so grand and far-seeing, that he built, nearly a century and a-half ago, a dock spacious enough for the vessels of the present day.

The earth-works, which lie along the side of the island exposed to the gulf, were thrown up during the late war. They are constructed on the most skilful plan, and seem to make it hopeless for troops to gain a footing in the face of them. The Russians have acted on the maxim, " Prevention is better than cure." Invasion is impossible now. On our return from them, we stopped to look at the English burying-ground. The graves are for the most part those of sailors. Three and four may be seen lying side-by-side, men of the same crew, all cut off within a few days by cholera or fever, and all in early manhood. A plain cross is the most common monument.

A very good general notion of the town and island is got

by viewing them from the tower of the English church. People, I suppose, need not be told that Kronstadt is ugly. The island is as flat and low as it can be, consistent with keeping itself out of the water. It is also a hot, dusty, wearisome place. But there is enough in it to interest a stranger, and it gives a better notion of what the Russians can and will do for self-preservation and self-aggrandizement, than the fine things one sees at Petersburg. And yet at Petersburg all the ships of the line are built, for the sake of the name rather than for the sake of convenience. For, in order to bring them over the bar to the sea, huge, but very ingenious contrivances have to be resorted to, namely, "camels," so called from the resemblance of their action to that of a camel, as it kneels down to receive its burthen, and then rises up and bears it away. The process has been often described.

From the balcony at Benson's one looks down upon a shed-like building, whence the steam-boats start for the country, *alias* Peterhoff, that phrase having very few aliases in St. Petersburg, and of the few Peterhoff being the most con-spicuous. An Englishman, who knows what is meant by " the country " at St. Petersburg, is a good deal amused at the fondness with which its citizens repeat the expression. On 'Change the desire is to shape business engagements so as to allow of getting into " the country." If a man seems to be disappointed, the chances are that it is of not being able to get into " the country." When a Petersburger, especially if he be of English blood, is drawing near to the end of his voyage to St. Petersburg, all his conjectures and calculations about the time of arrival turn upon the question, " Shall I be able to get into the country the same day ? " The delay at the custom house grows into the greatest grievance of a despotic government, if it threaten to hinder the traveller from getting into " the country." And yet all this anxiety is about what we should consider a very moderate advantage. It is merely about leaving a swamp with a town upon it for a swamp without a town upon it. The environs of St. Petersburg would be thought very small mercies by a London mechanic ; but they are all the mercies of the kind the Petersburgers have, and, like other men, they are thankful in an inverse ratio to the mercies. Indeed one quarter, called the Forest-corps (from an establishment there something after the manner of Cirencester Agricultural College), which, on account of its nearness to the city, is most frequented by those who have least leisure time, is so filled with houses, as well as dust, that one is surprised that anybody should consider it a good change from the wide, handsome streets of the city. But the truth is, dust and houses are not the only things from which the citizens fly. The canals, which do the drainage, are very offensive in the summer, and the Petersburgers believe in the unhealthiness of bad smells, Dr. Parkin "On the Causation and Prevention of Disease " to the contrary, notwithstanding.

As to Peterhoff, which heads the list of places,* Oraniembaum, Tsarskoe-selo, Pavlosky, the Forest Corps, and the rest, which comprise "the country" of the Petersburgers, I must say a few words. The English Quay, whence the Peterhoff boats start, is almost the only place in St. Petersburg where anything like bustle or crowding is to be seen. At the hours of arrival and departure, it is all alive with eager, noisy, isvostchiks. The little life that lingers in the deserted city dwells among the isvostchiks. Clear them, and their rattling droshkies, off the streets, and St. Petersburg would be empty indeed. On festivals (all holy days are holidays in Russia, Sunday with the rest) the tide of people flows unceasingly towards the English Quay, from early morning to well on in the afternoon. The boats are crowded to the gunwale, and yet late comers press into them, in spite of the remonstrances of the police, who waste much of the vernacular instead of hoisting the gang-way. An hour and a

---

* During the late war, British subjects were not allowed to live at Peterhoff, the Government having an odd fear of their communicating with the English Fleet ; a not very practicable feat, considering that Kronstadt lay between them and it.

half brings you to the pier at Peterhoff.  My first visit was on
a Sunday, and just as we landed, an imperial carriage, like an
Irish out-side car of a very large size, drove up with a party
of priests who had been officiating at the imperial church.
These reverend gentlemen looked, in all respects, very unlike
their brethren, the rustic popes, whom one often sees seated
in the wretched little market-carts behind the peasant women,
who drive into the towns to sell their commodities ; or, may
be, trudging it on foot.

Peterhoff is a very pretty place, albeit the houses stand, for
the most part, very close together.  But pretty is the only word
that can be applied to it.  Beautiful, grand, fine, are terms incon-
sistent with made scenery.*   Slight rises in the ground, which
pass for hills in this flat country, are the only favours which
Nature has shown to Peterhoff.  Art, in obedience to imperial will, has accomplished great things.  The best general
notion of the extent and beauty of its achievements is to
be had from Babigone, the highest point in the neighbourhood.  On this summit stands a building, the most extravagant
of the many extravagancies which the Emperor Nicholas has
left behind him at Peterhoff, to testify to his splendid selfish-
ness.  It is designed to represent a Grecian temple, and would
be perfect in its way, but for the violence that is done to the
proportions by having a basement storey which dips into the
side of the hill, and upon which the temple-like portion is
raised.  The ceiling of the principal apartment rests upon
beautiful white marble monoliths.  On the outside grey
granite monoliths support the projecting roof along the four
sides.  Nothing less than monoliths for the shafts of their
pillars seem to satisfy the Russians.  The four porticoes
which adorn the four faces of S. Izak's church, rest on stupendous monoliths of red granite.  And now let us look forth
upon the prospect which lies before us as we stand on the
gallery surrounding the building.  Peterhoff is spread out as

* As you go about the lakes you are unpleasantly reminded that they
are all artificial, by seeing, through the clear water, the pipes lying along
the bottom.

on a map; below are the lakes and islands—all made—whereon stand the pretty tea-houses. A strange whim has placed some sham ruins of Palmyra in the fore-ground. Beyond the islands lie the Palace, with its many accessories of courtiers' lodgings, chapel, stables, barracks, &c.; the village, like anything in the world but a Russian village; the country-houses of the Petersburgers, thickly lying together among the shrubs, like eggs packed in moss. The gulf stretches away beyond the green boundary of trees, melting into the sun-lit haze, that makes the horizon indistinguishable, but for the bright line which crosses the heaven, and which we know to be St. Petersburg. And most beautiful does the city look, like a long, narrow, fleecy cloud, resting on the sunny sky. It seems to have a sun of its own. For just above it shines and radiates with deep golden light the dome of S. Izak's. The spires of the Fortress Church and of the Admiralty, the other church-domes and minarets, are lost in the distance to the naked eye; for they are only gilded. But the dome of S. Izak's dazzles the beholder even here; for it only is gold.* If we turn our eyes to the right, and so sweep round the country behind Peterhoff, we see the slopes studded with the tents of some of the camps in which the soldiers, who are not required for town duty, pass the summer. It is altogether a sight not easily matched in the world.

A word about the *dacha*, or villa, may not be out of place here. Dachas are of various sizes, but all substantially on the same model. They are slight buildings, mostly of wood, and constructed with one prevailing purpose—coolness. Air and shade are courted in every way. The eaves of the roofs project far out, and cover spacious balconies, where the meals are generally taken, or, at any rate, where the fruit and the coffee are always served. The ice-well is a *sine quâ non* of a dacha. In the case of a hired house, the landlord always fills it for the season. Considering how near to one another, and to the road, most average dachas lie, it is wonderful how

---

* The plates are thin, but what there is of them is gold, and they have an appearance which no gilding can equal.

thoroughly private and secluded they are. The shrubs are arranged so skilfully as to leave you to imagine yourself quite in the country, until the sound of wheels and horse-steps reminds you that you are on the road-side, and the sound of voices that you are only N°. so-and-so, in a row of dachas. Through the trees you catch a glimpse of a Cossack as he gallops on some errand for the Imperials; or, may be, you see the Imperials themselves as they pass for a drive, or are on their way to take tea at one of the many little summer-houses which are scattered over the islands.

About the palaces at Peterhoff there is no need to say any-thing here. All princes must have palaces, and all palaces are very much alike. But the summer-houses which ornament the Peterhoff islands deserve notice. They are very pretty, very costly, very useless. Some are meant to represent Italian villas, having been built by Nicholas to surprise his wife on her return from Italy. Each consists of some three or four rooms, fitted up with great luxury and elegance. Now and then, in the summer season, the Emperor takes a fancy to have tea in one of them. Beyond this they are put to no useful purpose; but are merely kept, like a Dutch wife's best room, in idle, vacant order.

All visitors to Peterhoff have two objects to attain—to see the fountains play and to hear the band play. The former are very curious; many of them very beautiful, designed in divers ways to give effect and variety to the action of water. With regard to the band-playing, there is a custom worth while mentioning. Every summer's evening two military bands perform alternately before the palace. At nine o'clock a gun fires, the guard turns out, the two bands unite, and play the "Soldier's Evening Hymn." This ended, the soldiers (and after them the whole company) uncover and repeat, in a very subdued voice, the Lord's Prayer, crossing themselves at the conclusion; after which they fall out, and the company disperse. The idea of all this is very beautiful, and the effect (I speak of what I myself witnessed) would have been very impressive if the bugle-call, which

preceded and followed the devotions, had been clear and
vigorous instead of weak and squeaky. This is not the only
instance I met with in Russia of a fine sentiment being marred
in the practice by some blunder or want of taste on the part of
the performers. A richly-vestured deacon, standing on the
polished jasper floor of the gorgeous S. Izak's, and singing the
sweet-flowing Slavonic Liturgy to a plaintive chant, is all
very beautiful, and very solemnizing; but what becomes of
the beauty and solemnity when the said deacon stops to spit
on the said jasper floor?

A friend of mine, tutor to the son of Prince B——, was
with the prince's family at Tsarskoe-selo, and this gave me an
additional reason for visiting the place. It is a short run by
rail from St. Petersburg. My friend had no idea of my being
in Russia, and I had no one to interpret for me, so I had
misgivings about being able to find him out. I was told to
jump into a droshky on arriving at the station, and say to the
isvostchik, "Dom B——."* This I did, and I found myself
quite understood. To give the isvostchiks their due, I must
say, they are very sharp, ready fellows at catching one's
meaning. A drive through the broad clean roads of this
imperial village, over paving that would do credit to M'Adam,
was a very pleasant change to one who had been so much
jolted out of breath and temper at Petersburg and Moscow.
The isvostchik pulled up at the Prince's stable-yard, where I
found a Russian understrapper, to whom I pronounced, with
such emphasis as I thought would be most acceptable to the
Slavonic ear, the name of my friend; whereupon he took me
to the head groom, who turned out to be an Englishman.

In Prince B——'s house (which is only a larger and more
costly specimen of the common type of dacha, being a cottage
ornée by the road-side, half smothered in shrubs and hedges)
and also at the palace, I saw a *montagne*—a device for amusing

---

* *Dom*, domus, "house" is always coupled with the name of the owner in
giving addresses. Thus, if one's friend Smith rents his house from Nicholas,
the address would be: "Mr. Smith, at the house of Nicholas." This is quite
Eastern.

children. It consists of an inclined plane of the smoothest wood, down which the children slide, as their parents do down the ice-hills in winter.

Here it may be remarked how much this vast empire depends upon foreigners for all that requires talent and thought. One day I met a young man, an officer attached to the Etat-Major, whose duty it was to read over the despatches from the Caucasus, cut out the fine language, with which they are plentifully stuffed, and present them in a clear, concise form, for the Emperor's perusal; he was a German. The Astronomer Imperial is a German. The chief engineer at the Admiralty is a Scotchman. An English jockey went out in the same ship with us to ride a Russian prince's horse, at the Moscow races. Another passenger was the manager of a cotton fabric (or factory, as we should call it); I came home with the manager of a paper-fabric—both Englishmen. And here, this head-groom, who is an Englishman, guides me to my friend, an Englishman, whom I find giving a lesson to the son and heir of one of the noblest families in Russia.

To the hand-books I refer readers for a description of the palaces, only remarking by the way that in them the skill in making floors, for which the Russians are pre-eminent, is carried to its highest pitch. Elegant in design and beautiful in execution are these specimens. The art of in-laying is thoroughly mastered in this country. The Russian carpenter is famous for the precision with which he uses the common axe in cutting wood to whatever pattern he pleases; and the floors he produces are fine examples of Tunbridge ware, on a large scale. The Imperials are fond of out-of-the-way things, be they in or out of taste. The room, the walls of which are entirely covered with amber, looks far more strange than beautiful. The necessarily small pieces in which the amber is laid on, and the consequent want of uniformity in shade, give a queer, patched-up appearance to the walls. Far more pleasing and quite as curious is the floor, which is of ebony, inlaid with mother-o'-pearl.

Before leaving St. Petersburg, I must remark that the famous street, the Nevskoï Prospekt (or Perspektiff, as it is sometimes called) rather fell short of the notion I had formed of it from pictures and descriptions. In the first place, it loses much of the fine effect it would have if it were the centre one of the three streets which start from the Admiralty-Plain. In that case, a person walking up the street would have before him a full view of the mid-section of the Admiralty, surmounted by its beautiful gilded spire. As it is, he only catches a side-view of it. Then, again, the street is narrower from the Admiralty to the Moika Bridge than in the remainder of its length. Considering that St. Petersburg has been built, from the first, on a grand uniform plan; considering, too, that imperial will rules all private enterprises; it is astonishing that the finest street should be allowed to fall short of perfection by two such simple defects, as being placed in an inferior position, and having its grand perspective marred by unequal breadth.

The Nevskoï, though four versts (or three miles) long, is only carried about two-thirds of that distance in a right line; and it is only so far that fine shops and grand façades extend, even if they do so far, for some falling off is noticeable after one passess the Gostinoi Dvor. And when I speak of fine shops, I do not mean that they present immense fronts of plate-glass. The fact is, the windows are necessarily small, in order to leave enough wall-space, upon which pictures of the articles sold inside are painted for the information of the unlettered. The rest of the street is continued on at a slight angle to the former portion, till it reaches the monastery of S. Alexander Nevskoï. The moment you turn this angle you notice a tremendous come-down, from the grand and showy to the mean and shabby. No longer does the wood pavement afford a quiet, smooth passage to your droshky. Great holes, filled with dust, shake you from side to side, and send up a stifling, blinding cloud. Tumble-down houses, seedy cabarets, great blank spaces strewn with old, done-for droshkies and other used-up articles, show that even to the fine St. Petersburg there is a fag end. A visit to the new monastery of S. Alexander took us into this region. It was founded in 1724. The saint is surnamed " *Nevskoï,*" or, "of the Neva," from the victory in which he repulsed the Swedes on the banks of that river.* It ranks third among the Russian monasteries; that at Kieff and the Troitza taking precedence.

There was nothing going forward to call for remark. Though in appearance it is inexpressibly ugly, being simply a large collection of plain white-washed buildings, we found the quiet within its moated and high-walled inclosure, and the cool shade of its formally-set rows of trees, very refreshing after our dusty ride. We bought little pictures of the saint painted on bits of china. He is represented clothed in armour, with a red cloak on his shoulders, and his right hand pressed to his left side. One sees in this the intensely martial spirit of the Russian Church. He is not the only warrior enrolled in the calendar of saints. The churches, too, are filled with trophies, fortress-keys, marshals' batons, soldiers' coats, military standards. Soldiers, too, are the attendants in the churches—veterans, abundantly decorated with medals and stars. The keys of Adrianople hang over the massive silver shrine of S. Alexander.

At the bend in the Nevskoï, noticed above, stands the terminus of the Moscow railway. Here we will take leave of St. Petersburg and take tickets for Moscow. Very lofty and spacious are all railway stations in Russia; very handsome, too, in point of architecture. That at Peterhoff is one of the finest buildings in the place. The tickets are long slips of paper, bearing a list of all the stations on the line, with the times at which the train is due at them. Two trains each way (which direction is "up" and which "down," it would be difficult to say in travelling between two such cities as Petersburg and Moscow) in the 24 hours comprise all the traffic. One, the express so called, starts at 12 noon, and does the

---

* See Stanley's " Eastern Church."

journey of 400 miles in 20 hours.  The other, a luggage-train, with passenger-carriages attached, starts at 2 p.m. and performs the distance in 30 hours.  The carriages are of enormous length, carrying 60 or 80 passengers in each.  They are made on the American model.  A passage runs down the middle between the two entrances, which open at each end on a railed-in platform.  The seats hold two persons each, and are arranged like the boxes in a chop-house.  The road is straight enough to bear out the story commonly told, that the Emperor Nicholas decided upon the course the railway should take by ruling a line on the map between the two points, St. Petersburg and Moscow.  The consequence is that in the whole distance of 400 miles the road does not touch a single town except Tver, and Tver stands above a mile from the station of that name.  There are not many important places, it is true, through which it could have passed.  But the city of Novgorod might easily have been included in the route, and before St. Petersburg was built this was the capital of that part of Russia, and through it the old Moscow road used to run.

Anything so wearisome as the journey between St. Petersburg and Moscow I never experienced.  The heat was insufferable.  One could not lay one's hand upon the iron pillars of the station for two seconds.  Yet the Russians seem to think nothing of it.  Most of them wear great coats hanging loosely from their shoulders.  They stand in the scorching sun (though shade may be but a step from them) smoking their paparosses (cigarettes) with perfect *sang-froid*, if *sang-froid* there can be with the temperature at 81 Fahrenheit in the shade.  And those blue-coated, brass-helmeted, booted and spurred *gens-d'armes*, with their long swords, who (two of them) stand on the platform at every station and keep guard over the train, from its arrival to its departure—how they can endure, as they do, the sun's rays pouring down upon their helmets, passes understanding.  Then, again, the monotony of the country is tiresome.  For three-fourths of the distance the road runs through a wood, consisting of the only trees that seem to have any chance of life in this part of

Russia—birch and pine. They do not attain to any great size, and do not grow very near the railway; for, in order to supply fuel for the engines, a considerable space on each side is cleared, and stacks of felled timber stand ready for use at frequent intervals. In consequence of wood being used in the locomotives, the chimneys are of an inverted conical form, looking ugly and top-heavy. This kind of fuel also necessitates more frequent " coaling," as the bulk is so great and the consumption so quick.

The extent to which timber is used in Russia is enormous. During the summer the Neva and adjacent canals in Petersburg are crowded with huge barges filled with wood, cut in convenient lengths for fuel. These barges, built for the special purpose of floating the timber down, are themselves broken up and sold for fire-wood. The laying in of fuel for the winter is a good part of the summer's business. Along the quays this sort of work is continually going on, and the *gamins* of the place, who no doubt think that stolen wood burns brightest, are on the look out for plunder. One young rascal, apparently about six years old, I saw scampering from the quay as fast as he could with a log of wood in his arms as big as himself. A man was in full chase after him, yelling out Russian oaths and threats. The little thief, when he found his pursuer gaining on him, let the log drop and then got clear off. The price of fuel, I was told, had risen considerably this year. Likely enough: for as the forests get cleared, the distance whence it has to be brought increases, and therefore the cost. Moreover peasants' houses are all built of logs of wood, so in this direction there is a large out-going of timber. Villages of these barn-like cottages are the only signs of habitation one sees along the railway. They stand with the gable-end to the street. No chimneys diversify the uniform ridge-and-furrow appearance of rows of these huts; and one dingy-brown colour of roofs and walls makes a Russian village far from picturesque. The only thing that imparts variety to the scene is the church, which is always white-washed, and generally has a green dome or two.

Along the whole line of rail very little agriculture is to be seen, and that little a long way behind the farming of the Lothians. The labourers (mostly women) whom we caught sight of here and there, with wooden spades, and straight-handled scythes, looked like those pictures of "peasantry in the eleventh century," which we know so well in the school histories of England. Nevertheless, agricultural machinery is being largely imported into Russia. The ship I went out in was entirely laden with it. The fact is, the land-owners (and hitherto serf-owners) are casting about how they may render themselves independent of manual labour, now that the emancipation has set the serf free from compulsory work.

Although, as has been said, the country along the Moscow line is painfully ugly and monotonous, yet there are one or two exceptional spots. When the rail-road crosses a river, a pleasant and, by contrast, highly picturesque view opens out: *e.g.* the river Volokhof; and again the Volga at Tver, which gives good promise of the majestic breadth it attains at Nijni-Novgorod. The railway stations, with their pretty gardens, do their best to enliven the dull sameness of the journey. At every stoppage time enough is given for smoking one papaross at least, and ladies blow their little cloud with the rest. Smoking is not allowed in the carriages; sometimes the guard will, for a consideration, let a man smoke outside the carriage, on the gallery at the end; but not always. One passenger, an Englishman, who had come to Russia with a fixed belief that every official in the empire was on sale; that, in fact, there was a bribe-tariff, pushed a handful of cigars into the readily opened palm of the guard, and proceeded to smoke his weed, having, as he thought, duly purchased licence to do so. But no, the guard failed to connect the two ideas, and turned the Englishman into the carriage with a virtuous frown. Apropos of smoking, I may observe that it is not lawful to smoke on foot in the streets of Petersburg or Moscow. Riding or driving, on balconies or on steam-boats, it is allowed. This regulation is to prevent fires. It really promotes them; for the common people are driven to smoke in hay-lofts and other places, where a spark soon kindles a conflagration. At many stations very substantial refreshment is provided, and everywhere tea is to be had. In some cases the stations have something of the bazaar about them. Elegant trifles in silver, gold, and other materials are exposed for sale. At a station called Valdaïskaïa, bells, cast in all sorts of shapes of fruit, flowers, &c. are sold as knives are at Châtelrault.*  Nor are the claims of religion forgotten. At the doors of the refreshment rooms poor men are generally to be seen standing, holding plates to receive the alms of the faithful, for the sake of a neighbouring church or other pious use : and these plates are well filled by the devout travellers.

The most tedious journey comes to an end, and that to Moscow with the rest. Right glad were we to awake from a short snatch of unrefreshing sleep to find ourselves within an hour of the Holy City. At 8 A.M. we arrived, punctual to a moment. If the journey has been monotonous, the change of scene which it has brought about is the most complete. It may be described in two words—we have passed from the Western to the Eastern world. As we drive away from the terminus to M. E. Billo's Hotel, we feel that we are in totally different circumstances. We go down a hill, a thing which we could not do at St. Petersburg, because there are no hills to go down : we ascend another, an equally novel feat for the same reason. We see abundance of trees surrounding the houses, making Moscow look like a city in a garden. This is new, and the trees themselves are other than pine and birch, and therefore new. At St. Petersburg we had grown so accustomed to looking up at the lofty houses which line its streets, that now, when we see modest dwellings going no higher than one story above the basement, we seem literally to look down upon them. But the drive to Billo's does not show one all Moscow. Indeed, here is another point of contrast to St. Petersburg. You cannot pass through any quarter of

* They come from a famous foundry at Valdaï, a town near at hand, which takes its name from the adjacent hills. The general use of bells on the harness, in the sledging season, creates a large demand.

that city without gaining a notion of the general aspect of the whole. But, after our drive from the railway, we took another considerable drive about Moscow without having the least suspicion that there were a Chinese City and a Kremlin, and that churches were very numerous. This is in consequence of the extreme irregularity and absence of plan. The houses seem to have fallen from the clouds, and to have remained where they fell, and the streets to have been cut in and out amongst them, as best could be managed without disturbing them. Hence no thorough view is to be had. There is always some bend in a street that shuts out what is behind it. A first walk in Moscow, under proper guidance, is a wonderful series of surprises; you foresee nothing; you stumble upon new sights at every turn, and when you least expect them. Pass under that ancient gateway, and you find yourself in a narrow street, the appearance of which so strongly reminds you of Eastern towns that you look for turbans and flowing dresses, and bright-coloured garments, as matters of course. You have left the broad-ways and plentiful shrubs of the White City, and are in the closely-packed and most ancient Chinese City. The fires of 1812 left this quarter untouched. Walk on, and you come to a wide space—the Red Place, so called from the blood of Russians and Tartars which dyed it in those fierce, but obscure struggles, when Russia was only thought of by Europe as barbarous Muscovy. Before you is the Kremlin. To your left stands the " Church of the protection of Mary," otherwise called " S. Basil's," *—the most fantastic of the many fantastic examples of Russian church architecture. It has been elaborately described by travellers. Suffice it to say that if a man had time to look at only one church in Russia, and wished that one to embody the grotesquenesses of all the rest, S. Basil's is the church he ought to choose. Suppose twenty builders met together to erect a congeries of churches, side by side, one on another, without

---

* The name of the church in Russ is, " *Tserkov sv. Vassiliaia blazhennavo,*" ":the church of S. Basil the blessed." Basil, Vassili, William, are all the same name.

purpose, save to emulate each other in producing the greatest extravagance; and then suppose twenty painters and gilders assembled to colour the outsides of these churches, with the sole aim of laying on the greatest variety of colours in the most striking contrasts, then, as the result of these efforts, you may form a faint notion of the cathedral of S. Basil, the folly of Ivan the Terrible.

We cross the Red Place and pass through the Holy Gate. We uncover and remain bare-headed so long as we are under the sacred arch, having been warned of the custom, from observance of which no man is ever excused. A person stands by for the purpose of enforcing obedience. Indeed, the idea is extended beyond merely doffing one's hat or cap. One day I was about to pass through, having removed my hat, when I was stopped by the guard, who pointed to my umbrella, which I held down by my side open. He insisted upon my closing it. And now we are on the broad platform of the Kremlin.

Claudian, in his panegyric on the Sixth Consulship of Honorius, alluding to the view of Rome from the Palatine, speaks of

————" densum stipantibus æthera templis."

Lord Macaulay, in his essay on Madame d'Arblay, pointing to Oxford, imagines the delight with which Miss Burney would have "looked down from the dome of the Radcliffe Library on the magnificent sea of turrets and battlements below." If these expressions appear to be somewhat forced and unreal, look forth from the Kremlin over the city of Moscow, and you will then understand what is meant by the sky being crammed with churches, and by looking down on a sea of minarets and domes. The standing-place whence this wondrous sight is had, ought to be observed. You are on a spacious terrace, bounded by a low parapet. The sides slope precipitately to the massive wall which surrounds the Kremlin, and makes it what it is, a most remarkable Eastern fortress. This wall is topped with the leaf-like machicolations, distinctively oriental; and at the angles, and at intervals in its circuit, rise large square and round towers, surmounted by spires, coloured green, on the tops of which the ubiquitous Russian eagle spreads its gilded wings. The wall, on the side towards which we are looking, is skirted by the river Moskva, now sunk low down in its deep channel, and scarcely covering the whole of its bed, though in the winter it rises to overflowing the quays. And now, behold what lies spread out beyond the river. Numberless gilded crosses glitter in the sun. Every conceivable effect is produced by green, blue, red, gold, and silver; striped, starred, scaley, wavey, spiral, and dentated domes; domes bell-shaped and bulb-shaped; minarets, conical roofs, and spires. From what I had read of Moscow, I had prepared myself for a wonderful sight; but the reality far surpassed the expectation. The number of churches in Moscow is variously estimated. Some say 500, some 1,500. Whatever the exact figure may be it matters little: the general result is passing strange to an European eye. A notion of the multitude of domes and minarets, spires, towers, and belfries, may be formed when it is said that each church has generally five, one in the middle and one at each corner; besides, very often, others surmounting out-buildings, or stuck in here and there in addition to the regular complement.

A less marvellous sight, but more truly grateful to the eye, is that seen from the Sparrow Hills. We took an early opportunity of going thither. A pretty long drive carries us beyond the houses, though not beyond the boundaries of the city, for it is only at certain points that the buildings have stretched out far enough from the old centre to touch the line of fortification which describes the wide area of Moscow proper. A short distance after we have passed this line, a rough road, or rather track in the sand, brings us to the river side at a place where there is a ferry. Near the ferry are small wooden sheds, set up a little way out in the stream, and reached by planks. These are bathing places. From under them now and then appears a bather. There is no people that uses the bath more systematically than the Russians. It is a sort of religious

duty with them. No peasant will go to church on great
festivals, few on Sundays and other holy days, without having
previously taken the bath. And yet they do not impress one
as being a clean people.

The *perevostchik* (or "ferry-man") paddles us over the
*perevoss* (or "ferry"). This Russian word is easily remembered
by Englishmen, as it is pronounced almost exactly like the
very appropriate words "pair-of-oars." As soon as we land
we begin to ascend the Sparrow Hills, the steep slope of which
starts almost from the water's edge. They are not very high,
though they appeared so to us, who had seen nothing higher
than the gently rising ground at Peterhoff. A narrow footpath soon brings us up to the top. This reached, we turn
round and find that a noble view lies before us. We are on
the right bank of the Moskva, whence Moscow takes its name.
The course of the river is remarkably tortuous. Looking to
the north-west, we first catch sight of it flowing towards
the western side of the city, hardly touching it, and then
abruptly sweeping round till it returns upon the Sparrow
Hills, which bend its course once more, and send it back
again to the city, which it penetrates till it reaches the walls
of the Kremlin, at whose base it flows, and then once more
comes round upon its own course. We thus seem to stand
at the bend of a fetterlock, which grasps the city firmly in
the middle. On this side, the hills, the sides of which are
well wooded, run steeply down to the water. From the other
bank the ground stretches away with very slight undulations,
just enough to make the city, which is built upon it, rather
hilly.

The view hence of Moscow, as we find it, is very grand.
The houses, the walls of which are for the most part white, are
lit up brilliantly by the gorgeous sun. The many-coloured roofs
give richness and tone to the picture, and the infinite domes
spangle it with silver and gold. From the middle rises the
fortress of the Kremlin, its many churches sending up a
forest of dome-capped towers, among which stands highest
the lofty Ivan Veliki. In the south-west quarter of the city,

a white building, larger much than any other to be seen, and crowned with an enormous dome, catches the eye, as being something quite in advance of all the rest. It is the new cathedral, not yet completed. In the environs of the city stand the many monasteries and convents, each with its cluster of domes and minarets, like so many religious outworks to cover and defend the special sanctity of Moscow the holy.

We have been standing with our backs to the small village of Vorobief (the word means "sparrow"), which crowns the hill. Its little church rests on the brow, and from a seat, which overhangs the edge, we took our most easy and leisurely view of the prospect. The great heat and exertion of climbing the hill made us thirsty, and we were glad to learn from our guide that milk could be had at a cottage hard by. This gave us an opportunity of seeing the inside of a Russian peasant's dwelling. It was an average specimen, built of logs piled up, the interstices being filled in with tow. We found the inside bare enough. The best room had no furniture at all, unless sacred pictures be considered furniture; and, by a Russian, they would be· thought to be the most indispensable furniture. There were six hanging close together, in two rows of three, with little lamps suspended before them, one of which was burning. The subjects were the usual ones—the Saviour, the Virgin, and other saints. One was a group-picture, examples of which are often seen in the churches. In these, whole companies of apostles, and armies of martyrs, are marshalled in line, much after the manner of the prints, known as "Skilt's Characters," which children buy for their toy theatres. In an inner room, which seemed to be the "living-room" of the family, all the chattels, few and shabby, were collected. It was not a model cottage; but it would rank very respectably among English peasant dwellings for cleanliness and comfort. Doubtless, in the winter, when the *paich* sends forth its great heat, and the house is crowded, and kept tightly closed, the atmosphere is far from pleasant; but we found nothing to offend us. The milk, which was delightfully cool, was brought to us by a plain, healthy-looking girl, dressed tidily enough. It was poured from an earthen vessel, narrowed off to a very small base, so as scarcely to allow of its standing upright.

On our return we stopped at the convent, of Novo-devitcheï, whose minarets and domes especially strike the eye, as they stand in the foreground of the view from the Sparrow Hills. Its battlemented and loopholed walls, garnished with massive towers, and its moat crossed by a drawbridge, give it the appearance of a fortress. Time was when monasteries and convents had to do duty as refuges from the violence of men, as well as from the less palpable assaults of Satan. We went into the principal chapel and were almost driven out again by the horrible smell—that universal Russian smell, passing description, which haunts one, more or less, everywhere. Often is the traveller in Russia provoked to exclaim of her people, "Noses have they, and smell not!" Several nuns were performing their devotions. The conventual dress is a very disfiguring costume indeed—black gowns with tight sleeves, and on the head a black conical cap, with flaps falling over the ears, and tied under the chin. One contrasts these little black figures, bowing, and crossing, and prostrating before the pictures, with their sisters of the Roman Communion (*e.g.* at the *Beguinage* at Ghent), who, with their ample veils of spotless white mantling them completely as they kneel in prayer, look the very ideal of what a *religieuse* ought to be. On the other hand, the monks of the Greek Church, with their flowing robes, high caps and falls, and long hair and beards, have the advantage, in appearance, over their tonsured serge-clad brethren of the West.

The Kremlin, so rich in all that the devout, the loyal, the patriotic Russian holds dear ; to the history of which cling the most cherished associations of the good and ill fortunes of Muscovy ; may well tax the skill of the best hand-book writers to describe. I shall content myself with one or two points that came under my notice. Although, as a mere matter of antiquity, the Kremlin be one of the most precious relics the world has—all the more precious, because hardly saved from the ruin of fire and conquest—yet the Tsars and Tsarinas of Russia seem to have been little careful of preserving its primitive character. As one looks up at it from the opposite side of the river, the Winter Palace, handsome though it be in itself, and, as I submit, far superior in taste to that at St. Petersburg, stands out behind the Tartar battlements, and from among the spired and domed towers, very incongruously. Moreover, the barracks and other anachronistic buildings mar the effect. But if disposed to grumble at what has been done, we need to be thankful for what has been left undone. In the Treasury there is a model of the scheme Catherine II. had in contemplation, of surrounding the whole of this ancient citadel with modern buildings, in a tasteless, semi-classic style.

Of the many churches which stand in the Kremlin, English readers have no need to be ignorant, if they will turn to the graphic pages of Dr. Stanley's *" Lectures on the Eastern Church."* The Cathedral (they are all called cathedrals) of the Assumption I visited once when a grand episcopal office was being celebrated. The building was crowded. I made my way as near to the ikonostast as possible, and while standing before it I felt something pushing against the back of my leg. It was a woman on her knees, trying, as best she could in the press, to touch the ground with her forehead. She showed no impatience at my presence; and this leads me to say that one marked sign of the tolerant spirit of the Greek Church is the freedom with which a stranger may move among the worshippers, without being frowned at, as one often is in the Latin Church, with looks that say " heretic." As I left the cathedral I saw, lying crouching on the ground just outside the door, a very old, white-bearded man ; he was fast asleep ; his staff and his wallet showed him to be a pilgrim. Probably he had walked several hundred miles on a pious journey to Moscow, the bourn of many a devout and longsome pilgrimage. The windows of this, and other old Russian churches, are few and small, and the odd way in which they are stuck in here and there reminds one of what Sir Francis Head says of

those at the Tuileries, that they look as though they had
been knocked out by random cannon-shots. Excessively as
the Greek Church delights in pictures, painted windows have
no place in its decorations. I only noticed one in all the
churches I visited, and that was in S. Izak's, and therefore
quite modern. Colour without taste, costliness without beauty,
prevail everywhere. It is difficult to look with a serious
countenance at the queer faces that meet the eye at every
turn. The walls and pillars are not sufficient to display
these grotesque paintings. Many are exposed for osculation
on desks. The more highly venerated ikons are jewelled
with diamonds, rubies, sapphires, beyond all value ; but what
with bad setting, bad arrangement, and worse cutting, no
light beams from them, and you would not know they were
there, unless you went close up to them. Indeed, bad workmanship has spoilt many a precious stone in Moscow. In
the Treasury are exhibited ancient Tartar crowns, garnished
with gems no otherwise set than by being stuck, like beads,
on bits of wire. The Cathedral of the Annunciation is paved
with agate, carnelian, and jasper. The thought of the wealth
which is thus dedicated to religion may please the devout,
but the effect produced is only that of a dark-looking floor,
made of small irregular pieces, and rather slippery to
walk on.

Of the treasures, in stones and pearls, which the church
possesses, there is no end. The patriarchal sacristy, otherwise
called " The House of the Holy Synod," astonishes one with
its wealth. Perhaps the best notion of its riches may be
given by extracting from the catalogue, of eighty octavo pages,
drawn up by the Archimandrite Sabas, the description of one
of its gorgeous vestments :—

" L'omophore* du Patriarche *Nicon*, en étoffe de soie brochée d'or, richement
" ornée de perles fines, de rubis et d'émeraudes. Dessus, sur quatre croix,
" sont brodées en or et en soie les fêtes et la Passion du Seigneur, et au
" milieu, dans un cercle, l'image de la Sainte Trinité. Autour du cercle sont
" formés de perles fines ces mots : *Par l'ordre du Souverain Alexis Michaï-*

---

'Ωμοφόριον—pall.

"*lovitch, Czar et Grand-Duc de tout la Russie et de l'Orthodoxe Czarina Marie,*
"*cet omophore a été fait pour le très-Saint Patriarche Nicon, et il lui a été offert*
"*en 1655, le 1-er Octobre.*"

We were shown over this treasury by a monk, with the most courteous attention. I had been told that Russ was a beautiful, mellifluous language, but was disposed to doubt the fact, having chiefly heard it spoken by the isvostchiks, who are no smoother-tongued than our own cabmen. But when I heard it from the lips of this monk, I found it to be very soft and musical in its sounds. At the door of one room, that wherein the Synod holds its sittings, and on the table of which a richly-bound copy of the Gospels stood in a frame, was an old soldier as door-keeper. I noticed the eagerness with which he craved the monk's blessing.

While on Church subjects, I may here recount a most interesting episode in my visit to Moscow. I had the good fortune to be invited by a Russian gentleman to attend, in his company, the examination of the students (of whom at present there are about 350), at the Seminary for the education of the sons of priests.* We reached the college between one and two o'clock. On arriving, we saw the coach of the Metropolitan of Moscow, drawn by six black horses, standing in the court-yard. I was glad to learn from this that the venerable patriarch was in the college, and that I should have an opportunity of seeing the man who, as well for his personal character as for his ecclesiastical rank, is held in the highest esteem throughout Russia.

The buildings of the college, which are very plain in style and considerable in extent, form three sides of a square, having extensive abutments in the rear. The examination was going forward in an apartment, one end of which is divided off for use as a chapel by a curtain. As we entered, a priest, who knew my friend, showed us to seats, handing to

* There is a seminary in every government. The seminarial course extends over six years ; then the students pass on to the academies, of which there are four, viz. at Petersburg, Moscow (or rather, at the Troitza Lavra, forty miles distant), at Kieff, and at Kazan. The academical course is four years long, at the end of which period degrees are conferred.

each a manuscript syllabus of the subjects of examination.
A translation of it from the Russ may interest the reader :—

*" Summary of Subjects given out at the Public Examination of the Students in
the Moscow Seminary, at the close of the Collegiate Course,* 1860-1861.

### A.—In the Upper Class.

1. *In Dogmatic Theology.*—Of the Holy Trinity; of the Creation of the
   World ; of God's Providence ; of the Angels.
2. *Readings in Holy Scripture.*—The Book of the Acts of the Apostles;
   the Catholic Epistle of S. James the Apostle.
3. *In Moral Philosophy.*—Of our love to God and our neighbours.
4. *In Church History.*—About the Emperors Constantine, Constantius, and
   Julian ; on the false teaching of Arius ; of the first Œcumenical
   Council.

### B.—In the Middle Class.

1. *Readings in Holy Scripture.*—The Book of Ecclesiastes.
2. *Biblical Church History.*—The Judges of the People of Israel.
3. *Biblical Hermeneutics.*—Of the Mystical Sense.
4. *In Logic.*—On the logical completeness of the respective parts of the
   Science,—Explications, division, and arguments.
5. *Patristic Theology.*—About S. Clement of Rome, and S. Justin the
   Philosopher.
6. *In Russian Civil History.*—On the Mongolian Yoke ; on the Internal
   Condition of Russia up to the Muscovite Period.
7. *In Physics.*—On the Air ; from Natural History ; about Plants, which
   constitute the family of Grasses.

### C.—In the Lower Classes.

1. *Catechetical Lessons.*—On the Sacraments ; on the Lord's Prayer.
2. *In Rhetoric.*—Of the external and internal properties or meaning of
   Language.
3. *In General History.*—Of the history of Sparta and Athens.
4. *In Algebra.*—On Arithmetical and Geometrical Progression.   The examination in languages,—Hebrew, Greek, Latin, German, French,—is
   to be by Translations."

I was not sorry to find that we had come in for the latter
part of the last subject for the day—Rhetoric; and that I
had not long to wait through (to me) an unintelligible proceeding.

The room was very crowded.  Down the middle were set

two rows of chairs facing each other, occupied by ecclesiastics
of various ranks.   There were the archimandrites, or chiefs,
of the monasteries in and around Moscow.   There was an
Egyptian bishop, who had come to Russia to collect the alms
of the faithful for the benefit of his diocese.   There were many
secular priests holding benefices in Moscow, besides some who
filled professorships in the seminary.   At the head of all sat
the aged Patriarch, Philaret, Metropolitan of Moscow, and
Archimandrite of the Troitza Monastery.   Before him stood
a row of students, who were being examined *vivâ voce.*

A photographic portrait of the Metropolitan lies before me
to assist my memory, if that were necessary, in recalling his
appearance.   He is a very handsome man.   His features are
cast in that bold, well-defined mould which age cannot
mar, but only make venerable.   His brow shows intellectual
power, and his deep-set eye still keeps its brightness.   A full,
grey beard conceals his lips and chin, and rests on his breast.
He is under the middle height, slightly made, and bends
beneath the weight of fourscore years.   His dress may claim
a few words, both to complete the picture, and also to give
some idea of the costume worn by the Russian ecclesiastics.
He wore a long, flowing robe of purple silk, with large, hanging sleeves.   The usual cross hung from his neck by a chain,
besides several decorations of honour and distinction, which
were suspended by coloured ribbons.   Around his left wrist
was twisted a rosary.   On his head he wore a high cylindrical
cap, flat at top, with a fall hanging down behind—the mark
of the monks ; in his case the cap and fall are white, to distinguish his rank as metropolitan ; in all others they are black.
On the front of the cap was fixed a plain gold cross.

To a Western, and especially to an English eye, the
whole presented a very imposing sight.   The sombre garb
of the regulars, the becoming robes of the seculars, and the
venerable look imparted to all by the long, ample beards and
flowing hair, combined to form a vivid representation of what
one fancies to have been the aspect of a council of the early
Church.

The examination ended, the Metropolitan rose, all rising with him, and walked towards the curtain, in front of which he stood, and to which all present turned their faces. Bowing lowly and crossing himself, he began to chant a hymn, which was taken up by the rest of the assembly. The deep, rich tones of the priests rose in a volume of harmony such as I have never elsewhere heard. The chant, simple and plaintive as all music of the Greek Church is, swelling from the single note of the Patriarch into the chorus of the whole body of the clergy, and then sinking down to the one voice again, and again rising to its fulness, and all the while bearing on its waves the beautiful sounds of the Slavonic tongue, had a most awe-filling and devotional influence. At the conclusion of the hymn the Metropolitan turned round to the assembly, and gave the benediction, with the sign of the cross. As he passed out, the bystanders pressed forward, with eager reverence, to kiss his hand and receive his blessing. Two priests, as an act of respect, supported him up the stairs to a room where he took some refreshment. This done, he rose, and bowing towards the ikon, took his leave, proceeding slowly through the crowd of persons, who, bowing and touching the ground before him, put themselves in his path again to kiss his hand, and receive his blessing. No words can describe the reverence, one had almost said adoration, which is paid to the Patriarch. As he got into his coach, and was driven away, the bells of the college (which are hung in a low kind of shed or belfry in the quadrangle) clanged forth. I cannot say they rang a peal; for no regular cadence, or any orderly sequence of notes, was heard. But they simply were sounded as noisily and as discordantly as possible; and this may be said of all the bell-ringing I heard in Russia. No system of changes, that I could make out, is observed.

While we were waiting for dinner, the Professor of Logic, hearing, I suppose, that I was an English clergyman, brought me a copy of "Essays and Reviews." It was the eighth edition, uncut and unmutilated, and therefore unread, even by the censor, into whose hands I feel quite certain it had never fallen. I was not a little surprised to have this book, which had been the *bête-noire* of the English mind, lay and clerical, for the last eight months, put into my hands by a Russian priest at Moscow. The learned professor, who was unacquainted with English, inquired about the writers of the Essays, and of the position they held in this country; to which questions I replied through the interpretation of my friend.

We were now summoned to dinner. Between forty and fifty sat down, all of whom first crossed themselves by way of grace. The company consisted of ecclesiastics, with the exception of two or three lay-professors, and my friend. The high caps were now laid aside, and with them all dignity and reserve. Talk, and joke, and laughter, passed round briskly. But a word about the viands. In the first place, they were all of fish, no flesh-meat appearing because of the monks who were present, and who are forbidden so to indulge, except on certain great festivals. In the next place, they were all cold. The order of courses was this : 1. Pressed caviare, with a kind of cake cut in slices. 2. Cold soup, of a greenish colour, made (I believe) of qvass, and having cucumber chopped small into it. With this delightful *potage* slices of cold fish were handed round, to be put into and eaten with it. 3. Fish, another kind, jellied over. 4. Fish, with horse-radish and other garnishings. 5. Broiled fish. Then came the sweetmeats and fruits. Off this repast I cannot say that I dined. I certainly did taste the soup, or I could not speak of it in such condemnatory terms as I feel disposed to use, whenever I call it to mind. I also tasted one or two other dishes ; but it was only tasting. The bread was good, white and black (which latter has a pleasant, sharp flavour about it), and the wine was good ; and to these I confined my attention. The wines, indeed, were numerous and excellent, and their worth seemed to be fully appreciated by my brethren of the Greek rite. A decanter of qvass stood before me wonderfully fermenting. I tried it, but liked it no better than the cold soup. For-

tunately our good company were not given to after-dinner
speeches, and confined their toasts to the healths of the
Metropolitan, and the Rector of the Seminary, which were
given and responded to in champagne, without comment.
The merriment kept pace with the time; though I observed
that the regulars were more grave of countenance, and more
silent, than the seculars.  I was a good deal amused to see
one or two of the secular clerics put up some of the fruit into
their handkerchiefs, and these into their pockets—for the little
ones at home, I suppose.  I "inly smiled," too, when asked
by one of them whether I would drink any more of a luscious
red wine, a glass of which, just tasted, stood by me; and
when, on my declining, he took it and divided it between
himself and another.

After a reasonable time, all rose from the table and
dispersed, many tarrying by the way to give and receive
kisses on both cheeks, with many embraces.  My friend and
I were taken by the Professor of Russian History, a layman,
to his rooms, whither accompanied us the Archimandrite of
the Monastery of S. Daniel.  I was here shown some very
beautiful drawings of Russian churches, taken from ancient
examples in different parts of the country.  When I say the
drawings were beautiful, I mean as drawings, not as representing anything that would attract the student of church
architecture.  For Russian ecclesiology is a very narrow field
of research, in which the chief specimens are more remarkable
for their individual eccentricities than as developments of
any fixed style or period.  The painter has much more to do
with the matter than the architect or the sculptor, as will be
easily understood when it is remembered that all the old
churches are built of brick plastered over, and presenting a
surface for the brush, not for the chisel.  How far the colouring of the exteriors of Russian churches, which are often
daubed over like the outside of a travelling player's van, may
be reducible to a system, I know not.  But wash this colouring off and bare walls only remain.  There are exceptions,
but they prove the rule.

Our host, after a while, entertained us with snatches from Russian songs, accompanying himself on the piano. As a nation the Russians are without a rival for accuracy of musical ear. If one goes into a church at service-time, one is sure to meet with proofs of this. The music of the Greek Church (which is unaccompanied, instruments being un-orthodox)* is of the severest simplicity, and is only rescued from baldness by its finished execution. The choristers are carefully chosen and trained, and consequently the part they have to take in the service is perfectly performed. At the same time it should be remembered, that the congregational idea of worship is quite excluded from the Greek ritual. One never sees a service-book in the hands of the worshippers. They stand in reverent attention to the office that is being celebrated by the clergy and choir, and only indicate their participation in it by frequent crossings and bowings, and occasionally prostrating themselves till their foreheads touch the ground. The services are performed in a language—the Slavonic—which is not "understanded of the people ;" and is set to music, which one would also think to be not "under-standed of the people." Now all this might be expected to have the effect of keeping the people silent ; yet, when standing in the crowd in a Russian church, one often hears a man of the humbler class joining in with the choir. It needs attention to find it out ; for the voice is always so subdued as to be well-nigh drowned by the choristers. But listen, and you discover that not only is he singing, but also singing in harmony, and all by ear ; for probably he could not, if he had a book, read either words or notes. A striking example of the

---

* The principle which penetrates the Greek ritual is, that the whole man, body as well as spirit, ought to be offered to God in worship ; and to delegate any part of the service to an instrument is looked upon as a violation of this principle. It has, however, been violated of late in a new Greek church at Manchester, in a way amusingly characteristic of that mechanical city. A part of the ceremonial is to open the holy gates at certain places in the service, and this is always done by the hands of the priest. But in this church a machine is used for the purpose. Were this innovation introduced into Russia it would drive thousands into schism.

Russians having good ears for music came under my notice
one Sunday that I was visiting a gentleman in the environs
of St. Petersburg.   We were sitting in the garden, when the
sounds of many voices joining in a national air were heard
coming from a distance.   My friend bade me attend.   It was
a party of some dozen peasants, who were marching along
the road to the measure of their  song.   One of them
walked in front, and acted as conductor, keeping time by
waving his hand over his head.   He led off with a bar,
and the rest took it up, each singing his part, and all doing it
well.

After the music, we took a stroll in the college gardens.   I
cannot say much for their beauty, though they are quite as good
as Russian winters and summers will allow them to be.   Here
we met the Professor of Theology, who acknowledged my
introduction with much cordiality.   On being told that I was an
English clergyman, he put his arm through mine, and walked
forward, exclaiming, "*Sacerdotes !*" and then waving his hand to
our two companions (laymen), said with much drollery, " *Odi
profanum vulgus—et arceo !*"   He took us into the college, and
showed us some of the class-rooms and the library, where,
among other books, I saw the first Bible printed in Russia.   He
gave me a copy of the " *Holy Gospel of our Lord Jesus Christ
by Matthew, Mark, Luke, and John, in the Russian dialect.
Second Edition: St. Petersburg*, 1860 ;" put forth by authority.   On the wrapper is printed the cross in the usual Russian
form—that is to say, a short horizontal bar is introduced to
mark the place where the superscription was fixed, and a short,
oblique bar to indicate the support on which the feet rested.
The latter is put askew in conformity with an ancient tradition, which says, that during the agony of the crucifixion our
Saviour, by a convulsive effort, displaced the piece of wood to
which His feet were nailed.   The form of the Cross, like many
other matters equally trivial, is a subject of difference between
the orthodox and the dissenters.   The orthodox allow other
forms besides that here described ; but the dissenters, and of
these especially the " *Staroobriadzi*," or " Old-faith People,"

rigidly adhere to this, the eight-pointed cross, alone; and condemn the use of any other form.

That I might take with me another souvenir of my visit, the Professor gave me a copy of the Slavonic New Testament. The arrangement of the books in this version is peculiar. The Epistles of SS. James, Peter, John, and Jude, immediately follow the Acts, and then come the Epistles of St. Paul in the usual order. Here ended my pleasant visit to the Moscow Seminary, the professors at which have my very best thanks for their kindness and hospitality.

Hot and fatiguing as sight-seeing in Moscow is, one can always take refuge in a tea-room, where the most excellent tea (hardly rough enough, perhaps, for English tastes) is drunk, from morning to night, by the Russians in quantities that would have amazed even Dr. Johnson. These tea-rooms extend above the shops in long suites of apartments for a considerable distance down a street. The tea is served in a small pot, while in a larger one is the hot-water, which the Russians will add, from time to time, till the drink becomes so weak, as to be scarcely distinguishable from water. It is always drunk in tumblers, with slices of lemon instead of milk. One of the most interesting sights to be seen in the streets of Moscow, is the long trains of waggons coming into the city, laden with bales of tea (for it is packed up in a sort of painted canvass), which have travelled thousands of miles over-land from China.

In my strolls about the city, I went into the arcade where the jewellers' shops most abound. Half of them were closed and sealed up, and all approach to that part of the bazaar cut off by a rope across the passage. The tradesmen, I was told, had been detected in selling silver articles with the stamp of assay upon them, although they had little more than half of the due proportion of silver; and the authorities had come down upon them in this summary way. To match this fraud among the silversmiths, I heard of one among the tea-merchants, who had been found out by the Chinese to have paid them in bad money. The store kept by the Armenians is worth going to.  Ornaments in silver from the Caucasus, bracelets, brooches, girdles, are sold here.  The make is massive and rude, and the engraving bold and characteristic. To one girdle, for a lady, was hung a small dagger, the use of which the Armenian expatiated upon with many knowing looks and gestures.

The religion of Russia has pressed itself upon our notice a good deal in these pages; and there yet remain one or two points to be mentioned in connexion with Moscow.  As you ascend the hill towards the Sunday Gate, which leads into the Red Place, you see, no matter at what hour in the day, a crowd of people bowing, crossing, prostrating, in front of a small shed that stands between the two arches.  It is the chapel of the Iberian Mother, the Russian goddess of healing. Before her image the devout are in transports of adoration. With some difficulty I made my way up to the picture, and found it as large, as swarthy, and as plain, as any I had seen in the Kremlin.  A profusion of jewels of all kinds, and many of great size, studded the nimbus and the dress.  A forest of candles was burning before it.  The little chapel was crammed with worshippers, and many, who could approach no nearer, contented themselves with paying their devotions on the steps outside.  In the chapel are sold ribbons, inscribed with prayers for the saint's favour.  Here is one: "By thy holy " Image, O mighty Mother of God! being healed thyself, " cure those who give freely, and come with faith and love " to it.  My helplessness likewise visit with thy holy good- " ness, thou most pure!"

Although one cannot stir in St. Petersburg without seeing proofs of the national religiousness, still, among its handsome modern buildings, and with everything around speaking of the West, and of Europe, this demonstrative piety seems exotic.  At Moscow, however, which is to the Russian as Jerusalem to the Jew, as Mecca to the Mussulman, it looks quite at home.  In St. Petersburg there is something out of place in a man, as he turns out in the morning, bowing towards the four quarters of the compass, which may happen to be bounded by a railway-station, a steam-boat office, an hotel, or a barrack. In Moscow, however, where he, probably, can only turn from one holy church or picture to another equally holy or more holy still, all this is consistent.

But I must not keep the reader any longer in Moscow, though there be enough to detain him for many pages, or many days. The twenty-hours' journey back to St. Petersburg I looked forward to with much more dread than to the voyage home, which turned out, though far less uncomfortable, far more perilous. Our weather had been charming, saving the heat, which was perfectly tropical. But on the day of our leaving Russia, the rain came down in a style quite cheering to the spirits of a home-sick Englishman, from its likeness to the weather of his native land. We steamed down to Kronstadt in the " General Admiral." As we passed, we saw a fire raging in Oraniembaum. I wonder whether the good folks were trying to put it out by showing it the faces of their "ikons;" much more quenching, as the devout think, than water. I was told of a priest, whose mind was more common-sense than pious, having incurred a good deal of censure from his flock, because he advised them to fetch buckets of water, instead of standing round the burning houses with the useless pictures in their hands.

We leave Kronstadt for Hull in clouds and rain, and come in for heavy gales, which drive us miles out of our course, and head-winds which reduce our speed to four knots an hour. We reach Copenhagen two days late, and are glad to put in for twenty hours to let the weather blow itself out. While there we hear that a Hull steamer is missing, and when we reach England, we learn that the " Z. C. Pearson " has gone down, and that all on board have perished.

Vacation Tourists 1861
NORTH
The Country of Schamyl

CASPIAN SEA
Sulak R.
Terek R.
VLADIKAFKAZ
Andah Kin Suo R.
Batlaigh
Kin Suo R.
Chirkatt
Ghimb
Chirgher M.
Cal
Tando
Ko Suo R.
Gunib
DAGHESTAN
TCHETSCHNA
Telaw
Alazan R.
TIFLIS
Segnach
Bes Dagh
GEORGIA
R. Koor
L. GOKTSCHAI
Delidschan
Nucha
ERIVAN
Etschmiadzin

A Regiment Apscheronski under Colonel Baryatinski. — B Regiment Samour. — C 1st Regiment Fusiliers — D Daghestan Station under
General Tulhanoff. E Aoul. — F Schamyl's last wall and position it has two cannon at the mouth of Gnib
G Russian Works and Buildings. H Small Birch wood and Baryatinski's stone where he met Schamyl. T Line
of steep rocks. K Attack of Regiment Chamanski under General Komarovski.

Macmillan & Co. Cambridge & London

## 2. *THE COUNTRY OF SCHAMYL.*

BY WILLIAM MARSHALL, ESQ. F.R.G.S.

I HAD been travelling in Armenia and Koordistan, and had come up from Van under Ararat, and by the Lake Goktschai to Tiflis. The journey had been long and fatiguing, and the alternations of heat and cold in the valleys and highlands of Armenia particularly trying; but, on the whole, I felt repaid.

To the general circle of one's acquaintance, who can see no charm or advantage in travelling in any country where hotels and table-d'hôtes are wanting, it is better, when they ask your motive for going to a country where these and most other creature-comforts are scarce, to give an evasive answer; —say, that you mean to shoot there, or you understand that the kabobs are good, or you are in search of the remains of the Ark; anything positive and definite will do, but don't try to explain, don't dare to mention the charm you may find in the contemplation of nature, in her freshest and wildest forms, in difficulties met and overcome, in days spent in the saddle and nights watched by the stars, in strange voices hailing you and strange faces peering into your's, the change at every hour, and the novelty at every step; don't attempt this, save to an old friend or a young lady—the first will understand *you*, and ladies are the most enthusiastic travellers it has ever been my luck to meet.

To an old travelling companion I explained, that, from what I could gather upon the subject, I expected to find in Armenia the picturesque people and gorgeous costumes which we had seen together in the East, transplanted to a country which, in beauty and grandeur, might vie with Switzerland.

But how different places turn out from what one has been
led to expect, or permitted one's self to imagine! The mountains are, for the most part, round-topped, without peak or
crag, and the valleys wide and treeless; the towns generally
deficient in colour and character; and the people not only
inferior in costume, but utterly wanting in that dignified,
imposing demeanour which characterises the veritable Eastern.
Still, though it was not what I had expected, it was all very
new and strange: I travelled without any companion, except
my servant and the muleteers, and so was necessarily thrown
a good deal into the society of the people; and I had a
kindly feeling for a country where I had received open-
handed hospitality, alike in the palace of the Turkish Pasha
and the tent of the Koordish chief.

Coming up from the south, the Russian frontier is passed a
few hours before Igdyr, a pretty little village, surrounded by
vineyards and fruit-trees, and lying in that wide rich plain of
the Aras (Araxes) into which the Aghri-dagh, "the difficult
mountain," has poured his black streams of lava. Cossack
out-posts are pushed half a day further south; but here is the
custom-house, and here the examination of passports takes
place. The officials were glad to see a stranger; and I
was rejoiced to be again among Europeans; for though travelling alone gives ample time for reflection, it is apt to become
monotonous. The Convent of Etschmiadzin is situated at the
north end of this plain. I stayed a day there with the
Catholicos of the Armenian Church, whose residence it is;
but I will not enter into a description of this interesting
place, with its church of the third and its illuminated manuscripts of the fifth century, for I wish to pass on, as quickly
as possible, to the real object of this paper, and am merely
sketching this part of my journey to account for my being at
Tiflis, in order not to have the air of having dropped there
from the clouds.

At the large and increasing town of Erivan, which lies a
short way up the hills which bound the plain of the Aras to
the north, the Russian post begins; but I was warned that

the horses were at that moment a good deal employed by the Government (and anyone who has travelled in Russia knows what a nuisance it is to be kept a whole day or more in a miserable *stanitza* waiting for horses); so the only change I made in my mode of travelling was to put my baggage and servant into a covered waggon, instead of hiring pack-horses; and, retaining two riding-horses, which I had bought at Erzerúm, I started for Tiflis from Erivan, on the 26th of June. Villages of Russian colonists became more and more common along the road, and at the north-west end of the Lake Goktschai there is a large settlement, engaged in curing a large species of trout, which are caught in great numbers in the lake and are excellent eating.

From Erivan thus far the road passes over an elevated plateau, treeless and uninteresting; but after crossing the volcanic amphitheatre of hills which surround the lake (itself 5,000 feet above the sea), it descends through a ravine, into the soft, wooded, and most lovely valley of Delishan, by which I left, on the fourth day from Erivan, and on the last day of June, the highlands of Armenia for the sultry plains of Georgia. What a change, from green grass and young crops, to a baked soil and corn already being cut; from the fresh breeze of the mountains, to the burning breath which scorched me now!

For some time next day, I rode through a burnt-up uncultivated tract, by two villages now deserted; the upright stones in the graveyards seeming to be the only crop the pestilential air of the fever-blasted plain could nourish; but crossing over an irregular brick bridge, which tradition says was built by an Englishman seven hundred years ago, the road again traversed wide fields of yellow corn.

The horses drawing the waggon, though brisk enough before, could now only creep along, on account of the intense heat. I rode slowly, letting my horse graze and drink from time to time; but when we halted, in the afternoon, I found the other horse, which was merely fastened by his halter behind the waggon, and carrying no one, drenched with cold

sweat and altogether in a bad way. I bathed him, pulled his
ears, did all I could for him; but he could not look up; so
I threw him the end of his halter, and he lay down and died
almost directly. It was a regular case of sunstroke. The
one I had ridden was fresh and lively after he had been
groomed and fed; so I gave him four hours' rest, then
mounted him again, and rode all night, till, at daybreak, I
found myself on the banks of the Koor, and in sight of the
outskirts of Tiflis. It was too early to find any one up in the
town, so I lay down and slept for an hour or two before
entering the capital town of Georgia.

Entering Tiflis from this direction, it is necessary to pass
through the narrow dirty streets of the Asiatic quarter,
bazaars of arms, furs, slippers, &c., where the artizans carry
on their trades in small shops open to the street. The
Russian quarter lies higher, and has wide straight streets,
large houses, a pretty theatre, and a well-managed club, where
strangers are admitted simply on the nomination of a member:
it is altogether European. The shops are good, but everything
is dear; the hotels afford very poor accommodation. Bare,
sun-burnt, brick-coloured hills rise close behind the town,
retaining the heat of the sun, and emitting it again after he
has set. In these the hot sulphur springs, which were,
doubtless, the cause of the town being built in this unhealthy situation, take their rise and run down to the bath-
houses in the lower town. The temperature of the water is
so high as to require passing through two or three gradations
before it is even fit for the hottest bath. In the shallow
watercourse, which runs outside the baths and along the
public street, I have seen women bathing in a state of almost
perfect nudity, and without exciting much attention from the
passers by. I should be glad to be able to cite this as a
proof of primitive simplicity of manners; but, in truth, I
cannot ascribe to them any such quality—quite the reverse.

The general aspect of the town is singular; the houses rising
in terraces on both sides of the Koor, which flows through the
town in a broad turbid stream: the views from the bridges

are very striking. The polygonal towers of the churches, of which there are very many, the wooden balconies which shade the houses, the mixed population of Russians, Georgians, Tartars, and Persians, with their varieties of costume, give a character to Tiflis quite peculiar to itself. As a residence, it must be disagreeable: the climate is unhealthy, and fever is general; all the springs are impregnated with one foul flavour or another, and the muddy waters of the Koor are far from pleasant drinking; the dust in dry weather is a perfect plague, and penetrates everywhere—closed windows are no protection; and after rain the streets and squares of the Russian quarter are a perfect quagmire; the lower town is paved roughly. In summer it is dull enough, as every one who can, gets away to the baths at Pätigorsk or elsewhere; but in winter I am assured that there is plenty of amusement, an opera, balls, parties, and flirtation to any amount.

At this time I could only stay three days at Tiflis, for Baron Finot, the kind and accomplished French Consul, invited me to accompany him on an expedition to Elbruz. The Governor of Zugdidi, in Mingrelia, a province south of the Caucasus on the Black Sea, was waiting for him, with two hundred horsemen as escort, and it was an opportunity not to be lost. I had time, however, in the interval before the day fixed for starting with him, to see the great pass of Dariel, that stupendous cleft which divides the Caucasus in half, to its very foundations. The post-road connecting Tiflis with Moscow runs through this, passing close under the Kasbek, second in height only to Elbruz of all the mountains of the Caucasus, and follows the course of the Terek through the wildest scenery to Vladikankaz, a little way beyond the north mouth of the gorge.

I made this journey rather hastily by the post: to do justice to its beauty, it should be done on horseback. Subsequently I repented the haste with which I had passed by places, which might form head-quarters for most interesting excursions, when on my return, after six days' absence, I found that Baron Finot was detained at Nukha, (a town halfway between Tiflis and the Caspian) to look after the interests and lives of a number of Frenchmen, both of which were at that moment in rather a precarious condition.

A disease having attacked the silk-worms in France, as in other places, for the last two or three years, it has been the custom for a number of Frenchmen, who are engaged in the silk trade, to join company and travel to Nukha to buy the " graine," as the eggs are called. This year, these men, about a score in number, happened to come out in the same vessel as myself from Constantinople to Trebizond, and seemed decent well-conducted people. The native population, however, considered that they interfered with their trade ; and the French, it is said, gave offence by their conduct towards the women, a liberty which a Mahometan people will not allow. The end of the matter was that two mollahs were imported from Constantinople, who preached against the French in the mosques, and excited the people to that degree, that a number rushed out with the determination of destroying the offenders. There were four Frenchmen in the first house which they attacked : one escaped, the others defended themselves with resolution ; and though two were killed, and the third desperately wounded, an alarm was raised and the affair put an end to.

I waited some time, hoping Baron Finot would soon return, and that I should not lose my visit to Elbruz ; but I found there was no chance of it,* so I prepared to put in execution a plan, which I had long formed, of crossing Daghestan to Ghunib. There, it had always appeared to me, lay the crowning point of interest in the Caucasus, being the country which Schamyl so long successfully defended, and the natural fortress where he was at length taken prisoner. When, after ten more days at Tiflis, I was on the point of starting for my journey, I was rather embarrassed by my

---

* I regretted not having made this projected journey, when I afterwards passed by the mountains in that region of the Caucasus. They are rocky, serrated, and run into peaks, and are altogether of a more picturesque form than those in Daghestan ; they also rise to a much greater elevation.

servant declaring himself too ill to go. It was evidently the case, and I was at my wits' end to find another, when my friend, Mr. Rice, an Englishman, in whom a long residence in Russia has not destroyed a strong predilection for his country-men (a feeling which it is often the fashion for foreign residents to disclaim), came to my assistance, and lent me a servant. Speaking Russian, Georgian, and a little French, this man was of great service to me.

On Monday, the 22d of July, I started by the Russian post, along a fair road for Segnach. I was fortunate in finding horses at every station, and travelling rapidly, I arrived in about fourteen hours, including stoppages. The scenery thus far was tame, the road passing over the burnt-up undulating plain of the Jora river, divided by a low range of hills from the charming valley of the Alazan. Segnach lies along the top of this range, and commands a splendid view of the great chain of the Caucasus. It was too dark to see this overnight, but next morning it burst upon me in all its glory. I had not hitherto seen any view of the Caucasus which I could call comprehensive; for at Tiflis, and on the road to Vladikaukaz, inferior chains of hills and long spurs interfered, but here no obstacle intervenes, and the eye may range for many miles, both up and down the broad and fertile valley below, survey-ing the mountains from their very bases to their summits.

Early next morning I drove down into this valley of the Alazan, and still travelling by the post, kept just under the soft well-wooded hills, which hem it in on the south, to Telaw, where I arrived in good time. The Judge of this district, to whom I brought a letter of introduction, gave me a hearty welcome, and I stayed with him two days, while I made my plans for crossing the mountains. The Governor, however, hearing of my arrival in the town, sent me an invitation; he proved not only an agreeable acquaintance, but a most useful friend. He told me he was aware I had been trying to hire horses for my journey, but that was not the way to travel; I ought to ride Government horses and take a proper escort. Of course I had not the smallest objection, but I at once expressed my extreme surprise at the proposal, telling him how men in England, supposed to have the best information, had, with one accord, warned me that my chief obstacle to travelling in the Caucasus would be the jealousy of the Russian officials. How unfounded was this belief, will sufficiently appear in my account of this one expedition.

On the 25th of July, I left Telaw in a tröicka (a small cart without springs, drawn by three horses abreast), and crossed the valley of the Alazan, now through yellow corn-fields and vineyards, producing the famous Kakhetian wine; now by snug villages, nestling among walnut-trees,* knotted with age, and casting a most welcome shade; then through thickets of tall shrubs and low trees, so lovingly bound together by wild vines and flowering creepers, as to be impenetrable but by the axe; while in front lay the mysterious Caucasus. Its thickly wooded, lower slopes, were backed by successive ridges without rock or peak, but grassy to their summits, and towering like dark walls above the plain.

Some three hours of tolerably rapid driving, brought me across the valley to the village of Sabooi, scattered pleasantly about, between two spurs of the mountains, and I drove straight to the house of the principal proprietor, to whom the Governor of Telaw had given me a letter. He was a capital specimen of a Georgian gentleman, frank and hospitable, and his home was a fair type of a country-house, something like an old rambling farm-house in England, with the addition of a large wooden balcony running all along the front of the upper story. Before it was a piece of grass, where large dogs basked and a flock of turkeys pecked, with some out-buildings; the whole was surrounded by a strong fence of wattled boughs, about eight feet high.

My host and I dined alone at one o'clock, and then separated, to sleep through the hotter hours of the afternoon; but

---

* Hundreds of cartloads of the bosses and excrescences of the huge walnut-trees in these provinces are annually exported to Europe for ornamental furniture. These deformities of the tree are naturally more curiously veined than the trunk.

when I was summoned to tea on the lawn, I found four ladies
added to our party, all Georgians.  The wife and daughter of
my entertainer wore the white flowing veil, and the embroidered
coronet usual in Georgia, while I was surprised to find the
others, at the foot of the Caucasus, arrayed in the last Paris
fashions, and also, to my great delight, speaking excellent
French.  After tea, as we walked about, I found that it was
still considered dangerous to wander after sun-set more than
a couple of hundred yards from the house, and that three
years ago they would not have ventured beyond the gates, for
a forest runs down to the village, and may at any time
harbour a party of murderous Lesghian mountaineers.

At supper, which was also served out of doors, my friend
thought it right to follow the Georgian custom, and make me
drink as much Kakhetian wine as I could carry; and as bottle
after bottle disappeared, I saw with horror a fresh one placed
on the table.  I explained to my fair neighbour that a milk
diet among the Koords had ill prepared me for the contest,
when she kindly comforted me by the assurance that the
Prince, our host, was becoming rapidly drunk.  This restored
my courage, and though the measures were large and no heel-
taps allowed, to the Prince's Tartar challenge, oft repeated, of
Allah verdi, I steadily responded by the customary Yakshi
oul,* and an emptied tumbler: I felt considerable self-approval,
when I found myself capable of walking to my room.  The
ladies usually assist at these entertainments, and though of
course partaking with extreme moderation themselves, I don't
believe that they would consider a guest, who imitated them
in that respect, at all to be commended for his sobriety.

The wine of Kakhetie is justly celebrated throughout Georgia.
There are two kinds, red and white : the red much resembling
Burgundy, the white possessing a flavour peculiar to itself.
In private cellars, the wine is kept in large earthen jars, but
for transport and in wine-shops, it is put into ox-hides, which,
when they are distended, wobble about in such a plethoric

---

* Phonetic spelling.  "God gave it," and a "Happy journey ;" viz. to the
wine.

fashion, as to inspire one with an almost irresistible desire to ease them with a pen-knife; and these give a strong unpleasant flavour to their contents.

I was obliged to spend another day with these kind people, and the morning after I left them with regret. The Prince gave me four horses and a guide to convey me with my servant and baggage to Cadori, half a day's journey up the mountains.

A few versts up the valley, behind Sabooi, I came upon a Russian camp, employed in making a road, which, only lately begun, is eventually to cross the mountains to Ghunib. I dined and spent the hot afternoon with the officers here, and by great good luck, fell in with my friend Vinci, who I knew was somewhere in the neighbourhood, and who rode into camp while I was there.

An engineer officer of great repute, he had the whole military force in this part of the country working under his direction; and as I had travelled with him previously, and we had shared in a rather serious accident, I knew that his assistance, and none could be more valuable, would be freely rendered me He had come from Cadori, whither I was bound, and returned thither with me. We rode rapidly up the remainder of the valley; for the mountains, instead of approaching at the upper end, are joined by a steep ridge, the face of which is ascended by nearly eighty zigzags; and as the path is narrow and the corners are sharp, it was desirable to get up before nightfall. The summit of this pass, called Cadori, is upwards of 8,000 feet above the sea-level, and is defended by a small fort, whose garrison sustains, in winter, a severe siege from frost and snow. Four thousand men were under canvas here, and as the next day was Sunday, and there were no parties out at work, I had a good opportunity of seeing them.

The Russian troops in the Caucasus have few changes of quarters, and a soldier once drafted there may expect to remain during the whole time of his service. None but men of strong constitution could stand such a rigorous climate, and such hard work; and the Czar is supposed, I believe rightly, to possess no finer troops than these. Here and in other camps I was as much surprised at the size and robust appearance of the men, as I was charmed with their cheerfulness and contentment; for they really have few enjoyments. The Russian soldier receives his food and clothing from the Government; his actual pay in money amounts to only about eight shillings a year; but when he is employed on public works, he gets a few kopecks extra per day, and, in harvest time, is allowed to get wages from the farmers.

It has been discovered of late years, that in spite of the inclemency of the weather, winter is the best season for making expeditions, the rivers being then so much lower; but the sufferings of the troops are severe. Having seen the country, I could almost comprehend the bitterness of the recollections of a Russian officer, who, in my hearing, after describing a winter campaign, when he had barely seen the sun, but lay in the mud for a month, without a tent, under heavy rain, and engaged with an active enemy, added, " I have actually pitied myself, I have cursed the hour I was born and the mother who gave me birth."

The bands of the regiments do not go with them into the mountains; so the soldiers, having a taste for music, form themselves into companies of singers. In the afternoon Colonel Avinoff invited me to his tent with several of his officers, and treated us, of all things in the world, with English porter. It is much esteemed here, and from the length and difficulty of the land carriage, is very expensive. It is, therefore, only produced on high days, when a guest is to be entertained; Barclay and Perkins' is in point of fact the champagne of the Caucasus. The best singers in the regiment had been ordered before the tent, and sang in chorus, with great taste and spirit, songs of love and songs of war. They stood in a circle, directed by a tall, wiry fellow, whose animated countenance and energetic action expressed most perfectly the sentiment of the words. In a favourite song, " The siege of Kars," the preparation, the leave-taking, and the attack, were represented in unmistakeable pantomime. I was quite carried away by the genuine feeling with which

they sang, and regretted my inability, through ignorance of
the language, to express my thanks to the men; but fired by
enthusiasm and British porter, I holloaed out the universal
toast of *Allah verdi*, and drank their health in a bumper of
our national drink. There was a shout and a rush, and I
found myself hoisted in the air, balanced on the palms of
their hands—a mode of thanks novel and rather surprising.
We had interludes of dancing by some Lesghians who were
in the camp. They danced the Lesghinska, which is full of
life and movement, quite a different performance from the
posturing common in most eastern countries.

While this was still going on, drums suddenly beat all
over the camp, the men hurried to their ranks before their
tents, every head was bared, and four thousand voices chaunted
low the evening prayer. Those wild stern mountains resound-
ing with the sacred song, together with the reverent aspect of
the war-worn and weather-beaten men, made one of the most
elevating and affecting scenes I ever witnessed.

All the tribes of Daghestan have submitted to the Russians,
but outbreaks continually occur; and even the neighbourhood
of this large force did not deter the natives from occasional
acts of violence, whether with or without the prompting of
their chiefs it is difficult to determine. A very few days
before my arrival a party of seven men of the Grenadiers of
the Grand Duke Constantine, a battalion of the regiment which
Colonel Avinoff commanded, was sent out to a small lake in
the neighbourhood to fish for trout. Early the following
morning some of their comrades, going a short distance from
the camp, were horrified at finding the body of one of these
men, naked, cruelly hacked, and half-frozen, but still breathing.
He was of course immediately brought in, and everything
possible was done to restore him, but the poor fellow could
only smile his thanks, and died without speaking a word.
It was plain enough that something terrible had happened to
the party, but how, or by whom the deed had been done, was
left for the present to be surmised. However, a few hours
later another of the fishermen came in and told his tale. The

men were preparing their supper under the shelter of a high bank, covered with trees and brushwood, when suddenly a large party of Lesghians, who had approached silently and undiscovered, burst down upon them. The Russians were all fine strong men, and though they were soon overpowered by numbers, made a determined resistance. But it was a hopeless fight, six of them were almost cut in pieces by the terrible khangiars, the seventh rushed into the water and gained the opposite bank, and escaped by concealing himself in the underwood. The Lesghians stripped the bodies and departed. Then that wounded man, though left for dead, came to himself, and staggered, naked, through the freezing night, up a difficult path to a spot whence he might perhaps even see the tents of his comrades—a few yards further and he might have lived—but though his brave heart had not failed him, cold and loss of blood dragged him down.

The natives who perpetrated this deed were inhabitants of some outlying villages of the large tribe called Dido, on whose territory we were, a turbulent and bloodthirsty set, who are very difficult to manage. They are much given to cattle-stealing, and we had a little excitement from hearing that they had driven off several hundred head of our cattle during the night. This turned out to be a false alarm, they had only strayed : but a man of an adjacent tribe came in and complained that a number of theirs were really gone. The people who were the losers on this occasion were Christians, converted or planted here in some remote period, and though numerically weak, they are of the sect called "muscular," hit hard blows, and generally hold their own.

I stayed here one more day quietly as Colonel Avinoff's battalion was moving in the direction I meant to pursue, and it was considered better that I should go with them. On the third morning after my arrival, our tents were struck and the baggage horses laden with the quickness and precision attained by long and pretty constant practice. The troops marched twelve hundred strong with three hundred horses. These carried baggage, provisions, tents, and tools for road-making,

and though the number may appear excessive, it is not so in
fact, as they have to make toilsome journeys over difficult
paths, and it is better to have light loads and sound backs,
even though more horses are requisite ; especially in a country
like this, which is covered thickly with grass, and no fodder
requires to be cut. The routes which have been traced by the
Russians, do not follow the easiest or the most direct line. In
place of following the valleys and passing over the shoulders
of the mountains, they go in zigzags to their very summits, to
avoid the risk of being attacked at a disadvantage, and of
having rocks hurled on them from above. The main body of
the troops, therefore, passed by a path of this nature over a
mountain to our left, while the Colonel, Vinci and myself,
with a company of men as escort, went by a ravine, leading
nearly due north to the place appointed for camping. A thick
fog, which had covered everything in the morning, had now
turned to rain, and made a difficult path slippery and dangerous, so that it became necessary in ugly places for the colonel
and myself, who of course only carried side arms, having
secured a good foot-hold, to check the soldiers as they slid
down, encumbered by their rifles and accoutrements. We
could hardly believe that a dying man a few nights before
could have clambered up such places in the way I have
related.

Though the mountains around range from ten to twelve
thousand feet in height, their tops are free from snow in the
summer months, but we passed over and by some large
patches of snow hidden from the sun in this ravine. A small
level piece of ground had been selected for our camp, where
the stream which we had followed joined another, their united
waters running down a third valley. Dark forests surrounded
us on all sides, now and then opening into glades of thick
grass, across which a large herd of deer were seen leisurely
passing during our march. We arrived while the last of the
troops were descending the hill, and though we were crowded
into a very limited space, the horses were unladen and
picketed, and the tents pitched with a quietness and despatch

beyond all praise: The rain was falling in torrents, while
the peals of thuuder rolling from hill to hill, could not deafen
us to the roar of the swollen streams just below: the ground
too, was thoroughly saturated long before the tents were
pitched, but by some process almost miraculous we soon had
hot tea and a capital shislick before us.  Shislick is the great
mountain dish, deservedly esteemed for its excellence and the
readiness with which it is cooked: it consists of bits of
mutton threaded on a stick and frizzled over a fire, like
gigantic kabobs ; all its goodness depends on the cooking:
it is either very tender and good or else very tough and bad;
generally the latter.

During the night the storm continued, and the stream rose
to such a height as to flood that part of the camp where the
horses were picketed, carrying off two and drowning them—
two heavy iron cooking kettles were also floated off and seen
no more, to the great grief of the men.  The next day was
occupied in changing our position to one more secure in every
respect, on an elevated plateau across the stream.  Our tents
were pitched on a piece of ground, till that morning covered
by the forest, and as the Colonel was to remain here some
time, he thought it worth while to pay attention to the picturesque, and issued directions for small clumps of trees to
be left standing here and there about the camp.  This gave
a pleasant natural air to the otherwise stiff straight rows of
tents, which formed three sides of a square resting on the
edge of a precipitous ravine, and when at supper we lay full
length on carpets spread upon the soft grass, lighted and
warmed by large fires behind, the whole thing gave one
rather the idea of a magnified pic-nic.

We made a party next day to fish in the small lake, where
those poor fellows had been massacred shortly before, but
after the rain the water was too thick for any sport.  Sicken-
ing evidences of the fray still lay round the ashes of their
fire, aud in the long grass growing on the steep bank above
was a thin line, like the trail of a huge serpent, the path of the
Lesghians as they slid down in single file upon their victims.

I was still not quite through what is considered the dangerous part of this country; so when I started the following morning, Friday, August 22, Vinci kindly escorted me with one hundred and fifty men to a point just above a village called Khupro. From here I was to go on the same day to Beschat, under the guidance of a trustworthy native, and furnished with an order for one or two men from each village to serve me as escort. The scenery was wild, but not beautiful; the riding sufficiently bad, but nothing to what I found beyond Beschat: in a mountain country, one always has to walk the worst ascents and descents, if the horse is to last out the day. At a large village some hours beyond Khupro, I was met as I approached the place by a short, broad-shouldered fellow, of rather pleasant aspect if he could only have looked one in the face—he shook me by the hand, and taking my horse's rein led me off to his house, where he gave me some excellent tea, and pressed me hard to stay the night. I was really quite sorry to have to decline, but I had reasons for pushing on to Beschat, and so we parted with mutual protestations of regard. I did not know till some time afterwards that the man was Djabet, the naïb, the chief of the obnoxious Dido, reckoned an out-and-out villain. His eldest son, however, is a hostage at Petersburg, which is a sufficient guarantee from any overt act of violence on his part.

A great part of this district is under cultivation, and I was surprised by the abundance of the crops, which were now almost ripe for the sickle, not only down in the valleys, but a long way up their sides. The natural grasses are fine and luxuriant, and the wild flowers, though not singly remarkable, varied and abundant. Perhaps the most common among them is that pink and white flower, resembling the common daisy, were it not that several bloom on one stem, from which Persian powder is made, accounted a great preservative from fleas and other insects. The natives are quite aware of its properties, and prepare large quantities of the powder. In descending the last mountain into the valley which leads to Beschat, it was necessary in places to force our way through strong weeds, considerably higher than my head as I sat on horseback, a convincing proof of the fertility of the soil.

The village of Beschat is a mere heap of blackened walls, having been burnt by the Russians in their campaign, but the place of course retains its name. The tribe inhabiting the villages round are called Capucha. It was long past dark when I arrived at the spot where the valley widened out and formed a small level amphitheatre, where Prince Scheila-khoff had pitched his camp. The lights were out, and my only greeting was the challenge of the sentinel. My friend Vinci, to whose kindness I almost entirely owe the success of this journey, had given me a letter to the general, but he was asleep,, and I was rather puzzled what to do about supper. While I was stumbling among tent cords, and giving directions to my servant in French, I was hailed in the same language, and asked to come inside a tent close by. When I had groped my way in, I found two young men in their beds, the nephew of the Prince and his tutor, a Frenchman. They were soon up and dressed; and a hospitable major, who had not yet turned in, and who was rather celebrated for having everything about him very comfortable, nobly sustained his reputation, and gave us all an excellent supper. I found that the general meant to march early the next morning, bag and baggage, and I hardly expected that he would have time, even if he had the inclination, to attend to the wants of an utter stranger. But I had yet to learn how far the kindness and courtesy of a Georgian gentleman could go. Four horses were waiting for me at the tent door before I was up, and when I went to thank him, he gave me three of his native (Lesghian) body-guard for escort, and a muleteer, recommending to me especially one of the men, named Osman, a tall, gaunt, severe-looking soldier. He spoke a little Georgian, as did my servant. I treated him with a certain amount of consideration, and to him all my orders were given. I have always found it answer in travelling to throw the responsibility on one man, and hold as little communication as possible with the rest. It flatters him, and makes the rest fear you more. After a short acquaintance I had a real regard for this man, and I am sure he had the same for me. How is it that the half-civilized man has that soul of a gentleman which prevents him from offending one's ideas of propriety and fitness, while one of the same class, who has had the advantage of a Sunday-school in youth, and penny-papers in his maturer years, rubs you sore at every turn? I don't know why—but I am sure that anyone who has travelled both with Eastern and European servants will understand and agree with me.

Scheilakhoff started about eight in the direction from which I had come, and as soon as I could get my horses saddled, and the baggage properly managed—it is always necessary to see these things done oneself—I rode off in the other. For several hours the path lay up the valley of a clear broad stream, wide at first, and with wooded gently-sloping banks, which, as we advanced, grew narrower, more perpendicular and rocky, till the open, smiling valley became a dark contracted gorge. Before I was through it, I was overtaken by three horsemen, who had been sent by the general to ask me to return, and make the expedition with him, adding that I should go to Ghunib on my return. This was very perplexing. I got out of my saddle, and weighed it all for a few minutes. I did not like to refuse a man who had been so kind, and had given me everything I wanted; I should have agreeable society, and all the creature-comforts: but on the other hand I thought of the delays I had already experienced, and I felt that if I turned I should never see Ghunib. So I wrote a short note, excusing myself, and rode on again, hoping that Scheilakhoff would not think me ungrateful or discourteous.

Leaving the valley, a sharp pull brought us over a mountain, a short way down the further side of which are a few small villages, the habitations of the Ansuch people. Shaho the naïb of this clan, is a person of some consideration. He received me hospitably, and killed me a sheep. We had stopped at half-past four, for the horses, fed only on grass, were incapable of making a real good day's work. There were some hours of daylight, what was I to do with them?

Oh, shoot of course ; no game for miles round. Read ? I had only a " Bradshaw's Foreign Guide," having left all but indispensable baggage behind. I never thought of reading on a mountain excursion, my habit being to ride till dark, then sup and sleep, but the weakness of my cattle prevented that, and I don't believe I ever knew what ennui really meant till that afternoon. And the worst of it was, that the same thing frequently occurred, and I was obliged to put myself on a short allowance even of Bradshaw, and could only allow myself so many pages a day of his valuable information, concerning the population and hotels of the principal towns of France and Switzerland. Well, night came at last, and a certain amount of repose. Most of the villages in this district have been burned by the Russians, and this had not escaped. The naïb had only a few small rooms repaired amid the general ruin, but close by he had built the walls of a good-sized house. I chose to sleep there, thinking to be free from vermin ; but though there were no doors or windows, the fleas were already at home, and gave me the usual hearty welcome.

The villages in Daghestan present a sombre appearance, the houses being built of a dark-coloured stone, cemented with mud ; for though limestone abounds, the people appear to be ignorant of the art of burning it, and making mortar. Lines of these houses rise row above row against the sides of the hills, making it difficult to determine from below where each house begins, and whether the one above be or be not only an upper story of the one below. In every village some few houses have a plain square tower attached, intended for defence, and generally pierced with loop-holes for musketry. The roofs are flat, which is remarkable in so changeable a climate, resembling much, it appeared to me, that of Switzerland ; the windows, mere apertures in the wall, were closed by a shutter or a sliding door.

The generic name, which comprehends all these tribes, is Lesghian. They may speak different dialects, but they certainly understand one another without difficulty, over a large extent of country ; and this, though I know that very many distinct languages are spoken in the Caucasus, makes me believe that the number of them has been exaggerated.

The Lesghian is short, slight, generally without much beard, and with very ordinary features. His dress to an unpractised eye would probably appear almost identical with that of a Circassian, but it differs in many minor points. He wears on his head the sheep-skin papack, varying in height,—I have seen it often so low and shaggy as to mistake it for the wearer's hair; a long tunic, full about the chest and shoulders, with cartridge-cases sown on across the breast, comes down to his knees; it is pulled tight in round the waist by a leathern strap, studded with metal bosses; his trousers fit close to his ankles, and he wears either boots or shoes, the toes of which are turned up like an old-fashioned skate. In wet or cold weather, a hood, called beshlick, protects his head and shoulders, in shape resembling exactly the helmet with the cape of chain armour attached, which is still worn by the people near the Kasbek: and the bourka, a rough sheep-skin cloak with the wool outside, covers the rest of him. He never moves without his eternal khangiar, a strong, pointed, double-edged knife, generally about fourteen inches long, useful both for striking and stabbing, fastened to his belt by a small thong, not on one side, but right across him in front; while the shaska, a long, heavy, slightly curved sabre, without a guard, hangs loose from a thin black strap, passed over his right shoulder. The pistol is always stuck in the belt behind the back. Their rifles have long barrels with a small bore, the stock remarkably small, and often beautifully inlaid with ivory and mother-of-pearl. The shaskas, of their own manufacture, are of such excellent quality, and are so much esteemed by the Russians quartered here, that they prefer them infinitely to their ordinary regulation sword, and I never saw an officer on service carry any other. The scabbard is often ornamented with silver, upon which arabesque patterns of great beauty and variety are carved, and darkened so that they stand out in high relief from the bright ground.

I have said that the men are not handsome, but the women

are downright ugly.  They wear no veil over their faces—I
wished they did—so there can be no mistake about the matter.
The head-dress is a hood, fitting tight to the head, and falling
back a good deal below the waist.  It is frequently of red
cloth, and ornamented variously in different tribes with beads,
coins, and cowrie-shells ; an edging of thin iron scales over-
lapping one another is common.  Their short, ill-fitting robe
is open at the breast, to show a breast-plate of coins and thin
plates of metal, and coarse clumsy hose complete the costume.
Without being forward, they are not shy, at least not to that
degree one generally finds among Eastern women.  Poor creatures ! they have to do all the hard work out of doors as well
as in the house, so it is not fair to expect good looks.

The religion of the country is Mahometan.  I have travelled in many Mahometan countries, but I have never been
in any where the duties prescribed by the Koran were observed so religiously as in this.  I never saw a man touch
wine or spirits here, and even smoking is unusual.  The regularity with which my escort asked permission to stop to perform their ablutions and pray was sometimes embarrassing
when time was valuable, but it was of course a permission
which no man under any circumstances should refuse.
Among Turks and Arabs there is always, it appears to me, a
certain ostentation, or what at all events must seem to our
views an unbecoming publicity in their manner of praying.
A well-bred Turk has, while I have been sitting on his carpet,
and smoking with him, got up at the hour of prayer, and begging
me not to move, made his prostrations almost into my lap ;
but these men as carefully shunned observation, by which
they rose much in my esteem, for they were not the less religious, and they showed far better taste.  I did not see one
single mosque in the country, and I cannot assign a reason
for it.  Some of the villages in which I stayed were quite
large enough to require one.  But though no muezzin shrieked
it from a minaret, not the less did I hear in the morning a
sonorous voice proclaim aloud, "There is no God but God,
and Mahomet is the prophet of God."

I left Ansuch rather late, as the horses' shoes had to be looked to. I ought to have seen it done the night before, for if you don't look after those things yourself, no one else will—it rained hard, and the travelling was shockingly bad, so our progress was but slow. It was a pity it rained, for the scenery we passed through was fine, the mountains becoming more craggy and savage. The wildest combination of rock and wood was in the neighbourhood of a village called Kosto.

I found Tonsoda a collection of miserable villages, their naturally dull appearance made more melancholy by the rain which was falling plentifully. We were directed to the best of their poor habitations, and took possession of a large room, with a fire burning in the middle of the floor. The place was filthily dirty and swarmed with vermin : the people had nothing whatever to give us to eat—they cook their own messes and bread only in sufficient quantity for each meal— and the bread which we had brought with us was quite wet. Things did not look very cheerful at first, but we dried the bread; I had a quantity of milk boiled, and though it was smoked, it warmed us. I thought I knew the worst about vermin, but I never saw their ranks so serried as on this night. It was useless thinking of sleep, though I was very tired; and I know nothing more hopeless or depressing than sitting up cold and weary, waiting for the dawn. I roused my people up before sunrise, and after undressing, and having a cold bath, felt a man again. The constant use of an india-rubber bath which I carried always with me, was, I am convinced, my preservative against fever and other complaints with which those around me were visited from time to time. I have some-times, without ceremony, tumbled the people out of a Khan, in order that I might enjoy my bath. They always yielded, thinking, I verily believe, that it was a religious ceremony.

The storm, which soaked us yesterday, had fallen in snow upon the mountain-tops, which was seen to sparkle brightly in the morning sun, as after a sharp climb of two hours we gained the summit of the steep ridge behind Tonsoda. This is a very commanding height, and I was startled at the sudden change in the scenery, and at the wild character of the new country which was in one moment spread before me. In place of the dark mountains with gradual slopes of grass and shoulders clothed with forest which I left behind, I saw long perpendicular ridges of yellowish limestone, in horizontal strata without peak or cleft, eventopped as the battlements of a fortress and bare as its walls. In form and colour they resemble somewhat those hills which hem in the valley of the Nile, but they far outstrip them in grandeur and in height. Populous villages and cultivated fields fill the vallies at their feet, but now nothing was visible except the broad weather-beaten brows of the ridges.

Ratlough lay far below ; the way to it passed over a bleak upland and down a steep shady path through the forest. Two men, whom I met some miles from the village, had turned back and given warning of my approach ; so when I arrived about midday, several of the inhabitants came out to meet me, one of them leading me off with great demonstrations of friendship to his house, where preparations had been made for my reception. These attentions were due in a great measure to the natural kind feeling which people, uncorrupted by the blessings of civilization, generally entertain toward a stranger, but much of them must also undoubtedly be set down to the politic desire of a conquered race to stand well with the authorities set over them, under whose protection I was evidently travelling. I often tried to explain that I was an Englishman, but the word bore no meaning to their ears, and the utmost I could obtain was to be recognised as a Frank. The kind fellow, after he had given us of his best, pressed me hard to stay the night under his roof, promising, if I would let him, to ride on with me to Ghunib. I should have liked his company, though it is tedious holding com-munication through two interpreters—my servant repeating what I said to Osman in Georgian, who again translated into Lesghian—but I could not wait.

At the next stiff pull my servant's horse shut completely up. I was not surprised, for the man, though born at Tiflis,

was of French extraction, and the lively blood of that gallant
nation had asserted itself by gallops on his miserable mount,
when the nature of the ground permitted it.  I had warned
him of the inevitable result of that treatment of a grass-fed
horse making a long journey over a rough country, so I left
him without pity to drive his horse before him in company
with the baggage animals, and pushed on with Osman and
another to Heedatl, which is about five hours beyond Ratlough.  Between these two places the Avarski-koi-soo is
crossed by a wooden bridge, at a spot where the wide bed of
the river is contracted by the approach of the cliffs on each
side.  To the best of my recollection this bridge was between
eighty and one hundred feet long, and it was made in this
manner:—from each bank of the river solid beams of wood
had been laid in layers, each row projecting a little beyond
the one below, till they were sufficiently near for long thick
planks to reach across.  This is one of the four great rivers,
which, fed by the snows of the Berbala range and the Bus-
dagh, after watering Daghestan under the name of Koi-soo,
join their waters and flow into the Caspian under that of Sulak.

I got late into Heedatl, and my baggage did not come up
till two or three hours later.  The individual in whose house
I slept, promised to find me a fresh horse some time the
following day, so I determined to push on to Ghunib, leaving my
baggage to follow on as soon as the fresh horse should arrive.
The fellow was an intense snob in every respect, misinforming
me about the distances, and keeping out of the way after I
had left, in order that he might not have to produce his
horse.  On my return I rode through his village without
halting or noticing him or anybody else in it.

I remarked in the burial-ground at Heedatl, as in several
other places, that some of the tombs were built right on to the
path, as if purposely to catch the eye and force the passer by
to read their inscription, and that they had long poles rising
from them, surmounted sometimes by a crescent, sometimes
by a small flag torn to tatters by the wind.  I found that these
were the tombs of men who had met with a violent death in

war or by assassination, and until the friends of the dead man
shall have avenged his death by killing one of the tribe or
family who caused it, that pole stands ever before the eyes of
his people, a continual sign and memorial of a duty which
has to be performed.

I knew this last day would be a long one, so I took Osman
and another Lesghian with me, and left the rest of the men
and the baggage to come on quietly in two days.   Osman and
I had hardly a word in common, but he soon made me understand very plainly that he considered our getting to Ghunib
that day to be quite out of the question, and he made piteous
appeals to me to stop at every dirty little village we came
near.   After two or three steep climbs, and equally sharp
descents, we were in a wide valley opposite to Tilitl.   Instead
of crossing to that village, we kept on the other side, pursuing
a path which runs high up along the mountains.   The bare
sides of Ghunib were right in front ; the path was better than
usual ; so, in spite of the remonstrances of Osman, to which I
attended the less, as he did not know the road, I caught my
animal hard by the head and shoved him briskly on.   The
Lesghian was right, and I was wrong ; but the place seemed
so near, that I could not believe we should be benighted.   I
did not know that the only access to the top of these precipices was on the further side, and that a long circuit had
to be made.   After sunset the night closed in rapidly ; it
rained slightly, and was so dark that I was reduced to feeling
for my footing with a stick.   We none of us knew where we
were : my hopes of supper were fading away ; and I was on
the point of giving in, and sleeping in my bornous, which I
don't object to in fine, but am averse to in wet weather, when
I saw a light below, shining through the door of a tent.
Tents must be Russian ; so I hailed immediately, was
answered, and soon found myself in a small Russian camp.
The officer was in bed ; but he told me I had not far to go
and called out four of his men to show me the way ; then
groping our way up a long winding road, we arrived at our
destination in another hour and a half.

I spent two entire days at this singular place. Officers who took part in the siege, and were present at the capture of Schamyl, informed me of details which I think are new, and are at all events authentic; and my own notes were written on the spot.

In general aspect, Ghunib does not materially differ from many mountains in its neighbourhood. Some of these are even more escarped, but they want other advantages which Ghunib possesses. It is an isolated oval rock of limestone, rising in precipitous and almost inaccessible terraces, between three and four thousand feet from the valleys surrounding it. At one end—I will call it the north, for though, perhaps, it is not strictly so, it will make my description more simple—at the north end, then, the inclination is more gradual, and the Russians have here completed an excellent road as far as a plateau eleven hundred feet above the Kara-koi-soo,* which runs at its foot, and are preparing to erect upon this plateau a fortress, with hospital, store-houses, &c., and a house for General Lazaroff, the Commander-in-chief of Daghestan. Above this, again, is a steep range of rocks; and through a long gully in the middle of these a zig-zag road leads to the top of the mountain. The extreme length of it is stated to be six versts the extreme breadth four; but it has not been measured, and I believe it to be one-third more. The Tartar aoul, not far from the north end, has been ascertained to be 4,920 feet above the sea; thence there is a continual rise to the south end, which is 7,742 feet. The top of the mountain is not a plane surface, as I should have imagined from below, but very much hollowed out, in shape like a shell, the aoul lying in the bottom, and is diversified with rocks and valleys. What constitutes the prime excellence of Ghunib as a natural fortress is, that it is not only so escarped as to be, except at the north end, practically inaccessible, if held by even a moderate force; but that it contains abundantly within itself, everything necessary for the provision of its garrison for an

---

* Kara-koi-soo is Tartar, and means "the black cold water;" the native bridge which crosses it here is 2,900 feet above the sea. The Tartar element predominates in this part of the Caucasus. (It is hardly necessary to mention that the Tartar language differs very slightly from the Turkish.)

indefinite time. The soil is fertile, and produces, where it is cultivated, fine crops of corn; the rest is covered with long thick grass, upon which the Russian captors found three hundred horses and six thousand sheep at pasture. It is watered by two streams, which, rising in the high ground, join near the aoul; they find an exit to the west, where they pour over the rocks down to the valley below, and nourish the fruit-trees and gardens of Hindak. One little rivulet runs into the gulley at the north end, and forms a singular waterfall. It comes to the abrupt edge of a cleft in the rock with sufficient force to clear it at a bound, and falls from the opposite side of the cleft to a great depth in a shower of spray, a veritable Staubbach.

On the mountain itself there are very few trees, only one small clump of birches; but fuel abounds in the neighbourhood. Coal, of a fine quality, is plentiful; but, unfortunately, it lies between strata of such hard rock as not to pay for the working. On the other hand, large fields exist of an inferior kind, mixed with earth, which require little labour to utilize, and which afford the fuel that is generally burned. Capital turf, too, abounds in the district.

No natives are now allowed to live upon the mountain, and the aoul is already falling into decay. The house which Schamyl occupied is the only one kept in repair, and is used as a hospital. It was clean and in good order. One room was filled by Tartar invalids from the neighbourhood, who even in bed wore their shaggy caps upon their shaven heads. The kindness shown to them is only one instance of the conciliating treatment which I everywhere observed to be pursued by the Russians towards the inhabitants of the country.

When Schamyl finally retreated to Ghunib, Prince Baryatinski, the viceroy, with a vigour and decision, the happy result of which was the subjugation of the Eastern Caucasus, at once ordered the concentration of an overwhelming force at that spot. Schamyl had built three walls across the gully at the north end, which was considered the only possible passage, and defended them resolutely. He had only two small cannon, which he placed in position there. The Russians attempted to make regular approaches ; but the rocky nature of the ground rendered their progress exceedingly slow. When the Viceroy saw this, knowing that if time were given, Schamyl's weak force might receive an accession of strength—and the youngest soldier might see at a glance how hopeless an escalade must be, if strongly opposed—promptly commanded an instant attack. Schamyl had with him only four hundred men, it is true : they had a wonderful position to defend, but were opposed to the attack of twelve thousand.

Before dawn five columns advanced to the assault. The First Regiment of Fusiliers, and the Daghestan Militia, under General Takhanoff, came up on the west ; the first struggling up a desperate place, the latter finding less difficulty. On the east there were likewise two attacks, by the Regiment Samur and the Regiment Apcheronski. The Regiment Chervanski, under Colonel Ranonovitch, attacked the north end, where Schamyl and his handful of men fought behind their walls with desperation ; some were fanatics, who had vowed themselves to death ; some were Russian renegades, whose only hope lay in victory ; and the rest were proud to die for their prophet-king. But while the combat raged at its fiercest round him, shouts from the rear proclaimed to Schamyl that the place he deemed invincible was won, and that all was over, and he fled in despair to a tower in the aoul.

The Regiment Apcheronski, 2,000 strong, under Colonel Tergoukasoff, were the first to gain the summit, and Lieutenant Squarzoff was the first officer up. It was, indeed, a perilous climb, for their attack was at nearly the highest point of the rock. By the aid of ladders and grappling-irons, one or two of the most active passed the difficult spots ; these threw ropes, of which they had plenty, to others, who in their turn assisted, and the thing was done. They met with a trifling resistance from a few Tartars, who were immediately killed ; their women fought by their side, and shared their fate. An officer of this regiment, while showing me the ground, described well their bewilderment at finding themselves, on a dark night, at the top of a mountain on which none of them had placed foot before; how no one knew where the village was, or the enemy; and how they caught a horse for the Major, who, fat and out of breath, but full of pluck, rode him barebacked down the hill to seek the foe.

The rest of the columns of assault soon gained the summit, and surrounded the aoul. A storm of bullets poured upon it, (the stars made by them are still visible), and Schamyl, perceiving that further resistance was hopeless, showed a white flag and surrendered. Baryatinski's own position had been on Chegher, a mountain which commands the north end of Ghunib; but by this time he had arrived on the scene of action, and, seated on a large stone by the side of the clump of birches before-mentioned, he commanded that his active enemy, who had so long baffled him, and who at length was in his power, should be brought before him.

Schamyl was pale with fear, for he expected instant death; and his fingers closed round the hilt of his khangiar with a nervous clutch, a movement misinterpreted by the body-guard of the Viceroy, whose hands simultaneously grasped their weapons, ready to cut the prisoner in pieces at his first movement towards their general. But his fears were needless; he was treated with the courtesy which a brave enemy deserves, and he is still alive and well-treated in Russia.

With the taking of Schamyl ended the resistance of Daghestan. Fear of him, more than aversion to the Russians, had prolonged the war. The miserable natives were, indeed, in a sad dilemma; the Russians burned any villages which opposed them, and Schamyl visited those which yielded with a like punishment. New habitations are only now beginning to rise among the blackened walls.

I have often heard Schamyl's name used in connexion with the Circassians. He had no connexion whatever with them, and, in all probability, never was in their country. The Tcherkess, from which we derive Circassian, are a people inhabiting quite the other end of the Caucasus, and differing totally from the Lesghians in language and personal appear-
· ance. Allied with neighbouring tribes, they still wage active

war with the Russians. A few months ago two expeditions, which marched against them in force, were obliged to retreat after a heavy loss of officers and men ; and the chain of forts between Anapa and Suchum Kalé sustain a continual siege. Here are still seen fanatics, called " abreck," who, under a vow of death, rush single-handed upon the Russian ranks, and striking, regardless of their own safety, seldom strike in vain.

It is remarkable how the hill tribes differ from those which inhabit the plains, in their notions of morality. In any case where portions of the same tribe inhabit both the high and the low lands adjacent, the distinction is very striking and altogether in favour of the mountaineers.

As regards the sale of their offspring, revolting as the idea of traffic in human flesh must always be, the practice is not so brutal as may be imagined by those who are ignorant of Eastern customs. The purchasers are Turks, and their slaves, as we call them, are regarded as a portion more or less humble of the family, members whose dependence carries with it nothing that is degrading. An instance, which came in a manner under my own observation, though it presents a sad complication of misery, will show what I mean. When I was at the large town of E——, in Armenia, the Pasha governing that part of the country was changed. His successor was a Georgian, sold in his childhood to a wealthy Turk. The boy grew and prospered, and after passing through subordinate offices, he was, some years previous to the time I speak of, entrusted with the command of a district. On his departure from Constantinople, the Sultan was pleased to give him to wife, as is not unusual, a lady from the royal harem. With her he lived most happily for three years, when by some means, whether a mutual recollection of some incident which had happened, or some spot which had been seen in childhood, I know not what, these two, man and wife, discovered that they were brother and sister. The wife, like the husband, had been sold away from her country, and met her brother in this strange wretched manner. They fortunately had had no children, and the marriage was immediately dissolved, but they say that the Pasha has never smiled since the discovery.

. The engineer officer, to whom the fortifying of Ghunib has been confided, entertained a great idea of the strength of the position, and continually referred to it as the Russian Gibraltar; but the site fixed upon for the fortress, the plateau which I have already mentioned, a little more than half way up the northern side of the mountain, is ill-chosen, being completely commanded by the opposite heights of Chegher. Armstrong guns planted there, would render it quite untenable. But it is only intended to hold mountaineers in check, and as they are not likely ever to possess such weapons, the works about to be constructed will no doubt prove sufficient for that purpose. For regular strategical purposes the fortress would have been better placed on the summit immediately above this plateau, but the transport of fuel and other necessaries would have been very laborious, and the climate is much more rigorous, the summit being exposed to cold winds, from which the plateau is sheltered.

Other positions similar to Ghunib, as Ulikala and Achulgo, taken by General Grabbe, were great steps in advance when they fell into the hands of the Russians. An elevated tableland, a day and a half from here, more extensive than Ghunib, and the rocky sides of which are fully as precipitous (at least from the side on which I passed), is still called the mountain of Hadji Murad, a chief of the same class as Schamyl, who was taken prisoner a few years before him, decapitated, and his head (it is said) sent in pickle to Petersburg. But Ghunib was the strongest and last of these fortresses, and the taking of Schamyl gave it an additional éclat. On the walls of one of the reception-rooms, in the palace of the Viceroy at Tiflis, beside glittering trophies of arms, is hung up the plain leathern saddle, in which he rode to a conquest of which he might well be proud, for it terminated a long weary contest in which Russia had not always the advantage; and in a large plaster map, in the same room, where the whole chain of the Caucasus is shown in relief, a gilded spot marks the summit of Ghunib.

Having seen and heard all that was likely to be of interest

here, on Friday, the 9th of August, I started on my road back.
As I varied my journey very little, on my return, it would
be tedious to follow it day by day, recording merely how
the baggage got behind and left me destitute of even a cloak
to sleep in; how horses fell; how, though I got a fresh horse
at Ghunib, and handed over to my Frenchman the one which
had carried me there, he succeeded in thoroughly knocking
him up in two days, notwithstanding his being some stone
lighter than I; and how, when after waiting a considerable
time for him to come up, he ran in in his tall boots, pumped
but plucky, and remarked, with the most pleasing naïveté,
that he had left his horse in a wood—these little embarrass‑
ments would not interest the reader.

I found Shaho, the naïb of the Ansuch, ill, and saw nothing
of him the night I got to his village, but he sent to ask me to
come to his room next morning. I found him huddled up in
a corner looking very miserable, but, speaking through two
interpreters, it was impossible to find out what was the matter
with him, so I could not prescribe anything. Quinine, in a
solid form, is so very portable, that it is worth while taking a
good quantity of it into a country of this sort, where fever and
ague are prevalent, and are generally left to fight it out with
nature. In other cases, where the disease showed itself in a
decided form, I applied it freely, but I could not understand
Shaho's case, and he was too good a fellow to try experiments
on. I think he was only a little depressed from want of occu‑
pation, missing probably the excitement of an occasional brush
with the Russians. His eldest son is a hostage at Petersburg,
which debars him, poor fellow, from any amusement of the
sort. He seemed to think that a stranger must necessarily
come from Petersburg, and charged me with messages to his
son, Mahmouta, which I may some day deliver. He was
mightily pleased with a photographic portrait which I hap‑
pened to have in my pocket-book, and his remark upon it was
characteristic of a country where the beauty of the women
vanishes at an early‑age,—"How young she is."

I had to wait some time for a capital breakfast, which he

insisted on having prepared for me, and which it would have disappointed him to have refused; but at length, having said many a good-bye, we kissed first on one then on the other side of the mouth, and I got off rather late for Beschat. At sunset we were still some miles from our destination, and coming to a nice bit of long grass we turned our poor tired horses loose to graze a little. Near this spot I, for the first time, saw a Mahometan woman out of doors and in public (for the people were returning home to a neighbouring village from labouring in the harvest-fields) saying her prayers, and going through the usual prostrations like a man.

When I got to Beschat, August 13th, I found none of the officers there whose acquaintance I had made on my first visit. They were with General Scheilakoff, who had not yet returned from his expedition. It was too dark to see me, but the first who heard the trampling of my horses claimed me as a guest, and I desire no more frank ready hospitality than that of a Russian officer. After suggesting everything that was possible for my comfort, one of the officers quietly and seriously asked me if I did not want any money. I stared at first, thinking I had misunderstood him, or that he was joking; but there was not a symptom of a smile on his face, and he was evidently in earnest, so I thanked him and declined with an equally grave face, as if it were quite a natural thing, and I were perfectly used to it. Such implicit confidence in an utter stranger I certainly never met with.

In the morning I found my little Frenchman ill with the fever. The Russians told me plainly that their doctor was an ass, and that if the man got into his hands I might wait till doomsday before he got better, so I took the case into my own hands, and, giving him as much quinine as he could stand, cured him in two days. This time I spent very pleasantly in the camp. Prince Orbeliani was quartered there with a regiment of Georgian Militia, superb fellows, carrying the native arms and picturesque national costume, and with a capital fighting reputation. Some of them were directed to fire at a mark at 150 yards, that I might judge of their proficiency; but even at that distance their firing was not very accurate. The Russian powder which they used is coarse and dirty, and a rifle requires cleaning after firing three charges of it. We passed the afternoon watching the games and dances of the soldiers. The music for the latter consisted of drums, and the shrieking flageolets which the Georgians affect. For some slight fault or other, as the dance began, a man marched straight up to one of the drummers, a full-grown soldier, and smacked his face soundly and repeatedly, the drummer not moving a limb the while. This is the only occasion on which I saw a soldier struck. I had heard a good deal of the rough treatment which the Russian soldier experiences at the hand of his officers, but I don't believe it is the case: on the contrary, I was much struck with the kind feeling which I saw show itself on several occasions, on the part both of officers and men.

There was staying with Prince Orbeliani a Bavarian artist, named Horschelt, who has been three years in the Caucasus, and having been present at several engagements, has gained a medal and two crosses. His sketches are exceedingly spirited, but I saw none of his finished works: the Emperor takes all he does. I thought I should have a chance of begging or borrowing some books from him, but I was disappointed, for his library consisted of one book, those sentimental sonnets of Heine—a thoroughly German notion. We passed the best part of an evening reading them aloud alternately, while the others played whist: at a pinch even sentiment is amusing. Prince Sheilakhoff returned to the camp the day after I got back there and resumed the command. He stopped at once the excuses which I began to offer for not having turned back to accompany him; and showed me every possible kindness. His expedition, as I expected from the direction he took, had been meant as, and had proved, merely a military promenade, and no powder had been burnt. He is one of those men, whose amiable disposition and conciliating manner, joined to great activity and firmness of purpose, mark them out as peculiarly adapted for a command of this sort in the centre of a warlike and recently conquered population, among whom one spark of oppression might probably excite a blaze of rebellion. When I was at Cadori, just after the loss of those

soldiers before related, I had joined heartily in the general
wish to burn the villages which their murderers inhabited, and
which from the mountains near were plainly visible, and I
heard many a murmur from my friends at the hand which
held them in. Such a proceeding might have caused a revolt
through the whole country. The event showed me how much
wiser was the course which a calmer judgment and a wider
experience dictated. Sheilakhoff decided that the native
chiefs should be the instruments for the punishment of a
deed, the commission of which it was strongly suspected they
had themselves instigated. He therefore applied to them for
the production of the actual offenders. They could not take
offence at a demand so obviously just, and they had already
sent in half a dozen, and promised to produce the rest. These
six were placed on a small eminence in the camp. It was
extremely cold at night, so a friend of one of the prisoners
came in and asked leave to give him a great sheepskin bourka.
Permission was given. Towards morning the guard observed
this man fumbling in a suspicious manner under his bourka,
and on examination found that a knife had been cunningly
sown into the skin, and that the man had made good use of it
and cut his bonds. I suppose he meant to make one dash for
life towards the mountains, but he was happily prevented.

My servant being better, I started on the 16th, with fresh
horses and also with fresh men. I was sorry to part with
Osman. He and his horse had become very thin during the
short time we had been together, but nevertheless he seemed
anything but happy when he kissed my hand, and said good-
bye. The present head of my escort was one of that unpleasant tribe Dido, whose territory I had to pass through again.
On his introduction he drew his hand across his throat, and
said it should answer for mine : and in fact I could not be in
better hands. He was related to Djabot, the naïb of the clan,
whose acquaintance I had made before. I wished to see his
manner of life, so I decided upon passing a night at the place
where he resided. A man rode on in advance, to let the naïb
know I was coming, so he had time to get into his Sunday
clothes, a coat of fine blue cloth, edged with silver lace, and a

towering white papack. Supper was late, as he had to send
a long way for a sheep : it consisted entirely of fresh,
stringy mutton, boiled and grilled, and great cakes of bread,
stuffed with a white, tasteless cheese, served in hot honey, a
favourite dish all over the country. We supped *tête-à-tête*. He
ate enormously, and I—did likewise. I think he was the best
man at the mutton, but I know I beat him at the cheese-cakes.

The Lesghians took me next day by a shorter and more
difficult path than that by which I had come with Vinci to
Arnihoff's camp. He and several more of the officers had
left, and out of 1200 men who marched here, 100 were laid
up from one cause or another. I did not wish to keep Scheilakhoff's horses and men longer than was necessary ; so after
spending one night here, I rode past Cadori, where not a tent
remained of the large encampment I had left there, right down
to Sabooi. Prince Georgiadzi, with whom I stayed before,
and his family, were absent, and I was seeking another house
on which to quarter myself, when I fortunately met one of
the ladies, whose acquaintance I had made on my previous
visit, walking with her husband, and they soon found me
supper and lodging. The latter, however, I declined, for though
it is not a healthy practice, and may induce fever, sleeping
out in the soft air of these warm plains is exceedingly pleasant.

I believe it is only when a journey is over that you know
how much you have enjoyed it. The last days are always
regretful : though one has a great pleasure in looking back at
events which, having happened perhaps a week ago, seem to
be divided from one by a long lapse of time, as they are by
space gone over. It was certainly with sorrow that I turned
my back upon the mountains where I had seen so much that
interested me, and where I left men whom I may call friends
behind me ; but I was glad to rest awhile with the judge at
Telaw, sauntering in shady balconies and lounging about the
old palace of the Georgian kings. Its stout stone towers look
right across the valley of the Alazan, but the curtain had
dropped upon the stage,—a thick veil hung on the brows of
Kaphkaz, and I never again saw the summits of Daghestan.

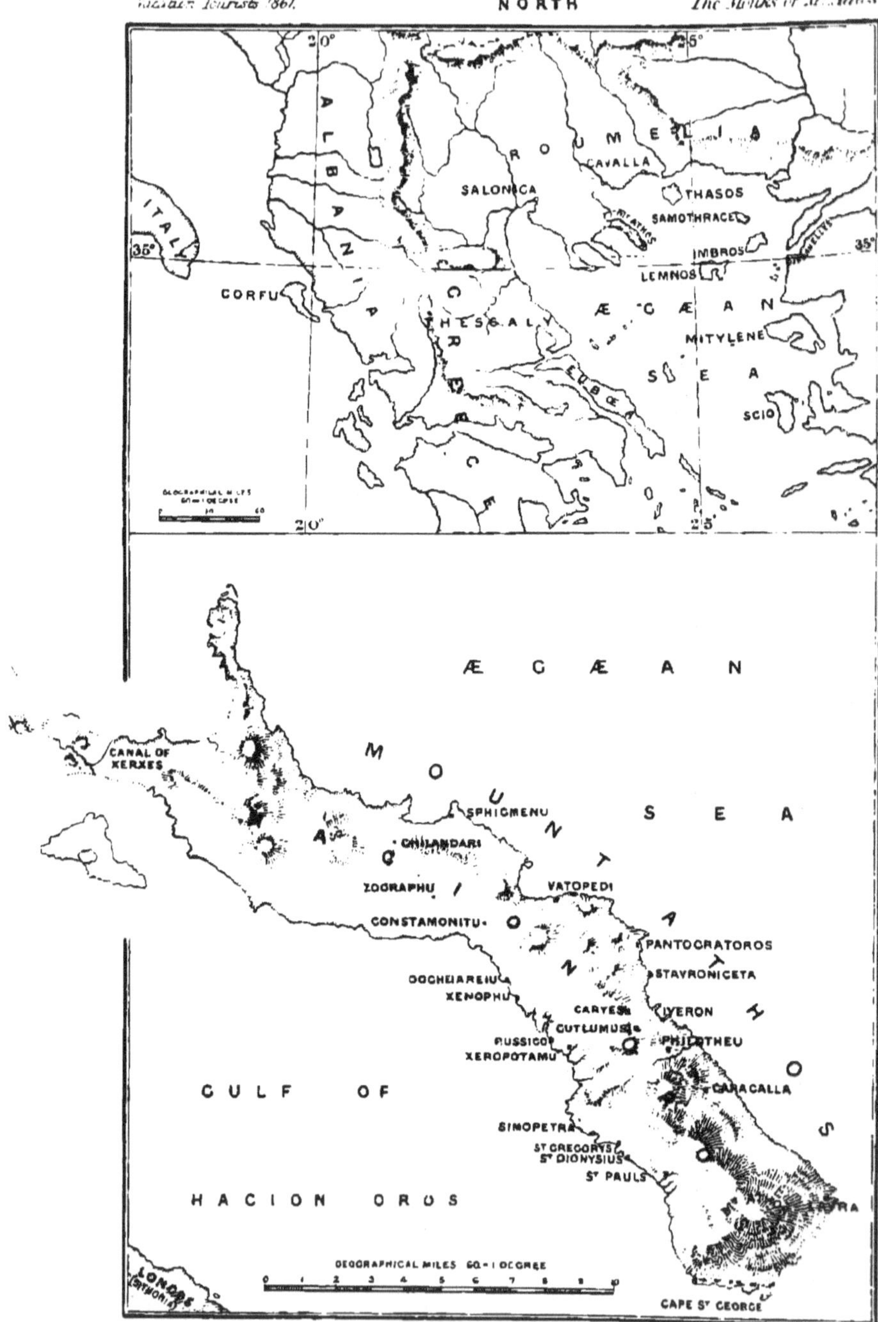
NORTH
20°
25°
ALBANIA
ITALY
ROUMELIA
CAVALLA
SALONICA
THASOS
SAMOTHRACE
MT ATHOS
IMBROS
35°
35°
LEMNOS
CORFU
GREECE
THESSALY
ÆGEAN
EUBŒA
MITYLENE
SEA
SCIO
GEOGRAPHICAL MILES
60 = 1 DEGREE
20°
25°
ÆGEAN
CANAL OF
XERXES
MOUNTAIN
SPHIGMENU
SEA
CHILANDARI
ZOGRAPHU
VATOPEDI
CONSTAMONITU
PANTOCRATOROS
STAVRONICETA
DOCHEIAREIU
XENOPHU
CARYES
IVERON
CUTLUMUS
RUSSICO
PHILOTHEU
XEROPOTAMU
GULF    OF
CARACALLA
SIMOPETRA
ST GREGORYS
ST DIONYSIUS
ST PAULS
HACION    OROS
LONGOS
SITHONIA
GEOGRAPHICAL MILES  60 = 1 DEGREE
0   1   2   3   4   5   6   7   8   9   10
CAPE ST GEORGE

## 3. *THE MONKS OF MOUNT ATHOS.*

BY H. F. TOZER, M.A.

THE easternmost of the three peninsulas, which stretch, like
a trident, from the coast of Macedonia into the north of
the Ægæan, notwithstanding its important position and
striking natural features, does not seem to have risen to
much importance before the Christian era.  On one occasion
it comes prominently forward, when Xerxes, warned by the
destruction of the fleet of Mardonius on its rocky coasts, cut
the canal through the isthmus, the traces of which, notwithstanding the soil which has accumulated in the course of
ages, are still distinctly visible.  At a later period the
architect Dinocrates proposed to carve its huge peak into a
statue of Alexander.  But the small towns that fringed its
shores never attained to opulence, and are seldom mentioned
in history.  In Christian times, however, this spot has
gradually become the seat of a community, which is probably
without a parallel in the world.  At what period monks
and anchorites first began to resort to Mount Athos, it is
difficult to determine.  Several of the monasteries possess
relics and ancient works of art, which are described as presents from the Empress Pulcheria ; some of them refer their
foundation to the time of Constantine ; and though we may
hesitate to accept these statements, and though a large
number of monks seem to have come over from Egypt, when
that country was overrun by the Mahometans, yet it is
highly probable that hermitages and retreats existed there
at a very early time.  It is in consequence of this antiquity
of the monastic community, and the freedom both from

attacks and from external influences which their isolated situation has secured to them, that Athos possesses so many features of interest at the present day. Nowhere in Europe, probably, can such a collection of ancient jewellery and gold-smith's work be found, as is presented by the relics preserved in the different monasteries; nowhere certainly can the Byzantine school of painting be studied with equal advantage; and some of the illuminated MSS. are inestimable treasures of art. The buildings of the monasteries are, with the sole exception of Pompeii, the most ancient existing specimens of domestic architecture; and within their walls the life of the Middle Ages is enacted before your eyes, with its manners and customs, dress, and modes of thought and belief, abso-lutely unchanged. And it is no slight addition to the pleasure of a visit, that in passing from one monastery to another you are surrounded by scenery, certainly not sur-passed, and hardly equalled, by any in Europe.

In the spring of 1853, I spent a week in this interesting place in company with my friend Mr. Crowder, of Wadham College; but as there were many interesting objects which we were obliged to leave unseen at that time, and many points in con-nexion with the life of the monks, which we were anxious further to investigate, we were glad to have an opportunity of revisiting it together in the summer of 1861. Accordingly, on the 11th of August, we left Gallipoli, on the Dardanelles, by the Austrian steamer, and following St. Paul's track, went "from Troas with a straight course to Samothrace, and the next day to Neapolis," the modern Cavalla, where we hired a boat to take us to one of the nearer monasteries on the east coast of the peninsula. We started at nightfall, and after tossing and tacking for a long time under the wooded heights of Thasos, with plentiful experience of the light and fickle winds of the Ægæan, about noon the following day we found ourselves approaching the great monastery of Vatopedi ($\mathrm{B}\alpha\tau o\pi\alpha i\delta\iota o\nu$); the name of which, according to the monks, is derived from the legend, that the Emperor Arcadius, when an infant, having been shipwrecked on the coast, was found miraculously preserved under a thornbush; and in acknowledgment of this, his father, Theodosius the Great, erected the monastery and called it Vatopedi, or "The bush of the child." The story is embodied in an extremely rude and quaint woodcut of the monastery, which was presented to us on our departure.

We had expected to find that the number of visitors to Athos would have greatly increased since our former stay, particularly as a Russian steamer from Constantinople had begun in the interval to touch on the western coast. We were consequently surprised to discover that fewer travellers came there now than formerly. At one monastery, when we asked the monk who waited on us, whether they saw many strangers: "Oh! yes," he replied, "they come from all the kingdoms of the world"—an instance of the Scripture phraseology, which not unfrequently occurs in the monks' conversation; however, when we questioned him more closely, he allowed that no one had been there for two years. On several occasions, when we asked what they supposed to be the reason of this change, we received almost identically the same answer; that they could not altogether account for it, but they thought "there was misfortune and poverty abroad in the world." Eight years had sufficed to work numerous changes. Many of the old superiors, whom we had seen in 1853, were now no more; parts of two monasteries had been shaken down by earthquakes; other buildings had suffered from the effects of fires; and one monastery had altered its constitution and form of government. We noticed also, what to us was particularly agreeable, a marked improvement in respect of cleanliness in the rooms we occupied. In one respect our visit was somewhat ill timed; for the day of our arrival coincided with the commencement of a fourteen days' fast, which precedes the festival of the Repose of the Virgin, the strictest in the year next to Lent. As the monks do not eat meat even on feast-days, we had not expected to have our carnivorous appetites satisfied; but we were rather dismayed at finding that we should not even get fish; not because the monks wished to make us conform to their rules, for they gave us the very best of what they had, but because they did not catch fish at that time. On one or two occasions they paid us the acceptable compliment of sending out a boat to take some for us; but the greater part of the twelve days of our sojourn there, we subsisted on rice, eggs, vegetables, and wine. We had, however, some compensation, in being able to observe the extreme rigour of an Athos fast.

Before we set foot on the Holy Mountain, let me endeavour briefly to sketch its general features. The peninsula, which in ancient times was called Acte, and now is known as Hagion Oros, or Monte Santo, is about forty miles in length, running from north-west to south-east, and on an average about four miles broad. At the isthmus, where are the remains of Xerxes' canal, its breadth is less than two miles, and the ground is comparatively level; but from this point it rises in undulations, until it forms a steep central ridge, which runs like a backbone through the whole peninsula. Towards the southern end it attains the elevation of about 4,000 feet, and then, after a slight depression, suddenly throws up a vast conical peak, 6,400 feet high, the base of which is washed on three sides by the sea. From the central ridge, lateral valleys and deep gorges run down to the coast; but the character of the ground on the two sides of the peninsula is entirely different, the western side being rugged and precipitous, while the eastern is comparatively soft, and clothed with magnificent trees. The vegetation of this part surpasses everything that I have seen elsewhere. On the ridge itself, and its steep declivities, are forests of beech and chestnut; below this oaks and plane-trees are found, together with the olive, cypress, arbutus, catalpa, and a plentiful undergrowth of heath and broom: in addition to which, as if the earth could never tire of pouring forth her stores, numerous creepers trail over the trees, and hang in festoons from the branches. The peak itself, to which the name of Athos is now restricted, is, from its height and solitary position, its conical form and delicate colour, a most impressive mountain. It rises several thousand feet above the region of firs in a steep mass of white marble, which, from exposure to the atmosphere, assumes a faint, tender tint of grey, of the strange beauty of which some idea may be formed by those who have seen the dolomite peaks of the Tyrol. I have seen its pyramidal outline from the plains of Troy, nearly one hundred miles off, towering up from the horizon, like a vast spirit of the waters, when the rest of the peninsula was concealed below. So great is the distance that it is only visible at sunset, when the faintness of the light allows it to appear. From its isolated position it is a centre of attraction to the storms in the north of the Ægæan; in consequence of which, the Greek sailors have so great a dread of rounding it in the winter, that it would be no unreasonable speculation for an enterprising government to renew the work of Xerxes.

It may easily be conceived from this, that the scenery is of the most magnificent description. Such combinations of rock, wood, and water can hardly be seen elsewhere. The deep blue expanse of the Ægæan forms a part of every view, and on the horizon, to the north and east, appear the heights of Mount Pangæus, and the magnificent outlines of the islands of Thasos, Samothrace, Imbros, and Lemnos. The slopes of the Holy Mountain itself are dotted with farms and monastic buildings, about which lie bright patches of cultivated land, which have been reclaimed by the hands of the monks. Perhaps the most beautiful ride is along the south-east coast of the peninsula. In this part you are sometimes in the midst of brushwood close to the sea, sometimes in shrubberies excluding the sun, through which, here and there, you get peeps of the Ægæan far below. From these, again, you penetrate inland, from time to time, into dells filled with planes and chestnuts, and embowered with creepers—a wilderness of leafy shade—places which Shelley would have delighted in; from the openings in which the majestic peak is frequently visible, its lower slopes melting into purple haze, while its summit assumes that unearthly, ethereal, lilac-grey tinge, which I have

before mentioned. The positions of the monasteries are singularly picturesque. A few are built in secluded situations on
the higher ridge; but the greater number of them are situated
on the sea-board, either at the mouths of gorges, or rising
from promontories of rock which project into the sea.

The principal exports are wood, charcoal, and nuts, of which
last article a large quantity is carried to Constantinople. The
climate is healthy, and the air extremely fine. The monasteries
which lie under the western precipices, are much exposed to
the summer heat, and on some of those higher up the mountain, snow often lies in winter for several days together; but,
on the whole, the temperature is equable, and epidemics are
almost unknown. In one or two of the larger monasteries
there are resident physicians; but many of the monks, partly,
perhaps, from being unaccustomed to medical treatment, seem
to take rather a fatalist view of diseases. At one place, where
there were lepers, I asked whether they came to Athos to be
cured. "No; not to be cured," was the reply; "they get well
whenever the Holy Virgin pleases;" and on another occasion
some of them said, "We have brethren in the monastery who
can treat slight maladies; the greater diseases we leave to
God." We shall not, perhaps, be far wrong in tracing here the
influence of Mahometanism. On one part of the coast we saw
a patient undergoing the sand-bath, a curious and primitive
cure for rheumatism. He was buried in the shingle up to his
chest, his head and shoulders alone appearing, and an umbrella
was spread over him, to protect him from the scorching rays of
the sun.

The day after our arrival, we proceeded on mules, lent to us
by the monks of Vatopedi, to Caryes, or "The Hazels," the
central and only village on Athos, where the Holy Synod of
the Mountain holds its sittings, and the Turkish governor
resides. This village, which lies in a lovely position, high up
on the eastern slopes of the central ridge, in the midst of the
trees from which it takes its name, consists mainly of one
long street, with open shops, forming a kind of bazaar; and
is remarkable for its cleanliness, and for the entire absence of

women and children. The exclusion of females from Athos is absolute. Not only are women prevented from landing on its sacred shores, but no cow, ewe, she-goat, sow, hen, or other creature of the forbidden sex is, under any circumstances, admitted. This restriction, which seems absurd at first sight, is in reality a singular parallel to some of the ordinances of the Mosaic law; such, for instance, as those in Lev. xix. 19, where garments of mixed linen and woollen texture are forbidden to be worn; the object in both cases being to enforce the main precept by keeping it before the minds of the people in a number of minor analogous cases. Even the Turkish governor is obliged to leave his harem behind him during his term of residence. This officer, the representative of the Porte, and the only Mahometan who is allowed to live here, is in reality of very little influence in the affairs of the monastic community, his duties being, for the most part, confined to the collection of taxes. The defence of the district is confided to a body of about twenty-five Christian soldiers, who may sometimes be seen in the monasteries, flaunting about in their gay Albanian dresses; but they are under the direction of the Holy Synod. The independence and immunities of Athos, in respect of which it is the most favoured part of the Turkish dominions, are of long standing. Shortly before the taking of Constantinople, the monks of that period agreed to submit to the rule of Mahomet II. on his guaranteeing them the privileges which they then enjoyed; and this engagement has been observed with tolerable fidelity by later sultans. The tribute, when divided among the different monasteries, amounts to about ten shillings a head, and they are not exposed to any irregular exactions.

The Holy Synod of the Mountain is a representative body, which, like the councils of our two English universities, manages the general affairs of the community at large, without interfering with the independent self-government of the different monasteries. Each of the twenty monasteries sends a representative (ἀντιπρόσωπος), who is maintained at Caryes at the expense of his society. Besides these, there are four presidents (ἐπιστάται), taken in rotation from the different monasteries who form the administrative body; and one of these again, according to a fixed cycle, takes precedence of the rest, and during his year of office is called "The First Man of Athos." After paying a visit to the Turkish governor, and presenting to him the *Firman* of the new sultan, which he kissed and reverently pressed to his forehead, we were introduced to the "First Man," who was a monk from Vatopedi, and gave him an introduction which we had brought from the Patriarch of Constantinople. We were then conducted to the chamber of meeting, a room of moderate size, with a divan running round three sides of it, where ten of the representatives were waiting to receive us. We were seated at the upper end, and after the usual refreshments, and some informal conversation, received a commendatory letter to the monasteries, written by the secretary in ancient Greek; a very curious document, stating the object of our visit, and requesting them to entertain us, and pay attention to our "creature comforts" (σωματικὴν ἀνάπαυσιν καὶ ἄνεσιν), to show us all we desired to see, and to "speed the parting guest" from place to place, by means of the mules of the monasteries (διὰ Μοναστηριακῶν ζώων). This letter serves as a passport, to show the monks that your visit is sanctioned by the authorities. As a stimulus to their hospitality, it certainly is not needed; for it would be hard to find elsewhere such unwearied kindness and liberal entertainment as the traveller meets with here. He is not expected, as in the smaller Greek monasteries, and the conventional establishments of the West, to defray the expenses of his entertainment by a donation; and the means of transit are provided for him *gratis*, both by land and water. A present to the servants, however, will generally be found acceptable.

After the assembly was dismissed, several of the caloyers, as the Greek monks are called (καλόγερος, a good old man), accompanied us to the school which has been established at Caryes for the education of some of the younger monks, two on an average being sent by each monastery. It is a commodious building, with well-arranged class-rooms, and a library containing editions of the classics, and standard authors in several European languages; but it had a deserted aspect, as the school was closed at this time, in consequence of a dispute which had arisen amongst the monasteries. The history of this I will now relate, not from any wish to expose the quarrels of my hospitable entertainers, but because it illustrates in a curious way the influence of the Great Powers, and of England in particular, in very remote districts. Who would imagine that Great Britain could be deeply involved in a dispute of the monks of Athos?

*Ab Jove principium:* we must begin from the Emperor Alexius Comnenus. That eminent personage founded the two monasteries of Cutlumusi and Pantocratoros, the former of which is close to Caryes on the mountain side, the latter on the sea-coast below. He endowed them with adjoining lands, and one farm belonging to Pantocratoros lies within the territory of Cutlumusi. A dispute arose about a water-course, that fruitful source of litigation, connected with this piece of ground. The Holy Synod took up the question, and cited the Warden of Cutlumusi to appear before them: this, however, he refused to do, as he knew beforehand that judgment would be given against him, and maintained that they had no authority in the matter. The Cutlumusi monks had a further story about a Russian general, who, during a long stay on Athos, had become enamoured of some MSS. in their library, and had fomented the quarrel for his own purposes; but it seemed to rest on a somewhat doubtful foundation. However, one morning a number of the members of the Synod, coming with soldiers, broke open the doors of the monastery, seized and imprisoned the most influential monks, and stripped the Warden naked, in order to search his clothes for papers, on a suspicion of treachery. Now it happened that these monks were from the Ionian islands, and therefore British subjects: so when they saw that they had no hopes of redress from other quarters, they appealed for protection to the consuls at Salonica and Cavalla. Mr. Wilkinson, the

English Consul at Salonica, laid the matter before the Pasha of that place, whom he found already preparing to pay a visit to the Holy Mountain; and accordingly, when he arrived there, and the case was put into his hands, he decided that the ejected monks should be reinstated. After procuring the acquiescence of the monks generally in various changes, such as the dismissal of the guard of soldiers, the Pasha returned home laden with presents, or, more properly speaking, plunder, in the shape of works of art, which he had obtained from the monasteries. At a later period, however, by means of representations from the Russian embassy at Constantinople, the decision of the Pasha was reversed in several points; in consequence of which five of the monasteries, which disapproved of the whole proceedings, seceded, and withdrew their representatives from the Synod. This was the state of things at the time of our visit, but there was some hope of a reconciliation being brought about by the good offices of Mr. Wilkinson.

We are so accustomed to look on the position of the inhabitants of the Ionian islands towards the English as one of undisguised opposition, that it seems curious to find them relying so much on the protection of England, when at a distance from home. But, as one of them frankly admitted, it is only in the islands, where the fact of the Protectorate is before their eyes, that they grumble, while here they enjoyed all the advantages of a powerful connexion. This, however, leads to much bitter feeling and jealousy of England on the part of the other caloyers. "Whenever fault is found with an Ionian monk," they would say, "he cries directly, 'Hands off! I'm a British subject; I shall appeal to the English consul.'" But I am bound to add, that the feeling of these Ionians towards an English traveller is of the most friendly description, and that the disinterested kindness which we received from many of them was remarkable, even in the midst of the hospitalities of the Holy Mountain.

One of the greatest sources of interest in a visit to Athos consists in this, that here can be seen in one view all the different phases of eastern monastic life. First of all there are the hermits, who dwell, like St. Anthony, the first anchorite, in perfect solitude, practising the sternest asceticism. In the retreats ($\kappa a\theta i\sigma\mu a\tau a$) we find small associations of monks living together in retirement, and working for a common stock. Again, when a number of these retreats are assembled round a central church, a skete ($\dot{a}\sigma\kappa\eta\tau\dot{\eta}\rho\iota o\nu$) is formed, which, in some cases, differs from a monastery only in not possessing an independent constitution. And lastly, there are the regular monasteries, each enjoying a separate corporate existence, possessing land on the mountain, and generally also beyond its limits, and having the right to be represented in the Synod. These again must be divided into two classes, according to their different forms of government; the one kind being *Cœnobite*, where there is one warden, or hegumen, and a common stock and common table; the other *Idiorrhythmic*, where "every man is a rule to himself," and the constitution is a sort of republic, the government being in the hands of two superiors annually elected: in these the inmates generally take their meals in their own cells, and both in respect of laying by money and the disposal of their time, are in a position of comparative freedom. Here, also, a wealthy monk, if he desires it, can have as many servants as he chooses to pay. The Idiorrhythmic rule is a departure from the original form, and of somewhat recent introduction; and it is a significant fact, that by far the greater number of the monasteries on the eastern slopes have adopted the less stringent discipline, while those which lie in more secluded positions, under the rugged precipices of the western side, have, with only two exceptions, remained Cœnobite. The lands which these monasteries possess out of Athos are partly in Macedonia, partly in Thasos, Lemnos, and other islands of the Ægæan; but by far the greatest part consists of estates in the Danubian Principalities, which have been given to them in former centuries by Hospodars of Moldavia and Wallachia. From these sources some of them derive large revenues; but of late years their prosperity has been considerably checked by debts incurred during the Greek War of Independence, when a large body of Turkish soldiers was quartered on them for nine years, from 1821 to 1830.

The whole number of monks on Athos is believed to be about 3,000; besides these there is a fluctuating population of *seculars* ($\kappa o \sigma \mu \iota \kappa o i$), some of whom reside permanently in the monasteries as servants or labourers, though without taking any monastic vows, while others come for a time from the adjoining country, and afterwards return to their homes. These may, perhaps, amount to 3,000 more. The number of monks in the separate monasteries varies from twenty-five to three hundred, but about one hundred is the commonest number. It seldom happens, however, that all are present at the same time, as a certain proportion are generally engaged in superintending the outlying farms. We found it extremely difficult to get any accurate information on these points, owing to that singular dislike of statistics which is so characteristic of orientals. A Turk, when asked a question of figures, to save himself further trouble, replies at once with a good round number: a Greek winces, utters a peculiar exclamation, expressing something between doubt and annoyance, and when he sees no means of escape, tells you as much as he knows himself. "How many monks are there in the monastery?" "Do you mean *this* monastery?" "Yes; how many are there in this monastery?" "Eigh! a great many." "But what do you suppose is the exact number?" "Eigh! I don't know; *about* eighty or ninety." We seldom arrived at anything more definite than this. By far the greater number of the monks are Greeks by race, natives of free Greece, the Ionian islands, or the Turkish dominions; two of the monasteries, however, Zographu and Chilandari, situated in the northern part of the peninsula, are exclusively inhabited by Bulgarians and Servians, and have the service in the Slavonic tongue; there are also a few Georgians in the Iberian monastery; and there are a great many Russians, who are found partly in the Russian

monastery and the sketes which they have founded, partly
scattered about among the other monasteries.  It was curious
to observe the contrast between the children of the north
and the south ; and I could not help fancying that the Greek
regarded the Russian as a large uncouth being, somewhat
like the Troll of the Norse tales, simple-minded and easily
outwitted.  The following incidents may serve to illustrate
what I mean.

On the evening of the day on which we were presented to
the Synod at Caryes, we had descended to the monastery of
Pantocratoros, or The Almighty, which stands on a rock on
the east coast of the peninsula, and were sitting with some
of the superiors in a room overlooking the sea, which was
dashing in below, when suddenly they exclaimed, " Ah ! here
he is ; here comes the Archimandrite * ! "  As we looked up
in expectation of some great dignitary, there walked, or
rather rolled, into the room, a burly man, whose light hair and
ruddy complexion formed a complete contrast to the appearance of the other monks.  He tumbled himself down on the
divan, and turning to us, exclaimed, laughing, " Good evening ;
you are welcome : I am a Muscovite—a barbarian ! " (καλε-
σπέρα σας· καλῶς ὡρίσατε· εἶμαι Μόσχοβ—εἶμαι βάρβαρος).
We returned his salutations, and then I asked, " As there are
so many monasteries in Russia, why do you come to Athos ?
Why do you not remain in one of the establishments in your
own country ? "  " It's because of the women, sir," he replied,
" It's the women !  In Russia there are women in the
monasteries, and I can't endure them ; and therefore I come
here where there are no women."†  And then he went off

* This name, which in Russia still retains its original sense of " head of
a monastery," in the Byzantine Church, is simply titular.

† In many of the Greek monasteries, as, for instance, the great monastery of
Megaspelæon in the Morea, women of advanced age are admitted as servants.
In 1853, we found a Greek gentleman and his daughter living in one of the
more accessible of the convents on the heights of Meteora, having taken
refuge there from the banditti, who infested the plains of Thessaly during the
summer : in the winter, when the severity of the climate dispersed those
gentry, they returned to their country seat.

into a rigmarole story in broken Greek, until the rest of the company told him in very plain terms that he was a bore and talked unintelligible nonsense ; on which he took himself off, but, before the evening was over, showed that he was not offended, by sending us some tea (τζάἰ), which is found wherever the Russians are.

At the Greek monastery of Simopetra there was an old Russian monk, who was evidently the butt of the others. Poor old fellow! five and twenty years he had been in the monastery, and yet he could hardly speak a word of Greek. " Two, three words, I know," he said, " wine, bread—no more." His principal companion was a clever tom-cat, which he had trained to turn most wonderful summersaults, and which was brought out into the court of the monastery to perform before us.   " Ah!" exclaimed a sharp-witted young Zantiote, who was standing by, with a look of compassion, " the Russians are thicksculled" (οἱ Ῥῶσσοι εἶναι χονδροκέφαλοι).   Yet for all this, as the Russian Church has been the progressive branch of the Eastern Church since the time of Peter the Great, so the Russian monks are the most progressive element in the society of the Holy Mountain.   The other monks are aware of this, and used to speak of their good bell-ringing and harmonious chanting, which is indeed an agreeable contrast to the dismal drone of the Greek services : in addition to this, the only printing-press on Athos is in the Russian monastery.

There is hardly one of the twenty monasteries which is not worth seeing, either on account of its position, or its buildings, or some precious work of art which it contains : but to avoid repetition, let me describe two of the most characteristic ; and first, the Idiorrhythmic convent of Iveron, that is, of the Iberians or Georgians, which ranks the third in numbers and importance.

This monastery, which was founded by three Georgians at the end of the 10th century, stands near the sea, between steep wooded hills, at the mouth of a deep valley, which runs down eastward from the central ridge.   In shape it is an irregular square, and its appearance is extremely imposing, as the high stone wall by which it is surrounded makes it resemble a vast castle.  The domestic buildings, however, by which this wall is surmounted, are entirely at variance with this military aspect: they are of wood, singularly picturesque, projecting at different levels and angles, and supported by sloping beams, which lean like brackets against the wall.  From the roofs of these houses rise numerous chimneys, many of which, like the house-fronts themselves, are painted with bright colours; behind these appear the domes of the church; while at the back of all a massive tower, which was probably used as a watch-tower in more troublous times,* forms a conspicuous object.  Close to a dry river-bed, which lies behind the monastery, is a poor-house, where distressed seculars are provided for, and on the heights above is a skete for lepers, who, as well as madmen, are sent to the Holy Mountain to be taken care of.  It is no slight praise to the monks, that they provide a refuge for these outcasts of society.  Again, on the hill to the north, is a skete for Georgians, to which nation also ten of the 200 inmates of the monastery belong.  The cemetery may generally be distinguished by a group of cypresses; but there are no tombstones, as the bones are removed a certain time after interment, and laid in a common heap.

Entering the monastery by the gateway, we pass through a dark and winding passage, intended apparently to baffle a besieging force, and find ourselves in the great court, in the centre of which, detached from the other buildings, stands the principal church.  What first attracts our attention on looking round, is the extreme irregularity of everything.  In one place you see a wooden cloister, in another an out-house;

---

* Abp. Georgirenes ("Description of the present state of Samos, Patmos, Nicaria, and Mount Athos") says, in A. D. 1678, speaking of the monastery of Lavra (p. 88), "They have a strong magazin, and a sentinel perpetually standing to give notice of any Corsair:" and of St. Gregory's (p. 95), that it is "near the sea, and much infested with pirates, for want of fortifications and men to defend it, having but sixty monks."

here a chapel appears, there a vine-covered trellis peeps out, and the mixed brick and stone work of the more regular buildings contributes to increase the variety. Not the least conspicuous objects are two magnificent cypresses with velvet foliage, which rise near the east end of the church. It is this picturesqueness which constitutes the charm of domestic buildings of the Byzantine style, to which all these monasteries belong ; for they cannot aspire to beauty, and the few which are built regularly are far from pleasing. As wood is so much used as a material for building, many parts of these structures must be of a comparatively late date ; but still they represent to us very fairly the original edifices, in consequence of the conservative and traditionary spirit of the Greek Church, which appears nowhere so strikingly as on Athos, in accordance with which every part, when it falls into decay, is repaired so as to correspond in style, even if it is not exactly similar, to the original design.

Let us now visit what in all the monasteries is the most important building, the central church, entering at the west end, and observing as we pass, the subjects of the frescoes, which are disposed in regular order along the walls. We first find ourselves in the proaulion or porch, a corridor, supported on the outside by light pillars, running the whole width of the building : in this part are represented scenes from the Apocalypse, especially the punishment of the wicked ; and in one place there are pictures of the Œcumenical Councils, that of Nice being particularly striking. In this, Athanasius is represented as a young man stooping down to write the Creed, while Arius is in the act of disputing between his two great adversaries, Spiridion and Nicholas, and on the right of this group is a band of Arians, dressed as philosophers, some of whom are coming into the council chamber to recant their errors, while the rest are being driven into a prison by a man armed with a club. Passing onward from the proaulion, we enter the first narthex or antechapel, which contains representations of various forms of martyrdom : on either side of the central door, which leads into the second narthex, are figures of SS. Peter and Paul. These narthekes, which are divided by walls from one another and from the body of the church, seem originally to have been intended for catechumens and penitents, and must have been introduced into the monastic churches more for the sake of maintaining the usual type, than with a view to actual use: as it is, they are employed for the celebration of the more ordinary services, and when the body of the church is too small for the number of worshippers, they serve to provide additional room. In the second narthex are frescoes of saints and hermits, who look down in grim solemnity from the walls; the hermits especially are most striking objects, being almost human skeletons, and stark naked, except for their long grey beards, which reach to the ground. From this we pass into the main body of the church, which is in the form of a Greek cross, with a central cupola supported on four pillars, which symbolize the four Evangelists. At the east end and in the transepts are semi-cupolas, but the whole of the sanctuary is concealed by the iconostase, a wooden screen, reaching nearly to the roof, and most elaborately carved and gilt, in which are set pictures of our Lord and saints. The position of two of the frescoes in this part is universally the same in all the monasteries: in the cupola is a colossal figure of the Saviour, and over the western door of entrance a representation of the Repose (κοίμησις) of the Virgin. Other parts of the walls are covered with Scripture subjects, and generally in one of the transepts is a group of young warrior saints, among whom St. George is always conspicuous. From the drum of the cupola hangs an elegant brass coronal, and from this are suspended silver lamps, small Byzantine pictures, and ostrich eggs, which are said to symbolize faith, according to a strange but beautiful fable, that the ostrich hatches its eggs by gazing steadfastly at them: within this coronal again is a large . chandelier. The floor is ornamented in parts with *opus Alexandrinum*, a kind of inlaid work in white marble, porphyry, and *verd antique;* and here and there are placed lecterns, elaborately decorated with mother of pearl and tortoiseshell.

Mosaic work is rare on Athos, though in some places, as at Vatopedi and Lavra, there are most curious specimens of it. Where it is found, it is a proof of great antiquity in the build-ing, for it was not used in edifices of the later Byzantine style. The stalls are ranged all round the sides, and are provided with *misereres*, which, however, are seldom used, as the monks generally stand during the whole service.

At first sight the general appearance of the building seems rather marred by the multiplicity of details crowded into so small a space; but when the eye is once accustomed to this, the effect is magnificent, from the brilliancy of the ornaments and the harmonious, though sober colours of the frescoes. In the Byzantine pictures, as well as the frescoes, which one sees on Athos, the drawing and perspective are generally bad, and when the description of strong passions or violent action is attempted, they are often indescribably grotesque; and we look in vain for the delicacy and spirituality of Fra Angelico: but the more passive feelings, such as humility, resignation, and devotion, are often admirably expressed, with a grace and sweetness which are rarely found in the specimens by which Byzantine art is represented in Western Europe.* There was, however, one artist of real power, some of whose frescoes still remain in the peninsula, called Panselenus, a name little known away from Athos. He lived in the 11th or 12th century, and is called by Didron "the Raphael, or rather the Giotto, of the Byzantine school." His most famous works are in the church at Caryes, and consist of single figures and groups of saints, the drapery and arrangement of which are excellent, and the faces full of originality and power. There are also frescoes attributed to him in the monasteries of Pantocratoros and Lavra, and though we are naturally suspi-cious of the indiscriminate use of a distinguished name, yet these are so superior to the ordinary pictures, as to make it probable that they are by his hand.

* M. Didron says ("Manuel d'Iconographie Chrétienne," p. xlv.): "La beauté des anciens ouvrages de cette école est incontestable." He attributes the oldest of the frescoes to the ninth century.

Returning to the external porch of the church, we see two *Semantra*, or instruments for calling the brethren to prayers. One of these is a long flat board, narrow in the centre, so that it may be grasped by one hand while it is struck with a wooden mallet by the other. The second is of iron, resembling a piece of the tire of a wheel, which is struck with a hammer. The monotonous sound of these instruments may often be heard in the dead of night, summoning the caloyers to the midnight service. Outside the west end of the church is an elegant cupola supported on pillars, inside which is a stone basin, in which the holy water is blessed, which is used in the ceremonies of the Epiphany, and in other rites of the Greek Church. Opposite this is the refectory ($\tau\rho\acute{a}\pi\epsilon\zeta a$), a building in the form of a Latin cross, along the walls of which inside are ranged small stone tables, one of which at the further end is placed so as to form a high table. At the angle where one of the transepts joins the nave, is a pulpit, attached to the wall, from which the homily is read during meals. Most of the refectories are decorated with frescoes of saints along the side walls, and a representation of the Last Supper over the high table ; but here the structure is of a recent date, and consequently plain, as the monks have not yet been able to afford the decorations. Over the entrance of the refectory is a bell-tower, in the lower story of which a new library has been constructed; to this some of the books are being removed from the old library, a confined room over the church porch. The contents of these libraries consist mainly of Greek ecclesiastical writings, together with a fair number of classical authors, and mathematical works : 1 noticed also a good many books published at Venice at the beginning of this century. In this library there is a curious Greek translation of Goldsmith's History of Greece, which was " well spoken of" by the monks. The best account of the libraries generally, will be found in Dr. Hunt's notice in Walpole's *Turkey;* of the MSS. a full description is given in Mr. Curzon's *Monasteries of the Levant.* Many of these are fine works of art; but the effects of damp and neglect are sadly visible. The most precious of all, however, which belongs to the monastery of Chilandari, is in perfect preservation, from having been kept in the church along with the sacred relics. It is a 4to Greek MS. of St. John's Gospel, of about the 12th century, written in gold letters on white vellum, and was presented to the monastery by the Emperor Andronicus Comnenus. But the finest *illuminated* MS. which we saw, is the property of the monks of Docheiareiu, and seems to have escaped the notice of Mr. Curzon. It is a book of Lives of Saints, of the 11th century, decorated with miniatures of the saints, most delicately executed, and initial letters bordered with exquisite arabesques. It is possible that unknown literary treasures may still be concealed in these libraries; but they have been so carefully examined by *savants* from Russia and elsewhere, that it is hardly likely.

Among the other buildings which are most worthy of notice, are the kitchen, a curious square building, in the centre of which is the hearth, and a large chimney running up through the roof; the underground cellars, which contain some huge tuns; and the numerous chapels and oratories which are found in all parts of the building. There are as many as twenty-two of these;* and one, which is built near the gateway, contains a miraculous picture of the Virgin, the story of which is worth relating, as a specimen of the numerous legends which abound on Athos, and are believed and told by the monks with the simplest faith. It was cast into the sea near Nicæa, but was carried safely to the Holy Mountain. When it had been brought to the monastery, and the monks were deliberating where they should place it, it knocked several times on a spot close to the gate, to signify that her chapel should be erected there; and from this circumstance she is called the Portaitissa, or Portress. In one part there is a scar, where an unbeliever stuck his lance into it; blood issued immediately, and the malefactor was converted, and died a saint. He is represented in a fresco in

* It is said that there are in all 935 churches, chapels, and oratories on the Holy Mountain.

the narthex of the chapel, where he is called " The Barbarian Saint." The face of the picture, like most of the sacred paintings of the Greek Church, is in the hardest style ; but it is surrounded by embossed work, or sheathing, of gold, which is covered with the most magnificent jewels. A copy of it was taken to Russia, in the 17th century, by order of the Patriarch Nicon, and is still to be seen at Moscow.*

As a description of the monasteries would be incomplete without a notice of the relics, I will add a few words about them. They are mainly composed of heads, limbs, and bones of saints, partially cased in silver, and pieces of the true cross, which are frequently surrounded by filigree and flower-work in metal, of great antiquity, and the most exquisite workmanship. The caskets in which these are kept are often superb specimens of the goldsmith's art, and ornamented with diamonds, extremely rare from their antiquity, and pearls, rubies, and emeralds of immense size, and for the most part uncut. As works of art, however, they are not appreciated by the monks, who value the relics themselves, and not their decorations. They are always kept behind the iconostase, near the holy table, and are brought out and arranged on a kind of desk, when they are to be shown to pilgrims and visitors. It was curious to observe the various degrees of respect with which they were treated in different monasteries. Generally the candles were lighted in their honour, and the priest who handled them put on his stole (ἐπιτραχήλιον) ; but in some places the caloyers treated them with the utmost veneration, keeping silence in their presence, and kissing them fervently ; in others they treated the exhibition more as a matter of course ; and here and there they knew very little about them. Actual carelessness or irreverence we never saw ; but at the Lavra, one of the superiors, named Melchizedech, a man of vast proportions, and overflowing with fun and humour, observed aside to our dragoman,

* See Stanley's " Eastern Church," p. 424. The legend, with some variations from the account given me by the monks, is related at length in the " Travels of Macarius," vol. ii. p. 172.

"When I am dead, and they preserve my relics, it will cost the monastery a *precious* lot to case my head with silver!"

As a specimen of one of the smaller convents, we will take the Cœnobite establishment of Simopetra, or the rock of Simon the Anchorite, which is built in a steep position about half-way down the cliffs of the western side. We approached it from the sea, for the precipices between this and the monastery of St. Paul, from which we came, are so tremendous, and the paths so bad, that the monks do not like their mules to go that way. Accordingly we were provided with a boat and two naval caloyers (ναυτικοὶ καλόγεροι), who rowed us to a tiny port, provided with a pier and landing-place, above which the monastery towers, perched on a rock, at a height of 800 feet. Shortly after our arrival a monk appeared, and finding that we wanted our saddle-bags carried up, took out a large speaking-trumpet, and shouted through it to the monastery, in Greek, "two mules," (δύο μυλάρια). He was answered from above, and not long after, as we sauntered up the zigzag path, we met the animals on their way down. Just below the monastery the ground is carefully made into terraces, where vegetables are grown, while vines and gourds trail over the high supporting walls. From these rises the perpendicular rock, on which the building stands, isolated on all sides from the surrounding ground, except at the back, where it is joined to the cliffs by an aqueduct with two rows of arches. The upper part of its high walls is lined with wooden balconies and corridors, which are supported on projecting brackets, and rise, tier above tier, to the roof, with the most picturesque irregularity. Inside, the buildings are most curiously packed away. In the lower part are the storehouses, between the side walls and the upper part of the rock, which crops out in the interior court; the court itself is so narrow, that the whole building has been roofed over, the light penetrating by side windows, and a variety of openings and crevices. In consequence of this, the church is not isolated as in most of the monasteries, but closely surrounded by the other buildings; and its walls are pierced with numerous windows for a Byzantine edifice, in order to admit more light into the interior.  The forms with which a traveller is received on his arrival are universally the same;  after delivering the letter of the Synod to the porter, who carries it to the Hegumen, he is conducted to the guest-chamber, one of the best rooms in the monastery, generally commanding a superb view, where he is regaled with sweetmeats, arrack, cold water, and coffee; and when he is supposed to be sufficiently rested, he receives a visit from the superiors and some of the more intelligent monks, who, before their departure, inquire if he would like to " eat bread."

Having thus taken a survey of the buildings of the monasteries, let us inquire what is the employment of the pale grave men, with long beards and flowing hair, dressed in dark blue serge gowns and high caps, who move about their courts and corridors.  But first, perhaps, it may be well for us to notice some of the points in which they differ from our ordinary ideas of monastic life.

In the first place, then, only a small proportion of these monks are *clergy*, and the clerical office is in no way connected with the monastic profession.  Even in the large establishments, such as Vatopedi and Iveron, it is not usual to find more than ten or twelve of the community in Holy Orders ; and at Philotheu, the smallest of the monasteries, there were but three priests, just enough to carry on the services.  Still less are they *teachers* or *missionaries*, except in one instance, the Bulgarian monastery of Chilandari, where of late years a system has been established of sending a number of ordained monks into Bulgaria on a sort of home mission, to assist the parish priests in extensive districts. This " Apostolic " system, as they call it, is said to have worked well, but it is wholly an excrescence from the monastic life of Athos.  Again, they are not *students* or *learned men*, though, from the way in which the books have been used and marked in the libraries, there is evidence that there were such among them in former times ; and they have traditions of a period, shortly before the taking of Constantinople, when teachers went out from this place, as a centre, to the whole of the Eastern Church: now, however, the libraries are rarely opened, and the monks do not pretend to make study a part of their occupations; though, at the same time, they profess a desire for learning, and take more care of their books; and some of the monasteries have lately sent some of their younger members to the University of Athens. A few of the monks we found to be acquainted with the ancient Greek authors. One remarkably intelligent young fellow, who had left his convent on a former occasion, against the will of the hegumen, in order to get instruction at Athens, amused us by remarking, "I don't get on particularly well with Hellenic (ancient Greek); Xenophon and some other authors I can read easily enough, but I find the speeches in Thucydides so very hard!" We consoled him by telling him that he was not singular in his difficulties. Modern languages are almost entirely unknown; only a very few could speak a little French or Italian; and theology, to which, at least, one would expect some time to be devoted, is hardly in a better condition. In fact, the great proportion of the caloyers are of the class of peasants and artisans, and are wholly uneducated and ignorant. But the ludicrous inexperience of ordinary things, which has been attributed to them, does not generally exist now; for in almost all the convents one of the Constantinople or Athens journals is taken in, and some of the monks read the Greek newspaper published in London, the *Bretannikos Aster*, so that they are able to talk about the ordinary subjects of the day, though regarding them from a very distant point of view.

But if the monks of Athos are neither clergy, nor missionaries, nor students, yet they realize the primitive idea of monasticism in a way in which it is not realized elsewhere. When Antony and his followers withdrew to the deserts of Egypt, their object was not the pursuit of learning or the benefit of their fellow men, but retirement from a dangerous and distracting world, and leisure for devotion and religious exercises. This idea of monastic life

is still maintained in the Eastern Church; and accordingly,
as in those early times there was no distinction of monastic
orders, so here one rule alone is followed, that established
by St. Basil.  Six or seven hours of every day, and more
on Sundays, are occupied by the Church services; and on
some of the greater festivals the almost incredible time of
from sixteen to twenty hours is spent in church.*  Their
life is one of the sternest bodily mortification.  In the
Cœnobite convents they never touch meat, and rarely in
the Idiorrhythmic.  Nearly half the days in the year are
fast days, and on these they take only one meal, which is
generally composed of bread, vegetables, and water; and
during the first three days of Lent, those whose constitutions
can stand it, eat *nothing*.  In addition to this, they never get
an unbroken night's rest, as the first service commences
between 1 and 2 A.M.  The remainder of their time which
is not occupied in public prayer, is spent by the superiors
in the management of the affairs of their society, and by the
lower monks in various menial occupations which are required of them.  There is, however, a class intermediate
between these two, whose time cannot be so easily accounted
for.  In the Idiorrhythmic convents any person who pays
on entrance a sum equal to about 45*l.* of our money, becomes
permanently free from any obligation to work in the monastery.  Those who are on this footing must have a considerable
amount of spare time, and, as far as we could discover, but
scanty means of employing it.  In some of the Cœnobite
monasteries the brethren work in the fields, but even in
these it is only for a few hours in the day; and in general
this kind of labour, and other outdoor employments, such
as fishing, are left to the seculars.

When we inquired what constituted the attractiveness of
this seemingly uninviting life, we constantly received the
same reply.  Tranquillity ($\dot{\eta}\sigma\upsilon\chi\acute{\iota}a$); rest of body and soul;

---

* For an account of the services, and other details connected with the
monasteries, the reader is referred to an elaborate and impartial article in the
*Christian Remembrancer* for April, 1851, to which I am much indebted.

which was valued by some as freeing them from temptation,
and giving them time for devotion, by others as securing
them comparative ease ; by the greater number, probably, from
a mixture of these two feelings. But to the Christian subjects
of the Porte, the great attraction is the security which they
enjoy here, and freedom from the ill-treatment and exactions
to which they are exposed elsewhere, as every one knows
who has travelled in the interior of European Turkey.

The most thoroughly monastic group that we saw, was in
the small and secluded Cœnobite monastery of Constamonitu,
one of the very few which do not command a sea view.    On
our arrival, we were ushered into the guest-chamber, a small
gloomy room, where we were soon after visited by the
Hegumen, a kind hearty old man, and very simple in his
ideas, having been very little away from Athos ; yet we soon
discovered that he knew everything of what was going on in
Europe and America ; he was even aware that in England we
used steam-machinery in agriculture ; and a smile of grim
satisfaction played over his features, as he spoke of the
probable downfall of the Papacy.* While we were talking
with him, there came in a very old man, so venerable in his
appearance, that the most thoughtless person could not but
have risen up in his presence. His flowing beard was snowy
white, his limbs spare and ascetic, so that he looked more like
one of the ancient hermits, than any one else that we saw.
He was born in Mitylene, and was employed in a merchant's
business in Egypt at the time of Napoleon's expedition :
after this he retired to the convent of Mount Sinai, and when
he had spent three years there, came in 1809 to Athos, where

---

* At Cutlumusi and other monasteries, there is a curious tradition, that they
were destroyed by the Pope of Rome, who came here " about the time of the
great schism." The foundation of this was, probably, some attack of the
crusaders at the time of the Fourth Crusade ; or the expedition of the
Emperor Michael Palæologus to force the monks to accept the terms of the
Concordat of Lyons, on which occasion they suffered great injury at his hands.
The name Caryes, which, as I have before mentioned, means " The Hazels," is
derived by many of the monks from Κάρα (a head), in accordance with a story
that the Pope cut off the heads of all the representatives of that period, and
placed them round the Protaton, or principal church of the place.

he had remained ever since. He had been tutor to the old Hegumen, with whom he had maintained a warm and unbroken friendship. The man who waited on us, was a tall gaunt caloyer, with a hard Scotch cast of features, who might have sat for a likeness of a Covenanter. He talked with fervour of the protection afforded to them by the sacred relics, of the devoted lives of some of the hermits, their prophetic power, and the need of sternly subjugating the passions, in order to gain an insight into the higher spiritual mysteries, until at last he looked almost like one inspired, and his utterance became so indistinct, that we could understand but little of what he said. The sight of these three men together in the dark monastic chamber was one not to be forgotten ; and it is a characteristic instance of the hospitality of the Holy Mountain, that, though they were sternly fasting, they pressed us to feast on the best of what they had, and the Covenanter replenished our wine-glasses.

The principal difference between the life in the sketes and retreats, and that in the monasteries, consists in the amount of manual labour which is performed in the former. In these reside most of the artisans, by whom the shops at Caryes, and through them the monasteries, are provided with clothing and other necessary articles. In consequence of their laborious occupations, their inmates are considered to live a very severe life, and I was certainly far more favourably impressed with these societies than with the convents. As a skete is an association of retreats, it may be sufficient to describe the sort of life that is met with in these.

As we were on our way to ascend the peak, we stopped to leave our baggage-mule at the Retreat of St. Demetrius, one of the few buildings which stand at the south end of the peninsula, where the ground descends with great steepness to the sea. It contained twelve monks, engaged in different occupations, but working for a common stock. The sloping hill-side below is covered with well-tended vineyards, which are cultivated by the monks themselves, and afford a proof of their careful husbandry. Outside, the building has nothing to distinguish it from an ordinary cottage ; in one part of the interior is a little chapel, and the rest is occupied by the cells and workshops of the inmates. Going into one of the rooms, I found a painter sitting by a window, which opened out on a lovely gorge, and engaged in painting on a thick block of wood a picture in exactly the same style as those from which the early Italian artists copied. He was a small emaciated delicate-looking man, with a pensive countenance, and quite realized my idea of a mediæval artist. He wore the Great Habit ($\mu\acute{e}\gamma a$ $\sigma\chi\tilde{\eta}\mu a$), a kind of breast-plate or stomacher of a woollen material, worked with a cross and other devices, which is a sign of the highest grade of monastic austerity. He was so intent on his work, that at first he hardly noticed me ; and I watched him for some time, as he worked on without a copy, and yet too rapidly and mechanically to allow me to suppose that he was painting from imagination. However, when I asked him some questions, and he saw that I was interested in his art, he put down his brush, and showed me the secret of his inspiration—the "Guide to Painting" of Dionysius of Agrapha, which has been translated into French by M. Didron, under the title of " Manuel d'Iconographie Chrétienne," from a MS. which he obtained from Athos. This remarkable book, compiled at an unknown, but very early period, by a man who professed himself a diligent student of the works of Panselenus, contains the explanation of the singular uniformity of design in the paintings, both ancient and modern, of the Greek Church, as it is composed of rules, very often of a minute description, for the treatment of all kinds of sacred subjects, specifying the position and attitudes of the figures, the expression of the faces, and the back-grounds and accompaniments. The art of painting has existed uninterruptedly on Athos, and it has possessed, and still possesses, so many artists, that we may say with M. Didron, " c'est veritablement l'Italie de l'Eglise Orientale." Another art which employs many of the monks, is that of wood-carving, an elaborate specimen of which was being prepared, at the time of our visit, to be sent to the Great Exhibition of 1862.

On one occasion I was fortunate enough to have an inter-
iew with a hermit.  In one part of the road between the
1onasteries of Docheiareiu and Constamonitu, where the
ath lies along the beach, we had stopped for my companion
ɔ gather some pebbles, when our dragoman, looking up the
teep cliffs, exclaimed that he saw a man standing at some
istance above us.  Guessing what he might be, I dismounted,
nd scrambled up twenty or thirty feet to the mouth of a
ave, where I found a dark hollow-cheeked man, clothed in a
ingle garment of rough cloth.  In the inner part of the cave,
vhich was divided off from the rest by a low wall, was his
ed of straw, and one book of prayers was lying on the wall.
n this place he lived both winter and summer.  He came
riginally from Argyro-Castro, in Albania, and had served for
ome years as a corporal in the army of the king of Greece;
iut after a time he was seized with a desire for the life of
etirement, and came as a caloyer to the skete of St. Anne.
Lfter remaining there for three years, he devoted himself to
he life of a hermit, in which he had passed his time for
even years.  His food was brought to him from the neigh-
ouring monasteries.  He spoke distinctly, like a man who
ιad had some education; and slowly, as one unaccustomed
o conversation.  As we were looking down on the tumbling
vaves, I said to him, before leaving, "Here you have near
rou God and the sea."  "Ah!" he replied, "we are all
inners;" as if to deprecate the idea that he was on a higher
piritual level than other men.  His answer illustrates the
ntire absence of pretension which we observed among the
nonks: they never represented themselves as more learned,
ir more religious, or having higher aims than was really the
ase; and when they had devoted themselves to the monastic
ifè from mixed motives, they did not hesitate to avow it.

One principal object which we had in view in visiting
Lthos at this time, was to be present at the festival of the
Transfiguration, which is celebrated on the summit of the
ieak on the 6th of August (Old Style).  Any monk from any
f the monasteries is welcome to attend it, though it is quite a

voluntary matter; and we found that they regarded the mountain expedition not by any means as a member of the Alpine Club would have regarded it, but in the light of a pilgrimage. We had arranged our plans so as to arrive at the Lavra,* which is the nearest monastery, two days before: the monks, however, we found, had already started, to make their preparations. On the afternoon of the day preceding the festival, we rode to the Retreat of St. Demetrius ; and from thence ascended through forests by an extremely steep mule-track, commanding views of indescribable beauty, until about sunset we arrived at a chapel of the Virgin, situated in the midst of grassy slopes, on a rocky projection of the mountain, just where the trees begin to cease. From this point, the two other peninsulas, which form the trident of Chalcidice, were visible, and to the south the line of small islands which run off from the north of Euboea ; far below us a steamer was making its way like a fly on the water. A few monks were here, preparing, in an immense stew-pan, the viands for the next day—a suspicious-looking mess of fish and vegetables, of which they gave us a dish for supper. After this repast, we commenced the ascent on foot, accompanied by two monks, one of whom was a sportsman, and carried his gun, a curious contrast to his monastic dress, and talked, with evident satisfaction, of the price which wild boars fetched, when killed and exported. Before long the other monk and our dragoman fell into the rear ; but our sporting friend was in training, and we soon found ourselves rapidly mounting by a rough, zigzag path, and scaling the white marble summits, which looked almost like snow-peaks in the light of the brilliant moon. After about an hour of this work, when we had almost reached the top, we sat down, to wait for our companions, to listen to the tinkling bells of the mules in the distance, and to watch the moonbeams streaming on the

* The name Lavra, or Laura, signifies a street of cells, the early form of a monastery (Smith's Gibbon, iv. 319; Kingsley's "Hypatia," 4). It is applied to this place, as being *the* monastery *par excellence :* it was once the largest on Athos, but has declined of late years.

water thousands of feet below us. Our sportsman whiled away the time by relating to us some of the legends of the mountain; how, before the birth of Christ, a heathen image had existed on the summit; * and how St. Athanasius, the founder of the Lavra, had destroyed it; and how, when he was building his monastery, the devil, according to the story so common throughout Christendom, had thrown down the stones by night which he had put together by day. Several other legends have at different times gathered round this peak, some of which, relating to the absence of wind, and the extraordinary dryness of the air, are mentioned by Sir John Maundeville in the fourteenth century.† Another tradition is said to have related, that it was on this mountain that Satan placed our Lord at the temptation; and here, in 1821, just before the Greek Revolution, a cross of light was seen by the monks, with the words—"In this conquer."‡ At present however, there is no trace remaining of these legends.

The summit of the mountain rises to so sharp a point, that it only just leaves room for a small chapel, dedicated to the Transfiguration, on the north side of which the crags descend in tremendous precipices, while to the south is a narrow platform of rock, a few feet wide, from which again the cliffs fall rapidly away. As we approached from the east, we first heard the sound of chaunting from within the chapel, and when we came round to the platform in front, a scene appeared which I shall never forget. Distinctly seen in the moonlight were the weird ghostly figures of the monks, closely wrapped in their gowns, with long dark beards, and unshorn locks, some sitting close to the window of the little chapel, where service was going on; some lying about in groups, like the figures of the three apostles in Raphael's picture of the Transfiguration; and on going about to different points, we could see them lying relieved against the white rocks, or dimly seen in the dark shadows—themselves "a shadowy band." There were about sixty of them, besides a number of

* There seems to have been an altar to Zeus here, as on many "high places" in Greece: see Pomp. Mela, ii. 2.        † Maundeville's "Travels," p. 20.
‡ Sir G. F. Bowen's "Mount Athos, Thessaly, and Albania," p. 52.

Russian pilgrims.  We were not less an object of wonder to
them than they were to us.  They even forgot the usual salutations.  "Where *do* you come from?" (ἀπὸ ποῦ εἶσθε) was
all that they could say.  We told them we were Englishmen,
and that we came from the Lavra; on learning which, they
brought us to the wood fire they had lighted, and made some
coffee for us.  In connexion with the fire, the classical reader
will remember that this peak was one of the stations of the
fire-beacons which carried Agamemnon's telegram to Clytem-
nestra.  At intervals, as we sat there, the priest came out, arrayed in gorgeous vestments, and swung the incense about us;
until at last, as the vigil service lasted the whole night, I betook
myself to a small cornice in the rock, where I slept, wrapped
in my plaid, for a couple of hours; after which I lay awake,
gazing up into the bright heaven, and feeling the strange sensation of being elevated on such a rocky pinnacle, with nothing
but sea and sky around—*cœlum undique et undique pontus.*
One could almost realize the feelings of Simeon Stylites.

At dawn the service ceased, and the monks kissed one
another, and were sprinkled with holy water.  When the sun
rose, the shadow of the peak was projected over sea and land
to the west, in a distinctly marked pyramid; but daylight
added little to the view, as the greater part of the peninsulas
of Athos and Sithonia had been visible during the night, and
the distance was hazy.  Eight of the monasteries, however,
could be distinguished, and the expanse of sea was an extraordinary sight.  On a clear day, both Ida and Olympus may be
seen.  Half an hour after sunrise, the Eucharistic service—
the Liturgy, as it is called—commenced; and at its conclusion,
a bunch of grapes was brought in and blessed, this being the
first day on which they are allowed to be eaten.  They then
descended the mountain by the zigzag path in companies,
singing psalms: and, after breakfasting on the grass by the
Chapel of the Virgin, we dispersed to our several destinations.*

---

* The theological dispute about the uncreated light of Tabor, to which this
festival carries us back (see Gibbon, vii. 404), is now wholly forgotten, and
the name of the monk Barlaam almost unknown.

Our estimate of these monasteries will vary, according as
we fix our thoughts on the present or the past.  Probably
a considerable number of the monks regard the monastic
system in no other light than as a source of personal benefit to
themselves.  The theory, however, which the more thoughtful
of them maintain, is this: that these bodies serve as an
example of holy life, as they contain a number of men devoted
to piety and religion; that they maintain intact the old customs
and principles; that their constant prayers are a support to
the Church; and that in prosperous times they become seats
of learning.  How far this theory, even supposing it to be
tenable, is carried out in practice, may be gathered from the
fact, that our dragoman, a trustworthy man, assured us, that
he had never heard so much foul and disgusting language as
in the conversation of the lower monks, among whom he was
thrown.  We are not to suppose that this applies to the
conversation of the ordinary monks, but to a certain number
of *mauvais sujets*, who are to be found in each monastery;
yet it is in part the result of the system.  Take a number
of uneducated peasants from any country, separate them
from female society, and give them a certain amount of
leisure; the result will be, that even the purest religious
influences, unalloyed by superstition, will not prevent a large
amount of evil from being fostered among them.  Notwithstanding that we find much that is pleasing in the life of
the monks, and that strict morality is enforced by their rigid
discipline, yet we cannot but draw the conclusion, that
Eastern monastic life has here been tried on a large scale, is
displayed to the greatest advantage—and has failed.

But, whatever may be their faults, and however false in a
healthy state of the Church the monastic system may be, yet,
looking to the past, we must remember, that they were once
to a certain extent strongholds of learning, and still more,
strongholds of faith in the midst of unbelievers.  To one who
reads, however cursorily, the history of the Greek Church,
the great source of wonder is, not that its faith has been
overlaid by superstition, but that it has retained its Chris-

tianity at all; and to this the monasteries have in no slight
degree contributed. Besides this, they have served as refuges
for the persecuted, and for those perplexed by the distractions
and confusions of the world. Thousands have been saved
from suicide by their means. And from this point of view,
the need of them cannot be said to have wholly passed
away; for as long as the Turks remain in Europe, the
Christians will be persecuted, and as long as they are persecuted, they will need a refuge.

It is a difficult matter to speculate on what may be the
future of the Holy Mountain. It was a subject on which we
often talked to the monks, and they invariably connected
their own future with the political future of Turkey. When
the happy period arrives, to which all Greeks look forward,
when they are to regain Constantinople, Athos, they think,
may once more become the learned place which they believe
it to have been in former times. Yet some of them were not
slow to see that freedom would open to men various sources of
occupation, which would cause them to be less disposed for
the monastic calling. It may also be doubted how far an
educational system can be engrafted on the present life of
the place, as the experiment was tried in the last century by
Eugenius Bulgaris, of Corfu, who built a school here, which
succeeded admirably for a time, and attracted students from
all parts of Greece, but failed at last, from various causes,
and now remains a ruin. Yet this is the best thing which
we can hope for them. We should not wish to see so
venerable an institution destroyed, root and branch, if it is
possible by any means to adapt it to the exigencies of a
coming time. Will any of us live to see the day, when the
Christian sovereign of an independent Byzantine empire will
issue a commission to inquire into the state, discipline, studies,
and revenues of the University and Colleges of Mount Athos?

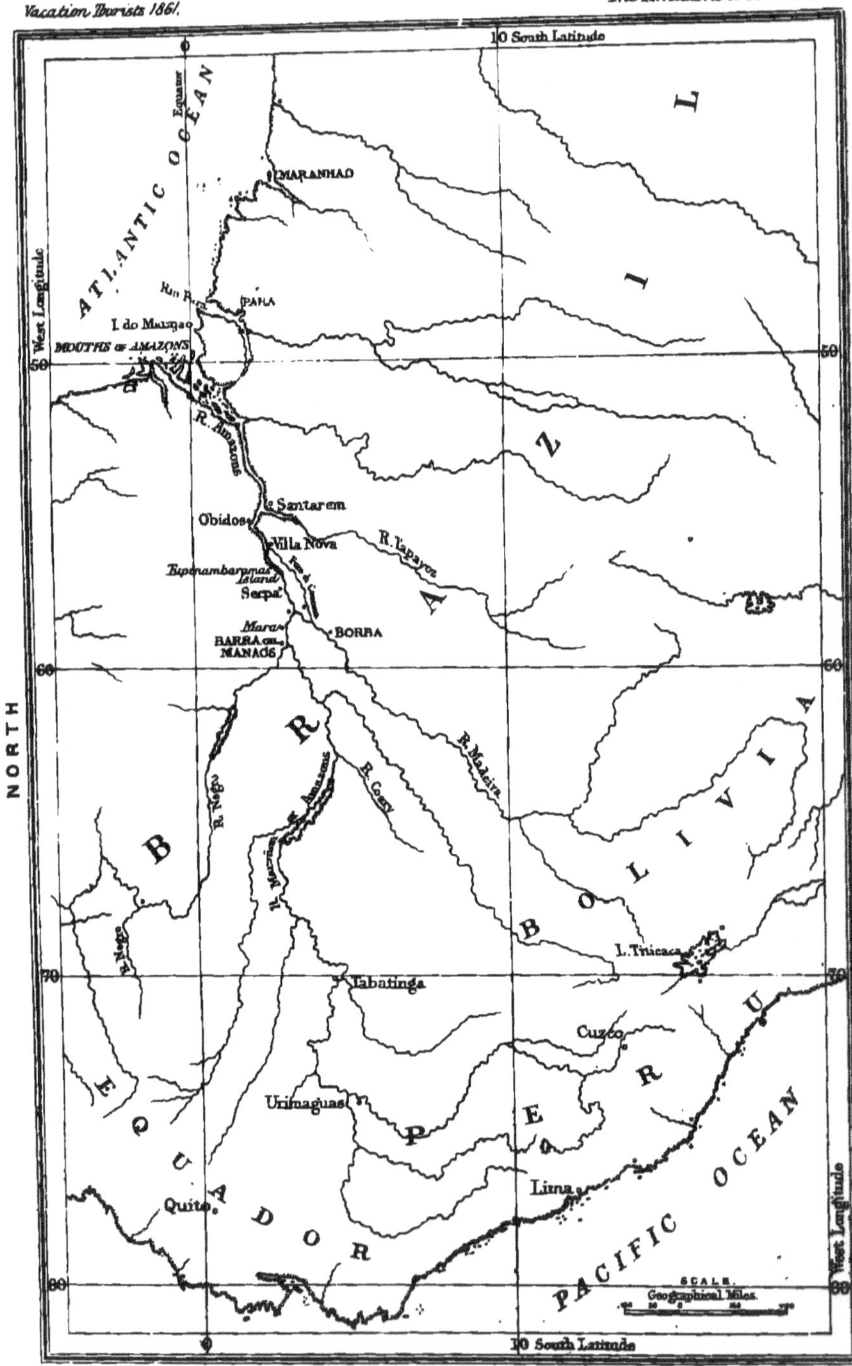

Vacation Tourists 1861.
The Amazons & R. Madera.
10 South Latitude
ATLANTIC OCEAN
Equator
West Longitude
BRAZIL
MARANHAO
Rio P.
PARA
I. do Marajo
MOUTHS OF AMAZONS
R. Amazons
Santarem
Obidos
Villa Nova
R. Tapayos
Tupenambaranas
Island
Serpa
Maras
BARRA or
MANAOS
BORBA
R. Negro
R. Madeira
R. Amazons
R. Guey
R. Madeira
NORTH
BOLIVIA
R. Negro
L. Triicaca
Tabatinga
PERU
Cuzco
Urimaguas
EQUADOR
Lima
Quito
PACIFIC OCEAN
West Longitude
SCALE.
Geographical Miles.
Macmillan & Co, Cambridge & London.

# 4. *THE AMAZON, AND RIO MADEIRA.*

## BY THE REV. CHARLES YOUNG.

HAD an opportunity last year of fulfilling a long cherished
project. From childhood nothing in nature has had a greater
attraction for me than trees, and a giant tree, such as that
of which the bark exists in the Crystal Palace, has been the
height of my ambition among the sights of nature. As far
as I could discover, the largest specimens were to be found
in California, but Humboldt's writings, and other works, led
me to believe, that also between the Amazon and Orinoco
were to be found trees which fifteen men with linked hands
could hardly embrace. Moreover, I was anxious to kill two
birds with one stone, and to see at the same time tropical
vegetation, and the abundant flowers of a South American
forest. I therefore made Brazil my goal rather than
California. In the dearth of precise information, concerning
the remote and untravelled parts to which I was going, I
was obliged to trust largely to what I should be able to learn
on arrival, as to the best point to make for, in order to find
trees of transcendent height and girth.

As I was to travel alone, I was anxious to procure some
letters of introduction; four or five came to my hands within
a few hours of the vessel's starting, a great consolation, certainly, though I was determined to have gone, had I had no
other letter of introduction but my passport. I may be
allowed to mention gratefully Mr. Nicholson, who gave me
a letter to Mr. Edward Ryder, an American merchant at
Pernambuco; Mr. Singlehurst, who sent me a letter to Mr.
Brocklehurst, his partner at Pará; Admiral Grenfell, who gave
me letters to the captains of the ports of Pernambuco and

Pará; and Sir Woodbine Parish, who not only introduced me to the consuls, but took the trouble to apply to the Foreign Office on my behalf.

My friends had universally reprobated my proceedings as rash; it was therefore with the exultation of a successful truant that I heard the parting cheers of the vessel's tender, and knew that there was no stopping one now.

The vessel on which I found myself was the *Milford Haven*, a screw steamer of the Anglo-Luso-Brazilian line, which has since, I am sorry to say, succumbed from want of a subsidy. It sailed under the Portuguese flag, so that besides the English captain there was a Portuguese captain, who, without disparaging my fellow-conntrymen, was really one of the finest men I ever saw, and with the most fascinating smile and address. The crew consisted of English, Portuguese, and negroes, a motley mixture which already introduced one to Brazil. As for my fellow-passengers, all were going for duty or business; one familiar with Brazil, who was going on business, told me that he would give a thousand pounds to avoid the journey. "Is there then so much risk?" I asked. "Oh yes," he said, "the climate used to be very healthy, but of late years the yellow fever has passed over from the west coast of Africa (which it has left healthy) to the coast of Brazil." One and all expressed themselves astonished at my going for pleasure, and to see big trees of all things in the world—"What an idea!" The yellow fever formed a frequent topic of conversation; one of the passengers told me that he had nursed a man through an attack of it for nine days, and the doctor had assured him that he had saved his life. This man met him afterwards, and—cut him! We lost four days in the Bay of Biscay, unable to make way against the waves and a head-wind. But it was a glorious sight, this free and mighty life of the floods lifting up their hands. One element of beauty in the storm was the prismatic light which hung upon the edge of every wave, like an emblem of hope in the midst of despair.

We had left Liverpool on August 25; on September 2

'e reached Lisbon, which broke the voyage agreeably ; it lies
little distance up the Tagus, amid a wilderness of reddish
ocks, as seen from the water, but their shapes are beautiful,
nd to its contrast with these, Cintra owes much of its
otoriety. There was no time to visit this place, and I con-
nted myself with getting a general idea of the city. It forms
sort of crescent, standing upon several hills on the left bank
f the river as you ascend it. The streets are as steep, many of
nem, as the roads of Linton, in Devonshire, if they are not
neeper. Among grey and respectable buildings, are huddled
ouses with as many colours as Harlequin's, and of all heights
nd elevations ; trellises of vines, with large oleanders, the
nyrtle, the acacia, the tamarisk, the olive, and the small
edar, appear as if in hanging gardens ; and up and down
he streets, or leaning from the balconies, or gazing through
ilousies, you see a swart brown people, whose eyes and
ress are alike staring. Red is a favourite colour.

Next afternoon we were off again, and I set myself in
arnest to study my Portuguese "Guide," and to learn the
rammar well, for the streets of Lisbon had convinced me
f the necessity of more exertion in that respect. The
anguage to a Latin scholar is exceedingly easy in grammar
nd construction ; the chief difficulty lies in the numerous
efinements of the pronunciation ; very necessary to be
ttended to, because a slight difference in the sound will
give to the same word an utterly different meaning ; and so
n thinking to pay a compliment, you perhaps insult a
erson grievously.

We seemed now to have bid adieu to foul skies ; the sea
eneath the bows had the deep colour of blue ink ; the
wning was put up on deck ; the trade winds began ; and one
ecame so absorbed in the little floating world with every
uxury of civilization, that it was not till dusk, when
tanding alone at the stern, and removing one's eyes from
he vessel, "shadowing with wings," like a majestic bird of
ight—it was not till then that one could realize we were
ff the coast of Africa.

In the morning haze, Patmos Isle loomed over us. A day we stopped at that desolate red rock of the Cape de Verde Islands. Leaving this, foul weather paid us a last visit. It was rougher than the Bay of Biscay, and we lost another four days.

The doctor believed, that with our doors and ports closed, we had slept in a heat of 100 degrees, which he frankly styled a Pandemonium. At this time we had our finest sunset—a palace of emerald decked with gold and purple. Fair weather returned; large flat purple fish sped along in front of the bows; and one adventurous passenger fished for them from the end of the bowsprit. He was a good swimmer; but I don't know how, in the event of falling, he would have contended with the sharks, whose dorsal fins we had seen not far from us. As we drew near the line, the heavens seemed lower, the stars larger and brighter; Mars, red and big, hung over the mast-head; the moon was surpassingly clear and gibbous, its dark body very distinctly seen. If one turned one's eyes upward, there lay over us the Milky Way, like a silver tissue; if downwards, there lay under us a golden tissue of fiery noctilucæ, a path of light, from which shapes like rockets fell away to right and left.

On the 20th we passed the line, and on the 23d I saw with keen delight the long low coast of South America, barely above the level of the sea, and gray with distant trees, steeped in the light of the sun of the equator. His heat had driven me to the use of a little quinine, but I soon became acclimatised and ceased to take it. At twelve o'clock we were off Pernambuco (the mouth of hell), so called from its frightful *recife*, a ridge of rock which runs 400 or 500 miles along the coast, and has few openings to admit vessels to the land. The boats charge £1 to come off and on, and double that in rough weather. Although the water was quite smooth, the surf was breaking with tremendous violence against the *recife*, and indicated what it might be on worse days.

I presented my letter of introduction to Mr. Ryder, thinking it would only procure me some advice; but to my agreeable

urprise he invited me to stop at his house, if I would rough.
—a very unnecessary addition, since I never was in greater
ixury.  I may mention for the sake of others who may be
ss fortunate, Widow Raymond's boarding-house, which seems
etter than the hotels, at four milrees per day (*i.e.* from
*s.* 8*d.* to 9*s.*), or 100 milrees per month.

I found I must wait here a week, for the next coasting
eamer.  A river divides the town.  The houses are coloured
rightly—yellow, red, chocolate, lilac, green; among them
tand grey churches and cathedrals.  In the streets you
eet the Portuguese, the merry negro (who seems to have a
ght existence here), and the fine thin Brazilian, together
ith all mixtures of all these in all proportions; but in
'ernambuco I saw nothing of the Indian race.  The negro
omen adorn themselves like peacocks, bright scarlet and
right green silk shawls, and a profusion of gold ornaments;
ut the green and gold lizard of the wall has a gayer mantle.

The fellow-passenger whom I mentioned in the opening of
his sketch, was to sleep at my host's; he drove us to his
ouse, which lay next the English clergyman's, about a mile
om the city.  The way lay among similar houses and
ardens, with the strange vegetation of a tropical climate.
'here were the grey plumes of the palm-tree, the massy
ango with long leaves of dark green, the bright green flags
f the banana, the feathery tamarisks and acacias, the
range and lemon trees, and the bushes of the cajoub, a
omewhat acid fruit, a pear in shape, a tomata in colour.
las! it was the end of the wet season, therefore but few
owers remained; yet there were some of a waxen texture,
ink and white; others scarlet; weeds with yellow and lilac
owers crept on the ground; the tree-top under my window
ore tufts of a lavender hue, over which the bees and
*emtivis* seemed busy.  These birds are so called from the
btrusive observation they seem to be always making, "Bem-
i-vi;"—"I saw you well."  They were a great annoyance
o my friend, an Irishman, who sounded an early alarum at
ay door, to inform me that "at four o'clock in the morning.

all the cocks in Pernambuco begin to crow, and those ——
bemtivis begin directly afterwards, so there's no sleeping
after that."

A strange country. Overnight I had fancied a bat had
flown in my eyes, but it was only an enormous butterfly. As
I strolled along in the moonlight, among low houses with
quaint stone devices, the firefly darting in the trees, and
coming on low, pale, squalid figures, whose endless shades of
complexion between black and brownish white told the tale
of their origin; and as they gazed at me with half shy, half
wild-beast eyes, I fancied myself in Milton's Limbo rather
than on earth.

In the early morning, and near sunset, I searched the
suburbs; there are some fine houses and gardens in the Rua
da Mondega. I remember a large white house with pale
green edgings, and a reddish brown roof. The garden was
divided by many rectangular paths running among beds
inclosed with squares of stone, decorated with blue and
white china vases. All the paths were covered with trellises
of vine, and in the beds I noticed a spiked plant like an aloe,
in hue like a copper beech, but much redder. A copper-
coloured negro lad and two large greyhounds completed the
picture. Horses passed in that extraordinary hobble which
they cultivate here, between a trot and a canter. In the Rua
da Bemfica were many fig-trees. Gardens with statues sloped
to the river. Brazilian ladies clad in white lay indolently in
rocking-chairs, with their arms lolled behind their heads.

On the last of September, I was fortunate in having the
*Cruzeira do Sul*, the largest and the fastest of the coast
steamers, to proceed by. A humming-bird, the first I had
seen, flew into the house, as if he were the herald of forest
glories. My host, jocosely asking if my friends seriously
expected to see me again, conducted me to the water. Indeed
they might have seen me rather earlier than I should have
liked, since, but for Providence, my tour would have been
now knocked on the head. The rascally negro to whom my
portmanteau had been confided, had detained it an hour

hilst he was adorning his person. My host promised to
lorn his person in a different manner, for had not the vessel
;arted half-an-hour late that day, I should have lost it. As
. was, indeed, a quarter of an hour after I was on board, it was
1 motion.

Hitherto I had heard English voices about me, now nothing
ut Portuguese. For the first time I began to feel that I was
lone, and cast upon my own resources. But it was a
leasant feeling, for *reasonable* self-reliance is, I have always
hought, reliance upon God. The moon was at the full; a
ool breeze freshened lungs and heart; and a woman's voice
rom the other end of the vessel sung some lulling song, in
rhich the words "*da Noite*" formed a constant refrain, the
oost musical version of the word night.

Unqualified Brazilian fare awaited me now. Beef cooked
n every imaginable way (mutton is unattainable), dishes of
aince and custard, meat and raisins—but nothing without
;arlic. However, no one could complain of the dessert—ripe
igs and bananas, cajoubs, bread-fruit and oranges, which in
his country are rivalled only by the pine-apples. There was
ı German on board who had been three times round the
vorld, his wife with him the last time, but it was for business
ıe had visited the towns, where he gave concerts, and did not
ınderstand going into the forests for pleasure. A priest, who
belonged to the Island of Marajao, at the mouth of the
Amazon, examined me with much curiosity on the subject of
;eligion, and displayed the profound ignorance of the genera-
ity of the Roman Catholic clergy in Brazil. "Was the
Senhor a pagan?" "No, a Christian." "But did the Senhor
believe in God?" "Certainly." "And in Jesus Christ?"
"Yes." "And in the Holy Ghost?" "Yes." "Oh si! and
that Christ was Son of God and Son of man?" "Yes."
"And that Mary was a Virgin?" "Yes." "Oh! there's not
much difference then," said he, addressing another who came
up, shook his finger warningly, and said with a frown, "*Naò
Senhor, é dogmatico, muito dogmatico*;" and detected that I
did not hold the doctrine of the Immaculate Conception.

However, the priest held by his opinion that there was no great difference. It is, probably, because there is great indifference to religion except for political purposes, that I found great liberality towards the English pagans. But then I imagine the English could not be made more of in Hungary than in Brazil. The vessel called at Parahiba do Norte, amid a cluster of mudbanks, from which the mangroves dipped their roots, like bony fingers, into the still bosom of the waters. Again it touched at Ciara, a fine white beach, behind which rise the tops of buildings, backed by a blue mountain. The last stoppage was at Maranhâm, a red town on an island, amongst smaller islands.

On October 7 (the most settled time of the year in these parts) we exchanged the green waves of the sea for the yellow flood of the Amazon; and the rocking, rolling, and tumbling, for a far steadier motion than that of the broad guage. At its mouth the river is a hundred and fifty miles broad. This mighty current runs into the sea, and flows upwards to the N.N.E., giving vessels two knots an hour for the first five or six hundred miles.

In the mouth of the river lies the island of Marajao, one hundred and twenty miles in length, in breadth sixty or eighty, dividing the river into two arms. We entered, of course, the most southern, the narrowest. Pará lies eighty miles up it. On the right the tree-tops of Marajao just fringed the water; on the left appeared a long line of low islands, to which as we advanced we drew nearer and nearer. My heart swelled with pleasure at the scene which now unfolded itself. The appearance of the water is like new bronze, and so opaque, that a hand dipped beneath it is obscured from sight. Although, therefore, it has not the beauty of clear streams, yet it has a beauty of its own, reflecting the trees and clouds. In shore I noticed that it had a crimson tint, which I was at a loss to account for, but think now that it must have been owing to the reflection of the flowering trees. These ascended in one dense mass of graceful, feathery foliage, the general colour being a light vivid metallic green, on which the sun scintillated with dazzling brightness. Even at that distance we could see masses of colour upon the trees which were in flower. Prodigal nature had draped living and dead trees alike with parasites; but here and there a tall trunk rose uninterrupted as a pillar into its dome of foliage above; and grassy nooks sloped back, and gave a glimpse of the forest shades. At such openings would be palm-trees and the roof of an Indian hut. The fort appeared on an island ahead. The Rio Magoary opened on the left; a whole archipelago of islands seemed floating on the right. Dinner was an unwelcome interruption, and when I rushed on deck again, there was Pará, the most picturesque combination of colours that I know after Venice: a long front of houses coloured crimson and yellow: on the right a small promontory hiding the older portion of the town; at its base the cathedral rears two steeples. It is the largest in Brazil. Both it and its sister churches—a large number— have collected upon their faces the pink dust of the streets, which contrasts finely with the dark, mouldy green of their tops, from which weeds and creepers wave in the air. Over- head vultures wheel slowly. They seem tame as fowls; for they are the scavengers of the city, and there is a fine of a hundred milrees (ten pounds) to be paid for destroy- ing one.

At the Punto da Pedras you see collected a specimen of the inhabitants. There is the European merchant, the Brazilian, the negro, and Indian half-breed—it is rare to see a perfectly pure Indian. Such have been driven into the interior of the country, and those who remained have so intermarried with the whites and negroes, that you seldom find unmixed Indian blood amongst them. And yet they call them by their original name—Tapuyos. These Tapuyos, then, may be seen floating about in boats of all sizes. There is the large galliota, with a deck, the small galliota, without deck (these have round bottoms), and the monterias, varying in size, but mere canoes with a flat bottom. These last are propelled by one or two paddles, and seem to fly over the water. Fruits are being exhibited for sale, and animals. The whole is

K

relieved against a lofty background of vivid green, and a foreground of the *bronzen* river dotted with fairy islands.

I presented my letter of introduction to Mr. Brocklehurst, who received me with such kindness as I can never forget. Overburdened with business himself, my unselfish and generous host made me perfectly ashamed by his attentions; and I am sure that it must have been owing chiefly to his treatment of his guest that I met with so much liberality and kindness from his neighbours. I say it must have been chiefly owing to himself; but it would not be giving the Brazilians their due, to say that nothing was owing to their own hospitable temper. Of this more afterwards.

His house overlooks the water. It is of three stories. The rooms are large, and exceedingly high, with as many windows as possible to circulate the air. A large telescope here, as in other houses, commands the wide expanse of islands and water, and gives early notice of the approach of a vessel. I must confess to having spent a somewhat astonished night. There was a bed and a hammock to choose between. I entered the hammock without the usual mishap which awaits the uninitiated; but I could not divest myself of the idea, that I should be enfolded by the boa constrictor of the establishment, an enormous fellow whom they encourage in the stores underneath for the suppression of rats and other vermin. They say he would never think of coming upstairs, unless his ordinary food ran short! The practice is not confined to this house. I visited an Irish merchant's, who told me, that on inquiring with what his clerk was busy one morning, he was answered; "Oh! I've only found a hundred dollars I had lost," in the shape of a young boa constrictor, who had turned up among the stores after some years' disappearance, and had, in the meantime, grown to be a valuable possession. He was to be shipped for the States. I saw him coiled in a large box, twenty feet long, with a body nearly as thick as the calf of a man's leg.

The pleasantest time of the day is from five till eight in the morning. Breakfast is at ten. The heat is too great till one

'clock for anything but sleep; but then the trade wind blows
strongly from the sea, and makes it quite possible to be about
in the afternoon; and the evenings during the dry season are
delightful.

I visited the cathedral one morning. Many Roman
Catholics complain of the unsatisfactory service here. The
singing is terribly nasal. I had some difficulty in preserving
my gravity. The youth who swung the censer nodded and
smiled to his friends on both sides of him. An under-current
of laughter and conversation was carried on under the defence
of the singing. An old ecclesiastic stepped up to a most
dolorous penitent, and seemed to be making a few half-jocose
remarks to him; then passing on, he looked about him with
a look of cheerful inquiry, spat on the ground sonorously, and
dropped upon his knees. The style in which the different
curtseys were made was curious. One young man bowed to
the saint with the air of being introduced to a gentleman for
the first time. A friend told me that he had trodden by
accident upon the dress of a Brazilian lady who knelt with
her face buried in her hands, and she, withdrawing them,
exclaimed, " *Ore Diabo.*"

My host took me to visit an American merchant in the
evening. He had a monkey very anxious to fondle us; we
kept him gently at a distance; but when his master addressed
him, he flung himself round his leg, which he embraced
passionately, and wept in a manner surprisingly human.
Whilst sitting at table in the verandah, I heard cries like a
child's voice; and soon after came pattering feet upon the
boards, and a young tapir stood before us. I saw him in the
flesh with keen interest, for I had often beheld him in the
spirit, in the dreams of boyhood, ascending and descending
with his relations upon my stomach in crowded nightmare.
He was very gentle and docile, and ate unweariedly the bananas we offered him. He was about the size of a hog, but
far heavier, and he had not attained his full growth. I was told
by his owner that his ponderosity exceeds that of any other
animal of the same stature, and in spite of his odd shape he is

very fleet. Hence his reputed mode of dealing with his great
enemy the jaguar. The jaguar, who is sometimes as long as the
Bengal tiger, though not so tall, leaps upon his back, but the
tapir runs off with him at full speed, and hurls his body with
such tremendous *aplomb* between two trees, where there is
barely room for himself to pass, that the larger animal is
squashed between them. He mentioned as another instance of
his great weight and strength that the captain of a vessel who
was taking a tapir to the States, had released him on deck, at
some distance from the shore, when he noticed the beast
making for the water, and knowing his powers, shouted,
"Four of you men lay hold of that tapir." They did so,
but were forced to let him go, or be pulled into the sea by
him ; and he regained his native forests.

The Rua da Mangabeiras is a great ornament to Pará. It
is a very long avenue of trees, so called, with a smooth bark
and large oval leaves. It is crossed at right angles by a
similar avenue. From this you reach the arsenal and botani-
cal gardens on the right hand, and on the left hand San
Nazaré. This is a chapel, small, but of wide celebrity,
standing in the forest about a mile from the city, and dedicated to our Lady of Nazareth. She has the reputation of
having delivered a noble huntsman from following a stag
over a precipice, and of having delivered the crew of a shipwrecked vessel in the ship's boat. About a mile farther into
the forest lives a Scotch gentleman of the name of Henderson.
With all the energy and independence of his countrymen, he
labours with his own hands in a land where no white man
is willing to do a stroke of work that can be done by men
of colour. He keeps cows, and sells the milk in the city, for
in Pará milk is far from plentiful. And he would gladly
introduce farming improvements upon the estate, if it were
not that he is compelled to hold it on most disadvantageous
terms, and might be turned out in a moment. The long road
to his house is all his own making. On one side are the
remains of an old wall, some building of the Jesuits. His
cottage lies in a small campo, surrounded by assai-palms. He

howed me round his campos, and through his bush, as he
called the thick wood.

In the campos the sensitive plant grew into a giant shrub,
nd the trees of the surrounding forest were covered with
ellow flowers.  Every one who leaves the open glades which
ave been cleared through the forests, is armed with a tre-
ado, a knife two or three feet long, with which he, or more
ften the guide who precedes him, clears the way with prac-
ised hand.  The undergrowth is not usually dense, and
much of it is so brittle as to be easily smitten away.  I saw
ere the seringa, from which india-rubber is made, to be
ent in large quantities to the United States.  It is a tree
which gives milk sweet and pleasant to the taste, but very
antalizing, because it coagulates almost immediately, even
efore you have swallowed it, into a number of those hard
urds from which india-rubber is made,—and even in these
lays of caoutchouc inventions no one desires an india-rubber
tomach.  The masseranduba, or cow-tree, gives milk also,
ut with the same drawback to its enjoyment.  And the
urve, whose milk is more delicious than any, is as disap-
ointing as the rest.  It bears, however, a very nice fruit
ike the medlar, and superior to it.

About the house were several of those curious air-plants,
rowing upon the palings, and deriving all their sustenance
rom the air.  I tasted here the alligator-pear ; it is eaten either
s a vegetable with salt, or as a fruit with wine and sugar.
t was dark when we returned down the forest glade toward
he city, and I was startled by bright flashes of light bearing
own upon me, and actually illuminating the path under my
eet.  This was the lantern-fly, not like the fire-fly, a mere
park, but a long ray.

On the following day I paid a visit to the rice mill at
Magoary.  It was once in American hands, but now belongs to
wealthy Portuguese.  It lay about fourteen miles off through
he forest, but at a distance of ten or twelve hours by water.
No drivers would venture with their cars, for the glade is
iable to be blocked by fallen trees ; and no horse could be

got to ride, because I should have had to provide my own saddle. I therefore took a negro as guide and porter, and drove to the forest, through which, though it was the hottest time of the day, it was easy to walk, owing to the dense shade. The trees here averaged 200 feet in height, sending out their branches at forty or fifty feet from the ground, and were chiefly masseranduba and seringa trees, and trees which exuded gum (not turpentine). The branches sent down segraws, sometimes a hundred feet long, from above to the ground; many of these had taken root, and grew up again. By these, and by parasites, the trees seemed bound together, and deeply I regretted that there were but a few lingerers, of different shades of red, among the flowers with which, at the end of the wet season, the forest is profusely garlanded. They, in the words of Spix and Martius, "are of every shade of colour into which the rays of light can be arranged."

It was curious to see the way in which a species of parasite had enveloped some trees, which it had gradually ruined by its embraces, until it reared its own trunk, flourishing on the decay of its supporter.

The leaves of the trees were various in shape, but few of them large; and the girth of the trunks, at the height of six feet from the ground, did not exceed fifteen feet. They tapered more gradually than an arrow. Large armies of ants passed and repassed, and the great egg-shaped nests of the cupim, or white ant, hung from the branches. Enormous butterflies, as large as a man's hand, dazzled the eye with the light which was reflected from their blue armour. These are difficult to catch without breaking them. Toucans and parrots screamed and chattered all round, but were too crafty to show themselves. Six streams were passed by narrow bridges, where the "Agoa da Matte" trickled over a deep red bottom; and my guide formed a "copo Brazilieno" from a kind of large dock-leaf—a twisted goblet secured by its stem. We then emerged upon the rice mill. It is worked by the water collected in two artificial lakes which lie to left and right of the mill, connected by a long igaripé (stream) running at a distance of a hundred rods in front of the building. The water runs from this through a pool and a mill-wheel, into a broader igaripé at right angles to the first, which widens continually into the Rio Magoary, and this again joins the Amazon. To my surprise, I found that I was described by my entertainer's letter as a naturalist, who would spend three or four days there; and, to my amusement, discovered that, not reckoning on an English appetite, he had empowered his factor to procure, for my sustenance, "three rolls, three eggs, and a fowl—with beans, butter, tea, and sugar—*e o senhor sera bem servido.*" What can the factor have thought of me for despatching this on the first afternoon—or the black rider, who rode so often to the city for more?

On the following day, with the negro from the city, and another, as guide, from the mill, I mounted a little rickety pony, and went in search of large trees: a humming-bird flew on before. I found the highest tree I had yet seen, about 250 feet. Whilst attempting to sketch it, my sable attendants held a gloomy conference, the burden of which seemed to be that I was a pagan, and that when I was dead I should go "ao inferno."

Next dawn, the factor took me in a small montaria, with a negro and half-breed to row us, down the igaripé to the entrance of the Rio Magoary. The glassy stream wound and turned incessantly; acacias dipped over it; and there were water-plants, bearing a large flower, six inches long, like a passion-flower with white radii tipped with crimson. At one of the bends of the stream, we met the large galliota of the mill, advancing with ghostly stillness, and propelled by copper-coloured Indians, who stood in the bows, and gazed listlessly upon us. Now we passed through low, sedgy banks; now they heightened again. A brawny, good-humoured Indian woman, paddling along, directed at us a deprecating look, and shrugged her shoulders, as if she begged to be excused for her existence; then shyly turned her canoe to the bank, and with one vigorous stroke of the paddle, which seemed to send the little bark almost out of the water, vanished in a creek. Indian casas appeared among palms, and the trees which bear yellow flowers; the Rio Magoary opened beyond. Under one of these casas I paused and sketched, while the factor gossipped with the old Indian dame, and returned laden with fruit of the ingá. This tree bears a white flower, of which the humming-birds are fond, and a pod, about a foot long and an inch wide, of which the Indians are as fond. The pod contains sweet, creamy pulp, of a white colour and viscous consistency, enveloping large, bean-like seeds, which, after stripping, you reject.

On reaching the mill again, I was introduced to a new delicacy. This was assai. It is made from the fruit of the assai-palm, a kind of purple cream not unlike raspberry-cream. It is thickened with farinha (which is the flour of the country, prepared from the manioc-root), and is both refreshing and strengthening, food and drink in one.

Being anxious to witness the festa on the 14th, I returned in the afternoon to Pará; and found out what a heavy tropical rain is. Yet this was the only rain by which I was incommoded during the whole time I was on the river. It came down like a shower-bath, and in a very few minutes changed the pleasant forest-glade into a pestilential drain, making one pale with the stench. We waded along ankle-deep.

On the morning of the 15th my host took me to the house of an Irish merchant, to see the procession of the Virgin go to Nazaré. On our way we called at the house of two German merchants; they had just had a visit from cupim (white ants), who had eaten up breeches, coats, shirts, the whole contents of a wardrobe.

From a summer-house over the road we witnessed the procession. Javelin-men and soldiers on horseback preceded; then followed the judge of the feast, in his carriage; next followed the prettiest part of the spectacle—little children decked out in fairy style, with blue gauze wings, as guardian angels. But it was a singular thing to see guardian angels conducted by men in top-boots! On a large car, Nossa

enhora succeeded, represented on a gigantic scale, in wax
nd tinsel, with the stag and its hunter, whom she had saved
rom following his chace over a precipice. After these, the
dentical boat was borne on the shoulders of the identical
rew, which were saved in it about fifteen years ago from
hipwreck, after prayers to the Lady of Nazaré. Besides
his large figure, which was intended to be widely seen, there
vas also carried, in a glass case, the small figure of the
Virgin which belongs to the shrine itself. This is taken
back secretly to the shrine at night, where they say it appears
by *miracle* next morning! A long line of carriages closed
he procession. The festa lasts nine days, and an astonishing
um of money is expended in the time. It is a saturnalia,
but a very orderly one. Amongst the vast crowds not a
brawl occurs, not a soldier or policeman is required.

On the 16th the steamer was to start up the river. It is
ne of a new company which has only existed for four or five
years, but has now carried its vessels even to Yurimaguas, on
he Huallaga, about 2,500 miles from the Atlantic. (The
Amazon itself is 3,200 miles long.) From Yurimaguas the
passage of the Andes is made to Lima on the Pacific, a journey
n mules of about fifty or sixty days at the most as I am told,
ncluding a break of a week at Barra, on the Rio Négro, and
another week at Tabatinga, on the frontier of Brazil. Thus
n about three months you may pass from ocean to ocean,
nd see both the Amazon and the Cordilleras. Six months
vould have been required formerly by the river craft to reach
Tabatinga alone. I imagine that it is owing to the increased
raffic on the river by this steam line, that a new province
as been formed round Barra do Rio Negro, with this town as
s centre. They call the province Amazonas, and prefer the
ame of Manáos to the old name of the town,

The first 1,200 miles of the river, *i. e.* from Pará to Manáos,
re styled the " Amazon ; " the next piece of the river as far as
Tatabinga, is called the Solimoëns, and the third and highest
vaters bear the name of Maranon. I believe that each of
hese stages of the river is served by a couple of steamers,

which ply only upon that stage, and proceed no further.
"The service of the first line" is supplied by the vessels
*Manáos* and *Tapajoz.* The *Manáos* is the largest and
fastest of the two, and burns coal; the other only wood. It
was the *Manáos* which was to sail that evening.

My acquaintance in Pará all came to wish me good-bye,
and made it something more than a visit of ceremony, by
furnishing me with letters of introduction. Mr. Campbell
furnished one to a friend of his up the river. Another was
given me to the captain of the steamer. Mr. Oreline, the
engineer of the company, did me the greatest service, without
which I could scarcely have proceeded. He made known my
wishes to Signor Henriquez Antonio, an Italian trader, who
has lived fifty years at Barra, and even now, in the improved
state of civilisation there, has more influence than the Government itself amongst the Indians. I had heard of this gentleman before leaving England, and was very grateful to be
introduced to him by Mr. Oreline. The senhor regretted
that he would not be at Barra himself, as he had visited
Pará with the intention of staying out the festa, but he gave
me a letter of introduction to his brother-in-law, the Portuguese vice-consul, and authorized him to put his own body-
servant, a Tapuyos Indian, at my service, as guide, &c. while
I was up the country. And in an hour or two I received a
letter from the consul, saying that he had spoken of me to
the president, who herewith sent me a letter of introduction
to the vice-president at Manáos (the presidency being
vacant), and had been pleased to order me a free passage up
the river, with the exception of my board, which I was to pay
for. And I must mention here, that on my return to Pará, I
discovered from Mr. Scully, a merchant of high position in Rio
Janeiro, and Government inspector of writing in the schools
of Brazil, that it was probably intended, that not only my
passage up the river, but down it again, as well as my travelling expenses up the country, should have been presented me.
However this may be, I had been, of course, unwilling to
spur a free horse; and to this day remain astonished at the

iberality and generosity of the Brazilians to an obscure and olitary stranger. I am not a Freemason; and I do not believe hat the letter from the Foreign Office reached the consul till ong afterwards. Indeed, when I told my host, he seemed much surprised, and said, "Well, I'm glad all this has appened, for people think we are half savages out here."

With many kind wishes for my safe return from my friends t Pará, and bearing two large hammocks which my host had ent me for use up the country, I put off to the vessel at ine o'clock in the evening. It was to start at midnight. I ound it a large, roomy, and clean vessel, built of teak, to esist the little boring insects which infest these waters, and vould soon destroy any other timber. There were two cabins ide by side, the chief one containing upwards of twenty erths in double tier. One of them had been reserved for ne; but I preferred to follow the prevailing fashion, and sleep n the deck, over which an awning was stretched, on the top of ron pillars; and from these pillars were already dangling ammocks in all directions. I found a vacant space in a orner, and with the assistance of the American mate, whose cquaintance I had previously made, slung my hammock, vhere in shirt, trousers, and poncho which guarded my head rom drafts, as the awning above from night-dew, I passed a very good night.

The cool morning air awoke me about four o'clock; I rose nd threaded my way through the hammocks and their sleep- ng occupants, to the outside of the awning. "The maiden plendours" (not " of the morning star," but) of the Southern Cross "shook in the steadfast blue." It was too early to liscern the objects about us, and I slept again till dawn. When I opened my eyes again, I thought I must be still lreaming, and lay entranced in my hammock, with fixed eyes lrinking in the endless variety of the leafage, rapidly chang- ug with the movement of the steamer. The sun was gradually lighting up the lovely islands which lay on every ide of us, and seemed to float upon the water. Our vessel lashed among them, often approaching within a hundred yards of the shore.  Although the river was from ten to twenty miles broad in this part, yet one never saw this breadth uninterrupted, because of the numerous islands. Their shores were low, and utterly without undulation, but covered with flowering trees.  Tea and coffee were brought to our hammocks by the boys of the steamer; breakfast, as usual, was not till ten o'clock.  It happened that there was a French Creole on board, who spoke English admirably; some of the Brazilians too spoke French, so that I was able to hold conversations with them.  The captain observed that it was a great voyage for " Padres."  We had already three or four on board, and others got in at the stoppages on the river; beside which there was myself, a puzzle to them, as a solitary traveller, who had no object but big trees, and was, nevertheless, a Padre.  One or two, I fancy, had suspicions that some political or religious purpose must be hidden behind this excuse.  However, I found great liberality of sentiment amongst them, my plea of, " Anglo-Catholico, non Romano-Catholico," was accepted, and they asked me if I was Episcopal, and at dinner the first dish was offered to the Padre Inglez. An old gentleman something like a friendly baboon, inquired if I would vote for priests marrying.  " Certainly."  He said they were going to petition the Pope for it.  In the afternoon we touched at Braves, on the island of Marajâo; a small village with a few general shops, or stores as they call them. There were folk here with their teeth chipped and filed to a point.

Next day we reached the fort of Gurupá, after which the vessel put on full speed, about ten miles an hour.  About dinner-time we were passing the Arayayates, low hills upon the northern bank, the sight of which was refreshing after so much low country.  We were now passing the mouth of the river Xingu, which flows in here from the south. After this I had been given to understand that the mosquitoes of the country, called cárapanás, would be " as mais feroces."  I was presently reminded of this by hearing on all sides (and with reason, as I felt) first one man, and then another, and each as if he alone had just discovered it,

ive vent to their surprise and wrath in rapid succession and
n varying tones. "Cárapaná!" observed the first. "Ah!
árapaná!" said the next with equal surprise. "Muito de
árapanás!" said a third. "Ah, bah, cárapaná!" complained
nother. "Agoa sta boâ, agoa!" cried several at once; and
rhilst they ran to the water-jars to thin their blood, the
ecure occupant of another hammock whom evil had at
ast found, roared out, "Cárapaná! oh, diā-bo!" These
ittle pests are the bane of enjoyment on these rivers while
hey last. They come on in troops at certain hours, and
raw off again for a while. They are, of course, worst in
hore, and least troublesome in the centre of the stream.
At Villa Nova the vessel stopped all night, which is more
han the cárapanás did, and we were glad enough to leave in
he morning. Noon found us at Santarem, once the largest
own on the Amazon, after Pará, but now rivalled by Manáos
he new capital of Amazonas.

The Tapajoz, which is one of the black-water rivers, pours
tself at this point into the yellow flood of the Amazon,
roducing a neutral green tint. We were to stay a couple
f hours here, so I visited the place in the boat of the
teamer along with the mate, who went to buy wine for the
essel. There was nothing to be seen, but I heard that seven
undred people had just died there of the low fever which
nfests the mouth of the river at this season of year.
Fruit here was plentiful and cheap; a large pine-apple was
nly threepence, and an alligator pear one halfpenny. I was
ike to have been left behind again, for I had broken my
ratch so that I could not tell the time, and missed seeing
he mate return to his boat; but thinking it unsafe to wait
onger, I had come off in another boat, and looking round
t a sound from the vessel, found that they were already
ripping the anchor.

We kept now along the southern bank of the river, which
eightened now and then into cliffs of sand and coloured
oams; the trees flowered with yellow, orange, brown,
rimson, and white flowers, like autumn embracing spring.

High up, and perched like nests among the branches, sitios, as they call the dwellings, appeared; and between the tall stems the naked forms of Indians sauntered along a wide path, and descended the alluvial terraces to the brink, over which tall ferns nodded and tamarisks waved, and lush green grasses changed the water there into a sheet of green, broken by the reflection of a canoe, with the scarlet bundle and white dresses of two small half-bred imps. We lay all night at Obidos, on the northern shore. It is at the mouth of the river Trombetas, from which is brought a great deal of fine timber. It was here that the Amazons were supposed to dwell. The bend of the river showed a semicircle of hills clad with forests, and along the water cacao plantations.

The next day was Sunday. As I sat reading my Bible, a young abbé, a much more intelligent and educated priest than I had yet met with, came up and examined me in French on the differences between the English and Roman Catholic Church. A military officer joined us at the close of the discussion, and on hearing me repudiate what were so many cardinal points of faith in his eyes, the worship of saints, &c. he asked anxiously, "Mas creias im Deo?" (but you believe in God?) and on hearing "Yes," seemed to think that that made all right.

A heavy squall set the Amazon boiling and foaming in the afternoon. At eleven at night we reached Manáos. There, the next day, I presented my letters of introduction. The Portuguese vice-consul was moving his quarters, but directed me to a house where I could swing my hammock at night, and received me during the day at his table. By the good offices of the French Creole, who was waiting here for a week until the departure of the *Inca* steamer to Peru, I spoke with Senhor Brandôa (the father-in-law of Senhor Henriquez Antonio before mentioned). He knows the whole country thoroughly well; but on hearing my object, he said that the largest trees were to be found by following up the igaripés in a canoe, and that the igaripés were at present all dry. This was a very great misfortune, as

hey are the only roads through the forests.  He discouraged
ie from going any higher up the Amazon, saying that I
hould find it all the same, and that I was as likely to find
irge trees here as anywhere else.  The Tapuyos Indian
lasimir was then placed at my orders.  This man was not
f pure Indian blood.  He was middle-aged, about five feet
ight or nine, and robust, brown rather than copper-coloured,
/ith small features and a sleepy air, good-humoured, and
·erfectly honest.  He could speak a little more Portuguese
han he would allow, and I had little difficulty in making
ıy wants known to him.  But he could not realize the size
/hich I sought in trees.  I think he had seen some larger
han those to which he conducted me, but could not find his
/ay to them again.

The town of Manáos (*i.q.* Barra) stands on the eastern
ank of the Rio Négro, a few miles from the mouth.  The
Négro here is about four miles, the Amazon about six miles
road.  The town stands on a series of undulations, which
ontinue along the water's edge.  Between these undulations
garipés draining the country run into the Négro; but inland,
t the back of the town and above it, rises a table-land,
leared of trees for some distance, and giving a wide view to
he north.

It was pleasant to snuff some fresh air here after the close
eat of the river.  At my feet was a steep descent to an
garipé below.  The ground here was covered with a tall
hrub of a bright yellow-green, bearing what resembled
rilliant scarlet flowers, so abrupt was the transition of colour,
ut which proved on nearer inspection to be leaves, which at
his season turn to this hue.  I did not see any at various
tages of change, but they were all of one uniform tint,
/hether green or scarlet.  Lower down were bowers of feathery
oliage, of an emerald green.  At the bottom Indians were
quatting in the pools and splashing water over their heads.
)n the opposite ascent stood the tamarisk, and the dark
ensitive plant, become a tree.  A fine rolling country suc-
·eeded, covered with trees of infinite variety in shape and

colour.  Over the first ridge lay the Lago Casuéris.  There
are two streams from one source, which flow out to the north
and south of the town, which are called the Casuéris, and
Casuerinha (or little Casuéris) ; both are favourite resorts for
bathing ; for though the Rio Négro is cool at sunrise, yet it
cannot boast the well-like coolness of these.  The streams
and pools of Scotland are winning in the heats of August,
but the greatest luxury I ever enjoyed in the way of a bath
was in the Casuerinha.  All the water everywhere else, even
the Rio Négro in which I had dipped before the morning star
was gone in, seemed even at that hour to retain something of
yesterday's warmth.  But on the same morning, just as I was
returning from the river, Doctor Duarte, the juiz de paz, and
his wife with bare head and hair streaming to her waist, came
up, and went off in a boat to this same stream for a bath.
They offered the boat to me for the next morning, at the same
hour.  Drawing its waters from profound shades, and trans-
parent as glass, it babbles now over a gravelly bottom, and
now widens into crystal pools, into which the traveller,
fevered by the heat of the day and the mosquitoes of the
night, may cast himself with equal gratitude and surprise at
the icy coolness of the Casuerinha.

I searched the banks of these streams in vain under the
guidance of the Tapuyos, for large trees.  I found a singular
insect here, hardly distinguishable from the plant to which it
clung.  It was two or three inches in length, and it had a
long neck resembling a twig, from which two bright green
wings, in the shape of leaves, bifurcated, and concealed the
body from its foes.  One would think it some relation of the
leaf butterfly, which, if pursued by a bird, darts to the
nearest tree, and *when it finds itself on a leaf,* dons a great-
coat, which makes it seem a *dead leaf,* and in that character
it drops to the ground.

One day we made a long journey toward the north-east, in
a direction suggested by Silva, a handsome Indian hunter,
whom we met in the forest.  His naked chest matched well
with the copper horn of powder slung across it; a shot

monkey dangled from his hand. After many ascents and
descents, we at length descended into a hollow, and found
there a tree which measured twenty-three feet round at the
greatest height which I could reach from the ground, and this
girth continued almost undiminished for a height of forty
feet; but there some accident had happened to the giant,
which was broken short off, yet had thrown out a large limb
on one side, and continued its life through that. Once it
must have been a splendid sight. Whilst here we saw the
tops of some palm-trees violently swung to and fro, and heard
a chattering sound; the guide told me it was a large monkey,
but we were unable to get a sight of him. Shortly afterwards
I was startled by the heavy rush of some animal through the
bushes, everything breaking and giving way before him. I
asked Casimir if it was a jaguar. " No," he said, " a tapir."
Then stooping down, he said that he saw an ant-bear. We
had no firearms with us that day, and my object was not sport,
but large trees. After sketching the tree through a camera
lucida which I had with me, I returned to the town, and
dined off one of the river turtles for the first time. It is
cooked in a savoury manner, but the meat itself is tough and
insipid.

My time was slipping away, and I did not find the big
trees which I had hoped for at Barra, so I determined to look
elsewhere. I had already made the acquaintance of Doctor
Duarte, the juiz de paiz, to whom the consul had given me a
letter. He told me very decidedly that I must not think of
going up the Rio Négro, as it was very unhealthy. Now the
works that I had read made out just the opposite. However,
he went with me to the captain of the *Inca*, which was on
the point of ascending the second stage of the river, and this
gentleman did not encourage me to believe that I should be
any better suited by going with himself. Senhor Duarte
then advised that I should procure from the vice-president a
galliota and search the banks of the river in the neighbourhood. He kindly accompanied me for this purpose, and the
result was, that the vice-president informed us that a galliota

should be at my service, to go where I pleased, and whenever
I pleased to apply for it through the Doctor.

I now went to the Secretario da Policia, and had my passport viséd for travelling in the district of Amazonas ; and he,
discovering my object, proposed to introduce me to Senhor
Brumaire, a French naturalist in the employ of the Brazilian Government, which gives him what is equivalent to
£600 sterling per annum. Rejoiced at so good an offer,
I repaired thither with the secretary. All these gentlemen to whom I have alluded, spoke French, but Senhor
Brumaire did better, he spoke English. A spare form, above
the middle height, a gaunt but handsome face, with a grave
expression, grizzled hair and beard, shaggy eyebrows, but
vivacious and keen eyes, and a Frenchman's blithe springy
step. Whilst dining at his table, a message came that a little
tiger, which was to have been delivered to him for a consideration that evening, had made his escape from his captor ;
and then an invitation from a neighbour, who was going to an
island at the mouth of the river to fish, for Senhor Brumaire
to go with him and shoot. I was asked to join the party, and
within an hour found myself lying side by side with the
naturalist at the end of a crowded boat. One of the crew was
overjoyous with drink, and the dog entertained us by the
droll howling songs with which he bayed the moon, until,
feeling sleepy, I told the senhor that I had heard it was dangerous to sleep exposed to the moonlight, and asked him if
there was truth in the opinion. He replied, that there was no
danger in the influence of the moonlight itself, but in the
dews with which it might be accompanied, and that if travellers protected themselves from the dews, they would suffer
nothing from the light.

At midnight we arrived at a cluster of islands at the junction of the rivers. Here we landed, and the boat was secured.
An Indian in the crew, being asked by the senhor whether
there were birds here, " Si—grande passaros," and so waggled
his head and flapped his arms, as to look very much like a
bird himself. He added that we could not sling our ham-

nocks from the trees about 300 yards off, because there were "tigres," as they call the jaguars. Therefore a fire was lit upon the sands ; and after the fire-arms had been set in order or the night, we lay down to sleep. Besides my hammock, I had brought with me Mr. Levinge's contrivance for protection of travellers in the East from mosquitoes, for a full description of which I must refer the reader to Murray's "Guide to the East." I had never used it before. Suffice it to say, that when it dangled from a pole erected in the sand, it resembled a crinoline of muslin roofed in at the top, and at the bottom sewn on to a linen bag nine feet long, which lay upon the sand at right angles to the crinoline, and had a kind of coffee-bag on one side of it, which opened so as to admit yourself, and then could be rapidly drawn together by tapes, so as to exclude the mosquitoes. I was well pleased with it that night, for the muslin swelled with the dews, and answered the purpose of a tent. It was about to become a really invaluable servant, as will be seen. I was awaked by the shouts and laughter of the crew, who were taking their morning bath, and screaming real or pretended alarms of " Jacaré ! Jacaré ! " as they call the alligators. As yet I had seen none of these animals ; they congregate about the mouth of the Amazon, but are rarely seen at this season higher up the river. A bowl of coffee was being prepared in gipsy fashion in one spot, in another strips of fish fastened into the cleft ends of long pieces of wood in-clined over a fire were being cooked. As we sat talking after breakfast, I told Senhor Brumaire of my ill-success in finding trees of large girth, and asked his advice. He knew the pro-vince of Pernambuco well, but had not been long in the pro-vince of Amazonas. However he invited me to go on with him up the Amazon to Alvellos on the Rio Coary, where he was going to remain for two months' hunting in the forests. I was obliged to refuse this tempting offer, from want of time. Hearing how little time I had to spend, he then suggested as the most probable way of finding large trees, that I should avail myself of the vice-president's offer of a galliota, descend the Amazon again to Mura, opposite the mouth of the Madeira (which is the largest tributary of the Amazon, and flows into it from the south), and that I should ascend the Madeira as far as the Furo di Canomá, and pursue that channel till it brought me out into the Amazon again at Villa Nova, where I might meet the steamer for Pará. I deeply regret not having followed this advice, instead of continuing up the Madeira to Borba; but I rejected it because I considered it would take a longer time, and that the risk of missing the steamer was too great. But I believe now, that I might have done it, and I mention it for the sake of any future traveller.

If the reader looks at the map, he will see that this furo or canal is a natural one, passing from the Madeira into the Amazon, and thus forming the long island of Tupinambaramas. Eight small rivers flow into it from the south, which are not represented, for want of space. A tract so abundantly broken up by watery paths would, I suppose, give nature a fair chance to produce here and there a monster tree upon the banks, for the great obstacle to girth in the timber is of course the crowded state of the trees, except at such openings. The Furo of Canomá is a natural channel of considerable breadth, but I am told that there are many artificial canals cut to join the rivers in various parts of the country, and these are described as being exceedingly narrow, so that you may travel for days together under a dense canopy of leaves, which sometimes scarcely allows room for the boat to pass beneath.

However, as it was, I told Senhor Brumaire that I feared I should have no time for more than to go to Borba, which he said I had better do under the circumstances, since the river Madeira would show me, at all events, a different vegetation from the Amazon, and I should probably find some large timber.

I then followed him round the island. Amongst other birds which he shot, were five or six huge fowls, very handsomely marked with blue and chestnut feathers. They saw each other drop, one after another, without moving from the spot; apparently never having had experience of a gun before. There was no dinner for us that day, and we returned in the evening o Manáos, which we reached at two o'clock in the morning. After a few hours' sleep, I set about preparations for my voyage without further loss of time. I called on Senhor Duarte, and acquainted him with my resolve. He thought I was crazy to venture so far with Indians alone, being unable o speak a word of their language. And even when he heard my plan, which was to make Casimir my captain and interpreter, he dissuaded me earnestly, said that I did not know what devils the Tapuyos were, and that they would as soon kill me or leave me, as not. Against this I urged, that Senhor Brumaire and some others had not thought it impracticable; next, that Casimir, the trusted Tapuyos of his master, would not dare show his face to him, if he cut my throat, or allowed t to be cut by the rest; and finally, that the arrangements of he Government seemed pretty good along the river, which was now constantly traversed by the steamers; and that the ndians would probably feel that if a white man were murdered, there would be some inquiry made after him, which might t least inconvenience them more than taking my life could benefit them. The juiz de paiz retorted, that when I was once dead, there would be no more inquiry made after me. But I owe him my thanks both for his well-meant advice, and for his assistance when he found I was still resolved to go. He first sent a letter to the vice-president, to see whether he would consent to let the galliota go so far as Borba, who wrote back word that I could have it, with two rowers beside Casimir, as far as Mura, and should have an order made out, to take in three or four more, when I should have to turn *up* stream. He then sent for Casimir, and asked him whether he knew the way to Borba, and would accept the responsibility of being Capitão do viagem." The poor fellow drawled out the word Pode," which was as much as to say that he was able, and added a slight sigh, which was as much as to say that he was unwilling.

I then sought out my acquaintance of the steamer, the French Creole before mentioned, who had not yet left Manáos, and requested him to aid me in storing a galliota with whatever might be necessary for the voyage.  I may as well mention what is needed.  The following is sufficient for a crew of six men for a week :—One arroba of salt-fish—strips of dried cow-fish tied together in a bundle (about fourteen shillings); one basket of farinha (an "arcade"), (about twelve. shillings); and a demi-john of cashaça (the rum of the country), a large glass jar, enclosed in a wicker case to protect it (eighteen shillings).  For my own use I got a tin of soda crackers (instead of bread), (eight shillings); eggs and oranges ; and placed in a large earthenware vessel, packets of coffee, sugar, salt, tapioca, and barley (for soup).  I had brought twelve 1 lb. tins of preserved beef from England, and tea ; and a portable tin kitchen, with spirit-lamp, for cooking. (Spirits of wine are dirt-cheap in this country.  You buy a quart for a shilling.)  I added a small lantern.

When I was ready, the vice-president had forgotten all about the order for fresh Indians at Mura, so I had to pay him a second visit ; and luckily found a priest there, to whom I told my wants in Latin, and he interpreted them for me. Armed with this order, I proceeded to the galliota, and found it was about twenty feet long, broad, and round-bottomed. The hinder part was boarded, and had benches running round it in the form of an oblong, and in these benches were holes, designed for the supports of the tolda ; but never a tolda was to be seen.  Nor could I persuade any of the occupants of the neighbouring galliotas to sell me one.  A tolda may be represented as the roof of a waggon, if you substitute plaited palm-leaves for sail-cloth ; and it is an absolute necessity, both as a shelter from the sun by day, and the dews by night.  I discovered, also, to my chagrin, that the two Indians were two lazy, thievish-looking lads, one of whom was lame.  They were unwilling to carry either my luggage or their own provisions to the boat ; therefore Casimir and I made several journeys for these articles ; and at last I shouldered my own portmanteau, which seemed to the natives a most unconscionable performance for a white man.  It was dark when I departed, amidst the laughter of the crowd, who vere much amused at the idea of my going to Borba with his inefficient crew, and without a tolda.

Wearied and excited by the last few days, I had now promised myself some sleep; but Casimir informed me that I must take the helm, if we were to make any progress. I obeyed, and found that steering a boat was not such a simple thing as in my ignorance I had supposed. We shot down the river rapidly; only the plash of the oars, and the directions esquerda—direita" (left—right), uttered by my guide, broke the silence, and it was with the greatest difficulty I could keep my eyes open. About midnight we passed the island where I had been with Senhor Brumaire, bid adieu to the river Negro, and proceeded into the centre of the Amazon. Somos na corrente d'agoa," said Casimir (We are in a current of water), "and may all lie down to sleep." Accordingly the boat was laid broadside to the descending stream, which is exceedingly powerful here, and would bear us far before the morning. The only fear was of overshooting the sitio of the Capitâo dos Trabalhadores (captain of the labourers), an officer whose business it is to furnish Indians for the service of the river. The moon was nearly full overhead; we should have light nights. I looked round; nothing was to be seen but a waste of waters, with a thin veil of mist rising from them, and turbulent currents hissing and foaming. The Indians had already flung themselves at length upon the seats. I wrapped myself in poncho and plaid, and stowed my head and feet away under the seats. But a perverse wakefulness now succeeded to my drowsiness, and I lay reflecting on my singular situation till the morning, when I found my wrappers soaked with the night-damps, and determined not to pass another day without a tolda, if I made them stop to weave one. About nine o'clock we arrived at the mouth of an igaripé, on the right bank of the river, where the officer before mentioned had one sitio; but he was not there. The men landed, and cooked their breakfast, and I was just thinking of bathing, when I saw gliding from the shore, at the distance of a hundred yards, an object about eight feet long, which looked like the skeleton of some animal. The Indians exclaimed "Jacaré!" It was an alligator, whose ribbed back had this strange appearance. We now crossed over to the left bank, where the officer's other sitio lay; but had much difficulty in reaching it, by reason of the current and wind turning against us, and my own bad steering. I became sick and faint from the intolerable heat, from which an umbrella was a very insufficient protection, and began to long for the rest of the crew. The sitio lay at the top of a precipitous bank, a hundred feet above the water. Hard by stood a large tree with an enormous spread of foliage. The officer, a shrewd, active man, received me with a hearty welcome. He had been surprised at our devious approach, and the absence of a tolda; but he speedily remedied this, gave a lecture to Casimir and Co. on the necessity of good behaviour, and would take nothing for the new tolda, saying that the Governor had ordered that my boat should be supplied with everything gratis, provisions included, if I had not enough. He gave me a letter to his lieutenant, the Salvador da Costa, at Mura, that he might supply me with three more Indians. At sundown we continued our route down a narrow, still side-stream. It was so dark that I could hardly see to steer the boat. The darkness brought an English fireside to mind, and I wondered what the friends at home were thinking of; yet I would have little thanked a genie for conveying me thither as yet. The moon was now rising over a tree, and drew from me all the songs I had ever heard or sung. The lame lad complained that he was ill, and unable to row any more, so I gave him the helm, and got some sleep, though the cárapanás were determined it should not be much. The others got the boat at last into a current of water, and then slept themselves.

Casimir woke me at dawn, and pointed out Mura, "debaixo do sol" (under the sun), which was just rising above it. As at our last stoppage, the bank rose precipitously here, and on the top was the village. The Mura tribe are accounted treacherous; but my Indians were, as usual, mongrels; and I must say, proved a very good-humoured set. There was a great deal of trouble in catching them ; for it was a festa, and every one was keeping holiday. The Salvador da Costa and the Captain of the National Guard could neither of them read, so I had to read them the order myself, which I did with much emphasis on the words "order of the Governor," and ' sem falta alguma " (without any fail). We lost four hours in this job. The sick lad was useless, therefore I discharged him, and paid him off here ; and demanded another man in his place. Accordingly four men were brought in from the woods ; but two disappeared again, and only one of them was reclaimed at last. It was impossible to get a fourth, so I agreed to take back the sick lad, who was much disconcerted at his discharge, as steersman. He came back improved by it, and worked better all the rest of the voyage. Casimir had been rather saucy in his manner, and jested with the others when I gave him orders, so I took him aside, and told him that his master had put him at my service ; that I was not bound to pay him a farthing, and would not do so, unless he altered his conduct ; besides which I would complain to his master on my return. On the other hand, if he gave me satisfaction, I would pay him double whatever I gave the others. After this he behaved admirably, and by my direction told the men seriously, that if we did not reach Borba on the fourth night I had been forewarned that the voyage ought not to be longer), would pay them no " gratificacâo ;" but that if they worked well their pay should be doubled. And now the authorities besieged me with abject entreaties for cashaça. I could not afford to part with any of this stuff, the influence of which over my crew was inferior only to the " order of the Governor." Such slaves are they of the present moment, that for cashaça they would have sacrificed any amount of pay, and almost their birthrights, like Esau for a mess of pottage.

The Salvador da Costa and the Captain of the National Guard had already had more of my cashaça than was good for them ; but would hardly let me depart. I was glad to get the crew away, on the promise of a drop presently, which operated like magic. They left their elders vociferating on the bank, and went off with me at a fine pace. I was fain to have recourse to the brandy flask myself; for there was a short chopping sea running (if I may be allowed the expression) at the Bocca da Madeira, and we were much knocked about by the waves. At twelve o'clock we got into smooth water. The wind, which had been dead against us, was now at right angles to us, and, of course, in our favour. The mast was raised, the sail hoisted, and the galliota went up stream famously. Poor Casimir had had hard work, and anxiety, so I bade him sleep now, and cooked a meal for him from my stores. We made but one stoppage in the day, when enough was cooked till next time. The men dined at sunset on a sandy island, which they supposed would be free from cárapanás; some lit the fire, and others hunted for turtles' eggs. These have no shell; but are inclosed in a skin a good deal thicker than the skin of a chicken's egg. When quite fresh, they are pleasant, but rather rich.

We had much deceived ourselves in supposing that this spot would be free from cárapanás; I never remember to have been so cruelly attacked. Besides, they had one at a fearful disadvantage, since, partly to accommodate myself to the climate, and partly to the society in which I found myself, I had just reduced my clothing to a minimum. In a dense cloud they literally darkened the air for a few feet round me; it was impossible to stroke them from my limbs as fast as they coated them. After all, I daresay these insects are beneficial, and phlebotomize a white man advantageously for his health (for they do not so much tease the coloured men); still, you may have too much of a good thing, and they certainly appear to you a real curse when they render your nights feverish and sleepless.

The little sleep which I got was due to that admirable contrivance of Mr. Levinge's before alluded to, which excited the envy and admiration of the Indians. I had affixed it to the inside of the tolda; here it was secured by day, and at night let down round me as I lay on my wrappers in the bottom of the boat. It was merely owing to the narrow quarters, that

ie sides of the " machina" (as Casimir styled it) could not
e sufficiently extended, and therefore the cárapanás were
ble to sting me through the muslin here and there. Still, the
ɔmparative superiority of my position gave me many a laugh
t the Indians, who often exclaimed "Muito bonito" (Very
retty), and "Sta bôa" (That's a good plan), and often
nxiously inquired whether uot a single cárapaná had got in.
thought them a good-natured set of fellows, and considering
ieir natural indolence, they responded industriously to my
ressing and repeated demands for speed. In short, I did not
ɔnsider it a position for wearing my revolver ostentatiously,
nd thought it wisest to *trust* to my companions, and Casimir
ɪ particular. And then for the rest I felt it no presumption
ɔ trust to the Wings *beneath which if we remain*, it little
iatters to some of us whether we live or die.

At dawn we drew to land for bathing, since the Jacaré,
rho has to turn on his back to bite, rarely attempts it in
hallow water, or near a whole boatful of men. The rowers
lept little at night, but during the day, when the wind blew
trongly from nine A. M. until two P. M., at other times from one
ill six P.M. As soon as the wind sunk they rowed close in
hore in ascending the river, and where the bank permitted
t, two of them by turns got out and towed the boat by a rope.

The Madeira presented a different vegetation from the
ᴀmazon. On the Amazou there were no trees of dark hue—
iothing of the fir tribe; but here, the greater number of the
rees were cedar-trecs and mulatto-trees (so called from their
rellow-brown bark). The cedar has not the beauty of the
:edar of Lebanon; it is more like its kinsman of North
ᴀmerica, but richer in foliage and odorous in its wood.
Waking often at night, I saw them bending over the boat,
oaded with the fantastic drapery of parasites, and glistening
with the silvery sheen of dews in the moonlight.

On this day, we passed an island to which the turtles
:esort in great numbers; and here the Government has
placed a guarda to monopolize them. We pulled alongside to
purchase one, but it was given us.

In the evening I had landed to sketch a tree, and whilst thus engaged, observed winks and signs going on among the crew, and fancied from these and a few words which I caught, that they regarded me as a great nuisance, and thought it would be a good plan to leave me on the bank, and make off with my effects.  It was a joke, I believe, but then it was an ugly joke ; so I got into the boat as if I had forgotten something, and removed my stick and waistcoat, which had some bank-notes of the country in it, intending, if they played me false, to return along the bank for fifty miles, in which it was likely I should reach one of the very rare sitios, which would give me a chance for life.  I own that I did not fall asleep at once that night.

Next morning, at five o'clock, we passed the mouth of the Furo di Canomá (before mentioned).  The wind was doing the work now, and not only the rowers, but the men at the prow and helm, had fallen asleep, so that the boat ran into the trees, and nearly had the tolda knocked away.  I blew them up well, and told them, for such another fault, I would take off half their gratificacâo from the men at the prow and the helm.  This had a good effect for a while ; but, the men being tired and sleepy, a second accident took place, in a few hours. The wind shifted suddenly ; we were nearly pitched into the water on the right ; and my barley-soup, which was just ready, after three hours' cooking, was bestowed altogether on the wrong place, scalding me soundly and roundly, so that I could not sit or lie on that side for some days.  The men laughed, of course, and I muttered the threat, " Calaboose at Borba."

In the evening, just as they were landing for dinner, a squall burst upon us—" Embarca, embarca !" shouted Casimir, clutching the sail only just in time ; and, for ten minutes, we shot on like a " botte do vapor."

At eleven o'clock next morning we reached Borba, half a day before time ; thanks to the good wind.  It lay on the top of a steep bank, at the foot of which stood a Yankee trader, firing away at the motionless nose of an alligator.

A few hours before our arrival, I had met with a vexatious
isappointment.   My revolver, inserted in a stock, which
hanged it into a carbine, lay ready on the bench at my side ;
 had shown its efficiency to Casimir, and bidden him, in
ase he saw any large animal on the banks, to let me know.
'his morning, I saw him lift his hand and arm above his
ead, and heard him raise a shout, after which he kept his
yes fixed for a few seconds on the bank.   On my asking
rhat it was, he replied, at his leisure, "Um grande preto
igre ;" a great black tiger, or, to speak more correctly,
 jaguar.   He told me it was standing on the bank,
ratching us, and did not move till he raised the shout.
'he boat was close in shore, the beast only about thirty
ards off.   If I had but wounded him, he would pos-
ibly have turned to bay ; and then it would have been
trange if, with six shots and a boatful of six men, I could
ot have either secured the beast, or our own escape : of
ourse a sportsman would shudder with disgust at this
onfession.

On going to present my letter of introduction to the senhor
rho was to aid me in my search for trees, I found him gone
way for three months, and (as might be expected in this
ountry, where every other person seems unwell in the head)
he senhora was incommodada ; but she would see me later in
he day.   So we went a little higher up the river, out of sight
f the Yankee, and there o Senhor Tartaroga (turtle) was slain
y my companions, I grieve to say it, with every disgusting
ircumstance of barbarity and cannibal ferocity.   However,
e made very good soup.

The Indians scooped a little hole in the gravelly bank, and
t was immediately filled with cool spring-water.

I then paid my respects to the senhora, who lodged me in
he house of the military commandant at Borba.   Like all
ther houses here, it had only one story, with two or three
arge, lofty rooms, and an open ceiling, much traversed by
ats.   It was delicious to swing one's hammock again in airy
egions above the level of the cárapanás.   My host and I

lay in opposite corners, slowly oscillating, and studying each other.

He was a handsome man, with large, soft, dewy eyes, and glossy black hair and beard; but he also was incommodado, and feared he was going to die. The place did not seem a healthy one for residents, though far cooler than the river.

He praised the goodness of his neighbour, who sent us our meals, and visited him continually.

Sleepless, bitten, and sore from head to foot, I found Sunday a welcome rest. In the evening, when the senhora's musical clock was sounding, the traders of the place dropped in, and promised to arrange an expedition, and find big trees for me; but their efforts were unsuccessful; and, since the chief man of the place was absent, I determined to make a search alone, and return at once. The commandant wished to return with me. It certainly was rather an inconvenience to have a dying man in an already crowded boat. But I could not refuse my poor host, and agreed to it. I waited for him one or two days; but he changed his mind, and never went, after all.

I have already mentioned that the Brazilians make a more abundant use of the devil's name than I ever heard from any people; and my companion amused me a good deal by this habit. He spoke, at first, of having a "comrade" in the next room, and, judging from Damon, I expected that Pythias would be worthy of him. But this comrade proved a servant as different from his master as Friday from Robinson Crusoe. The commandant, wearily swinging himself in his hammock, exclaims, faintly, "Cesario, oh, Ces-á-rio!" The comrade, cleaning boots audibly, makes no reply. After a few more movements of the hammock, "Ces-á-rio!" says the officer, loudly. No sound returns but the cleaning of boots. "Oh, Cesário!" languishes the officer, in despair. To him, in his own time, the comrade entered slowly—a human rat, with twinkling eyes, low forehead, and short, glossy, black bristles all over his head. He draws himself up, to do him justice, in military position, with his hands by his sides, and looks at his master like a sly rat. That gentleman's turn was now come;

e kept Cesario waiting till he had accomplished his pre-
etermined number of oscillations, when he checked the
ammock, spat upon the ground, shook off dull sloth, and
assionately accosted him: "Cesārio, porque non vem?
iābo; tu es um demōnio, diabo di-ā-bo; non faz nada,
iabo diabo diabo di-ā-bo." The servant replied, that he
idn't hear. "Mentiroso, diabo—Um soldado! diabo. Um
ıldado de ser mentiroso!" And then, like lightning, "Diabo
iabo, diabo diabo, diabo diabo, diabo di-ā-bo."

(Cesariô, why do you not come? . . . You are a demon!
. . You do nothing, &c. . . . Liar! . . . A soldier! . . . A
ıldier to be a liar!! &c. &c.)

It was impossible to keep a grave face; but I affected to be
mused at the stupidity of Cesario.

I paid a visit to the first igaripé on the left bank, a little
bove Borba, and, under the guidance of Casimir and Chris-
ɔrao, one of the boat's crew, discovered, at last, a tree 300
ɛet high, but of no great girth. For the first hundred feet
: was utterly without branches, a pillar of light red wood,
omewhat redder than brown madder, and very hard. Then
wo-thirds of the tree above sent out branches, and a light
ɔliage quivering like the leaves of the aspen. Near this
pot, Casimir brought me a piece of wood from which he
queezed clear water into my mouth: he called it pao d'agoa
wood of water).

It took only two days to return to Serpa, on the Amazon,
he boat keeping the middle of the stream in descending.

Nothing of interest occurred, except that on the morning of
he second day I was awoke at dawn by a most execrable
ıowling from the long Isle of Tupirambos, on the right. As
egularly as Memnon, but with far other sounds, the guaribas
or howling monkeys) thus greet the rising sun.

There is a colony at Serpa of liberated slaves. The big
ree of Serpa is celebrated along the river. An English
ɔlerk, who lives here, told me that it measured thirty or forty
ɛet round, and 250 feet high; but it is deceptive, and does
ıot look so much. He showed me a Tapuyos Indian of

pure breed; the man's skin was of a sallow hue, like the mud of the Amazon.

After waiting here a couple of days, I went on down the river in the steamer *Tapayoz.* The vessel burned wood instead of coal, and therefore no hammocks could be slung on deck, the awning of which was burnt everywhere in holes by the falling sparks. These vessels take up a quantity of salt-fish and farinha, which is the staple food of the lower class; and bring down turtles, india-rubber, grass hammocks, and Chili hats from Peru. The hats are made neither* of leaves nor of grass, nor of bark, but of the wood of a small palm-tree, split into thin strips, and then plaited.

After a voyage of five days I reached Pará again, and received a kind welcome from my friends, who seemed surprised at my solitary trip in the galliota to Borba.

To my great chagrin, I now heard, from a most reliable eye-witness, of trees within five days' journey from Pará, which twelve persons could scarcely embrace. This gentleman offered to send a guide with me; but I was to go to sea in ten days' time, and the risk of losing my vessel was too great to be incurred. I was therefore obliged to relinquish the idea; and paid a visit during the remainder of my stay to Taüaü, the estate of Mr. Campbell, thirty miles south of Pará on the Rio Acará. Taüaü signifies red clay, of which the soil is composed, and from this a large quantity of pottery-ware is manufactured by negroes for the proprietor.

It was a curious sight to see them coming to their young master and his Brazilian assistants, and to myself, for an evening blessing. They seem to have been indoctrinated to believe that every white man is capable of conferring a blessing on his brother.

My entertainer rode with me into the forest, and showed me several trees from twenty to twenty-three feet in girth, and one 250 feet high. On our return, we killed a yellow snake, about three feet long, which is called the " mother of ants," because they are necessary to her existence. The next evening I witnessed a tropical thunderstorm. The thunder cept up a continuous roll, and one clap startled even my companions, who were accustomed to such storms. The vivid lightning was reflected in the rain-drops which streamed from he roof of the long balcony in which we sat, presenting the appearance of a rain of fire.

As we returned from Taüaü to Pará, we passed the public slaughter-house on the outskirts of the city, where more than a thousand vultures were feeding. Hard by is the arsenal, and a specimen of that curious tree the fan-palm.

My time was now up. I intended to return to England by way of New York, to see Niagara in its winter garb.

Yet, before turning from Brazil, I must mention, first, a few ' skeleton tours " which the lover of nature might adopt, and also a few facts of social interest.

First, then, as to skeleton tours. That which I took may be done in four months and a half;—accidents protracted it to five months in my case. But for the following, six months would be needed :—

Route 1. By steamer in three weeks from Southampton to Isthmus of Panamá. Cross it by railroad in one day. Go on by the Pacific Steam Line to Lima in about four or five days. Thence ride over the Andes to Yurimaguas on the Huallaga, about six weeks' journey through the magnificent scenery of the Andes (which, according to Humboldt, combines all the beauties of all the mountain scenery in the world, and transcends it all). Thence by the Amazon steamers to Pará, in three or four weeks. Home by the West Indies or Pernambuco, in five or six weeks. This makes five months. Allow one month for accidents. This might be safely done by a man travelling alone, and taking proper precautions.

Route 2. Niagara, and California (in order to see the Wellingtonia) * might be visited, and the port of Choco reached by steamer in three months from Liverpool. Thence by three weeks' riding to Santa Fé de Bogotá, in order to see the cataract of Tequendama, a river descending 650 feet 574 at one bound), and draped with heliconias, palms, and

* The last discovered is 112 feet in girth, and 450 feet high.

arborescent ferns. Thence down the Rio Meta, by canoe, in about fifteen days into the Orinoco; for the Meta is the swiftest of the American rivers. Allow a week to reach and visit the rapids of Atures and Maypures.* Thence down the river in sixteen days (Humboldt's reckoning here) to Angostura. It is probable that some steamers, French or others, ply between this and Trinadad. Thence home in fifteen days, by steamer. A companion would be almost needed here, for this country is disturbed by contending parties; and it would be well to have letters of introduction to both of the combatants.

Route 3. The same, starting from Quito to Santa Fé de Bogotá, and leaving out North America altogether. This would also occupy six months.

Route 4. Humboldt's round from Trinadad to Atures, &c.; and thence by the Casiquiare Canal (where the forests are thickest, the trees largest, and the animals most plentiful) into the Rio Négro; descend that river to Barra, and thence by the Amazon steamers to Pará. Home by West Indies or Pernambuco. This might be done by a man travelling alone.

Route 5. This last route would be highly interesting, and is almost unexplored country; but a companion would be absolutely necessary, and it would take eight or nine months. Ascend the Amazon to Barra. There, if not at Pará, study the Lingoa Geral (or Lingua Franca of the Indians) enough at least to carry you along; and if Casimir could be secured as a guide, all the better. Then, provided, of course, with letters of introduction, and small trinkets to propitiate the Indians, ascend the Madeira to its head-waters, passing through the Matto Grosso, and its utterly wild tribes of Indians. And then by a short land-portage reach the head-waters of the Rio Paraná, and descend into Paraguay. Steamers run up the river Plate into that country. There

---

* Of these, Humboldt says: "Neither the fall of the Tequendama, nor the magnificent scenes of the Cordilleras, could weaken the impression produced on my mind by the first view of the rapids of Atures and of Maypures. When you are so stationed that the eye can, at once, take in the long succession of cataracts, the immense sheet of foam and vapours illumined by the rays of the setting sun, it seems as if you saw the whole river suspended over its bed."

would be most danger in this unusual route, which, however,
is now and then taken by merchants who pass through with
an armed party ; but have not published any account of their
travels.

Next, as regards matters of general interest. It is noticeable that Brazil, though once the most backward of the
South American States, has, since its freedom from the Portuguese yoke, and since abolishing the slave trade, become the
most promising, and certainly the most tranquil. I suppose
this is greatly owing to the contentment of the negro population, who seem to form a power in the State. Thus there are
black doctors, priests, and even presidents of provinces ; and
no man thinks worse of his wife that her ancestors came
from over the water. The Indians, on the other hand, being
still disunited and uncivilized, are more oppressed ; for
though the Brazilian laws are good, they are often badly
administered.

I may mention, as an instance of credulity on the part of
negroes, that when a master cannot procure a service from
his slave by beating *him,* he can always procure it from him
by beating *a figure of San Antonio* in his presence. To save
the saint, the slave will not spare himself.

There seem to be many staunch Roman Catholics in
Brazil, who nevertheless disapprove highly of the administra-
tion of that religion by the ecclesiastics ; and they have a
great opinion of *English* Protestants, on account of English
morality. Hence I was told by a Roman Catholic, that in
Rio Janeiro a Protestant place of worship is crowded ; and
that a mission to Brazil would be well received by the
people. The same gentleman informed me that there is a
school in Rio Janeiro kept by an Englishman ; and that the
best families in the country send their children there, on the
condition, however, that no Brazilian ecclesiastic be admitted
to confess them, nor even Brazilian tutors to teach them.
They will have English masters and mistresses.

There is also a great request for English governesses, and
female servants, who might command there double the salary

they receive in England, and in both cases far more consideration, and excellent matrimonial prospects.

The English character stands so high with the Brazilians at present, that if an Englishman misbehaves himself when trusted, they say, "Oh! he can't be an Englishman—he must be a Frenchman or an American." I heard that the Yankees have been sharp customers to the Brazilians. I was told, also, that an English gentleman of the middle class, bearing letters of introduction to Brazilians, and conducting himself properly in their society, might ally himself with the very first families in Brazil.

As an instance of this, a Scotch gentleman married the sister of the largest landowner in the province of Pará; but then *he* was such a man of his word, and had, therefore, so great influence, that my host at Pará told me he was regarded "almost as a demi-god." For the Brazilians are not eminent for truth, yet they can appreciate it in others ; and when they wish it to be understood that they are really telling the truth, and no lie, they say, " E palabra Inglez " (It is an English word).

The emperor and empress are distinguished for their courtesy and accessibility, and the latter esteemed for her virtues as a saint.

The nobility is not hereditary ; the highest rank, that of marquis, as well as the inferior grades, is only conferred for distinguished public services ; and with the exception of *prestige*, the son has no further benefit from the father's title.

Their hospitality is universal, but unbounded towards Englishmen ; and Senhor Brumaire informed me that, with one or two letters of introduction to Brazilian families, I might have passed through Brazil from end to end, with houses, horses, guides at my service, and no expense beyond my passage out and back to England.

A highly-paid class is that of the working-engineer—that is to say, one who knows what should be done, and can set the example of doing it with his own hands.

The public instructor of writing receives more than the
prime minister.  He is an Irishman, and was the last, but
not the least, of those who befriended me in America.

I left Pará at daybreak on December 1st, in the brig
*Sea-Foam*, 280 tons burthen, for New York ; and right glad I
was to get the first breath of sea-air, although it produced
symptoms which an old hand, a fellow-passenger, assured me
would have turned to yellow fever, if I had remained longer
in the country.

The voyage was interesting in itself, and agreeable from
my companions ; and I cordially recommend Captain
Theodore Boreham, and any vessel he commands, to future
travellers.

But the passage was eventful, since the pilot left us in
shoals coming out of the river.  We sprung our mainmast, and
were knocked about between a headwind and sea from behind
for nine days, over a space of one day's sail north of Cape
Hatteras.

New York was already excited with the firing of guns, and
telegraphic messages from the South.  But I will neither
trench on ground to which matters of late occurrence have
given a new and absorbing interest, nor will I venture to
describe Niagara, already hackneyed, but never done justice
to.  I will only say that its icy trappings shone under the sun
like silver ; that Goat's Island looked like a fairy palace ;
that rainbows decked the whole ; that, standing underneath
the Horse-shoe Fall, between it and the rock, and gazing down-
ward into the abyss, one was reminded, now of the deluge,
now of Milton's fall of the angels from heaven ; now, again,
of the voice of ascending praise to God from all creation,
which is like the voice of many waters, and of mighty
thunderings.  And looking upward, where the water came
over the edge of the precipice in sparkling diamonds, one
thought, with Dickens, of " angels' tears."  But looking
forward to the Terrapin Cliff, shaped so like a watery altar,
one was reminded of that streaming altar of Elijah which
the fire of heaven burned up, as this one, too, must be,

when the elements themselves shall be dissolved with fervent heat.

I reached Liverpool again on January 20, 1861. Thus ended what might seem in many eyes to have been a rash journey for a country clergyman to have undertaken; exemption from the dangers of which, the writer ascribes entirely to God's indulgence.

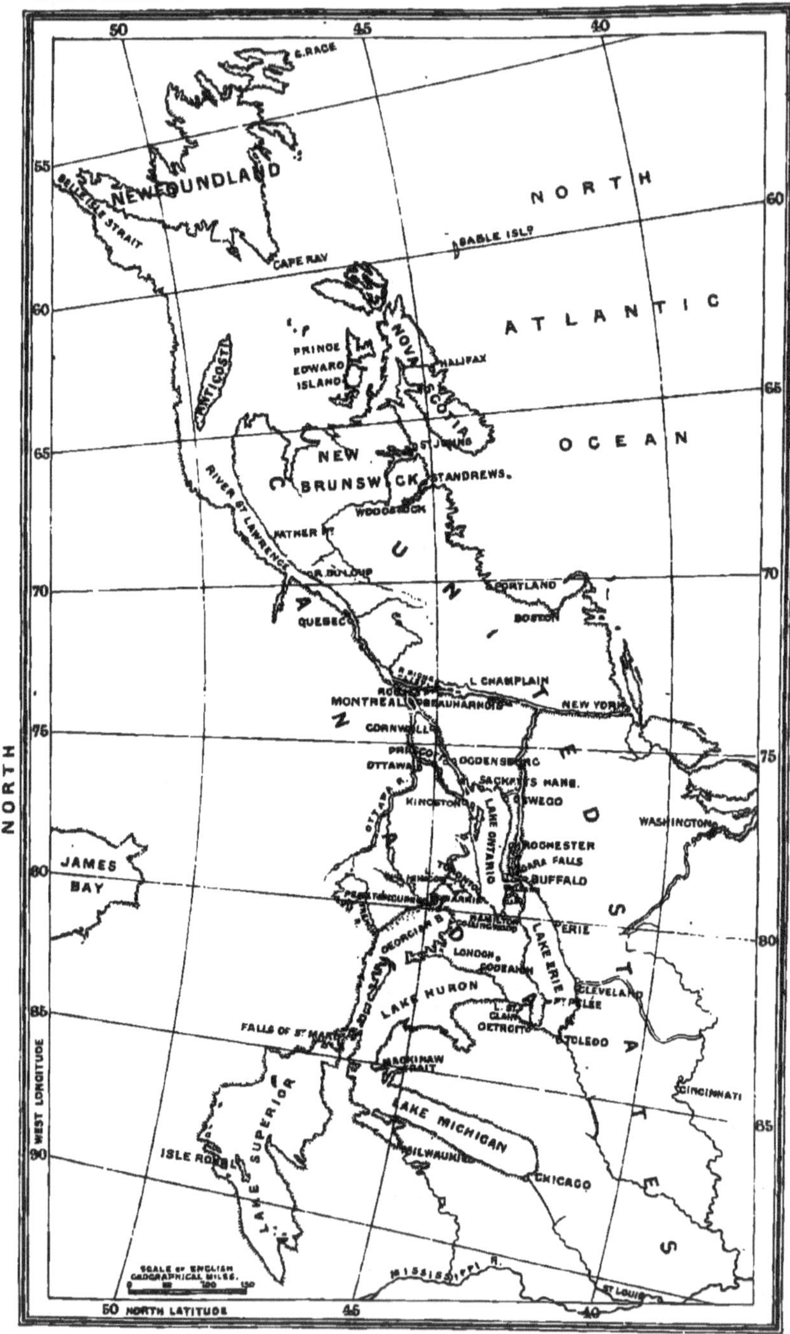
NORTH
WEST LONGITUDE
NORTH LATITUDE
50
45
40
55
60
65
70
75
80
85
90
60
65
70
75
80
85
S.RACE
NEWFOUNDLAND
BELLISLE STRAIT
CAPE RAY
SABLE ISL?
NORTH
ATLANTIC
OCEAN
ANTICOSTI
PRINCE
EDWARD
ISLAND
NOVA SCOTIA
HALIFAX
RIVER ST LAWRENCE
NEW
BRUNSWICK
ST ANDREWS.
ST JOHNS
WOODSTOCK
FATHER PT
R. DU LOUP
QUEBEC
PORTLAND
BOSTON
MONTREAL
BEAUHARNOIS
L CHAMPLAIN
NEW YORK
CORNWALL
PRESCOTT
OGDENSBURG
OTTAWA
SACKET'S HARB.
OSWEGO
KINGSTON
LAKE ONTARIO
ROCHESTER
NIAGARA FALLS
BUFFALO
WASHINGTON
JAMES
BAY
GEORGIAN B.
HAMILTON
LONDON
GODERICH
LAKE ERIE
ERIE
CLEVELAND
PT PELEE
LAKE HURON
L. ST
CLAIR
DETROIT
TOLEDO
FALLS OF ST MARYS
MACKINAW
STRAIT
LAKE SUPERIOR
ISLE ROYAL
LAKE MICHIGAN
MILWAUKEE
CHICAGO
CINCINNATI
MISSISSIPPI R.
ST LOUIS
UNITED STATES
SCALE OF ENGLISH
GEOGRAPHICAL MILES.
0      50     100     150

## 5. *NINE WEEKS IN CANADA.*

### BY CAPT. RICHARD COLLINSON, R.N. C.B.

SITTING in my arm-chair one day last June, I was disturbed
in the perusal of a novel by an unexpected offer of a temporary
appointment in Canada. As that was a part of the world I had
never seen, I at once accepted the attached conditions, that I
should depart by the next mail; so I engaged my passage in
the *Canadian.* But in that vessel I was not fated to go, as on
my reaching Liverpool she had not arrived, and the *Nova
Scotian* was substituted. On our passage to Derry, we fell in
with the *North Briton,* and heard from her of the loss of the
*Canadian* in the ice. A few words may be admissible here
in reference to that disaster. Much has been said in blame
of the *Canadian* having taken the Belleisle Straits so early in
the season, and the period for using this passage (which is 226
miles shorter than that to the southward of Newfoundland)
has been changed, in consequence, from the 20th of May to
the 20th of June. But two seasons are seldom alike, and
observations show that fogs are less frequent in the Belleisle Straits than to the southward. The average number
of days of fog at the Belleisle lighthouse in 1859 was eight
per month; while to the southward the fogs sometimes
extend for 800 to 1,000 miles without a break. It also
appears that field-ice was fallen in with, in the parallel of
Cape Race and 300 miles east of it, twenty-three days after
the loss of the *Canadian.* With respect to this unfortunate

occurrence, it may be remarked that, as the gale was coming on from the southward, it would have been more prudent to have taken the southern channel, for the loose pack was sure to be closed by the effect of the wind; and, again, that four to five knots is too great a speed for an iron vessel with ice in close vicinity. I also think that half a dozen wooden fenders, strung together five feet apart, with a guy forward, to keep them in their place while the vessel was going through the water, would in all probability have obviated the calamity.

The Company, hitherto, have been very unfortunate, this being the fourth vessel they have lost. Fog, no doubt, is the great difficulty in preventing the ascertainment of the ship's position by observation. Could an artificial horizon be devised, it would lessen the risk one-half.*

Our passage was a favourable one, so far as wind and weather were concerned; but on coming upon the Newfoundland banks we fell in with the fog, which compelled us to go slowly; and on the evening of the 29th, just as we had completed our last rubber, came the cry, "Ice ahead!" whereupon we rushed on deck, in time to feel the cold, clammy atmosphere, and to satisfy ourselves that there was a huge mass of something, more palpable than the air, towering high above our heads within 200 feet of us. Falling in with these floating islands is not a pleasant sensation; but I did what I advise all passengers to do under similar circumstances: go to bed prepared for a sudden rise, and lay in a stock of sleep for any emergency. When the fog cleared off in the morning, we were able to resume our speed; eight bergs were revealed, for the benefit of those who had not seen ice before, and to satisfy the curiosity of those who were not content with the opaque glimmer last evening.

Our enemy, the fog, closed again around us, compelling us to reduce our speed, and to grope our way by the lead, so that it was not until the afternoon of the 2d of July that we were

---

* Since writing the above, another vessel, the *North Briton*, has been lost.

nabled to comprehend our position positively. The opening
f the fog then disclosed the summit of the land; but we
vere in doubt for some time, not being able to recognise its
ontour. It will, probably, be found advantageous to crown
he summits of the hills with different-shaped beacons, as
s done on the coast of Norway, so that a glimpse will be
ufficient to identify them. In a little time, however, the
and to the northward appeared, and we were enabled to fix
ur position nearly midway between Cape Race and St. Paul's
sland, and shaped our course for Anticosti, which we passed
n the dark, and picked up our pilot at Father Point, at
ive A.M. on the 4th. Favoured with a fine day, we had an
pportunity of admiring this, the most beautiful of all rivers
have seen. The mountains, on either side, rise to the
eight of near 4,000 feet in successive slopes clothed with
orest, while the shore-line is ornamented with villages,
pproaching nearer and nearer to each other as you ascend
he river, until they become one continuous street, studded
rith churches, whose bright tinned spires and red roofs
parkle in the sun, and give a pleasing foreground to the
learings and cultivation in the rear. The river itself, studded
rith islands, and ornamented with vessels, boats, white
orpoises, and birds, is of a width sufficient to impress you
rith its grandeur, and maintain its claim as the noblest
utlet to the most wonderful water system in the globe.
.ighthouse after lighthouse, buoys and beacons, all proclaim
he use to which man has turned it, and give an inkling of
hat vast internal communication which, bringing a vessel
rom 2,000 miles inland, here launches her upon the ocean to
erform her voyage to another continent.

Night closed in upon us before we reached our destination,
nd, sorry though we were to lose the view of Quebec, we had
he comet to console us for our disappointment and excite our
dmiration by its sudden appearance.

Midnight found us alongside the Grand Trunk Railway
ier at Point Levi; and, taking a hurried but friendly leave of
hose of our fellow-passengers who were bound to Montreal,

we embarked, after the usual custom-house difficulties, in the ferry-boat, and were carried over to Quebec. If this city is beautiful in its approach by daylight, no one who ever enters it for the first time in the dark will deny that it is wonderful: such a pavement, such a jolting, and such a hill, made one anxious for daylight to see what the streets were made of and how the horses ever got up them.

Six the next morning found me doing the town. Its quaint architecture at once attracts sympathy and veneration: large collegiate buildings, numerous churches, and a class of well-to-do houses, proclaim its civic position, while the predominance of wood gives it a strange character. There are wooden trottoirs, wooden crossings (which accounted for the jolting of last night), wooden steeples, wooden gutters, shingled roofs. Many of the stone houses are also coated with wood, as a protection from the frost. The cliff rises abruptly on the south-east side, leaving barely space between it and the river for one street; the bastions follow the brow of the hill, separating the city from the suburb of St. Roche on the north-west; while the Plains of Abraham, which are nearly on a level with the citadel, are free from houses, and protected by Martello towers to the south-west. The citadel rises to the height of 320 feet above the river, and commands a most magnificent prospect. Mountain ranges terminate it in every direction, while the intervening spaces are strewed with villages and clearings. Beneath, the river is separated by the Isle d'Orleans into two branches, and forms a grand object, with its numerous shipping, its steamboats, and its rafts; the steep pitched roofs of the houses, many of them glittering with their tin covers, combine to render the scene more effective. Though the wall which surrounds the town shows unmistakeable signs of decay, the casemates on the summit of the hill form an entirely independent position, and would require siege operations to effect their capture. Breakfast introduced me, for the first time, into American hotel life, about which so much has been written that I will only add my name to the general English verdict of its discomfort. I

uppose the general habit of living in hotels and feeding
t a common table has come upon the Americans by
ecessity; but to us it is a strange contrast, and leaves
nything but the impression of "taking mine ease at my inn."
he system of the bar, and its universal concomitant, the
arber's shop, require to be seen to be thoroughly realized:
hy they should be in close connexion, it is difficult to
magine, as it certainly cannot add to the zest of Jones
iquoring up, to witness Smith, with his legs on high, under-
oing tonsure by the hands of a black artist. Perhaps it may
e, that at the one any gentleman can relieve himself of the
emblance of being so, and at the other any ruffian may have
is personal appearance improved upon.

The general off-hand manner in which matters are conducted
n these establishments may be exemplified by the following
necdote. In the course of our travels, one of my colleagues,
eing dissatisfied with his room, made application for another,
hereon he was referred by the waiter to the chambermaid,
n these words: "Miss, this man says he wants another
partment."

My business not being likely to be forwarded at present at
Quebec, I took the steamboat to Montreal on the afternoon
f the 5th. The excellent accommodation of these vessels
nabled us to take on board two companies of the 47th
Regiment in addition to the usual passengers. The lower
leck, into which you step from the wharf, is ten feet high.
A staircase leads up to the saloon, which occupies the
whole length of the vessel, and is surrounded, except at the
ow and stern, by sleeping cabins. Here there are spacious
alconies, whence the scenery can be viewed with great
omfort and pleasure. The width of the river at Quebec is
,400 yards, a breadth which it maintains generally, all the
vay to Lake St. Peter's, ninety-seven miles, where it
xpands to six miles and a half. The lake is shallow (ten
o twelve feet); but a navigable channel of eighteen feet
as been dredged through it; and, though the course of the
iver is obstructed by rocks and shoals in many places, it is

so well lighted that vessels of that draught are enabled to perform the voyage to Montreal by night as well as by day. The river banks rise usually at once to two hundred feet; but there is no longer the noble background of mountains that was seen at the entrance to the river. The houses still continue their street-like appearance, a proof of the value of river frontage, as well as of the gregariousness of the French Canadian, who does not appear to be happy unless he has a neighbour within hail of him. We reached Trois Rivières after nightfall, which is at the embouchure of the St. Maurice, an important river on the left bank. The rivers St. Francis, Yamaska, and Richelieu, also empty themselves into the lake on the southern shore. The town of Richmond is situated forty miles up the former, and is of importance, as here the Quebec and Montreal railroad joins the branch to Portland. The latter, before the introduction of railways, was the main communication between the river St. Lawrence and New York. There are rapids on it at Chambly; but this obstruction has been overcome by locks, which are capable of taking vessels of seven feet draught of water.

Montreal, though lacking the grandeur of site which contributes so much to the look of Quebec, has a noble appearance from the river. Spacious, well-built quays, with a depth of water sufficient to admit large vessels to lay alongside, are backed by a row of buildings which would do honour to any city in the world. Nor is this impression at all impaired on landing. Well-paved, broad streets, with many public and private edifices of dark grey limestone, are seen; while a bustling thoroughfare and handsome shops pronounce undoubtedly that Montreal is the commercial, if not political, capital of the Canadas. Here the navigation of the St. Lawrence used to terminate; but the energy of man has overcome the obstruction of nature; and by means of the Lachine, and other canals, the farther end of Lake Superior may be reached by vessels of nine feet draught of water, twenty-six feet broad, and a hundred and forty feet long, thus opening out a communication which has called into play, up to the present me, a shipping of 390,000 tons, four-fifths of which are in ne hands of the United States.

The river opposite to Montreal attains a width of 2,600 ards; but of this, the navigable channel comprises only our hundred.

The island of St. Helen's, opposite the town, has no avigable channel between it and the right bank of the iver; and though Montreal may not be so clever a strategic osition, in a military point of view, as Quebec, yet the ossession of this island, and of the Mont Real, affords means f deterring an enemy from any attack that has no other object han plunder. They are 5,000 yards apart, and the latter s 760 feet above the river.

No one can approach Montreal without talking of that vonder of our time, "The Bridge." Tremendous as it is, t falls far below expectation. The straight line has done way with that grand conception of man's genius, the key-tone of the arch, and the bridge is a matter-of-fact affair, ooking like a gigantic fence to keep in mammoth cattle. With a tribute of great respect to the engineer who over-ame the difficulties of rapid current and overwhelming ice, nd raised from a Yankee friend of mine one of the few cknowledgments I have ever heard one of their nation bestow n a Britisher, "Well, sir, I calculate you beat us there;" it annot be looked upon otherwise than as a work before its ime, and, unless it be the link forged to connect Maine more ntimately with Canada, the money it has cost had better never have been spent.

Having accomplished the object of my visit, I returned o Quebec by the rail, through the most dreary country, I think, I ever saw. There were miles upon miles of forest, vith an occasional opening of blackened stumps and barked trees. But that the soil has got in it that which will repay or these clearings, was amply proved by the luxuriant growth of clover which has sprung up along the edges of the railway. Richmond appeared an oasis in the desert, with its undulating nills, flowing river, and cleared tracts, and would have been a much greater place than it is, but for the fear of war; for here surely, one of these days, will be a frontier fight.

A general election for the Houses of Parliament having summoned Canadian ministers to their constituents, it was ten days before my provincial colleague could be appointed, and I had, therefore, time to look about me at Quebec. The Houses of Parliament are contained in a large block, built of brick, with a flat roof, situated on the east bastion. The Chambers for the Legislative Council and the Legislative Assembly are very convenient, and there is an excellent library. Since the junction of the two provinces, Parliament has met alternately at Toronto and Quebec, involving a change of residences as well as a shifting of public documents, books, and papers, every four years. It is, however, understood that the new buildings at Ottawa will be complete in time to prevent another adjournment to Toronto, and Ottawa will become the political capital. The elections were looked forward to with much interest, parties being nearly equal, and the platform of the Opposition being a cry for representation by population, which would involve a preponderance to the upper province. The census of 1861 gives as follows:—

CANADA WEST, 1,395,222 ; CANADA EAST, 1,103,666.

The population of the large towns is in—

CANADA WEST : Hamilton, 19,096 ; Kingston, 13,743 ; Toronto, 44,743.

CANADA EAST : Montreal, 90,498 ; Quebec, 51,109.

The buildings connected with the Romish Church, as well as the general appearance of the priesthood, betoken a prosperous condition. The priests, in particular, appeared to me to be selected from a higher class than those I have seen in other countries; and I have good authority for stating that their general conduct is as irreproachable as their appearance is good.

The city at this period of the year is at the height of its commercial activity; but it was crammed on this occasion

nore than was usual, by the arrival of the *Great Eastern*;
.nd I was heartily glad when arrangements were made which
.nabled me to leave on the afternoon of the 20th.   After
·icking up one of my colleagues at Montreal, we left by the
vening train for Toronto on the 22d, journeying in a
leeping car, where the accommodation is very simply
.dapted for lying at full length, and a pillow and a rug are
upplied.   There is also a washing-closet at one end; but
 would recommend the traveller to provide his own towel.
Ve reached Kingston at 7.15 A.M., and, halting a short time
or breakfast, proceeded on to Toronto, where we arrived
.t 3 P.M., performing the journey of 333 miles in fifteen
.ours and a half.   The crops in Upper Canada were ten days
n advance of the lower province; and we passed numerous
.learings with large fields of yellow corn.   The contrast of
he two races of inhabitants showed itself in a remarkable
vay.   Instead of the continuous street and cluster of houses,
.ere every man appeared to have set up for himself, and
solated homesteads in lieu of dense forest bounded the view,
vhile the progress of prosperity was strongly marked.   First
ame the shanty alone; then the shanty and log-hut; again
.hanty, log-hut, and boarded house.   At length the summit
.f prosperity was reached by brick or stone houses, with
.arden and orchard; the boarded house becoming the barn;
he log-hut, the stable; and the shanty, the pig-stye.   The
ecurrence of these homesteads in each stage of their progress,
.ogether with an occasional peep of the lake, made our day's
.ourney a very enjoyable one.

Toronto does not give the impression of a commercial city,
hough it owes its locality to its excellent harbour.   This is
.ormed by what was formerly a long tongue of shingle, but
.i now an island, the lake having, in the course of the
.ast two years, broken through a passage at its eastern
.xtremity, in which there is now a depth of eight feet
vater.   The timber brought by the Northern Railway from
.akes Simcoe and Huron is here formed into rafts for
ransmission to Quebec; but all the commerce is represented

by a few schooners and steamboats.  There are, however, important manufactories, and a well-endowed university; and as it is the terminus of the Great Western as well as of the Great Northern Railway, and as the Grand Trunk passes through it, it will, doubtless, retain its position as the metropolis of Upper Canada.  Though not so well built as Montreal, the streets have a handsome appearance; and besides handsome public buildings, there are many private houses indicating a prosperous condition.  Following the example of the United States, the railway passes through the town.  Accustomed as we are to fences and gates, it is a matter of astonishment to the European that accidents should not occur more frequently than they do, upon the unguarded railway.

Here we were joined by the third commissioner, and on consultation it was agreed that we should commence our labours from the westward (our farthest point in that direction being the island of St. Joseph); but as no vessel proceeded straight to that island, it was determined to take advantage of the weekly packet from Collingwood to the Sault St. Marie.  We left Toronto on Thursday morning, passing through a beautiful country, the clearings extending on each side as far as the eye could reach, and getting glimpses of Lake Simcoe at Bell, Ewart, and Barry.  Near the former place are steam saw-mills, but at present they have little occupation, and there is upwards of a million feet of boarding stacked ready for use.  Formerly grain from Chicago was landed at Collingwood, and the vessels that brought it took back boards; but, in the last year, the trade has been diverted to Goderich.  The war no doubt has also put a great check upon house building in the far west.

Collingwood is a small, but rising town, in the bottom of Nottawasaga Bay, on Lake Huron.  There is a small harbour protected by a breakwater, which will admit vessels of nine feet; but the commerce is represented by two steamers, one of which finds occupation in visiting the settlements in the Georgian Bay, and the other, *The Ploughboy*, has the contract for carrying the mails to and from Sault St. Marie.

Embarking in this vessel, we put into Owen Sound, at the
bottom of which is the thriving settlement of Sydenham,
and then struck across for the east end of Manitoulin Island,
off which we arrived at daylight the following morning, and
where we were met by two boats, into which were put barrels
of flour and groceries.   Manitoulin Island is one of our
large Indian reserves, and here are collected the remnants of
a tribe whom we have dispossessed of their country : only
one or two white men now reside on the island.   One of
my companions told, as an instance of how much the
Indian desires to cultivate civilization, that when he had
passed up here a few weeks ago, he had seen a young
English girl put into the canoe, just as we had witnessed the
discharge of our cargo : she had accepted a situation as
governess to the family of an Indian chief.   Poor thing, he
told us, she said nothing, but she looked back to the steamer,
as if she knew she had severed every tie.   The navigation
to the north of the Manitoulin group is exceedingly intri-
cate : the channels are so narrow, and the islands so numerous, that you feel you want a clue to the labyrinth, while
to enhance the gratification of contrast between rock and
tree, you now and then come upon the canoe and the wigwam.
One place, where we stopped for wood, the Indian children
were prepared with baskets of raspberries and strawberries,
and took back as payment the broken victuals of our break-
fast-table.   Towards evening, our engine broke down ; but we
were fortunately in a position where there was room enough
to admit of the vessel's drift, during repairs ; and though I
had been greatly charmed with the accommodation I had on
board the American steamers, I could not help admiring the
wisdom which gives to the Margate steamer some control
over her proceedings in the event of accident to her engine.
We reached the Bruce Mines at 3.30 A.M. and hastily got rid
of our despatches : the settlement did not look inviting, and
from the wharf had the appearance of an " every-one for
himself place."   The copper mines have ceased to be profitable, but a good lode has been found in the adjoining bay.

N

We had a continuance of our beautiful scenery of yesterday, and reached the Sault St. Marie at 11.30 A.M.  On our passage up, we stopped at two places on the United States shore ; one of which was the celebrated manufactory of Mr. Church, of raspberry jam, and were told that he had made no less than twelve tons that year ; at the other, was the following novel machine for fly-fishing.  In the eddy caused by the jetty was fixed an upright post, across the top of which were two sticks, at right angles to each other ; at the end of each of the four arms was the model of a vessel under sail, which caused the sticks to revolve, and to each arm was attached a line with a fly on it.

The village on the Canadian side of the Sault St. Marie consists of a few scattered houses, but is likely to become of importance, as the Canadian government, with a view to attract settlers, have declared it a free port.  The houses on the American side have much more the appearance of a town ; but, since the opening of the canal, there is no longer a necessity for a portage, and the place now appears to be going to decay.  The canal is 17.8 miles in length, and is capable of taking vessels 48 feet wide, 290 feet long, and 12 feet draught of water.  It has had the effect of completely opening out Lake Superior.  The value of the merchandise annually passing through it exceeds a million sterling, and the tonnage is upwards of 300,000 tons.  The height of the fall is $17\frac{1}{2}$ feet ; and it is a beautiful sight to watch the canoes running the fall, bringing up in an eddy, and catching fish with a poke-net at the end of a pole.  The Comptroller of the Customs not only granted us the loan of his boat, to go to the south end of St. Joseph's Island, but also promised to accompany us.  We procured tent equipage, &c., from the Hudson's Bay Company's post, but did not get away until 9.15 on the morning of the 29th.  Favoured with a fine breeze, we ran down to the west of Sugar Island, through the Neebish Channel, round the north end of St. Joseph's, to Milford Haven, at its south-east point, where we arrived at 3.45.  While the tent was pitching, we visited the only

nhabited house on the point, and found a man who had been
ettled here twenty-eight years: formerly it was a calling-
lace for the steamers, for wood, but latterly he has very little
ommunication with the outside world. Understanding from
iim that the property we had come to look at would be
ound by following the path, I induced one of my com-
anions to accompany me. We, however, soon lost our way;
nd, after wandering through rotten wood and swamp, tor-
nented by mosquitoes and in dread of snakes, we were
ieartily glad when our boat rescued us from the bough of a
ree overhanging the lake. There are but few settlers as yet
n St. Joseph's Island, and their numbers are declining; some
f them have been attracted by the offer of employment at
he Bruce Mines. Leaving Milford Haven, we touched at
he Hudson's Bay Company's old post, and at the Fort at
he south point of the island; the latter was captured by
he Americans and destroyed during the last war. Then we
rossed over to the Detour Channel, where we were picked
p at noon by the American steamer, *Planet*, a fine vessel of
,000 tons, trading between Lake Superior and Detroit. Our
riend, the Comptroller, had amused us much with his
imerican antipathies. I was told, after he had left us, that,
n the execution of his duty, he seized an American boat,
ttempting to smuggle a cargo on the Canadian side.
onathan with his usual effrontery, however, decided that
he boat, in the course of the chase, had crossed the boundary
ne, and our friend, the first time he put his foot on the
round of the United States, was seized and incarcerated for
aving violated the territory of the stars and stripes; after
e had been kept some time in gaol, he was told he might go
bout his business. He, however, being imbued with a
*ivis Romanus sum* feeling, refused to be liberated without
n apology; whereupon the judge ordered his cell to be
nlocked and his provisions stopped; an effectual way of
etting rid of a troublesome prisoner. On board the *Planet*
iere two companies of western volunteers bound to the war.
he men appeared in very good spirits, and, when we got

into the St. Clair River, commenced a fusilade at the ducks
with their revolvers.

About ten at night we were visited by one of those electric
storms for which this region is famous.  It came up from
the south-west in a dense black cloud, illumined by vivid
sheet lightning, which was answered in the north-east with
forked lightning, and burst upon us in a torrent of rain,
which came down in such quantities that the scuppers
were unable to free the decks.  We arrived, after daylight,
at the entrance of the St. Clair River, which is 600 yards
wide; the land on both sides is low.  Here there is a
steam ferry which connects the Grand Junction, as well
as the Great Western Railway, with the Port Huron and
Detroit Railway.  We reached Detroit at noon, when,
finding that the *Planet* was going on to Cleveland, and
the captain being civil enough to consent to put us on
board the steamboat, that is attending the erection of the
lighthouse at Point Pelee, we determined to continue our
voyage.

Detroit is one of those towns which has sprung up with
wonderful activity; and a quay, crowded with shipping,
extends all along the river-side, quite throwing into the
shade our village of Windsor, opposite.  On reaching Point
Pelee we found that the steamer had been damaged and
gone away for repairs; we had, therefore, no alternative
but to go on to Cleveland, which we reached just in time
to save the train to Buffaloe, and arrived at that place at
2.30 A.M., when my companions determined on perambulating
the town, until the starting of the early train to Port
Colborne.

Very few of the shops were wholly closed by shutters;
not that we saw much property of value exposed to tempt
the housebreaker, but the custom forms a curious contrast
to our European notions, and says a great deal for the
morality of the people.  On arriving at Port Colborne we
took the train to St. Catherine's, and, after inspecting Port
Dalhousie, drove back to Port Colborne, along the banks

)f the Welland Canal. We found them busy deepening it, 30 as to admit of Lake Erie becoming the feeder instead )f the Grand River. The locks, both at the entrances to ;he canal on Lake Erie and Ontario, will admit vessels of 45 feet wide, but, in the centre, they are only 26 feet wide; ;hey are twenty-seven in number, and lift the vessels 330 feet above Lake Ontario. The country round about the Welland )anal is more open than usual, the forest having been cleared away long ago.

After sleeping at Port Colborne, we drove early the next morning to the Grand River, by the lake shore, passing through a park-like country. The under-bush in many places had been cleared away, letting air and light into the forest, and exposing the bolls of the trees for our admiration. The farmers complained that the army-worm had made its appearance in the wheat and was committing great devastation. The Grand River was originally intended as the outlet of the Welland Canal, but it turned out an unhealthy place, owing to the swampy character of the land, and it is now almost abandoned; few vessels frequent the harbour, which is a very good one. We drove up to )unville, a flourishing little town, where the river is dammed, for the purpose of supplying the Welland Canal, and where the water power has caused several factories to be erected. Here we took the train to Thorold, a village beautifully situated near the highest part of the Welland Canal, and whence there is a magnificent view of the low plateau between it and Lake Ontario. Here we separated; one of my companions returned to Toronto, while the other kindly undertook to show me the Falls, as we purposed remaining Saturday and Sunday at Niagara. Neither the roar of the cataract nor the appearance of spray warned me of its presence, and, though upon the look-out, the first view I had of the Falls came upon me by surprise. The eye wanders from one fall to the other, doubtful whether it will be most attracted by the broad line of feathery spray of the American side, or by the blue of that mass of water

going over the horse-shoe; the latter prevails, for wonder
has more effect upon the brain than admiration. The whole
effect of wonder and astonishment is greatly enhanced by
the narrow and precipitous gorge through which the water,
after it has fallen, makes its escape. It is difficult to imagine
that the only outlet for all this volume exists between you
and the opposite bank; yet such is not only the case, but
there is a safe ferry, for small boats, but a short distance
below the Falls.

The immense power of such a stream ought to undermine
the adjoining banks, but the masses of rock along the shore
have the effect of a rubble embankment, and the cliffs
retain their perpendicular character, with only a pathway
here and there to the bottom. The recession of the horse-
shoe is calculated, from measurements extending over twenty
years, to be at the rate of one foot per annum; but it is
impossible not to contemplate that, if the river once wears
its way to a serious fault in the Laurentian dyke, the whole
character of the Falls may be completely altered in the
course of twenty-four hours. I do not wonder at its attraction, for no one can have seen it without an anxious desire
to look at it again. Besides the Falls, the adjoining country
is full of historical associations, and you can go from the
scene of one battle-field to another. The suspension bridge
is remarkable for its light appearance; wire rope is used
instead of chains, as with us; the span is 1,045 feet, and
its extreme capacity is estimated at 835 tons. After two
days of great delight, we took our departure by rail to the
town of Niagara, where we embarked on board the steamboat to Toronto, passing between Forts Niagara and Missa-
sauga, the former of which is upon the United States shore,
and does not appear to be a modern work. On the 7th of
July we again left for Collingwood, on our way to the
harbour of Penetanguishene. We found, however, on our
arrival, that the steamer we had engaged had that morning
deposited a party of school-children midway between Owen
Sound and Collingwood; and, as it was evident they could

ιot be left in the woods all night, we were obliged to go
ut of our way to pick them up and restore them to their
aothers; they had evidently enjoyed themselves notwith-
tanding a little drizzle, and came on board laden with wild
.owers and raspberries.  So school feasts have made their
ιay to the backwoods of Canada as well as to the rural
istricts of England !  Penetanguishene is one of the most
onvenient harbours upon the coast of Lake Huron, and
ιas one of our dockyards in the last war.  At present
; has lost much of its importance, the railway having
ιeen carried to Collingwood instead of to it.  We found
, flourishing reformatory under an active superintendent,
vho was turning the services of the boys to good account,
a clearing the land, making roads, and building jetties.
'he place appears admirably suited for this purpose, as the
ιoys are out of the way of temptation, and can have more
iberty given them, in consequence of the difficulty of getting
.way.  On our way back to Toronto we stopped at Barrie,
o inspect the old means of communication between Lakes
)ntario and Huron.  The goods were carted from Toronto to
he head waters of the Holland River, on which they were
mbarked in flats, and carried across Lake Simcoe to Barrie,
vhence they were transported to an affluent of the Nottawasaga
Ĝiver, by which they reached Lake Huron.  Though only five
·ears had elapsed since this had been the usual route, we had
ome difficulty in getting a guide, but at length started off for
. drive through the forest ; every here and there we came to
. fresh clearing, and the crops, as well as the timber, showed
hat there is a great deal of good land in this neighbourhood.
ι.fter losing our way, and having to drive back two miles, we
eached the length our carriage could go, and, setting off on
oot along a decayed corduroy road, we reached our destination
.fter an uncomfortable tramp of three miles, the greater part
ιf which was in swampy ground, where the mosquitoes were
n legions.  Since the construction of the railway, the lower
ʒround here has been abandoned for more healthy localities
n the undulating country adjoining.  The cattle find their

way into the cleared land from the neighbouring farms, and we found a good deal of hay cut and stacked; but the habitations had all been removed.

On our return to our carriage, we got a hospitable invitation to tea, from the mother of a large family, in a shanty. She gave us capital bread and butter and raspberry jam, and tendered eggs and bacon; but these we would not wait for. They had been there five years, and were getting on; but it was a long way to send the crops to market. The orchard was planted and the garden fenced in, and, next year, she hoped, the house would be begun. Happy and contented with her lot, the children's schooling appeared to be her only trouble.

In the course of this journey we went over a considerable portion of the route of the contemplated ship canal, which is intended to connect Lake Huron with Lake Ontario. The principal engineering difficulty appears to be the supply of water for feeding the upper lock. No doubt that could be overcome, in these days of steam-power, by pumps; but it is questionable whether a work of such magnitude would pay, until the shores of the Georgian Bay become more thickly populated. The ores from Lake Superior require to be taken to the coal district on Lake Erie; and, though this would be a direct route for the grain from Chicago to Oswego, the grain merchants, I am told, would prefer the grain being transferred, as it is at present, at Goderich and Port Colborne, where there are elevators which pump it out of the hold of the vessels into the railway cars, in the course of which process, it is in a measure ventilated and dried. The canal would, no doubt, admit of the rafts from the Georgian Bay being taken at once to Quebec for exportation, instead of being, as they are now, broken up at Collingwood and carried by rail to Toronto, and there re-formed for the transit to Quebec, by way of the St. Lawrence.

Having failed in our arrangements, on a former occasion, for visiting Pelee Island, we determined on hiring a small steamboat at Detroit. We left Toronto for Sarnia on Monday,

.2th, and, after sleeping at that quiet little town, we drove
ibout eleven miles along the banks of the St. Clair River, and
hrough a portion of the Indian reserves.  It is wonderful how
lowly the Indians fall into the habits of civilization ; but it
s to be hoped that a great advance may be made in the next
;eneration.  At present, their fences are in bad order, their
'illage rude, and their huts anything but comfortable in
.ppearance.  The river banks are elevated not more than
wenty feet above the water, and the general aspect of the
:ountry is level.

Sleeping at Detroit, we embarked on board our steamer,
.arly in the morning ; and, after taking in wood at Amherst-
)urgh, started for our destination, which appeared to our
:aptain to be a matter of some concern.  He had traded
egularly, for the last three years, from Detroit to Sandusky ;
.nd, as he told us, a Britisher had calculated for him that, in
;oing to and fro, he had sailed the distance of twice round
he globe.  But this he looked upon as a voyage of discovery ;
.nd, when I intimated to him that very likely we might have
o anchor, he was alarmed, and suggested drifting about the
ake all night.  " I have got an anchor and cable, sir, but I
lever use 'em ; I lay alongside a wharf always."  The owner
.f the vessel, a black man, was also on board, and the captain
.onfided to us that we should have good " fixings," as he had
.een major-domo to President Harrison.  We had a long
alk about the war, which he summed up with, " Well, sir,
ve must whip them some, and then turn them out of the
Jnion."

Point Pelee Island is low, with a good deal of swampy
round ; but there is a considerable quantity of valuable
imber upon it.  It is inhabited at present by eight families
nly ; but, as the adjoining island to the southward (Kelly's
sland), which is within the United States' boundary-line, has
. population of 400, and is famous for its vineyards, Point
'elee will also, probably, become settled.  After steaming
ound the island, we went up to the caisson for the new

lighthouse at Point Pelee. The site was one of great difficulty to overcome, being a shifting sand going off suddenly into deep water. The caisson, an octagon of forty feet, with a capacity of 350 tons, was put together at the Welland Canal Works, whence it was towed to its destination, and sunk upon the spot, by the admission of water; the interior has been filled up with stones from Pelee Island; and, after three years' trial, it has been found so firm in its foundation, as to admit of the permanent lighthouse being erected on it. We found the schooner in attendance on the workpeople, at anchor under the point, and, the night being fine, her captain consented to our being lashed alongside, and ours was saved from "letting go his anchor," of which he had such a horror.

We put in the next morning into the harbour of Rondeau, where we found a carriage waiting for us, in which we drove through a very fine country, and along a capital road, to Chatham. This is a pleasant-looking little town, with a good many Indians settled around it; we saw some very picturesque groups of them, men who had come on horseback to attend the market. We took the rail from Chatham to London; the latter town is well built, with numerous shops, and the Tecumseh hotel is one of the best in Canada. The railway between London and Toronto passes through the best land in the upper province, and through some very picturesque spots. The town of Hamilton is beautifully situated in Burlington Bay, and is becoming a place of considerable importance, from its iron and other factories; the census of 1861 giving it a population of 19,096. After a short sojourn at Kingston, we proceeded to Montreal, by way of the St. Lawrence. The thousand isles well merit all the encomiums bestowed upon them; the scenery on both banks, the excitement of the running rapids, all combine to render this a most pleasurable excursion. Our labours concluded by a visit to Isle au Noir, on the River Richelieu, a post of great importance, formerly, as it guarded the approach to the province from ake Champlain.  The railways have, in a great measure, iverted this traffic into more direct channels, and the island i at present occupied as a juvenile reformatory.  The mericans were busy completing a strong military work at Louse's Point, which, when complete, will protect the floating ridge that carries the trains across the River Richelieu, at s junction with Lake Champlain, and maintains the comiunication by rail between Ogdensburgh and the Eastern eaboard.

While our own Government, satisfied with the excellent urveys (as far as they go) of the lakes, by Bayfield and )wen, have of late years confined their attention to the urvey of the lower part of the St. Lawrence—a survey which as been most admirably executed—the Government of the Jnited States have taken in hand an elaborate and most areful survey of their own shores.  In the annual report or last year, I find that eighteen charts and plans have een published, and that the estimated expense for the nsuing year amounts to $125,000.  In addition to valuable aeteorological and magnetical observations, together with a letailed report of the survey, the report contains some mportant diagrams of the comparative height of water in he different lakes, as well as an account of the means aken to fix the longitude of several positions with extreme iccuracy.

By a return made to the Provincial Parliament, dated )ecember, 1859, the gross amount of tonnage on the lakes s 390,000 tons, four-fifths of which is owned by the United States.  In addition to the great passenger traffic, the grain rade from Lake Michigan, and the transport of copper and ron ore from Lake Superior, have called forth great mercantile ictivity, the centres of which may be deemed the cities of )etroit and Buffaloe.  On Lake Erie, the cities of Toledo, Cleveland, and Erie, are places of great importance : the ormer from its direct communication with the far west, and Cleveland from its vicinity to the coal region.  On Lake

Ontario, Rochester and Oswego are the places whence Canadian timber, and grain from the westward, are shipped from the lakes to the Atlantic seaboard.

To conclude.  In the course of my sojourn of fifty-eight days, I travelled with great convenience over 3,000 miles, and have great reason to be extremely grateful for much kindness and attention.

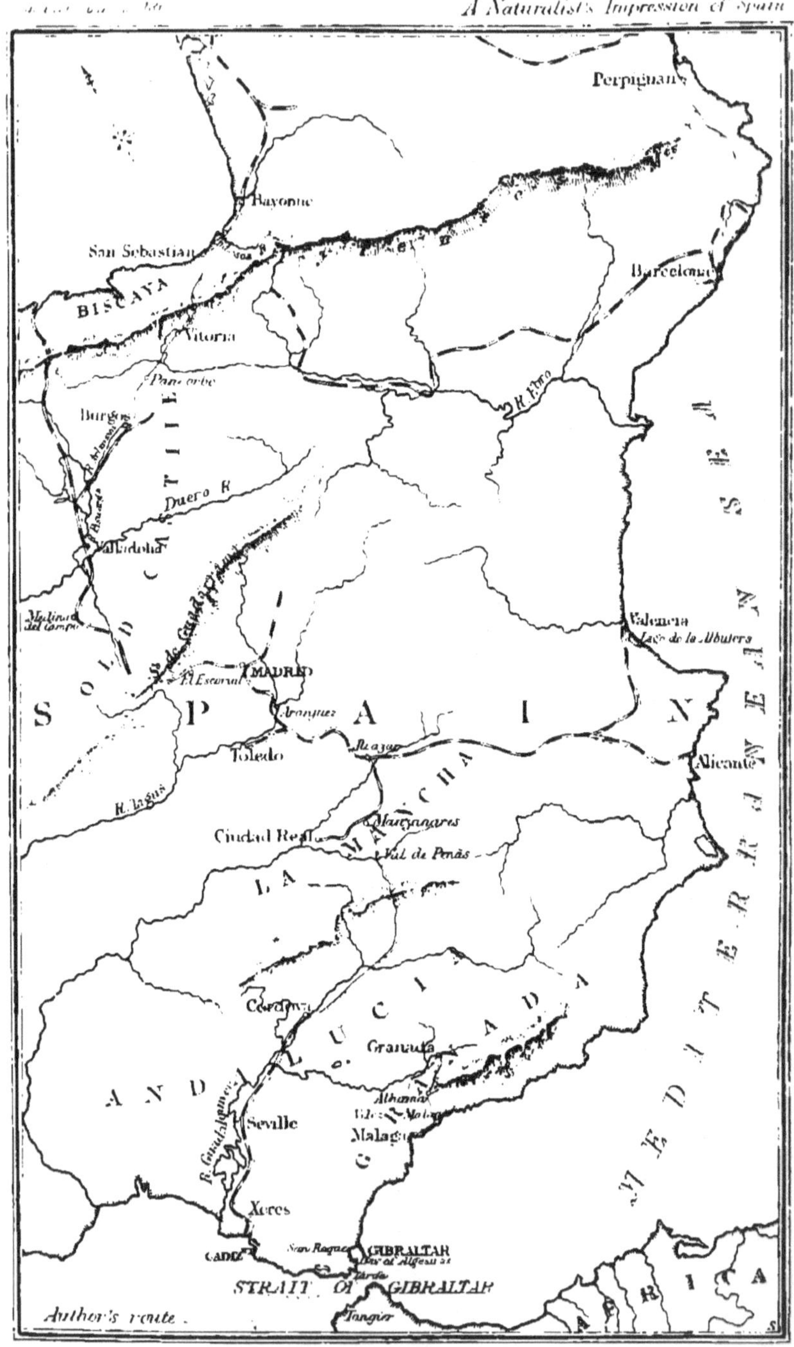

A Naturalist's Impression of Spain
Perpignan
Bayonne
San Sebastian
BISCAYA
Barcelona
Vitoria
Pancorbo
R. Ebro
Burgos
Duero R.
Valladolid
Molina del Campo
S. de Guadarrama
El Escorial
MADRID
Valencia
Lac de la Albufera
SPAIN
Aranjuez
Toledo
Alcazar
Alicante
R. Tagus
LA MANCHA
Manzanares
Ciudad Real
Val de Peñas
ANDALUCIA
Cordova
Granada
Alhama
Vélez-Malaga
R. Guadalquivir
Seville
Malaga
Xeres
San Roque
GIBRALTAR
Bay of Algeciras
CADIZ
Tarifa
STRAIT OF GIBRALTAR
AFRICA
Tangier
Author's route
MEDITERRANEAN
Scale                    English Miles
50  40  30  20  10  0                60
Macmillan & Co. Cambridge & London

# 6. *A NATURALIST'S IMPRESSIONS OF SPAIN.*

## BY PHILIP LUTLEY SCLATER, M.A., Ph.D. F.R.S.

)F all the dry, bare, barren, ugly countries I have ever
isited in the course of my travels, Northern Spain, *in
utumn*, must certainly be placed at the head of the list.   I
.ad been in Sicily, in Tunis, and in Algeria, and had pre-
iously formed some ideas as to the results which might be
roduced by the united efforts of a minimum of rainfall and
 maximum of sunshine continued for several months toge-
her; but when the sun arose on the morning of the 28th
f September last, and I took my first glimpse at the plains
f Castile from the *banquète* of a diligence half-way between
'ittoria and Burgos, I must confess I was surprised.   "Es ist
in *hässliches* Land," said a patriotic German to me a few days
fterwards, when we were comparing notes together upon the
ubject; and I know of no other word than that hissing
ompound of "hate," which so well expresses my ideas on
his occasion.   We had started from San Sebastian early on
he previous day.   Now, San Sebastian is a great point of
ttraction for the Pyrenean tourist.   You go there one day,
nd return to Bayonne the next, and fancy you have been in
pain, or, at all events, are entitled to tell your friends so
ithout equivocation.   But "La Viscaya" is not really Spain.
'xcept that our diligence was dragged along by a combination
f fourteen mules taken two and two together, instead of a
eries of nine horses taken three and three together, and that
he driver cursed them in Spanish, and called them nasty
ames in that harsh language, instead of French, I had seen

and heard, since crossing the Bidassoa, but little to remind me that we had quitted "la belle France." Leaving San Sebastian early, we had passed the day winding slowly up the northern slopes of the continuation of the Pyrenean chain, which borders the coast-line of Northern Spain. But the physical features of the country gave no signs of a change of ownership. The ranges of contorted limestones belonging to the cretaceous series, that have here been so twisted and toasted as scarcely to allow one to recognise the, most familiar fossils, produced nothing but what might be found in the adjoining districts of France. The oaks and chestnuts clothed, though somewhat scantily, the elevated slopes; patches of maize were to be seen alongside the river bottoms; and all looked as green as could be expected, considering the latitude and the time of the year. So passed the day. During the night we had rolled along through Vittoria, and over the tertiary plain of the Ebro, unfortunately missing the fine view over the valley of that river, of which Mr. Galton has spoken in such high terms. Next morning we were passing the defile of Pancorvo and meeting the groups of labourers returning to their work, on the unfinished railway between Burgos and Vittoria. It was not, therefore, until the sun arose, and the landscape cleared, that I realized the change of scene to which a night's travel had introduced me, and, as I have already stated, began to understand for the first time in my life the terrors of a dry and thirsty land, where no water is. The road was following the bottom of a wide and shallow valley. A dry watercourse appeared on our right, with not even the remnants of an occasional pool to testify that it was ever in the habit of conveying fluid. A low range of hills, composed of bare and naked limestone rocks, was on either side, through the intervals of which we could see the dreary plains beyond. There was not a tree, not a shrub, not a blade of grass, hardly even a dry weed, to vary the unlovely prospect. A barren plain, without signs of cultivation, lay around us; a road, some inches deep in dust, before and behind; and a wind, at this early period in the day, dry, chilly, and cutting, blew in our faces. Such was my first introduction to Spain, which, at all events, had the merit of novelty, being equally different from anything I had seen before and from what I had expected to find it.

As we drew nearer Burgos the prospect barely improved, though there were occasional signs of cultivation, and some rows of trees in the valley to the left. The temperature, however, rose rapidly as the sun heightened, so that when, shortly after midday, we arrived at our destination—the *Parador de las diligencias*—in that city, it was very pleasant to take refuge in the shade of our hotel. Having achieved, with an amount of success of which we were pardonably proud, the task of making ourselves understood in an unknown tongue, we devoted a day and a night to repose and to the lions of Burgos. In my own case, I must confess, a somewhat unequal division was made of these twenty-four hours, greatly, I fear, to the disadvantage of the lions. I managed, however, to see the cathedral—one of the finest ecclesiastical buildings in Spain, and in its exterior appearance, perhaps, superior even to those of Toledo and Seville. I also made a pilgrimage on the following morning, in company with my friend Mr. Taylor, to the Carthusian convent of Miraflores—the second orthodox sight of Burgos. The building is situated on the slope of the hills a mile from the city, on the left bank of what is commonly called the *river* Arlanzon, though, at this time of the year at least, it has certainly but slight pretensions to that title, consisting merely of some dirty pools, which the citizens of Burgos render dirtier as the summer advances. An avenue of seedy limes and stunted sycamores, constituting one of the Alamedas of the city, led us towards it. But these trees, with their scanty foliage and crisped-up leaves, did not suffice to protect our heads from the solar rays, and though carefully watered by artificial irrigation, betrayed the manifest effects of a long-continued "struggle for existence." My companion and I were always on the look-out for birds. But the country, I suppose, was literally too hot to hold them, for we saw but few. The Pied Flycatcher (*Muscicapa luctuosa*)—rare certainly in most parts of England—was here the most plentiful species. It had evidently been breeding in abundance in the neighbourhood, as those we saw were mostly young birds of the year. They were behaving pretty much as other flycatchers do, catching an insect in the air every few minutes, and returning, after a short flight, to the post whence they had started—just in the way that even the most unobservant must have noticed our common Grey Flycatcher acting; but not quite so absurdly regular in returning invariably to the perch, as our familiar bird often shows itself. Besides these, we noticed an occasional Chaffinch and a few Pied Wagtails, and, on reaching the open plains, larks of several species—the Calandra and the Crested Lark. But the ornithology of the neighbourhood of Burgos, and indeed of the high interior plateau of Spain generally, is rather meagre, and, if we except that of the mountain ranges, not very tempting to the naturalist.

In the afternoon we left Burgos for Valladolid, a journey of some six hours—our first experience of a Spanish railway. Although I believe the earliest railways laid down in the Peninsula, as in most parts of the Continent, were undertaken by English companies and English contractors, and though English engineers are still at work on several of the lines now under construction, the railways of Spain are, mostly, in the hands of French capitalists, and are managed entirely according to the French system. There are the same formalities observed as to locking up passengers in separate waiting-rooms, and carefully weighing and registering their baggage; the carriages are constructed and the lines worked exactly according to the French fashion; and there is, I believe, the same complicated system of accounts. The head officials and the engine-drivers are also mostly French. Our Gallic neighbours employed us to make their earliest railways, but quickly learnt how to build them for other people.

The railway from Burgos to Valladolid is a section of the great *Linea del Norte*, which will eventually connect Madrid with France by one branch, and with Santander—the principal seaport of Spain on the north—by another. The line between Madrid and Santander is already open, with the exception of two breaks—one near the seaboard, caused by the intersection of the railway with the mountain range that edges the coast, and the other about thirty miles north of the capital, where the Sierra de Guaderrama is crossed. The latter obstacle offers a very serious hindrance to the early completion of the works of this line throughout. To pierce through the crest of this granitic range, which shuts off the approach to Madrid from the north, a tunnel of nearly seven kilomètres in length is required. This is an operation of greater magnitude than any that has as yet been performed in the annals of tunnelling, and will require several years for its accomplishment. In the meanwhile, both the breaks are filled up by services of diligences ; and the route, *via* Santander to Madrid, is very convenient for those who do not dread the journey by sea from Bayonne, or the longer passage in one of the fine screw-steamers which now run regularly between Liverpool and Santander. The still more important branch of the Linea del Norte, which is intended to connect the Spanish capital with France, was only open to a little beyond Burgos in September last, but we saw visible signs of its further progress towards the north ; and next summer, we believe there is little doubt that the line will be finished to Vittoria. This will leave a gap of only about twelve or fourteen hours to be filled up by diligence between Bayonne and the latter city, and greatly increase the facilities for tourists who visit the Spanish capital.

The railway between Burgos and Valladolid follows the valley of the Arlanzon until its junction with the Pisuerga, and thence continues alongside the latter river to Valladolid. The country greatly improves in appearance shortly after quitting Burgos, and is mostly under cultivation, though varied with huge gaps of unsightly waste. The plains of the Pisuerga and the Duero which we now entered upon, particularly those in the neighbourhood of Medina del Campo, a little further to the south, are, in fact, of extraordinary fertility, and produce wheat in large quantities. The enormous cost of the long land-carriage has hitherto checked the growth for exportation; but the railway, if once completed to Santander, will effect a great change in this respect.

Valladolid occupies a large area, but appeared to me to contain more ruins than inhabited houses within its circumference. It is also remarkable, even amongst Spanish cities, for its *dirt*. In many, perhaps I might say in most of the cities of Southern Europe, the streets too often fulfil the ordinary purpose of sewers, and the unsavoury refuse with which London is now ashamed to pollute even the Thames, is deposited in the highways *coram publico*. But the citizens of Valladolid appeared to me to carry out this practice to an excess of development, which the stranger who walks their streets will not fail to appreciate in its proper light. This is the less excusable as the Pisuerga runs most conveniently by, and certainly could hardly be rendered dirtier by any additional amount of colouring matter poured into it. The description of the wonders of the city occupies twelve or fourteen pages in Murray's Handbook, but I found the people in the streets, and their habits and manners, more interesting than Mr. Ford's long list of second-rate antiquities. I accordingly stuck to the open air, while my more energetic companion went the prescribed round of sights.

We quitted Valladolid after our day's sojourn, and again had the advantage of being able to use the Linea del Norte as far as its present termination—a few miles north of the Sierra de Guaderrama. Our route lay over a flat tertiary plain, intersected by the Pisuerga, the Duero, and their various branches. We passed through Medina del Campo, the chief town of this rich corn-growing district. On leaving the railway, and taking our places on the roof of one of the diligences that run in connexion with the trains, and fill up the break caused by the interruption of the Guaderrama, we saw the mountain range rising like a wall before us; and after a short hour's drive, found ourselves on the granite, and in a totally different style of country.  The undulating surface of the land was mostly covered with large naked blocks of stone ; and in the place of corn-fields we beheld a rough open country, varied only by small shrubs and heather, and by occasional groups of the Umbrella Pine.  We gradually approached the mountain range, and wound slowly up the steep slope.  A large number of birds of prey were soaring around us—consisting chiefly of kites (*Milvus regalis*) and buzzards (*Buteo vulgaris*).  But we also discriminated several eagles at a distance, and other species of the falcon family, to which a range of rocky mountains is always attractive. It is a grand sight for an ornithologist to see ten or twelve of these fine birds on the wing together.  In no other country, except in Algeria and Tunis, have I ever seen the Kite so abundant.  In England, it must be recollected, this formerly common bird is, owing to the increase of population and *game*-preserving, nearly extinct, and is looked upon as an extraordinary rarity even by the most energetic gamekeeper.

It was late in the afternoon before we reached the summit of the Guaderrama, which is here more than 5,000 feet above the sea-level, although, from the great elevation of the interior table-land of Spain, it does not give one the idea of being nearly so high.  The view was not extensive, and, moreover, darkened by an approaching thunderstorm, which came up from the left, rolling along the range of the Sierra.  Before this had cleared off the sun had set, and it was dark when we reached *Villa Alba*, the station of the lately opened Madrid and Escorial section of the Northern Railway, whence the train conveyed us to the capital.

Madrid is not a very attractive place for a naturalist, and I shall not weary my readers with many observations on its peculiarities, which are, perhaps, less characteristic of the nation than those of any other city in the peninsula.  As in duty bound, I visited the Gabinete de Storia Naturale, and the Giardino Botanico, but saw little in either to induce me to wish to repeat the experiment.  The most conspicuous object in the *Gabinete* is the skeleton of the *Megatherium*, obtained in 1789 near Buenos Ayres, and celebrated as that upon which Cuvier based his description of this animal in his "Ossemenes Fossiles." Although, since that period, portions of other skeletons have been discovered, which would all together make a more complete specimen, the Spanish skeleton, taken as a whole, still, I believe, remains the most perfect example of this gigantic sloth that has yet been discovered. I did not succeed in meeting with Señor Mariano de la Paz Graels, the director of the museum, and one of the few people in Spain who are interested in such subjects; but I had the pleasure of making the personal acquaintance of Dr. Reinhold Brehm, a German physician resident at Madrid, son of the well-known ornithologist, Herr Pastor Brehm, who has imbibed much of his father's love for birds. Dr. Brehm introduced me, in his drawing-room, on the occasion of my first visit to him, to three fine examples of the diminutive eagle, commonly known as the Booted, or Little eagle (*Aquila pennata*). This is a scarce bird in Northern Europe, and one which I had not previously seen in captivity, but is not unfrequent in some parts of Spain. I persuaded Dr. Brehm to part with his favourites in favour of the Zoological Society of London, to whose gardens in the Regent's Park they were shortly afterwards transferred. Dr. Brehm also showed to me a fine series of specimens of rapacious birds, which he had obtained in the neighbourhood of Madrid, including the Egyptian Vulture (*Neophron percnopterus*), the Griffin Vulture (*Gyps fulvus*), and the Black Vulture (*Vultur cinereus*), some eagles (*Aquila chrysaetos* and *A. nævioides*), and several other interesting species. An egg of the Black Vulture which Dr. Brehm had obtained, along with a pair of old birds, from a nest placed, as he informed me, on the summit of one of the flat-topped umbrella pines in one of the neighbouring mountain ranges, was the first really well-authenticated example I had seen of the egg of this species. It much resembled, in general appearance, the egg of the Griffon (with which I was well acquainted from having

visited the nesting-places of this bird in the Western Atlas),
but was of considerably larger dimensions.

I was particularly anxious to see, in a living state, the little
Blue-winged Pie of Spain (*Cyanopica cooki*).   This bird is
very remarkable from being found only in the peninsula, and
not occurring elsewhere in Europe.   Its nearest analogue is
the Blue Pie of Siberia (*Cyanopica cyanea*), a very closely
allied, though distinct form, with which the Spanish bird was
formerly confounded.   As the valley of the Wealden, between
the North and South Downs, was once covered by the chalk,
so to my mind there is no doubt that the intervening area of
Europe was formerly occupied by the common progenitors of
this little bird, whose descendants still linger in the more
secluded parts of the peninsula, and of its Siberian representative.   Dr. Brehm told me that the Blue-winged Pie was
far from uncommon in the plantations adjoining some of the
royal palaces near Madrid ; but in the only one of these that
I visited—the Escorial—I was unsuccessful in my efforts to
get a sight of it.   I have, however, hopes that Dr. Brehm will
be able to fulfil his kind promise of endeavouring to procure
living examples of the Spanish Blue-winged Pie for the
Zoological Society's collection, and that we may thus obtain
a more intimate knowledge of the habits and peculiarities
of this interesting bird.

No one, whether naturalist or otherwise, would think of
visiting Spain without seeing a bull-fight ; and, though it was
rather late in the season, we were on two occasions so fortunate
as to fall in with opportunities of attending fights of this description of the best quality.   The first of these was on French
soil, at Bayonne, where the favourite matador Don Auguste
de Vicente—commonly called EL TATO—brought his entire
troop of bull-fighters and six victims, warranted fierce and of
the primest quality for pluck, direct from Madrid, to delight
the eyes of the Empress of the French.   The fair Eugénie
takes the opportunity of her autumnal residence at Biarritz to
gratify her taste for seeing bulls slaughtered—a passion which
eems ineradicable from a breast wherein Spanish blood flows.

At Madrid, again, one fine Sunday afternoon we drove up to the Plaza de Toros, provided with tickets which certified that we were entitled to occupy a certain number of square inches on the ninth bench of the Plaza (in the shade), and that we had each paid 18 reals (about 3*s.* 8*d.*) for this privilege. El Tato was again the hero of the day, and despatched his victims, as long as I remained looking on, in his usual masterly way. The details of a bull-fight have been so often described that it would be only tiresome to repeat them. Having been in the habit of inspecting the entrails of large animals in dissecting-rooms, and also of occasionally seeing horses slaughtered, I do not pretend to have been much disgusted by what occurred, though I cannot say that it is a pleasing sight to witness horses cantering about with their *viscera* dragging after them. But there appeared to me to be a "slowness" about the whole affair, and, after the first two or three bulls and half-dozen horses had been despatched, a sameness that was rather wearying. If the bystanders themselves were allowed to participate personally in the fun of tormenting the bulls, I could have realized the devoted attachment of the Spaniards to the Plaza de Toros. But it seemed to me to be, what I can best express by the slang term, rather *mild* to sit still and look on at feats of agility such as any Englishman with a cool head and active habits would without much difficulty accomplish. As regards the cruelty of the Spanish amusement, it does not become one who indulges in field sports to say over much. I may, however, remark, that having occasionally seen English ladies riding " to hounds " and present at " the death," I have always observed that the spectacle of " breaking up " the fox was rather shirked by the fair equestrians, who generally retire to a little distance to re-cover their breath and wait for the brush, whilst *man*-kind crowds around to witness the exciting spectacle. I did not, however, remark that the Spanish ladies turned their heads away or hid their faces with their fans on corresponding occasions at the bull-fight. On the contrary, they seemed to " smile and smile " more sweetly, and to shoot forth the most brilliant glances from their dark eyes at the more critical periods of the entertainment.

On the 8th of October we left Madrid, by the Saragossa and Alicante Railway, for Toledo.   Having passed some agreeable hours in lionizing that ancient and decaying city, we returned to Aranjuez, where the Toledo branch leaves the main line, to sleep.   The country traversed by the southern railway is not strikingly different in appearance from Old Castile.   There are the same dry open arid plains, which everywhere characterise the high interior table-land of Spain, partially in cultivation, it is true, but capable, they say, of yielding wheat to any amount, if labour and irrigation were applied to them. From Madrid the railway descends at first the valley of the Manzanares, then turns to the left, and crosses the main stream of the Tagus at Aranjuez.   The extensive plantations, which here surround the Royal Palace, offer a contrast so marked to anything to be seen in the immediate neighbourhood of the capital, that Spaniards may well be excused for the somewhat exaggerated enthusiasm with which they regard them.   Had I courage to incur the odium of suspected Cockneyism, I should give the preference to the groves of Hampton Court.   Leaving Aranjuez by the morning train from Madrid, we continued over the upland plains, and taking the branch line at Alcazar, which leads to Ciudad Real, and will eventually connect the Spanish and Portuguese capitals, arrived about two P.M. at Manzanares.   Two hours afterwards we were traversing in our diligence the streets of Val de Peñas, so celebrated for its red wine.   The vintage was at its height, and we passed a long string of carts, horses, donkeys, men, women, and children, all engaged in transporting the ripe produce of the surrounding vineyards into the town.   The abundance and the *vileness* (in its original sense) of the  raw material seemed strange enough to our Northern eyes.   Rich clusters were flung at the postilion's head and into the driver's lap as we passed, and the passengers purchased enormous bunches of grapes of the first quality for the smallest coppers.   It was unfortunately night before we took leave of the plains of La Mancha and descended

into the great valley of the Guadalquiver, through the Puerto
of Despeña-perros, which here opens a passage through the
Sierra Morena.    What a different scene met us next morning !
Olive-groves had taken the place of the open upland plains,
and the cactus and aloe, which grew in every hedgerow, at
once betrayed the change of soil and the presence of a more
genial climate.    How strange it is that the two *most* characteristic plants of Southern Europe should be exotics introduced
at a very recent date from the New World !  Is not this fact
alone sufficient to lead us to question the ordinary doctrine of
the separate creation of species ?   Why was it left to mankind
to import the *Cactus opuntia* into a region so admirably
adapted for it, and where it luxuriates so freely, as the shores
of the Mediterranean ?   Why was it reserved for the same
agency to reintroduce the horse into a country so palpably
fitted for its occupation as the Pampas of South America ?
Such facts as these cannot, I think, be explained in accordance with the popular theory, without in some degree calling
into question the most ordinary attributes of a Divine Creator.

We were not sorry to reach Cordova after our long journey
from Manzanares.   Twenty hours in a railway-carriage may
be passed without much inconvenience, but in a diligence
the corresponding operation is detestable.  Until these vehicles
are altogether replaced by the more commodious railway-
carriage, there will be little material increase of travellers in
Spain. Let me, however, assure my readers that this salutary
change will very shortly be brought about.   On my journey
from London, *via* Madrid to Gibraltar, I had only occasion to
enter a diligence three times.   One of these breaks in the
nearly completed railway system through Spain is of very
short duration, and the two others will be materially reduced
in length before next summer arrives.   So let those who are
tired of the beaten highways of Central Europe turn to Spain.
They will find a new people, a strange language, and a most
interesting country very conveniently situated for a few weeks'
excursion.   The hotels in all the principal cities are well
conducted, the rooms clean, and the *cuisine* excellent ;

well-appointed steamboats connect the many attractive cities
on the Mediterranean coast, and the lumbering diligences, as
I have already stated, on the main routes, are fast disappear-
ing as the railways advance.

At Cordova, the great object of interest is the Mosque—
*La Mezquita*—one of the most striking buildings I have ever
beheld.  The extensive area of the interior, crowded with
rows of splendid marble pillars, gives one such grand ideas
of its former magnificence, that the ill-assorted Christian choir
erected in the middle of it, barely destroys the effect.  The
adjoining Court of Oranges, and the magnificent trees laden
with golden fruit, is hardly less impressive, and the whole
forms a worthy relique of a city which once boasted of its
millions of inhabitants, and to be the capital of a great empire.

At Cordova we had the happiness of finding the railway
again, and a short journey down the banks of the Guadalquiver brought us to Seville.  Here we passed a week
pleasantly enough, being comfortably lodged in the Fonda
de Europa.  We spent our days chiefly in the streets of the
Andalusian capital, glad even at this season of the year to
skulk along on the shady side, and to hoist our umbrellas for
protection when compelled to stand the fire of the sun's rays.
Mindful of the complaints of my friend Dr. Günther as to
the deficiency of Spanish fresh-water fishes in the British
Museum, I visited the fish-market every day to see what
specimens of the scaly tribe I could procure for him from the
Guadalquiver. The supply was not very plentiful. I obtained
*Barbos* (a species of Barbel different from ours); *Alburos*
(Grey Mullets, probably from the brackish water lower down);
*Ropillos* (*Labrax lupus*), also strictly a marine fish, but ascending into fresh water ; and *Anguillas* (eels).  I heard also of
*Pesregios* and *Lampreas* (no doubt a lamprey of some sort),
but could not procure any for love or money.  Much interest
was taken by my Spanish friends in the process of packing
these fishes in rags and aguardiente, and soldering them up
in tin cases.  So often as we arrived at one of the Douanes
which environ the Spanish cities, no small amount of

explanation was requisite to persuade the officials to allow my cargo of spirits and flesh to pass untaxed. They could not understand how a mixture of two exciseable articles could make free goods.

The courtyard of our hotel at Seville, which had been an old Moorish palace, was filled with orange-trees, and a beautiful white-flowering *Cestrum* (*C. vespertinum*, as Mr. Bentham has kindly informed me) expanded its petals at night and diffused a most delicious odour around. It is called by the Spaniards the *Dama del Noche*, having been introduced into this country from South America, along with several other tropical exotics.* We did not fail to pay the accustomed visit to a *baile*, where some Spanish ballerinas danced very much as Londoners may have seen them perform in the Haymarket, and to her Catholic Majesty's tobacco manufactory, which is carried on exclusively by women's labour. About 4,000 young ladies are here crowded round small tables, in a series of large rooms, occupied in rolling cigars. As the temperature is high, and space is rather at a premium, the crinolines (which have penetrated even to Seville) are taken off and placed out of the way on the shelves surrounding the rooms, where they form a curious spectacle, of which I was at first unable to penetrate the meaning.

From Seville we again took the Andalusian railway to its terminus at Cadiz. Here to our disgust a violent southeast wind was blowing, which made us fear for our passage to Gibraltar. We made the usual day's excursion to Xerez, and visited the Bodegas or vaults belonging to one of the largest sherry exporters. Here the mysteries of the manufacture of brown sherry were duly explained to us, and we tasted a series of pale Amontillados and Manzanillas, and two excellent sweet wines called Pedro Ximenez and Paxarete.

I must also not forget to mention the pleasure we experienced at Xeres in watching the flights of the Southern or

---

* Amongst these we particularly noticed, as forming an ornamental tree, the yellow-flowered *Nicotiana glauca*, which is planted in rows along the ramparts of Cadiz.

Lesser Kestrel, the *Falco cenchris* of systematists. This pretty falcon is extremely abundant at Xerez, inhabiting the church-towers, and hovering just before sunset in numerous flights over the city. We could at first hardly believe our eyes when we saw these scarce birds in such profusion, but by watching them settle on the turrets, where they entered the holes and niches in innocent converse with the pigeons, we soon convinced ourselves of what they really were.

Xerez must be a most unpleasant residence during the prevalence of the high wind which blew at the time of our visit. The city lies much exposed, and the violent gusts, being unaccompanied by rain, force clouds of dust into your eyes and down your teeth as you struggle along the streets. This charming autumnal *divertissement* is often continued, as we were informed, for several days together.

Fortunately, on the day we were anxious to leave Cadiz the south-easter abated. This welcome incident gave us a choice of three weather-bound steamers, which all started off the same morning for Gibraltar. Four hours after quitting our anchorage in the harbour of Cadiz we were under the guns of Tarifa, being just able to distinguish the position of Tangier on the African coast. By four o'clock in the afternoon we had cast anchor in the roadstead opposite Gibraltar, and were admiring the bold sharp outlines of " The Rock " and the blueness of the calm sunlit sea, which together constitute the charms of the Bay of Algeciras. The beauty of Gibraltar and its surrounding scenery has been much too little appreciated by writers, who have, I suppose, rather occupied themselves in wondering at the galleries and counting the guns, than in comparing the adjoining bay to that of Naples, which they might well have done. One's first thought is certainly what a nuisance it must all be for the Spaniards. No one will hesitate to indorse Napoleon le Grand's *mot*, that the possession of Gibraltar secures to England the perpetual hostility of the Peninsula. Fancy an enormous military garrison of foreigners, speaking a strange language, and not *too* forbearing in their intercourse with their neighbours quartered in the strongest natural position on the whole coast. No nation would stand this if they could help it. The Spaniards have become used to it to a certain extent; but should ever an opportunity occur and England be hard pressed, they will not be slow in endeavouring to regain possession of what, by every law human and divine, ought most certainly to belong to them.

It is a great satisfaction for an Englishman to march into Gibraltar, with his portmanteau behind him, and no questions asked. The porters who carry the baggage, too, look with deference on the new arrivals, and suppose, as a matter of course, that they are officers come to join their regiments, or to visit their companions in arms. It is less satisfactory, however, when you put up at one of the indifferent hotels, which the civilian is compelled to resort to, to find a second-rate English inn, instead of the really excellent accommodation left behind at Cadiz, Seville, or Malaga. But no one should go to Gibraltar unless he has relations or acquaintances in the garrison, or has at least supplied himself with a letter or two of introduction. We were fortunate enough to find a military acquaintance on the spot, who not only fed us sumptuously at his mess, but mounted us one morning (out of the few days to which our stay was limited), and took us out to the celebrated *"cork forest."* Leaving Gibraltar about ten o'clock, we cantered over the neutral ground, taking great care, however, to pull up as we passed through the line of Spanish sentries. I am always inclined to be circumspect in dealing with armed foreigners. A British soldier I do not so much care about. I have no idea that he would shoot at me, even though I were to tread on forbidden ground, or run when I ought to walk—unless, indeed, I were his sergeant, or his adjutant, in which case, as it appears, from recent events, my confidence might prove to be misplaced. But an Austrian, or a Frenchman, or even a Spaniard (in these latter days), with a musket in his hands, is a different sort of being. I have no sort of confidence that he will give me the time I should require to explain to him, in his native tongue, that I am merely an inoffensive Englishman, and I therefore make it a rule to be on my best behaviour in his presence. On the present occasion, however, we passed the line of sentries without a word—hardly even a look—being vouchsafed to us, and resumed our gallop along the sands of the Bay of Algeciras. Turning over the hill to the left, we descended into the valley, and kept along the sandy tracks until we reached the "Second venta," at the edge of the cork forest, said to be a favourite "fixture" of the "Calpe Hunt." This scenery is decidedly pretty. The Spanish cork-tree, and another species of oak, are scattered singly, and in groups, through some wild-looking, bush-covered ground, which is broken up by numerous open spaces, and reminded me somewhat of a favourite English common. We returned by another route, halting at San Roque, and feasting on pork-chops and bitter beer at a little English inn there, which I can conscientiously recommend to the notice of visitors to Gibraltar.

Another day was devoted to the galleries and the batteries, which, in spite of the contrary opinions lately put forward by the Professor of Modern History in the University of Oxford, the military authorities on the spot seem to think still render Gibraltar quite secure from assault. After the galleries had been duly traversed, we ascended to the signal station. The signal station occupies the middle of the three elevations, into which the ridge of the Rock of Gibraltar culminates, and is inhabited by a party of her Majesty's Royal Artillery, who signal all vessels passing in or out during the daytime, and perform other duties. We did not fail to notice such examples of animal life as came across us during our walk. A party of swallows attracted my attention by peculiarities in their flight, which, though difficult to express in words, at once convinced me that they did not belong to any of our well-known English *Hirundines.* Upon their nearer approach, I recognised them as the rock-swallow (*Hirundo rupestris*) of Southern Europe —a species allied to our Bank-swallow or Sand-martin. I was told they were here all the year round. Towards the summit, the fine black Rock-chat (*Saxicola leucura*) was frequently to be seen, running over the bare stones, and elevating and depressing its tail like our wheat-ears and stone-chats. Similar to a great extent in its habits is the Blue Rock-thrush (*Petrocincla cyanea*), which, however, does not confine itself to the summits, but is found somewhat sparingly all over the Rock. Few visitors to the Coliseum at Rome can have been so unobservant as not to have noticed this beautiful bird on the walls of that building, which appear to suit him equally well with his native rocks. This Rock-thrush is called the *Passere solitario* by the Italians, and here ·I was given the same name for it—the popular idea being that this is the bird alluded to by the Psalmist as "sitting alone upon the housetops." Whether this is so or not, is somewhat doubtful; but a recent authority* on the birds of Palestine tells us that it is often seen perched on the half-ruined buildings of the villages and towns of the Holy Land, and it is certainly more entitled to the epithet of "solitary" than any ordinary sparrow. Besides the three birds already mentioned, we noticed Ravens, Tithys-redstarts, and Rock-doves. The Red-legged Partridge is likewise said to be numerous. But no gun is allowed to be fired on "the Rock," so the 1st of September brings them no trouble.

The Rock of Gibraltar is, as is well known, the only locality in Europe where monkeys are now found in a state of nature. The Barbary ape (*Inuus sylvanus*) has penetrated here from the opposite coast of Marocco, where it is abundant, and was formerly tolerably numerous on the Rock, though now nearly extinct. We made careful inquiries of the artillerymen at the signal station, one of whom had resided there ten or twelve years, on this subject. They all agreed that there are now only three apes left on the Rock, all of which are females. Some time ago the troop had been headed by a large and fierce male, who was supposed to have destroyed all the younger males, and had himself lately disappeared, leaving his wives husbandless. As we have,

---

* Rev. H. B. Tristram, in "The Ibis," vol. i. p. 30 (1859).

at present, no authority for believing that the phenomenon of *Parthenogenesis* takes place amongst the Vertebrates, it is, therefore, evident that the Barbary Ape will become extinct in Europe, unless steps are taken to supply an individual of the deficient sex. Ought not her Majesty's Government, or the Acclimatization Society, to interfere and prevent such a scandal as this coming to pass? Will it be fair to the Spaniards, for whose benefit, whilst in *statu pupillari*, according to a recent authority, we have been holding Gibraltar, to render it back to them again deprived of one of its best known causes of celebrity?

The fish-market at Gibraltar was another source of attraction to us—the extent and the variety of the supply here being perfectly astonishing. The whole stock is also fresh every morning, that which remains after gun-fire being inexorably destroyed. As the hours wax, therefore, prices diminish; and so abundant is the supply, that the ichthyologist may always select the specimen he requires for a mere trifle. I cannot fancy a better residence than Gibraltar for any one wishing to study the Mediterranean fishes, and I have no doubt that many novelties might be procured here.*

We left Gibraltar by a steamer one evening, and at the following daybreak found ourselves in the harbour of Malaga. We lost no time in making arrangements to ride up to Granada, and started on horseback the following morning, with a mule to carry our luggage. Our *arriero* was a Crimean hero, having been sent to the war with Spanish mules by the English consul at Malaga, and afterwards, as he informed us, taken to drive an omnibus between Balaklava

* No attempt, as far as I know, has been made to give a connected account of the Zoology of Gibraltar; but the Botany of the Rock and its vicinity has been carefully studied by the late Dr. Kelaart, and the results arrived at published in his work called " Flora Calpensis : Contributions to the Botany and Topography of Gibraltar." London, 1846, 8vo. A paper by Mr. J. Smith, on the Geology of Gibraltar, which presents many features of interest, will be found in the second volume of " The Quarterly Journal of the Geological Society of London."

and the camp.   Our route lay along the coast to Velez Malaga —dusty and hot—though there were evident signs, in the unwonted masses of clouds that covered the sky, of a coming storm.   The strip of land along the seashore here is chiefly devoted to growing the celebrated Malaga raisins, which, as we all know, are so *good ;* though it has been remarked, we believe, that those of Smyrna are better !   We were much edified at meeting continual strings of mules and donkeys carrying the aforesaid raisins, all ready packed in their well-known square boxes, into Malaga, whence the greater portion of them find their way to the English market.   I was also greatly pleased to see the sugar-cane in cultivation for the first time in my life.   It is grown in several spots in the valley near Velez Malaga, and here alone in Europe, I believe, are two steam-mills devoted to the manufacture of sugar from this plant.   From this locality the *Saccharum officinale* was introduced by the Spaniards into the American continent, and this Eastern grass is now become one of the most abundant cultivated products of the New World.   Let my readers, who ride from Malaga to Granada by this route (which I most sincerely recommend them to do), follow Mr. Ford's advice and start early.   Let them also not linger by the way, for, after the midday's halt at Velez, more than seven hours are required over an infamous road before Alhama is reached. Let them also not flatter themselves because they have found good hotels at Malaga, and in nearly every other city of Spain, that there is anything worthy of that name at Alhama. The Posada Grande of the Moorish city has taken no part in the recent progress of Spain, and is evidently in just the same condition as that which Mr. Ford so well describes in his Handbook.   Food uneatable, beds untenantable, charges unconscionable, is the state of the case now, as then.

Our next day's journey from Alhama to La Granada was short and easy enough ; and, although we waited several hours for the fag-end of the rainstorm which had threatened us the day before, but kindly " evaporated " during the night, we reached the Fonda de la Alameda in good time.   The weather was chilly at Granada at this season (October 27th)—not, perhaps, more than what one might expect at an elevation of 2,200 feet above the sea level. I need not describe the Alhambra. Has not every one seen it at the Crystal Palace more perfect than the original? That, however, it is true, cannot give them any idea of the lovely view over the *Vega* to be seen from its turrets. But I must not forget to record my disappointment at the Sierra Nevada. That a mountain claiming to be 12,459 feet in height should present such an insignificant appearance as the Picacho de la Veleta from Granada is certainly worthy of remark. It is a slightly elevated point in a high ridge of mountains, which, instead of being covered with snow, as I had expected to find, has merely, as far as one can see, a few white patches here and there, and these of no great extent. The quantity of snow, however, is, it is said, really large, though melted off all the more exposed parts of the mountain by the summer suns.

After a few days at Granada, I found my holiday time was nearly over, and the weather too chilly to be pleasant. I returned by diligence to Malaga, and thence by an excellent steamer—one of Lopez and Co's *Vapores Correos*—to Alicante. Here it rained all day—an event which seemed rather to gratify the Alicantians, who assured me that such an event as real rain had not happened before for the last three years. There is, however, nothing to detain one at Alicante, and I took advantage of the railway to proceed without delay to Valençia. The district round Valençia, called the *Huerta*, presents such a contrast to Spain in general, that even the most hasty traveller cannot but stop to admire its appearance. The vegetation is most luxuriant; every yard of soil having been brought, by means of irrigation, into splendid cultivation, The oranges grow more thickly on the trees than even in the celebrated Concha d'Oro, near Palermo, and the whole country seems flourishing, financially as well as physically. The railway passes the margin of the large fresh-water lake called the Lago de la Albufera—a favourite resort of aquatic birds of many species. This is quasi-classical ground to the naturalist, having been sedulously watched for many years by the late Don Ignacio Vidal, of Valençia' (one of the few ornithologists Spain has produced), who has recorded the occurrence of many ornithological rarities in his favourite sporting-ground.*

Arriving at Valençia by the morning train, I devoted the day to the sights of that city, having, however, a struggle to effect an entrance into the Botanic Gardens, as it was a feast day, and the Professor of Botany not at his post. In the evening I hired a *tartana*, as I was told it was the correct thing to do, to convey me to the Grao or harbour of Valençia, whence the steamer started for Barcelona. A *tartana*, I may observe, means, according to my dictionary, " a small coasting vessel," but in reality it is an utterly springless cart, and a very uncomfortable vehicle indeed; particularly unsuitable for any one whose bones are fragile. Luckily the distance was not great, and my driver did not hurry himself.

The railway from Barcelona to Gerona is not quite finished, but the whole journey through to Perpignan may be easily accomplished in about sixteen hours. Here the French railway system is joined, and express trains convey one quickly to Paris and London. Six weeks is certainly not so much time as even in these days of fast-living one might well devote to a country like Spain. A few years ago it would have been simply ridiculous to attempt a journey in that country without a much larger margin of time to draw upon. But travelling in Spain is now so improved, and the access to its frontiers so easy, that I can conscientiously recommend those who have "used up" Central Europe, and have only even that limited time to spare, to devote their six weeks to the Spanish peninsula.

* See this gentleman's " Catalogo de las Aves de la Albufera," in the " Memorias de la R. Academia de Ciencias de Madrid," vols. i. and ii.

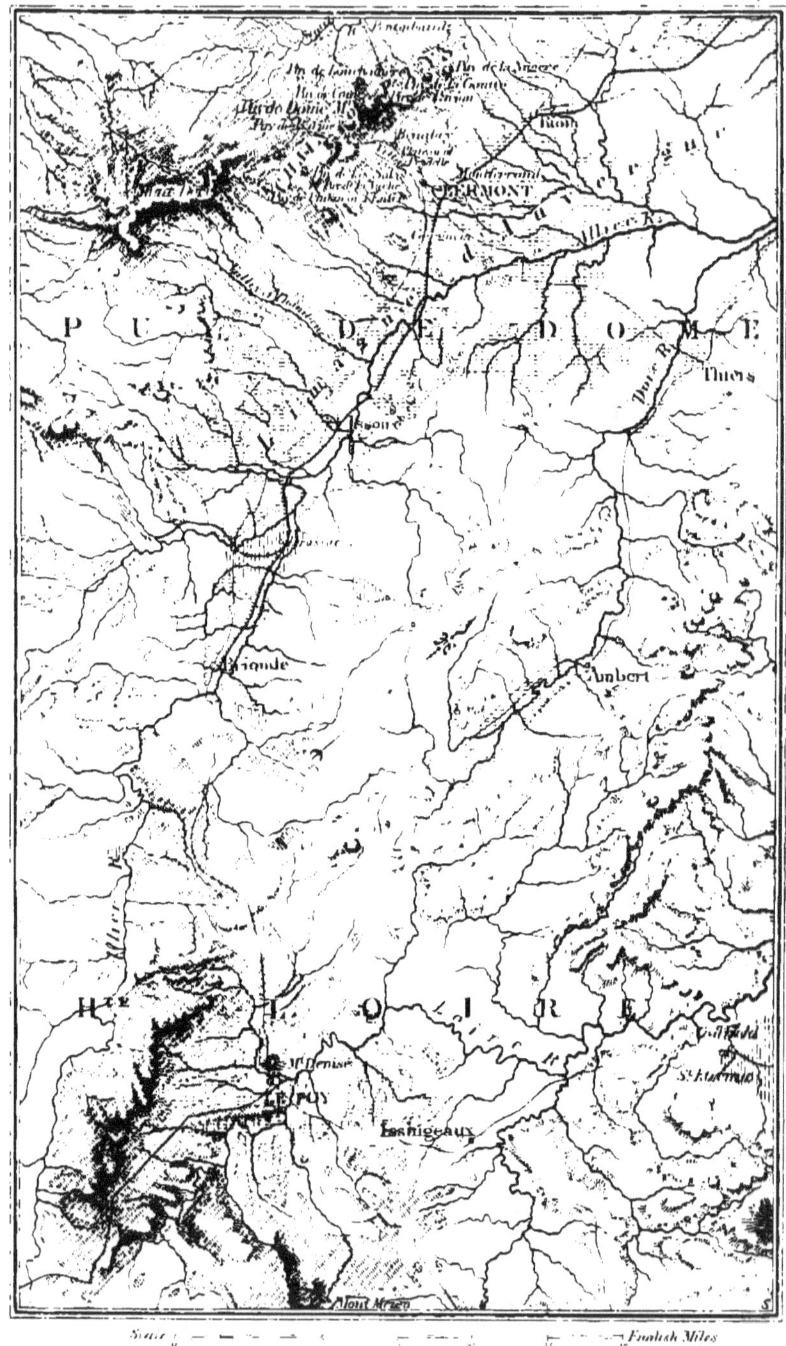
CLERMONT
Montferrand
Riom
Thiers
Issoire
Brioude
Ambert
HTE LOIRE
PUY DE DOME
Le Puy
St Denise
Montmée
Scale
English Miles

# 7. *GEOLOGICAL NOTES ON AUVERGNE.*

BY ARCHIBALD GEIKIE, F.R.S.E., F.G.S.

IT had been my good fortune to spend several years in a more or less continuous examination of those volcanic hills and crags which form so characteristic a feature in the scenery of the great central valley of Scotland. I had traced them in their changes and gradations over many hundreds of square miles, sometimes among the very streets and squares of a town, sometimes across the richly cultivated fields of the Lothians, and sometimes away inland among lonely moors and mosses. I had studied their association with the stratified rocks of that old era of this country's history known as the Carboniferous Period, and had marked, too, their relation to the strange plants and animals which then lived on the site of what is now Britain. As the result of these labours I had been enabled, in some measure, to realize the scenery of that ancient time—its wide jungles and lagoons, crowded with graceful trees, and dotted here and there with volcanic cones that sent out their columns of steam and showers of ashes, or rolled their streams of lava hissing and glowing among the waters. There were many things, however, which I could not explain, and which no book that had yet come in my way could explain for me. My restorations of the old Carboniferous landscapes were still very incomplete ; indeed, they could be regarded as little more than mere outlines. They had cost such an amount of labour, too, that it was by no means easy to divest them of the appearance of study and effort, and to regard them as truly representing, so far at least as they went, a former condition of this country. They wanted spirit and life, even more than the plaster model of some extinct monster constructed from the hints that may be suggested by a tooth and a few bones. They needed to be compared with some region of recent volcanoes, where, like the dry bones in the field of old, they might straightway be touched into life.

As the Scottish volcanoes had been of small extent, as well as eminently sporadic in their distribution, it seemed to promise more success to compare them with a district where similar phenomena had been manifested, than with such regions as those of Etna or Vesuvius, where the eruptions had been on a much larger scale, and had proceeded from the different vents of one great volcano. There were two districts in Europe that appeared likely to throw light on the subject— one of these lay in the Eifel, the other in the high grounds of Auvergne and the Haute-Loire. The latter covers a much greater area than the German tract, and presents besides a more extensive variety of volcanic phenomena. It had been described in detail in the admirable volume of Mr. Poulett Scrope, as well as in several works and memoirs by some of the ablest geologists of England and France. These writings did not, indeed, treat the geological structure of the country from the particular point of view which chiefly interested me at the time, but they formed an invaluable guide to one who wished to acquire as rapidly as possible a general knowledge of the district. So it was resolved by an old schoolfellow and myself to go to Auvergne, and enlarge our ideas in one department of British geology. Between two countries that were once so closely linked together in peace and war, it seemed as if there might be a closer relationship than that of mere State policy, and so with some such fanciful notion we set out to see how far we could succeed in establishing a harmony between Central Scotland and Central France.

Not many years ago it was a matter of no little discomfort to reach the high grounds of the Puy de Dôme and the other departments in the interior of France. Several days of diligence travelling, and inns none of the best, were hindrances seldom surmounted save by enthusiastic geologists, or by valetudinarians who risked all peril to spend a few weeks at the Baths of Mont Dore.   Now, however, this state of things has changed.   Railways penetrate far into the upland districts, and although this part of France is still comparatively little known to English tourists, it can be visited with even more ease, and in a shorter time, than the remoter parts of Scotland.   You may dine on a summer evening in London, take your seat in the Dover express about nine o'clock, and by next evening at the same hour you may see the sun set behind the long chain of *puys* that dot the granitic plateau of Auvergne.   The journey from Paris southward, indeed, is a dreary and monotonous one, even if you make it at the rate of thirty-five or forty miles an hour. Wide uninteresting plains occupy hundreds of square miles, and it is not until towards the close of the day, as you approach the department of Allier, that the ground begins to undulate, amid hedgerows of acacias and patches of woodland.   From the quaint old town of Moulins the scenery becomes hourly more interesting.   A vast, richly cultivated plain, several miles broad, and known as the Limagne d'Auvergne, widens out southward and stretches as far in that direction as the eye can reach.   On the east lies the chain of granite hills which separates this plain of the Allier from the basin of the Loire, while to the west the eye rests with increasing wonder upon a long line of conical hills, sometimes bare. and grey, sometimes dark with foliage, and grouped like a series of colossal forts and earthworks along the summit of a long swelling ridge.   Beyond these, and seemingly rising out of them, towers the grand cone of the Puy de Dôme, now flushed, perhaps, with the last rays of the sinking sun.   As the train advances southward these cones become still more defined, standing up dark and clear against the evening sky, until, halting at last at Clermont, we seem to rest almost at the feet of the giant Puy.

The ancient province of Auvergne—now parcelled out into

the departments of Cantal, Puy de Dôme and Haute-Loire—
comprises a considerable part of the high ground in central
France, and from the variety of its geological structure contains a diversity of outline that contrasts well with the
monotonous scenery of so much of the lower parts of the
country.   Granite and other metamorphic rocks rise from
under encircling plains of secondary and tertiary strata, and
form elevated hilly ground in the central districts, through
which run the valleys of the Loire, the Allier, the Dore, the
Sioule, and other minor rivers.

At a comparatively recent geological period there were
some large lakes in these uplands, one of them extending
over the modern Limagne d'Auvergne in a north and south
direction between granitic hills for a distance of fully forty
miles, and with a breadth of sometimes twenty.   But the
lakes have long since disappeared, though their site is still
marked by broad plains, which are formed of lacustrine strata,
containing the remains of the shells that lived by millions in
these waters.   It was in this region of high ground, among
hills of granite, gneiss, and schist, watered by large rivers and
by broad lakes, that those volcanic erruptions broke forth, to
some of whose features it is the object of the present paper to
direct attention.   To such protrusions of igneous matter, the
great altitude of some parts of the district is due.   Lava,
ashes, and scoriæ, have been thrown out upon the older
granitic hills, so as to rise even into great mountains, where,
as in the higher and deeper recesses of Mont Dore, snow
may be seen gleaming white among the crags under the glare
of a July sun.

The easiest point from which to commence the examination
of this region is probably Clermont, the chief town of the
department of Puy de Dôme.   Built round a small hill on
the west side of the Limagne, where that broad valley attains
its greatest width, Clermont rises conspicuously above the
general level of the plain (which is about 1,200 feet above
the sea-level), and seems to nestle at the base of the long
granitic ridge that supports the chain of Puys.   The hill on

which the town is placed is of volcanic origin, so too are similar gentle eminences that rise above the level country towards the east; north and south at the distance of a mile or two are remnants of ancient lava-beds, now forming flat-topped hills; while to the west, down some of the narrow gullies that descend through the granitic ridge, currents of lava have forced their way from the volcanic vents of the Puys almost to the very gates of the town. Here, then, the traveller may rest for a little, with plenty of geological interest around him if he care to ply his hammer, and with not less of varied and curious scenery if he be only in search of the novel and picturesque. Let no man, however, whether geologist or not, visit Auvergne in July, unless fully prepared to eat, drink, and be merry with the thermometer at 82° in the shade. During the hotter part of last summer, at least, the only way to geologize was, to start by daybreak, and, after a five or six hours' work, to get back in time for a *table d'hôte* breakfast. Towards the afternoon it was sometimes cool enough to undertake another expedition.

Our first ramble was begun in this way soon after sunrise. Passing through a labyrinth of lanes and by-ways, we succeeded in reaching the base of the hills, and began to wind upwards among the vineyards that cluster along the slopes and look down upon the rich plain of the Limagne. It was a glorious morning. A light mist hung over the valley, concealing its features as completely as if the lake which once filled it had been again restored; while some twenty miles to the eastward, on the further side of this sheet of phantom water, rose the purple hills of the Forez that separate the basins of the Allier and the Loire. Behind us, as we looked across the plain, lay the great granitic ridge or plateau, rising to a height of somewhere about 1,600 feet above the plain, and nearly 3,000 feet above the sea. Its base, up which we were slowly ascending, had a varied mantle of corn-fields and vineyards; narrow, well-wooded valleys had been cut by streamlets down its flanks, but the higher slopes became barer by degrees as they approached the range of volcanic cones that crowns the summit of the ridge.   It was with no slight interest that, among the little runnels and cart-tracks which were crossed in the ascent, we watched for indications of the nature of the rocks below. Sometimes a chalky marl was noticed; and, as we drew nearer to the granite, we found ourselves upon pebbly sandstone that had evidently been formed out of the waste of the granite hills.   But how could the formation of such a deposit have been effected here?   Foot by foot as we crept up the acclivity this sandstone accompanied us, until at last, at a height of probably of not less than a thousand feet above the level of the plain, we reached the granite.   The gravel and sand, out of which this sandstone had been made, must have been deposited in a lake—the old lake, in short, which once occupied the site of the Limagne.   The water must, therefore, have reached up as far as to the point to which we had traced the sandstone; and thus, in the course of an hour's ramble, we ascertained for ourselves the somewhat startling fact, that unless later subterranean movements had altered the relative levels, the fertile plain below was formerly covered by a lake at least a thousand feet deep.   Once on the granite we were free from the entanglements of enclosures and fences.   As this rock crumbles away with rapidity, like some of the granite of Arran, its surface is characterized by a smoothness of outline and an absence of those rugged features which mark the surrounding basaltic rocks.   It is coated with a short scrubby grass, save in those places where the amount of waste is too great and rapid to allow the vegetation to take root.   Crossing a short interval of this ground, at the height of about 2,400 feet above the sea, we arrived at the basalt that caps the ridge of Prudelle.

From this height, we commanded a wide view of the Limagne, from which the morning sun had now dispelled the floating mists; we could judge better of the disposition of the volcanic cones, or puys, and of the aspect of some of the basaltic plateaux and lava streams.   But the most impressive part of the scene was not in the traces of old igneous eruptions, but in the evidence of the power of running water.

I had wandered long among the basalt hills of the Hebrides, and now recognised many features of the landscape; but nothing I had seen or read had prepared me for such a stupendous manifestation of the power of rains and rivers. No one, indeed, who has confined his observations to a country which has been above the sea, only since the glacial period, can form any adequate idea of the denuding effect of water flowing over the surface of the land. Standing on the plateau of Prudelle, with its remnant of a lava-current, and looking down into the valley of Villar—a deep gorge, excavated by a rivulet through that lava current, and partially choked up by a later coulée of lava which the stream is now wearing away—I received a kind of new revelation, so utterly above and beyond all my previous conceptions was the impression which the sight of this landscape now conveyed. The ridge of Prudelle is a narrow promontory of granite, extending eastward from the main granitic chain, and cut down on either side, but more especially to the south, by a deep ravine. It is capped with a cake of columnar basalt, which of course was once in a melted state, and, like all lava streams, rolled along the ground ever seeking its lowest levels. A first glance is enough to convince us that this basaltic cake is a mere fragment, that its eastern and southern edges have been largely cut away, and that it once extended southwards across what is now the deep gorge of Villar. Since the eruption of the basalt, therefore, the whole of this gorge has been excavated. But what agent could have worked so mighty a change? We bethink us, perhaps, of the sea; and picture the breakers working their way steadily inland through the softer granite. But this supposition is untenable, for it can be shown on good grounds that, since the volcanic eruptions of this district began, the country has never been below the sea. It is with a feeling almost of reluctance that we are compelled to admit, in default of any other possible explanation, that the erosion of the valley has been the work of the stream, that seems to run in a mere rut at the end of the slopes. How tardy must be the working of such an agent, and how immeasurably far into the past does the contemplation of such an operation carry us ! This illustration of the power of running water, however, though the first, was by no means the most striking which occurred in the course of my rambles in Auvergne. The same fact stood out with a kind of oppressive reality in the Haute-Loire, to which reference will be made on a subsequent page.

The basalt of Prudelle recalled many of the basaltic hills in various parts of Scotland. I could have supposed myself under one of the cliffs that look out upon the deep fiords of Skye, or below the range of crags on the shores of the Forth, over which Alexander III. lost his life, or even among some of the ridges that form the eastern part of Arthur's Seat, at Edinburgh. The French basalt had, indeed, a greyer colour and a finely cavernous structure, which distinguished it from the hard black compact rock which is known as basalt in Scotland ; but they were columned both in the same way, traversed by similar transverse joints, and, above all, resembled each other in their mode of yielding to the weather, and in their general aspect in the landscape.

Quitting this ridge, we walked westwards towards the Puy de Dôme, until we reached the hostelry of Bonabry, where the road splits into two, one branch crossing the hilly ground for Pont Gibaud, the other striking south-west for Mont Dore. Here, finding the morning too far advanced for further breakfastless exploration, we struck down for the valley of Villar, with the view of examining more narrowly what had appeared from the distance to be a later current of lava descending the bottom of the ravine. Hardly had we left the highway and crossed some fields that sloped southwards, than we found ourselves in front of a barren expanse of black rugged scoriæ rising into the most fantastic forms, and nearly destitute of vegetation. It was, in truth, the surface of a lava current greatly more recent than that of Prudelle, for it had been erupted after the excavation of the ravine. We were able afterwards, as had been done many years before by

Mr. Scrope and others, to trace up this current of melted rock to the very crater from which it had flowed. But in the meantime, *fame compulsi*, we were content to follow its course down the valley. Few walks in Auvergne are in their way more instructive than this. The valley itself, with its impressive lesson of river action, becomes still more striking when seen from below. The Prudelle basalt hanging over the ravine stands as a silent witness at once of the antiquity of the earlier volcanic eruptions, and of the changes of after time. The great river of lava, too, is an object of unceasing interest to a geological eye, winding as it does with all the curvings of the valley, now sinking down beneath a mass of tangled copsewood, and now rising up into black craggy masses, where some projecting rock of granite had formed a temporary impediment to its course. It would be tedious to tell how much light the examination of this lava current threw upon points of structure in those igneous rocks of Scotland to which I have already alluded : how some conjectures were verified, not a few doubts were solved, and certain questions were suggested for future study. Descending the valley along the old Roman road, or *chemin ferré*, which partly runs on the surface of the lava, we found that the rivulet had actually cut in places a second narrow gorge through the lava, sometimes of considerable depth. But part of the stream still appears to flow down the old channel beneath the lava by which that channel has been usurped, for at the abrupt termination of the lava current an abundant gush of water issues from under the black rugged masses. We reached Clermont before eleven o'clock, highly satisfied with the results of our morning's work, and, despite the heat, ready for a hearty breakfast.

In the town of Clermont itself there is not much of interest. It is built round the sides of a gently sloping hill, and thus the towers of the old church, rising to a considerable height above the surrounding plain, can be seen from a great distance. This church, like most of the rest of the town, is built of a dark compact lava, that gives a somewhat sombre hue to the building. The same tone of colouring would also characterize the street architecture, but for a plentiful use of whitewash.   One cannot but admire the sharpness with which this lava has retained for centuries its chisel-marks and sculpturings; even staircases, that have been trodden so long day after day, seem well-nigh as fresh as ever.   So black and dingy, indeed, and so sharp in outline, are some of the tall pillars, that they might readily be mistaken for so many shafts of cast-iron.   Along the roadsides, too, you constantly pass crosses made of the same material—black, sombre things, rising sometimes from the edge of a vineyard, sometimes standing up alone in a solitary part of the way, among broken walls and thickets of brushwood.   It was not un-interesting to remember that some three hundred years ago, when Popery held sway in Scotland, the roadsides were studded with similar crosses, of which the pedestals and parts of the stems may still, here and there, be seen; and that these were in many cases made of an old lava, just as in Auvergne. The Scottish rock, however, had been erupted many a long geological period ere the Auvergne volcanoes broke forth; and though the crosses hewn out of it may not have dated further back than some of these French ones, yet Nature has dealt kindlier with them, crusting them over with lichen and moss, till they look as grey and venerable as the crags and hill-sides that rise around them.   The Auvergne lava, on the other hand, is a singularly barren stone; it gives no harbour-age to vegetation, and its chiselled surfaces stand up now as bare and blank as they have done for centuries.

Clermont being the chief town of the department, there is always plenty of stir and bustle in its great central *place;* so in the evenings we used to sit in front of the hotel, and watch the constantly changing groups that passed to and fro until dusk.   A large proportion of the visitors to Clermont come for the sake of the mineral waters which abound in the district.   Of these, the wells of Royat, only a few miles away, form a continual source of attraction.   From sunrise to dark, voitures, diligences, and conveyances of all sorts and sizes, go and come in a noisy never-ending succession.   The din of drivers, whips, passengers, and horse-bells, fills the market-place all day long; then there are the drums and bugle-calls of the regiments of infantry and cavalry stationed in the town, the ringing of the church bells, the chattering and laughing of men and women, and the games of the children. When one had done a good day's work under a fierce sun, pleasant was the hour or two spent in the cool of the evening, watching and listening to this motley array of sights and sounds. Our landlord was a chatty little fellow, never without his cap on and a cigar in his mouth. Under his tuition we were initiated into the nature of not a few of the groups that were clustered together in the square. He entertained a great respect for Englishmen; but it was, we found, a respect inseparably interwoven with an admiration of the length of their purses. He had long yarns to spin of Englishmen who had been his guests, especially one—a huge man and a great poet, who had been with him shortly before, but had gone up to Mont Dore. In our subsequent journeyings we kept a watchful eye for such a tall, hairy-visaged countryman, with a sugar-loaf hat, answering to the merry description of mine host; but we failed to discover him; and to this hour neither of us have learned the name of the "great English poet" who, last summer, visited Auvergne.

No one should leave Clermont without looking at the baths of Saint Alyre. A spring, highly charged with carbonate of lime, issues from the side of the hill of Clermont, and deposits along its course a constantly increasing mass of white travertin. In this way, it has formed for itself a natural aqueduct, running for a considerable distance, and terminating in a rude but picturesque arch of the same material, below which flows a small stream. The water that trickles over this bridge undergoes in its progress more or less evaporation, and hence leaves behind a proportionate amount of its mineral matter as a thin pellicle of carbonate of lime, which gathers into rugged masses, or hangs down in long stone icicles or stalactites. Such a *fontaine pétrifiante* could not remain a mere curiosity: it has been turned into a source of considerable profit, and manufactures for the good of visitors an endless stock of brooches, casts, alto-relievos, basso-relievos, baskets, birds' nests, groups of flowers, leaves, fruit, and such like. A portion of the water is diverted into a series of sheds, where it is made to run over flights of narrow steps, on which are placed the objects to be " petrified." By varying the position of these objects, and removing them further and further from the first dash of the water, they become uniformly coated over with a fine hard crust of white carbonate of lime, which retains all the inequalities of the surface on which it is deposited. There is here, of course, no real *petrifaction;* the substances operated upon retain all their original structure, and are only *incrusted* with the calcareous sediment. When once covered with this stony crust, they may remain unchanged for a long period, being thus hermetically sealed and protected from the influences of the air.

It formed no part of our plan to attempt to enter into the details of the geological structure of Auvergne. For this we neither had time nor did the heat of the season permit of such prolonged fatigue as would have been necessary. Having mastered the leading features of the country from the admirable volume of Mr. Scrope (which, moreover, we carried with us as a constant hand-book), our chief aim was, in the first place, to carry away such a vivid impression of the general aspect of the volcanic districts as might help in the investigation of the older volcanic tracts of Scotland, and in the next place to note for ourselves the form and structure of the cones, the disposition of the lava streams, and such points of detail as our previous explorations in Scotland had rendered it advisable to examine on the spot. I shall not weary the reader with a jotting of what were merely geological rambles. Let him suppose himself, however, on the top of the Puy de Dôme, 4,842 feet above the sea level. Seated on the greensward which covers that elevated cone, he has the volcanic district spread out as in a map below him—cones, craters, and lava currents—clear and distinct for many miles to the north and south.   While he rests there, let me try to sketch to him the noble panorama that stretches out around us.

The Puy de Dôme stands about midway between the northern and southern ends of the chain of the Puys. It rises out of the centre of that long granitic ridge or plateau which I have described as bounding the western edge of the valley of the Allier. Its position, therefore, is eminently favourable for obtaining a bird's eye view of the country. Below us, to the eastward, lies the broad plain of the Limagne like a vast garden, dotted here and there with hamlets and villages and towns.   Yonder, for instance, are the sloping streets of Clermont, with their dingy red-tiled houses, and the sombre spires of the old church; further eastward is Mont-ferrand, and others of lesser note lie in the district beyond. The eastern horizon is bounded by the range of the granitic hills of the Forez, which have been already referred to as rising from the level of the Limagne on the one side, and descending into the basin of the Loire on the other.   They look grey and parched in the glare of the summer afternoon, though softened a little by the purple light of distance, till their base seems to melt into the subdued verdure of the valley.   Westward, the eye wanders over a dreary region of broken and barren ground which stretches far to the north, while southward, some fifteen or twenty miles away, it sweeps round into the mountains of Mont Dore that terminate the southern landscape.

It is the nearer prospect, however, which forms the chief source of wonder as we look from the summit of the Puy de Dôme.   Between us and the great plain of the Limagne lies a strip of the elevated granitic plateau—a tract of bare uneven ground, traversed by some deep valleys that descend towards the east.   On this plateau rises a chain of isolated conical hills, stretching due north and south from the Puy de Dôme, which is the highest point in the district.   You probably never saw such heights anywhere else.   They are not connected by ridges and water-sheds into a regular chain, like a common range of hills.   From a dark sombre kind of table-land they

shoot up at a steep angle into cones which seem to be completely separated from each other.  Cone behind cone, from a
mere hillock up to a good hill, rises from the brown waste for
some twenty miles to the north and south of the great Puy.
Some of them are partially clothed with beechwoods, but most
have a coating of coarse grass and heath, intermingled here
and there with numerous wild flowers.  Yet some are partially
devoid of vegetation, and their slopes then consist of loose
dust and stones, like parts of the table-land on which they
stand.  A more lonely and desolate scene could hardly be
than round these conical Puys.  Wolves still harbour in their
solitudes, among the dense woods that clothe some of the
slopes, and the shepherds have to keep a good look-out after
their flocks.  At the top of the Puy de Dôme I found a stout
boy, of ten or twelve years, armed with a club-headed staff,
which he told me was used against the audacious wolves, and
he pointed to a thick forest on a neighbouring hill whence the
animals made their forays.  He was accompanied by two
active dogs ; a wide-awake hat, immensely too wide for the
wearer, covered his head ; his clothes, also, made with due
regard to his future growth, were of a coarse grey woollen,
his bare feet were thrust into a pair of huge wooden shoes,
while over his shoulders hung a scrip, containing some fragments of sour brown bread and cheese.  He was sadly at a
loss for the names of the surrounding hills, and not a little
greedy withal, for, having stood for three minutes till I
sketched him in my note-book, he seemed mightily indig-
nant at the sum with which he was presented ; nor did his
equanimity appear to be much restored by the gift of an
English penny which my companion, with great gravity, added
to his previous donation.  The little fellow probably drives a
pretty good trade by acting as *cicerone* to the French tourists
who come to the mountain.  At least, he must make more by
misinforming his visitors as to the names of the hills than by
defending a few sheep from the wolves of the Puy de Dôme.

Not the least singular feature of these conical hills is, that
nearly all of them look as if they had had their tops shaved

off. Nay, they even seem in the distance to have been more or less scooped out, as if some old Titan had taken a huge spadeful out of the summit of each hill. The reason of this structure may be guessed, but it becomes strikingly apparent on a closer inspection of the ground. Each cone, with four or five exceptions,* is found on examination to be an actual volcano, extinct indeed, but still well-nigh as fresh as if the internal fires had burnt out only yesterday. The truncated, hollowed summit thus turns out to be a true crater—the vent, in short, from which the hill itself was erupted. Upwards of fifty such volcanoes dot the ridge to the north and south of the Puy de Dôme, each formed from an independent orifice, and sometimes containing, as in the Puy de Montchié, no fewer than four separate craters in one hill. They consist of loose ashes, dust, and scoriæ, still so lightly aggregated that, where the rain has bared off long strips of the grassy covering, one may slide rapidly ancle-deep in *débris* from the top of a cone to its base. Many of the cones have had one of their sides removed, and from the broken part a current of dark rugged lava has issued, flowing out over the table-land, sometimes for several miles, and even descending the valleys that slope into the Limagne. The main mass of lava, in many different streams, has gone down the western side of the chain towards the valley of the Sioule, and hence the strange, sombre, arid aspect of that tract. From the summit of the Puy

* These exceptions are the Puy de Dôme itself, the Puy de Chopine, Le Grand Sarcoui, and one or two others of lesser size. They consist of a white felspathic rock, to which the name *Domite* has been given. It resembles some of the decomposing claystones of Scotland, and, like them, is undoubtedly an igneous rock. Mr. Scrope supposes it to have been protruded among the craters with a low degree of fluidity, so as to accumulate in great dome-shaped hills. I do not pretend to criticise this deduction, though my own observations certainly incline me to regard those white trachytic domes as older than the surrounding craters, which have actually thrown bombs of scoriæ upon the Puy de Dôme. It appeared to me that they were fragments of a sheet or sheets of white trachyte, like that of Mont Dore, and that the Puys had broken out in long subsequent times. But a more extended examination of the whole district would have been necessary to enable me to speak with any confidence on this subject.

de Dôme you can trace some of the lava streams, marking whence they issued and how they flowed across the country. That of the Villar valley, already described, is especially noticeable, breaking from the Puy de Pariou, and descending towards the east in a black rugged current, like a river of frozen icebergs.

Such, then, is the general landscape that stretches around the great Puy de Dôme. It is eminently dreary and desolate in the nearer parts, while in the eastern distance the eye rests on the bright corn-clad Limagne. The long line of volcanic cones stretching to the north and south affords every facility to the geologist, and presents him, moreover, with a class of phenomena not found round the larger active volcanoes of Europe. The independence, small extent, number, and local distribution of the cones are features that help in no small degree to explain certain ancient volcanic rocks in the British isles. Especially did they throw light on what must have been the character and aspect of the carboniferous volcanoes of central Scotland, to illustrate which had been the prime object of my visit to Auvergne. Nor was a closer examination of the district less instructive in its results, as may be seen if we take one of the cones as an illustration. For this purpose the Puy de Pariou offers itself as one of the most accessible, and at the same time one of the most perfect, cones of the chain.

This Puy lies somewhat more than a mile due north of the Puy de Dôme. It consists, in reality, of two craters, but only a portion of the northern rim of the older one is now visible, the rest being occupied by the newer crater, which is still in a perfect state of preservation. Ascending, as is usual, from the east side, the visitor first passes over a part of the lava current, which will be immediately described. From the foot of the cone the ascent is tolerably steep, among coarse grass, violets, martagon lilies, yellow gentians, and many other flowers, until the top of the older cone is reached. Here we look down into the first crater, with the gap which the lava current has made in it. Walking southward along its rim, we nd it passing under a later cone, which reaches a height of

738 feet above the plateau from which the southern side of
the hill rises.   After a second ascent, we arrive at last at the
top of the Puy, and find that the newer cone has been erupted
over the southern half of the older one, and that it contains
a beautifully perfect crater.   Hence, from the top of the Puy
there is on the south side an unbroken declivity sloping at
about 35° down to the surface of the table-land, while on the
north side the inner cone descends first into the older crater,
which half encircles it.   The last-formed crater measures
3,000 feet in circumference.   It is an inverted cone ; its sides
are smooth and grassy, and shelve steeply down to a depth of
300 feet.   They have been indented by a series of cattle-
tracks, rising in successive steps above each other, which
Mr. Scrope aptly compares to the seats of an amphitheatre.
Nothing can be more complete or regular than this part of
the Puy.   While ascending the outer slopes, you look forward
to reach a broad flat table-land on the top, carpeted perchance
with the same coarse heather and wild flowers as clothe the
sides of the hill ; but, instead of level ground, you find a
deep, round, smooth-sided crater, covered with grass to the
bottom.   Between the inward slope of this hollow and the
outward slopes of the sides of the Puy, the rim is at times
so narrow that you may almost sit astride on it, one foot
dangling into the crater, the other pointing down to the
plateau from which the hill rises.   And there you may rest,
if you like, undisturbed for a whole summer's day, with wild
flowers clustering around you, butterflies hovering past, cattle
browsing leisurely down the sides of the crater below, while
the tinkle of the sheep-bells ever and anon comes up with
the scented breeze from the outer slopes of the Puy.   In a
scene so peaceful and still, one cannot without an effort
picture the turmoil and violence to which the Puy owes its
rise, when the ground was rent by subterranean explosions,
and when showers of dust and stones were thrown out from
the orifice.   It is one of those contrasts which abound in
nature, but which are never truly realized until geology has
traced their origin.

Q 2

From the northern edge of this later cone the spectator looks down into the older crater, now more than half-filled up by the last eruptions. A stream of lava passes out northwards, through a great gap in the outer and earlier cone, trending at once to the east, over the plateau and down the valley of Villar. Here the history of the whole Puy is at once apparent. First of all, after some underground movements, a fracture was made, through which gas, steam, ashes, and scoriæ were vomited forth. The ejected material fell back again, partly into the vent, partly round its margin. Such portions as dropt into the orifice would be once more thrown out, and by this process would become still further triturated and pulverised. The dust and stones which fell round the verge of the hole would gather by degrees into a cone with a crater in its centre. As the eruptions went on the cone would, of course, increase in width and height until it reached the size indicated by the older cone of Pariou. And now a column of lava rose through the vent, and began to fill the bowl-like cavity of the crater. It continued to well upward until the loosely compacted sides of the hill were no longer able to withstand the pressure of the increasing mass of melted rock. The northern side, being probably the weakest, gave way, and then the lava, like a great river, burst out into the plain below. Taking at once an easterly course, owing to the general slope of the ground, it descended in a sheet of dark rugged rock, now swelling up against ridges that opposed its progress, and then sweeping past them until it reached the beginning of the hill of Prudelle already noticed. Here, in a scene of singular confusion, it broke into two streams, one leaping like a torrent down the valley of Villar, the other plunging into the valley of Gresinier.* But the emission of this vast body of melted rock did not conclude the eruptions of the Puy de Pariou. When the lava had perhaps ceased to flow, the vapour and gases still continued to escape with violence. By their means another cone was in

* Mr. Scrope's description of these lava streams is a model of graphic and accurate description.

time produced, not quite on the former site, but a little to the south, so as to cover the southern half of the older cone, and leave visible that northern segment of it from which the lava issued. Thus arose the later cone of Pariou. No subsequent eruptions have disturbed its regularity or filled up its crater. The hand of time has not effaced its smooth curves and slopes, but has covered them with vegetation, whereby the loose dust and scoriæ are protected from the destructive effects of heavy rains. After the lapse of many a long century this little volcano is still as perfect as when the last shower of ashes fell over its sides, and it promises to remain so for as many centuries to come.

The Puy de Pariou is only one of a series of similar cones. Some have but one crater, others have two, three, or even, as in the instance already cited, four. Each crater is of course the product of a different eruption or series of eruptions, as the Puy de Pariou so well explains. Sometimes the whole of one side of a cone has been broken down by a stream of lava issuing from the bottom of the crater. Several striking examples of this singular structure occur among the cones to the south of the Puy de Dôme, as in the Puy de las Solas and the Puy de la Vache. These two hills, when seen from the south, look like the mouths of two yawning chasms. Their southern sides have been swept away by a black rugged river of lava, which, issuing from the bottom of each crater, flows eastward in a united stream for twelve miles down a deep narrow valley. The scenery round these hills is even more desolate than among those to the north of the Puy de Dôme. The cones and craters are in many places devoid of all verdure, and have still much of the blackened and burnt aspect of active volcanoes. The lava, too, which has spread out over most of the intermediate ground, is dark, bristling, and sterile. The whole landscape leaves an impression, not easily effaced, of the vigour of volcanic agency, and of its power to modify, and even altogether change the general aspect of a district.

To one who had been at work for some years among a set

of old and fragmentary volcanic rocks, trying to piece together greenstones, and basalts, and ash-beds, the sight of these Puys, with their fresh cones and craters of ash and scoriæ, and their still perfect floods of lava, was inexpressibly instructive. I cannot hope to convey to the reader a notion of how much I learnt by merely casting the eye over the landscape. It was exactly the scene that was needed to enable one to fill in the missing portions of the Scottish series, and fully to realize the character of those old carboniferous volcanoes of which only such mere fragments now remain. High among the uplands of Central France, my eye was ever instinctively recalling the hills and valleys of Central Scotland, and picturing their earliest scenery by transferring to them some of the main features in the landscapes of Auvergne. The imagination easily filled again with a sheet of deep blue water the broad expanse of yonder Limagne. Vines, and acacias, and mulberry-trees seemed to melt of their own accord into stately *sigillariæ, lepidodendra,* and *calamites;* the orchards and corn-fields along the slopes began to wave with a dense underwood of ferns and shrubby vegetation, and there, with but little further change, lay a landscape in the central valley of Scotland during an early part of the great Carboniferous Period. Nor did a more extended examination of other parts of the Volcanic District weaken this comparison. The general outward resemblance of the present volcanic rocks of France, to what must have been the original aspect of those of Scotland at the geological era just named, holds good, even when traced into detail. It is, indeed, pleasant to find that the operations of nature throughout all time have been so uniform in character. Physical conditions have varied in the course of long ages ; but the difference has been one of degree, not of kind. Of the harmony with which the phenomena of one cycle may be dove-tailed into those of another, a better instance could hardly be given than this close agreement between the results of volcanic action at so recent a date as to be almost within the human era, and those which stretch far back into the dim twilight of the Carboniferous Period.

One of the most interesting excursions from Clermont, is to the hill of Gergovia, about six miles to the south. We started off early one morning, while the sky, which had been remarkably clear for some days, began to grow dusky with heavy clouds that kept trooping up from the south-west. Puy de Dôme had his head wrapped in mist, and giant shadows chased each other across the range of Puys until, as the clouds thickened, all the uplands were shrouded in an ominous gloom. Ere we had gone half-way rain began to fall in large round drops, and a distant muttering of thunder was heard rolling away northward. But the morning was fresh and cool, and even at the risk of a good drenching we persevered. The road, like all the French military highways, is excellently made and well kept. It passes through endless vineyards, many of which lie among the broken ruins of lava-flows that have descended from the heights to the westward. At one point the road has even been cut through a part of one of these lavas, the surface of which has all that dark, rugged, scoriform aspect already described.

The hill of Gergovia is famous in history as the site of a town long and successfully defended by the Arverni (people of Auvergne) against Cæsar's legions. Some interesting antiquarian remains had been found shortly before our visit, and we learnt that excavations were about to be renewed in search of more. But the hill is not less interesting to the geologist than to the antiquary. Seen from the east, it looks like a broad truncated cone ; but it differs altogether in appearance and origin from the true volcanic cones of the Puys. It consists, in fact, of horizontal strata of marl and limestone ; about two-thirds of the way up lies a bed of basalt, which forms a marked feature along the hillside ; some calcareous and ashy strata next occur, while the summit is formed by a capping of basalt. These marls and limestones are of lacustrine origin, as is shown by their fresh-water shells, and by the caddis-worm cases which they contain. They are parts of the deposits of the old lake of the Limagne, and they attain in this hill a thickness of probably not less than 1,200 or 1,500 feet. Ascending one of the ravines which deeply furrow the east side of the hill, we passed over these thinly laminated strata, piled over each other in successive layers, and crumbling away like chalk. Every yard of the ascent deepened the impression of the exceedingly slow rate at which these strata must have been formed, and, therefore, of the prodigious lapse of time which their entire thickness represents. Slowly we threaded the ravine, which is in places tolerably steep. The morning, after clearing up for a brief space, had again overcast, and rain began to fall as heavily as before. We sheltered for a little under the lower basalt, and gained information there for which it was worth our while to have come all the way to Auvergne. Had we been suddenly spirited away unawares from some of the Scottish glens, and set down at the side of this rock, we should hardly have recognised the change of scene. The basalt is a true bed, some thirty or forty feet thick, and is scarcely distinguishable from certain carboniferous basalts of the Lothians. It is a hard, dark, compact rock, somewhat rough and scoriaceous towards the bottom, like the greenstones and basalts along the magnificent coast-section near Kinghorn in Fife. But what especially interested me was, to find that the upper surface of the bed was even and smooth, and that the marls rested on it unaltered, the line of demarcation being sharp and clear. Many a time, among the moorlands of Scotland, had I been led to reflect on the difference of aspect between a lava-current which cools in the open air, and one which solidifies under water. Theoretically, of course, the rock ought to part with its heat less quickly in the latter element; and hence, the surface of a submarine lava should present a smoother outline than that of a subaerial one. It was in this way that I endeavoured to account for the even and unbroken surface of many of the Scottish trap-rocks, which could hardly be regarded as sheets of melted matter subsequently thrust among the strata, but which gave good evidence of having been erupted as true lava-flows. Here, then, in this ravine of Gergovia, an example occurred that seemed to justify the inference. The basalt had undoubtedly rolled over the bottom of the old lake ; it rested on lacustrine marls, and strata of the same kind covered it. But its upper surface, so far from rising up into black bristling masses, like the subaerial currents of the Puys, was smooth and even, like the top of a bed of sandstone or limestone, and the marls which succeeded gave no sign of alteration or disturbance. I had thus no longer any doubt that the evenness of the upper surface of certain greenstones and basalts in Scotland was no valid objection to their being of the nature of true lava-currents.

Ascending beyond the prominent zone of basalt, we soon reached a bed of calcareous peperino, or ash. This rock strongly resembled some of the ash-beds associated with parts of the mountain-limestone of Linlithgowshire and Fife. Its stratification was a good deal confused, the inclination appearing sometimes to be at a high angle, while a short way off it changed its direction, or traces of bedding disappeared altogether. Similar ashy materials, mingled with calcareous matter, occupy the remainder of the hill up to the cake of basalt which crowns the summit.

We intended to make a circuit of Gergovia, descending on the north-west side towards the strange isolated castle-crowned crag of Montrognon. But the rain, which had fallen with scarcely an intermission since we began the ascent, now came down in torrents. We took refuge in a little cave in the calcareous peperino, which looked eastward across the Limagne to the distant mountains of the Loire and southward to the volcanic heights of the Velay. But the landscape was blotted out in one thick veil of falling water, and we could hardly distinguish the form of the trees at but a short distance down the slopes. I had seen many a day of mist and shower among the Hebrides, where it rains as it does scarcely anywhere else in the British Islands ; but the clouds of Skye are certainly no match for those of Auvergne. It was an instructive lesson to sit at the mouth of the cave and watch the increase of the rills and runnels. Over ground which in

the morning was as dry and parched as a drought of some
weeks' duration could make it, water now poured in hundreds
of rivulets, acquiring a milky colour from the marl which it
partially decomposed in its progress. One could see how
comparatively rapid must be the waste of these soft calcareous
rocks. Every shower loosens and removes portions of their
substance and prepares the way for the action of the shower
that succeeds. It is by this means, joined with the under-
mining agency of streams and rivers, that the deep and wide
valleys of these districts have been excavated.

Sitting in the cave while the deluge continued outside, we
had leisure to reflect on the geological history of the hill.
We could picture the time when these strata, now existing in
so fragmentary a state, were elaborated at the bottom of that
old lake which filled the broad valley of the Limagne. Leaf
after leaf, and layer after layer, were slowly laid down, derived mainly from the crumbling remains of shells, cyprides,
and other living creatures that tenanted the water. The rate
of growth of these deposits must have been inconceivably
slow, perhaps like that of the dust which gathers on the floor
of some deserted hall. When in this way a thickness of at
least a thousand feet had been formed, a volcano sprang up
in the neighbourhood, and rolled into the lake the stream of
lava represented by the lower bed of basalt. The fine calcareous sediment however began to be deposited anew over
the floor of lava, yet the volcanic forces had not become
wholly quiescent, for from time to time showers of ashes
were thrown out, which, falling into the lake, gave rise to
those beds of peperino, in one of which we were now taking
refuge from the storm. Afterwards another stream of lava
was erupted, forming the present summit of the hill. How
much further the series may have originally extended cannot
now be discovered, since if anything was deposited on the
surface of the second basalt it has been subsequently removed.

While the rain still continued to fall heavily, an old
peasant took refuge with us in the cave. He wore a broad-
brimmed felt hat and a long brown coat that reached nearly

to his heels. A wooden bottle of water and a small scrip containing some fragments of brown bread were slung across his shoulders. His sallow emaciated cheeks contrasted painfully with the large goitrous swelling round his neck, and his eyes, bleared and bloodshot, sent rheumy streams down the deep furrows that traversed his features. He had not been seated half a minute, however, ere he monopolized the conversation of the cavern. In the peculiar dialect of Auvergne, which it is by no means easy to follow, he rattled away with true French volubility. Nothing came amiss. In one of the lulls of the storm the clouds lifted a little and we saw a railway-train far below us moving along the plain of the Limagne. Our friend had instantly a world to say about the *chemin-de-fer*. By and by a lovely green lizard darted across the mouth of the cave, and off went the peasant into a disquisition on the lizards and other kindred animals of Auvergne. In vain my companion occasionally put in a question by way of getting him to repeat some of his rapid utterances. We might as well have tried to arrest some of the rain-swollen streams that were rushing and foaming before us down the hillside. After continuing his discourse until he had well-nigh run himself out of breath, he came to a halt and asked with infinite nonchalance if we understood the patois. We came from Paris, he presumed. No, we came from England. " England," he repeated after us with an incredulous smile, " Where's England?" It was a hopeless task to tell him, so he was allowed to begin another torrent of talk. Ere he had brought it to an end, however, the scarcely more portentous torrents outside began to slacken, and in a few minutes we were all on our way, he southwards towards the valley of Channonat, we northwards for Clermout.

Water in a thousand rills and runnels was rushing down the slopes of Gergovia. A narrow footpath into which we stumbled had been partly converted by the rain into the bed of an impetuous rivulet. Along this track we made our way for some time until it began to bend so much to the left as to take us far out of what appeared to be a straight line for Clermont. Discarding it, therefore, we struck down through tangled brushwood dripping with rain, until another track was reached, which seemed to lead more directly to our goal. It soon joined a rough cart-road, bordered here and there with cherry-trees in fruit, and before many minutes had passed, we found ourselves at the entrance of the little village of Perpignat. The entrance of two strangers, the effect of whose foreign garments was considerably heightened by a copious drenching of rain-water, seemed to afford no little amusement to the secluded peasantry. In the belief that the road would lead us right through the village, we entered boldly, but soon found ourselves in a labyrinth of narrow lanes from which at last we found it fairly impossible to emerge in any direction. On asking the way, we were told to take " the high-road," which leads straight to Clermont. But it was no easy task to decide to which of the lanes that sounding name should be given. This same " high-road " we found at last to be a narrow dirty lane, in no respect different from its neighbours, save, perhaps, in being still more narrow and crooked. It led us by an endless series of turnings and windings to a tree-shaded road through corn-fields, now heavy with their golden crop. Away to the left we could see the Château de Montrognon—a ruined fortalice perched on the summit of a narrow and precipitous basaltic hill. Further over lay the high ground of the Puys, with the rain-clouds still floating over it. As we advanced, however, the sky began to clear, patches of deep blue could now and then be seen through gaps in the driving clouds, until the last mist-wreath rose from the great Puy de Dôme, and amid gleams of bright sunshine we re-entered Clermont about noon, with a goodly appetite for breakfast.

One of the greatest luxuries in travelling is to have no luggage to look after. My companion and myself carried each a small knapsack, which contained the whole of our spare wardrobe. Our geological accoutrements were of the simplest kind—a hammer strapped round the waist, a compass and clinometer, a small lens, and a note-book. These instruments, with the exception of the hammer, slipped easily into the pocket. Hence we went unencumbered with baggage and unfettered by the annoyances with which it is accompanied. At the custom-houses we passed through the official scrutiny at once, while our fellow-travellers were sometimes detained for hours in a state of frenzy and indignation. At each town where an *octroi* is charged, our little bags acted as a charm, and again we were bowed through with expedition. At railway stations, too, we fortunately never experienced the suspense of waiting on for a weary hour or more until a portmanteau or valise could be rescued from the fangs of guards and porters. Nor away in the remoter districts, to which railways have not reached, were we ever compelled to delay a journey because the conductor either could not or would not make room for our baggage on the top of his diligence. No feature of these rambles was fraught with greater interest than the contemplation of the evils of baggage. Fully nine-tenths of the annoyance and vexation, surliness and high words which one sees and hears at railway-stations and elsewhere, spring from those hapless packages that crowd the dark recesses of the luggage-van. What a depressing thought is it that one's comfort and happiness should be bound up in a little leather trunk, that this same object should be watched over with the most tender solicitude, that its due labelling and numbering should take up so much time and care, that its detention should keep us in a state of fret and fume, and that its loss should cause us first to break out into a universal indignation against everything and everybody foreign, and then to return, perhaps, to our own land in unutterable disgust.

It was with such a train of thought passing through my head that I took my seat one bright morning on the diligence which runs between Clermont and Mont Dore. A stout Frenchman, by dint of not a little exertion, had worked himself into a fury of excitement. His wife and he, along with a maid-servant, were bound for the baths of Mont Dore, and had engaged their places in the coach. They had unfortunately omitted, however, to inquire whether there was also room for two portmanteaux, three large trunks, a couple of band-boxes, and a little regiment of smaller packages. Long and loud was the altercation between Monsieur and the conductor; the clerk of the booking-office was soon summoned to the fray, the landlord of the hotel next joined the combatants, then came the driver and some supernumeraries from the stables, until a goodly crowd had collected in the market-place. In vain did the conductor point to the top of the coach, already loaded to the full with boxes and bags of all sizes. Monsieur had paid his fare, and was entitled to room for his luggage. "*Bagage !*" shouted the *cocher*, as with a look of ineffable contempt he turned from the injured traveller to the array of boxes with which the latter proposed to crown the diligence. In vain did mine host attempt to mediate and to suggest the propriety of the travellers going on at once, while he undertook to see their luggage sent by the next coach. Too much time had been lost in this debate, and so at last we started off with a lumbering speed over the causewayed track that traverses the square of Clermont. Looking back, we could see the enraged gentleman still in fierce contest with the clerk and landlord, surrounded by an admiring audience of stable-boys, until a turn of the street hid him from the view.

My comrade and myself had secured places in the banquette, where, screened from the sun, we could yet see the landscape as we rolled along. Our only companion on the way, was a gentleman of apparently about fifty years of age pale and sallow, as if from bad health. To a few words of French which we addressed to him, he replied in such English, as to show at once that he was himself an Englishman. We found that he had been residing in the north of Italy for the benefit of his health, and that he was now, like ourselves, on his way to Mont Dore les Bains, where he said he meant to drink the mineral waters for a month. No one was with him; he knew not a soul at the baths, and looked forward to spend there four weeks of dulness and *ennui*.

The journey to Mont Dore, being uphill nearly all the way, takes the greater part of a day. The first half of the road winding up the side of the granitic plateau, crosses several of the lava-streams which have descended the valleys, like that from the cone of Parion, and at last reaches the desolate table-land on which runs the chain of the Puys. A good view is obtained of several of the cones on the south side of the Puy de Dôme, the ruined yawning craters of the Puy de las Solas and the Puy de la Vache being especially noticeable, with their now silent rivers of black rugged lava. From the half-way house the road runs southward over the undulating surface of the plateau, until it begins the ascent of the Mont Dore hills. These heights, in their lower portions, are tolerably green, and constantly recalled to my memory parts of the trappean scenery of Skye and Mull. Numerous blocks of basalt, sometimes of considerable size, are scattered over the surface, and often lie in such positions that it is difficult to see how the action of the atmosphere, or of running water, could have placed them there. I kept au eye on the alert to detect a striated or polished surface, but there is little rock exposed in places along the road, and I was unsuccessful. It seemed at the time, however, to be far from unlikely that some of these great blocks of stone had been ice-borne. When the glaciers of the Alps filled the valley of the Lake of Geneva, at a height of no more than 1200 feet above the sea, there seems no reason why glaciers should not have descended from the Mont Dore mountains, which now form the highest ground in Central France, rising in the Pic de Sancy to a height of 6,217 feet. At this day, indeed, snow remains unmelted in the higher recessos of these mountains even in midsummer. I am not aware, however, that the existence of glaciers has ever been recognised here, and I had no time even to make a beginning in the attempt to solve the question for myself. The occurrence of the scattered blocks, and of some coarse unstratified detritus, in the steep defile that descends from the east into the valley of the Dordogne, was at least sufficient to suggest

the possibility of a partially glacial origin to some of the
deep valleys of the Mont Dore.

The Baths lie in a valley of surpassing loveliness, hemmed
in by lofty mountains and huge precipices. The climate is
delicious as a contrast to the scorching sultriness of the lower
plains, and hence the locality has been a watering-place since
the days of the Roman occupation of Gaul. We had time
only to get a peep at the conglomerates and trachytes of this
great volcanic district. Everything is on a scale so much
vaster than in the country of the Puy de Dôme, that the first
impression of the geologist is one of bewilderment. We did
not remain long enough to get rid of this feeling, and at this
moment I have a confused remembrance of vast, irregular
sheets of trachytic lava, separated by piles of volcanic ash and
conglomerate, the whole thrown together in a way which at
the time it seemed hopeless to attempt to unravel; of dykes
and veins of basalt, and currents of lava, belonging to a
greatly more recent set of eruptions, for they flowed down
the deep valleys which had been excavated out of the more
ancient lavas.

Contenting ourselves with a mere survey of its external
features, we left the Mont Dore district by the road which,
on re-ascending from the valley of the Dordogne, strikes
towards the east and then sweeps down into the valley of
Chambon. The Baths, after lying for some hours under the
shade of the great hills, were now bathed in sunlight, and full
of bustle, as we drove through the streets. Invalids, valetudinarians, and folks of fashion, were passing to and fro between
the hotels and the central building where the waters are dis-
pensed. Some were borne in sedan-chairs, but the greater
number performed the short journey on foot. It was a
ludicrous sight to watch men and women, as soon as they
imbibed their draught, hurry home holding their mouths.
The effect, indeed, became irresistibly comic when the patient
happened to be one of the numerous ecclesiastics who frequent
the place—a portly priest, perhaps, of some threescore, wad-
dling back to his hotel with the ends of his dress muffled

round his mouth and nose.  On inquiry, we learnt that the design of this proceeding was to prevent the gas from escaping after the morning dose of water had been taken—a precaution without which it was held impossible to derive the full benefits of *les eaux minerales.*

The journey from Mont Dore les Bains to the plain of the Allier at Issoire, is one of the most varied and interesting in Central France.  From the summit level of the road the eye wanders over a wide sweep of mountains of volcanic origin, traversed by wide valleys and narrow gorges.  Southward, in the dark shady rifts of the higher peaks, we saw several gleaming patches of snow, and the breeze that played about these uplands, even in the bright sunshine, was cool and re-freshing.  But as we descended, mile after mile, the temperature increased, until when we gained once more the valley of the Allier, the heat was as stifling as it had been at Clermont. In spite of the sweltering sun, however, we succeeded in learning not a little by the way.  We could see evidence of lava-flows of several distinct ages, some of them high up along the sides of the valleys, which had since been excavated through them ; old river gravels, too, far above the channels of the present streams ; while down the bottom of the valley, and following all its curves like a river, ran a current of black rugged lava, which in one or two places rose up into the most fantastic masses, as if it had flowed only a few years ago. The impression of the immense lapse of time represented by these tertiary formations was deepened tenfold as we threaded this Valley of Chambon.  The stream which meanders through the broader meadow-lands, and leaps down the narrower defiles, has undoubtedly been the main agent in scooping out this great indentation in the flanks of Mont Dore.  Here and there, in the centre of the valley, it has left isolated patches of the beds of rock that occur on either side, such as the picturesque conical crag on which stands the ruinous castle of Murol. These outliers are silent witnesses of the reality of the abrasion. But how incalculably slow must this process be.  The lava-current at the bottom of the valley has certainly not been erupted since the time of the Romans. It must, therefore, be at least 2,000 years old, and may, for aught we can tell, be ten or a hundred times older. Yet since its eruption, the action of the river, though it has here and there cut its way through the lava, has nevertheless been, on the whole, but trifling ; indeed the amount of excavation effected since the eruption of this lava probably falls far short of a thousandth part of the general erosion of the valley. How quickly is a million of years exhausted in such a calculation, and how far is it from carrying us back even to the beginning of the excavation of the Valley of Chambon. And when we do reach that beginning, we find ourselves only at the dawn of the latest and perhaps the shortest, of all the stages which the geology of the district indicates. How vast must have been that earlier period wherein were deposited those fine alternations of lime and clay which form hills, such as Mont Perrier, several hundred feet in height, divisible into distinct zones, each characterised by peculiar assemblages of fossils. The mind fails to realize these infinitely protracted ages. And yet, after all, the geological records of this part of France do not carry us to the commencement of the tertiary formations. There was an earlier time, during which the country was inhabited by that family of pachydermatous animals whose bones lie buried in the strata of the Paris basin. It is only by thus advancing, step by step, backward into the remote past, that we begin to appreciate the antiquity of the tertiary group of strata, and to realize, in some measure, the extent of that long history of physical and organic changes, of which the Tertiaries contain only the last chapter.

We hurried onward from Issoire up the plain of the Allier, catching a glimpse of the little contorted coalfield of Brassac — an outlier of true carboniferous strata, resting in a hollow of the metamorphic rocks, and over-lapped by the tertiary marls and limestones which stretch southward from the Limagne. Here and there in the valley were volcanic mounds, sometimes capped with little towns, so that, although we had quitted the district of great lava-streams, we were far from having reached the limits of the volcanic district. The town of Brioude lies at the southern extremity of that great lacustrine deposit of the valley of the Allier, so conspicuously displayed in the Limagne d'Auvergne. The granitic hills close in upon the river, and thence swell southwards into the mountains of La Margeride and the uplands of the Haute-Loire. Of Brioude itself I have a pleasant recollection as a quaint rambling town with some large decayed houses that seem to have once been tenanted by a better class of inmates. The hotel at which we stayed was one of these. From a retired street we entered a low archway, and found ourselves in a dark room with a large fire-place, now used as a kitchen. A number of doors opened out of the further side of the room, and through one of them we were ushered into a lobby with broad staircase and carved banisters. Up and down, through one passage into another, we at last halted at a recess on one of the landings, and were shown into a large wainscotted bedroom. Its tarnished mirrors, faded green-velvet chairs, old-fashioned cabinets and tables, were certainly not the kind of furniture one would have expected to see in a quiet hotel in a remote little town. There was a taste and harmony about the whole, and they fitted so well with the character of the rest of the house, as to suggest that the place had been the residence of some decayed family, and that not many years could have elapsed since it passed into the hands of an innkeeper. While here, a severe thunder-storm passed over the town, killing a young man only about quarter of a mile from where we were. The heat, which for some days had been intense, was now somewhat modified, and next day the sky remained more or less cloudy. A pleasant breeze came down from the high grounds to the west, and under such favourable auspices we started for Le Puy.

Crossing the Allier by the fine bridge at Old Brioude, we bade adieu to that noble river. Our course now lay towards the south-east, up a range of rising grounds, traversed by numerous narrow and deep, but often thickly wooded ravines. The ground for the first part of the journey was formed of granite ; but fragments of ancient basalt could now and then be seen by the roadside, or along the upper edge of a steep bank.   The country, however, remained somewhat bare and uninteresting ; nor until we began to descend towards the basin of the Loire, and caught sight of the range of volcanic hills and cones that encircle Le Puy, did its interest revive.

Le Puy was by far the most picturesque town we saw anywhere in France.   It is built round a conical hill, which rises in the valley between the river Borne and another tributary of the Loire.   An abrupt crag of breccia, crowned with a bronze statue of the Virgin, overhangs it on the north ; while lower down in the plain, a tall massive column of the same rock supports the little and seemingly inacessible church of St. Michel.   The country rises rapidly on all sides, so that Le Puy lies embosomed among hills—vast piles of lava, and cones of ash formed by many different eruptions, sweep away south into the heights of Mont Mezen and the long plateau which here separates the waters of the Allier from those of the Loire.

The geologist could hardly pitch upon a locality where more may be learned in so narrow a compass.   Le Puy lies in the centre of what, during a part of the tertiary periods, was a lake, some twenty miles long, and twelve or fourteen broad.   This lake occupied a hollow in the great granitic framework of the country, and, like the Limagne d'Auvergne, gave rise to the slow accumulation of fine marls, limestones, and sandstones, which attained a united thickness of hundreds of feet.   Over the top of these horizontal strata, the lavas and ashes were erupted to a depth of three or four hundred feet more, so as wholly to cover up the lacustrine deposits, and obliterate the site of the lake.   Since these events, the Loire and its tributaries have been ceaselessly at work in deepening and widening their channels.   And now, incredible as it may seem, these streams have actually cut their way down through the solid basalt, and a great part of the old lake formations. They have, in short, excavated a series of valleys, several hundred feet deep, and sometimes of considerable width, along the sides of which are exposed the remaining edges of the strata that have been borne away.  Standing on the summit of the Mont Denize, and looking round upon the valleys and ravines on every side, each traversed by what seemed such a tiny stream, I felt as if a new geological agent were for the first time made known to me.  Striking as are the proofs of fluviatile and pluvial action in the country of the Limagne, they fall far short of these in the Haute-Loire.  To be actually realized, such a scene must be visited in person. No amount of verbal description, not even the most careful drawings, will convey a full sense of the magnitude of the changes to one who is acquainted only with the rivers of a glaciated country such as Britain.  His first impression, when he looks with his own eyes on a landscape like that round Le Puy, will be one of utter bewilderment.  The upsetting of all his previous notions of the power of rain and rivers is so sudden, and so complete, that for a few minutes he can hardly shake himself free from a feeling of vague discomfort, almost bordering, perhaps, on despair.  It is not without an effort, and after having analysed the scene, feature by feature, that he can take it all in.  But when he has done so, his views of the effects of subaerial disintegration become permanently altered, and he quits the district with a rooted conviction that there is almost no amount of waste and erosion of the solid framework of our islands and continents, which may not be brought about in time by the combined influence of springs, frost, rain, and rivers.

The volcanic phenomena of the neighbourhood of Le Puy are likewise full of interest, and, owing to the numerous deep ravines, they can be easily studied along admirable natural sections.  The beds of lava, often beautifully columnar, recall many of the basalts of Scotland.  The beds of peperino, or ash, likewise bear the strongest resemblance to some of the trap-tuffs of the Lothians.  Indeed, many parts of the scenery differ but little from some of the Scottish trappean districts.  We found the cones of scoriæ more numerous, but less perfect than round the Puy de Dome ; as if they belonged to an earlier era, and had consequently been longer exposed to the wasting effects of time. But this greater antiquity is occasionally productive of much advantage to the geologist, for it presents him with chasms and cliffs, without which he would miss many incidents in the geological history of the district. Thus, near Le Puy, the volcanic cone of Mont Denize, so well known for the interesting fossils which have been found in its underlying gravels, has had its western front exposed partly by nature, and partly by man. By this means are laid bare the strata of volcanic breccia that rest on the marls of the old lake ; on a worn surface of the breccia comes a band of true river gravel now several hundred feet above the present bed of the Borne, while associated with this gravel there is sometimes a newer ash. Through these various deposits the volcano of Mont Denize has broken out, piling up the mound of loose scoriæ and ashes that form the hill. Here we saw, what it had not been our good fortune to meet with in the Puy de Dôme— the actual section of a volcanic vent. The sides were smooth and worn, and the bed of hard breccia, which had been perforated nearly vertically, still retained the grooving and polishing produced by the friction of the ejected scoriæ. The vent was filled up with a black scoriaceous lava, while several lava *coulées* that had rolled down the hillside, now formed dark masses of prominent crag and cliff. This little volcano, in short, bore a close resemblance to the upper part of Arthur's Seat at Edinburgh. In each case, a column of lava is surrounded by an outer envelope of loose ashes, over which various currents of lava have rolled down from the crater.

With no little reluctance, and not until the sun had dipped behind the western hills, did we quit the slopes of Mont Denize. The evening, after a day of mingled storm and sunshine, was passing fair, and the whole of that wondrous landscape lay bright and clear around. It was the last evening, too, which we spent in the volcanic region of Central France ; nor could we have happened upon a more auspicious

sky, or a more favourable locality for taking a last view of
the scenery, and summing up the results of our tour. Sitting
on a pile of loose cinders, on the top of the hill, we watched
the level rays lighting up the vast basalt plateau that
stretched away for miles to the west, while each of the many
cones that dotted the plain cast its long shadow towards us.
With undiminished wonder we gazed again at the deep ravines
and valleys by which the plateau is broken up, each with its
streamlet meandering like a silver thread between the slopes.
The sunlight lay warm and bright on the town of Le Puy in
the valley below, with its isolated crag of La Vièrge, and its
church-crowned pinnacle of St. Michel—two rocks that
remain to record the enormous erosion of these valleys. The
castle of Polignac—built on another outlying crag further
down the plain—stood up in the deep shadow of Mont
Denize. Eastward, the gorges that open into the Loire
gleamed white as the sunset fell along their bars of pale
marls and limestones, and their capping of basalt. Beyond
these, cone rose behind cone, amid piles of lava currents of
many different ages ; each sunward slope and crest was
now flushed with a rosy hue deepening into purple in the
distance, until, far away as the eye could reach, the mountains
of Mont Mezen were steeped in the softest violet, that melted
into the twilight of the eastern sky.

And here we took leave of the volcanoes of Central France.
We had come simply to learn, and without the least idea of
attempting to make any original discoveries in a district
which had been so often and so carefully explored. Despite
an unusually fierce summer, and somewhat indifferent health,
we saw what we had resolved to see. We gained that vivid
impression of the phenomena of a country which can only be
obtained from an actual visit. We were now able to realize,
with a clearness till then unlooked-for, the original features
of those ancient Scottish igneous rocks, among whose fragmentary relics we had been at work for years. In the form
of their cones, their distribution, their aspect in the landscape,
the limited extension of their ashes, the form and disposition

of their lava currents, the structure of their craters, and their relation to the underlying and to the contemporaneous stratified deposits, these extinct tertiary volcanoes of France cast a flood of what to us was new light upon the long-extinct carboniferous volcanoes of Scotland. We seemed no longer to be dealing with conjectures, but with sober truths. To the igneous rocks of our own country there was now imparted a freshness and reality such as they did not possess before. More than ever did we feel them to be not mere mineral masses to be described in text-books as occupying definite areas of ground, and to be arranged by hand-specimens in a museum as so many mineralogical compounds. They had a story to tell if they were only questioned in the right way. And the main result of our wanderings in the Auvergne and Velay was to shew us how this questioning should be carried on. The lesson was one too precious ever to be forgotten.

Nor did we value less the new and enlarged views which those rambles gave us of the potency of rains, rivers, and other atmospheric agencies, in effecting the degradation of the land. Nothing we had read in geological literature, not even the descriptions of this very region, had prepared us for the contemplation of changes so stupendous as those of the erosion of the ravines and valleys of Le Puy. To look upon them for the first time was, as I have said, like a new revelation, which in an instant uprooted a host of narrow long-cherished conceptions, and supplanted them with a profound respect for the power of the terrestrial agencies of waste. Broader, and truer, and fresher views of nature are worth the trouble of a long journey, and in gaining them, we felt ourselves abundantly repaid for our toil under a fierce sun among the uplands of Central France.

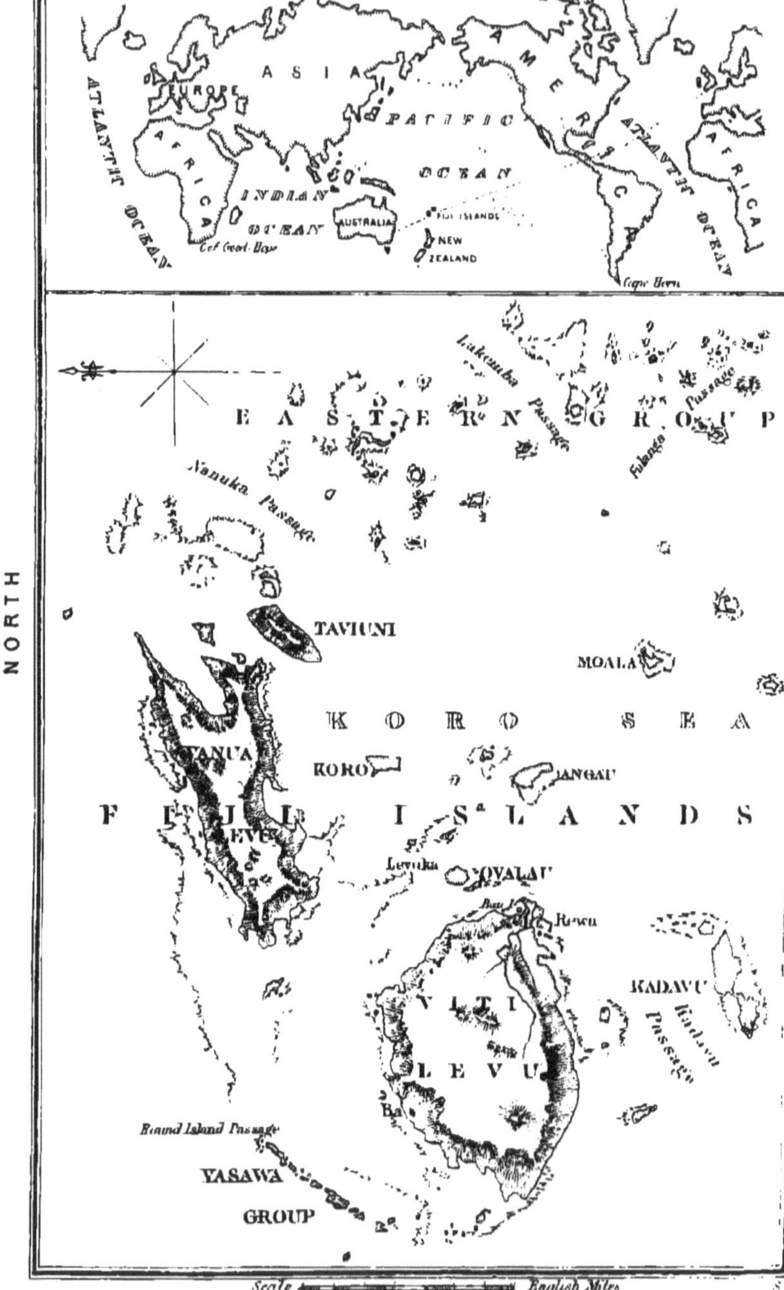

Vacation Tourists 1861.
Fiji & its Inhabitants
ASIA
AMERICA
EUROPE
ATLANTIC OCEAN
PACIFIC
OCEAN
AFRICA
INDIAN
OCEAN
AUSTRALIA
FIJI ISLANDS
NEW ZEALAND
AFRICA
ATLANTIC OCEAN
Cape Good Hope
Cape Horn
NORTH
EASTERN GROUP
Lakemba Passage
Fulanga Passage
Nanuka Passage
TAVIUNI
MOALA
KORO SEA
VANUA
KORO
NGAU
LEVU
FIJI ISLANDS
Levuka
OVALAU
Bau
Rewa
VITI
KADAVU
Kadavu Passage
LEVU
Ba
Round Island Passage
YASAWA
GROUP
Scale
English Miles
20  10  0  10  20  30  40  50
Macmillan & Co Cambridge & London

# 8. *FIJI AND ITS INHABITANTS.**

BY BERTHOLD SEEMANN, Ph. D., F.L.S.

The veil of obscurity in which the Fiji islands have been shrouded, from the time Captain Cook sighted the southern-most one to the present day, have induced Europeans to associate with them and their inhabitants all that is repulsive, and nothing that appeals to human sympathies. I must own that, after leaving the luxuries of the Peninsular and Oriental steamers behind at Sydney, and fairly embarked on board the *John Wesley* for the Cannibal Islands, reading every scrap of information relating to them, and hearing from my fellow-voyagers, few of whom had visited the group previously, none save stories about the cruelties and bloodthirstiness of the natives, a feeling crept over me somewhat akin to that taking possession of the soldier or sailor when the first boom of cannon announces that battle has actually commenced. From being the whole day entertained with anecdotes and stories relating to those subjects, my dreams at night were far from pleasant. For breakfast there were, as our jokers have it, missionary pies and a cold shoulder of a clergyman on the sideboard. Barnum's mermaid from the Fijis, at one time, looking like an old boot, as I had seen it a few years previously in the Museum at Boston, U.S., at another like the lovely creature imagination .paints it, half flesh, half fish combing golden tresses of luxuriant hair, was swimming from isle to isle, and trying to practise on me the same arts as the

* All the native names are spelt according to Fijian orthography, as laid down in D. Hazelwood's Dictionary. (Viwa, Fiji, 1850.)

Sirens did on Ulysses, or that dangerous Lorely does on unwary boatmen of the Rhine.

I felt quite relieved when, after a passage of more than three weeks from Sydney, the Fijis hove in sight, and an opportunity was offered for judging of the country and people for myself. All voyagers have been enraptured with the South-Sea Islands, scattered over the broad Pacific Ocean like stars over the firmament of heaven ; and, indeed, they exercise a spell over every visitor, be he from whatever country he may. In my wanderings over the greater portion of the globe, I have beheld grander sights, bolder scenery, but never prettier or more captivating. In the first instance, there is the gently wafting trade-wind and the fleecy clouds to set off the deep blue of the sky ; the heavy surf breaking upon the long lines of reef encircling every island, and acting like so many natural breakwaters. Then there are the fine white beaches of decomposed coral, densely crowded with feathery cocoa-nut palms, followed by forests of breadfruit-trees, with their deeply-cut leaves and heavy loads of nutritious fruit. Finally, the natives, paddling or sailing in their single or double canoes, a cheerful, fine-looking race, certainly not too much encumbered with articles of clothing, but, nevertheless, free from every approach to that indecency which impure minds might fancy intimately associated with so scanty a garb.

Is it safe to land ? Certainly. Land whereon nature has profusely supplied the necessaries of life ; but avoid, carefully avoid, as a general rule, all spots where provisions are scarce, and the arrival of new-comers must ever be regarded as a public calamity rather than a matter of general rejoicing. Why hesitate ? The quick eye of the natives has already observed your hesitation. They assume the initiative in establishing friendly relations. Look! they bring their wives and children on the beach in proof that no hostilities are intended, and the young men run to fetch green boughs, genuine flags of truce, though their colour be not white. Confidence begets confidence. You hasten on shore. Don't be frightened by

people crowding near in order to *sniffle* you. It is their way
of salutation and expression of good-will. In Rome you must
do as Rome does. To be on intimate terms with the Esqui-
maux you must rub noses, with the Spaniards embrace, French
kiss, English shake hands. Why object to be sniffled at here?

Step inside a house, the sun is too hot to stand long exposed
to its direct rays. How cool and pleasant, how well-con-
structed these huts are, with their thatch of sugar-cane leaves
and posts of tree-ferns! Sit down on the floor; there *are* no
chairs, sofas, or tables, but plenty of good mats, laid double
and treble over each other, all well shaken in the morning, and free from every kind of dirt. Flies are collecting on
you? Ah, that is certainly a drawback to all the South-Sea
Islands, but let those two dark-eyed boys fan you; they do it
with pleasure, and your stock of jew's-harps, soon to be distributed amongst the lads and lasses, will amply repay them for
their little trouble. Now out with your foreign tobacco.
Give a few sticks of it to the man you fancy the biggest
amongst them, and see how carefully he will divide it
amongst all who are present, and how pleased every one will
look when the precious weed is fairly lit.

But here comes the dinner, breakfast, luncheon, or supper—
whatever you like to consider it. Don't appear to notice
the way in which it is brought in. It may not be quite in
accordance with your notions; but don't quarrel with all
mankind because they are not of your way of thinking. Unless you allow the women to crawl on their knees and elbows
when they are serving up the food, you may retard your
meal, or, perhaps, have to go without it altogether. You
have the satisfaction of knowing that all the plates and
dishes are new, and that they will never be used again by
anybody. Every meal new plates and dishes! Here would
be an unpardonable extravagance, unless Dame Nature kept up
the supply with unsparing hand. The trays are fine wicker-
work, made of cocoa-nut or screw-pines, and the plates and
dishes large smooth leaves fresh from the bush. Let us
see what we have got. In the first instance, there is baked

taro, yam, and bread-fruit, with plenty of pork, all done in the way Captain Cook described it nearly a century ago, on heated stones, and covered with a thick layer of mould. All has been so well wrapped up in leaves, that not a grain of earth has been able to get at the food. Those "greens," looking like spinach, are taro-tops ; very good eating, and by boiling, quite free from that acridity which makes them, in a raw state, taste like so many pins and needles. Yonder greyish-looking stuff is salt, made by the islanders themselves, and partly owing its appearance to its being always kept near the fire-places. Forks you must dispense with ; they are never used in Fiji, except at cannibal feasts, all other food being eaten with the fingers ; but the stalk of a banana will be handed to you after the meal, to remove with its juice any impurities adhering to them. Knives you can be supplied with ; and that thin, soup-like looking dish, the *kaile*, prepared from a wild yam, you will have to eat with the leaves of the spoon-tree. I am glad to hear you are quite of my opinion, that the islanders know how to cook. Suspend your judgment a little longer, and it may be even more favourable. Here comes the pudding ; two different kinds to begin with. If you stay a few weeks, you shall be introduced to the whole series ; and if there should happen to be a grand public festival you may hope to see a monster pudding from eighteen to. twenty-one feet round. Don't laugh ! I am really telling no traveller's tale. Taste this ; it is *vaka lolo*, very good eating, and made of bananas filled with ripe rasped cocoa-nut ; the white, milk-like sauce, is the juice of the nut. Not bad, is it ? One might, with advantage, introduce it into Europe. Few foreigners dislike it, and a good European cook would, doubtless, by a few finishing touches set it off to a great advantage. These little jelly-like cakes are made of South-Sea arrow-root, sweetened with rasped sugar-cane, and boiled in the juice squeezed from a ripe cocoa-nut. All you see before you has been produced in the country. If you are fond of curry, you can have it whenever you please. There are plenty of fowls, though they be rather difficult to catch,

and the sea and rivers swarm with an endless variety
of fish, whilst you need not trouble yourself with dry
curry powder, all the ingredients of it grow here wild, and
you can have the genuine article by simply asking for
it.  You wish to drink?  Well, you can have spring water ;
but take care your lips don't touch that long bamboo in
which it is kept.  In order not to offend the delicacy of the
people, you must pour it out into your mouth ; and as I don't
think you could do that without spilling and wetting yourself
all over, you had better have a cocoa-nut or two.  The boys
have just brought in a great number, all tied in a bunch, and
already husked.  You can have your milk in all stages of
development, from the most insipid stage, tasting like *eau-
de-sucré* you get at a French or German restaurant, to those
of slightly acid by fermentation.  Every native has got a
stage of which he is particularly fond, and as all have different names, and are easily known by tapping the nut with
the fingers and listening to the sound, it is readily picked
out.  Ere long your taste will have fixed upon a particular
sort, and you will care little for any other.

Meal concluded, and the sun still high, let us take a stroll
through the town.  The youngest children will scream terribly
on seeing your white face ; but don't mind that.  We must
inspect the *bures*.  There are two kinds ; those in which the
men sleep (*Bure ni sa*), and those dedicated to the gods (*Bure
Kalou*).  The sleeping bures may aptly be compared to our
clubs.  There are several in the larger towns, and that
which the ruling chiefs frequent does not seem visited
much by the lower class of people.  There is one nearly a
hundred feet long, and forty broad.  All along the sides are
sleeping-places, covered with fine mats large enough for two
persons, and between each is a fire-place, and stages to put
the legs on.  Overhead a good supply of fire-wood is stored.
The centre of the building is covered with loose grass.  There
are no windows, only low doors, which may be closed by
means of thick mats.  A large kava-bowl, and bamboo
vessels filled with spring water, seem to be the only utensils

admitted. In buildings or bures like these, all the male population, married and unmarried, sleeps. The boys, until they have come of age, erect a bure of their own, often built on raised stages over the water, and approachable only by a long narrow trunk of a tree. The women and girls sleep at home, and it is quite against Fijian etiquette for a husband to take his night's repose anywhere except at one of the public bures of his town or village, though he will go to his family soon after dawn.

In the daytime the bures are generally deserted. Towards four o'clock people begin to pour in, and if any strangers arrive, they will invariably take up their quarters at these places. Here politics and all events of the day are discussed, and when talking, the men, even high chiefs, will be plaiting cocoa-nut fibre into *sinnet*, so much used in the construction of houses, canoes, and arms. And a great deal these people have to talk about. The politics of the groups, independent of the new element introduced by the cession of the country to England, and the never-ending intrigues of the Tonguese immigration, are rather complicated, and give rise to a good deal of discussion and speculation. Fiji is divided into a number of petty states, all of which acknowledge vassalage to Bau, by paying either a direct tribute to that state, or being tributary to other states which have to pay it. It seems highly probable, however, that at one time all Fijians were under one head, and formed a more compact nation than they do at present. Of course the title " *Tui Viti* " (or King of Fiji), has been revived only lately, owing, it is stated, to a letter which General Miller, formerly H.B.M. Consul-General at the Hawaiian or Sandwich Islands, addressed to " Tui Viti," and which Cakobau (or Thakombau), as the powerful chief of the leading state, thought it right to open. But the title, " Tui Viti," occurs in many ancient legends, current in various groups of Polynesia, and could scarcely have originated with such close neighbours, who would rather be apt to detract than to magnify the power of a foreign nation already far above them in the exercise of various useful arts and manufactures. Old traditions further state the Fijians to have been an unwarlike people, until they had established a more intimate and frequent intercourse with the light-coloured races of the eastern groups, when sanguinary intratribal quarrels became almost their normal condition. These traditions would be favourable to the existence of a powerful monarchy in Fiji, such as legendary evidence represents it as being at one time, and also its ultimate extinction by the growing power of petty chiefs, skilful in new practices of war acquired whilst abroad. The hypothesis advanced derives additional strength from the fact of all Fijians, though scattered over a group of two hundred and fifty different islands having a powerfully developed sense of nationality, and feeling as one people. No ancient Roman could have felt greater pride in pronouncing the words "*Romanus sum*," than a modern Fijian in informing you that he is a "*Kai Viti*" (a Fijian). We can scarcely conceive these general sentiments to have taken hold of the popular mind with such force, if the people had always been as divided, or spoken as many different dialects as at present.

Cakobau, or Thakombau, as his name may be written in English orthography, has been described repeatedly as a man of almost gigantic dimensions. But he is only of fair proportions, and does not measure more than six feet in height. I can speak very positively on this point, having often seen his majesty with nothing more than a few yards of native cloth on, as well as in a blue naval uniform. When dressed in uniform, people would scarcely believe him to be the same man whose powerful build excited their attention. When one day in his company, I got quite close to him, in order to take his measure without his becoming aware of the attempt. But his quick eye had detected the study of comparative anatomy in which I was engaged, and very good-naturedly he offered to stand close to me, when it was found that he was more than two inches shorter than I am, without his shoes and socks. I measure exactly six feet two inches, so that he is after all only six feet high. It is not difficult to reconcile the statement relating to his gigantic stature with what I have ascertained. People not accustomed to move much amongst natives almost in an absolute state of nudity, are generally deceived about the size of the person they see before them. Moreover, the king, previous to his conversion to Christianity, wore a large head of hair, all frizzled and curled in such a way as to stand literally at an end, and covered with a piece of white native cloth ; a device which must have greatly added to his height, and induced foreigners to believe him much taller than he really is. He has of late years suffered a little from elephantiasis, but generally enjoys very good health. None of the portraits that have been published do justice to him, and he feels rather annoyed that Europeans should think him as ugly as those representations make him. His face expresses great shrewdness and good-humour. His bearing is very dignified, especially on public occasions, and it was gratifying to see him at church behaving in a manner that no reasonable man could find the slightest fault with.

The Queen of Fiji, to whom Cakobau has been married according to Christian rites ever since he abandoned heathenism, is a rather stout quiet woman, about five feet two inches in height. I have only seen her once *dressed*, and that at the time of our first official interview about the cession. She then wore a neat bonnet, latest Parisian fashion, a coloured silk dress, and a black mantilla trimmed with lace. I need scarcely add that the use of crinoline was not unknown even in this remote quarter of the globe. The queen, at the interview alluded to, was rather bashful, owing to a wish expressed by the British Consul that she should sit at her husband's side, instead of, as the rules of the country demanded, behind him. However, she comported herself very well indeed, but, I daresay, was very glad to get her clothes off, as soon as the official interview was over.

Away from the capital, some of the Fijian chiefs talk very boastfully of their total independence, and wish you to believe the suzerainty of Bau merely applies to certain inferior chieftains; whilst the *social* supremacy of that state

is seldom disputed. The court-dialect is understood by all
the chiefs, even those living in the remotest parts of the
group, and has, therefore, very properly been adopted by
the Wesleyan missionaries in their translation of the
Bible. Each of these states or principalities has its ambassador at Bau (*Mataki Bau*), who, however, does not
constantly reside in the capital, but only when there is
any business to transact, which may occasionally last for
weeks or months. On arriving at Bau, he takes up his
abode at the house of the Bauan "minister," if he may
be called so, charged with the affairs of the district from
which he comes as ambassador, and he is by his host
introduced to the king of Fiji. When Bau has any business to transact abroad, the ambassador selected is invariably
the minister of the affairs of the district to which he
is sent, and his place at the capital is temporarily filled
by a relative. The office of these diplomatic agents is
hereditary in certain families, and they are appointed by the
ruling chiefs. Title and office are quite as much valued as
they are in Europe by ourselves—human nature being human
nature all the world over.

Evening is coming on, the bure is beginning to fill, most of
the fires between the sleeping-places are lit, and the natives
are leisurely stretched on the mats, their legs cocked up on the
stages, like Yankees in a tavern—all smoking their cigarettos
made of self-grown tobacco and dry banana-leaves. Here
come the kava-chewers, two comely-looking youngsters, carrying the large wooden bowl, a cocoa-nut shell for drinking the
beverage, the bamboo water-vessel, a handful of fibre for
straining the kava, and the root of the South-Sea pepper, from
which it is prepared. No sooner have they taken their seat
and began chewing, taking care to throw the rope affixed to
the kava-bowl toward the person highest in rank, than a
leading man, perhaps a heathen priest, begins chanting a song,
in which the whole assembly joins, and two young fellows
beat time with little sticks, applied on a bamboo or any other
sounding wood that happens to be handy. The leader of

the chant does not sit motionless, but waves his body, arms, and hands in such a variety of ways, and with such extreme ease, that you fancy you can imitate him as readily as the whole assembly. But the very first time you fail, to the great delight of your native spectators. The motions which he makes are not difficult, but you never know what they are going to be until it is too late to imitate, and he has already passed on to something else. The interest of this by-play is thus well kept up, and the Fijians deserve full credit of having obtained hold of one of the great secrets of fixing the attention on an object, or making it, in other words interesting. They know the art of concealing the end as long as possible. What would our novelists do without the use of this machinery! How dull would life itself be if the future was unveiled to us!

The lads have by this time chewed a sufficient quantity of the root, and placed the masticated mass into the bowl; now water is poured on, the whole yellowish-looking fluid strained through fibres, and a cup filled. Whilst the cup-bearer is holding it to hand to the chief or highest personage present, an old man gives the toast of the evening. It is pathetic or humorous as occasion demands, and listened to with attention, all singing and beating with sticks having ceased the moment the cup was filled. A general shout follows the conclusion of this toast, the cup is emptied in one draft, and thrown by the drinker on the mat, to be filled again and handed to the next in rank, until the whole assembly has been served.

The song becomes less and less hearty, the conversation slackens, and one by one the men drop off to sleep. Strange sight! Their pillows are made of a thick stick, have four legs, and are put just under the neck, so that the hair of the sleepers may not be deranged. They have had it only recently newly done up, washed with lime to make it frizzed like that of negroes, dyed in various colours, and arranged in many different ways. Several days must have been spent to get some of these extraordinary heads dressed. And for

this reason—no other—they are ready to sleep all their lives
on a pillow made of a stick of wood, and so constructed that
a European could not rest his neck five minutes upon it
without suffering dreadful pain.  It is very fine talking about
the ease of living in a state of nature, but the inconveniences
to which savages put themselves in order to gratify their
vanity are quite as great, if not greater, than those forced
upon us by our fashions and dictates of our own society.
Think of the agonies of tatooing!  What would the natives
give to escape it, if society would let them?  But there
is no escape.  The stern laws of fashion allow of no exception.  In Fiji this practice is confined to the women, the
operation being performed by members of their own sex, and
applied solely to the corners of the mouth, and those parts
of the body covered by the scanty clothing worn by them.
The skin is punctured by an instrument made of bone, or by
the spines of the shaddock-tree, whilst the dye injected into
the punctures is obtained chiefly from the candle-nut.  No
reason is given for the adoption of the custom, beyond its
being commanded by Degei, their supreme god.  Neglect of
this divine commandment is believed to be punished after
death.  The men, probably, refrain from tatooing, because
their skin, generally speaking, is so dark that the designs
would not be seen, and the painful operation undergone
would be mere labour thrown away.  In Polynesia the
practice seems to have attained its culminating point in the
Society Islands, and the Marquesas, where both men and
women submitted to it; proceeding thence eastward to
Samoa and Tonga, we find it restricted to the men; in Fiji
to the women, and altogether ceasing in the New Hebrides.
Yet, strange to add, tradition asserts that the custom was
known in Fiji before its being adopted in Samoa or Tonga.
Two goddesses, Taema and Tilafainga, swam from Fiji to
Samoa, and on reaching the latter group, commenced singing,
" Tatoo the men, but not the women."*  Hence, the two were
worshipped as the presiding deities by those who followed

* Turner's " Nineteen Years in Polynesia," p. 112.

tatooing as a trade ; for a trade it was and is, quite as much as tailoring is in our own country, and requiring, by far, greater care and caution.  The blue tracery once made, cannot, like a coat or pair of trousers, be thrown aside when spoilt in the cut, but has to be worn for life, exposed to all the remarks which good and ill-natured friends may be disposed to make.  A tradition, current in Tonga and Fiji, corroborates the fact of tatooing having been derived from the latter group.  It is stated, that at a remote period the king of Tonga (Tui Toga) sent a mission to Fiji, in order to ascertain whether, as had been reported, the women of these islands were tatooed.  On reaching the island of Ogea, in the eastern part of Fiji, the mission, with some difficulty, made the natives comprehend that they wished to find out what sex was tatooed (qia) ; to which the Fijians replied, " Qia na alewa " (women are tatooed).  In obedience to orders, the first person met had been asked, and as a plain answer to a plain question had been obtained, the mission departed homewards.  There were no other means of remembering the answer than by repeating it continually.  This was done without interruption, until their canoe reached the Ogea passage ; where, the sea becoming rough, apprehensions about the safety of the canoe began to be entertained, and in the ensuing excitement the repetition of the precious words was neglected.  Suddenly the neglect was perceived, and it was asked all round what the words were.  Somebody replied, " Qia na tagane " (men are tatooed), instead of " Qia na alewa " (women are tatooed), which mistake, passing unnoticed, was repeated until the crew reached Tonga ; and on being reported to the king, he exclaimed, " Oh, it is men, not women, that are tatooed ! well, then, I will be tatooed at once."  The example set was speedily followed ; hence the custom, that in Fiji the women, in Tonga the men are tatooed ; hence, also, adds the tradition, the name of the Ogea passage, " Qia na tagane."*

* Another version of the tradition is given by Williams, " Fiji and Fijians," vol. i. p. 160, where a man, repeating the intelligence, violently strikes his foot against a stump of a tree, and in the confusion ensuing changes its tenor.

If you look into that corner, you will see an old man, who is telling one of the innumerable stories current in the islands, in which the people may be said to photograph themselves, and which no traveller worthy of the name should neglect to write down. He does it in a business-like way, because those crowded around him are going to pay him handsomely for his trouble. He may get a couple of fat pigs, a supply of kava-root, a few bales of bark-cloth, or a quantity of yams, but of his pay he is more certain than many a poor author with us. The story is a long one, and takes hours in telling ; and, as several of his hearers have listened to it more than once, no poetical licence can be taken with it, and all must be narrated as tradition has handed it down. Well, you may as well hear it, and be content when, in translating, I simply give you the pith of the whole, leaving out those details which, without ample explanation, would be quite unintelligible :—

" Once upon a time there dwelt at Rewa a powerful god, whose name was Ravovonicakaugawa,* and along with him his friend the God of the Winds, from Wairua.† Ravovonica-kaugawa was leading a solitary life, and had long been think-ing of taking a wife to himself. At last his mind seemed to be made up. 'Put mast and sail in the canoe,' he said, ' and let us take some women from Rokoua, the God of Naicobocobo.'‡ 'When do you think of starting ?' inquired his friend. ' I shall go in broad daylight,' was the reply, ' or do you think I am a coward to choose the night for my work ?' All things being ready, the two friends set sail, and anchored towards

* Ravovonicakaugawa—" A long way off."

† This god was and is supposed to reside at a little brook in the lovely valley of Namosi, on Viti Levu, pointed out to us when we visited the interior of that island in September, 1860. When the Rewa people come to the Namosi valley, they never fail to make sacrificial offerings at Wairua (which is both the name of the locality and its god). Even some of those that have become Christians continue this practice.

‡ Naicobocobo, the west end of Vanua Levu, and the supposed starting-place of departed spirits for *Bulu*, the abode of life hereafter.

sunset off Naicobocobo. There they waited one, two, three days, without, contrary to Fijian customs, any friendly communication from the shore reaching them, for Rokoua, probably guessing their intentions, had strictly forbidden his people to take any food to the canoe. Rokoua's repugnance, however, was not shared by his household. His daughter, the lovely Naiogabui,* who diffused so sweet and powerful a perfume, that if the wind blew from the east, the perfume could be perceived in the west, and if it blew from the west, it could be perceived in the east—in consequence of which, and on account of her great personal beauty, all the young men fell in love with her. Naiogabui ordered one of her female slaves to cook a yam, and take it to the foreign canoe, and at the same time inform its owner that she would be with him at the first opportunity. To give a further proof of her affection, she ordered all the women in Naicobocobo to have a day's fishing. This order having been promptly executed, and the fish cooked, Naiogabui herself swam off with it during the night, and presented it to the Rewa God.

"Ravovonicakaugawa was charmed with the princess, and ready to start with her at once. She, however, begged him to wait another night, to enable Naimilamila, one of Rokoua's young wives, to accompany them. Naimilamila was a native of Naicobocobo, and against her will united to Rokoua, who had no affection whatever for her, and kept her exclusively to scratch his head or play with his locks, hence her name. Dissatisfied with her sad lot, she had concocted a plan for escape with her step-daughter, and was making active preparations to carry it into execution. On the night agreed upon, Naimilamila was true to her engagement. 'Who are you?' asked the god as she stepped on the deck. 'I am Rokoua's wife,' she rejoined, 'get your canoe under weigh. My lord may follow closely on my heels, and Naiogabui will be with us immediately.' Almost directly after a splash in the water was heard. 'There she comes,' cried Naimilamila,

---

* Naiogabui—" that which smells sweetly."

'make sail;' and instantly the canoe, with Ravovonicakaugawa,
his friend, and the two women, departed for Rewa.

"Next morning, when Rokoua discovered the elopement,
he determined to pursue the fugitives, and for that purpose
embarked in the 'Vatutulali,' a canoe deriving its name from
his large drum, the sound of which was so powerful that it
could be heard all over Fiji. His club and spear were put on
board, both of which were of such gigantic dimensions and
weight, that it took ten men to lift either of them. Rokoua
soon reached Nukuilailai, where he took the spear out,
and making a kind of bridge of it, walked over it on shore.
Taking spear and club in his hand, he musingly walked
along. 'It will never do to be at once discovered,' he said to
himself; 'I must disguise myself. But what shape shall I
assume? That of a hog or a dog? As a hog, I should not
be allowed to come near the door; and, as a dog, I should
have to fetch the bones thrown outside. Neither will answer
my purpose. I shall, therefore, assume the shape of a woman.'
Continuing his walk along the beach, he met an old woman,
carrying a basket of taro and puddings, all ready cooked,
and, without letting her be at all aware of it, he exchanged
figures with her. He then inquired whither she was going,
and, being informed to the house of the God of Rewa, he
took the basket from her, and, leaving club and spear on the
beach, proceeded to his destination. His disguise was so
complete, that even his own daughter did not recognise him.
'Who is that?' she asked, as he was about to enter. 'It is I,'
replied Rokoua, in a feigned voice; 'I have come from
Monisa with food.' 'Come in, old lady,' said Naiogabui, 'and
sit down.' Rokoua accordingly entered, and took care to sit
like a Fijian woman would do, so that his disguise might not
be discovered. 'Are you going back to-night?' he was asked.
'No,' the disguised god replied; 'there is no occasion for
that.' Finding it very close in the house, Rokoua proposed
a walk and a bath, to which both Naiogabui and Naimilamila agreed. When getting the women to that spot of the
beach where club and spear had been left, he threw off his

disguise, and exclaimed, 'You little knew who I was; I am Rokoua, your lord and master,' and, at the same time taking hold of their hands, he dragged the runaways to the canoe, and immediately departed homewards.

"When the Rewa God found his women gone, he again started for Naicobocobo, where, as he wore no disguise, he was instantly recognised, his canoe taken and dragged on shore by Rokoua's men, while he himself and his faithful friend, who again accompanied him, were seized and made pig-drivers. They were kept in this degrading position a long time, until a great festival took place in Vanua Levu, which Rokoua and his party attended. Arrived at the destination, the Rewa God and his friend were left in charge of the two canoes that had carried the party thither, whilst all the others went on shore to enjoy themselves; but as both friends were liked by all the women, they were kept amply supplied with food and other good things during the festival. Nevertheless Ravovonicakaugawa was very much cast down, and taking a kava-root (Yaqona), he offered it as a sacrifice, and despairingly exclaimed, 'Have none of the mighty gods of Rewa pity on my misfortune?' His friend's body became instantly possessed by a god, and began to tremble violently. 'What do you want?' asked the god within. 'A gale to frighten my oppressors out of their wits.' 'It shall be granted,' replied the god, and departed.

" The festival being over, Rokoua's party embarked for Naicobocobo. But it had hardly set sail when a strong northerly gale sprang up, which nearly destroyed the canoes, and terribly frightened those on board. Still they reached Naicobocobo, where the Rewa God prayed for an easterly wind to carry him home. All Rokoua's men having landed, and left the women behind to carry the luggage and goods on shore, the desired wind sprang up, and the two canoes, with sails set, started for Rewa, where they safely arrived, and the goods and other property were landed and distributed as presents among the people.

"But Rokoua was not to be beaten thus. Although his

two canoes had been taken, there was still the one captured from Ravovonicakaugawa on his second visit to
Naicobocobo. That was launched without delay, and the
fugitives pursued. Arriving at Nukuilailai, Rokoua laid
his spear on the deck of the canoe and walked over it on
shore, as he had done on a previous occasion. Landed,
he dropped his heavy club, thereby causing so loud a
noise that it woke all the people on Viti Levu. This noise
did not escape the quick ears of Naimilamila. 'Be on your
guard,' she said to her new lord, 'Rokoua is coming; I heard
his club fall; he can assume any shape he pleases; be a dog,
or a pig, or a woman; he can command even solid rocks to
split open and admit him, so be on your guard.' Rokoua
meanwhile met a young girl from Nadoi on the road, carrying
shrimps, landcrabs, and taro to the house of the God of Rewa,
and without hesitation he assumed her shape, and she took
his without being herself aware of it. Arriving with his
basket at his destination, Naiogabui asked, Who is there? To
which Rokoua replied, 'It is me; I am from Nadoi, bringing
food for your husband.' The supposed messenger was asked
into the house, and sitting down, he imprudently assumed a
position not proper to Fijian women. This, and the shape of his
limbs, was noticed by Naiogabui, who whispered the discovery
made into her husband's ear. Ravovonicakaugawa stole out
of the house, assembled his people, recalled to their minds
the indignities heaped upon him by Rokoua, and having
worked them up to a high pitch of excitement, he informed
them that the offender was now in their power. All rushed
to arms, and entering the house they demanded the young
girl from Nadoi. 'There she sits,' replied Naiogabui, pointing
to her father, and no sooner had the words been spoken, than
a heavy blow with a club felled Rokoua to the ground. A
general onset followed, in which the head of the victim was
beaten to atoms. This was the end of Rokoua."

This story finished, all the natives retire to sleep, and we
ourselves must now creep under the large mosquito-curtain
provided for us. It consists of native cloth, made of the bark

of the paper-mulberry by the women, and must have taken
many days and weeks to complete.  Observe, it is thirty feet
long, and ornamented all over with many choice patterns and
colours, all *printed* on it; aye printed—for the Fijians, long
previous to their intercourse with Europeans, perfectly well
understood that art.  They did not print books certainly,
but they had got hold of the principle it involves, and may
fairly claim, with the Chinese, Dutch, and Germans, the
honour of the invention.  Be careful in entering the screen
not to lift it up too high, or more than you can help.
The mosquitoes will get in, and their sting to new-comers
is so irritating, that it will keep them awake the greater
part of the night.  They do not seem to care for people
who have been in the tropics any length of time, or rather
Europeans so circumstanced do not seem to be affected by
the bites very much.  The air is rather confined under
these screens; yet you will not find it too warm, as you
have to lay down on the mats, dispense with blankets,
and use for your pillow a stone or piece of wood, covered
with the coat taken of your back.  If you wish to travel
in Fiji, you must learn to "rough it," and not lose your
temper.  There are only four men more to sleep under
this screen, so there will be plenty of room for all, and some
to spare for kicking.

Morn commenced, we must take a look at the outside of
the strange building in which we have passed the night.
You see these savages have some taste.  They have made a
nice green lawn around it, and planted a number of what our
gardeners term leaf-plants—shrubs and herbs distinguished
for their gay-coloured or variously-shaped foliage.  This
phyllomania, as I call it, is a predilection they share not only
with Europeans, but also with the Chinese and the Japanese.
There are besides a few kava-shrubs, of the root of which you
saw them make that yellow-looking beverage last night, and
on the preparation of which the boys are again engaged this
morning.  Those trees so frequently seen about the Fijian
bures, are "Tavolas," known to botanists by the name of

*Terminalia Catappa.* The horizontal growth of their branches, and the great change of colour which their foliage undergoes, very much like that of a North American forest in the autumn, is given as the reason for this predilection. The long rows of erect stones encircling the building have a more ominous meaning. Every one of them, and you may count several hundred, denotes a human body eaten on the premises, and the largest stones represent the bodies of chiefs. A little further off you see the ovens in which dead men are baked, and those bones suspended in the trees overgrown with ferns, are those of human victims. All this, and even the vegetables eaten with human flesh, it may be ethnologically important to notice, since—thanks to the influence of commerce, Christian teaching, and the presence of a British Consul!—cannabalism survives only in a few localities, and is daily becoming more and more a matter of history. Human flesh, Fijians have repeatedly assured me, is extremely difficult to digest; and even the healthiest suffer from confined bowels for two or three days after partaking of it. Probably, in order to assist the process of digestion, *Bokola*, as dead man's flesh is technically termed, is always eaten with an addition of vegetables. There are principally three kinds, which, in Fijian estimation, ought to accompany bokola—the leaves of the Malawaci (*Trophis anthropophagorum*, Seem.), the Tudano (*Omalanthus pedicellatus*, Bth), and the Boro dina (*Solanum anthropophagorum*, Seem.). The two former are middle-sized trees, growing wild in many parts of the group, but the Boro dina is cultivated, and there are generally several large bushes of it near every *bure ni sa* (or stranger's house), where the bodies are always taken. The Boro dina is a bushy shrub, seldom higher than six feet, with a dark, glossy foliage, and berries of the shape and colour of tomatoes. This fruit has a faint aromatic smell, and is occasionally prepared like tomato-sauce. The leaves of these three plants are wrapped around the bokola, as those of the taro are around pork, and baked with it on heated stones. Salt is not forgotten; for

the Fijians, unlike most South-Sea Islanders, were familiar
with the use and preparation of salt long before their intercourse with Europeans. Whilst every other kind of vegetable and meat is eaten with the fingers, cannibal food is
touched only with forks, generally made of the wood of the
Nokonoko (*Casuarina equisetifolia*, Forst.), or the Vesi (*Afzelia bijuga*, A. Gray), bearing curious, often obscene names,
and having three or four long prongs. The reason given for
this deviation from the general mode of eating is a widely
spread belief, that fingers which have touched bokola are
apt to generate cutaneous diseases when coming in contact
with the tender skin of children; and as the Fijians are
very fond of their offspring, they are most scrupulous in using
forks on the above occasions.

Besides these three plants, some kinds of yams and taro
are deemed fit accompaniments at a dish of bokola. The yams
are hung up in the bure ni sa for a certain time, having previously been covered with turmeric, to preserve them, it
would seem, from rapid decay—our own sailors effecting the
same end by whitewashing the yams when taking them
on board. A peculiar kind of taro (*Caladium esculentum*,
Schott. var.), called *Kurilagi*, was pointed out as having
been eaten with a whole tribe of people. The story sounds
strange, but as a number of natives were present when it
was told, several of whom corroborated the various statements, or corrected the proper names that occurred, its truth
appears unimpeachable. In the centre of Viti Levu, about
three miles N.N.E. from Namosi, there dwelt a tribe, known
by the name of Kai na loca, who in days of yore gave great
offence to the ruling chief of the Namosi district, and, as
a punishment of their misdeeds, the whole tribe was condemned to die. Every year the inmates of *one* house were
baked and eaten, fire was set to the empty dwelling, and
its foundation planted with kurilagi. In the following year,
as soon as this taro was ripe, it became the signal for the
destruction of the next house and its inhabitants, and the
planting of a fresh field of taro. Thus house after house,

family after family, disappeared, until Rutuibuna, the father
of the present chief, Kuruduadua, pardoned the remaining
few, and allowed them to die a natural death. In 1860,
only one old woman, living at Cagina, was the sole survivor of
the Na loca people. Picture the feelings of these unfortunate
wretches, as they watched the growth of the ominous taro!
Throughout the dominions of the powerful chief whose
authority they had insulted, their lives were forfeited, and to
escape into territories where they were strangers would, in
those days, only have been to hasten the awful doom awaiting
them in their own country. Nothing remained save to watch,
watch, watch, the rapid development of the kurilagi. As leaf
after leaf unfolded, the tubers increased in size and substance,
how their hearts must have trembled, their courage forsaken
them! and when at last the foliage began to turn yellow, the
taro was ripe, what agonies they must have undergone! what
torture could have equalled theirs?

We must now take a look at the *bure kalou*, or temple.
All Fijian temples have a pyramidal form, and are often
erected on terraced mounds; in this respect reminding us
of the ancient Central American structures. We meet the
same terraced mounds also in Eastern Polynesia, with which
Fiji, and all other groups of the South Sea, shares the
principal features of its religious belief. The supreme
god in Fiji is Degei (pronounced Ndengei), known in the
other groups as Tanga-roa, or Taa-roa, Tanga being his proper
name, "roa" an adjective, signifying "the far removed,"
perhaps, also, the "most high." To him is attributed the
creation and government of the world ; and there are no images
of him, nor of any of the minor gods, collectively termed
"kalou." His sway is universally acknowledged by the
natives, and no attempts are ever made to elevate any local
gods above him. The inside of the temples is scarcely worth
looking at. There is in most of them a shrine where the god
is supposed to descend when holding communication with
the priests, and there is also a long piece of native cloth
hung at one end of the building, and from the very ceiling,

which is also connected with the arrival of the god invoked. The revelations, however, are made by means of the spirit of the god entering the body of the priest, who, having become possessed, begins to tremble most violently ; and in this excited state utters disjointed sentences, supposed to be the revelations which the god wishes to make by the mouth of his servant. It is the oracle at Delphi over again. Mankind will be deceived, whether by a Fijian priest, a Phythia, or an American spirit-rapper.

The conceptions which the Fijians have of the origin of their islands is, that they were made and peopled by Degei. This god, when walking along the beaches, wore long trains of native cloth, like great chiefs do at the present day ; and whenever he allowed them to drag the ground, the beach, becoming free from vegetation, showed the white sand ; whenever he took them up, the trees and shrubs remained undisturbed. Degei was roused every morning by the cooing of a monstrous bird, called "Tarukawa," who performed his duty well until two youths accidentally killed it with bow and arrow, and, in order to conceal their deed, buried it. Degei, fond of being roused at sunrise by his favourite bird, was greatly annoyed on finding him disappeared, and he at once despatched his messenger, Uto, to go all over the island in search of it ; but all endeavours to discover any traces of the lost one proved unsuccessful. The messenger declared that it could nowhere be found. Degei, had a fresh search instituted, which led to the discovery of the body of the dead bird, and that of the deed which had deprived him of life. The two youths, fearing Degei's anger, fled to the mountains to take refuge with a powerful tribe of carpenters, who willingly agreed to build a fence strong enough to keep Degei and his messengers at bay. They little knew the power they had attempted to baulk. Degei caused violent rains to fall, and the waters rose to such a height, that at last they reached the place where the two youths and their abettors had fortified themselves. To save themselves from drowning, they jumped into large bowls that happened to be at hand, and

in these they were scattered in various directions.   When
the waters subsided, some landed at Suva, some at Navua;
and it is from these people that the present race of carpenters
and canoe-builders claim to be descended.   The story is silent
about the fate of the two youths who provoked Degei's anger,
and it appears to have been after this time that Degei turned
himself into a serpent, the world-wide symbol of eternity, and
lay coiled up in a cave of a mountain, indicating his turning
about by occasional shocks of earthquake felt all over Fiji.
The mountain is on the Rakiraki coast of Viti Levu, and
called " Na Vatu " (*i. e.* the stone).

One of the most universal beliefs of all mankind is, doubtless, that in the aid or protection departed ancestors are able
to afford.   All nations participate in it more or less, and even
Christianity has not been able to uproot an idea which Poetry
and Art have rivalled to perpetuate.  What educated man could
be so cruel as to wish to prove to an orphan child, left alone
in the wide world, that, according to strict orthodoxy, the spirit
of its mother could not possibly watch over it, because the
lost one would quietly slumber in her grave till the great day
of judgment?   The Chinese, Japanese, South African tribes,
and Polynesians, do not clothe their ideas in so poetical a
garb, or banish admiration for the mighty deeds of their
ancestors from the region of religious sentiment.   They
supplicate their formidable shades when misfortune befalls
them, or fear of the future takes possession of their minds.
With the Fijians, as soon as beloved parents expire, they
take their place amongst the family gods.   " Bures " or
temples are erected to their memory, and offerings deposited
either on their graves or on rudely constructed altars—
mere stages in the form of tables, the legs of which are
driven in the ground, and the top of which is covered with
pieces of native cloth.   The construction of these altars
is identical with that observed by Turner in Tanna, and
only differs in its inferior finish from the altars formerly
erected in Tahiti and the adjacent islands.   The offerings,
consisting of the choicest articles of food, are left exposed to

wind and weather, and firmly believed by the mass of Fijians
to be consumed by the spirits of departed friends and
relations; but, if not eaten by animals, they are often
stolen by the more enlightened class of their countrymen,
and even some of the foreigners do not disdain occasionally to help themselves freely to them. However, it is
not only on tombs or on altars that offerings are made.
Often, when the natives eat or drink anything, they throw
portions of it away, stating them to be for their departed
ancestors. I remember ordering a young chief to empty a
bowl containing kava, which he did, muttering to himself,
"There, father, is some kava for you. Protect me from illness
or breaking any of my limbs whilst in the mountains."

The Fijians fully believe in a life hereafter, and the souls
are supposed to take their departure from the extreme west
point of the island of Vanua Levu. It is from this conviction
that on the death of a man, be he chief or commoner, all his
wives are strangled, so that he may not have to go alone on
his journey, or arrive at the future abode of bliss without
anybody near and dear about him. Only in the Christianized
districts has this cruel custom been abolished. At Mua i
Vudu, as the eastern extremity of Vanua Levu is termed,
there stood, until lately, an old screw-pine, to which a strange
superstition attached. A man who could hit any part of this
tree between the root and the crown with a stone, made sure
that at his death all his wives would be strangled. Ratu
Mara, a chief well known in the annals of Fiji as a frequent
disturber of the public peace, vainly tried to hit the tree.
Enraged at his continued failures, he cut it down. But what
use is it to wrangle with fate? Ratu Mara ended his restless
career at Bau, where, for repeated treacheries, the king
thought fit to hang him, and all his wives escaped the fearful doom of strangulation.

Sacred groves and trees form as prominent a feature in the
paganism of the Fijians as they did in that of the Indo-
Germanic nations. Several celebrated groves were destroyed
on the introduction of Christianity, and a large one, near Bau,

was felled the day after King Cakobau had embraced the new faith, the native carpenters trembling when they had to lay the axe on objects so long sacred to them by all the laws of "*taboo*." A fine grove of this kind still exists in the Rewa district, near the Mission Station of Mataisuva, and at a point of the coast termed Na Vadra Tolu (the three Screw-pines), probably from three specimens of the *Pandanus odoratissimus*, still a common plant in that locality, having stood there. Leaving the Mission premises, and keeping along the sandy beach, an enormous Yevuyevu tree (*Hernandia Sonora*, Linn.) presents itself, forming a complete bower, which leads to a curious group of vegetable giants. A venerable Vutu rakaraka (*Barringtonia speciosa*, Linn.), more than sixty feet high, has thrown out several huge branches, two of which form, in connexion with the stem, bold arches. The large aërial roots of epiphytical fig-trees are holding this monster in close embrace. Several kinds of fern, and climbing *Aroideæ* and wax-flowers interlace the straggling masses, and tend to increase the wildness of this fantastic scene. The dense foliage of surrounding Vesi, Ivi, and other fine trees, insures a constant gloom and sombreness to the place, and only through the bower, serving for an entrance, does the eye obtain a glance at the open sea, and perchance the sight of a passing canoe, with its large triangular sail. It was at this lonely spot, far away from human habitations, where, in the depth of night, the heathen priest used to consult the gods whether it was to be war or peace. If at dawn of day blood was found on the path, more blood was to be spilt; if no such sign was discoverable, peace was the watchword.

Besides these groves there were isolated trees, which were held sacred, and in days of yore European sawyers came occasionally in unpleasant contact with the natives, when, unknowingly, they had cut them down for timber. Vesi (*Afzelia bijuga*, A. Gray) and Baka (*Ficus*) seemed to have been those principally selected. The Vesi furnishes the best timber of the islands, and may, as the most valued tree, have been thought the fit residence of a god, as there is nothing in its appearance that is extraordinary, our beech most nearly resembling it in look. The Baka is not famous for its timber, but its habit is as remarkable as that of the banyan-tree of India, aërial roots propping up its branches and forming a fantastic maze, which no words can describe. At first living as an epiphyte on other trees, it soon acquires such dimensions, that, as in the fable of the Goose with the golden eggs, it kills its benefactor, and henceforward must draw its nourishment from the soil. There are fine specimens of the Baka on the Isthmus of Kadava, and on an islet belonging to Mr. Hennigs. The aërial root of the latter form a cabin, in which Mr. Pritchard, myself, and all our boat's crew, took shelter during a heavy tropical shower ; and twenty persons might have found room there. The crown of this tree was 152 feet in diameter, or 456 feet in circumference. The horizontal branches, and the large roots issuing from all parts of the stem, and more sparingly from the branches, rendered this tree a noble object, well calculated to inspire pleasure or awe. The Rev. W. Moore lamented the destruction of one of these fine trees near Rewa, committed by a sick man, in hopes that it might be pleasing to the Christian God and incline him to favour his convalescence. These sacred' groves and trees were not worshipped as gods, but as in the Odin religion of our ancestors, looked upon as places where certain gods had taken up their abode.

Sacred stones, to which the natives pay reverence, exist in Fiji ; for instance, near Vuna and Bau, as well as in many other parts of Polynesia. Fully granting their being the supposed abode of certain gods and goddesses, as has been contended, we can only hope to arrive at their real meaning and primary origin, by considering them in connexion with the ideas associated with, or represented by other monoliths. I would particularly direct attention to their peculiar shape, of which the missionaries Williams * and Turner † have published some good illustrations. Compared with certain

* Williams's "Fiji and Fijians," p. 220.
† Turner's "Nineteen Years in Polynesia," p. 347.

remnants of Priapus worship, as found at Indian temples, the Museo segreto of Naples, and in the obelisks of Egypt, their nature becomes evident. More or less the object of these monoliths was to represent the generative principle ; and, if the subject were one that admitted of popular treatment, it would not be difficult to show that the Polynesian stones, their shape, the reverence paid to them, their decoration, and the results expected from this worship, are quite in accordance with a widely-spread superstition, which assumed such offensive forms in ancient Rome, and found vent in the noblest monuments of which the land of the Pharaohs can boast. Turner, after stating that he had in his possession several smooth stones from the New Hebrides, says that some of the Polynesian stone-gods were supposed to cause fecundity in pigs, rain, and sunshine. A stone at Mayo, according to the Earl of Roden, was carefully wrapped up in flannel, periodically worshipped, and supplicated to send wrecks on the coast. Two large stones, lying at the bottom of a moat, are said to have given birth to Degei, the supreme god of Fiji. In all instances, an addition to objects already existing was expected from these monoliths. There was a stone near Bau, which, whenever a lady of rank at Fiji capital was confined, also gave birth to a little stone. It argues nothing that these stony offsprings were fraudulently placed there. The ideas floating in the minds of the bulk of the people absolutely tended towards the unbiassed conviction that some mysterious connexion existed between the larger stones and the Bauan ladies. Since the introduction of Christianity to these districts, it has been found necessary to remove the large stone, leaving its numerous posterity behind to get on as best it may.

In order to uphold the whole fabric of heathen superstition, the priests had recourse to the same means which all religions have had in dealing with doubting minds. Punishment was sure to overtake the sceptic, let his station in life be what it might. What could be more terrible than that which was inflicted upon Koroika? He, a chief high in rank at Bau, made bold to doubt the existence of the god Ratumaibulu ; and, as the god was then enshrined in a serpent of a neighbouring cave, he determined to put the question to the test. Embarking in a canoe, with a cargo of fish, he steered for the very spot where the god was reported to be. On arriving, a serpent issued from the cave ; and the chief asked, " Please, good sir, are you the god Ratumaibulu ? " " No, I am not," was the reply ; " I am his son." The chief made him a present of fish, and requested an interview with his father. Presently another serpent appeared, but that proved to be the grandson, and the same present and request were made to him as had been made to the son. At length there issued a serpent, so large, so noble and commanding, as to leave little doubt in the mind of the chief that the god himself was now before him. Fish was presented to him ; and just as the god was retiring with it to his cave, Koroika hit him with an arrow, and then retreated in all possible haste. But the voice of the god followed him, exclaiming, "Nought but serpents !—nought but serpents ! " Arrived at home, and scarcely recovered from his state of agitation, he ordered dinner to be brought. The cover was removed from the pot, when, oh ! horror, it was full of serpents ! The chief seized a jug of water, saying, "At any rate, I will drink." But, instead of the limpid fluid, he poured out crawling serpents. Unable to eat or drink, he sought comfort in sleep. He unrolled his mat, and was in the act of laying down upon it, when innumerable serpents appeared. Mad with excitement, he rushes out of doors, and, passing a temple, hears, to his dismay, a priest revealing that the god has been wounded by the hand of a citizen, and that punishment will overtake the city. There is now no escape but to make a suitable atonement for the terrible offence committed. He returns home, collects all the valuables he can lay his hands on, presents them to the god, is pardoned, and his name handed down to unborn generations as a sceptic, and a fit example of the danger to which all men of his disposition expose themselves.*

* Compare Waterhouse, " Vah-ta-ah," p. 46.

We have now seen the ins and outs of a Fijian town.
Finally, let us visit that lonely hut erected on the very outskirts.  You hear the shrieks proceeding from it?  They are
curing a man of leprosy, by burning the poisonous sinu-wood,
the smoke of which, when entering the eyes, causes as great a
pain as that of the manchineal-tree of America, to which the
sinu is otherwise closely related.  It is an awful process to
undergo, and one which our medical men at home would consider of doubtful benefit.  Nevertheless, many Fijians submit to
it.  Mr. Moore, of Rewa, a worthy missionary, gave me full
particulars of a young man, named Wiliami Lawaleou.  After
stating that he knew Wiliami as a fine, healthy lad, Mr.
Moore was surprised to find him one day so much altered by
the effects of leprosy.  Some time after he again met him
full of health, and, on inquiry, learnt the treatment adopted
to bring about this change.  Taken to a small empty house,
the leper is stripped of every particle of clothing, his body
rubbed all over with green leaves, and then buried in them.
A small fire is then kindled, and a few pieces of the poison-
sinu laid on it.  As soon as the thick black smoke begins to
ascend, the leper is bound hand and foot, a rope fastened to
his heels, by means of which he is drawn up over the fire, so
that his head is some fifteen inches from the ground, in the
midst of the poisonous smoke.  The door is then closed, and
his friends retire a little distance, whilst the poor sufferer
is left to cry, and shout, and plead from the midst of the
suffocating stream ; but he is often allowed to remain for
hours, and finally faints away.  When he is thought sufficiently smoked, the fire is removed, the slime scraped from
the body, and deep gashes cut into the skin, until the blood
flows freely.  The leper is now taken down, and laid on his
mat to await the result—in some cases death, in many life
and health.  Wiliami had undergone this fearful process.
He had taken some of the youths of the place, and, on the
way to the smoking house, told them his pitiable condition,
his shame as an outcast, his willingness to suffer anything to obtain a cure, and much would depend on their

firmness.  They were not to be moved by his groans and cries ; and, for the love they bore him, he begged them to do the operation well, and threatened to punish them if they performed it only half.  Imagine the scene !  They proceed to the lonely house.  Wiliami's companions, as much afraid of overdoing as underdoing their sad task, leave the poor leper drawn up by his heels in the midst of a thick black smoke ; they retire to some distance, and presently are horrified by his piteous cries and groans.  Some weep, some run home, others rush into the smoking-house to take him down ; but, with Spartan-like endurance, he commands them not to terminate his suffering until the process is complete.  At last they take him down.  He is faint and exhausted.  The operation has been successful.  Wiliami is no longer a leper, but again walks God's earth a healthy man.

For fear that I may be accused of drawing mere fancy pictures of Fiji and its inhabitants, I must give an outline of some of my actual proceedings in the group.  First, I should state what brought me there.  In 1859, Mr. W. T. Pritchard, son of the Rev. George Pritchard, formerly British Consul at Tahiti at the time of the French troubles, came to England in order to communicate to Her Majesty's Government, that Cakobau (= Thakombau), king of Fiji, had ceded the whole group over which his sway extended, a country about as large as Wales, or eight times that of the Ionian Islands, to the British Crown.  One of the conditions was that a fine of 45,000 dollars, fastened upon him by the Government of the United States, as an indemnity for various outrages alleged to have been committed against American citizens, be liquidated for an equivalent of 200,000 acres of land, to be selected by two English and two Fijian commissioners ; also that he (Cakobau) should retain his title of king, and receive an annual pension for life.  There being little reliable information respecting the Fijis, her Majesty's Government determined to send Colonel Smythe, R.A., and myself, for the purpose of inquiry, every one of us having special duties assigned to him.  On the 12th of February, 1860, I took the Peninsular and Oriental steamer for Sydney.  Colonel Smythe had preceded me by the previous mail, and we communicated at Sydney, whence he went to New Zealand by the mail-boat, in hopes of getting there a man-of-war to take him to Fiji, whilst I preferred to take advantage of the kind offer of the missionaries, to proceed direct in their vessel, the *John Wesley*, to my destination.  Colonel Smythe was unsuccessful in getting a man-of-war, as the insurrection of the Maoris kept all the available naval force employed, and he had to charter a schooner, in which he arrived two months after me in Fiji.

We made Lakeba, in the eastern part of the group, on the 12th of May.  That day being a Sunday, the captain of the *John Wesley* did not think it desirable to land; but the next morning a whale-boat was sent, of which I took advantage to get on shore.  We had some difficulty in finding the entrance to the little harbour through the coral reef, on which the surf was breaking violently.  A lot of Christian natives and Tonguese, as well as Mr. Fletcher, one of the resident missionaries of that place, were on the beach to welcome us.  Mr. Fletcher conducted us to his house, which we found substantially built, surrounded by a large court-yard, and a neatly kept little garden, in which various tropical and other flowers were flourishing luxuriantly.  Leaving him and his family to read their home letters, I hastened in the bush to collect what plants and curiosities I could.  A troop of boys followed me, who eagerly assisted in gathering whatever they thought worth taking home.  They pointed out a ravine in which Professor Harvey, of Trinity College, Dublin, the celebrated botanist, found, a few years previously, one of the finest ferns in the islands, the large fan-leaved *Polypodium Horsfieldi*.

Amongst my followers was Charles, the son of the Tongan chief, Maafu, so famous for having very nearly succeeded in conquering the whole Fijis, and descended from the ancient royal house of Tonga (Finau).  Charles Maafu—young rascal!—had been up to some pranks, and his father had sent him to Lakeba, as a kind of punishment.  I don't wonder that all the girls should have fallen in love with him, or he with them, as the case may be; for he was certainly one of the finest young men I have ever seen anywhere, both in figure and face. He wore nothing save two yards of white calico, and a native ornament made of mother-of-pearl. King George, of Tonga, had wished to send him to Sydney, to be educated there with his own son, but to this his father would not agree, and the young chief was left to pick up such information as the missionary establishments offer.

The Tonguese are a much lighter race than the Fijians; in fact, they are real Polynesians, whilst the Fijians are of Papuan origin. They are also a much handsomer and taller people. This physical superiority which, independent of the difference of race, the Tonguese enjoy over the Fijians, may partly result from the different treatment to which the women are subjected amongst these two nations. Whilst in Tonga the women have been treated from time immemorial with all the consideration demanded by their weaker and more delicate constitution—not been allowed to perform any hard work—the women of Fiji are little better than beasts of burden, having to carry heavy loads, do actual field-work, go out fishing, and, besides, attend to all the domestic arrangements devolving upon their sex in other countries. Indeed, their position is almost identical with that enjoyed, or rather endured, by their poor Indian sisters in North and South America. They have to work hard, and cheerfully go through all the drudgery forced upon them by the lords of creation. I remember an eccentric friend of mine once remonstrating with a Fijian who allowed his wife to carry a large bundle of sugar-cane whilst he leisurely walked by her side. The native thought the remonstrance simply a piece of impertinence, and did not see why an inferior being should not be made to contribute to the comforts of a superior.

To the Fijians the Tonguese have been a source of great trouble. They first came over as peaceful traders for sandal wood and timber, two articles of which Tonga is deficient; and they paid handsomely for permission to build canoes, principally in and about Lakeba, which, from its proximity to their own country, offered peculiar advantages.   Gradually, they established more intimate connexions in Fiji, and as the latter is far superior to Tonga in fertility and productiveness, and as, also, owing to the prevalence of the trade wind, it was far easier for their canoes to make the sea passage from Tonga to Fiji, than *vice versa,* Tongan settlers increased every year in numbers.  Being athletic men, the Fijian chiefs courted their assistance in intra-tribal fights, paying them well for their services.   Finding themselves strong, as well as feared, the Tonguese commenced making war on their own account, and thus gradually obtained a permanent footing in the eastern parts of Fiji.  When, after the suppressed rebellion against King George of Tonga, Maafu, as a dangerous ringleader, was banished to Fiji, he at once set about subduing parts not as yet under Tongan influences, and he formed a clever plan for conquering the whole group, which would doubtless have been successful, if his little game had not been spoiled by Mr. Consul Pritchard.   The Tonguese behaved to the Fijians with all the airs of insolent conquerors ; and the hatred with which a Fijian regards a Tongan is, therefore, pardonable. One of the many reasons which induced the king and all the chiefs of Fiji to cede their beautiful islands to the British crown was, undoubtedly, the hope that Great Britain would be able to protect them against the insolence of these Ton-gamen.   Captain Cook called them the Friendly Islanders, and all voyagers have spoken so highly of their good looks and fine physical development, and they are undoubtedly the flower of the Polynesian race, that they have become quite con-ceited and spoiled.  An unlucky affair, long forgotten in England, but well remembered in Tonga, has greatly con-tributed towards making them assume airs, even over Europeans, and look down upon us as we do upon negroes, or aborigines of Australia.   When, in 1840, Captain Croker of H.M.S. *Favourite,* visited Tonga, the heathen and Christian parties of that group carried on an open warfare.  Captain Croker was persuaded to join the Christian party ; quite against the better judgment of his officers, he landed, rushed up to a native fort, and was struck down by a bullet. The officer succeeding him in command thought it advisable to beat a retreat, and one or two guns were left behind. As the case stood, the British Government did not deem it advisable to ask for any reparation, and simply contented itself with recovering the guns. However, the Tonguese magnified this affair into a grand victory obtained over a British man-of-war; and, though their chiefs know better, all the lower classes firmly believe that they can beat Great Britain any day they wish to make the attempt.

The next place we called at was the island of Taviuni, or, as most of our maps erroneously call it, Vuna. One of the passengers on board the *John Wesley*, Captain Wilson, had planted there a cocoa-nut oil establishment, and as he kindly invited me to make use of such accommodation as his place afforded, I determined to stay there a month. Mr. William Coxon, his nephew, had charge of it during his absence, and no sooner had our vessel entered the Strait of Somosomo, than he came on board. His boat's crew consisted of eight natives of Rotuma, an island to the north of Fiji, belonging to its consulate, and useful as likely to furnish an ample supply of labour whenever any large agricultural operations are attempted in Fiji. It has been found that the Polynesians will work much better in islands not their home. The Rotuma men were really very industrious fellows, and would work hard in making cocoa-nut oil. There were also some natives of Tahiti, the Sandwich Islands, Were, Roratonga, and others, who were much preferred by the white settlers to the Fijians. And yet the Fijians cannot be called an idle race. The peculiar position in which the Tonguese are placed, probably accounts for their being an exception to this rule.

For more than a month I remained at Somosomo, the town in which Captain Wilson had settled, making excursions in all directions, and now and then going to Wairiki to have a chat with the mission families of that place. I obtained material assistance from the mission, by their lending me their boat and crew to cross the Strait of Somosomo, or sending men when I ascended the heights of Taviuni. Somosomo itself was quite deserted. All the men had gone on a fighting expedition to Vanua Levu, headed by Golia, the younger brother of Tui Cakau, king of Cakadrove. Eleanor, Golia's wife, remained at home, and often paid us a visit, or accompanied us on excursions in the mountains, never, however without her maids of honour. She was the niece of Cakobau, the king of Bau, and had been converted to Christianity in the capital; but Golia, her husband, was still a heathen, and whilst she held the rank of queen, he was only a younger brother of a king, tributary to Bau, and bore no such title. She was ladylike and dignified in her bearing, and never allowed any other wife of Golia's, and he had a great many, to take any liberties with her or refuse her proper respect. On the other hand, she would always be at the head of any work which the women had to do. I often saw her on the reefs fishing, and one evening, it was quite dark, she and another woman had caught a large turtle in their net, to which they managed to hold on until her calls brought assistance, the animal flapping and splashing with all its might.

We had been some time in Somosomo, when one fine morning a little hunchback belonging to the court came running breathless to our place, to ask Mr. Coxon to fire off a pop-gun, which he and the women had managed to load, but of which nobody had the courage to pull the trigger. It was to be discharged the moment Golia stepped on shore from his victorious expedition, and the large war canoes, all sails set, were already close to; the men dancing on board, and giving occasional blasts on the conch-shell. All the women had gathered on the beach, singing songs of welcome and in praise of victory, and no sooner had the chief set foot on *terra firma*, than off went the pop-gun. All the warriors were in war costume; their faces blackened with charcoal, their hair done up in white turbans, and their arms and legs decorated with bleached leaves of screw-pines. Many of them had fire-arms, and all short and long clubs, spears, bows and arrows.

Chief Golia paid us a visit soon after landing, and was particularly anxious to learn who I and my assistants were, and what objects we had in view. He was a tall well-made man, scarcely older than twenty years, with a fine cast of countenance, and a rich melodious voice. This was the first time he was engaged on his own account in a military expedition, and he was very circumstantial in giving us an account of his doings. The object was to punish a people who had a few years ago murdered one of his elder brothers. He had burnt several towns and villages, but, as all the inhabitants had thought it prudent to fly at his approach, only two were knocked down, and one of them, added scandal, was an old woman.

The Strait of Somosomo, as the sea between Taviuni and Vanua Levu is termed, is more subject to rain than any other part of the group. The consequence is that the vegetation is more luxuriant and dense. I thought it a good place for establishing an experimental cotton plantation, and as the suitableness of Fiji for cotton growing was one of the objects I was directed to investigate, it may not be out of place to subjoin here some of the general results I arrived at.

If I understand the nature and requirements of cotton aright, the Fijis seem to be as if made for it. In the whole group there is scarcely a rod of ground that might not be cultivated, or that has not, at one time or other, produced a crop of some kind, the soil being of an average amount of fertility, and in some parts rich in the extreme. Cotton requires a gently undulated surface, slopes of hill, rather than flat land. The whole country, the deltas of the great rivers excepted, is a succession of hills and dales, covered on the weather side with a luxuriant herbage or a dense forest ; on the lee side with grass, and isolated screw-pines—more immediately available for planting. Cotton wants sea air. What country would answer to this requirement better than a group of more than 200 islands, surrounded by the ocean, as a convenient highway to even small boats and canoes, since the force of winds and waves are broken by the natural breakwater, presented by the

reefs which encircle nearly the whole ? Cotton requires further
to be fanned by gentle breezes when growing, and rather a
comparatively low temperature.   There is scarcely ever a calm
in Fiji, either the north-east or south-east trade winds blowing
over the islands, keep up a constant current, and the thermometer for months vacillates between 62° and 80° Fahrenheit,
and never rises to the height attained in tropical parts of Asia,
Africa, or America. In fine, every condition required to favour
the growth of this important article seems to be provided ;
and it is hardly possible to add anything more in order to
impress those best qualified to judge, with a better idea of
Fiji as a first-rate cotton growing country.

Notwithstanding cotton being undoubtedly an introduced
plant, and although, until lately, no attention whatever was
paid to its cultivation, it has spread over all the littoral parts
of Fiji, and become in some localities perfectly naturalized.
Six different kinds have come to my knowledge, all of which
are shrubby, and produce flower and fruit throughout the
whole year, though the greater number of pods arrive at
maturity during the dry season, from June to September.
There is scarcely any difference in the look of the four first-
mentioned kinds, which a person not botanically trained
could readily detect.   Left to themselves, and never subjected
to the pruning-knife, these cotton shrubs become as high as a
tall man can reach, and each shrub spreads over a surface of
about fourteen feet square.   I have had no. opportunity of
counting the number of pods produced throughout the year
by a single specimen, but that found in July was on an
average 700 per plant.   Twenty pods of cleaned cotton
weighed 1oz. ; thus, each plant would yield 2lb. 3oz.   Allowing fourteen feet square for every plant, an acre would hold
222 plants, yielding, at the rate of 2lb. 3oz. per individual
plant, 485lb. 10oz.   Even fixing the price of sorts worth more
than 12$d$. at Manchester as low as 6$d$. per lb. on the spot,
an acre would realize £12 2$s$. 9$\frac{1}{4}d$.   When it is borne in
mind that Fijian cotton brings forth ripe fruit without intermission throughout the year, but that this calculation is based

*solely* upon the number of pods *found at one time only*, and that the pods were gathered from plants upon which *no attention whatsoever had been bestowed*, the result will be still more striking ; double, even treble the above quantity may safely be calculated upon as their annual crop.　When it is further remembered that Fijian cotton is not an annual, and that the plants will continue to yield for several years, without requiring any other attention than keeping them free from weedy creepers, and pruning them periodically, the encouragement held out to cultivators will be pronounced very great.

Until the excellence of Fijian cotton had been acknowledged at Manchester, and the mercantile value of the different sorts been ascertained to be 7*d.* to 7½*d.*, 8*d.*, 9*d.*, 11*d.*, and even 12*d.* to 12½*d.* per lb. respectively, no attempt had been made to cultivate the plant.　It was almost entirely left to itself, and, perhaps, only here and there disseminated by the natives, in order to furnish materials for wicks.　But when, in November, 1859, Mr. Pritchard returned from England to Fiji with the valuation printed in the *Manchester Cotton Supply Reporter* for March, 1859, he induced the most influential chiefs to give orders for planting it, and the Wesleyan missionaries, without any exception, zealously aided in these endeavours, by recommending the cultivation both personally and through the agency of their native teachers.　Thus, cotton has been thickly spread over all the Christianized districts, and imparts to them a characteristic feature, occasionally very striking in places having a mixed religious population.　In Navua, for instance, that part of the town inhabited by Christians is full of cotton, whilst that inhabited by the heathens destitute of it.

On leaving England, the " Manchester Cotton Supply Association," through their able secretary, Mr. Haywood, furnished me with a large quantity of New Orleans cotton seeds, together with printed instructions for their cultivation. Distributing a fair share of the seeds and papers amongst white settlers, who I felt persuaded would make use of them, I, myself, was enabled to establish a small plantation on the Somosomo estate of Captain Wilson and M. Joubert of

Sydney. My New Orleans cotton readily grew. Seeds set on the 9th of June, began to *yield ripe pods* within *three* months, and I was thus enabled to take home a crop from the very seeds I brought out, though my absence from England amounted to only thirteen months altogether. This may truly be termed growing cotton by steam. When I paid a second visit to Somosomo on the 18th of October, my plants were from four to seven feet high, full of ripe pods and flowers. A Rotuma native, whom I had begged to look after the plantation, said, that the field only required weeding once; after that the cotton plants grew so rapidly, that they kept down the weeds, and he had no farther trouble. Simultaneously, Dr. Brower, United States Vice Consul, had succeeded in raising New Orleans cotton on his estate in the island of Wakaya, twelve pods of which weighed an ounce, whilst the seeds distributed by me amongst various people had evidently not fallen on barren soil. Of course my plantation could only be a small one, but, nevertheless, it proved so far beneficial that it convinced those white settlers who had lately repaired to the group, what quick returns cotton would yield, and some of them resolutely set about establishing plantations.

The fact that cotton will grow, and will grow well, being established, the success of this and similar attempts will chiefly depend upon the supply of manual labour. Those best acquainted with the condition of the group, and the character of its people, confidently look forward to a steady supply of it. In Rewa, Ovalau, and other districts longest frequented by whites, the natives go round asking for employment. This is quite an innovation, and shows that the Fijian is gradually becoming accustomed to labour for fixed wages; and when the chiefs shall have either voluntarily relinquished, or been compelled to give up their claim to all the property accumulated by the lower classes, a favourable result will be the immediate consequence, and a fresh impulse be imparted to all branches of industry. Let the common people once be assured that nobody can legally take their fair earnings away from them, and that the little comforts with which they have managed to surround themselves may be openly displayed without the danger of being coveted by the chiefs and their favourites, and they will doubtless be eager to engage in any work that does not require any great mechanical skill or violent exertion, and at the same time will yield them reasonable returns.

On the 20th of June, the *Paul Jones*, a little schooner, arrived from Ovalau, whence it had been sent by Mr. Pritchard to fetch us, in accordance with my request. Having had to beat up, it had been several days on the voyage.

On the 22d, I reached Levuka, the capital of the island of Ovalau, where I was hospitably received by Mr. W. Pritchard, her Majesty's Consul for Fiji. Mr. Pritchard had long wished to pay a visit to Kuruduadua, a powerful chief of Viti Levu, who had hitherto been inaccessible to all missionary influence. We started in the Consul's gig, and calling at Bau, Rewa, Nigau, reached the mouth of the Navua river on the 5th of July. Kuruduadua received us well, and pledged himself, that cannibalism should henceforward be discontinued in his dominions. We had an opportunity of seeing the large iron pot, originally intended for curing *biche-de-mer*, but, as McDonald has correctly stated in the Royal Geographical Society's Journal, occasionally used for boiling human flesh. We succeeded in establishing the most friendly relations with this chief, and should have proceeded to the very heart of Viti Levu, that unknown centre of the largest island of the group, if the weather had permitted. Continued rain, however, made us postpone our trip until the arrival of Colonel Smythe. After a week's stay, we returned to Ovalau. On the road, a native messenger, who had been sent by the Consulate, met us with the glad tidings that Colonel Smythe had safely arrived at Levuka.

Conjointly with Colonel Smythe, who had chartered the schooner *Pegasus*, at New Zealand, an extremely slow vessel, Mr. Pritchard and I, on board the *Paul Jones*, a smaller, but faster-sailing schooner, built in the islands, visited the greater

part of the group.   The first official meeting was held at Bau, as
the capital of Fiji.   It took place on the 27th of July, at 11
A.M., and in the house of the king.   As it may be considered
typical of all the other meetings, I may as well record what
took place.

The king's residence is close to the beach, and a large native-
built house, around which several out-houses are clustered,
one of which is inhabited by Peter, a Tonguese, who fills the
office of prime minister, and seems much attached to the king.
In front of the house is a fine lawn of couch-grass, and groups
of iron-wood and other native shrubs and trees, the whole, I
believe, a creation of Mrs. Collis, the wife of the resident
schoolmaster of Bau, who will ever live in my memory for
having, amongst other great acts of kindness conferred, never
failed to supply me in this land of pork and yams, with bread,
cakes, and other acceptable presents whenever I came in that
neighbourhood.   Precisely at eleven o'clock the king fired a
salute, and when we arrived at the place of meeting, we found
most of the chiefs and landed proprietors assembled, squatted
on the matted floor, whilst the king and the queen, both
dressed in European fashion, the former in a blue uniform,
were seated in chairs, of which there had been arranged a
semicircle.   Ratu Abel, the king's eldest son, a fine-looking
fellow, was absent, but sent for.   There were present, besides
Colonel Smythe, Mr. Pritchard, and myself—not to mention
the ladies—Messrs. Collis and Fordham from the mission.
Mr. Fordham interpreted for Colonel Smythe, and Mr. Charles
Wise for Mr. Pritchard.   I wrote all down at the time, and
the following, obtained from both sources, may be regarded
as a faithful *résumé* of what occurred.

"It having been represented to her Britannic Majesty,"
said Colonel Smythe, addressing King Cacobau, "that the
king and chiefs of Fiji are disposed to become British
subjects, her Majesty has directed an inquiry to be made
into the matter, and hear what king and chiefs have to say
on the subject, in order that it may be reported to her."

The king replied : "The arrangement respecting the cession

entered into with Mr. Consul Pritchard is still in full force, and shall not be disturbed by any foreign power."

"Great Britain," continued Colonel Smythe, " produces many things that Fiji does not, and *vice versâ,* so that by an exchange of products, the two countries may be mutually benefited. I refer, especially, to cotton, which grows luxuriantly in Fiji, and is valuable in England."

The king replied : "I am fully aware of it ; and in consequence of what Mr. Consul Pritchard told me, at the interview at Levuka, about the desirableness of cultivating cotton, I have directed it to be planted, and my commands have been carried out to some extent."

"In ceding the country," Colonel Smythe resumed, "every man will retain his own property and land, and everybody will be protected, so that a stop will be put to the fearful feuds that have decimated the population."

The king rejoined : "There may be people in the group who at present cannot fully appreciate that idea, but it is somewhat like Christianity, which, though a blessing, is looked upon with prejudicial eyes by many not familiar with its beneficial tendency."

When the chiefs and landholders were asked whether they had any observation to make, they remained mute, and at the conclusion of the whole raised shouts of approval.

Afterwards we visited all the large islands, Kadavu, Viti Levu, and Vanua Levu, but want of space prevents me from entering into details. It must suffice to say, that at every place chiefs and people expressed themselves unanimously in favour of the cession brought about by Mr. Pritchard, expressing at the same time an ardent wish that the British flag might be hoisted as soon as possible. At the time I am penning these lines, the Government has not made up its mind whether to accept or finally reject the cession of these beautiful islands. England, it is contended, had already too much land in hand to long for more. So had the Roman Empire at the time of Augustus, yet force of circumstances constantly compelled it to extend its territory, and the same power may ultimately induce England to take the Fijis. Thanks to Mr. Pritchard's efforts, the path has been made perfectly smooth, and nothing now remains to be done than to hoist the flag. The subject is free from every kind of complication; but who can foresee the difficulties that may arise if over-cautious hesitation usurps the place of prompt action? The Americans will probably insist upon the payment of their debt, rapidly growing larger by unpaid interest. The Tonguese, now with difficulty kept in bounds by the British representative, will again open hostilities against the natives. Other nations may take what England thinks fit to reject, and I have already heard of two distinct schemes tending in that direction, which would greatly annoy the Australian colonies, one of whom, through their Parliament, has already recommended to her Majesty's Government that the Fijian offer be accepted. Finally, the white population of the islands, now numbering about 2,000 souls, would probably endeavour to form a government of their own, as was done in New Zealand years ago, and thought to lead to such complications, that England, at the eleventh hour, made up its mind to hoist the flag in the country of the Maories; which would have been frustrated by the French, if a sharp-witted and patriotic lady had not succeeded in worming out the plan and detaining the French commander at a ball given at her house, whilst her own countrymen slipped out of the rooms to hoist the English flag.

In a direct steam communication between England, Central America, and Australia, the Fijis would offer a suitable place for coaling and taking in supplies. Starting from Brisbane, the capital of the new and flourishing colony of Queensland, steamers, having touched at the French settlement of New Caledonia, could call at Kadavu, one of the southernmost islands, which on the southern side has the fine harbour of Galoa, protected from all winds, and easy of access. They would thence proceed, almost in a straight line, to the northernmost of the Marquesas islands, and to either Panama, or to Salinas Bay or San Juan del Sur [Captain Bedford

Pim's transit], by which means the passage from Southampton to eastern Australia, now accomplished never under fifty-five days, could be made in eleven, perhaps in thirteen, days less than at present.

Unless great expenses are incurred in sending out a large staff of officials, Fiji, if properly managed, could be made a self-supporting colony. At present the government and jurisdiction have been made over to Mr. Pritchard; and he, with one or two clerks, and taking due advantage of the government of the chiefs, and the occasional visits of English men-of-war, has been able to keep the country straight, and afford protection to the constantly increasing white population, some of whom have turned cotton and sugar planters, some sheep farmers or traders. Until the white population has become more numerous, scarcely anything more would be wanted than an efficient British Resident, well trained in native modes of thought, who would be able to keep the peace between natives and foreigners, and see neither takes undue advantage of the other.

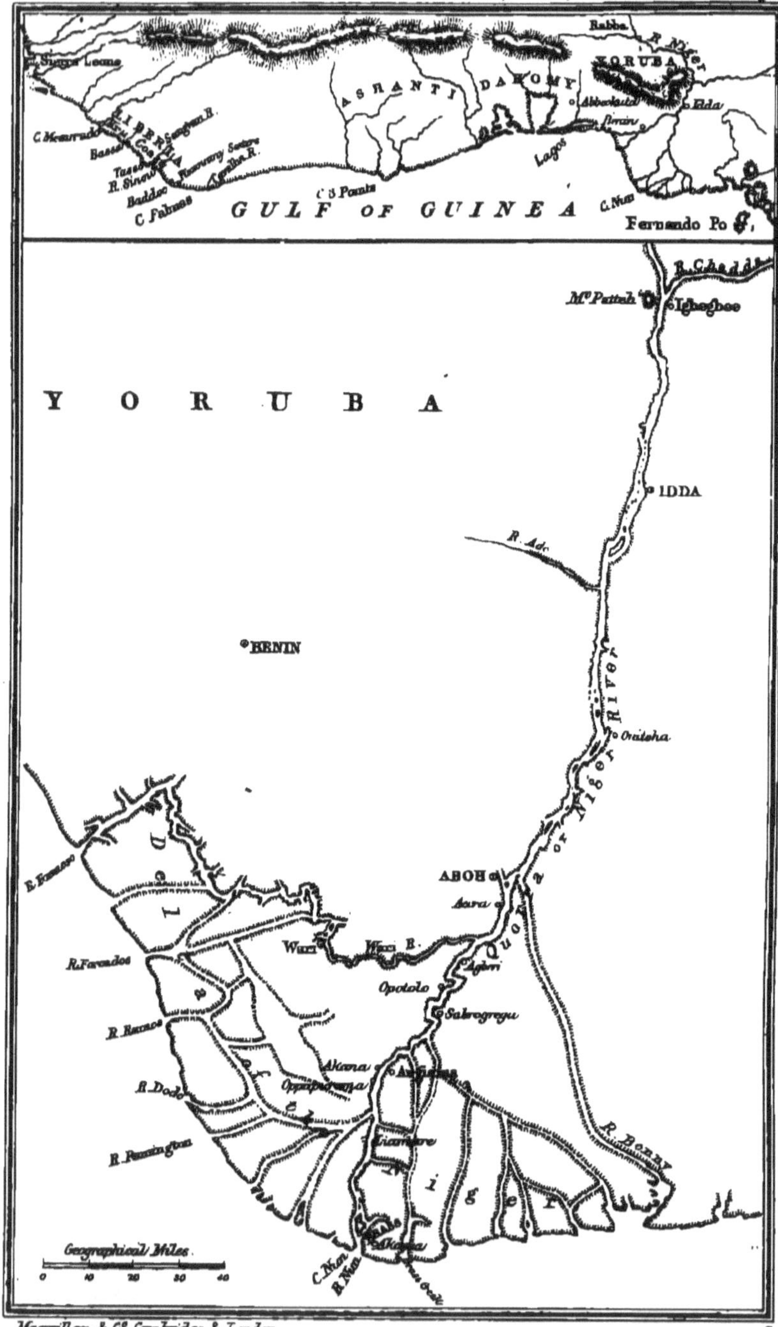
Sierra Leone
ASHANTI
DAHOMY
YORUBA
Rabba
R. Niger
Abbeokuta
Eda
Benin
Lagos
LIBERIA
C. Mesurado
Bassa
Tase
R. Sino
Baddoe
C. Palmas
R.
C. 3 Points
GULF OF GUINEA
C. Nun
Fernando Po
R. Chadda
M? Patteh
Igbegbee
Y O R U B A
IDDA
R. Ad
BENIN
Niger River
Quorra or
Onitsha
ABOH
Asaba
R. Formoso
DEL
Agberi
Warri
Warri R.
Opotolo
R. Farcados
Sabrogregu
R. Ramos
Akara
Angiama
R. Dodo
Oppaparoppa
Liamwre
R. Bonny
R. Pennington
N i g e r
Geographical Miles
0    10    20    30    40
C. Nun
R. Nun
Akassa

# 9. *THE KRU COAST, CAPE PALMAS, AND THE NIGER.*

## BY WILLIAM DURRANT, M.D.

I SAILED in the capacity of medical officer to the most recent of the many expeditions which were despatched by the late Mr. McGregor Laird, of the African Steam Navigation Company, to trade up the Niger for palm oil and cotton. This expedition was made with the aid of a subsidy from her Majesty's Government, who also supplied two gunboats for our protection, as Mr. Laird's vessels, on a previous occasion, had been attacked by the natives at Sabogrega, two days' sail above the Delta.

It was on June 16, 1860, that I embarked at Liverpool on board my vessel, the *Sunbeam*, an iron screw-steamer, for a voyage whence I did not return until January, 1862. We left England under sail, reserving our coals for the African coast.

On the 16th of July we sighted Cape Mesurado, in Liberia, which gave us a point of departure for the Kru Coast, where we intended to make a stay off the town of Bassa, in order to engage Krumen sailors to assist us in the Niger. The next day we lowered our screw and stood in for the Sangurin river, anchoring about two miles from its mouth. Here we fired a gun as a signal to the natives, but were not able to induce any of them to join us. We therefore continued to run along the coast, touching at different villages.

The inhabitants on the Kru Coast are intelligent and muscular; they are employed both by merchant-vessels and men-of-war to perform the rougher duties of the service, which are too trying to the constitution of European sailors in these climates. On arriving off any one of their villages an ensign is hoisted, which they understand as a signal to ask for their services, a number of canoes are soon seen to come from the shore, crowded with men, who when they are on board are well watched, for they are sad thieves; and have been known, even within the last few years, to murder the crews of becalmed merchant-vessels, for the purpose of obtaining their cargoes.

After considerable palaver, seven Krumen were obtained at the second place where we tried, and then we proceeded under steam and sail to the next village, Tasso. Having fired our salute, we remained at anchor; but after a great many natives had visited us, who crowded on board begging tobacco, rum, and anything they could get, we found the people on shore had become suspicious and took our vessel for a slaver; we were told, "Dey tink you Jamaica ship;" so we proceeded to the Sinon river, where we engaged three Krumen.

The next place was Baddoo, where we received a visit from the officers of the Liberian war schooner which lay there. She had been presented to that infant republic of blacks by our own Government. The crew of the schooner formed a motley group of whites, half-breeds, and Liberians, whose occupation is to prevent slave trade on this coast. Her lieutenant came to scrutinize our vessel; he was a young West Indian Mulatto, of gentlemanly manners, who had been educated in England, and he performed his duty in a way which passed for a complimentary visit.

On the 21st a great many canoes came off to us, and a deafening amount of jargon took place, on the part of the African headmen, as to the quantity of calico, gunpowder, and rum which was to be paid in advance. All were anxious to speak first, and what with the confusion of their bad English, our utter ignorance of their tongue, and their crowding down into the cabin to look at the goods, we were utterly bewildered. There was a concourse of naked Africans, young and old, of all shades, from dark coffee-colour to a light coppery tint; but very few of them could be strictly called black. We contrived to engage seventeen men, and immediately after proceeded to a village called Piccanniny Sesters, where we anchored on the same day. At this place I went ashore in one of their canoes, being desirous of seeing the character of a Kru town. The natives seemed surprised to find I was willing to go, and my visit was thought somewhat hazardous by our crew.

I went in one of the native canoes, which average from eighteen inches to two feet in width, and from twenty-five to thirty feet in length. These little craft are easily capsized, and require those who are in them to accommodate themselves to their motion in order to maintain equilibrium. It is not practicable to stand erect, but the passenger must kneel and sit on his haunches, as the natives invariably do. I felt this position extremely irksome, but as there was a considerable sea running I found it dangerous to move; however, at last, being compelled by pain to do so, I stretched out my legs before me and supported myself by holding on to each side. The sea came over us continually and the canoe was half filled with water, but one man is always kept baling with a wooden scoop. It is amusing to see the dexterity of the natives when they get capsized and their canoe turns upside down; for as they swim they roll it round, and rid it of the water inside by suddenly pushing the canoe backwards and forwards, and at last, with a single spring from the top of a wave, they alight safely in the emptied boat. The canoes are constructed of a crescentic form, and when they are filled with water there is such a disparity between the hollow space occupied by the fluid and the massive wood-work of the canoe, that several men would be easily supported above water, even by one that was waterlogged, and though they are often split, and very leaky, their utility is not destroyed. These canoes are all one piece, formed by hollowing trees. This is accomplished by heaping lighted charcoal along the centre of the trunk, which being burned is easily chipped out. The natives are obliged to resort to this plan because they have no suitable axes.

When we approached the beach I observed a reef of rocks running far along the coast, over which the breakers bounded furiously. However, as we neared them I perceived a narrow channel where, watching a favourable opportunity, the Krumen set their paddles to work with such rapidity, that we darted past all danger and arrived safely on a beautiful sandy beach.

Crowds of natives watched us from shore with the greatest curiosity. I was surrounded by men, youths, and children, who looked at me with a wonder for which I was quite unprepared. I approached, and cordially offered my hand to several of the men, who hesitated, and walked back from me; others allowed me to take their hands, but surveyed my appearance with a puzzled and very serious air. But Pimoonah, the man to whom the canoe belonged, could speak a little English, and had been to London. He stepped through the crowd, and, taking my hand, led me up the beach, and past a rude tent, beneath which three or four natives sat around a fire, wearing bracelets of ivory and leopard's teeth. They were squatting on their haunches, and one was smoking lustily. At my approach, they gazed in mute amazement. Passing on we struck into a path between some dense shrubs and cocoa-nut trees. At a few hundred yards' distance we came upon the town, and soon reached a large bamboo-hut, square built, and roofed with palm-leaves. Pimoonah and myself passed through an aperture which required me to bend chin and knee together, and then I found myself in a commodious room. The floor was composed of closely inter-woven bamboo, and very clean, and on one side was a wood-fire, laid upon hard baked clay. A large shallow pan was supported on three short columns, and contained a quantity of rice and fish. Four females were sitting round the fire, and Pimoonah said these were his mother and his three wives. I put myself into the same posture as they, sitting cross-legged upon the floor. A crowd of persons had followed us

into his house, and their reek and crowding soon became so
overpowering that I was obliged to go out, and I sauntered
away, followed by a multitude.   I proceeded over soft sandy
paths, between numerous huts of various sizes, at equal
distances apart.  Some of the natives darted back as if I were
venomous to the touch.   Some women, who were pounding
corn, and others who were sitting at their doors, dropped
their utensils, and fled screaming away.   At last, when I
halted for a few minutes to survey a group, a woman
approached and took my hand, and made signs to me to
pull up the sleeve of my shirt.   This I did ; and when the
crowd saw my white arm, they threw up their hands, and
shouted with delight or surprise.

The women wore no clothing, except a few strings of different coloured beads around the loins.   Some wore ivory,
or brass, or iron bracelets and anklets ; others had small
necklaces, while most of the men had several ivory ornaments
of that kind, accompanied with one or more leopard's teeth.
Besides that they wore some small carved object in wood, bone,
or shells, called dju-dju, or charms, and many had a string of
cowrie-shells around both ankles.   Their tatooed marks were
mostly one broad black line from the hair down the centre of
the forehead to the tip of the nose, and a triangular mark at
the external angle of each eye.   Their teeth were filed to a
point, and some had a small cloth round the waist, carried
between the legs, and fastened in front.   I went to the
residence of the chief, an old man, who wore nothing but a
blue Guernsey frock, and a very shabby one, and an old black
English hat, and carried a rude short sword.  He gave me
dinner ; a hot earthen dish of rice and meat was brought, and
a large bowl of soup.   Of this I was desired to partake, which
I did gladly enough, for I was getting faint with my four or
five-mile canoe ride, and the bewilderment of the novel scene
around me.   The food was frightfully hot with pepper, and
all tasted strongly of tainted meat.   A woman lifted up a
baby in her arms for me to look at, or for it to see me, but no
sooner did the child cast its eyes upon my face than it yelled

most lustily, and clung back upon its mother.   Now and then
I took the hands of the children, patted some, and made
a face at a few of the most good-natured looking men, at
which they laughed immoderately.   A fat woman, of about
thirty, approached me boldly, but very kindly, and desired
me by signs to take off my shirt.   To this, however, I for
some time paid no regard, but others soon seconded her, and
at last became so urgent that, supposing they were anxious
to know if my body were as white as my face, I opened my
shirt-bosom, and the look of amazement and loud expressions
of surprise quite perplexed me.   These people are, indeed, in
the habit of selling palm oil to merchant-vessels which trade
along the coast.   But it seems the whites rarely or never
land, and it is only a few of the men who are engaged in
conveying the oil to the ships, anchored some miles from the
shore, who become accustomed to the whites.   I had a good
night's rest at Pimoonah's house.   His three wives were
sitting up for us, smoking tobacco.   They furnished a pipe
for me, and Pimoonah brought a calabash of water, and,
sitting round the fire, told me his history with a vocabulary of
about twenty words of English, assisted by capital pantomime.   I made out that the village was his birth-place;
that when quite a youth, and a canoe-paddler, a palm oil
trader gave his father some cloth, rum, gunpowder, and a
flint-musket, to allow him to go down the coast and act as
pilot, adding that he should then go to white man's country,
and be brought back with "plenty everything to buy wife
and be genl'um."   All this was accomplished in two years,
and he showed me mementos of his visit to London in several
small articles, such as a little dressing-case of the Lowther
Arcade style, worth about 2*s.* 6*d.*, several tin cups, a few
pewter spoons, knife and fork, and some sailor's clothing,
besides which he had a good flint-gun, and a lot of cotton
cloth.   Having finished his story, he stripped himself,
and well lubricated his body with agreeably scented oil,
which he proceeded to rub in till it was all absorbed by the
skin.   Throwing down the usual bed for me before the fire,

simply a large mat, and a flat stone, wrapped in another mat, for a pillow, he entered the next apartment with one wife, while the other two went to sleep on the opposite side of the room from me. Altogether, Pimoonah was a very superior specimen of a Kruman.

Lying on my mat, tired out as I was, sleep was long in visiting me. I lay reflecting upon the oddity of my situation, and the contrast of a society which existed within a few weeks' sail from my own land.

Shortly after daylight there was a movement among the inmates, and the fire was crackling away, while a large bowl of fish and rice was prepared for our breakfasts. Pimoonah brought me hot water, soap, a large red and yellow cotton bandana to wipe with, and the London cheap dressing-case, containing a comb and brush. After breakfast I made ready to depart. It was evident nothing but the simplest kindness and respect had been entertained by my hosts towards their white guest, and Pimoonah, myself, and our paddlers, followed by a small crowd of men, and children, male and female, proceeded to the beach, and were soon launched through the surf upon a considerable sea, which continually made a breach over us, and made me feel somewhat anxious for my safety, but one hour's paddling brought me once more on board our ship. These Krumen seem to be nearly amphibious, as they are frequently known to swim for miles from the ship to the beach, a feat which I myself have witnessed. On one occasion a canoe leaving the vessel was capsized some distance from the ship; the crew dived quickly for their sinking goods, and then swam towards the canoe. Two of them righted it, emptied it of water, received the things on board, and then all took their seats again, as if it were quite an unimportant occurrence.

All these Kru people file their teeth to a point, and have a disagreeable habit of gritting them, so that they set one's teeth on edge, like the sharpening of a saw. They are cleanly in their habits, washing their bodies thoroughly every day, and their teeth after every meal.

After making Pimoonah a present, and sending the chief a pilot-cloth coat, I took leave of my goodnatured host.

We afterwards proceeded to Cape Palmas, the Liberian colony lately annexed to this state. Here we arrived about nine o'clock the following morning, and myself and the second mate went ashore. We were met on our way by a native canoe, whose headman presented a note, requesting we would call on Mr. Marshall, an agent of the African Mail Company.

Cape Palmas has a lighthouse at its extremity, a hundred feet elevation from the sea, and close by is a comfortable residence, called the Orphan Asylum, under the patronage of some benevolent ladies of Philadelphia, in the charge of an American Missionary, Mr. Trumbold, and his lady, assisted by two ladies as schoolmistresses, one of which, Miss Ball, is English. Having first paid a visit to the agent, who is at the same time landlord of the only hotel there, where we were most hospitably entertained, a gentleman volunteered to escort me to Mount Vaughan, three miles from the Cape, to the residence of the Rev. Mr. Crummel. We passed along a sandy pathway through a continuous natural grove of the tamarind, orange, lime, date, cocoa-palms, pine-apples, cotton-bushes, and India-rubber trees. Here the thermometer rarely exceeds 85°, and from the appearance of the residents, and their own testimony, I believe it to be a healthy spot. On arrival at the reverend gentleman's house, we were very cordially welcomed, and he took great interest in my history of the proposed expedition. There was a good view of the surrounding country from this spot; a fine cluster of cocoanut trees, swarming with the pretty weaver-birds, stood on the hill opposite his large and well-built house. Fields of rice, and dense intertropical foliage, stretching gradually upwards from the shore towards the Mount, were the foreground to an African village in the distance, and a fine sandy beach upon the south of the Cape, and a lagoon some three miles in length. The river Cavalha, about three hundred yards broad, not, however, navigable for any considerable distance, lay on the northern side.

Returning by the same sandy path, we met a few native females loaded with cassava, bananas, and palm-nuts, and occasionally passed a frame-house, consisting only of one floor divided into apartments. As we neared the Cape, a wheelwright's shop attracted my attention, where two or three coloured men were busily engaged constructing a small four-wheeled carriage. Farther on were more pretending-looking buildings, one of which, the property of Mr. Gibson, the Governor, was handsome, and elegantly furnished. This gentleman stands high in the estimation of the colonists, and his hospitable kindness was warmly evinced towards all of us. Arriving at the hotel, we found a most acceptable dinner prepared. This over, I paid a visit to the Orphan Asylum for young coloured females. A group assembled near the gates, for the most part girls whose blood had been intermingled with the whites, formed an interesting and handsome bevy. The Rev. Mr. Trumbold and his lady were evidently pleased with our visit, and an hour with them passed most agreeably.

Preparing now to return on board, Mr. Marshall said he had been desired to invite our party to celebrate the Anniversary of the Liberian Republic, which occurred on the morrow, and we left him anticipating much pleasure on the next day. Nor were we disappointed. As morning broke, we hoisted all our flags; the day was beautiful, and early after breakfast we went ashore. Service was performed by the Rev. Mr. Crummel at the Episcopal Church, and an address delivered by him, on the " Advantages they enjoyed by speaking the English tongue." It was redolent of encomiums on the great destiny of the Anglo-Saxon race, who were now preparing to open up the broad highway of the Niger, for the regeneration of Africans. It was certainly a clever and original harangue, and gained marked admiration from all its auditors.

After dinner fourteen rounds were fired from our ship for the occasion; and it so happened that ours was the first to confer that compliment since the annexation of Cape Palmas to the republic.

In the evening my surprise was most agreeably excited by
the appearance of a great many handsome and tastefully
dressed quadroon ladies. They were tall, delicate in features,
and graceful in bearing. There was a softness of expression
in their large hazel eyes, conjoined with a simplicity of
manner, without insipidity, which was charming to me.

Liberia is inhabited principally by Kru people, who live in
scattered villages around Cape Palmas, which has now become
a colony of free blacks from America. The natives tried, some
few years ago, to expel them by force of arms, but were
repulsed by the energy of the colonists. The population of
the cape is about 1,500 blacks. There are no resident white
persons excepting the missionaries, who are held in much
esteem. The people are sober and industrious in their habits,
but from their limited means have not been able to take
such advantage of their beautiful and fertile soil as a larger
capital might enable them to secure.

The night wore on; next day came departure; and for
many days I dwelt in thought upon the peaceful happiness of
Cape Palmas.

We took with us two passengers for the town of Cavalha,
which is a few hours' sail from Cape Palmas. They were
Mr. Messenger, an American missionary, and an American
governess. Myself and the captain, with a boat's crew, took
them ashore through a dangerous reef of rocks which line this
coast. The Bishop of Liberia, Mr. Payne, resides here, and
his church and house stand near the beach. It presented
an interesting appearance among the thatched bamboo huts of
the naked Africans, who watched us from the shore.

Shortly after leaving Cavalha a very novel and extraordinary
spectacle occurred. Our attention was attracted by a tremendous splashing in the water a considerable distance from
the ship, which we set down as an attack upon a whale by
his adversary, the thrasher or sword-fish; but our astonishment rose with a vociferous exclamation from the whole ship's
crew, when two enormous whales jumped almost perpendicularly out of the water to the height of ten feet. They

were at least forty feet long, and continued leaping side by side, all the while nearing our vessel. Though I had seen many whales in the Arctic regions, I never witnessed or heard of such an occurrence as this before.

Six Krumen were engaged at Cavalla, making forty-eight in all from the various villages along the coast. Those you have the good fortune to engage, are but poorly paid according to their services, which are indispensably necessary on the coast. They get about 1*l.* per month and their food, consisting of two pints of rice and two salt herrings per day, and salt meat once or twice a week. When they engage, they have advances to the extent of from two to four cloths, from half to one gallon of rum, and ten to twenty pounds of powder. The last they use for celebrating the deaths of relatives, on which events much powder is fired away, and much grog is drunk.

On the 31st of July, we arrived off Accra, and anchored three miles from the shore. This old and interesting military station stands upon a bluff height, and the blending of its buildings of a half European, half Oriental character, with those of a large native village, has a bizarre effect, which is not at all diminished on landing, and threading one's way among its scattered abodes. The beach is dangerous from its heavy surf; nevertheless, the peculiar flat-bottomed canoes used here, worked by the dusky natives with great skill, pass and repass to the vessels off the place, in weather which our English seamen do not care to risk.

Myself and our purser went ashore, and a messenger came to us with an invitation from Captain Duvergue, of the English fort, where we spent a very pleasant evening, and then retired to the hotel kept by a native, whose name is Ado; a man much respected, who though entirely illiterate, has realized considerable property, and carries on a large trade with the natives for gold, gums, ivory, &c. Accra being one of the chief ports of the Ashantee, or Gold Coast Kingdom, this metal is continually brought into the town in dust or small particles for the purchase of goods of English manufacture. The natives are ingenious in adulterating the gold, and traders have occasionally been considerably cheated by such means.  They manufacture ornaments, and especially rings, of the purest gold, which display considerable taste in their design, and are executed in good style.  The faces of these people indicate intelligence, and they are rather elegant in general appearance, their costume consisting of long tobes of native cotton, mostly woven with broad blue stripes.

On landing, we passed through a long street of disconnected wattle-and-daub huts, where young women were sitting behind small baskets of goods for sale.  The street was much crowded with people, and the market wares consisted of aromatic herbs, cigars, copal, and sweet-scented gums, fruits, beads, and various small articles of native manufacture, the uses of which were a puzzle to me.  The people were civil, and laughed and talked with volubility.  The currency among themselves is the cowrie-shell, heaps of which lay on the floors of their small warehouses, in every one of which the most prominent article was a British rum cask—that fatal liquid which West Africans appear to prize beyond any-thing else.  The heat was oppressive, and we soon returned to the hotel, where we remained all night.  It was a com-modious building, and everything, from Bass's ale to cham-pagne, was of good quality, and supplied at charges about the same as those at home.

Six coopers were engaged at Accra, which completed the complement we were able to obtain on the coast, before arriving off the Niger, where we dropped anchor on Sunday, the 5th of August.  Here we lay for three days, awaiting the steamer *Rainbow* and one of her Majesty's gunboats, which was to accompany us up the river.  The height of the thermometer had averaged, up to this time 85° Fahr. in the shade ; and on one occasion had risen to 100°.

The next day we observed smoke upon the horizon, but the weather soon became so thick, that we feared, if it were the African Mail, from which we expected letters, that she would miss us ; but at the expiration of two hours the weather cleared, when we saw three steamers making towards us ;

and most welcome and cheering it was to our party.  The first was the *Cleopatra*, with the mails for England ; she only waited a few minutes to receive our letters, being three days behind time.   Of the other steamboats, one was the *Retriever*, a branch mail-boat, and the other the *Rainbow*, in tow by her, she having met with an accident to her boilers which totally disabled them.   We now proceeded to follow the latter vessels over the Bar of the Nun, one of the several mouths by which the Niger disgorges itself into the sea.   After entering the river, and proceeding a short distance, we came to anchor off the native town of Akassa.   We found a gunboat in the river, which had been previously reported to be there.

The Niger is remarkable for its powerful current, and large trees are continually floating down, which the swelling stream has ripped from the dense forests that grow close upon the water's edge, on a sandy soil, but a very few feet above the water-mark.

The 12th of August was our first Sunday in the Niger, and there were two African clergymen on board the *Rainbow*, passengers on their way to their Mission stations up the river.   One of these gentlemen was the Rev. Mr. Crowther, and the other the Rev. Mr. Taylor.   The former is a native of Yoruba, a large, important, and advanced nation of Africa, bordering upon the lower course of the Niger.   His history is well known to all who are interested in Western Africa ; he was, when a boy, sold as a slave from his native country, and embarked on board a slaver, which was seized by a British man-of-war, and taken to Sierra Leone, where he was educated. He was afterwards sent to England, and was finally ordained as a minister of the Church of England.   He chose his native country as the proper field for his labours, and was chaplain, interpreter, and guide in several expeditions up this river. Mr. Crowther is a little man, about sixty years of age, and though his face is characteristic of his race, the head is extremely well proportioned, the forehead and general expression indicating a man of no ordinary qualities.   He and the Rev. Mr. Taylor have conjointly written an interesting work, entitled "Expedition up the River Niger," embodying an account of their missions, and of the general character of the districts bordering upon the Niger.

This gentleman came on board the *Sunbeam*, and performed the Church Service. The half-naked Krumen we had on board flocked into the cabin as the ship-bell tolled, and squatted upon the floor and every spare place. It was unusually interesting to watch the air of mingled wonder and perplexity with which the poor natives looked upon one of their own colour preaching to the whites. For the most part, they could not possibly comprehend what the performance meant; while the canoes which came alongside from the shore, to barter their palm wine, cocoa-nuts, and fish, were, no doubt, sorely puzzled that they met with no attention, so different to the noisy reception which they usually encounter.

The months of July, August, and September, constitute the rainy season in the Niger, and about every two days we got a brisk and heavy shower, sometimes continuing for twenty-four hours. The rain was of course inconvenient for the time, but its result was an agreeable freshness. The intervening periods were delightful, but still sufficiently hot to produce lassitude and depression from comparatively little exertion.

The natives came alongside in the early part of the day to exchange their cassava, palm wine, cocoa-nuts, bananas, fish, and sometimes a few fowls, for tobacco, pipes, or some article of dress, and were greedy and exorbitant in their bartering. They prized a flannel jacket, Guernsey frock, or small shot, tobacco, and rum, more than anything else: a piece of "white man's chop" as they call it, such as salt beef, pork, or biscuit, is also a great luxury to them.

Myself and two young men took the boat, with a few Krumen, to go ashore on several occasions, with our guns and cutlasses, in search of birds, curiosities, or anything which could afford us an additional idea of the character of the locality or the natives. As it was necessary for the ships to procure wood for the engine fires, a large party of Krumen were also sent ashore in the boats to fell old trees for fuel. Under our

directions they made their way through the dense woods, and
in two or three hours some very tall withered trees fell under
the blows of American axes, crushing the surrounding
growth, and affording a week's work to cut them up in pieces
fit to be carried on board. While this was going on, a few
natives would lounge up along the beach, and through mazes
of narrow pathway here and there in the bush, and watch us
with considerable curiosity.

Availing ourselves of the delay, we made several expeditions. One day, on strolling along the beach, we came
upon a spot, where was placed a large earthen jar, such as are
manufactured in the interior, and a cocoa-nut shell fashioned
for a drinking-cup, and an old calabash for containing water,
as well as a broad dish of wood—close to them was a narrow
trail of a leopard leading far into the jungle, and the articles
were deposited with food and water as an offering to propitiate
the animal's favour. In many parts of the river this beast is
held sacred and never molested.

Half a mile farther on, we saw within the bush two or three
small huts of palm-leaves, which were now deserted. Scattered around lay great numbers of the shells of a very large
snail which they use as a common food. Continuing our walk
on a narrow pathway, a venomous green serpent wriggled close
to my feet, and as I recognised its character, a shudder passed
over my frame. A man has been known to die from the bite
of this serpent in three hours. We then came upon a path
which brought us to a stagnant marsh, and returning homeward
by another, found two boys engaged burning out an old trunk
of a tree to form a canoe. They were alarmed; one fled in
fright and the other quickly followed, though we endeavoured
by signs to be friendly. We soon after met a woman with
a child fastened on her back, just over her hips; its head was
daubed over with some kind of red paint, which looked like a
red woollen cap in the distance. She carried a small burden
on her head, and a little boy of about eight years of age
who followed her, ran away, in great alarm. The woman
regarded us very intently and then ran away also. After

picking up a few shells and some large brown speckled beans, which were very numerous, we returned to the ship, resolved on a more extensive acquaintance with the shore. A day or two after, we landed at the same spot and trudged a long way up the beach towards the town of Akassa, but ere we could arrive at the point proposed, having been delayed shooting snipes and kingfishers, which abound here, the tide began to come in with great rapidity, and before we got to the boats, the water had covered the beach. It being impossible to make our way through the wood on the banks, we were compelled to wade up to the waist along the river side, the tide driving in upon us with considerable force. Suddenly our attention was fearfully attracted by the sight of a human foot upon the bank, which had evidently been but a short time cut with some sharp instrument from the body. Our horror was increased by the belief that it was a white person's foot, and apparently a female's. The tendons were hanging loose, as if divided higher up. I put it in a handkerchief and carried it away. Upon arriving at our boat, the Krumen told us their dead always became white after having laid for some time in the water; but this foot did not appear to have been in water long enough, moreover it had not the proportions of a negro's foot, and indeed, in spite of the improbabilities, I felt doubtful as to its black origin. A variety of suppositions passed through my mind as to whence it came, which doubts, however, were cleared up by Mr. Mann, a German botanist and a passenger in the *Rainbow*. He had been botanizing on the banks and came upon the remains of a body there; his account was that the trunk was tatooed after the manner of the natives, it was however white; still his impression was in favour of its being a native's body, and as these people make slaves from other tribes who, in case of death, are cast upon the beach, we concluded it to be part of the corpse of some wretched slave.

On a subsequent visit to the northern bank, I picked up the saw with part of the skull of a saw-fish, one of the largest I have ever seen. Farther on in our walk, under a group of plantain-trees, squatted one or two men and women smoking outside a good-sized hut, the residence of a family. One of the women went into the hut, and brought out some mats for us to sit upon, and a large calabash of palm wine, which was very refreshing. The palm-tree is tapped for it, and the wine exudes into the vessel placed to catch it. The flavour is more like ginger beer than anything else I can compare it to. A pint of well-made palm wine is a good cure for a taciturn humour. We gave them some congreve matches that cracked a good deal, and when I rubbed one on the doorway to show their use, one of the women jumped briskly away in a fright.

These people are not by any means good-looking, and there is a wild expression of cunning about their features, which makes a man suspicious when he suddenly finds himself alone with them. The Rev. Mr. Crowther tells me that these natives at the mouth of the Niger may be classed among the most ignoble of any tribes in Africa. The women have long pendulous breasts, and are otherwise repulsive in appearance. The faces of the men present considerable variety, some few having regular features, and an aquiline nose.

Our vessel had now been detained within the Nun mouth of the Niger for nearly four weeks, in company with the *Rainbow;* their crews being engaged in cutting down dense bush, and palms, and mangrove-trees, which here grow in unusual proximity. The latter is only found on mud-swamps, while the palm requires a drier soil; but here we had good dry sandy soil upon the banks, and in a few minutes' walk we came to a mud-swamp, where one saw the mangrove in all its fantastic vagaries, its branches growing downwards till they reached the earth, then taking root, and growing upwards and then downwards again, and so on, *ad infinitum.* They formed a formidable barrier to one's progress; indeed, they were impassable unless our pioneer was the axe. Occasionally, after the branches have taken root, they grow into a series of arches, and form a complete bridge over the watery marsh, which enables the traveller to walk dryshod across. This clearing of trees and bush was done by us with the intention of building cask-sheds for palm oil, which it might be necessary to deposit here.

Fortunately, up to this date, the health of the crew had continued good, in spite of the wearisome monotony of delay and suspense. On the evening of the 7th August the mail-boat, *Armenian*, arrived off the Nun river, and met the branch-mail *Retriever*, both vessels joined us, and we obtained letters and newspapers, which were a source of great joy to the recipients. The sheds for depositing goods were now being roofed. The natives visited us every day, and were apparently pleased with our visits in return. They watched all our proceedings with great interest, but, as it appeared to me, with some degree of uneasiness. Some of them were continually on board, vending fowls, &c. We obtained a bullock from the *Retriever*, which was most welcome, for the continual appearance of salt beef and pork at our table had made us almost sick. The entire animal, however, only weighed seventy-five pounds, when ready for cooking, so small are the bullocks here. On the 10th, the Chiefs of Akassa, a town under the King of Brass, assembled on shore at the ground where the sheds were being constructed, where they met the Captain of the *Rainbow* to negotiate for our occupation of it. Presents were finally given to the chiefs, after some palaver, consisting of Arabian tobes of the gayest colours, with flaunting silk tassels, and including the invariable keg of rum, and then the right to occupation was ceded. It was a matter of course, for these poor people are totally incapable of resistance.

On the succeeding day I passed on to the beach, late in the afternoon; a canoe, containing two natives, passed close by us. We hailed them, and asked to be rowed up to their village, about half a mile distant. This they very willingly agreed to, and landed us where six or seven canoes lay drawn up upon the banks. We then proceeded up a footpath through the woods, and came suddenly and noiselessly upon a small square, formed by several huts. A group of natives, men, women, and children, were at their ordinary meal of palm oil and cassava out of doors; and our quiet approach, within a few yards of them, gave such alarm that all the women and children set up a scream. Several of the men, however, knew me from having visited the vessel, and one of them took my hand, while another brought stools, and others palm wine, which was very acceptable. Scarcely had we taken our seats, refreshed ourselves with the palm wine, and distributed a little tobacco, when my attention was arrested by a fine large-built man, about forty years of age, sitting just within the hut opposite us. He held in one hand a long mahogany club, divided off in white transverse lines, and in the other some small white fragments, which he appeared to be counting. His manner was so peculiar that I first thought he was a maniac. Under the encouragement of some of the men, the women and children had at this time emerged from their huts, and sat huddled together looking on; but while contemplating the scene, we were startled by the man rushing wildly out of the hut, then, striking the ground violently, he dashed up the earth with his club, roared and howled like a wild beast, and rushed through the thicket, beating down the bushes before him with Herculean strength. He now disappeared, but his roars were not a whit abated, and after a few minutes he emerged from the bush on the opposite side, foaming at the mouth, and with perspiration running from him like rain, evidently having worked himself into a frenzy. Running back against some young plantain-trees, he crushed one down, and addressed one of the bystanders, with an alarming savageness of aspect. A few words having passed between them, he moved towards us with his club advanced before him. Though two of our party urged a retreat, I begged them to keep their seats, and held out my hand towards the man, which he took with a hesitating and reluctant air. But the tempest had passed, and I suspected that this performance was merely made for the purpose of frightening us, or that it was, perhaps, a wild appeal to their gods for protection against the white man. I turned to a native and, pointing to him, said, "dju-dju?" and he replied, "Him dju-

dju; him dju-dju man;" and, as this term signifies charmer, or priest, I concluded that my last supposition was possibly the right one.

As we returned towards the canoe, on the beach, we were obliged, by the narrowness of the way, to pass in single file along the winding path, when one of our party, who lingered behind, was overtaken by the dju-dju man, who put his arm round his waist apparently to throw him, but desisted on resistance being made. This alarmed us a little, but the two natives who accompanied us back were very civil. and paddled us to the new sheds with great good will. These people cut their woolly hair into patterns resembling *parterres*, very various in design, and accurately cut; but this is a common practice throughout Western Africa. Our Krumen were very superior to them in every respect, and I think the natives here were fully aware that their black brothers are in advance of them.

The Kru people are quick and vivacious. After their day's work is over and supper finished, one takes a stick, and beats a monotonous tune on an iron plate, which sets them all dancing, in the most grotesque and ludicrous style, while the vehemence of their action shows how much they enjoy the recreation. They are not remarkable for industry, and though they work pretty steadily when watched, yet when they are left to themselves, they soon show how little addicted they are to systematic and regular labour. A party of Krumen will go into the woods for the purpose of hewing wood; presently they commence hacking while one chants, and their axes keep time. After a little work has been done, one strolls listlessly off into the bush, another squats upon the ground and lights his pipe, while another plays some antics, to the amusement of the ~ rest. When these *divertissements* are used up, they pick up the tools and again set to work; perhaps one or two are despatched in search of fruits, water, land-crabs, peppers, &c., the latter condiment being largely mixed with their food. All these people are most ingenious in their appliance of nature's gifts. I saw excellent rope

manufactured by hand out of strips of bark, and they exhibit
a good deal of taste in carving wood. Their women work
hard and perform the more tedious labours, while the men
take to their canoes, and fish, or shoulder their guns in search
of game. When a Kruman returns home, as the day de-
clines, he bathes outside his door from head to foot, rubs
himself dry, and sits down to his palm oil and fish, with rice
or cassava, and, as an occasional luxury, a piece of meat.
The repast finished, he washes his teeth most scrupulously,
squats himself close to the fire, and talks and smokes till
midnight. The guana, a large lizard, sometimes as thick as
a man's leg, is a favourite dish, and is simply boiled, and
eaten with palm oil and cassava. I once partook of a piece
with a native, who was sitting down to it in the bush, and
I thought it like veal.

As we were still delayed by the continued absence of her
Majesty's gunboat, the men's time on board was occupied
in repainting the vessel, getting up cargo, &c. The powder-
magazine was found to have admitted some water and several
kegs of gunpowder were damaged; they were sent on shore to
be dried in the sun. About this time the Krumen had built
themselves some nice little huts of the bamboo-palm, where
they cooked their own food, and slept at night. A great
quantity of the brush was being burnt, to clear the banks in
the locality of the new warehouses. When our powder
(which had been exposed for a day or two, and had become
caked) was being broken up, a few sparks were carried to it
by the wind, and the whole exploded, to the great con-
sternation of the workmen. Fortunately, only one person
was slightly injured. About this time, I was called on shore
to see a fine, powerful Kruman, who was said to be suddenly
seized with a violent frenzy. The expression of his face, as
described to me, assumed a wild, savage aspect. He jumped
five feet from the ground, rushed through the gable-end of a
hut, breaking down several strong stakes, and dashing himself
upon the ground, performed some convulsive evolutions which
astonished and alarmed the bystanders. This was succeeded

by great depression, as well as by the pain of some severe contusions which he had inflicted upon himself. It was explained to me by his comrades that these attacks were periodic, occurring at intervals of a month. With the exception of a few cases of injuries, and of slight ordinary attacks of illness, I had little to occupy my time professionally, and had ample leisure to make farther visits among the natives. Several serpents were caught while clearing the ground, two of which were amphisbenæ, having, apparently, an ill-developed head at each end of its body. Two of the venomous green vipers were taken, and also two serpents, with black and yellow stripes, and ring-like scales, which were by far the largest of them all, being about five feet long and three or four inches in diameter: both of these were caught swimming on the surface of the Niger. I found the natives here distributed about the bush in considerable numbers, but in societies, never exceeding six or seven huts together. They appeared always pleased with a visit, inviting me freely into their little residences, and placing before me their rare dishes of snake, guana, land-crabs, and fish, and abundance of "tumbo," as they call their palm wine. The women were always reserved and shy; they are fond of painting their neck and shoulders with red-wood dye, and sometimes the entire body is daubed with it. They have a little bundle of red-wood sticks, tied together, and, fixing it on the ground, take a lump of the same wood, which they dip in water; they then rub the latter on the end of the bundle, till a red paste forms upon the surface: it is afterwards applied to the body, where it presently dries, leaving a bright red brick-colour. They were much pleased with a few papers of pins which I distributed among them; but did not understand their use, till I caught hold of a man's waist-cloth and pinned the ends together. A look of gratification followed, and they examined the pins curiously. A few skeins of thread were also much prized. One young native seemed to take quite a fancy to my company, and insisted upon carrying me on his back through the occasional pools of water in our track, and paddled me about in his canoe, to and from the vessel, with great goodwill.

One of these villages lay about a mile up a small creek, through a dismal mangrove-swamp, close upon the sea, which was very audible as it beat upon the beach. Here the water-newts, lizards, and land-crabs, coursed rampant and unheeded. Arriving at the way that led to the village, always discoverable by the many canoes drawn up upon the banks adjacent to it, and after half a mile's walk through a rich field for an adventurous botanist, and across several little rivulets, we emerged on a square patch of ground surrounded by the huts. Then ensued the usual frightened rush of children and women, and exclamations of surprise at the first visit of the white man, soon overcome by holding up a bauble of blue or white beads to their delighted eyes. We distributed a little tobacco, the clay pipes were lighted, and one by one the women and children gathered round, while we tried by means of dumb show to inform them of our willingness to see their chief men on board; and examined their weapons, fishing apparatus, and the internal appliances of their rude dwellings, amid the wild, tangled, island-forests of this great river's delta. These sort of visits were often repeated, and every one of them would develop some new fact regarding their habits, though mostly relating to trivial matters. One day my accustomed guide observed me stoop to pick up a mass of spiral shells at the root of a tree upon the beach; each of the shells I found inhabited by the little timorous "hermit crab," and was about to draw one from his dwelling, when the man seized my hand, and begged me by his gestures to leave it alone, whispering, "dju-dju!" with a serious air.

There is scarcely a man, woman, or child, in these parts, that has not some patch of cutaneous disease, or else the scars of former eruptions upon their person. Lepra is common among them, and also a pustular eruption of an ecthymatous character on the leg, which is frequently covered with large, indolent, pouting sores. Nor do they appear to apply anything for their cure, though one or two permitted me to touch them with blue-stone. When these sores heal, they leave the surface streaked with white mottled patches upon the natural black surface, showing that the pigmentary layer of the skin is destroyed by the disease.

I utterly despaired of acquiring their tongue, and took more than ordinary pains with pantomimic signs, which I found well appreciated. Whenever I was about to take my leave, one would put a dried fish in my pocket, and another bring a pint of palm wine just before starting, which I drank out of the dried rind of something like a vegetable-marrow, hollowed out and polished on the outside, forming a very light, and not inelegant drinking-cup. Of these they gave me several in exchange for a black waistcoat.

The month of September was now drawing to a close, and despondency was visibly creeping over the minds of us all, arising from the suspense and disappointment we had been subjected to since our arrival, and the perplexity felt as to our probable destiny; for the water of the Niger commences to fall about the 5th of October, and all chance of ascending the river appeared to be at an end. The prospect of remaining in the mouth of the Nun during the dry season was indeed gloomy. Fever seized our engineer, who remained ill for some weeks, and the dread of sickness in a locality called "The Gates of the Cemetery," by an English writer, was another cause of depression.

The natives were extremely troublesome to deal with, and expected double, and often treble the value of their articles. They were avaricious and grasping, and never tired of begging from us, though they rarely gave us anything; and, indeed, if they give a "dash," as it is called—*i.e.* a present—they expect one in return of the full value, if not more.

Myself and others had frequently bathed in the river, and could not help remarking that the natives were never seen in the water, which was explained about this time by the capture of a good-sized shark, close in shore, by a man, who brought it to our vessels to dispose of. They would not even

enter the water to capture an unmoored canoe, which happened
to be carried down the stream ; and when I urged one of
them to swim for it, he absolutely refused to enter the water,
We saw several sharks since, and considered it fortunate to
have escaped them.

Our factory on the beach being partly completed, and the
captain of the *Rainbow* having despatched a canoe, about a
week since, to communicate to Brass our readiness for trade,
the king, Arishima, sent one of his war canoes to inform us
he would pay a visit shortly ; and early on a Sunday morning
we were attracted by the noisy clatter of their " tum tum,"
a hollow cylinder of wood, similar to those used on the Kru
Coast.    This announced the passage from the Brass creek
into the river Nun, of Arishima, king of Brass, within whose
territories we then were.

He came in a large canoe, made from one gigantic tree ; it
contained several puncheons of palm oil, and was covered in
from stem to stern with an awning of mats ; about the centre
a space was left, where we descried his Majesty, in a light
blue cocked-hat and a naval suit, but no shirt, seated on a
mat, drinking rum, and administering it to his suite.    These
kings are tenacious of their dignity, and after passing round
our vessels, with his flag flying, containing the word
" Arishima " and some mysterious figures, the King of Brass
passed on to the *Rainbow*.    It being Sunday, the captain and
missionaries had concluded not to receive him till after Divine
Service ; so he and his men adjourned to the shore, but
were presently sent for with a view of allowing them to
hear our service.    They speedily came, but were evidently
chagrined at their cold and serious reception.    His Majesty
having been seated in an arm-chair, after the ordinary
salutation of shaking hands, was subjected to three hours'
praying and preaching in a language he did not understand,
and was obviously in a state of torture at the prolonged
service, which his suite participated in, as was too clearly
evinced by the looks they exchanged together.    Others
laughed outright, not being able to contain themselves, at

this unexpected delay, while they were anticipating a speedy and rapid consumption of rum.   Before the service was completed, however, it was thought prudent to send his Majesty below for refreshment ; but the office of escort was consigned to a coloured man from Sierra Leone, who executed his mission so badly, that his Majesty preferred betaking himself to his canoe, where he remained till prayers were concluded.   The king being now asked, through the interpreter, what he thought of it, replied, " Dat be very good for little boy, same as dat (holding his hand about two feet from deck) ; man no want him.   Suppose we sabby, we stop ashore."   As Arishima had come on a Sunday, no business was transacted until the next day.   He requested some rum to be given to his men while he was taken below and entertained.   Presently some of his Majesty's officers descried a canoe, and hailed it.   But as it hastily fled, the king's men followed in pursuit, and overtook it, and, drawing it up on the beach, overhauled it.   After considerable palaver, the canoe was released.   I was told that the custom is for the king, when travelling, to seize upon any canoe he might meet, and to supply himself with anything he wanted that he might find on board.

About this period, the 1st of October, several vipers were captured ashore, including many specimens of the green viper and slow-worm.   A spider of very large size, weighing about three ounces, was taken by the Government botanist, Herr Mann.   Ascending the river two miles, I came upon a creek, across the mouth of which was passed a bark rope, twenty feet above the water-level, and in the centre a mysterious bundle was suspended on it, tied with twigs, which was supposed to act as a charm upon all who passed beneath.   A mile's walk brought us to a large village (which I estimated as containing, at least, two thousand inhabitants) of the usual character ; but the residents were quite surprised to see us, and it appeared to me no white man had been before among them.

A vessel which we had been daily expecting at this time arrived.   It was the barque *Bessy* of London, intended as a hulk for the reception of palm oil ; and our new visitors were a source of much interest to us, being fresh arrivals from home. The *Sunbeam* proceeded over the bar and towed her to the anchorage ground opposite our newly-constructed warehouse and trading-house.  The king, Arishima, having agreed before his departure to send oil, and having taken his " comey," or impost for permission to trade, caused several canoes to come from Brass with oil ; but the supply soon diminished, and after a lapse of several weeks only fifteen puncheons were mustered. In the last few days of November, a man-of-war arrived off the bar, and turned out to be the *Bloodhound,* sent to our assistance.  The *Bloodhound* had previously been at Brass to settle all difficulties with the traders there, who were supposed to instigate the natives against our trading up the river. The commander wished to take the person of Arishima and carry him off as a hostage ; but the messenger sent to bring the king returned without him.  His Majesty, however, forwarded an ivory bracelet upon which his name was engraved, as his representative—not an uncommon practice among the kings of the Niger.

It was now resolved we should proceed up the Niger, as far as the depth of water permitted at this season of the year (December), and accordingly the *Bloodhound* steamed ahead, and our vessel, the *Sunbeam,* followed in her wake.  For twenty miles, the river banks present one monotonous outline of mangrove-trees shooting forth their myriads of descending branches, which, touching the earth, take root and grow again in a continuous network of huge loops as if to hide the pestiferous mud soil from which they spring.  Having passed this lower part of the Nun branch of the Niger, the soil gradually rises till we see a small village, on the verge of a high clay bank.  The plantain and cocoa-nut trees became visible once more, and at this point we anchored all night and remained the succeeding day (Sunday).

We had some doubts as to our reception at this part of the river, as on a former voyage the *Sunbeam* had here received a salute of musketry which resulted in the death of two young men on board. There did not appear, however, at this period to be any hostile intentions; and in the afternoon the commander of the *Bloodhound*, Mr. Laird's agent, the surgeon of the man-of-war, myself, and the chief engineer of the latter vessel, went ashore, visiting the king, and sauntering among their rude wattle-and-daub huts. I found the air peculiarly oppressive, notwithstanding the thermometer stood only at 85° Fahrenheit; this feeling was also expressed by my companions, and we were very glad to return to our ships.

The village of Angiama was now only four miles distant. This town, containing a population set down as 500 in number, in the nautical charts, had also shown itself hostile on a former occasion; and arriving off the village a number of the inhabitants stood upon its banks; but there was no appearance of hostility, and the king (since dead) came on board.

Our interpreter, Appah, formerly a slave in Brass, having informed him of our intentions, he contracted to give us a piece of woodland above the village, bordering the river, for the establishment of a factory, or trading-house and premises. The document was drawn up on board, and signed with the king's mark, the commander of the *Bloodhound* and Mr. Laird's agent becoming parties to the contract, which contained a clause, binding the king to protect us and our property, and not to molest us in the way of trade or otherwise.

The papers were duly signed, and a piece of ground, of about two acres, but without any defined boundaries, was at once appropriated. The only line of demarcation consisted in one drawn at right angles from the river, to prevent any encroachment from or towards the town which lay immediately in contact with the land chosen. The one source of possible misunderstanding appeared to me to lie in the fact of no consideration being paid for these privileges; it could not be said the land was purchased; nor could it be called a "grant from the king;" for in reality the so-called king is a sort of viceroy or chief under the King of Brass, who is the sovereign of all the territory as far as the "Eboe country;"

and this affair was executed entirely without his concurrence. However, for this grant, if we may so term it, which within a year or two will be expected to realize thousands sterling annually, the poor king Dower received "the munificent present" as follows :—

One velvet cap ; one red cotton gig-umbrella ; one case of gin ; two pieces of cotton-velvet cloth ; five pieces of commonest cloth, such as is used in workhouses for bed-hangings ; one dozen clay pipes ; ten heads of tobacco.

On the other hand, the land was of no use to him, being mere forest ; and the labour of clearing it must be considered.

The king and suite were then conducted upon the paddle-box of the man-of-war, and desired to observe the distance which one of our rockets would be able to reach a refractory town or people, and sundry pleasant reminders were made as to its being made "all right about that factory." The poor king returned into his canoe with a look and manner reminding one of a helpless child who had just received a severe reprimand from a very stern master. Two days after, the ground, which was covered with brushwood, was cleared to a considerable extent by our Krumen, and the *Bloodhound* took her departure, leaving the *Sunbeam* to continue the arrangements, and land such things as might be necessary for the factory, and for the agent and two clerks, who were to be left behind to carry on the business of the place.

Next morning, we were attracted by the shouts of some of our men on shore, and hastening into a boat, rowed off to the fresh-cleared ground, to find the cause of alarm was a python, curled between the brushwood at the foot of a bamboo-palm tree. It was proposed at once to shoot the monster, but the natives begged us to desist, saying that Appah, the Brass interpreter we had brought with us, had told them that if they killed it, the King of Brass would hear of it, and punish them for its destruction. It is regarded as a dju-dju by the Brass people, but it appears every province or district has its own ideas upon the subject, and it is no dju-dju at Angiama, nor even in the town of Akassa, within seven miles of Brass and belonging to the same dominion. However, we persisted upon its being killed ; and sending for our Brass interpreter at once, told him, that should he make any difficulty with the natives on the subject, he would receive chastisement from us forthwith. Still the natives were not satisfied without Appah's consent to its being killed, and thereupon they proposed it should be caught alive, and carried to the other side of the river, and freed. This we acceded to, and awaited with much interest the manner in which the feat was to be accomplished. At this moment I approached within two yards of the large reptile, to get a good view of it, when my eyes caught sight of his head, which he protruded from the brushwood, darting out in quick succession his forked tongue ; and his eyes fixed on me, with fearful intensity, caused me to recoil hastily.

By this time five or six natives had cut out pronged staves about as thick as a man's arm, and nearly six feet in length, and surrounding the animal, when within a yard or so of him, they pinned him to the ground with the prongs, thus holding his body secure from his head downwards. The animal lashed its tail, and extending his mouth to its greatest extent, endeavoured to get free ; but two other natives had by this time made strong nooses from the stems of the creeping plants, so numerous here, and affording them for all purposes an artificial rope, which they slipped over the head and tail, and made tight, one close round the neck, and the other round the middle of the body. Thus he was speedily dragged to the river-side, and some natives springing into a canoe, towed him swiftly to the opposite shore, where he was allowed to make the best of it. The side of the reptile was torn open in the operation, but he had to be repelled, notwithstanding, from the canoe's side, being pushed under water with a prong by one of the natives, to prevent his attacking them in the canoe, while the other paddled away.

Notwithstanding the pleasure of these adventures and novel situations, they were poor compensations for the sleepless nights of anguish which I here endured from the

persecution of mosquitos and sand-flies.  I came on board
just before tea on the day we anchored at this place.  It had
been hot during the day, though endurable in the shade and
in the open air.  Descending into the cabin (unfortunately
our boilers formed the forward extremity of our cabin), the
heat was fearfully oppressive ;  my clothes were fairly wet
through with perspiration, and it poured from the whole body
in streams.   Night was closing in, and ascending to the deck,
we threw our weary bodies upon our hammocks or our
mattresses beneath the awning, when a vicious, wiry, sharp,
unmusical, *buz, buz!  uz, uz!  wuz, wuz!* saluted the ear, and
forehead, nose, face, hands, arms, feet—in short, every superficial exposed inch of the body became feeding-ground for
the· blood-sucking mosquitos, and the irritating sting of the
sand-flies.  "Why didn't you bring a mosquito curtain?" said
one, and forthwith arranged his prudent piece of netting, and
prepared for a good night's rest; but the ingenuity of man is
not always equal to shield him from these tormentors.  Presently, after various attempts to bury myself securely beneath
the counterpane, I fled from the spot in dismay, to be
equally wretched in another; and pacing the deck in a state
bordering on madness, ran against a fellow-sufferer, and was
ultimately joined by every soul on board, scratching, smarting.
swearing, tearing, and wondering what the devil mosquitos
were invented for.  Now, in a climate like that of the Niger,
this state of things is still more alarming, for rest is more
essential here, perhaps, than anywhere else.  The next night
there was a similar scene, but, fortunately, after this the
weather changed, and there was a marked falling off in the
number of these vicious flies of Africa.

The natives here were friendly, and presented me with food
and palm oil whenever I visited them.  Indeed, I soon found
I was a favourite guest, and was regarded as a dju-dju man, or
priest.  A small piece of blue-stone, applied to an ulcer, and
afterwards presented to them for use, secured great good-will.
The king's son, Bagua, is a shrewd, humorous fellow, extremely
avaricious, but evidently appreciating the white man.  Indeed,

he was a specimen of "Young Africa" in a favourable point of view, always remembering that the love of rum and intemperance is sure to graft itself upon these people, wherever the white man sets his foot.

Threading my way through the narrow lanes of the town, I was dismayed at the sight of two women, whose bodies were daubed over with wood-ashes, sitting at the further end of a small hut, and of a hole at their feet, about three feet deep, containing the remains of their husband, which were lying in the most revolting and disgusting state. Some pieces of cloth were wrapped around the body, but the face of the corpse was exposed, and in the last stage of decomposition. I found that it was the custom for the wives not to quit the body for nine days after the decease of their husband.

It is a common practice among the chieftains of the various nations in the Niger, upon the settlement of any commercial or friendly relations between themselves and the white man, to present one of their young sons as an attendant upon the person of the principal negotiator during pleasure, as a pledge of confidence. Accordingly, the king offered his son, and another chief offered a Houssa slave—a boy of fourteen years of age, with a good countenance and a robust person. The latter was accepted and came on board, and descended the Niger upon the *Bloodhound* as far as the Nun mouth, where he was transferred to the hulk. The boy was well fed and kindly treated, more as a guest than as a menial. Accordingly, on a boat-excursion to Akassa, he was taken in the boat. As many of the Akassa people were well known to us, they rushed into the water to pull our boat more swiftly on shore, screaming with delight at our visit. Now the Mahometan Houssa youth held the pagan in horror and disdain. His mind was full of visions of chains and slavery, to which many of his captive brothers had been led, and tales of the big water, "the ocean," as it broke for the first time upon his view, filled his heart with terror, combined with the yelling of the pagan tribes upon the beach. Overcome with these thoughts, he broke out into lamentations of grief which penetrated our hearts, lifting his hands above his head, and sinking upon his knees at the bottom of the boat; his loud and piteous appeals to "Allah" were distressing to witness, nor could any kind or caressing act pacify him; and, sooner than continue his distress, we hastened back to our vessel, much chagrined by this unexpected ebullition of feeling. Arrived at the ship, he appeared more tranquil, but bursts of agony still broke forth. It was clear he thought our intention was to sell him; and, as it is a common superstition among his people to suppose the white man dyes his brilliant red cloth with the blood of slaves, his misery may easily be conceived. On the next day, after scarcely an intermission to his distress, we sent him back to his master; and, at Angiama, when the latter came on board, he became apparently reconciled.

The moral characteristics and natural feelings of the Niger tribes are in many respects not inferior to those of the whites, in spite of their paganism; and certain it is that the missionaries engaged in Christianizing them cannot hope to produce any really advantageous effect, unless their minds are prepared for their influence by that knowledge of the whites which actual intercourse can alone give, and commerce bring about. Moreover, these missionaries are sometimes introduced by blacks who are despised by the tribes whom they visit, and who would be made slaves, were it not for the protection of the Englishman. These men are injurious to the missionary cause by the contempt in which they are themselves held, and with which they reciprocally treat the natives—a fact which I have myself observed. Besides, the assistant missionaries are sometimes totally unfit for their office. Among them are ill-educated, raw, unsophisticated young men, who neither speak their own language properly, nor that of the natives. It is extravagant to expect any Christianizing influence to arise from such sources.

We now descended the river in the *Sunbeam* from Angiama, and the petty villages which lay between this town and the Nun expected a " dash " as a sort of due for passing along in safety. Sometimes they would come on board, and show their letters or "books," received from previous expeditions. It was at a place called Liambre that I saw one in the possession of a chief, written by the unfortunate Richard Lander, who was shot near Angiama while endeavouring to proceed up the river, and who died at Fernando Po from his wound. This enterprising man, together with his brother, since dead, were the well-known discoverers of the exit of the Niger into the ocean.

During our stay in Angiama we were awakened in the middle of the night by the watch on deck, who told us he could hear the well-known chant of Kruboys. This assured us our letters were arriving from the Nun, a distance of sixty miles. We exhibited a blue light for their direction, as the night was quite dark, and had the satisfaction of receiving our mail. Having completed amicable arrangements with the natives, we left three white men and fourteen Kruboys to complete a building for the reception of goods.

In the interval of two weeks, between this period and our return to Angiama, Christmas and New Year's-day were celebrated with much glee, and these days ended with a grand finale of song, dance, and laughter, which, for a time, made all forget the reputed terrors of a sojourn in the Delta.

It was in this month that the Harmattan winds from the north-east set in pretty regularly, *i.e.* about every ten days, and continued for one or two days. Coming, as they do, across the land over the desert, a most disagreeable dryness over the whole surface of the body takes place, which I can compare to nothing so much as to the idea of a bath in a strong solution of alum, and being dried in the sun afterwards.

About the latter end of November the inhabitants on the right bank of the river remove *en masse* to the town of Akassa, on the opposite bank. Here the natives remain during all the dry season, which commences in January, and lasts to the end of March, when they commence removing back to their old habitations. In the interval Akassa is crowded, and the people celebrate certain days as sacred, or dju-dju days. Offerings are made to their gods in the places set apart for that purpose, and the remainder of the day is passed in a general jubilee. The women and men turn out decorated in their best beads and waist-cloths, their faces painted in curious and fantastic patterns. Considerable amount of gun-powder is expended, which has been all the year hoarded for the purpose, and rum issues from secret places.

It became necessary soon after our first visit to Angiama, that the oil collected and purchased in that place should be con-veyed by our own ship to Bonny, as the branch mail-boat of the African Steam Ship Company had broken down. It requires about thirty-six hours of steaming to reach this place. Before taking our departure for Bonny, a serious incident occurred, developing the thieving characteristics of the Kru people, a distinction which is universally acknowledged by all narrators respecting that tribe. The Krumen in our employ had had, some months before, a building erected for their habitation close to the factory. In the exercise of my professional duties I daily visited their abode. Within the entry was a small chamber, separated from their sleeping room, large enough for twenty men. The door of this inner apartment I found at all hours barred, and had invariably to wait some four or five minutes before it was opened to me by the men within. It had struck me as somewhat singular, that four or five Krumen were always engaged trimming and cutting the variegated muslin, or calico prints, used for trading among the natives, more especially as they affected to be ill, when I believed them to be well. Knowing that their pay consists, in great measure, of these articles, my suspicions were for a long time lulled.

I at last observed articles which I suspected could not be justly in their possession; and ventured to suggest to our captain that something was wrong. When I heard him announce the disappearance of a great many axe-blades, I said, " You will find them in the Krumen's house." In the afternoon we visited the shore in company, and proceeded to their dwelling, where we found a large amount of valuable property, stolen from the factory stores.   Returning to our ship, the head Kruman was sent for, and he refused to come off.   Another messenger went, but the Kruman still refused, declaring his men should not come till he was told who the man was that had informed the captain.   His bold reply was followed by a missive from our captain to the effect, that if he and his men did not come, force would be used.   They still refused, and forthwith the white men were ordered to arm themselves, and proceed on shore.   This done, we walked to the Krumen's house.   Their alarm at this demonstration was great, and when ordered into the boats, they immediately complied, excepting three, who rushed through the side of the building, and hid themselves in the bush, where they remained several days, till hunger induced them to return.   The party being examined, accounted for their possession of the stolen goods by most ridiculous statements, and we took them to Fernando Po, the nearest port where a British Consul resides, to be disposed of according to law.

This island is enticing to look at, bright as a glowworm. Its mountains of foliage, neglected, yet capable of yielding the produce of almost every clime; its bluff, yet peaceful shores; the purity of its water, romantic glens, brilliant fountains, and cascades fresh from Nature's hand, and the simplicity of the aborigines, attract the visitor.   We landed early in the morning under a scorching sun.   A few respectable buildings of wood, with broad verandahs, facing the sea, are the residences of the important personages of the island.   The English ex-governor, Mr. Lynslager, was the first person we visited.   The island is a Spanish possession, but was a few years ago abandoned, on account of the great mortality which occurred among the Spanish colonists.   Our Government then adopted it as a rendezvous for men-of-war, and Mr. Lynslager, from his long residence and extensive knowledge of the coast, was appointed governor by the Spaniards, after the decease of Governor Beecroft, an Englishman, who was previously governor, and at the same time acted as

Britannic Consul. The latter gentleman was among the first who ascended the Niger as far as Rabbah, and twenty miles beyond that place. Three years ago the Spaniards reclaimed possession, and appointed a Spanish governor and judge. They also established a garrison. The plenitude of their infirmary exhibits painfully the baneful character of the climate.

Three days having elapsed, our prisoners were placed on board a Spanish man-of-war, to be remitted to the English authorities at Cape Coast for trial, and we again returned to the 'River Nun. It was necessary that we should forward provisions to our comrades in Angiama; but we had yet to wait the arrival of another gunboat—the *Bloodhound* not being adapted for au ascent of the river so far.

On the 6th of April the mail from England brought us the unwelcome news of the decease of Mr. McGregor Laird, the father of our enterprise. During the period which elapsed before the arrival of the gunboat *Espoir,* which was despatched to us from Lagos, much sickness prevailed among our crew, and several of our black men died. We also lost our cook and the carpenter.

Fortunately the *Espoir* arrived in time to enable us to reach the confluence before the low water. No time was lost in arranging for our departure up the river, under her escort. On our ascent, Commander Douglas made inquiries of the natives respecting the outrages which I mentioned had occurred at Sabogrega on a former voyage, when the *Sunbeam* was fired upon from that place, and a nephew of Captain Walker killed. We found that village strongly protected by wooden stockades and earth-works, and defended by cannon.

A few miles above Sabogrega, we anchored off the villages Oloberi, Kiamah, and Opotolo. Captain Douglas despatched a boat with an interpreter, and required the chiefs to give explanations respecting the outrage in question. Some canoes, with about a hundred natives, after considerable delay, came alongside, and two chiefs, with their followers, were received on deck. They, however, denied all knowledge of the affair.

Captain Douglas, entertaining no doubt of their complicity, ordered one of the chiefs to be taken below. The natives on board forming his suite then became very uneasy, and the chief having jumped through a port-hole into the river, the other natives dashed over the bulwarks, and being good swimmers, reached the shore in safety, amid the cries of the women and children, who watched them from the banks.

The *Espoir* guns then fired upon the town, and the boats having been manned to attack it, I went on shore to assist the surgeon of the *Espoir*. We burnt the village to the ground. The natives secreted themselves in the bush, and kept up a steady fire upon us as we returned to the ship's boats. Two English seamen were killed, and two others slightly wounded. After bombarding another inimical town, which was quickly vacated by the inhabitants, we steamed up to Aboh, where Mr. McGregor Laird had formerly established a factory. We found that the floods of the rainy season had washed away the building, which had previously been plundered by the inhabitants. The clerk in charge had been made prisoner; but after much suffering, was allowed to go to Onitsha, where another European factory existed. From the latter place he reached us, and was sent home by Captain Walker.

Next day we proceeded on our way to Onitsha, which is a considerable town, and has a mission-house and school, and on the bank of the river, a mile below the town, McGregor Laird's trading-house, which was then in charge of a black man from Sierra Leone.

The country here is both magnificent and picturesque. The town of Onitsha is built within a delightful grove, rich in tropical fruits. The avenues leading to it are broad, and covered with grass, surrounded by a thick and beautifully wooded country. The town contains a large population, but of unknown amount. The people are favourable to the whites, and send a number of children to be educated at the mission school.

We remained at Onitsha for several days, and during that time made a picnic party to Bassa, a town in the interior about

seven miles distant. Our way there was upon the crest of
several hills, affording a view of the river Inam and a delightfully varied tract of a rich and fertile land.

The heat of the day was so great, that several of our party
were carried in palanquins, not being able to sustain the
fatigue of walking. Arriving at the town, it presented more
pleasing characteristics than Onitsha. We learned from a
native the residence of one of their chief men, who was
evidently pleased with our visit. Having presented him with
a few pieces of cloth and some tobacco, we looked out for a
quiet nook about the village where we might enjoy our picnic
dinner, in privacy, but we had no sooner spread our mats,
than (as it seemed to me) the whole population—men, women,
and children—all in a complete state of nudity, flocked to the
spot. We were obliged to pass a rope from one tree to
another, and employed several of our Krumen to keep them
from crowding on us. They exhibited great curiosity, and
goodnature, and I could not but observe the beauty of both
face and form in both sexes.

Soon after our repast, we returned to Onitsha, and on the
succeeding day heard that the king would present himself to
his people, in a large open space set apart for such displays,
on the morrow. The king, in this part of the country, does
not quit his house or grounds, nor is he seen by the populace
but once in the year, so that we prepared ourselves for a scene
of interest and excitement, and early on the following morning
walked into the town. Arriving upon the spot set apart for
the ceremony, we found a concourse of about 2,000 men and
women ; the latter were separated from the men, facing
each other, from either side of the grass-covered space,
in front of a long low building, under which sat the king and
his chiefs upon handsome mats, worked in fantastic designs
of different coloured grass. The king was a weak-minded
individual in the general expression of his features, and spoke
scarcely a word during the three hours that I remained near
him ; but his officers would not permit any of us to sit under the

same building, and showed us places some twenty yards from royalty. I took it into my head to pass over the square, and survey the female part of the population, but a man was despatched to stop my vagrancy, and he signified, to the best of my apprehension, that no men were permitted among them in this public display.

Presently a number of men appeared, armed with guns and spears, and went through evolutions, which would have formed a rich burlesque of a review in England. The affair was concluded by some most laughable war-dances, and we returned to our ships. The influential men of this community carry an elephant's tusk, carved and polished, with an aperture at both ends, and hollow throughout; this is used as a trumpet. Many of them also carry the skin of some wild animal under the arm, which is also a mark of distinction, not permitted to be worn by all classes.

Large quantities of palm oil are obtained here, and after embarking several tons, we left Onitsha, and proceeded on our way to Idda, situate on the top of a cliff of sandstone, rising perpendicularly from the river bank. Here, for the first time, we saw some horses grazing outside their huts. A great many of the natives came on board, but, unlike the people of Onitsha, the men wore long loose cotton tobes of native manufacture, some made of long white strips about four inches wide, sewn together. They have not the art to weave their cloth of any great width.

The inhabitants here have better and more solid huts to live in, and behaved with courtesy and showed much willingness to please. The town was divided into three sections. This division into sections appears to be a general practice among the inhabitants of the Niger. A young native was deputed to conduct me over their town, and I was frequently invited into their huts, and offered food and palm-wine on my way. The population numbered about 3,000. Here the country becomes mountainous, and covered with rich vegetation.

The water was too shallow beyond Onitsha to permit the *Espoir* to proceed, but the *Sunbeam* continued on her course to the confluence of the Niger with the Chadda, where we arrived in twenty-four hours from Idda.

Dr. Baikie's residence is in a locality at Locojee, which he has selected not far from the river, at the foot of Mount Patteh. He has an inclosure of about one acre of ground, within which are several huts, built after the native fashion. The entrance of his ground is built over, so as to form a waiting place for the slaves and attendants of chiefs, while on a visit to the doctor. His hut and its arrangements were indicative of his character and pursuits, and everything was carried on within the narrow circle of that single apartment.

On one side were arranged a few chemicals, and enormous piles of manuscripts closely packed. At a small table in the centre sat the doctor, habited in the native tobe and turban, his bed was stretched upon a few leopard skins close by, and various prepared specimens in natural history and botany hung around ; some of which, recently obtained, lay upon a floor of a hard dry concrete of earth and pebble. Here he was busily engaged in recording his experience among the natives, and gathering from their own lips such information as they could give of their various tribes, their powers, and relative positions, and the routes that connect them ; and accumulating a general knowledge of the country and people. At the same time he is conducting negotiations with Dasaba, which will be of extreme importance to future trading operations in oil, cotton, and ivory, and I believe his exertions will ultimately lead to a just appreciation of the vast commercial wealth of this country, hidden now, though surely to be reaped at no distant period.

The cotton grows here spontaneously, and might be cultivated over a beautiful and most extensive region. The inhabitants are Mahomedans, and friendly to Europeans ; but they carry on deadly wars with the pagan tribes who surround them. About two miles from Locojee there is an encampment, where the powerful Fellattah chief, Dasaba, keeps an armed force of horse and foot, of several hundred men, to protect the country from the incursions of neighbouring tribes. He took possession of this part of the river and drove the inhabitants across the Niger, where they built the town of Igbegbe. I ascended Mount Patteh, which is infested with wild beasts, and my guide, a native procured for me by Dr. Baikie, occasionally stopped, as we stood on a ledge of rock, over the high grass, and pointed for me to look, when I observed a wavy motion, which he gave me to understand was made by the trail of some brute of the mountain. At noon we arrived upon its summit, 1,160 feet above the level of the sea. The flat top was covered with luxurious grass and picturesque clumps of noble trees, reminding one of some old park in England. The further side was precipitous and thickly wooded, but broken by a line of bare rock reaching to the bottom of the ravine, which sloped gradually towards a wide tributary stream, whose clear waters reflected upon their bosom this wild mountain scene. My guide then conducted me to the ruins of a village from which Dasaba drove its inhabitants and burnt it to the ground, leaving only its blackened walls remaining. From this point the surrounding country was magnificent in mountain scenery, and beautiful in the variety of its woodlands and deep valleys sloping towards the Niger, and presented a view of its wide affluent, the Chadda, wending its way from the far and unknown interior.

I descended Mount Patteh and reached Dr. Baikie's establishment towards evening, exhausted with my day's toil, but fortunately in time to witness the entry of a part of Dasaba's cavalry into the town, on their way to the camp. If the reader will recall to mind the picture of a wandering tribe of Arabs in the desert, he will form a sufficiently correct notion of the scene.

Next day I visited some of the Mahomedan priests, who were courteous in their manner towards me. Several of them had two or three scriveners at work, writing upon wood and paper, copies of the Koran and books of prayer. I purchased a copy of some chapters from the Koran, for a piece of cloth worth about five shillings. We were just two weeks at this place, and during our stay I was much pleased with the people—surprised at their intelligence, and delighted with the faithful gentleness of disposition displayed by their tawny wives and daughters.

Dr. Baikie declined returning with us on account of some engagements he had with Dasaba, not being completed. He sent, however, both his white companions, Mr. Dalton, the naturalist, and McGregor Laird's trader, home by our vessel. We then returned down the river and closed our business at the several trading stations. I was the only person who suffered severely from fever during our return, which I attributed to injudicious exposure, and over-exertion ; and upon our arrival in the Nun, it was thought necessary for my safety that I should return by the mail to England, and I landed in Liverpool a day or two after the advent of the new year of 1862.

Before concluding with an allusion to what is to be done, and to what is now established on the Niger, I must again remind the reader how largely the development of its trade hereafter will have been due to the untiring and ill-remunerated efforts of the late Mr. McGregor Laird.

The articles of commerce in the Niger at present are palm oil, shea butter, cotton, lead ore, red pepper, camwood, indigo, and ivory,—palm oil and cotton are obtainable along the whole course of the Niger in inexhaustible amount,—and all these products may be purchased for cowries, cloth, and particularly salt. The trading stations in the Niger are established at the mouth of the Nun, at Angiama, Onitsha, and Locojee. At present there are no trading vessels in the Niger.

Lastly, I should mention the fact, that from among two hundred Europeans, or thereabouts, belonging to Mr. Laird's three ships, only two died during an absence of nearly two years on the coast and in the Niger, the greater part of which time was spent in the Delta, the most malarious part of the river, among the mud-swamps and mangroves. This remarkable absence of mortality well deserves to be borne in mind, as showing that the diseases originating in the peculiar climatical influences of the coast, are not so intractable as earlier experiences seemed to prove.

# 10. *NABLOOS AND THE SAMARITANS.*

BY GEORGE GROVE, ESQ.

FEW places in Palestine are more interesting than the town of Nabloos. To begin with, there is something unusual about its name. Nábloos—or Naplouse, as the French write it—is the Arabic attempt to pronounce the Greek name Neapolis, the "new city," the title given to the old Canaanite town of Shechem when it was restored or rebuilt, probably during Vespasian's reign. It is rare to find a modern or foreign name in the East that has succeeded in supplanting the ancient home-born Semitic one. In Egypt, at one time, almost every town of any importance was called Heliopolis, Lycopolis, or some other Greek or Roman name. Now, hardly one is to be found along the whole length of the Nile. In Palestine itself, Ptolemais, Diospolis, Antipatris, Ælia, have all completely disappeared, and the old names, which existed before these high-sounding titles were conferred—Akka (Acre), Lydd, Kefer-Saba, Jerusalem, have re-established themselves as firmly as if they had never been displaced. Sebaste and Neapolis have, however, succeeded in maintaining themselves, and preventing the return of Samaria and Shechem.

In its situation there is something still more unusual. It lies in a valley, between two lofty hills, while nineteen-twentieths of the towns of the Holy Land—at least those in the highlands—are perched on the top of eminences. The reason for the prevalent custom is obvious. In a country so open to the incursions of marauders of all sorts as Palestine has always been, it is important to seize any little natural advantage of situation which can assist the peasant against

the robber, be he Philistine, Midianite, Roman, Crusader,
Frenchman, or modern Bedouin Arab. And this, amongst other
reasons, explains why the villages are so often put in the most
inaccessible spots possible. Why Shechem should have been
an exception to this rule is not obvious. It was one of the
most ancient places of the country, and also powerful. Possibly
it was founded before there were any marauders to attack it,
or was built so strong that it did not fear their attacks.

Another thing impresses it without trouble on the favourable recollection of the traveller. It is usually the first place
he reaches which has any natural charm or beauty about
it. After riding the whole day in the burning sun over the
hills north of Jerusalem, often as bare and nearly as hard as
the foot-pavement of the Strand, the springs and brooks of the
valley of Nábloos, its green trees and vegetation, soft moist
atmosphere and twittering birds, are naturally very pleasant
and refreshing.

But besides this, it is one of the most characteristic examples of a Moslem town in the whole of the country. Compared with Damascus, or even Jerusalem, it is but a small place
—some 12 to 15,000 inhabitants. But what its people want in
numbers, they make up in independence and spirit. The district of the Jebel Nábloos is now—as it was when it bore the
name of Mount Ephraim—one of the most difficult to manage
in the whole of Syria. If an Englishman wants to know
something of a sphere of human life about as diametrically
opposite to his own as can be imagined, he cannot have a
better opportunity in all Syria of doing so than he will have
in the bazaars of Nábloos. He will see less of the grace and
charm of Oriental life than is to be found at Damascus or
Cairo; but he will see more of the fanaticism of Islam,
and it is but fair to warn him that there is no place where
he will be more soundly cursed as he works his way
through the bazaar, or stands a better chance of being mobbed
and illtreated. Native Christians are sadly. at a discount.
There are very few of them, and they have a furtive anxious
look about their thin sallow visages, contrasting very disad-

vantageously with the noble countenances and lofty figures of some of the other inhabitants.

But there is more than all this in Nábloos. Its archæology is indisputable. Not even Dr. Robinson doubts the tradition which identifies the two long, rough, lofty, ridgy hills, that rise so steeply on either side of the valley, with Ebal and Gerizim, or which sees in the ruined well at its eastern end, the well of Jacob. It would puzzle even Mr. Fergusson to find any arguments with which to assail the genuineness of the flat sheet of rock on the summit of Gerizim, which has been the holy place of the Samaritans for more than 2,000 years.

We have now arrived at that which gives its great charm to this place—the little community of Samaritans, who inhabit one corner of it.

Interesting they will always be for their own sake, as the smallest and oldest sect in the world, occupying the same spot, and clinging to the same identical sanctuary, through nearly twenty-five centuries, and that sanctuary not improbably the very earliest holy place in the Holy Land. The bare platform of rock on the summit of Mount Gerizim they bélieve to be the place on which Abraham was commanded to sacrifice Isaac, and arguments are to be found (not few or feeble to those who will consider them dispassionately) in favour of that spot, instead of the so-called Mount Moriah at Jerusalem.

Of persecution, the Samaritans have had plenty. From the time when Vespasian slaughtered 11,000 of them on their holy mountain, to the petty oppressions of the Turkish Beys, so touchingly described by Jacob esh-Shelaby, the hand and tongue of every dweller in the East—Heathen, Jew, Mahometan—seem to have been against them. This persecution has had its usual effect. It has attached them more closely than ever to their faith, and has perpetuated their peculiarities —their rites and their books—to a degree of minute conservatism, which at first sight is almost incredible. To name only two instances of this. Justin Martyr—himself a native of Neapolis—writing in the middle of the second century, mentions that the Samaritans roasted their Passover lambs on a spit *in the form of a cross.* They still do the very same thing after the lapse of 1,700 years. The second is, that they use the ancient Hebrew alphabet instead of the ordinary square letters introduced after the captivity by Ezra. These square letters they vehemently repudiate, and it almost takes one's breath away to hear an act of Ezra's, dating from five centuries before the Christian era, still denounced as an absurd and wicked innovation. I brought away a primer from which the little Samaritans are taught in their school at Nábloos, and it is covered with the thin sprawling forms of the venerable letters, much more rude and complicated than the usual Samaritan type of the Polyglotts.

And this is shown in many other things. Their copies of the Pentateuch differ in many grave (if not material) points from the Hebrew one. That these differences are at least 2,000 years old is rendered very probable, by many of them being found also in the translation of the Septuagint, which is known to have been made in the third century before Christ. Their mode of chanting (as we shall see afterwards) is peculiar and archaic. Their laws of marriage are most strict; they never marry out of their own people. With the Jews, the Passover has long ceased to be anything but the feast of unleavened bread; but the Samaritans encamp on the mountain for a whole week, and slay, roast, and eat the lambs, with their loins girt and staves in their hands, and with every minutest particular of the Mosaic ritual observed. And so in purification and other small enactments, they observe the regulations of the law in a far stricter manner than the Jews of Palestine or any other country. Now we know from their letters to Scaliger, in 1589, that they kept all these things as strictly three centuries ago as they now do, and this is a strong evidence that they have preserved a great deal from a still earlier age.*

* Those who would like to pursue this interesting subject farther, may be referred to the following sources :—The letters from the Samaritans to Scaliger (A. D. 1589), are given by Dé Sacy in Eichhorn's " Repertorium," &c. vol. xiii.

Indeed, that they are conservative there can be no doubt. But then comes the question, " What do they conserve ?" Are they Israelites ? or are they—as usually seems to be taken for granted—mere heathens, who adopted a bastard Jewish religion for their own ends, and whose whole system is an imposture ? This is obviously not the place for the discussion of such a question as this. I will content myself with naming one or two circumstances which seem strongly to favour the idea that the Samaritans have, to say the least, a very strong Israelite element in their composition, and which incline me to the belief, that in their seclusion they may have preserved some traits of the Israel of the Bible, and of the ancient worship of Jehovah, which the Jews (properly so called) have lost during their close intercourse with nations and institutions differing so extremely from their own.

I use the words " Israel " and " Israelite " advisedly ; because, though the Jews were Israelites, yet the Israelites were not Jews. The word " Jew " (*Judæus*) is really " Judæan," and dates only from the return from Babylon, when Judah became the head and representative of the nation. The Samaritans always call themselves the children of Joseph, and the Jews *Yehudhim*, or Judathites. Perhaps, of all the ancient practices of the Samaritans, none is more startling than this habit of insisting, in the nineteenth century of the Christian era, on the distinction between " Judah and Ephraim," with all the strength and animosity that can have been thrown into the terms in the days of · Jeroboam or

p. 257. Those to Ludolf, with others to De Sacy himself, and with a *resumé* of the whole correspondence, in his Paper in the " Notices et Extracts," tom. xii. See also Schnurrer in the " Repertorium," vol. ix. p. 1. On the whole, the fullest report of the existing community is that of Dr. Wilson (" Lands of the Bible," ii. 46—78, and 687—701.) He gives lists of their names, a copy and translation of a marriage covenant, their Creed, and other information, which his knowledge of Hebrew and Arabic enabled him to obtain. The narrative of the Abbé Bargès (" Les Samaritains de Naplouse ") is worth reading. But the most interesting of all is a small book called " Notices of the Modern Samaritans," the personal history of the family of Jacob esh-Shelaby, as dictated by himself to Mr. Rogers our excellent Consul at Damascus, who was formerly stationed in the neighbourhood of Nabloos.

Amaziah. The same distinction occurs constantly in their letters to Scaliger.

But to return. It is usually assumed that the kingdom of Samaria was completely cleared of its Israelite population before the Assyrian colonists were sent there. Was this so? Subsequent occurrences seem to show that it is at least doubtful.

The " remnant of Israel " are mentioned in the reign of Josiah as being sufficiently numerous to make it worth while to collect their subscriptions for the repair of the temple at Jerusalem.* That some considerable affinity existed between these people and Jerusalem is evident from a remarkable narrative of Jeremiah, which shows that large caravans of devotees from the chief cities of Samaria were in the habit of making pilgrimage to the ruins of the Temple after its destruction by Nebuchadnezzar, for the purpose of lamenting over it.† After Judah returned from captivity, the Samaritans showed their anxiety to join in the worship of Jehovah, and to assist in rebuilding the temple. This, however, the leaders of Judah would not hear of. They repulsed the offer with scorn as made, not by friends, but by " adversaries of Judah and Benjamin." ‡ This was the beginning of the strife. But that very strife was, perhaps, destined to cause a stronger infusion of the Jehovah element into the Samaritan community than would have been the case had they remained at peace with the Jews. For it so happened that Manasseh, son of the high-priest at Jerusalem, and himself acting high-priest, having married a daughter or grand-daughter of Sanballat, the Samaritan chief, was expelled from Jerusalem by Nehemiah, upon which he went over to his father-in-law, with a large number both of priests and laymen, and became the first priest of the sanctuary on Gerizim.§ Thus, the religious establishment of the Samaritans was actually inaugurated by a high-priest of Jehovah directly descended from Aaron, in a city, the

* 2 Chron. xxiv. 9.

† Jer. xli. 5, and the article on Ishmael, son of Nethaniah, in Smith's Dictionary of the Bible, vol. i. p. 895.

‡ Ezra iv. 1—3.        § Josephus, Antiquities, xi. 8, § 2—7.

inhabitants of which, to use the words of Josephus, were
chiefly "deserters from the nation of the Jews." These facts
certainly seem to indicate a much stronger connexion between
the Samaritan people and Israel, and a much broader Jehovistic
element in their religion, than is commonly assumed. They
certainly had the true succession in their priesthood. The
political animosity which began with Zerubbabel's rude re-
pulse (or rather, perhaps, centuries earlier, before the separation
of the northern and southern kingdoms), was fanned by the
constant secessions of discontented and turbulent Jews from
the Holy City, and is quite enough to account for the exag-
geration and ill-will which have existed on both sides with
such virulence and pertinacity.

I will now endeavour to describe the rites of the *Yôm
kippoor*, or Day of Atonement, of the Samaritans, as I witnessed it at Nabloos in 1861—in an extract from a letter
written at the time.

I arrived at the town on Friday, October 11. One of
the first persons I encountered was a Samaritan, who was
well known in England some years back, Jacob esh-Shelaby.
In his house I remained during my stay, and to him I
am indebted for all that I saw and heard. From sunset
of Thursday, the 11th, to that of Friday, the 12th, was
the Sabbath of the Samaritans, and from the sunset of
the 12th to that of the 13th, the *yom kippoor*. This is, I
believe, about a month later than the date at which the day is
kept by the Jews. The reason of this I could not discover,
either from the Samaritans, or from some learned Jews of whom
I inquired in Damascus: I can only conjecture that it arises
from a difference in the calculation of the days which have to be
added to adjust the difference between solar and lunar years.

The Samaritans, who number between ninety and a hundred
souls, besides women and children, inhabit a quarter of their
own at the south-west angle of the town. The Synagogue is
situated within the quarter. I entered it first on the evening
of the Sabbath, at 5 o'clock, so as to see the conclusion of the

ordinary service, and the commencement of that of the Fast.
They tell you that the building is 600 years old; and though
this is probably exaggerated, it has no ornamentation or other
evidence to contradict it, and it is a venerable edifice, quite in
keeping with the venerable sect who worship within it. Through
a little garden, shut in by high walls, I entered a small square
covered court, which at that time was filled with women and
children. From thence two low steps lead up into the church.
Here I put off my boots, and left them amongst the numerous
slippers of the community who had already entered. The

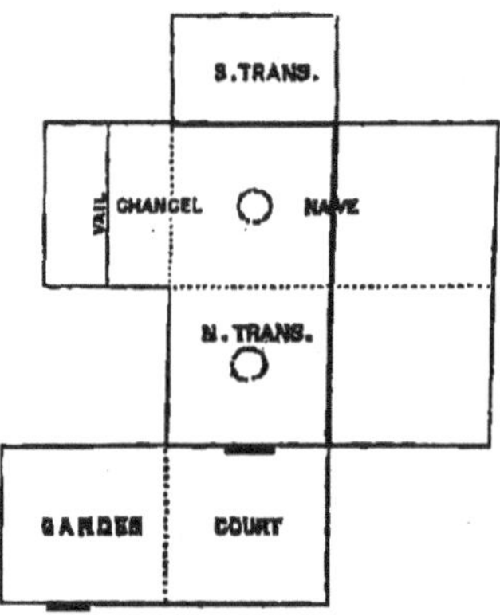


N.B.—The points of the compass are only used relatively, for description's sake. The
building did not point E. and W.

building may be best described as a nave of two bays, with
chancel and north and south transepts of one bay each, and
a chapel between the north transept and the west end of the
nave. The three last-named portions are raised one step.
Each bay is groined, and there are two small round apertures
in the roof. Besides these the only opening is the door. The
walls are white, and from the vaults hang two quaint glass-
chandeliers, and one small glass oil-lamp. The door is in the
north transept, so that on entering, the recess for the Torah,
or Book of the Law, answering to the chancel, was on the
left. Directly opposite the door hung a European clock.
I retreated to the corner immediately on my right, from
whence, being raised a step, I could overlook the rest, without
being myself too prominent.

It was a striking scene. The floor was covered with carpets. Except a space left up the transepts the whole building was nearly filled by about eighty persons, of whom fifteen or twenty were women and children, the rest men. All were in white surplices or gowns, with white turbans round their red tarbooshes. All were squatted on the ground, and looking towards the recess of the Torah, which points in the direction of the Kibleh on Mount Gerizim, the one holy place of the community. The back of this recess was hung with a veil of dull red and gold—the one piece of colour on the walls— behind which, among other similar, but less precious treasures, was the Book, or rather Roll of the Law, which the Samaritans affirm to be by the actual hand of Abishua, the son of Phinehas, the grandson of Aaron. The only articles of furniture in the chancel were a stool, and something which looked like a high-backed chair—a stand for the exhibition of the sacred rolls. On the stool lay a bundle in blue silk. It was a famous book of the Pentateuch (not a roll) wrapped in handkerchiefs, the offerings of the pious.

In front of the chancel, a little towards the right, was the priest, erect. He was dressed exactly like the others, and was reading some service in a loud, harsh, monotonous chant or plainsong, varied by occasional jerks or *barks*, and by strange gestures, as if he were trying to bite violently something immediately in front of him, producing altogether not exactly a ludicrous, but a most disagreeable and discordant effect. Every here and there the congregation joined in with him, with no concord, but the most extreme discord.

I soon discovered that there was a division in the congregation. Between the door and the corner of the chancel was a single row of figures squatting against the wall. These were the learned. They also filled the recess of the further transept, and one was even within the line of the chancel itself. This single individual, I afterwards learned, was the younger of the two priests of the community. After the minister had proceeded for some time with his violent ministrations he stopped, and this second priest began in a different tone, much quieter, and evidently different matter. Presently all rose, and, prostrating themselves in the Moslem fashion, with their faces to the ground, uttered a sort of booming sound—the only approach to concord or an agreeable noise which I heard during the whole evening. This I took to be the general Amen at the conclusion of the regular service. So it was. It was sunset. The Sabbath had ended; but the rites of the *yom kippoor* commenced without an instant's interval. I had noticed water-bottles circulating freely amongst the worshippers for several minutes before this. They were now emptied and placed on a shelf over my head. The fast had begun, and till the next sunset neither meat, drink, smoke, or even medicine will be tasted (however grave the case) by man, woman, child, infant, or suckling.

That the service had changed was quickly evident. The elder priest re-commenced reading, and *now* the whole congregation with him. It was the first chapter of the law—the first verse of Genesis—*Barashit bara Elooim.** The services of this great day, the only fast in the Samaritan calendar—which, from its severity, is looked forward to with uneasiness for the whole year—consist of the recital of the whole Pentateuch by priests and people, interspersed with common prayers, of the kind already described, and creeds, or professions of faith. A few of the congregation had books; but if all had possessed them it would have been of no avail for a considerable part of the time, for the service is continued through the night, without even the feeble lamp, which, on every other night of the year but this, burns in front of the holy books. The two priests and a few of the people know the whole of the Torah by heart; others know a single book; others a few chapters; so that there are always respondents. All stood up, and the storm of harsh voices raged around. They seemed to repeat very fast, and with a metrical, jumping sort of measure, which converted it almost into a gallop. Now and then—at what particular passages I could not discover—they roared or

* This is the Samaritan pronounciation of the words which in Hebrew are pronounced *Bereshith bara Elohim.*

barked still more loudly; now and then they prostrated themselves. The prostrations are made at certain solemn portions of the law, such as the Ten Commandments. They are made by rising from the squatting posture to the knees, then the two hands are placed flat on the floor, the palms down, and the forehead (not the nose, as in the Moslem prostrations) is brought to the floor between them.

After going in this way through two or three chapters, they stopped; and the younger priest re-commenced prayers in the plain chant, with occasional responses. His part was very similar to the old Gregorian plainsong of the Roman Church, but even more archaic in its turns. After a quarter of an hour of this, an aged man, seated next the door, began to read the Law. His peculiarity seemed to be the repetition, four or five times over, of the last syllable of each sentence, with a rumbling, mouthing sound, inexpressibly tedious to hear, but which evidently afforded him the greatest satisfaction. Then the reading in chorus began again, and then I came out. A good deal of private devotion had gone on during the general service. For instance: my host and several others came in, and, taking their places here and there, went through a series of prostrations and elevations, of the same kind as the ordinary prayers of the Moslems, except the small gestures of touching the ears, turning right and left, &c: and during these, it is only right to say, they were most devout and entirely absorbed. But there was also a good deal of talking amongst the general body in my neighbourhood, arising, in some measure, from the presence of the children, who pushed in and out, and already began whimpering and teasing for water. It was not, however, the talking or minor interruptions that struck me, so much as the hard, un-devotional, violent character of the proceedings. Not a soul seemed to be touched or interested. It was not disorderly, nor undignified, but seemed a service without worship.

I have already spoken of the extreme strictness with which the fast is kept. The wails and screams of the unfortunate infants in the neighbouring houses during the whole of the evening and night, testify that this part of my statement is not exaggerated.

The next morning was occupied in a visit to a village called Awertah, a few miles off, which contains the traditional sepulchres of Eleazar and Phinehas, the son and grandson of Aaron; and a cave, reputed to have been the residence of Elijah. In the afternoon, I returned to the synagogue. It was 3·45 P.M.: more than two hours of this weary day still remained to be passed before the twelfth hour should release the worshippers. The reading of the law was going on in earnest. They were deep in Deuteronomy. The church was not quite so full as when I first saw it; but there were still a large number present. The divan on the right was occupied as before by the unlearned, who looked on with a listless air, and shouted a verse or two now and then, as memory served; and by sleepers, taking a short rest before the final scenes. Two or three women kept their ground in my corner; and several children and youths, completely exhausted, were stretched like dogs on the mattings. On the other hand, the initiated on the lower part of the floor had gathered closer, and were formed into a wide circle, facing the chancel, squatting round with books of the law open on their knees, or supported on low stands. Some of these books were very large, written apparently with great beauty and width of margin—some of them still in separate sheets. The priests were taking no part, but seemed to have relinquished the reading altogether to the congregation, reserving themselves, no doubt, for what was coming. The younger man occupied himself in wrapping up, in its hundred and twenty handkerchiefs, the book of which I have already spoken, and which had been used during the morning.

The *sound* of the service was much the same as it had been last night, only, if possible, more discordant; but the *aspect* of the scene was most pleasing, and struck me even more than at first. Many of the men were models of manly beauty, tall and dignified in form, and with lofty, open, and most engaging countenances. There is no posture in the world

more noble and graceful than that in which Orientals sit on
the ground. But all these were not sitting. A few were
standing, if possible, in a still more striking posture ; propped
up against the wall, like Belisarius in the well-known picture,
on long staves, and holding out both hands in an attitude of
deprecation, or adoration. Then, the pure white dresses, just
relieved by the little dash of colour in the red caps emerging
from the turbans, or of a red or yellow scarf escaping here
and there ; the quaint charm and glister of the antique
chandeliers, the venerable vaults above, and the rich solid
hue of the carpets underfoot, all tempered by the sweet soft
light of the Eastern afternoon as it flowed in at the door, or
wavered down from the apertures overhead, these things
combined to form a picture which, to a *deaf* man, would have
been without alloy, and which was so beautiful as to make
even me (who am not deaf) forget the discordant voices for
a few moments as I contemplated it.

But I was not long in coming to myself ; and then I found
that the speed of the recitation was increasing. At last t
became a perfect race. Then they fell as before, only more
decidedly, into a metrical pace

&c. but with a concord of *measure* only, not of *pitch*. This
sort of metre was constantly varied during the rest of the
service ; now it was

and now

&c. When at length the two great songs, with which Deuteronomy concludes, had been reached, there was a general
stir, and a movement towards the front of the sanctuary.
The priests came forth from behind the red veil, clad in

dresses of very light green satin down to the feet, and the
recitations proceeded with greater clamour and impetuosity
than ever.    Then the two great rolls, which, according to the
Samaritans themselves, have stood to them in the place of the
ancient glories of their temple since its destruction, and have
certainly been the desire and the despair of European scholars
since Scaliger's time, were brought forth, enveloped in coverings of light blue velvet, and placed on the sloping stand in
the centre of the recess.    At last the law was ended, amidst a
perfect tumult, by the reiteration of one syllable—*ah* or *lah*—
at least thirty times.    Then the two priests again emerged
from behind the curtain, this time with a white cloth, or
shawl, covering the head and reaching nearly to the knees ;
they put off the velvet coverings, and exposed the cases of the
rolls to view.    That to the right was bright silver, and evidently of modern make ; the other puzzled me more.    It was
too distant for me to see any of its details, but the whole
effect struck me as that of Veneto-oriental work, of the time
of those fine silver and silver-gilt articles which have been
lately reproduced by Elkington.    The sequel will show what
it really is.    This was the signal for prostrations, fresh prayers,
and fresh responses, which lasted at least a quarter of an
hour.    And now came the great event of the day—nay, of
the year.    The priests opened the cases so as to expose their
contents to view ; and then, with their backs to the congregation, and their faces towards the Holy Place on Gerizim,
held them up over their heads, with the sacred parchments
full in view of the whole synagogue.    Every one prostrated
himself, and that not once, but repeatedly, and for a length of
time.    Then the devout pressed forwards to kiss, to stroke
fondly, to touch, or, if none of these were possible, to gaze on
the precious treasures.    Several children were allowed to
kiss.    It was past five ; and now commenced, if indeed
they can ever be said to have ceased, a succession of prayers
and catechisms between priest and congregation ; he intoning,
and they vociferating, after him, with him, before him, apparently in the wildest confusion.    His chant had a strong

resemblance to the ordinary plainsong in the Roman Church, and was tuneable enough, with the exception of a sort of jerk or *hiccup* which occasionally occurred, and which threw an individual, and quite a savage character into it.  *Their* part I can compare to nothing but the psalms for the day as performed at St. George's-in-the-East during the riots, when a majority *said*, and a minority *sung* them ; and even that wanted the force and energy which here lent such a dreadful life to the discord.  These responses—which I was afterwards were told were avowals of their belief in Jehovah and in Moses—were accompanied by constant sudden prostrations, the effect of which was most remarkable, and by frequently rubbing down the whole face and beard with the right hand, a gesture which I had not noticed till now.*  At intervals during this time, the kissing and stroking of the rolls, as they lay in state on the sloping stand, was going on to an extent which must seriously injure them, and would be fatal if it happened oftener.  The one in the old case was the favourite.  Had I not been present this day, I doubt if, even with Jacob's influence, I should have seen it ; for it is brought out with great reluctance, and all kinds of subterfuges are resorted to, to avoid showing it to travellers. One little episode of this part of the proceedings struck me.  There was a youth, whom I caught sight of timidly hovering behind the bolder spirits who pressed round the rolls, as if anxious, yet afraid, to come forward.

> " Still pressing, longing, to be right,
>     Yet fearing to be wrong."

Poor fellow ! after all he missed his opportunity and only succeeded in summoning his courage when the roll was shut, and it was too late to do more than touch the silver

---

* I afterwards saw this gesture frequently used by the Moslems.  " It signifies blessing," I was told.  It is used when any sacred name or form of words is said, and seems to be an attempt actually to catch the grace of the words, residing in the breath of the speaker himself, and communicate it to his countenance.

case. I pitied him from my heart, and longed that such modest, *Christian* diffidence in sacred things, might have a worthier object for its exercise. It was a pretty little incident, and was one of the few touches of human feeling which softened the harshness of this most singular service.

This kind of catechising went on for nearly an hour, till it seemed positively interminable. My weariness now became extreme. The length, the discordance, the noise, perhaps more than anything the unintelligibility of the whole—and also my anxiety for the poor fainting children strewed around, like so many Ishmaels in the last stage of existence for want of water and food—all combined to make me heartily wish it over. At length came an indication that the end was near. An elder advanced towards the door and put a *plate* on the ground for contributions. It was the only part of the whole in which I could find any connecting link with the services of our Church. It may have been a customary thing; but I fear it was aimed at the Nazarene stranger. At any rate, the sums put in by others were so exceedingly minute, that I feel pretty confident they were only deposited as baits for me. I did not disappoint the expectations of my friends, though it required some nerve to drop my mite, as the plate was taken in charge by two ancients, who seized my coin, almost before it left my fingers, and scrutinized its look and weight with the greatest care. At last the Holy Books were consigned to their retirement behind the veil, there to remain for another year. By degrees all went out. The little lamp was lowered from the ceiling, lighted, and left burning in the twilight before the sanctuary, and the *yom kippoor* for the year 1270 (as the Samaritans reckon, according to the Mahometan era) was at an end.

I confess that I was fairly exhausted. And if this was my case—a mere spectator of a small portion only of the proceedings—how must it have been with those who had gone through the whole labour of the day and night? the priests, the weak, the old, the women, who to the severe privations of the fast had added the pain of twenty-four hours almost incessant vociferation? For a few there were, such as the old man by the door, and some in the transept at the end, who had shouted the whole time. Any one who has taken part in the chorus of an oratorio knows how fatiguing that is, even for the two hours and a half or three hours of its duration, and how absolutely necessary refreshment becomes between the parts, even to those who are in the habit of singing regularly and frequently. But here were people who had been undergoing a similar exertion for twenty-four hours, after the interval of a twelvemonth, with no refreshment whatever, beyond an occasional expectoration! Strange to say, they were not nearly so exhausted as I imagined. I made my host take me to the elder just mentioned, and he really seemed neither hoarse nor weary. Smoke was the refreshment most immediately in request, and food only later in the evening, when the wants of the children and women had been satisfied.

And so finished this most curious and suggestive scene. My chief desire throughout—as far as the strange sights and sounds left me any room for reflection—had been, as you will imagine, to see if any illustration could be gained from it of the ancient Jewish ritual—the general ritual I mean, not that of the day of atonement only. If the Samaritan community be, as Stanley seems to believe, the most faithful representative of the old nation of Israel, is there not some reason for believing it possible that the services of Nábloos may retain a likeness to those of the times of the monarchy? I do not pretend to have examined the subject at all sufficiently to have come to any conclusion upon it. But what I saw and heard certainly threw a new light upon it in my mind, and as it is an interesting question, I will name one or two points which seem to me worth further consideration.

1. There is the fact of the undeniable likeness which I have noticed between the chant or plainsong of the priest, and that which is always considered to be the oldest part of the music of the Christian Church, and the eastern origin of

which is now, I believe, pretty generally admitted. 2. The probability that a small persecuted sect like the Samaritans would retain such a thing without material change, as they certainly have retained other trifling usages ; such, for instance, as the cross on the spit of the passover lambs (of which more anon). 3. The dissimilarity between the method of responding of the Samaritans, and that in the *zikkrs* or common worship of the Moslems ; which, wild, repulsive, and heathenish as they are, are of an entirely different character, for instance, are always in concord both of time and tune with the leader. 4. The sentiment or sacredness of the words of the Psalms employed in the ancient Jewish liturgy, would be no argument against their having been sung in the discordant tumultuous manner of the Samaritans ; for what can be more sacred or pathetic than some of the passages in the Pentateuch, which I actually heard so sung ? 5. On the other hand, may there not be some positive indications of the existence of similar discord in the ancient services, in the constant mention of " horns " (nothing but horns of animals, recollect), and "cymbals ;" of " mighty men" (that is great, strong persons) chosen as singers and players ; the frequent use, in describing these services, of such expressions as "loud noise," "make a noise," "shout," "roar," &c. The predominance of wind instruments—the " horns " just mentioned, as well as " cornets " and " trumpets" of metal—in the displays of which David was so fond, is in itself an evidence of the discord which must have reigned in them ; for those instruments are still the great difficulty of our orchestras, and with all the modern resources are extremely difficult to keep, and still more to play, in tune. But it would be premature to argue the question on such slender grounds, and, indeed, I should be almost reluctant to pursue it further, for it would be a real calamity, for which even the truth could hardly console one, to discover that the " Songs of Zion," which the Christian world has always regarded as the perfection of beauty (according to the modern ideas of beauty in music), at all resembled the harsh vociferations of the Samaritans, or that

the " services of the sanctuary " were so bereft of enthusiasm
and feeling as theirs are, and so exactly like the repetition
of a very hard and very uninteresting lesson.

There was one reflection, however, which forced itself on
me continually, without my having the least doubt whether I
should entertain it or not. I could not help recollecting the
great Christian Spectacle at which my wife and I had been
present last autumn at Ammergau, and wondering at the
force of the principle, which had been sufficient to raise that
miracle of ordered beauty, fitness, reverence, and intelligence,
out of such chaotic beginnings as those before me.


I must not forget to tell you that later in the evening, when
all the rest of the quarter were in bed, through the good
offices of my host, he and I met the priest at the synagogue,
and in consideration of a liberal backsheesh, and the present
of my knife, I was allowed to examine the case of the Great
Roll, and even to make some rubbings of parts of it—very
imperfect, for I had not at all the proper things with me. He
began by assuring me that it was 1,400 years old. I told him
if he took away the 1,000, I thought he would not be far
from the truth, and so it proved, for not only was my former
conjecture confirmed, but on examination, the priest himself
found a date which he read as equivalent to A.D. 1420.* It is
a beautiful and curious piece of work; a cylinder of about
two feet six inches long and ten or twelve inches diameter,
opening down the middle. One of the halves is engraved with
a ground-plan of the Tabernacle, showing every post, tenon,
veil, piece of furniture, vessel, &c. with a legend attached to
each—all in raised work. The other half is covered with ornament only, also raised. It is silver, and I think—but the light
was very imperfect—parcel-gilt. My visit would, no doubt,
have been very much resented by the community, if they had
known of it; and the feeling of this added a curious zest to it;

* These rubbings have since been shown to the authorities of the South
Kensington Museum, and pronounced to be Venetian work of the fourteenth
or fifteenth century.

as it was, I could not help fancying I was committing sacri-
lege; stealing in the dark and thus handling holy things.
Of the roll itself I say nothing, partly because, knowing
nothing of the subject, I hardly looked at it; and, partly
because it has been thoroughly examined by, and, I believe,
copied by, or for, a Russian Jew named Levisohn, at Jerusalem, who is devoting himself to the Samaritan Pentateuch,
and will very soon publish his discoveries.*

One thing more, and I have finished. I have solved the
mystery of the *cross-spit*. The Passover lambs (they require six
for the community now) are roasted all together, by stuffing
them vertically, head downwards, into an oven, which is like a
small well, about three feet diameter and four or five feet
deep, roughly steined, in which a fire has been kept up for
several hours. After the lambs are thrust in, the top of the
hole is covered with bushes and earth, to confine the heat till
the lambs are done. Each lamb has a stake or spit run
through him to draw him up by; and, to prevent the spit
from tearing away through the roast meat with the weight, a
cross piece is put through the lower end of it. This is all.
But it is still a curious thing, and must have startled the first
Christian who noticed it in modern times, though he may
not have drawn the same inference from it as old Justin.

* A short acount of these discoveries was published in the papers not long
since; and among other statements it was said that 24,000 variations had been
discovered between this and the ordinary Hebrew Pentateuch. I have very
lately heard from Jerusalem that Mr. Levisohn's progress is stopped for want
of funds—a want common enough in that part of the world, but one which
surely might be remedied without difficulty.

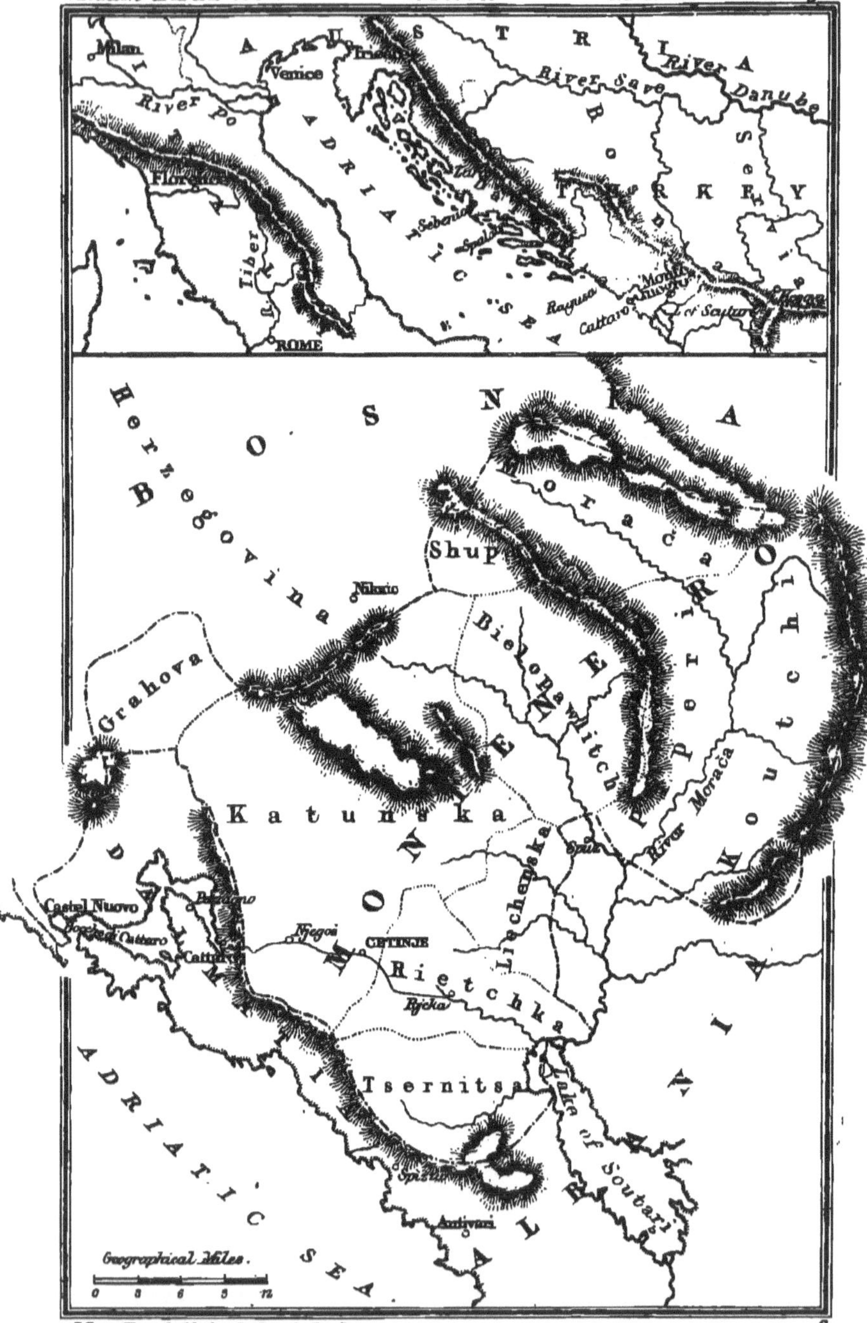

Vacation Tourists 1861.
NORTH
Christmas in Montenegro.
Milan
Venice
Trieste
River Po
River Save
River Danube
AUSTRIA
ADRIATIC SEA
Tiber
Florence
ROME
Sebenico
Spalato
Ragusa
Cattaro
Mostar
L. of Scutari
TURKEY
Servia
BOSNIA
Herzegovina
Grahova
Nikzic
Shup
Oraca
Bielopawlitch
Katunska
Pepera
Koutchi
River Moraca
Castel Nuovo
Risano
Bocca di Cattaro
Cattaro
Njegos
CETINJE
Rietchka
Rjeka
Llachanska
Tsernitsa
Lake of Scutari
Spiz
Antivari
ADRIATIC SEA
ALBANIA
Geographical Miles
0   3   6   9   12
Macmillan & Co Cambridge & London
S.

# 11. *CHRISTMAS IN MONTENEGRO.*

## BY I. M.

TOWARDS the end of December, 1861, during that fortnight which intervenes between the Latin Christmas and the Greek, we found ourselves on board an Austrian Lloyd steamer, entering the Bocche di Cattaro. As we approached the head of the gulf, the rock-walls on each side drew closer, and we could discern the town of Cattaro crouched under the shadow of its citadel. From the Austrian fortress upwards a white path winds over the face of the cliff; your eye can follow it to the mountain's brow, where it vanishes between two crags; it has reached the gates of the fortress of Montenegro.

"Look there," cried the old captain of the steamer, "that is the ladder you must climb to-morrow, if you mean to go to Cetinje." An individual in a soiled white uniform, who had been put on board at Castel Nuovo, here observed—"It is very dangerous to go to Montenegro." "You have been there?" said my aunt, inquiringly. "No, madame, we may not." "They may not," explained the captain; "for, since Prince Danilo was shot in Cattaro, the Montenegrins do not choose to see Austrians at Cetinje."*

The steamer stopped at a short distance from the shore, and boats came to take off the passengers. There was a numerous second class pressing out, and we expected to be met by the Prince of Montenegro's agent, so we remained seated on the deck, trying to identify the localities about us with those scenes to which the captain had alluded when he spoke of Prince Danilo being shot in Cattaro.

* Pronounce "Tzetinye," accent on the second syllable.

Immediately in front, the gulf runs into the land, forming a point, so narrow that it may be rounded in a few minutes' walk. A short way down the left shore lies the village Perzagno, and on our right, the Marine Platz of Cattaro, with an incipient public garden, and a free space where the band plays. It was at Perzagno that the late Prince and Princess of Montenegro resided, during that visit which terminated so fatally. The health of the princess required sea-baths, and her husband insisted on accompanying her to Cattaro, contrary to the advice of many of his counsellors, who did not consider his life safe on Austrian ground. At first, all went well; deputations from the various parts of the Bocche waited on Danilo, and among the inhabitants of Cattaro, including the chief Austrian officials and their families, the Montenegrin prince and princess soon became objects of affection and respect. On fine summer evenings, when the band played on the Marine Platz, Princess Darinka liked to come and hear it; and it was at the close of one of these entertainments that the murder took place. The scene was described to us by eye-witnesses. It was already twilight, and Danilo was in the act of handing the princess into the boat, when a pistol, fired from behind, shot him in the back, and he fell. The confusion that ensued was terrible. The Montenegrin attendants of the prince, deeming themselves betrayed by the Austrians, fired upon the crowd; the crowd, expecting to be massacred by the Highlanders, fled in the wildest terror. Strange to say, no one was hurt; even the assassin escaped to a distance, where he was arrested by the Austrian sentinels. At length, a guard of soldiers formed round the body of Danilo, and the princess herself assisting to support him, he was carried into Cattaro to the house of his agent. There, next day at the same hour, he died.*

The assassin was executed in Cattaro; but not till on the way to execution did he confess the crime: it is said, that he confessed also to having been instigated by Austria. Certain is it that this version of the story is believed by the

* August, 1860.

Montenegrins; nor is the other version, that of a private quarrel between the prince and his murderer, likely to unsettle their opinion. The assassin belonged to a faction, banished from Montenegro for opposing Danilo's reforms: the chiefs of that party reside at Zara, the Austrian capital of Dalmatia, and subsist on pensions from the Austrian Government. The murdered prince had lived on good terms with Austria; and, in 1848, he offered to support the Croats, rising in defence of the monarchy; but, in 1859, Montenegro was the ally of France; and, in case of a national movement among the Southern Slavs, talents, policy, and position, marked Danilo as its leader.

Signor B——, under whose roof Danilo died, was the person who came on board to meet us. He brought the welcome tidings that tolerable quarters were in readiness,* and conducted us through the narrow lanes and small dark squares of Cattaro to a house that had seen better days. Its present owners, an elderly widow and her daughter, let us our lodging as a sort of favour. Signor B—— advised us, by all means, to take advantage of the present mild and lovely weather, since, in the middle of winter, we must not count on its continuance. There had not as yet been snow to speak of, so the road to Cetinje would present few difficulties; he was afraid we should get miserable horses, but he would make our bargain, and secure good attendants. He then left us to get our passports viséd for Montenegro.

Our next care was to inquire about a "courier," whom we had been prepared to find at Cattaro. This was no other than a Montenegrin, adopted in childhood and educated by an Austrian officer, who intended to have made him his heir—now, by his patron's sudden death, left destitute. Great was our disappointment to learn that this accomplished

* We here remark, for the benefit of future travellers, that the inns of Dalmatia are now worse than ever. At Zara we found in the hotel both food and fire; at Sebenico, food but no fire; in Spalato, fire but no food. In Ragusa the best inn afforded neither food nor fire, the rooms were barely furnished, and the woman to whom they belonged constituted the sole attendance In Cattaro there is no inn at all.

person had just gone to seek his fortune in Constantinople: we did not like undertaking the next day's journey without some one who could speak Italian, and on whom we might rely to order our cavalcade. Count N—— went to find us another escort, and returned, followed by a tall Montenegrin. " I bring you," said Signor N——, " a friend of mine, who is going home to spend Christmas with his family, and agrees to start two days earlier than he intended, in order to be of use to you. He is a merchant, and speaks Italian ; he has made more than one voyage to Trieste, and has an idea of what civilized travellers require." The Montenegrin added, that " if, after we had visited Cetinje, we chose to go on to Rjeka, and would so far honour his humble home, he cordially invited us for the Christmas feast." Hereupon followed some arrangements for the journey, and then our intended escort begged to ask whether the large book before us was not a " travelling book," and if it gave an account of Crnagora. It happened to be a translation of Sir Gardner Wilkinson's valuable work on Dalmatia and Montenegro,* and we made haste to show him the portrait of the last Vladika. But when the Crnagorac found that the account of his country was written in a language he could not read, a cloud came over his face, and he remarked that, had he not neglected his opportunities, he might have understood German.

As on this occasion we only spent one night at Cattaro, we did not then make the acquaintance of a family who afterwards treated us with hospitable kindness—the family of the Austrian Commandant. This officer had been some years at his post, and expressed liberal opinions towards two bodies not generally favourites with Austrian *employés*—the Slavs of

---

* For comparatively recent accounts of Montenegro and its history, see Sir Gardner Wilkinson's "Dalmatia and Montenegro," "Montenegro and the Slavonians of Turkey," by Count Krasinsky, and Paton's "Highlands and Islands of the Adriatic." An interesting record of a visit to Montenegro is given by the German traveller Kohl, "Reise nach Istrien, Dalmatien und Montenegro." Just published, "Le Montenegro," par Henri Delarue. Duprat, Paris. 1862—contains the annals of Danilo's reign, and a description of the battle of Grahova. These accounts, one and all, speak in high terms of the Montenegrins.

the Greek Church, and the Montenegrins. To our question whether he did not find the latter unruly neighbours, he replied that on no one occasion had they given him trouble. In the town they never disagreed with the citizens, and in the country, where bickerings did take place, he thought the fault lay quite as often with the Bocchese as with the mountaineers. "I should never think," he continued, " of describing the Montenegrins as a robber nation; those raids on the Turkish frontiers are no more than border forays, such as, according to your own history, went on between the English and Scotch. A great deal is said about their cutting off the heads of their enemies; but who are their enemies?—the Turks and Albanians, whose warfare comprehends barbarities rather greater than the cutting off of heads. Besides, fighting against enormous odds, as the Montenegrins always do, how could they let their prisoners go? and how bestow their food and time on nursing wounded Turks? To kill them at once is much less cruel than to leave them perishing on the field, and the Montenegrin beheads his own companion rather than let him fall into the hands of the enemy. The Montenegrins are accused of making raids in time of peace; at least the Turks have no right to complain of this, for they do it themselves, not only on the Montenegrins, but even on us, in the military frontier." The Commandant also affirmed, what we had previously been assured of, that since the time of the last Vladika, perfect security of person and property exists within the Montenegrin boundary, while even in their wildest days, these Highlanders never molested a woman.

On the subject of the Slavs of the Greek Church, we had a question to ask, Had they kept open shops on the Latin Christmas-day? Till lately, in the Austrian empire, all sects must needs honour the Roman festival; but henceforth, no religious community is obliged to keep any feast but its own. In the Bocche, more than half the population are members of the Greek Church, but the Latins, long supreme, had not quite made up their minds to see their Christmas disregarded. It was said, "the Government would take it as an insult." However, the Greeks made use of their privilege, and kept open shops on the holiday of their rivals.   When the Commandant spoke to us about this, he added, "Many people were scandalized, but what could we expect ?   We Romanists have never thought of shutting our shops on the Greek Christmas.   The other day I was placed in a difficult position.   The Greeks required our soldiers to figure in their ecclesiastical processions, as they figure in those of the Latin Church.   Now I have orders to let the soldiers march in the Latin processions, and I have no orders with regard to the Greek.   I answered that I would write for instructions ; but, unluckily, they have little reason to expect that the Government will take their view of the matter."

Next morning our party assembled soon after sunrise, that is to say, a little past eight.   Three horses, of which one was for the luggage, small weak animals, the three men who led them far better able to carry us than they ; but the men carried nothing save their arms, two pistols and a kangiar stuck in the girdle.   Two boys from the Bocche followed with extra baggage.   Besides these, our regular attendants, we had as escort, Giorgio the merchant, and the Cetinje postman.   The latter was a splendid fellow, some six foot four in height, and with as honest and kindly a face as ever I saw.   His weapons were beautifully ornamented with silver, and on his bonnet he wore the Servian double eagle, a badge which constitutes in itself the uniform of the Montenegrin guard.   This postman had orders to keep by us half the way, and then, passing onwards, to announce our approach, and deliver our letters of introduction at Cetinje.

Our starting point was the so-called bazaar, an open space flanked by a single row of stone sheds ; it lies immediately at the foot of the rock, and outside the gate of the town.   Hither, thrice in the week, the mountaineers bring their produce, and hold their market ; for, except the Prince and the senators, the Montenegrins are not allowed to enter Cattaro armed, and rather than go in unarmed, they mostly prefer not to go in at all.   But for the Montenegrin bazaar the citizens of Cattaro must often hunger.   Their coast-strip between rocks and sea gives them little but wine and oil ; the mutton, the poultry, the scoranze (dried fish from the Lake of Scutari), the eggs, the milk that store their market come from Montenegro. Besides these products, the southern valleys of the Black Mountain yield corn, wine, silk, tobacco, and a wood called sumac, valued for its yellow dye. These the mountaineer wants to exchange for manufactured goods, weapons and ammunition. But here he feels the inconvenience of a political arrangement, which gives the national port of his country into Austria's keeping. The duties levied in the Austrian custom-house are found excessive even by Austrians residing in Cattaro; and worse than these, is an embargo laid on the sale of arms, whenever it suits Austria to leave Montenegro defenceless. At this moment there is peace between the Austrian Government and that of Montenegro, and yet, with Omer Pasha on the Montenegrin frontier, Austria forbids that arms and ammunition be sold at Cattaro to Montenegrins. Of course arms, ammunition, and everything else, finds its way to Cetinje so long as Prince Nicolas can pay those who bring them. But in order to have money for payment, Montenegro is kept dependent on Russia, and a hardy population is taught to smuggle, when it desires no better than to trade.

The bazaar used to be the place where strangers went to see the rich and warlike costumes of the mountaineers; but since the death of Danilo, his people are in mourning—the men carry their arms reversed, and turn the golden embroidery on their vests inside.

On the morning after Danilo's assassination, 8,000 Montenegrins gathered in the open space before the bazaar, swearing that if their Gospodar were not given up to them, they would burn Cattaro. The prince was dying; no one could be admitted to his chamber; but the princess sent his secretary with a message: " Children, as soon as your Gospodar* can be

* Gospodar, " Lord," title given by the Montenegrins to their secular sovereign. " Vladika" was the title of their ecclesiastical sovereigns or metropolitans, of whom the last, Peter II., died in 1851. His nephew, Danilo, separated the ecclesiastical from the secular dignity, and, as the head of an independent principality, definitely emancipated Montenegro from all claims of Russian suzerainty.

moved without pain, we will bring him up to Cetinje; meanwhile his bidding to every one of you is, Go home." "And like children," said an eye-witness, "they went home, with downcast heads; and in silence that terrible gathering melted away."

When without pain the prince could be moved, they did bring him up to Cetinje, and it was here, at the foot of the rock, that his body was delivered to his own people. By order of the emperor, Danilo was to receive the funeral of an Austrian marshal; the cannons sounded, the troops were drawn out, Austrian soldiers bore him through the streets of Cattaro. To the beginning of the ascent, Princess Darinka followed the bier on foot; up the mountain she followed it on horseback. To picture that funeral procession one must have mounted the Ladder of Cattaro.

Up a rock 4,000 feet high the path climbs, an endless series of zigzags. As far as the Montenegrin frontier it is kept up by Austria; but even on this, the best part of the road, in rainy weather it serves for a torrent's course, and is covered with large and pointed stones. Its windings exhaust the patience of the mountaineers, who most of them bound straight down the hill; while to escape its roughness, those who, driving mules or cattle, are obliged to follow the track, walk along the smooth flags which bind it on the verge of the precipice. Our horses also preferred easy footing. Whenever for a moment we ceased pulling at their heads, we found ourselves in a perpendicular line above the harbour and roofs of Cattaro. Riding up the hill, this made us rather giddy; but when it came to walking down, we were ourselves glad to step along the edge-stones, without giving a thought of the house-tops.

Although it was not market-day, the Ladder of Cattaro swarmed with Montenegrins, as the ladder of a bee-hive with bees. Such as were going the same way as ourselves would for a time join our party, and walk by our horses. Among the women we remarked one very tall, with fine features and brilliant eyes. Most were middle-sized, thick-set, and with weather-beaten complexions. However weighty their burdens, they walked under them with an elastic tread, talking, laughing, and often knitting the while.  However rough their work, not one had a coarse or brazen expression.  Indeed, the countenance of the Montenegrin woman is in itself enough for beauty, so cheerful and intelligent, so truly innocent and modest.  These women still wear mourning ; the long coat of coarse white cloth over the white chemise and petticoat, black apron, and black serge veil hanging behind like that of a nun ; no crimson embroideries, and no ornaments, except in a few instances the ponderous belt, comprising three rows of large cornelians massively set in silver or brass.

The men were also dressed in white.  Their coat is no longer than the knee, open in front, and girt round the waist with a sash, and with the leathern belt which supports their weapons.  Each carried also a long gun swinging behind. They had dark blue trousers, short and full, rather like knickerbockers, white gaiters, and the shoes called "Opanké," made of ox-hide, and said to be the best for rock-walking. The lofty stature of these sons of the mountain, their athletic proportions and warlike air, did not strike us more than the square brow, the intelligent eye, the frank smile.  They wear moustache, but not beard; the mouth and chin are firmly moulded; the teeth fine; the nose short, but high; hair brown, eyes brown or blue—we seldom saw either black; and the complexion is of a sunburnt red, not the dark yellow of the south.  It is remarkable how distinctly the northern origin of his race comes out in the Southern Slav. He has neither the grace of the Latin and Greek, nor the owl-like pose of Oriental dignity.  He is a great manly fellow, with a certain martial stateliness of his own.

Men and women walked and talked together, the conversation proceeding in a most lively style ; and in their intercourse we remarked, as did the German Kohl, the total absence of embarrassment, rudeness, or coquetry.  The decorum and simplicity of manners in Montenegro must favourably impress every stranger.  A less pleasing characteristic is the loudness of their voices in the open air.  To speak continuously, so as to be heard for miles off, is a highly valued Crnagoracan accomplishment.

As we approached the entrance to Montenegro, the way became rougher—there is no object in making it too easy—and the path was slippery with the unsunned frost of the morning. We had been obliged to dismount, when down came a drove of cattle, solemnly marching in the midst of the road, leaving us to choose between the cliff and the precipice. The mountaineers were eager to help; the women almost lifting us on to the ledges of rock, where we were out of harm's way. They were pleased when we tried some words in their tongue, and a man asked us if "Yes," the affirmative in their language, was not also an English word. At the same time they appeared disappointed unless we constantly halted, and admired the landscape.

Truly at every stage of the ascent the view becomes more striking. First, you look right down on Cattaro, into the squares of the city, upon the decks of the ships. Gradually, bend after bend of the winding fiord becomes visible, as like a silver way it threads the passes of the rocks. At last, the rocks themselves no longer shut out the sea, and when you gain the topmost step of the Ladder, the Adriatic lies before you unrolled to the horizon. At this point we turned our backs on the world, and passed into the Black Mountain. Giorgio, the travelled merchant, exclaimed, with a half-stifled sigh, "Ecco il Montenero;" and another member of the party, who scarcely knew Italian enough to make himself intelligible, pointed to the crags speckled with snow, and called out, "Now, Signora, you are in Montenegro; now you are in a free country; here you may go where you like, and do what you like by day or night; here no one will do you harm."

That this was a free country was its recommendation to its first settlers, who, forsaking the fertile but enslaved Herzegovina, where they had dwelt under the hill Njegos,* became the defenders of this rock-walled fortress, and called their new home after their old one. Of this band of freemen come the

* Pronounced "Nyégush;" *j* before *e* pronounced like *y*; *š* like *sh*.

reigning family of Montenegro, and his own patronymic
suffices to remind a prince of the house of Petrović de Njegos,*
that the land of his ancestor serves the oppressor, and that,
till he conquers it back, he is an exile.

The district of Njegos comprehends two or three villages
dotted over a small, broken plain. We here found the "half-
way house," an inn affording at one end a counter where
raki is sold, and at the other a room without windows. or
chimney, wherein passengers who wish for a fire may light
it in the middle of the floor. Giorgio managed the raki-
drinking part of the company, and we sat by the fire, and ate
the luncheon we had brought from Cattaro.

Recollecting that at Njegos a former traveller was assailed
by dogs, we asked what had become of the garrison? "Oh,"
answered our guide, "there used to be dogs in every village,
but since the Vladika and the late prince brought things into
order, we have no need of dogs, and many a house has not
even one."

The road between Njegos and Cetinje is merely a pathway,
crossing, one after another, ridges, the slopes of which are
clothed with low wood. Here the ground was covered with
snow, waxing deeper as we proceeded. We heard that much
had fallen during the night, and testified our regret at the
circumstance. But our escort was of a different mind. "How
I do like snow," quoth Giorgio, "it prevents one slipping,
and then it is so clean, if you do fall you are not dirtied;"
and, again, turning up a bit of earth; "See, this is good
black earth, and here every spot that is not rock is cultivated;
during the winter it is the snow that keeps it warm."

We came on a troop of small hill-cattle, and their herd, a
lad, armed like the rest. Afterwards we met people bringing
home wood. The women carried bundles of branches, and
the men dragged the heavier stems after them, sticking the
hatchet into the log, and fastening a cord to the hatchet.
Hereabouts, we were accosted by a beggar. We asked Giorgio
what became of those who were too old and sick to work.

.* Pronounce ć like *ch* in our word *each* ; c unaccented like *ts.*

"What becomes of them?" cried he, "why, if in the family there are a few who cannot work, there are always plenty of strong ones who can." These words reminded us that the old Slavonic family organization continues in Montenegro, whereby labour and gain are divided, and each member has his task assigned to him by the head-father. By this system, each family supports its own poor; widows are not left without protection, and as some one said to us, "there are no orphans." We afterwards learned that in Montenegro individuals who have well deserved of their country are, in old age, supported by the community; also, that there are a few licensed beggars, mostly cripples or idiots, who live from house to house, every one giving to them.

It is a fact, that while in his rich empire the Mahometan Turk is dying out,* the Christian population of the Black Mountain increases from year to year; is strong in its family affections, and sends forth vigorous offshoots. Kohl alludes to the many vigorous families on the Bocche and in Dalmatia, who derive their lineage from Crnagora; and since the Principality of Servia has recovered its freedom, the surplus inhabitants of Montenegro emigrate thither cheerfully, regarding this as a return to their ancient homes. It is, however, on the Herzegovina, as part of the old principality of Zeta,†

---

* See unanimous evidence in Mr. Senior's "Journal."

† See an interesting account of the sympathy of the Montenegrins with Servia—Sir Gardner Wilkinson's "Dalmatia and Montenegro," vol. i. 425 ; also his genealogical table of the Serb monarchs. Servia, Bosnia, Bulgaria, Herzegovina, Montenegro, &c. &c. are all peopled by a race which calls itself and its language Serb. This race is the southern division of the great Slav family, whereof the northern branch inhabits the Russias, and the western branch forms the majority of the population in the Austrian empire. The emigration of the Serbs from beyond the Carpathians happened in the reign of Emperor Heraclius, and is recorded by Constantine Porphyrogennetus. The Serb empire was at its greatest under Car Dushan (1333-1356). Afterwards some of its provinces were detached under princes of the royal family, and Montenegro is the Highlands of Zeta, or Zenta, a principality comprehending the Herzegovina, the north of Albania. The Serb monarchy fell (like Byzantium, Spain, Russia, and all those European countries which, by position, were similarly exposed) under the Mahometan deluge. Servia Proper held out till 1389, Zenta till 1485, and the Highlands of Zeta have never been subdued.

that the Montenegrins look as especially their own. Last autumn some thousand Crnagorki were on the point of emigrating to Servia ; the breaking out of the insurrection in the Herzegovina decided them to stay through another winter, rather than forego the hope of aiding to free their fathers' land.

That the road from Njegos looks grand in a snowstorm, we had occasion to know when we next traversed it ; in ordinary circumstances its only fine point is a view. This shows you Montenegro, as it were a rocky sea, whose waves thrown up " mountains high," culminate in the great Albanian chain. In the midst lies a sheet of snow—a fairy ring fenced about on all sides with jutting crags. This is the plain of Cetinje, the last fortress of the Serb empire, the stronghold where Christianity and freedom have stood a siege of nearly four hundred years.

The village, palace, and convent of Cetinje, situated behind a promontory of rock, are not visible until one is close upon them. From Cattaro the journey is counted six hours ; we took seven, but our horses were miserable, mine so ricketty that I must recall with discontent having been obliged to walk the last miles in the snow. Very tired, we arrived at the locanda of Cetinje, which, in the days of Sir Gardner Wilkinson and Kohl, seems to have been a creditable inn. Unluckily, " since the prince's death," so few strangers have visited it, that the landlord means to go away, and has not of late repaired his window-panes. The upper chamber to which we were conducted was, however, better furnished than in many Dalmatian inns ; and that the floor and tables had lately undergone a washing, was evident from the fact that they were not yet dry.

We were not long left to make observations. So soon as the prince knew we had arrived, he sent his French doctor to offer us better quarters. " His Highness regrets," said the doctor, " that he cannot accommodate you *chez lui*, but he has taken his whole family to live with him, and one wing of the palace is under repair. He has ordered a lodging to be prepared for you in the house of his cousin, Kerco Petrovic, Vice-President of the Senate. We soon found ourselves in a warm comfortable room, and heard with satisfaction that there was settled at Cetinje a Bocchese woman who spoke Italian, and had been trained as a servant in Cattaro. She acted housemaid to the doctor's family, and would be happy to wait upon us.

That evening we dined at the palace, "*en bourgeois*," as the invitation ran, and "to save us the trouble of ordering supper." To ensure our getting supper was the real meaning of the last part of the message; and we learned to thank the prince's consideration on discovering that the strict Greek fast before Christmas had begun, and that it would have been difficult for us to procure animal food. Equal kindness provisioned us throughout our sojourn, and from the next day forward our meals were sent from the palace kitchen. The French doctor congratulated us. "In virtue of my office," said he, "my wife and daughter and I dine every day with the prince, but in bad weather it is no joke plodding through the snow. As for the fare at the locanda, I can tell you, from the experience of a friend of mine, that had you been dependent on that, *vous auriez mangé des choses impossibles.*"

The doctor at Cetinje is no longer M. Tedeschi, who took many photographic views, and wrote an interesting little account of Montenegro. His successor has only filled his post eight months; being a married man, he does not live in the palace, and as he makes no attempt to learn the language, he is cut off from intercourse with the people. On the other hand, the light of his science is scarcely appreciated by the Montenegrins. "He may be a good man," said one of them, "but it seems to us that the prince pays a great deal of money for a doctor to give medicine to his people, and his people do not like medicine." Then said another, " a foreign doctor may know something about physic, but do you think a Montenegrin would let him meddle with broken bones? In the world there are no such surgeons as our own—if you had seen the wounds they healed after the battle of Grahova!"

This is not altogether a vain boast; many travellers allude to the surgical skill of the Southern Slavs. They can even *trepan*, and are in the habit of trepanning as a cure for madness—even for neuralgia!

Since Sir Gardner Wilkinson visited the Vladika, the interior of the palace of Cetinje has undergone transformation; its transformer was the first lady who has ruled society in Cetinje since the Venetian consort of Prince George Crnovic (1516). Out of the bachelor quarters of a warrior bishop, Princess Darinka succeeded in forming a comfortable, almost an elegant residence; and coming on such among the rocks of Montenegro, we, as British travellers, were reminded of a first-rate shooting-lodge in the Highlands of Scotland. This analogy was carried out by the dinner, which, well-cooked and served in the European style, was plain, and owed its chief delicacy to a splendid trout from the Lake of Scutari. As in our Highlands too, master and servants alike wore the Highland dress.

In the drawing-room of the palace at Cetinje hang two large portraits of the Emperor and Empress of the French, presented by themselves; also smaller ones of the Emperor and Empress of Austria, and of Danilo and the Princess Darinka. The best picture is that of the Vladika Peter II., wherein the expression, the attitude, and the hand recall the likeness of a Venetian Doge. This Vladika was the national poet; his songs are in the mouth of every Montenegrin.

The customs of the Greek Fast prevented our meeting several members of the palace circle. Neither the mother nor the sister of the prince were present; and as soon as dinner was announced, Princess Miljena took the arm of her father-in-law, and both withdrew. But even this glimpse of the young Montenegrin princess was enough to impress us favourably. She is only fifteen, yet her little figure is not less marked by dignity than simple grace, and I never met any one who had seen her without being struck with the bright intelligence of her eyes. She wears the Montenegrin dress with little difference from that of the other women, except that under the white coat appears a black silk skirt, that the cloth of the coat is exquisitely fine, and that in front it is adorned with gold. Princess Miljena is the daughter of one of the most respected Voyvodes of Montenegro; she has never been beyond her own mountains, and, unfortunately for foreigners, speaks no language but the Serb. This, together with her extreme youth, is unfavourable to society in Cetinje, and the return of Princess Darinka* is eagerly desired.

Grand Voyvode Mirko Petrovic, who led the princess from the drawing-room, is the elder brother of the late prince, and father of the present. A chief esteemed in council and in war, he has twice stood aside in the succession to power, and been content to give place to a younger because he did not receive a European education. Mirko is the hero of Gra-hova; and with respect to his sagacity, we were told that had Danilo listened to its suggestions he would not have perished as he did. " Mirko," said a Montenegrin to us, "is a simple Highlander; he cannot speak any foreign tongue, he can read and write nothing but a little Serb, but not in Paris, not in Vienna will you find a man with more head." (Here the speaker tapped his own.) "With the good Mirko is good, but his eye knows the wicked, and the wicked know that they cannot deceive Mirko, therefore do they hate and fear him." That is to say, Mirko has many enemies, and when we add that he is close-fisted in money matters, it may be guessed what colour for evil stories his character lends to Austrian journalists. We had heard that he wished to close Montenegro against civilization and foreign intercourse; nay more, that corn sent from Odessa for distribution among the poor had been sold and its price pocketed by Mirko. The more impatient spirits among the Austrian Slavs who wish Montenegro to back the insurrection in the Herzegovina, are

---

* Princess Darinka belongs to a Serb family of the Bocche, but received a careful education at Trieste. In her day, foreign ladies were constant visitors at the palace, and, had her reign lasted, it would have done much for society in Montenegro. Since her husband's death, she has resided with her infant daughter Olga at the courts of Paris and St. Petersburg. She is expected to return to Cetinje this summer.

also foes to Mirko, and at one time accused him of taking
a bribe from Omer Pasha to abandon the hapless Christians.
All these imputations have lately met with refutation, and
the corn which Mirko was represented to have sold is found
never to have left the magazine.

Some idea of Mirko may be formed from an anecdote.
When last autumn it was rumoured that Montenegro was
about openly to head the rising of the Christians in Turkey, a
young Servian officer gave up his commission at home, and
came to offer his services to the cause. Prince Nicolas
happened to be out riding, so the volunteer was brought to
Mirko, and the person who told us the story was present at
his introduction. The Grand Voyvode was walking up and
down before the palace, smoking his long pipe ; he received
the Servian graciously, and asked him his object in visiting
Montenegro. The young soldier stated it, and all around
smiled approval. Mirko answered, and his voice made the
hearers tremble. "Are there not many thousand Turks still
in Servia ? Turn them out, and then come and help us with
the Turks in the Herzegovina."

When Princess Miljena and her father-in-law had quitted
us, the only member of the family left was the prince himself,
who as host, remained, and did the honours of the dinner-
table. Prince Nicolas is only twenty years of age, but already
one of the largest men in his dominions ; though dark, almost
southern-looking, he has the fine stature, fine head, and frank
smile of the true Montenegrin. In case of Danilo leaving no son,
his nephew had been designated as his successor, and was the
first of his dynasty sent for education, not to St. Petersburg, but
to Paris. He speaks French like a native, understands German,
Italian, and Russian, and is a good poet in his own tongue.

In consideration of our ignorance of the Serb language, no
one spoke at dinner who could not speak in French. The conversation thus lost much in interest. But in no company in
Montenegro could one topic pass untouched, the topic of
Danilo's loss. The young prince spoke thereon with much
feeling. "If you had seen the country before my uncle died,"

said he, " you would not know it again. In former times, only because you are strangers, the population of Njegos, would have come out to meet you, and offered you fruits, and sung songs, and fired pistols ; now, though it is Christmas time, you will not hear a shot fired, or a song sung. I do not believe you will even see a fine garment. It is more than a year since the whole population went into mourning, but there are still no signs of its being laid aside." At another part of the conversation, the French doctor related that on board the steamer in which he came to Cetinje, there were several Montenegrins, who appeared quite delighted to return to their Black Mountain. He added "your highness would scarcely believe it." " I not believe it ?" exclaimed the prince. " Have I not felt the same myself ? Why, when I left Montenegro, to go to Paris, I climbed on the highest part of the deck to catch the last sight of the mountains ; and when I came back, I climbed up again to catch the first glimpse of them. *Allez !* I at least know what *that* is."

How far young Prince Nicolas may be expected ever to fill the place of Danilo is at present an anxious question in Montenegro, and an important one for the Christians of Turkey. It is satisfactory to know that Danilo himself, as successor to Peter II., and even Peter II., as successor to Peter I. were each, at the commencement of their respective reigns, the object of a similar discussion.

The party which describes Mirko as a grasping barbarian, sets down Prince Nicolas as his puppet ; those who justify the father from other accusations, deny that he holds an undue sway over his son. We, of course, could form no opinion, but we quote that of persons whose dearest interests were involved in knowing the truth, and who had ample means of knowing. it. In the senate, when judging the people, in family life, they had seen father and son together, and had convinced themselves that the prince's character is that of a man who will be ruled by none. At the same time, say they, " he is young, and new to his post ; he keeps quiet till he can feel his way, and get his hold on the trust of the people." In an all but republican * state, like Montenegro, the power of the sovereign depends chiefly on the degree of confidence wherewith his personal character inspires the nation.

But the greatest embarrassment of Prince Nicolas is his position towards the insurgents in the Herzegovina. As Slav against Turk, as European against Oriental, as Christian against Mussulman—the free Serb of Montenegro is bound to support his brethren now in arms against the oppressor. Moreover, the Prince of Montenegro, as representative of the Princes of Zeta, regards the Herzegovina as a part of his dominions only kept separate from the rest by force. The Christian Slavs, insurgent against Turkey, urge these pleas and beg for assistance; their petition is backed by that faction among the Western Slavs whom I have described as the impatient spirits; both parties speak as if the support of Montenegro were alone needed to make the Herzegovina free. For Prince Nicolas to refuse that support imperils his popularity at home, and his influence in the Slavonic world. On the other hand, France and Russia bid him wait. For a rising of the Slavs to be successful it must be general. Bosnia and Servia are not ready. For the interference of Montenegro in behalf of the Christians not to be worse than useless, it must be certain that Austria will not take this as an excuse for her own interference on behalf of Turkey.... While we were at Cetinje the government of Montenegro was reported neutral; in the Herzegovina, Luka Vukalovic and his desperate band †

---

* For an account of the government of Montenegro, see Sir Gardner Wilkinson's "Dalmatia and Montenegro," vol. i. 454.

† "Last time," said one of the insurgents to the French consul at Scutari, "you persuaded us to lay down our arms on the promise of the Turkish Government to redress our grievances; *you know* how that promise has been kept. You know how we are treated, and how our women are treated by the Mahometans. It is useless for France and England to get promises of redress made to us by the Turk; he never keeps them, and we will never again trust them. We may die with arms in our hands; we will not be trampled to death like worms." A French officer, who had visited Omer Pasha's camp in the Herzegovine, told us: "I believe this insurrection will be put down, but what will Turkey gain? L'Herzegovine lui coute les yeux de la tête; les popula-

held out against Omer Pasha, and not a day passed but volunteers went from Montenegro to join the "Forlorn Hope."

How gladly prince and people would welcome a release from this passive attitude, may be guessed from the following story.  Last autumn, a report. reached Cetinje that Omer Pasha had attacked the Montenegrin frontier.  That morning the prince's secretary was awakened by the sudden entrance of the young Gospodar, crying out, "Hurrah!  The Turk has attacked the frontier, now we *must* fight."  When the secretary went out, he found the great flag waving over the palace—no flag had waved there since Danilo's death.  All day the prince and the people were busy together with preparations for war; and in the evening, the prince sat under the great tree on the plain, the people stood round him, and he read them national war-songs out of the book of the Vladika's poems.  Some hundred men started at once; as they set out the prince said to them, "This day our war with the Turks begins; our national mourning is at an end."  And now comes a despatch from Omer Pasha.  The infringement of the Montenegrin territory is a mistake; he trusts that the good understanding with Montenegro will continue.  It was as if some great calamity had befallen the nation.  The warriors who had departed with songs, returned carrying their arms reversed; the national mourning continues to this day.

*       *       *       *       *       *

We now, and afterwards, saw some of the leading men in Montenegro.  It is scarcely necessary to say, that the difference between them and their poorer countrymen was nothing that indicated mastery on the one side, or servility on the other.  In Montenegro there is no distinction between class and class, like those of noble and peasant in most Continental countries.  Every Montenegrin is equal before law; every one has a right to wear arms, and to give his voice in the Assembly of the people.  Except in the family of the

tions seront écrasés, mais non domptés; il faudra pour les contenir dans la paix, autant de troupes, autant de sacrifice, que dans la guerre; c'est une sangsue qui sévera les dernières gouttes de sang turc."

sovereign, there is no such thing as hereditary office; and, except the sovereign himself, every one, even Mirko, is called simply by his Christian name. Superiority in the social scale can only be attained in three ways—by the industry which makes a family rich; by the sagacity or courage which procures for the individual election to the post of senator, voyvode, judge; and, thirdly, by a European education; which last is, as we have seen, a *sine quâ non* in a candidate for the throne.

It is easy to know if a Montenegrin is rich, for he carries a a good part of his wealth on his person, in the form of splendidly mounted arms. Also, under the white coat, he wears a crimson waistcoat, embroidered with gold, and over the coat, a crimson jacket without sleeves, handsomely worked, and adorned with massive buttons. Some have, besides, a sort of breastplate, or collar of silver; and in cold weather, surcoats with fur, and fur caps. It is a rich dress, and, from its contrasts of white and crimson, beautiful; but, as compared with that of the Scottish Highlander, I thought it lacking in drapery. Even the strooka, a sort of plaid, is stiff and narrow, and not wrapped about the figure, but left to trail in a straight line from one shoulder to the ground.

At the time we were in Montenegro, an air of troubled thought and sadness might be observed in most of the leading men. To sit with arms crossed, while their brethren in the Herzegovina call for aid, is a hard trial for the old chiefs, who have beaten the Turks again and again. Then, too, Danilo's loss fell heaviest on those who stood nearest to him. Many a one, we were told, had never looked up since. It was enough to see the cloud of gloom that settled on the face of our landlord, Kerco,* when he showed us a likeness of Danilo. With a sigh, almost a groan, he pressed the portrait to his lips, and spoke not a word.

Kerco is a Montenegrin of the old school: simple, kindly, even child-like in all circumstances but the heat of battle,

---

* Pronounce "Kertso."

and absolutely unconscious that any idea of horror can be associated with cutting off the head of a Turk. He is, to use the phrase of his country, one of the "best heroes" of the present generation ; and he alone, besides the Gospodar, may wear the plume of honour in his cap. Kerco has lately acquired a yataghan, mounted in silver and coral; he is very fond and rather vain of it. One day, he bade the prince's secretary tell us, that he hoped we did not mind his coming into our presence armed : "there was no need to be afraid of him, though he had, with his own hand, killed fifteen Turks." Then, drawing his beautiful yataghan, he passed his finger slowly along its edge, and observed, that it had already cut off two Turkish heads.

There are at present several young Montenegrins at college in St. Petersburg and Paris, and when their education is finished, they will travel. We just missed the son of a senator, who had been giving the prince an account of his voyage. No place had made such an impression on him as London. "Ah !" said an old Montenegrin to us (by the mouth of an interpreter), "when we get a sea-port, learning will come to us in our own country; now, we must send away our children, if they are to see foreigners, and know what goes on in the world; and few among us are rich enough to give them such an education as that."

*   *   *   *   *

The morrow of our arrival in Crnagora, and often subsequently during our stay, we walked on the mountain plain, and climbed its sides to various points of view. The best of the latter we did not indeed reach, the snow lying too deep on the hill; but we recommend no visitor to leave Cetinje without having seen it from the Rjeka road, and from the rock above the convent. The former commands the greater part of the valley, and the hamlets that stud its grey circlet of crag. Hence, too, appears, in most picturesque grouping, the village of Cetinje, with palace and convent lying at the foot of a rocky promontory, and surmounted by a round tower.

Tower, convent, palace, and village, all are modern, forming
the third encampment where two have been burnt by their
own inhabitants at the approach of the foe.   It is in the rock-
wreathed plain itself that you behold the capital of Montenegro.   There, while the surrounding lands have been groaning
under Moslem yoke, the last free Serbs have met in their
national parliament, a Christian bishop has held his see.
Twice, indeed, during the history of Montenegro have the
Turkish armies penetrated to Cetinje—the second time by
means of a treacherous stratagem.*   No sooner, however, was
the main force withdrawn, than the mountaineers came forth
from their rocks, massacred every Turk that remained, and set
up their independent state as before.   The Turks have never
won from Montenegro one year's tribute, or the acknowledgment of submission from one Vladika.   For the Sublime Porte
to call Montenegro an integral part of its dominions, is of
a piece with the belief of the common Osmanli, that all the
kings of Frangistan are vassals of their sultan ; that the queen
of Great Britain, and the emperor of France, hold their crowns
of his good will.

The tower on the rock appears never to have been finished
and can never have been inhabited, for it has no door.   On its
walls used to hang a bloody garland of Turkish heads, trophies
which so shocked Sir Gardner Wilkinson, that he urged the
Vladika to have them removed.   This the Vladika was himself
forward to do, and his moral influence effected thus much ;

---

* Thirty-seven Montenegrin chiefs, being invited to the Turkish camp to
settle conditions of peace, were treacherously put to death, and this was the
signal for the Turkish army to cross the Montenegrin frontier.   This is a
favourite stratagem with the Turk, and a Montenegrin leader was entrapped
by it only the other day.   Hence the refusal of the Montenegrins to allow
their Gospodar to accept similar invitations—a refusal which, by those who do
not know its origin, seems merely an excuse for declining to negotiate.   Besides
this, of late, on several occasions the Turkish forces have been headed by
*Renegades ;* and whatever tolerance modern philosophy may have for the
position of such individuals, it is fancied by an uncivilized people that a man
who, to advance his worldly prospects, has been false to his baptism, is not
likely to be scrupulous about adherence to an engagement with poor mountaineers when the Ottoman empire might benefit by his treason.

that, although in battle the Montenegrins still decapitate their enemies, the heads, instead of being exposed, are rolled into a pit of water. The Vladika excused the barbarism of his people, by pointing out that they have barbarians to deal with; and, in fact, when Sir Gardner Wilkinson reached Mostar, he found that the Turks not only stuck on the castle the heads of their slain foes, but tortured their captives, and impaled them alive.

Between the tower and the convent rears itself a stone house, three stories high, and no broader than a single room. This was the dwelling of the Vladikas before the present residence was built. Certainly architecture does not flourish at Cetinje. The only edifice of interest is the convent, and that boasts little save a row of double arches. The original monastery stood on the plain, and is said to have been a larger, finer building. In it were preserved jewels and church valuables belonging to the princes and primates of Zeta. But when the Turks approached Cetinje, the old convent was blown up by its own monks, and its treasures have never re-appeared. A store of valuable objects and of trophies are now kept in the palace. Among the latter, as we were told, may be seen English medals, taken at the battle of Grahova from Turks, who, having earned them before Sebastopol, lost them before Crnagora.

The convent of Cetinje contains the principal church and school of Montenegro; it is also the residence of an archimandrite, who will shortly receive consecration as Vladika. On our second visit we were shown into the apartments of the Rev. Father—very comfortable rooms, furnished in the European style. The archimandrite himself has the long hair and flowing robes of a Greek monk; but the parish priests or popes of Montenegro wear the national dress, and carry arms, which they only lay aside while reading service. They are generally " good heroes," the first at a gathering, the leaders of their flocks in war.

In the apartments of the archimandrite we met the " Minister " of Montenegro; a Dalmatian educated in Trieste;

also the Bohemian secretary of the prince; a Bosnian come
to Cetinje on a mission from the Christians in Turkey; and a
little Siberian engineer, engaged on a strategical map of
Montenegro.   These persons, natives of lands so distant, were
all of them Slavs, and each, speaking the dialect of his own
country, was able to converse with the rest.

As to the school of Cetinje: our visit happened in the
Christmas holidays, when regular lessons were not going on;
but one afternoon, hearing from without the voices of children
singing hymns, we entered, and found scholars but no teacher.
It appeared that rather than sit at home idle, the boys of the
first class were met to sing and read together.   Their song was
rough-voiced, as that in a Scotch kirk, the books they had just
laid down were church books; we were told that the Montenegrin dialect of the Serb is so near to the ancient Slavonic,
that the Cyrillic translation of the Bible can be read with ease
by a Montenegrin child.   Reading, writing, arithmetic, history,
geography, are taught at Cetinje; but the master not being
present, there was no one to put the class through its
manœuvres.   The boys showed their copy-books, in which the
writing was very fair; they use the Cyrillic characters, and
their favourite exercise is letters on given subjects.   Like the
rest of the race, the Slavs of Montenegro show much eagerness
for historical knowledge, and quickness in picking up foreign
languages.   At present the poetic talent is highly developed
among them, and a poem on the death of the last prince was
produced by the Cetinje scholars.   Schools were established
by Danilo in every village; but since his death the unsettled
state of the surrounding country has gone much against their
progress.   In case of a Turkish inroad, the people know that
their villages will be burnt, and everything like civilization
put an end to for years; and in the meantime, we heard of
schoolmasters forsaking their desks for the more congenial
post of volunteers in the Herzegovina.

The church in the monastery of Cetinje is in form and
adornment an ordinary Greek chapel, but it contains the tomb
of Danilo, and the mummy of St. Peter.   The secretary told

us that for eight weeks after the late prince's death the chapel was filled day and night with people, lamenting over his grave. " And not women alone," added he, " but huge, sunburnt warriors, weeping like very children."

Homage of another kind is rendered to the body of St. Peter, which lies displayed in priestly robes, with nothing but the face covered. St. Peter was in his lifetime Vladika Peter I. ; now he is the patron saint of Montenegro, and has a good title to his post, which is more than can be said of his neighbour, St. Blasius of Ragusa. When, in the cathedral of the Slavic Athens, we were shown the skull of its protector, magnificently set in jewels, we asked by what benefit to the city St. Blasius had entitled himself to a higher place in her homage than those great Dalmatians, St. Hilary and St. Jerome. " When the Venetians bombarded our city," was the answer, " the image of St. Blasius caught the balls in its hands ; and once he saved Ragusa from being taken, by revealing the enemy's project in a vision to a priest." Ask a Montenegrin what St. Peter did for Montenegro, and he tells you : " There are still with us men who lived under St. Peter's rule, heard his words, and saw his life. For fifty years he governed us, and fought and negotiated for us, and walked before us in pureness and uprightness from day to day. He gave us good laws, and put an end to the disorderly state of the country ; he enlarged our frontier, and drove away our enemies ; even on his deathbed he spoke words to our Elders which have kept peace among us since he is gone. While he yet lived, we swore by his name; we felt his smile a blessing, and his anger a curse ; we do so still."

St. Peter was the fourth ruler of the line of Njegos. Daniele, its founder, was the deliverer of Montenegro in the worst danger it ever ran from the Turks, and it was in consideration of his services that the office of Vladika was made hereditary in his family. The fifth, Petrovic, was the last Vladika—the national poet of Crnagora ; the sixth was Danilo, who resuscitated the princely dignity, and obtained a recognised frontier for Montenegro.

When the Serbs shall have freed their land from the oppressor, and have the crown of Car* Dusan to bestow, they need not ask the diplomats of West Europe to send them a king to wear it. Among the rocks of Montenegro a line of patriotic and talented rulers has grown up with the nation through its centuries of struggle.

Perhaps, however, the greatest benefit Danilo rendered to the cause was, when for himself and his descendants he disclaimed every right that could endanger the unity of the nation. From Prague to Bosnia are repeated the noble words with which he parted from the Servian Milos : "Prince, go forward, and I also will go forward. When our ways meet, trust me for being the first to hail you as Car of the Serbs."

From the convent at Cetinje a few steps bring you to the palace—a long one-storied building in the centre of an open court, flanked by four towers. Close by is soon to be erected a hall for the Senate, which now assembles in a room of the palace. The Parliament, or General National Assembly of Montenegro, meets in the open air, and has gone on meeting there for centuries, without ever finding the want of a parliament house. How different from the Austrians ! A civilized people begin things at the right end ; they put up a fine wooden parliament-house last year, and now lack nothing but the Parliament.

From the gates of the palace-court starts that line of street which, crossed at its further end by another line, forms the little village of Cetinje. "You think there are but few stone houses in Cetinje," said a Montenegrin to us ; "you would think there are a great many if you had seen Cetinje twenty years ago, when there were only two."

Most of the houses at Cetinje have an upper story, and in many of the private dwellings this is well furnished, and even carpeted, the rarest luxury being a stove. There are also several small locandas, and in summer a stranger accustomed to rough it would easily find tolerable quarters ; in winter this

* "Pronounced Tzar."

is more difficult, the absence of fire rendering most locandas intolerable.   At this season the kitchen is the only warm part of the house.   There, on a slight elevation at one end of the floor, you find not only fire but company, and, if you understand the language, more instruction and entertainment than anywhere else.   It is round the kitchen fire that those songs are sung and stories told wherein the Serbs of Montenegro hold intercourse with their brethren in Servia, Herzegovina, and even Bosnia and Dalmatia.   Centuries of separation have not loosed this tie, and Kara George, the liberator of Servia in our own day, is not less a national hero of the whole southern Slavonic race than Milos Obilic in the fourteenth century.

As for the resources of Cetinje, food—that is to say, fish, dried mutton, bread, and cheese—can be obtained in the locandas ; and, in the way of apparel, we bought a good woollen strooka from the household where it was made.   For a trifle any girl will undertake the six hours' walk to Cattaro, and bring you back whatever its dear and ill-supplied shops afford.   Still, the little daughter of the French doctor was not far wrong in describing Cetinje as " une ville où les ressources sont rares, et l'on ne trouve qu'un bon air."   · The air is indeed " bon "—even with snow on the ground it never felt chilly—the sunshine was bright, the atmosphere clear, and then " si les ressources sont rares," sickness is rare also, drunkenness still rarer, vice almost unknown.

To us the great grievance of Cetinje was the street.   There the snow lay, and to use the expression—" Got leave to lie," drift, freeze, crack or melt under the eyes of all those great fellows, who at this season have nothing to do.   For their negligence two excuses were alleged.   First, that at any moment the wind might change, and clear the valley in a few hours.  Secondly, that the inhabitants of Cetinje do not themselves fear the snow, and that in winter they are not accustomed to visitors.   But what excuse is admissible when one is hobbling and plunging from hole to hole where giant footsteps have trod before? ·

Every day, as we went out walking, we could see the crowd gathered round Mirko, where, sitting at the door of a house, he judged the people and gave ear to their petitions. This is his office as president of the senate. To the senate are referred cases which the judge of each separate village has failed to settle satisfactorily; and from the senate a last appeal lies to the Gospodar. Therefore, while causes are pleaded before Mirko, the Prince is often present, and, as it was described to us, "walks up and down, listening to what goes on, and frequently explaining the decisions to the people."

Another office is discharged by Mirko. Last year there was drought in Montenegro—cattle died, and the harvest suffered—to keep the poor alive, the government has had to buy Indian corn—and of this Mirko is the distributor. To swell his store, supplies have been sent from Russia and France—from Russia, as by race and creed the natural ally of the Montenegrins—from France, in order to save them from being wholly dependent on Russia. The Montenegrins are duly grateful, but still they feel that he is badly off who depends for daily bread on charity; and rather than live on the subsidies of foreign powers, they ask if it were not better to return to the old Highland fashion, and gain winter provision by a *tcheta* on the low country. These *tchetas* are plundering excursions on the Turkish territory, and the perpetrators being, as suggested by M. Broniewski, unacquainted with the high-sounding epithets of contribution, requisition, forced loans, &c., call pillage by its own name, and excuse it by such arguments as the following :—By force the Turk took that country from us, by force he keeps it from us ; have we not the right in our turn to take its produce by force from him ?

It was the late Vladika, and Danilo, who being resolved to elevate Montenegro into the community of civilized states, ordered *tchetas* to be given up. What then ? Comes a bad harvest in the Mountain, how are the inhabitants to live ? The answer is, that while the sovereigns of Montenegro were teaching their people to keep within the border, they looked to an arrangement with the Great Powers whereby Montenegro should receive a territory within which civilized beings could live. They had in view, first, that Turkey should be obliged to acquiesce in a definition of the Montenegrin frontier; and, secondly, an extension of that frontier to the coast at Antivari; or, at least, as far as Spizza. Such an extension would take from Turkey but a narrow strip of land, while it would give Montenegro access to the sea—the first step necessary for her prosperity and civilization.* The territory claimed is a part of the principality of Zeta, to which the sovereigns of Montenegro have never renounced their right—the inhabitants of the territory are Christians and Slavs.

In 1859, after Mirko's victory at Grahova, and when the Herzegovina only waited the signal to join him, the Porte did find itself obliged to recognize Montenegro as a separate state, and agree to the delineation of a Montenegrin boundary. The Great Powers sent their emissaries to draw the line; it was drawn, and on every side fell short of the sea. This was a terrible disappointment for the Montenegrins; they impute it partly to the influence of Austria, whose own frontier lies close to Spizza, and whose jealous policy it is to exclude the southern Slavs from the Adriatic. But even Russia is not too anxious to assist them in this matter. Why should she wish them to become independent of her subsidies? Why help them to a port, when this would bring them into direct communication with England, and open a path for English influence among the Slavs of the interior?

*     *     *     *

Sir Gardner Wilkinson complains that most travellers who ascend to Montenegro from the Bocche, go no further than Cetinje, and then come back, saying, that in the Ladder of

---

* "Let Montenegro receive, *nolens volens*, some accession of territory on her north-west, west, and east frontiers, and let her be acknowledged by the world, as she is by Russia, an independent principality, with consuls at her capital. . . . . While things exist as at present, the development of these countries in agriculture or commerce is as impossible as in civilization and Christianity."—*Times*, Oct. 3, 1861.

Cattaro they have found the secret of Montenegrin independence. He advises those who desire to learn the real secret of Montenegrin freedom, to prolong their expedition to the Turkish frontier at Niksic and at Spuz. There, on each side, valleys run into the mountain, and the Montenegrin territory is only twelve miles broad. Yet there the Highlanders dwell fearlessly, without rampart or defence of any kind save their individual valour.

Nothing would have pleased us better than to obey the injunction of the great traveller, but our visit falling in the depth of winter, the roads to Niksic and Spuz were blockaded by snow. We did our best in making out Rjeka, which lies not far from the Turkish border, in a valley opening to the Lake of Scutari. Rjeka was the home of our good friend, Giorgio; but he had kindly halted at Cetinje while we did, and although we had declined his invitation for the Christmas feast, we accepted of his escort with thankfulness. Another welcome companion was the Bosniak, on an embassy from the convent party to buy their Christmas desert at the Rjeka Bazaar. I have already alluded to the graver mission which brought this gentleman to Cetinje—besides his experience of Montenegro, he had much to tell us about the Slav populations in Austria and Turkey.

Our "equipage," on this expedition, was worse than ever. My aunt obtained a reddish-coloured pony, and a leathern saddle; but I had to put up with a lame mule, and a seat formed by wooden bars; an end of rope, fastened to one side of the bit, served for bridle.

Our road led, first, across the plain, in a direction opposite to that by which we had reached Cetinje; soon it began to climb the rocks, and brought us, on their further side, to the point called Granitza, or the boundary. Thence the view is beautiful and singular. Cetinje lies in the Katunska, or Alpine canton, Rjeka, in the River canton. Between the two, you stand as on a rampart, and look, on the one hand, into the court of the citadel; on the other, down the castle rock to the valley, and the enemies' country. Eastward, the Albanian Mountains stretch chain after chain of snow-covered summits; at their foot, the Lake of Scutari receives the streams, Rjeka and Moraca, and spreads its waters, blue and sunlit, as far as the eye can reach.

On the shores of the Lake of Scutari dwelt the Serb princes of Zeta, and ruled the fertile lands around till 1485. At that date, John the Black, finding he could no longer defend the level country against the overwhelming hordes of the Turk, called around him his best heroes, and took of them an oath on the New Testament to abide true to their faith and nation, and rather die than accept terms of the infidel. Whoever broke this oath, should be invested with a woman's apron, and hooted from the ranks of men. Then the Prince of Zeta turned his back on his "white castle" and smiling realm, and led his devoted band into the mountains. On the rock-girt plain of Cetinje he planted the eagle-banner of Servia, and erected a Christian church: thither he transferred the throne of the princes of Zeta, and the see of the metropolitans.

Soon after this, the plains of Zeta became the province of a Turkish pasha; and the Highlands of Zeta acquired their distinctive name of "Black Mountain;" in Serb, Crnagora; in the Venetian dialect, Montenegro.

Black John was succeeded by his son, George, who fought valiantly against the Turks; but, having no children, and wishing to end his days in peace, eventually abdicated, and withdrew to Venice. But first, in the Assembly of the Nation, he solemnly made over his power to the metropolitan; and from the date of his departure, 1516, till 1852, Montenegro was ruled by a vladika, or bishop. Under its vladikas, the Black Mountain weathered the severest storms of its history; and the fidelity of the Montenegrins to the Christian religion, at a time when so many other tribes "fell off," may, at least in part, have been owing to the character of their government. A Christian priest would surely be the last to sanction partnership with the Mahometan; and the uncompromising policy of the Montenegrin vladikas has come down to us in the declaration of their last representative.   He was a youth of twenty, and but lately come to the throne.   Grand Vizier, Mehemet Redschid Pasha, invited him to make submission to the Sultan, promising to reward him with the Berat.   Peter II. answered; " So long as Montenegro is independent, no Berat is needed to constitute me its ruler: should the independence of Montenegro be surrendered, the Berat were but a mockery."*

We have already told that, since 1711, the office of vladika was hereditary in the Petrovic family; also, that, in 1852, Danilo, the sixth Petrovic, separated the secular from the ecclesiastic dignity, and revived the original title of Prince. Had Danilo lived another year, he would have retraced the steps of Black John, and transferred his residence from Cetinje to the shores of the Lake of Scutari.

At the Granitza we began to descend, winding down the side of a long hill; the path was rough, and at first coated with ice, which grew less and less frequent as we proceeded.

In those gorges of the Black Mountain which open on the east and south, the climate is that of Central Italy—as spring to winter, compared with the climate of Cetinje.   The valleys yield in abundance fruits, tobacco, vines, and mulberry-trees ; the wine produced is red, and considered to be more wholesome than any in Dalmatia, and the Montenegrin cocoons of silk are of a superior quality.   But in the more mountainous regions culture is very laborious, and on the way to Rjeka we remarked patches no larger than flower-beds dotted about in the very clefts of the rock.

The Bosniak remarked them too, and exclaimed, "Every inch of soil turned to account; verily, it is an industrious people."

"Is it not then true," we asked, "that good land on the plain of Cetinje lies neglected ?"

He answered, "Whoever told you so knows nothing of

* On the foundation and history of Montenegro as a state, see "La Souveraineté du Monténégro et le Droit des Gens Moderne de l'Europe," par Jean Vaclik, Secretary to the Prince of Montenegro.

Montenegro.  It is astonishing, with their constant warfare and their few resources, what these poor people get out of their ground.  Where the plain of Cetinje is not worked, it is either necessary as pasture for the cattle, or the soil is not deep enough for cultivation."

We then inquired if he thought that the industry of the Montenegrins in eking out a subsistence from their barren mountains might be taken as a sign that they were naturally diligent and persevering, and would prove these qualities if tried on a wider stage.  We had been told that in the Montenegrin territory lay coal only waiting to be worked till they had a seaport of their own.  Was it likely that the Highlanders would accommodate themselves to continuous labour like that of working coal?  Would they know how to make a civilized use of a seaport, supposing they had one.

"That," said he, "need never be a question.  When Montenegro has a port on the Adriatic, as a free port under a Serb Government, it will attract to it the Serb merchants who now trade in Trieste and elsewhere.  If the coal is worth anything, there would soon be a company to undertake it.  You must observe, that in the present state of matters not Montenegro alone—all the Serb countries are cut off from the sea—a port given to one would be a benefit to all."

We here quoted the remark of a Dalmatian, given by Mr. Paton in his " Highlands and Islands of the Adriatic":— " Dalmatia without Bosnia is a face without a head."

"To be sure it is," answered the Bosniak, "and Bosnia without Dalmatia is a head without a face.  Bosnia has the produce, Dalmatia has the ports; to part them, as for ages they have been parted, is to bar the natural development of both."

"Did not Austria at one time hope to add Bosnia and Herzegovina to her empire?"

" Indeed she did, but in the meantime, instead of annexing, she has been losing provinces.  For the future, we may expect to see, not Bosnia and the Herzegovina added to Dalmatia, but Dalmatia added to Bosnia and the Herzegovina.  All three countries are peopled by the same race, and should ever a Christian and a Serb Government be firmly established in the inland regions, there can be little doubt but that the coast will make out her junction with them."

"But surely," we said, "though the population in Dalmatia and Bosnia are of one race with those in Serbia, the Herzegovina, and Montenegro, they are divided from them as to religion. We have heard that in Bosnia the descendants of those who, 400 years ago, renegaded from Christianity, hate the Christians more and are more hateful to them than the original Turks."

" The story of the Mussulman Bosniaks is this :—When, at the time of the Turkish conquest, the nobles of Bosnia found that rank and riches were continued to those who apostatized, rather than forfeit their wealth they changed their religion. The poor, who had less to lose, remained faithful; it was a case of the camel and the needle's eye. Further, I can tell you as a fact, that 400 years of apostasy has not obliterated among the Bosnian Mussulmans a sort of superstitious trust in the efficacy of their fathers' faith. In case of desperate illness they call in a Christian priest, and they will cause Christian prayers to be said over their parents' graves. There lingers among them even a tradition that their fathers' race will resume empire, and *lettres de noblesse* and title-deeds of estates received from Serb and Christian monarchs have been handed down in renegade families from an idea that they will be of advantage to the possessors when the Christian kingdom is restored."

" But are not the Dalmatian and other Christian Slavs Romanists, and as such divided from the Slavs of the Greek Church ?"

" They are, and at one time their sectarian jealousies drove many a brave man into the ranks of the Mahometan. But now-a-days influences are at work, whose tendency is to absorb such differences as separate Christians into Latin and Greek. You may have remarked that the Bohemians, who are Catholics, do not therefore wish the less kindly to us, and

among the lower classes, even in Dalmatia, religious pre-
judices do not prevent the Romanist from singing songs about
national heroes who are Greek. I am pretty sure that the
national sympathy will prove too strong for the sectarian
antipathy, at least where, as in the case of Bosnia and
Dalmatia, the material interests of the populations demand
their union."

After a while the Bosniak resumed : " Talking of agriculture, do you know that I was very near spending this
winter in Scotland ? I wish to see the Scotch farms, for
of all systems of farming none pleases me like the
Scotch."

We exclaimed, " It surprises us to hear that Scotch farming
is understood in Bosnia."

" I call myself a Bosniak," he answered, " because my
father was one; but he left the Turkish provinces and settled
within the Austrian frontier. My little property is in Slavonia.
I was one of those employed by the late Ban Jelacic to bring
out plans for improving agriculture."

" Perhaps then you can tell us if the Slavs on the military
frontier are inclined to assist their brethren against Turkey."

He replied, " Were they not, I should not be here;" and
then, at our request, proceeded further to explain the state of
matters. " To have a clear idea you must begin at the
beginning. The military frontier was originally organized to
defend Christendom against the Turks. Such a barrier was
then needed, and the Slav populations of which it was chiefly
composed, lent themselves gladly to any system which had
for its aim to keep out the Mahometan. It was on the lands
of the Slav, as those lying nearest to Asia, that the Mahometan swarm principally settled ; and while the Mahometan
remains in Europe he remains on Slavonic ground. The
Russian has already driven out the Tartar, the Serbian must
drive out the Turk ; and till the Turk is gone, northern and
southern Slav are alike bound never to lay down arms.
Well, now-a-days, the Turkish power is broken, in so far that
it can no longer molest the portion of Christendom com-

prehended in the Austrian empire.  At this point Austria
bids us halt.  She does not abolish the military frontier
although she has been much pressed to do so, and although
it is not needed for defence, she insists on retaining it, but
she refuses to let the Slavs who form it, come to the aid of
their southern brethren now finishing the common work."

" Perhaps," we suggested, " she thinks it a bad example for
the subjects of different governments to meddle in each
others' quarrels."

" She had no'such scruples in 1848-49, when, during her
own quarrel with the Magyars, Slavs from the Turkish
provinces crossed the frontier to join us in fighting for her.
But now that the Turkish Slavs are fighting for their freedom
and nationality, now that it is our turn to help, we may not
even give house-room to their stores, shelter to their women
and children.  Because I was discovered giving shelter to
such fugitives and house-room to such stores, the ammunition
and provisions on my premises were seized, and I myself
was to be made prisoner.  Instead of that I went to Bosnia,
and then came here to try what could be done for my people
in another way."

" But if," said we, " the Serbs have an enemy in Austria,
they have powerful friends in France and Russia."

" Powerful friends who, when their service is rendered,
will take care to repay themselves at our expense, while, in
the meantime, their friendship draws on us the hostility of
Austria and of England.  We do not want foreign inter-
vention ; what we want is *non-intervention* applied to our
cause as it was to the Italian.  We can do without France
and Russia, if we are certain that Austria will not co-operate
with Turkey, and that England will not pay the Turkish
troops.  Leave the Serb to fight it out with the Turk.
European against Asiatic, Christian against Mahometan,
freeman against oppressor ; surely it cannot be doubted that
we shall gain the day."

" And when you have gained the day, are we still to
practise non-intervention while you effect a junction with

your northern brethren, and inaugurate the kingdom of Panslavism ?"

He laughed. " You English people are too clever by hal You can look forward to the union of the whole Slavonic race under one government, but you do not recognize that at this moment the southern division of that race is struggling to assert an independent nationality. You can discern champions against Panslavism in the Austrian and Turk; you do not see that in order to render Panslavism impossible, you have only to balance Slav against Slav."

I thought this argument sounded very like those in Count Krasinski's treatise on Panslavism; and certainly we had heard almost the same words from the lips of Slavs of various nationalities, in Dalmatia, and Vienna, and Prague.

As we descended the rock-gorge to Rjeka, a wailing cry broke on our ears; it ended in a sustained drone. " Hark !" quoth Giorgio, "that is the lament. Women who have lost a relative in the Herzegovina, will gather to the bazaar to-morrow to mourn him, sing his exploits, and how he fell." Again the wail rang through the hills; it startled us painfully, and the tone of the last long note was heart-rending. Giorgio said, "When we are at Rjeka, I will show you one of these laments written in a book." The book proved to be that of the Vladika's poems, and we found therein a lamentation full of wild and touching poetry. It is the bewailment of a sister over her brother.

" My falcon, my eagle !" she calls the departed, using the Montenegrin epithet for a hero; "whither hast thou flown from me? Didst thou not know the treacherous Turks? didst thou not know that they would deceive thee? Oh ! my deep wound, my wound without cure ! Alas ! for my lost world, my world dearer than the sun ! Thou pride of brothers ! Had thy place been at the side of the emperor, thou wouldst have become his chief minister. If thy place had been at the side of the king, he would have made thee his general. Oh ! my brother, where is thy beautiful head? Could I but kiss it ! could I but comb its long hair ! But the enemy will desecrate thy beloved head; he will deck with it the walls of Travnik!" The singer frequently speaks of herself as a "poor cuckoo" (kukawiza); for, according to Serb legend, the voice of the cuckoo is that of a sister calling on her lost brother, and who will not be comforted, because he answers not.

But for the general mourning for Danilo, we should, at the bazaar, have heard something better than laments. Ballads celebrating the feats of national heroes, chanted by minstrels who are heroes themselves. Travellers, more fortunate than us, describe these Montenegrin singers as realizing the bards in Homer's Odyssey.

From Cetinje to Rjeka is a three hours' journey; but we had been late in setting out, and now arrived when it was too dark for a good view of the valley. We could just see that the houses of the village were surrounded by a verandah, and altogether in a different style to those of Cetinje; and we also caught the outline of Danilo's stone bridge, which spans the river below the town.

Above Rjeka stands a small fort; its story is curious. George Crnovic here erected a printing-press, where Church books were printed, as early as 1494. Specimens of these still exist, and are among the oldest printed works in Cyrillic character. Eventually, the printing establishment was turned into a fort; and the types, melted into bullets, were shot off against the Turks.

At Rjeka, we had been promised quarters better than at Cetinje; great, therefore, was our chagrin to find the one lodging with a stove already taken. The guest-chamber of the inn was fireless, and had broken windows; against each of its walls stood a bed large enough for the accommodation of half a dozen giants; one corner displayed a cupboard with glass doors, of which every pane was cracked; a gaily painted chest occupied the other. Between the windows hung a daub, representing the Emperor and Empress of the French, with their son. Even here, we only obtained a resting-place by the courtesy of persons who resigned their prior claim;

and we certainly never should have got meat for supper, had
not our companions insisted on our behalf. We felt a little
out of countenance when the landlady, bringing in our fowl,
made the remark: " It was plain we did not belong to their
religion, or we never should have asked meat during the
Christmas-fast." No one else touched even milk or cheese.

But though we did eat meat during the Christmas fast,
every one gave themselves the utmost trouble to make us
comfortable ; as for Giorgio, no sooner had he seen his wife
and child, than he returned to the inn, and there remained
till he had taken all necessary care for our well-being. I
must further note that, when it came to preparing our
chamber for the night, we were struck with the careful
decency of the female attendants—very different to what one
meets with in Italy, or even France.

That night, the wind changed; and the bright, mild
weather that had favoured us since we left Cattaro, gave way
to a snow-storm. This, at the moment of the Christmas fair,
was a real calamity; hundreds of people were prevented
from attending; others suffered much on the journey. The
show of stalls was proportionately small; and of all the good
things in requisition for the Convent-feast, nothing was to be
found but walnuts, strung together in long necklaces.

The bazaar was held in an open court, surrounded by
houses, of which the lower story served for a shop; the
upper, ascended by an outer stair, for dwellings. To see
about some specimens of costume, we paid a visit to the
court tailor, whose achievements we had admired in the
dress of the prince, and the crimson and gold jacket of the
Bosniak. It appeared, however, that he sold nothing ready
made, and could make nothing to order within three or
four months. We therefore left with him three dolls to be
dressed, one as a Montenegrin; one as a woman in her
holiday garb; the other, in the mourning costume worn
while we were in Crnagora. We also bought a cap, on the
subject of which we still feel puzzled.

Sir G. Wilkinson says that the Montenegrin head-dress is

a fez, surrounded by a turban : we never saw a Montenegrin
in either. Instead, they wore a round crimson bonnet,
without tassel, worked aslant the crown with gold, and
trimmed round the rim with a black silk band. These
Montenegrin bonnets have become fashionable in Corfu, as
smoking-caps ; and some of them may be seen, this year, in
the London Exhibition, among the things sent from the
Ionian Islands. We were repeatedly assured that they were
the characteristic Montenegrin head-gear, and were told,
further, that the black band round them is worn as mourning
for the occupation of the Serb Lands by the Turk. "When
the Turks are gone back to Asia, we shall throw the black
bands after them, and wear the red cap unveiled." *

After this Giorgio invited us to see his dwelling, and led
the way to a tidy upper chamber. "Had my room contained
a stove," said he, "I should have offered it to you for last
night." We could not help asking, why he, who evidently
knew the comfort of a fire-place, did not put up one for himself. "We Montenegrins," he answered, "do not require
warm houses. In winter evenings it is enough for us to sit
together in the kitchen. We are healthy and strong, even
our infants † do not need to be swaddled or coddled, we just
wrap them in a cloth, and if it is cold weather, we set them
near the fire." Coffee was brought to us by Giorgio's wife, a
pretty young woman, on whom the mourning costume looked
quite tasteful—we were shown some of her holiday garb,
jackets in form like the Greek, crimson and purple velvet,
embroidered in gold.

As we left the house we caught sight of Giorgio's little

* Red and white are the terms used among Slavonic tribes to designate
all that is beautiful, prosperous, and free—black signifies unfortunate or
enslaved.

† "Le défaut de soins médicaux fait que peu d'enfants faibles arrivent à
l'adolescence, de manière que ceux qui y parviennent sont tous forts et bien
constitués. L'absence de travaux d'esprit, la vie en plein air, leur rudes
labeurs par le grand soleil et le froid, l'influence de l'hérédité, la sobriété et la
tempérance sensuelle viennent encore ajouter à ces causes de vigueur."—*Notice
médicale sur le Monténégro, par M. Tedeschi.*

boy; he was not quite well that day, but seemed to us a fine chubby little fellow. After all the father had been telling us about hardiness, his only son appeared warmly clad.

We then returned to the inn, and for some time sat round the kitchen fire. The changing society was sufficiently amusing. Now entered a voyvode grandly attired, now quite a poor man in vile raiment, but the richest appeared not to think he had a superior right to a seat, nor did the poorest give up his place, or seem abashed at the neighbourhood of finer clothes than his own. As regards ourselves, we were never in any place where the presence of strangers was so quietly taken, no one noticed us except so far as to make room for us by the fire. On the other hand, if we chose to commence a conversation, it was sure to be continued with liveliness and courtesy.

And now the question began to be mooted, should we or should we not return to Cetinje that day? The snow was falling thick; crossing the hill would not be pleasant, but then if frost set in to-morrow, the road would become impassable for horses, and here we were at Rjeka, in a fireless room with broken windows. At present many people were leaving the bazaar for Cetinje, if we started at once we should have company, and, if need be, assistance by the way.

We started. Giorgio brought his great capote for an extra wrap, and engaged two stout fellows to take his place with us. He said he would have himself seen us safe back to Cattaro, but for the Christmas feast, and the illness of his child. We bade him good-bye with great regret; he had left his business in order to accompany us, and had undertaken all the trouble of the journey, yet he made no charge for his services, and seemed quite taken aback when, at parting, we gave him something for his little boy.

We have since learnt that the day we crossed the hill from Rjeka was the worst of all last winter. Now that it is well over, we are glad to know what the Black Mountain looks like in bad weather. The snow fell in thick flakes, all around was snow, and the Montenegrins in their white garments, and heads enveloped in their *strookas*, hurried past us, filling the air with their shrill voices. As evening drew on, the scene became unearthly, like the ghost of the scene of yesterday. Winding up the mountains the path was very steep, and as our beasts grew tired they frequently came to a dead halt. My luckless mule was lamer than ever, and more than once fell down on its nose. So long, however, as it did not roll over on its side, my best chance was to stick to it, seeing that I could not have hoped to walk, where the Montenegrins themselves were scarcely able to keep their feet. How we looked forward to the top of the hill! Alas! it proved the commencement of worse troubles. Descending to Cetinje, the snow lay thick, and a tremendous wind had sprung up, not a north wind, that would have finished us, but a wind that melted the snow, so that every step was a plunge. Here the mule did better than the pony; its sagacity in choosing sure footing was marvellous, and, at any rate, we were well off in comparison of the walkers. The women, who had hitherto been trudging along, talking, laughing, and encouraging each other, now tumbled down repeatedly, and under their burdens it was not so easy to rise. At length one of these hardy, patient creatures began to cry; she was not as strong-looking as the rest. I am glad to say we saw her again next day all right, and brave and merry as ever.

How we looked forward to the house of Kerco! But here, once more, we were doomed to disappointment. The men who had escorted us from Rjeka knocked, our hostess herself opened, spoke to the guides, then turned and shut us out. We supposed she was gone for a light, and, in fact, soon the door reopened. This time it was Kerco himself, he also spoke to the guides—we distinguished the word "locanda"—then again the door clapped to, and we were shut out again. What to do did not at first appear; the Bosniak, having seen us to the entrance of Kerco's house, had departed to his own, and with the guides we could not speak. They were dragging our beasts to the comfortless locanda, when, from the further line of street a light streamed over the snow, and a loud cheery voice hailed us. Again our poor beasts were pulled along ; and arrived at the light, we this time found an open house, and hosts who bade us welcome. A young woman assisted us to dismount, and an old woman led us into a large kitchen, where she made us sit by the fire.

We found ourselves in a regular Montenegrin house, and unable to make a soul understand us ; but our hosts were of the kindest, they took off our cloaks, spoke coaxingly to us, and pitied us as if we were children. And now a known tongue sounded behind us, and the Bosnian entered. He apologized for having taken for granted that when we got to Kerco's door we were all right ; and added, " This also is a little locanda, and upstairs there is a chamber with a stove, the person who rents it is at present in Cattaro, and you must take possession of it till you can get a better. I have ordered the stove to be lighted, but till the room becomes warm, I am afraid you must remain here." So there we sat round the fire, and the old woman brought us coffee. But soon the kitchen began to fill with water, which at first content with coming in at the door, ere long poured through a hole in the wall—wider and wider grew the pools, closer and closer the circle by the hearth—at length a hissing sound announced that the logs would soon cease to blaze. The women lifted what they could out of harm's way, but viewed the mishap calmly, as if accustomed to it ; meanwhile the landlord was telling a long story to the Bosniak. " Ha !" cried the latter, " water has burst into the house of Kerco, and the rooms are flooded. I know that last summer the roof wanted repairs, which it did not get ; no doubt it has broken in. Well for you that you were not there." At last the room upstairs was reputed habitable, and retiring thither we inquired into the state of our carpet-bag—thanks to the gallant bearing of the maiden who carried it over the mountain, some part of its contents were dry. The old woman came to us, and when she had otherwise helped us as much as she could, seated herself before the fire, and held up various of our articles to dry. Of her talk we could only understand a word or two, but the tone was intelligible enough.

And now it was the stove's turn to exhibit alarming peculiarities; it soon let us know that unless carefully attended to, it might be expected to set the house on fire. Meanwhile, without, the storm increased in fury, the wind was tremendous, there was thunder and lightning; we were told that the inmates thought it likely their roof would follow the example of Kerco's. Altogether the chances were that we should be disturbed that night, so we lay down without undressing. Tired as we were, we slept at once, only awakened at intervals by crashes and flashes.

At dawn the tumult ceased, and when we arose and asked after our neighbours, we heard that the floor of the kitchen was once more dry land,* and that such inhabitants of Cetinje as had been storm-stayed at Rjeka, came now trooping across the hill unscathed. Of course, no one had expected us the preceding evening, but so soon as our return and its attendant circumstances were known, the prince sent to tell us that arrangements had been made for our occupying the upper story of a house whose proprietor was in the Herzegovina. The abode was in charge of the Bocchese housemaid and her husband, an Austrian deserter, who made himself generally

---

* " Le sol fendillé et caillouté des montagnes calcaires absorbe l'eau des pluies et . des neiges qui se réunit après avoir parcouru des labyrinthes souterrains, et finit par se faire jour à travers les rochers sous forme de torrents impétueux. La rapidité avec laquelle elle parcourt ces méandres a donné lieu à un phenomène qui parâit de prime abord étonnant. L'existence de ces torrents est intermittente, elle est soumise au caprice des vents. L'eau ne s'échappe que lorsque soufflent les vents du sud-ouest. Aussitôt que ceux-ci sont remplacés par les vents du nord-est, toutes les sources sont taries. Ce phénomène s'explique cependant si l'on réfléchit que ce sont les vents du sud-ouest qui passent sur l'Adriatique, se chargent de vapeurs, lesquelles se résolvent en pluies sur les montagnes, et que ces mêmes vents fondent les neiges.

" Le 20 du courant, à la suite d'un coup de vent très-violent du sud-ouest qui dura toute une nuit et qui fit disparâitre plusieurs pieds de neige tout d'un coup, le bassin où se trouve Cettigné a été inondé au point que l'eau a pénétré dans le rez-de-chaussée de presque toutes les maisons; mais vingt-quatre heures après, ce vaste lac n'existait plus."—M. TEDESCHI, *Notice Médicale sur le Monténégro.*

useful. Extra furniture was sent from the Palace, and the Princess's maid, a purpose-like Bohemian, came to see that we were all right. Before evening we were installed in two (water-tight) rooms, with a spring arm-chair, a sofa, and a stove that had a good idea of its functions.

And now began the most enjoyable part of our stay in Montenegro. Frost had set in, and the road to Cattaro was impassable for horses, so there we were with time to rest and to pick up information. We did not want for society, nor, after the first day, for exercise, and the little girl of the French doctor showed us some capital walks about Cetinje.

The doctor himself came to see us the morning after our ride from Rjeka, and having ascertained that we were none the worse, poured forth the recital of his own grievances. "Je vous dirai, mesdames," he began, "that you must have excellent constitutions not to have suffered from the effects of that storm. For myself, I confess that life in Montenegro does not suit me; for the last three weeks I have had a cold. I am lodged with my wife and child in a single room. When it is bad weather, we cannot go to dinner at the Palace. Yesterday evening, for example, it was impossible to cross the road. During last night, from the violence of the tempest, the house rocked to its foundations." We could not resist answering, that his experience of life in Montenegro must increase his admiration for the Montenegrins, who, during centuries, had borne what he bore, and worse, rather than submit to the Turk. "Pardon," interrupted he; "that is a sentiment to which I do not aspire. Often I ask myself, Qu'est-ce que c'est que la liberté Monténégrine? Cannot any one be independent who chooses to dwell on the top of a rock? I avow, that rather than cultivate such liberty, I would a thousand times be subject to the Turk." Thus the quick-tempered little Frenchman: the Bosniak answered him—"Do you suppose you would better your condition by exchanging it for subjection to the Turk? Try life in the Herzegovina, and see if you find it pleasanter than life in Montenegro. The Montenegrin bears privations; the Chrisian subjects of the Turk must be content to bear cruelties, insults, shame. You see yourself that at the end of four centuries it is he that can endure his position no longer; that with hands folded, the subject of the Turk begs for help of the Montenegrin." The doctor hastily changed the subject. "If you knew," he said to us afterwards, "how monotonous is the conversation of these Slavs! It is the fashion, chez nous, to find them clever and witty; to me they seem to have but one idea—to think and talk of nothing but their eternal nationality and freedom."

When the prince's secretary and the Bosniak visited us, the text of discourse was usually some published account of Montenegro. They would point out wherein its statements seemed to them inaccurate, and what changes had taken place since it was written. Many were the anecdotes related; the life and work of Danilo became better known to us; the information about country and people would fill a book; it is difficult to select what may find space in a few pages.

One day we said to the secretary—"Do you know what a travelled and accomplished Englishman told us, 'That at this hour, in Montenegro there is no code but revenge'?" "Indeed!" answered he; "then to-morrow I had better bring our code to show you." He brought it, and translated for us some articles from the Serb. I believe there is a published translation in Italian, and a French translation may be found in M. Delarue's Memoir.

The code now in force in Montenegro is that of Danilo. It comprises ninety-five articles, and has for its basis the ordinances of St. Peter. A third, and somewhat less primitive code, rendered necessary by the more civilized state of the people, is now in process of compilation. Even by St. Peter's law—the first *written* Crnagora—private feuds and the vendetta are abolished, but at that time there were no regular officers of justice, and it was necessary to hold out rewards to private persons who would punish an offender caught in the act. Now-a-days the corps of Perjaniks, or National Guard of

Montenegro, undertakes the duty of police, and each company in its own village brings criminals before the judge, and sees to the execution of sentences. Capital offenders are shot, and for smaller transgressions there are fines and a state prison at Cetinje. But the prison is often empty, and has never more than two or three tenants; indeed, in a poor country like Montenegro precautions are taken not to let captivity become a resource for the improvident or the lazy. The victuals of the prisoners are paid for by themselves, and an article of the code provides that criminals sentenced to prison shall be employed in mending the roads, or on other works of public utility.

The ordinance abolishing vendetta runs thus—"Whereas, in Montenegro and Brda there exists a custom of vendetta, by which vengeance falls not only on the murderer or guilty individual, but also on his innocent relatives, these vendette are rigorously prohibited. No one shall dare to molest the brother or other guiltless relatives of the criminal, and he who kills an innocent person shall himself be put to death. The murderer alone, who shall be sought for and brought to justice, shall atone for the murder with his head."

Articles 24, 25, 26 are directed against tchetas and all infringement of the enemy's country in time of truce. "In order to preserve with neighbouring countries the tranquillity needful to our reciprocal interests and the welfare of the State, theft, brigandage, and depredations of what kind soever, are prohibited in time of peace. . . . In time of peace or of truce (*bessa*) with the parts of Turkey bordering on our country, brigandage, theft, and all depredations are forbidden, and should they occur, the booty shall be returned to those from whom it has been taken, and the guilty parties shall be punished. In case of transgression on the territory of a neighbouring country, the culprit shall receive the same punishment as if his offence had been committed against a brother Montenegrin."

Other sentences are primitive enough; one has come down unaltered from the days of Black John. The man who does

not take arms when his country is attacked, shall be deprived
of his weapons, and never may he again wear them. He can
never hold any place of honour in his country's service, and
he shall be condemned to wear a woman's apron, that every
one may be informed that he has not the heart of a man.

Several articles are directed against insults—not only
insulting actions, such as a kick, or a blow with the pipe, for
which it is lawful to retaliate by killing the offender on
the spot, but also against insulting words. We were told
that such abusive epithets as are commonly bandied about
among the lower ranks of other countries, would be held
to sully the mouth and the honour of the poorest Montenegrin. In the spirit of Crnagoracan equality, it is enacted,
"That the Montenegrin who insults a judge, voyvode, or
elder, shall pay a fine of twenty talari, and that a fine of
twenty talari shall be paid by any judge, voyvode, or elder
who insults a common Montenegrin."

A thief, for his first offence, is fined—for his third offence,
is shot. During the year 1859, there were fifteen thefts
committed in Montenegro; in the course of 1861, there
were only two crimes, and one of these was a theft to
the amount of a few pence.

The second case puzzled the criminal court of Cetinje. A
false prophet was brought up for trial. At first no one could
decide how far his offence came under Montenegrin law,
but after a while it transpired that his imposture had taken
the turn of squeezing money from his votaries. On this he
was found guilty of stealing. Now, for a thief convicted the
second time, Danilo had instituted the following punishment—
In presence of the senate and of the assembled people, the
culprit was to be led forth by an old idiotic beggar; then he
was to lie down at full length on a cannon, and the idiot with
a light rod gave him a whipping. After this manner they
dealt with the false prophet.

We will next quote one or two articles of the code of
Montenegro, which may help to answer the doctor's question—
" Qu'est-ce que c'est que la liberté Monténégrine ? "

" Article 1. All Montenegrins are equal before law.

" Article 2. (I quote the French translation.)   En vertu de la liberté héréditaire jusqu'ici conservée, l'honneur, la probité, la vie, et la liberté demeurent assurés à tout Monténégrin, et personne ne peut toucher à ces choses sacrées qu'en vertu d'un jugement."

On the question of religious toleration, it is written—

" Article 90. Although in our State there is no nationality but the Slavic-Serbian, and no religion but the non-united Greek, nevertheless the professor of any other religion may live among us freely, and enjoy the same privileges as a brother Montenegrin."

On the right of asylum—

" According to the will and testament of St. Peter, who was our Sovereign, every fugitive setting foot in our free State shall there be safe, and no one shall dare to molest him, so long as he behaves peaceably. He shall enjoy the same rights as a native Montenegrin, and if he does evil, he shall be chastised according to this code."

We asked the secretary if any persons not members of the Greek Church resided in Montenegro. He answered—" I myself am a Roman Catholic ; the servants who occupy this house are Roman Catholics.   There are at this moment Mahometans residing within our territory, and at their request the prince has given them permission to erect a place of worship.   For fear they should not have full confidence in his sanction, he has offered them money to assist the building, and not even Mirko has a word to say against it."

As for St. Peter's ordinance respecting the right of asylum, it was elicited by the following incident.—An Austrian soldier escaped hither in order to avoid a flogging.   The Austrians demanded that he should be given up.   St. Peter, who knew that the man's offence had been slight, and that his superior officer was cruel, refused, except on condition that his punishment should be remitted.   The Austrians promised this—they gave the promise in writing, still St. Peter would not turn out the fugitive, he only showed him the written promise, and left him to take his own way. The fugitive gave himself up, and no sooner did the Austrians see him in their power, than they had him flogged to death.

Dreadful was the wrath of St. Peter; he beheld in this incident a stain on the honour of Montenegro, and in his will he laid a curse on every Montenegrin who, on any plea or consideration whatever, should give up a fugitive to his persecutors.

We were anxious to learn what sort of position the law of Montenegro assigns to women.

According to Danilo's Code, the Montenegrin woman has, in every respect, the same legal rights as a man, and especial provision is made to secure her a full share in the division of property. When a father's possessions are parted among his children, daughters inherit as well as sons, and an only daughter can succeed to the whole property of both her parents. When a woman marries, she receives a dowry which passes to her husband's family, but in return, should she be left a widow, she is entitled to her husband's share in the common stock, and, should she marry again, the family of her first husband must continue her a certain pension. In cases of domestic quarrel, where the man refuses to dwell with his wife, they are at liberty to separate, but not to break the marriage. Neither of them may wed any one else, and the maintenance of the wife must be provided for by the husband. Farther, care is taken by law that no woman be married against her inclination. When, as is usual, persons have been affianced in childhood, the priest is forbidden to marry them without having ascertained that the bride is a willing party; and if a girl should dislike the spouse chosen for her by her parents, and choose one for herself, the family is not allowed to interfere. "Such couples," so runs the sentence, "are united by love."

"A woman who murders her husband shall be put to death like any other murderer, only no weapon may be employed in her execution, for it is shameful to use arms against one who cannot take arms in defence." By what agency a woman shall be executed is not provided by the code of Danilo, but, according to ancient usage, in cases of gross crime she is stoned, her father casting the first missile. With this fearful doom was visited every transgression of social purity, and though Danilo's code sanctions capital punishment only in the case of a married woman, by popular custom there is no exception. Nor, according to Montenegrin standard, is crime less degrading to the stronger than to the weaker culprit; the male offender equally forfeits his life, the honour of his family receives as deep a stain; while her father undertakes the punishment of the girl, the man is shot by his own relatives. Thus have they " put the evil away from among them ;" it is fact the Montenegrin spurns vice as unworthy of his manhood, and even when dealing with their Mahometan enemies, even in their wildest tchetas, with *these* "barbarians" a woman is safe.

It has been remarked that the social virtue of the Montenegrin is not less admirable in itself than as an evidence of what the precepts of Christianity can do for the moral life of a people even when its material life has been reduced to the verge of barbarism.

That the Montenegrin considers it as below him to offer violence to the defenceless, sufficed for the protection of women and their property even before the establishment of law and police. Through any part of the country they might walk unguarded and carry what they would, without fear of molestation, and it was even sufficient for the security of any person, be he stranger or fugitive, that a woman should take him under her charge. It is not, however, to be denied, that in a country where war is the business of life, the very fact of being defenceless is considered the mark of an inferior being. The vast, the immeasurable superiority of one who can take care of himself and others, over one who requires to be taken care of, needs no demonstration, it is taken for granted; and so long in Montenegro as war shall continue to be the business of life, this feeling cannot change. In the meantime there is no desire for selfish purposes to retain a woman in her position of inferiority. " Why should they not do as we do if they have the spirit?" These words we heard from the lips of a Montenegrin. A woman who has ever taken her part in the defence of the country is highly prized, and made the subject of national poems; a former traveller records having seen a Montenegrin girl, who had by some exploit acquired the right to wear arms; and we were ourselves witnesses of the honour in which all Montenegrins hold the sister of Prince Nicolas, because last autumn she asserted the resolution of accompanying her father to the seat of war.

Some conventional usages, more or less characteristic of the whole Southern Sclavonic race, appear in the behaviour of the Montenegrin woman. Her salutation to her husband and her husband's guest is the same as that generally offered to the Gospodar; she kisses the hand and the hem of the tunic. A more curious custom is that which regards it as indelicate for a young married woman to address her husband before company; from a like feeling, the husband avoids mention of his wife; and if he cannot help speaking of her, premises her name with a sort of apology.

Of a different character is the use of the invocation, " My brother, or my sister, in God." To claim the assistance of the most absolute stranger, it is only necessary to address him by this term. " Are we not all His offspring?" is the original idea; and in Serb poetry, the sun, the moon, the bird, the tree, every creature of the One Father, is called on to aid the sufferer as " a brother or sister in God." From her greater weakness, it is the woman who most frequently makes appeals of this nature; and the vengeance of Heaven would instantly overtake him who should either refuse aid thus invoked, or abuse his office of protector.

Another custom, still in force in Montenegro, is that of swearing " brotherhood." Two individuals bind themselves by solemn oaths to mutual aid, attachment, fidelity: their tie is stronger and more sacred than that of blood. The idea of such a relationship is not Montenegrin; it is human, world-old; we have world-famous instances of it in Achilles and Patroclus, in David and Jonathan. But what would seem to be characteristic of the Southern Sclavonic "friendship bond" is, that women, as well as men, are accustomed to engage in it. Two women may, and do, thus bind themselves, and solemnly receive the Church's blessing on their contract; or, a woman pledges herself as "bond-sister" to a man; and it is said, that there never was an instance of the association degenerating from its fraternal character.

As for the material existence of the Montenegrin woman, one need scarcely say that it has its full share of the toil and hardship of life on the mountain. War and agriculture are the employments of man; on woman devolves the work of the household, the manufacture of clothing, and the carriage of produce to market. By the latter arrangement, a great part of the commerce of Montenegro passes through the hands of women; but strangers riding up to Cetinje from Cattaro, and meeting the Highlanders on their way to the Bazaar, are not favourably impressed by the sight of heavy burdens on female shoulders. As for the Montenegrin warrior, even when not otherwise engaged, he has a natural aversion to be seen acting as porter; for it is one of the regulations of the Montenegrin army, that a man, who is by cowardice or crime incapacitated from bearing arms, shall be turned to account as a carrier of provisions.

Laborious as are the vocations of woman in Montenegro, they are not such as to impair her health, or debase her social character. Would that the same could be said of the life of women in more civilized countries! On this head, we have the testimony of one who ought to be a good judge—a physician, and a Frenchman. The Montenegrin women, he says, work more than the men. "On les voit portant des fardeaux énormes, cheminer lestement aux bords des précipices; souvent, comme si elles ne sentaient pas le poids qui les charge, elles tiennent à la main leurs fuseaux ou leurs chaussettes, et, tout en filant ou en tricoant, elles causent ensemble. Mais ces travaux n'humilient pas la femme; elle est inviolable, elle ne conçoit point l'amour sans le mariage ou sans le meurtre du séducteur. Si les rudes labeurs lui enlèvent vite certains charmes, ils lui procurent aussi des dédommagements : une santé toujours florissante, une grande vigueur et l'innocence des mœurs, bienfaits dont sont privées beaucoup de filles de nos grandes villes, dont la vie sédentaire et souvent oisive les livre à tous les écarts de leur imagination et à tous les égarements des passions qui flétrissent la beauté avant l'heure."*

And now the long Christmas-fast was drawing to a close ; the Christmas-feast was to begin.  It was high time ; for, by reason of abstinence, every face had grown thin and yellow ; but joy had fled from the coming holiday ; it was, like the last, to be celebrated in mourning—without songs, without shooting, without any of its festive characteristics, saving only the quasi-religious ceremony of the " Badnjak."

A few days after our arrival at Cetinje, the prince, with his "following," had gone into the mountains to cut down the yule log ; on Christmas-eve it was to be brought home.  He now sent us a message, to the effect that he would have asked us to witness the ceremony were it not contrary to the custom of the country that a foreigner should be present. A like pretext served for the banishment of the French doctor.  Considering that the Christmas party at the palace was to be a family gathering, and that very few of the prince's relatives speak any language but Serb, we did not find anything mysterious in a custom which excluded foreigners from their circle.

But it would have been vexatious on this account to miss witnessing the Badnjak, and with no small satisfaction we heard of the following arrangement :—It happened that the proprietors of the locanda in which we passed the night of the storm belonged to a family not resident in Cetinje, and had but lately set up for themselves.  For the young couple and their mother to keep Christmas alone seemed dolorous enough, and already old Yovana had been crying

* M. Tedeschi, " Notice Médicale sur le Monténégro."

over it; therefore it was agreed that the bringing home of the
log should be duly held in Andrea's kitchen, and that we and
some others, who, like our hosts, were passing the Christmas
away from our own fire-side, should be present at the ceremony. "You will excuse me," said the tall young landlord,
"if I am awkward and cannot make fine speeches; for this
is the first time I have acted house-father." "Ah," quoth
another of the party, "you should see the log brought home
in some of our large houses. We have here a family
numbering seventy guns, besides old men, women and
children."

About half-past six o'clock on Christmas-eve (Jan. 5th,
New Style), Andrea came for us, and with his assistance,
united to that of the Bocchese maid, we steered clear of the
snow-drifts and pool of water that lay between his door and
our own. Arrived in the locanda, we found the kitchen
swept clean and the kitchen fire in a cheery blaze. Around
the hearth was a row of seats, and at one end of this circle
places were assigned to us. By degrees our "scratch" party
gathered, and then the ceremony began. First entered old
Yovana. I never shall forget the gravity of her aspect; she
carried a lighted taper, and took her station in front of the
fire. Then came the house-father, bringing in the badnjak,
three logs, or rather trees, their stems protruding from under
his arms, their branches trailing behind him along the floor.
At the entrance of the badnjak all rose, and the men, taking
off their caps, greeted it in words like these:—" Welcome,
oh log; God save thee!" The badnjak was then placed on
the fire, and the house-father sprinkled them with raki,
uttering the while benedictions on all friends, and wishes for
the coming year. Glasses of raki were then handed round,
and each guest drank to his host. When it came to the turn
of the Bosniak, he being a Serb, and accustomed to the
ceremony, made a speech of some length, wishing Andrea a
house of his own and a son. The Montenegrin answered,
" May God give our prince a long arm and a sharp sword
from the field of Kosovo." The field of Kosovo was that in

which the Serb empire fell; the swords that there fought for freedom are those that shall retrieve its cause—this has been the Serb toast for four hundred and seventy-two years.

In a rich family we should now have set down to table, but Andrea's house boasted no table, and supper was represented by two plates of cakes brought in by the mistress, and set on the floor before the fire. These cakes were made of apple, and really delicious; unluckily, we have forgotten how they are called, but they take the place of plumcake, and shortbread, and bun, in Montenegro. Before the cakes were presented to the company, a portion of them was thrown upon the logs, the house-father making an invocation. Herewith the ceremonies ended. All sat round the fire and chatted, old Yovana especially distinguishing herself. The Prince's secretary translated to us the conversation. Meanwhile the young house-father, released from his difficult duties, slipped into a seat behind the blaze, and began confidential discourse with the Bosniak. Their talk was of the next campaign, and Andrea proposed that they should be brothers and fight side by side. The mutual obligation of such brothers is this: should one of them be slightly wounded, it is his friend who carries him out of the battle; should one of them be desperately wounded, and no chance remain of saving him from the enemy, it is his friend who strikes off his head.

Properly speaking, the evening of the badnjak should conclude with a grand letting-off of firearms, wherein families of seventy guns come out to great advantage. Because of the national mourning, not a shot was heard in Cetinje, and our little party separated in quiet, our friends promising to call for us next day on their way to the ten o'clock mass.

On Christmas morning before dawn we were awakened by the ringing of bells, and, for the first time since our arrival, beheld the sun rise on Cetinje. After that day we never missed the sight, so beautiful was the effect of the grey rocks and snowy field, tinged first with a pallid blue and then with a glowing blush. But while we enjoyed this scene of our Christmas morn, we little thought of what we were losing. Contrary to custom, the prince and his family attended mass, not at ten, but at six A.M.; and as the sun rose on the plain, the young "Gospodar," in kalpak and plume, issued from the door of the convent chapel, and received the Christmas greeting of his people. Hundreds of the white-robed mountain warriors— those old unconquerable champions of Christendom—gathered round their chief with the salutation, "Truly, this day Christ is born!"

Our ill luck was shared by those who had taught us to rely on mass taking place at the usual hour, and at first no one could account for the change. Afterwards it was explained as a kindly device on the part of the archimandrite to hasten the hour of breakfast for the exhausted people. Some of our friends were roused from their slumbers by a summons to keep their feast with the prince. Said one of these, "I do not feel as if it were Christmas-day, for I have had no mass." Others, whose duty bound them to be, at least, as alert as their sovereign, received no bidding to the palace, and lost both mass and breakfast.

We were honoured with various calls, every visitor dressed in his best; and on this occasion we were able to assure ourselves that, with the Montenegrins, at least, it is not "fine feathers that make the fine bird." The white, close-fitting coat and gaiter form an unmerciful costume for any but the athletic mountaineer. Later in the day we paid our respects at the palace, and after dinner came the palace servants, and the two women from the locanda. Each brought us something—an orange, an apple, a pomegranate—gifts too small to be offered in any capital except Cetinje; but there, owing to the absolute dearth of luxuries, more acceptable than can readily be conceived. (Some time afterwards a hamper of oranges and lemons came as a present to one of the convent party; and "galanteries," consisting of one orange and one lemon, were forthwith sent round to his principal acquaintance.) These compliments of the season we returned as well as we could, and made the discovery that maraschino is the refreshment conventionally offered to Christmas callers. Last of all the visitors appeared our young host of the preceding evening. His errand was to thank us for a Christmas gift made to his wife, and to renew his apologies for having awkwardly acted the part of house-father. "Besides all that," said he, "you must forgive the poverty of the feast. I know well that many a one would have spent sixty or seventy guldens to have entertained you properly, but at present, as you may be aware, we in Montenegro are poor."

The disappointment on Christmas morn was in some sort made up to us by another opportunity of seeing the Gospodar, with his senators, voyvodes, and heroes of many fights. Every day, about three P.M., this goodly company used to take its station in front of the palace-court, and there to practise shooting at the target. One afternoon we were invited to look on.

We found together some hundred warriors—picked men they would be anywhere—the poorer, with white garments; the wealthy, in picturesque and richly-coloured attire. Distinctive uniform they had none, saving the badge of the Servian Eagle; many wore splendid weapons, not a few Turkish spoil.* Contemplating this assemblage, and contrasting it with similar assemblies in other lands, we could not but recognise the words of the old Serb ballad to be as true to-day as in the time of Ivan Crnovic : "The Latins are rich ; they have gold and silver, and the skill of workmen ; but the Serbs have the proud and princely bearing, and the glad, fearless eye of heroes."

Among his "following," the Gospodar is distinguished by his lofty stature and tunic of green and gold. Eagerly watching the marksmen stands his sister—a dame of resolute mien, with loaded pistols at her girdle—and from a window in one of the court-towers looks forth the sweet face of little Princess Miljena.

The gun used by the shooters was long and slender, its stock inlaid with mother-of-pearl ; the target was set, at first,

---

* A number of good arms of European manufacture were taken by the Montenegrins from the Turk at the battle of Grahova.

a short way off, afterwards much farther; but the differences
between foreign and English measurements prevented us
from ascertaining the distance in yards. As for the skill of
the Montenegrin marksmen, we, of course, could be no judges;
such opinions as we have heard or read are in its favour.
The shooters stood in a throng; we could perceive no sort of
military formality in their practice; a good deal of talking
went on, but not cheering, or any demonstration, which might
have told us what we afterwards learnt, that they were
shooting for a prize. The winner was the patriarch of a large
family, and reputed the most honest man in Montenegro;
as such, chosen for the state-treasurer.

The Gospodar advanced to meet us, and then returned to
take his turn with the rest. His shot seemed invariably to hit
the target; and we were told that, like his two predecessors, he
is one of the best marksmen in the realm. Presently, the
Grand Voyvode, Mirko, came up, and held a conversation
through the medium of the secretary. As Mirko, not to
mention being the hero of Grahova, is himself a bard, a
singer of valorous exploits, we appealed to him to point out
some of the most distinguished warriors present. Casting
his eye round the circle, he indicated a Montenegrin, poorly
dressed, shorter of stature than the rest, of especially simple
and unpretending aspect. "That man," said Mirko, "has
with his own hand killed twenty-five Turks; his cousin has
killed thirty-five, but he is in the Herzegovina." The secretary added: "In a hand-to-hand combat the mountaineers
reckon ten Turks for each Montenegrin; the cousins noted by
Mirko are therefore really something more than common, for
they are still young, and can between them answer for sixty
Turks. In this computation foes merely shot down do not
count—to gain credit for having slain a Turk, a Montenegrin
must have struck off his head."

Perhaps it is as well to add, that while the Montenegrin
regards the slaughter of Turks as pleasing in the sight of
Heaven and of all good men, he does not, like a Mahometan
or a Crusader, practise war with the infidel as a short cut to

Paradise. He requires no such stimulus: the Turk is to him the trampler of his religion, the oppressor of his nation, the robber of his country, the abuser of his women—he fights not to destroy, but to defend or revenge.

" Thou knowest," says the old ballad, " the fierce sons of Montenegro; they are all of one race and stand as one man. They follow the banner of one chief: where he cries war, they all cry war; where he falls, they will fall." But even for the foreigner who does know the sons of Montenegro and their history, the contest that now lies before them must seem dangerous, if not desperate. A large Turkish army, under the best general the Turks have—inasmuch as he is not a Turk, but a Serb*—is congregating on the Montenegrin frontier; and on the side of Christian Europe, where, in her hardest struggles of old, Montenegro was sure of sympathy, now-a-days she sees herself blockaded by Austria. That the Montenegrins themselves have no fear—that they look forward to the signal for war as the signal for freedom to their brethren and their ancient homes—may arise from a depreciation of their adversary's strength. It may arise, also, from long experience of that adversary and of themselves.† Certain it is that they have hope—the same hope which, from century to century of ceaseless wrestle, has spoken to them of ultimate victory. In their own words, " He who knows how long we have held out for freedom and our faith on this barren mountain—He who sees what havoc the enemy has made of the fair countries that once were ours—God—will not much longer delay to give us back our fatherland."

The sun was setting, and we turned to leave the shooters, when a cavalcade was seen crossing the plain. The French and Russian consuls from Ragusa, whom the storm had

* Omar Pacha is a Croat.

† History testifies how often larger Turkish armies in their best days have been beaten by the Montenegrins. A European officer, who had often been in command of Mussulman troops, told us that unless the Turks had improved amazingly in the last few years—since the battle of Grahova—he should be sorry to find himself at the head of a Turkish battalion opposed to one hundred Montenegrins.

prevented from coming earlier, brought the young Gospodar of Montenegro a Christmas greeting and their good wishes for the coming year.

*　　*　　*　　*

Before that year began, we had bade farewell to Crnagora; and having run some risk in a snow-storm between Cetinje and Njegos, found ourselves once more at the gates of the rock-citadel, looking down on the olive-woods and white villages of the Bocche. A Montenegrin who had been charged to escort us pointed beyond the barrier mountains to the blue waters of the Adriatic; he stretched out his arm to the sea and called out " England."

To the dweller on the Black Mountain the sea is England, and the day that opens his country to the sea opens it to intercourse with England—to English sympathy, to English commerce. The subsidies of foreign Powers will never stand him in stead of a sea-port of his own, the alliance of military empires will never give him his place among civilized nations, until he receives the right hand of fellowship from the great commercial people of the West. Also, it is a fixed idea with the Montenegrin, that if England really knew that what he wants is access to the ocean—to 'that great world-highway, on which the ships of England are the carriers—she would be the first to admit and to advocate his claim. We cannot close this record of a Christmas spent in Crnagora without delivering the message intrusted to us by an old Highlandman, " Tell your great English Queen—for the power is hers—that we Montenegrins can live no longer without a bit of sea."


THE END.

*Early in May will be published,*

**PRICE ONE SHILLING,**

# HAND BOOK

## TO THE

# FINE ART COLLECTIONS

### IN THE

## INTERNATIONAL EXHIBITION.

BY

## FRANCIS TURNER PALGRAVE,

FELLOW OF EXETER COLLEGE, OXFORD.

" Nature never did betray
The heart that loved her."
W. WORDSWORTH.

PUBLISHED BY

## MACMILLAN & CO.

### LONDON AND CAMBRIDGE.

**SOLD WITHIN THE BUILDING UNDER THE SANCTION OF
HER MAJESTY'S COMMISSIONERS.**

# LIST OF BOOKS

PUBLISHED BY

## MACMILLAN AND CO.

Cambridge,

AND 23, HENRIETTA STREET, COVENT GARDEN, LONDON.

**ABDY.—A Historical Sketch of Civil Procedure among the**
Romans. By J. T. ABDY, LL.D. Regius Professor of Civil Law in the
University of Cambridge. Crown 8vo. cloth, 4s. 8d.

**ÆSCHYLI Eumenides.**
The Greek Text with English Notes, and an Introduction, containing an
Analysis of Müller's Dissertations. By BERNARD DRAKE, M.A., late
Fellow of King's College, Cambridge. 8vo. cloth, 7s. 6d.

**AGNES HOPETOUN'S SCHOOLS AND HOLIDAYS.**
The Experiences of a Little Girl. A Story for Girls. By Mrs. OLIPHANT,
Author of "Margaret Maitland." Royal 18mo. cloth, gilt leaves, 5s.

**AIRY.—Mathematical Tracts on the Lunar and Planetary**
Theories. The Figure of the Earth, Precession and Nutation, the Calculus
of Variations, and the Undulatory Theory of Optics. By G. B. AIRY, M.A.,
Astronomer Royal. **Fourth Edition**, revised and improved. 8vo. cloth, 15s.

**AIRY.—Treatise on the Algebraical and Numerical Theory of**
Errors of Observations, and the Combination of Observations. By G. B.
AIRY, M.A. Crown 8vo. cloth, 6s. 6d.

**ARISTOTLE on the Vital Principle.**
Translated, with Notes. By CHARLES COLLIER, M.D., F.R.S., Fellow
of the Royal College of Physicians. Crown 8vo. cloth, 8s. 6d.

**ARTIST AND CRAFTSMAN; A Novel.**
Crown 8vo. cloth, 10s. 6d.

**BAKER.—Military Education in connexion with the Univer-**
sities. By JAMES BAKER, Lieutenant-Colonel, Cambridge University
Volunteers. 8vo. 8d.

**BAKER.—Our Volunteer Army; a Plan for its Organization.**
By JAMES BAKER, B.A. late 8th Huzzars, Lieutenant-Colonel, Cambridge
University Volunteers. Crown 8vo. boards, 2s. With a Map of Volunteer
Rendezvous in the United Kingdom.

**BAXTER.—The Volunteer Movement; its Progress and**
Wants. With Tables of all the Volunteer Corps in Great Britain, and of
their Expenses. By R. DUDLEY BAXTER. 8vo. 1s.

**BEAMONT.—Catherine, the Egyptian Slave of 1852. A Tale**
of Eastern Life. By W. J. BEAMONT, M.A. Fellow of Trinity College.
Cambridge, late Principal of the English College, Jerusalem. Fcap. 8vo.
cloth 5s. 6d.

**BEASLEY.—An Elementary Treatise on Plane Trigonometry:**
with a numerous Collection of Examples. By R. D. BEASLEY, M.A., Fellow
of St. John's College, Cambridge, Head-Master of Grantham Grammar School.
Crown 8vo. cloth, 3s. 6d.

**BERKELEY.—The Theory of Vision Vindicated and Ex-**
plained. By the Right Rev. G. BERKELEY, Lord Bishop of Cloyne.
Edited, with Annotations, by H. V. H. COWELL, Associate of King's College,
London. Fcap. 8vo. cloth, red leaves, 4s. 6d.

**BIRKS.—The Difficulties of Belief in connexion with the**
Creation and the Fall. By THOMAS RAWSON BIRKS, M.A., Rector of
Kelshall, and Author of "The Life of the Rev. E. Bickersteth." Crown 8vo.
cloth, 4s. 6d.

**BLANCHE LISLE, and Other Poems.**
Fcap. 8vo. cloth, 4s. 6d.

**BOOLE.—The Mathematical Analysis of Logic.**
By GEORGE BOOLE, D.C.L. Professor of Mathematics in the Queen's
University, Ireland. 8vo. sewed, 5s.

**BOOLE.—A Treatise on Differential Equations.**
By GEORGE BOOLE, D.C.L. Crown 8vo. cloth, 14s.

**BOOLE.—A Treatise on the Calculus of Finite Differences.**
By GEORGE BOOLE, D.C.L. Crown 8vo. cloth, 10s. 6d.

**BRAVE WORDS for BRAVE SOLDIERS and SAILORS.**
**Tenth Thousand.** 16mo. sewed, 2d.; or 10s. per 100.

**BRETT. — Suggestions relative to the Restoration of**
Suffragan Bishops and Rural Deans. By THOMAS BRETT (A.D. 1711).
Edited by JAMES FENDALL, M.A., Procter in Convocation for the Clergy
of Ely. Crown 8vo. cloth, 2s. 6d.

**BRIMLEY.—Essays, by the late GEORGE BRIMLEY, M.A.**
Edited by W. G. CLARK, M.A., Tutor of Trinity College, and Public Orator
in the University of Cambridge. With Portrait. **Second Edition.**
Fcap. 8vo. cloth, 5s.

**BROCK.—Daily Readings on the Passion of Our Lord.**
By Mrs. H. F. BROCK. Fcap. 8vo. cloth, red leaves, 4s.

**BROKEN TROTH, The.—A Tale of Tuscan Life. From the**
Italian. By Philip Ireton. 2 vols. Fcap. 8vo. cloth, 12s.

**BROOK SMITH.—Arithmetic in Theory and Practice.**
For Advanced Pupils. Part First. By J. BROOK SMITH, M.A., of St.
John's College, Cambridge. Crown 8vo. cloth, 3s. 6d.

**BUNYAN.—The Pilgrim's Progress from this World to that**
which is to Come. By JOHN BUNYAN. With Vignette after a Design
by W. HOLMAN HUNT, engraved by C. H. JEENS. 18mo. cloth, 4s. 6d.
morocco plain, 7s. 6d. extra, 10s. 6d. The same on large paper, crown
8vo. half-morocco, 10s. 6d.

**BUTLER (Archer).—Sermons, Doctrinal and Practical.**
By the Rev. WILLIAM ARCHER BUTLER, M.A. late Professor of Moral
Philosophy in the University of Dublin. Edited, with a Memoir of the
Author's Life, by the Very Rev. THOMAS WOODWARD, M.A. Dean of Down.
With Portrait. **Fifth Edition.** 8vo. cloth, 12s.

**BUTLER (Archer).—A Second Series of Sermons.**
Edited by J. A. JEREMIE, D.D. Regius Professor of Divinity in the University of Cambridge. **Third Edition.** 8vo. cloth, 10s. 6d.

**BUTLER (Archer).—History of Ancient Philosophy.**
A Series of Lectures. Edited by WILLIAM HEPWORTH THOMPSON, M.A.
Regius Professor of Greek in the University of Cambridge. 2 vols. 8vo.
cloth, 1*l*. 5*s*.

**BUTLER (Archer).—Letters on Romanism, in Reply to Mr.**
NEWMAN's Essay on Development. Edited by the Very Rev. T. WOODWARD,
Dean of Down. **Second Edition**, revised by the Ven. Archdeacon HARD-
WICK. 8vo. cloth, 10*s*. 6*d*.

**BUTLER (Montagu).—Sermons Preached in the Chapel of**
Harrow School. By the Rev. H. MONTAGU BUTLER, Head Master of
Harrow School, and late Fellow of Trinity College, Cambridge. Crown 8vo.
cloth, 7*s*. 6*d*.

**CALDERWOOD.—Philosophy of the Infinite. A Treatise on**
Man's Knowledge of the Infinite Being, in answer to Sir W. Hamilton and
Dr. Mansel. By the Rev. HENRY CALDERWOOD, M.A. **Second
Edition**, 8vo. cloth, 14*s*.

**CAMBRIDGE. – Cambridge Scrap Book: containing in a**
Pictorial Form a Report on the Manners, Customs, Humours, and Pastimes
of the University of Cambridge. With nearly 300 Illustrations Second
Edition. Crown 4to. half-bound, 7*s*. 6*d*.

**CAMBRIDGE.—Cambridge Theological Papers. Comprising**
those given at the Voluntary Theological and Crosse Scholarship Examina-
tions. Edited, with References and Indices, by A. P. MOOR, M.A. of Trinity
College, Cambridge, and Sub-warden of St. Augustine's College, Canterbury.
8vo. cloth, 7*s*. 8*d*.

**CAMBRIDGE SENATE-HOUSE PROBLEMS and RIDERS,**
**with SOLUTIONS:—**

| | |
|---|---|
| 1848—1851.—Problems. | By N. M. FERRERS, M.A. and J. S. JACK-SON, M.A. of Caius College. 15*s*. 6*d*. |
| 1848—1851.—Riders. | By F. J. JAMESON, M.A. of Caius College. 7*s*. 6*d*. |
| 1854—Problems and Riders. | By W. WALTON, M.A. of Trinity College, and C. F. MACKENZIE, M.A. of Caius College. 10*s*. 8*d*. |
| 1857—Problems and Riders. | By W. M. CAMPION, M.A. of Queen's College, and W. WALTON, M.A. of Trinity College. 8*s*. 6*d*. |
| 1860—Problems and Riders. | By H. W. WATSON, M.A. Trinity College, and E. J. ROUTH, M.A. St. Peter's College. 7*s*. 6*d*. |

**CAMBRIDGE ENGLISH PRIZE POEMS, which have**
obtained the Chancellor's Gold Medal from the institution of the Prize to
1858. Crown 8vo. cloth, 7*s*. 6*d*.

**CAMBRIDGE.—Cambridge and Dublin Mathematical Journal.**
*The Complete Work*, in Nine Vols. 8vo. cloth, 7*l*. 4*s*.
ONLY A FEW COPIES OF THE COMPLETE WORK REMAIN ON HAND.

**CAMBRIDGE SENATE-HOUSE EXAMINATION PAPERS**
1860-61. Being a Collection of all the Papers set at the Examination for the
Degrees, the various Triposes and the Theological Examination. Crown 8vo.
limp cloth, 2*s*. 6*d*.

**CAMBRIDGE YEAR-BOOK and UNIVERSITY ALMANACK,**
FOR 1862. Edited by WILLIAM WHITE, Sub-Librarian of Trinity College.
Crown 8vo. limp cloth, 2*s*. 6*d*.

A 2

**CAMPBELL.**—The Nature of the Atonement and its Relation to Remission of Sins and Eternal Life. By JOHN M'LEOD CAMPBELL, formerly Minister of Row. 8vo. cloth, 10s. 8d.

**CHALLIS.**—Creation in Plan and in Progress: Being an Essay on the First Chapter of Genesis. By the Rev. JAMES CHALLIS, M.A. F.R.S., F.R.A.S. Crown 8vo. cloth, 3s. 6d.

**CHILDE.**—The Singular Properties of the Ellipsoid and Associated Surfaces of the Ninth Degree. By the Rev. G. F. CHILDE, M.A. Author of "Ray Surfaces," "Related Caustics." 8vo. half-bound, 10s. 6d.

**CHILDREN'S GARLAND.** From the Best Poets. Selected and Arranged by COVENTRY PATMORE. With a vignette after a Design by T. WOOLNER, engraved by C. H. JEENS. 18mo. cloth, 4s. 6d. morocco plain, 7s. 6d. extra, 10s. 6d.

**CHRETIEN.**—The Letter and the Spirit. Six Sermons on the Inspiration of Holy Scripture, Preached before the University of Oxford. By the Rev. CHARLES P. CHRETIEN, Rector of Cholderton. Fellow and late Tutor of Oriel College. Crown 8vo. cloth, 5s.

**CICERO.**—Old Age and Friendship. Translated into English. Two Parts. 12mo. sewed, 2s. 8d. each.

**CICERO.**—THE SECOND PHILIPPIC ORATION. With an Introduction and Notes, translated from Karl Halm. Edited with corrections and additions. By JOHN E. B. MAYOR, M.A. Fellow and Classical Lecturer of St. John's College, Cambridge. Fcap. 8vo. cloth, 5s.

**CLARK.**—Four Sermons Preached in the Chapel of Trinity College, Cambridge. By W. G. CLARK, M.A. Fellow and Tutor of Trinity College, and Public Orator in the University of Cambridge. Fcap. 8vo. limp cloth, red leaves, 2s. 6d.

**CLAY.**—The Prison Chaplain. A Memoir of the Rev. John CLAY, B.D. late Chaplain of the Preston Gaol. With Selections from his Reports and Correspondence, and a Sketch of Prison-Discipline in England. By his Son, the Rev. W. L. CLAY, M.A. 8vo. cloth, 15s.

**CLOUGH.**—The Bothie of Toper-Na-Fuosich. A long Vacation Pastoral. By ARTHUR HUGH CLOUGH. Royal 8vo. cloth limp, 3s.

**COLENSO.**—The Colony of Natal. A Journal of Ten Weeks' Tour of Visitation among the Colonists and Zulu Kafirs of Natal. By the Right Rev. JOHN WILLIAM COLENSO, D.D. Lord Bishop of Natal, with a Map and Illustrations. Fcap. 8vo. cloth, 5s.

**COLENSO.**—Village Sermons. Second Edition. Fcap. 8vo. cloth, 2s. 6d.

**COLENSO.**—Four Sermons on Ordination, and on Missions. 18mo. sewed, 1s.

**COLENSO.**—Companion to the Holy Communion, containing the Service, and Select Readings from the writings of Mr. MAURICE. Edited by the Lord Bishop of Natal. *Fine Edition*, rubricated and bound in morocco, antique style, 6s.; or in cloth, 2s. 6d. *Common Paper*, limp cloth, 1s.

**COLENSO.**—St. Paul's Epistle to the Romans. Newly Translated and Explained, from a Missionary point of View. By the LORD BISHOP OF NATAL. Crown 8vo. cloth, 7s. 6d.

**COLENSO.—A Letter to His Grace the Archbishop of**
Canterbury, upon the Question of the Proper Treatment of Cases of Polygamy,
as found already existing in Converts from Heathenism. From the Right
Rev. J. W. COLENSO, D.D. Bishop of Natal. Crown 8vo. sewed, 1s. 8d.

**COTTON.—Sermons and Addresses delivered in Marlborough**
College during Six Years by GEORGE EDWARD LYNCH COTTON, D.D.
Lord Bishop of Calcutta, and Metropolitan of India. Crown 8vo. cloth, 10s. 6d.

**COTTON.—Sermons: chiefly connected with Public Events**
of 1854. Fcap. 8vo. cloth, 3s.

**COTTON QUESTION, THE.—Where are the Spoils of the**
Slave? Addressed to the Upper and Middle Classes of Great Britain. By λ.
8vo. sewed, 1s.

**CRAIK.—My First Journal. A Book for Children.**
By GEORGIANA M. CRAIK, Author of "Riverston," &c. Royal 16mo.
cloth, gilt leaves, 4s. 6d.

**CROSSE.—An Analysis of Paley's Evidences.**
By C H. CROSSE, M.A. of Caius College, Cambridge. 24mo. boards, 3s. 6d.

**DAVIES.—St. Paul and Modern Thought:**
Remarks on some of the Views advanced in Professor Jowett's Commentary
on St. Paul. By Rev. J. LL. DAVIES, M.A.; Rector of Christ Church,
Marylebone. 8vo. sewed, 2s. 6d.

**DAVIES.—The Work of Christ; or the World Reconciled to**
God. Sermons Preached in Christ Church, St. Marylebone. With a Preface
on the Atonement Controversy. By the Rev. J. LL. DAVIES, M.A. Fcap.
8vo. cloth, 6s.

**DAYS OF OLD: Stories from Old English History of the**
Druids, the Anglo-Saxons, and the Crusades. By the Author of "Ruth and
her Friends." Royal 16mo. cloth, gilt leaves, 5s.

**DEMOSTHENES DE CORONA.**
The Greek Text with English Notes. By B. DRAKE, M.A. late Fellow of
King's College, Cambridge. **Second Edition,** to which is prefixed
AESCHINES AGAINST CTESIPHON, with English Notes. Fcap. 8vo.
cloth, 5s.

**DICEY.—Rome in 1860.**
By EDWARD DICEY. Crown 8vo. cloth, 6s. 6d.

**DICEY.—Cavour. A Memoir. With Portrait. Second Edition.**
Crown 8vo. cloth, 6s. 6d.

**DREW.—A Geometrical Treatise on Conic Sections, with**
Copious Examples from the Cambridge Senate House Papers. By W. H.
DREW, M.A. of St. John's College, Cambridge, Second Master of Black-
heath Proprietary School. **Second Edition.** Crown 8vo. cloth, 4s. 6d.

**DREW.—Solutions to Problems contained in "A Geometrical**
Treatise on Conic Sections." Crown 8vo. cloth, 4s. 6d.

**EARLY EGYPTIAN HISTORY FOR THE YOUNG. With**
Descriptions of the Tombs and Monuments. By the Author of "Sidney
Grey," etc. Fcap. 8vo. cloth, 5s.

**FAWCETT.—Leading Clauses of a new Reform Bill.**
By HENRY FAWCETT, Fellow of Trinity Hall, Cambridge. 8vo. sewed, 1s.

**FENDALL.—Exemption from Church Rates on Personal**
Grounds, considered in a Letter to J. G. Hubbard, M.P.: together with Suggestions. By JAMES FENDALL, M.A. Proctor for the Diocese of Ely. 8vo. sewed, 6d.

**FERRERS.—A Treatise on Trilinear Co-ordinates, the**
Method of Reciprocal Polars, and the Theory of Projections. By the Rev. N. M. FERRERS, M.A. Fellow of Gonville and Caius College. Crown 8vo. cloth, 6s. 6d.

**FISHER.—The Goth and the Saracen: a Comparison**
between the Historical Effect produced upon the Condition of Mankind by the Mahometan Conquests and those of the Northern Barbarians. By E. H. FISHER, B.A. Scholar of Trinity College, Cambridge. Crown 8vo. 1s. 6d.

**FORBES.—Life of Edward Forbes, F.R.S.**
Late Regius Professor of Natural History in the University of Edinburgh. By GEORGE WILSON, M.D. P.R.S.E. and ARCHIBALD GEIKIE, F.G.S. of the Geological Survey of Great Britain, 8vo. cloth, with Portrait, 14s.

**FROST.—The First Three Sections of Newton's Principia.**
With Notes and Problems in illustration of the subject. By PERCIVAL FROST, M.A. late Fellow of St. John's College, Cambridge, and Mathematical Lecturer of Jesus College. Crown 8vo. cloth, 10s. 6d.

**GARIBALDI AT CAPRERA. By COLONEL VECCHJ.**
Translated from the Italian. With Preface by Mrs. GASKELL. Fcap. 8vo. 3s. 6d.

**GILL.—The Anniversaries. Poems in Commemoration of**
Great Men and Great Events. By T. H. GILL. Fcap. 8vo. cloth, 6s.

**GOLDEN TREASURY of the BEST SONGS and LYRICAL**
Poems in the English Language. Selected and arranged, with Notes, by F. T. PALGRAVE, Fellow of Exeter College, Oxford. With a Vignette after a Design by T. WOOLNER, engraved by C. H. JEENS. 18mo. cloth, 4s. 6d. morocco, 7s. 6d. extra, 10s. 6d.

**GRANT.—Plane Astronomy.**
Including Explanations of Celestial Phenomena, and Descriptions of Astronomical Instruments. By A. R. GRANT, M.A., one of Her Majesty's Inspectors of Schools, late Fellow of Trinity College, Cambridge. 8vo. boards, 6s.

**GRANT.—Remarks on the Revised Code. By the Rev. A. R.**
GRANT, Rector of Hitcham, Late Her Majesty's Inspector of Schools, Formerly Fellow of Trinity College, Cambridge. 8vo. sewed, 1s.

**GROTE.—A Few Words on Criticism. Being an Examination**
of the Article in the *Saturday Review* of April 20, 1861. upon "Dr. Whewell's Platonic Dialogues for English Readers." By JOHN GROTE, B.D. Professor of Moral Philosophy in the University of Cambridge. 8vo. paper cover, 1s. 6d.

**GROVES.—A Commentary on the Book of Genesis.**
For the Use of Students and Readers of the English Version of the Bible. By the Rev. H. C. GROVES, M.A. Perpetual Curate of Mullavilly, Armagh. Crown 8vo. cloth, 9s.

**HAMILTON.—On Truth and Error: Thoughts, in Prose and**
Verse, on the Principles of Truth, and the Causes and Effects of Error.
By JOHN HAMILTON, Esq. (of St. Ernan's), M.A. St. John's College, Cambridge. Crown 8vo. cloth, 5s.

**HARE.—Charges delivered during the Years 1840 to 1854.**
With Notes on the Principal Events affecting the Church during that period.
By JULIUS CHARLES HARE, M.A. sometime Archdeacon of Lewes, and
Chaplain in Ordinary to the Queen. With an Introduction, explanatory
of his position in the Church with reference to the parties which divide it
3 vols. 8vo. cloth, 1l. 11s. 6d.

**HARE.—Miscellaneous Pamphlets on some of the Leading**
Questions agitated in the Church during the Years 1845—51. 8vo. cloth, 12s.

**HARE.—The Victory of Faith.**
Second Edition. 8vo. cloth, 5s.

**HARE.—The Mission of the Comforter.**
Second Edition. With Notes. 8vo. cloth, 12s.

**HARE.—Vindication of Luther from his English Assailants.**
Second Edition. 8vo. cloth, 7s.

**HARE.—Parish Sermons.**
Second Series. 8vo. cloth, 12s.

**HARE.—Sermons Preacht on Particular Occasions.**
8vo. cloth, 12s.

*** The two following Books are included in the Three Volumes of Charges, and
may still be had separately.

**HARE.—The Contest with Rome.**
With Notes, especially in answer to Dr. Newman's Lectures on Present Position
of Catholics. Second Edition. 8vo. cloth, 10s. 8d.

**HARE.—Charges delivered in the Years 1843, 1845, 1846.**
Never before published. With an Introduction, explanatory of his position
in the Church with reference to the parties which divide it. 8s. 6d.

**HARE.—Portions of the Psalms in English Verse.**
Selected for Public Worship. 18mo. cloth, 2s. 6d.

**HARE.—Two Sermons preached in Herstmonceux Church,**
on Septuagesima Sunday, 1855, being the Sunday after the Funeral of the
Venerable Archdeacon Hare. By the Rev. H. VENN ELLIOTT, Perpetual
Curate of St. Mary's, Brighton, late Fellow of Trinity College, Cambridge,
and the Rev. J. N. SIMPKINSON, Rector of Brington, Northampton,
formerly Curate of Herstmonceux. 8vo. 1s. 6d.

**HARDWICK.—Christ and other Masters.**
A Historical Inquiry Into some of the chief Parallelisms and Contrasts
between Christianity and the Religious Systems of the Ancient World. With
special reference to prevailing Difficulties and Objections. By the Ven.
ARCHDEACON HARDWICK. The Religions of China, America,
and Oceanica, in one part. Religions of Egypt and Medo-Persia,
in one part. 8vo. cloth. 7s. 6d. each part.

**HARDWICK.—A History of the Christian Church, during the Middle Ages and the Reformation.  (A.D. 590–1600.)**
By Archdeacon Hardwick.  Two vols. crown 8vo. cloth, 21*s.*
Vol. I.  **Second Edition.**  Edited by FRANCIS PROCTER, M.A. Vicar of Witton, Norfolk.  History from Gregory the Great to the Excommunication of Luther.  With Maps.
Vol. II.  History of the Reformation of the Church.
Each volume may be had separately.  Price 10*s.* 6*d.*
*** These Volumes form part of the Series of Theological Manuals.

**HARDWICK.—Twenty Sermons for Town Congregations.**
Crown 8vo. cloth, 6*s.* 6*d.*

**HAYNES.—Outlines of Equity.  By FREEMAN OLIVER**
HAYNES, Barrister-at-Law, late Fellow of Caius College, Cambridge. Crown 8vo. cloth, 10*s.*

**HEALY. — God is Light.  A Sermon preached at Great**
Waldingfield, Suffolk.  By J. B. HEALY, B.A. late Curate.  Fcp. 8vo, sewed, 8*d.*

**HEDDERWICK.—Lays of Middle Age, and other Poems.**
By JAMES HEDDERWICK.  Fcp. 8vo. 5*s.*

**HEMMING.—An Elementary Treatise on the Differential**
and Integral Calculus.  By G. W. HEMMING, M.A. Fellow of St. John's College, Cambridge.  **Second Edition.**  8vo. cloth, 9*s.*

**HERVEY.—The Genealogies of our Lord and Saviour Jesus**
Christ, as contained in the Gospels of St. Matthew and St. Luke, reconciled with each other and with the Genealogy of the House of David, from Adam to the close of the Canon of the Old Testament, and shown to be in harmony with the true Chronology of the Times.  By Lord ARTHUR HERVEY, M.A. Rector of Ickworth.  8vo. cloth, 10*s.* 6*d.*

**HERVEY.—The Inspiration of Holy Scripture.**
Five Sermons preached before the University of Cambridge. 8vo. cloth, 3*s.* 6*d.*

**HOMER.—The Iliad of Homer Translated into English Verse.**
By I. C. WRIGHT, M.A. Translator of "Dante."  Vol. I. containing Books I—XII.  Crown 8vo. cloth, 10*s.* 8*d.*  Books I—VI. in Printed Cover, price 5*s.* also, Books VII—XII, price 5*s.*

**HORT.—Thoughts on the Revised Code of Education.  Its**
Purposes and Probable Effects.  By FENTON J. A. HORT, M.A. Vicar of St. Ippolyts, Herts, and late Fellow of Trinity College, Cambridge.  8vo. sewed, 1*s.*

**HOWARD.—The Pentateuch; or, the Five Books of Moses.**
Translated into English from the Version of the LXX.  With Notes on its Omissions and Insertions, and also on the Passages in which it differs from the Authorised Version.  By the Hon. HENRY HOWARD, D.D. Dean of Lichfield.  Crown 8vo. cloth.  GENESIS, 1 vol. 8*s.* 6*d.*; EXODUS AND LEVITICUS, 1 vol. 10*s.* 6*d.*; NUMBERS AND DEUTERONOMY, 1 vol. 10*s.* 6*d.*

**HUGHES.—Account of the Lock-Out of Engineers, &c.**
1851-2.  Prepared for the Social Science Association.  By THOMAS HUGHES, Author of "Tom Brown."  8vo. sewed, 1*s.*

**HUMPHRY.—The Human Skeleton (including the Joints).**
By GEORGE MURRAY HUMPHRY, M.D. F.R.S., Surgeon to
Addenbrooke's Hospital, Lecturer on Surgery and Anatomy in the Cambridge
University Medical School. With Two Hundred and Sixty Illustrations
drawn from Nature. Medium 8vo. cloth, 1*l*. 8*s*.

**HUMPHRY.—On the Coagulation of the Blood in the Venous**
System during Life. 8vo. 2*s*. 6*d*.

**HUMPHRY.—Observations on the Limbs of Vertebrate**
Animals, the Plan of their Construction, their Homology, and the Comparison
of the Fore and Hind Limbs. 4to. 5*s*.

**HUMPHRY.—The Human Hand and the Human Foot.**
With Numerous Illustrations. Fcap. 8vo. cloth. 4*s*. 6*d*.

**INGLEBY.—Outlines of Theoretical Logic.**
Founded on the New Analytic of SIR WILLIAM HAMILTON. Designed for a
Text-book in Schools and Colleges. By C. MANSFIELD INGLEBY, M.A.,
of Trinity College, Cambridge. In fcap. 8vo. cloth, 3*s*. 6*d*.

**IRETON.—The Broken Troth, a Tale of Tuscan Life, from**
the Italian. By PHILIP IRETON. 2 vols. Fcap. 8vo. 12*s*.

**JAMESON.—Analogy between the Miracles and Doctrines**
of Scripture. By F. J. JAMESON, M.A., Fellow of St. Catharine's College,
Cambridge. Fcap. 8vo. cloth, 2*s*.

**JAMESON.—Brotherly Counsels to Students. Four Sermons**
preached in the Chapel of St. Catharine's College, Cambridge. By F. J.
JAMESON, M.A. Fcap. 8vo. limp cloth, red edges, 1*s*. 6*d*.

**JONES.—A Sermon preached at St. Luke's, Berwick Street,**
Oxford Street, to the St. Luke's Artisan Rifles (Sixth Company of the Nine-
teenth Middlesex), on Sunday, October 28, 1860. By the Rev. HARRY
JONES, M.A. Incumbent of St. Luke's. 8vo. 1*d*.

**JUVENAL.—Juvenal, for Schools.**
With English Notes. By J. E. B. MAYOR, M.A. Fellow and Classical
Lecturer of St. John's College, Cambridge. Crown 8vo. cloth, 10*s*. 6*d*.

**KINGSLEY.—Two Years Ago.**
By CHARLES KINGSLEY, M.A. Rector of Eversley, Chaplain in Ordinary
to the Queen, and Professor of Modern History in the University of Cambridge.
**Third Edition.** Crown 8vo. cloth, 6*s*.

**KINGSLEY.—"Westward Ho!" or, the Voyages and Adven-**
tures of Sir Amyas Leigh, Knight of Burrough, in the County of Devon, in
the Reign of Her Most Glorious Majesty Queen Elizabeth. **Fourth
Edition.** Crown 8vo. cloth, 6*s*.

**KINGSLEY.—Alton Locke, Tailor and Poet. New Edition,**
with a New Preface. Crown 8vo. cloth, 4*s*. 6*d*.

**KINGSLEY.—Glaucus; or, the Wonders of the Shore.**
**New and Illustrated Edition,** corrected and enlarged. Containing
beautifully Coloured Illustrations of the Objects mentioned in the Work.
Elegantly bound in cloth, with gilt leaves. 7*s*. 6*d*.

**KINGSLEY.—The Limits of Exact Science as Applied to**
History. An Inaugural Lecture delivered before the University of Cambridge. By CHARLES KINGSLEY, M.A. Crown 8vo. boards, 2*s.*

**KINGSLEY.—The Heroes: or, Greek Fairy Tales for my**
Children. With Eight Illustrations, Engraved by WHYMPER. **New Edition,** printed on toned paper, and elegantly bound in cloth, with gilt leaves, Imp. 16mo. 5*s.*

**KINGSLEY.—Alexandria and Her Schools: being Four Lec-**
tures delivered at the Philosophical Institution, Edinburgh. With a Preface. Crown 8vo. cloth, 5*s.*

**KINGSLEY.—Phaethon; or Loose Thoughts for Loose**
Thinkers. **Third Edition.** Crown 8vo. boards, 2*s.*

**KINGSLEY.—The Recollections of Geoffry Hamlyn.**
By HENRY KINGSLEY, Esq. **Second Edition,** crown 8vo. cloth, 6*s.*

**KIRCHHOFF.—Researches on the Solar Spectrum and the**
Spectra of the Chemical Elements. By G. KIRCHHOFF, Professor of Physics in the University of Heidelberg. Translated by HENRY E. ROSCOE, B.A. Professor of Chemistry in Owen's College, Manchester. 4to. boards, 5*s.*

**LATHAM.—The Construction of Wrought-Iron Bridges,**
embracing the Practical Application of the Principles of Mechanics to Wrought-Iron Girder Work. By J. H. LATHAM, Esq. Civil Engineer. 8vo. cloth. With numerous detail Plates. 15*s.*

**LECTURES TO LADIES ON PRACTICAL SUBJECTS.**
**Third Edition,** revised. Crown 8vo. cloth, 7*s.* 6*d.* By Reverends F. D. MAURICE, PROFESSOR KINGSLEY, J. Ll. DAVIES, ARCHDEACON ALLEN, DEAN TRENCH, PROFESSOR BREWER, DR. GEORGE JOHNSON, DR. SIEVEKING, DR. CHAMBERS, F. J. STEPHEN, Esq., and TOM TAYLOR, Esq.

**LIGHTFOOT.—Christian Progress. A Sermon preached in**
the Chapel of Trinity College, Cambridge, at the Commemoration of Benefactors, December 15, 1860. By J. B. LIGHTFOOT, M.A. Fellow and Tutor of Trinity College. 8vo. sewed, 1*s.*

**LITTLE ESTELLA, and other TALES FOR THE**
YOUNG. With Frontispiece. Royal 16mo. extra cloth, gilt leaves, 5*s.*

**LONGE.—An Inquiry into the Law of "Strikes."**
By F. D. LONGE, Barrister-at-Law. 8vo. sewed, 1*s.*

**LORD.—The Highway of the Seas in Time of War. By**
HENRY W. LORD, M.A. Barrister-at-Law, Fellow of Trinity College, Cambridge. Crown 8vo. stiff cover, 1*s.*

**LUDLOW and HUGHES.—A Sketch of the History of the**
United States from Independence to Secession. By J. M. LUDLOW, Author of "British India, its Races and its History," "The Policy of the Crown towards India,"&c.

To which is added, **The Struggle for Kansas.** By THOMAS HUGHES, Author of "Tom Brown's School Days," "Tom Brown at Oxford," &c. Crown 8vo. cloth, 8*s.* 6*d.*

**LUDLOW.—British India; its Races, and its History,**
down to 1857. By JOHN MALCOLM LUDLOW, Barrister-at-Law. 2 vols. fcap. 8vo. cloth, 9*s.*

**LUSHINGTON.—La Nation Boutiquière: and other Poems**
chiefly Political. With a Preface. By the late HENRY LUSHINGTON,
Chief Secretary to the Government of Malta. **Points of War.** By
FRANKLIN LUSHINGTON. In 1 vol. fcap 8vo. cloth, 3s.

**LUSHINGTON.—The Italian War 1848-9, and the Last**
Italian Poet. By the late HENRY LUSHINGTON. With a Biographical
Preface by G. S. VENABLES. Crown 8vo. cloth, 6s. 6d.

**MACKENZIE.—The Christian Clergy of the first Ten Cen-**
turies, and their Influence on European Civilization. By HENRY
MACKENZIE, B.A. Scholar of Trinity College, Cambridge. Crown 6vo.
cloth, 8s. 6d.

**MACMILLAN'S MAGAZINE. Published Monthly, Price**
One Shilling. Volume I. to V. are now ready, handsomely bound in cloth,
7s. 6d. each.

**MANSFIELD.—Paraguay, Brazil, and the Plate.**
With a Map, and numerous Woodcuts. By CHARLES MANSFIELD, M.A.
of Clare College, Cambridge. With a Sketch of his Life. By the Rev.
CHARLES KINGSLEY. Crown 8vo. cloth, 12s. 8d.

**MACMILLAN.—Footnotes from the Page of Nature.  A**
Popular Work on Algæ, Fungi, Mosses, and Lichens. By the Rev. HUGH
MACMILLAN, F.R.S.E. With numerous Illustrations, and a Coloured
Frontispiece. Fcap. 8vo. cloth, 5s.

**MACMILLAN'S SERIES OF BOOKS FOR THE YOUNG.**
Handsomely bound in cloth, Five Shillings each.

1. **Tom Brown's School days. Seventh Edition.**
2. **Our Year. By the Author of "John Halifax."  With**
Numerous Illustrations. Gilt leaves.
3. **Professor Kingsley's Heroes; or Greek Fairy Tales.**
With Eight Illustrations. Gilt leaves.
4. **Ruth and Her Friends. A Story for Girls. Gilt leaves.**
5. **Days of Old. Stories from Old English History. By the**
Author of "Ruth and Her Friends." Gilt leaves.
6. **Agnes Hopetoun's Schools and Holidays. By the Author**
of "Margaret Maitland." Gilt leaves.
7. **Little Estella, and other Fairy Tales. Gilt leaves.**
8. **David, King of Israel. A History for the Young. By**
J. WRIGHT, M.A. Gilt leaves.
9. **Early Egyptian History for the Young.**

**My First Journal. By G. M. Craik. Gilt leaves, 4s. 6d.**

**McCOSH.—The Supernatural in Relation to the Natural.**
By the Rev. JAMES McCOSH, LL.D. Crown 6vo. cloth, 7s. 6d.

**McCOSH.—The Method of the Divine Government, Physical**
and Moral. By JAMES McCOSH, LL.D. Professor of Logic and Meta-
physics in the Queen's University for Ireland. **Seventh Edition.** 8vo.
cloth, 10s. 6d.

**M'COY.**—Contributions to British Palæontology; or, First Descriptions of several hundred Fossil Radiata, Articulata, Mollusca, and Pisces, from the Tertiary, Cretaceous, Oolitic, and Palæozoic Strata of Great Britain. With numerous Woodcuts. By FREDERICK M'COY, F.G.S., Professor of Natural History in the University of Melbourne. 8vo. cloth, 9s.

**MARSTON.**—A Lady in Her Own Right. By WESTLAND MARSTON. Crown 8vo. cloth, 10s. 8d.

**MASSON.**—Essays, Biographical and Critical; chiefly on the English Poets. By DAVID MASSON, M.A. Professor of English Literature in University College, London. 8vo. cloth, 12s. 6d.

**MASSON.**—British Novelists and their Styles; being a Critical Sketch of the History of British Prose Fiction. By DAVID MASSON, M.A. Crown 8vo. cloth, 7s. 8d.

**MASSON.**—Life of John Milton, narrated in Connexion with the Political, Ecclesiastical, and Literary History of his Time. Vol. I. with Portraits. 18s.

**MAURICE.**—Expository Works on the Holy Scriptures. By FREDERICK DENISON MAURICE, M.A. Incumbent of St. Peter's, Vere Street, and late Chaplain of Lincoln's Inn.

    I.—The Patriarchs and Lawgivers of the Old Testament. Second Edition. Crown 8vo. cloth, 6s. This volume contains Discourses on the Pentateuch, Joshua, Judges, and the beginning of the First Book of Samuel.

    II.—The Prophets and Kings of the Old Testament. Second Edition. Crown 8vo. cloth, 10s. 6d. This volume contains Discourses on Samuel I. and II., Kings I. and II., Amos, Joel, Hosea, Isaiah, Micah, Nahum, Habakkuk, Jeremiah, and Ezekiel.

    III.—The Gospel of St. John; a Series of Discourses. Second Edition. Crown 8vo. cloth, 10s. 6d.

    IV.—The Epistles of St. John; a Series of Lectures on Christian Ethics. Crown 8vo. cloth, 7s. 6d.

**MAURICE.**—Lectures on the Apocalypse, or, Book of the Revelation of St. John the Divine. Crown 8vo. cloth, 16s. 6d.

**MAURICE.**—Expository Works on the Prayer-Book.
    I.—The Ordinary Services. Second Edition. Fcap. 8vo. cloth, 5s. 8d.

    II.—The Church a Family. Twelve Sermons on the Occasional Services. Fcap. 8vo. cloth, 4s. 6d.

**MAURICE.**—What is Revelation? A Series of Sermons on the Epiphany; to which are added Letters to a Theological Student on the Bampton Lectures of Mr. MANSEL. Crown 8vo. cloth, 10s. 6d.

**MAURICE.**—Sequel to the Inquiry, "What is Revelation?" Letters in Reply to Mr. Mansel's Examination of "Strictures on the Bampton Lectures." Crown 8vo. cloth, 6s.

**MAURICE.**—Lectures on Ecclesiastical History.
8vo. cloth, 10s. 6d.

**MAURICE.**—Theological Essays.
Second Edition, with a new Preface and other additions. Crown 8vo.
cloth, 10s. 6d.

**MAURICE.**—The Doctrine of Sacrifice deduced from the
Scriptures. With a Dedicatory Letter to the Young Men's Christian Association. Crown 8vo. cloth, 7s. 6d.

**MAURICE.**—The Religions of the World, and their Relations
to Christianity. Fourth Edition. Fcap. 8vo. cloth, 5s.

**MAURICE.**—On the Lord's Prayer.
Fourth Edition. Fcap. 8vo. cloth, 2s. 6d.

**MAURICE.**—On the Sabbath Day: the Character of the
Warrior; and on the Interpretation of History. Fcap. 8vo. cloth, 2s. 6d.

**MAURICE.**—Learning and Working.—Six Lectures on the
Foundation of Colleges for Working Men, delivered in Willis's Rooms,
London, in June and July, 1854. Crown 8vo. cloth, 5s.

**MAURICE.**—The Indian Crisis. Five Sermons.
Crown 8vo. cloth, 2s. 6d.

**MAURICE.**—Law's Remarks on the Fable of the Bees.
Edited, with an Introduction of Eighty Pages, by FREDERICK DENISON
MAURICE, M.A. Chaplain of Lincoln's Inn. Fcp. 8vo. cloth, 4s. 6d.

**MAURICE.**—Miscellaneous Pamphlets:—

    I.—War; How to Prepare Ourselves for It.  A Sermon.
     Fcap. 8vo. sewed, 2d.

    II.—Death and Life.  A Sermon.  In Memoriam C. B. M.
     6vo. sewed, 1s.

    III.—Plan of a Female College for the Help of the Rich
     and of the Poor. 8vo. 6d.

    IV.—Administrative Reform.
     Crown 8vo. 3d.

    V.—Sermon preached to the 19th Middlesex Rifle
     Volunteers. Fcap. 8vo. sewed, 2d.

    VI.—The Name "Protestant:" and the English Bishopric
     at Jerusalem. Second Edition. 8vo. 3s.

    VII.—Thoughts on the Oxford Election of 1847.
     8vo. 1s.

    VIII.—The Case of Queen's College, London.
     8vo. 1s. 6d.

    IX.—The Worship of the Church a Witness for the
     Redemption of the World. 8vo. sewed, 1s.

    X.—The Faith of the Liturgy and the Doctrine of the
     XXXIX Articles. Two Sermons. Crown 8vo. sewed, 2s. 6d.

**MAXWELL.—The Stability of the Motion of Saturn's Rings.**
By J. C. MAXWELL, M.A. Professor of Natural Philosophy in the University of Aberdeen. 4to. sewed, 6s.

**MAYOR.—Cambridge in the Seventeenth Century.**
2 vols. fcap. 8vo. cloth, 13s.
    Vol. I. Lives of Nicholas Ferrar.
    Vol. II. Autobiography of Matthew Robinson.
By JOHN E. B. MAYOR, M.A. Fellow and Classical Lecturer of St. John's College, Cambridge.

*** The Autobiography of Matthew Robinson may be had separately, price 6s. 6d.

**MAYOR.—Early Statutes of St. John's College, Cambridge.**
Now first edited with Notes. Royal 8vo. 18s.

    *** The First Part is now ready for delivery.

**MAYOR.—Juvenal for Schools.**
With English Notes. By JOHN E. B. MAYOR, M.A. Crown 8vo. cloth, 10s. 6d.

**MAYOR.—Cicero's Second Philippic.**
With English Notes and Introduction translated from Halm, with Corrections and Additions. By JOHN E. B. MAYOR, M.A. Fcap. 8vo. cloth, 5s.

**MERIVALE.—Sallust for Schools.**
By C. MERIVALE, B.D. Author of "History of Rome." Second Edition. Fcap. 8vo. cloth, 4s. 6d.

*** The Jugurtha and the Catilina may be had separately, price 2s. 6d. each, bound in cloth.

**MOORE.—A New Proof of the Method of Algebra commonly**
called "Greatest Common Measure." By B. T. MOORE, B.A., Fellow of Pembroke College, Cambridge. Crown 8vo. 8d.

**MOOR COTTAGE.—A Tale of Home Life.**
By the Author of "Little Estella." Crown 8vo. cloth, 10s. 6d.

**MOORHOUSE. — Some Modern Difficulties respecting the**
Facts of Nature and Revelation. Considered in Four Sermons preached before the University of Cambridge, in Lent, 1861. By JAMES MOORHOUSE, M.A. of St. John's College, Cambridge, Curate of Hornsey. Fcap. 8vo. cloth, 2s. 6d.

**MORGAN.—A Collection of Mathematical Problems and**
Examples. Arranged in the Different Subjects progressively, with Answers to all the Questions. By H. A. MORGAN, M.A., Fellow of Jesus College. Crown 8vo. cloth, 6s. 6d.

**MORSE.—Working for God, and other Practical Sermons.**
By FRANCIS MORSE, M.A. Incumbent of St. John's, Ladywood, Birmingham. **Second Edition.** Fcap. 8vo. cloth, 5s.

**MORTLOCK.—Christianity agreeable to Reason. To which**
is added Baptism from the Bible. By the Rev. EDMUND MORTLOCK, B.D. Rector of Moulton, Newmarket. **Second Edition.** Fcap. 8vo. cloth, 3s. 6d.

**NAPIER.—Lord Bacon and Sir Walter Raleigh.**
Critical and Biographical Essays. By MACVEY NAPIER, late Editor of the *Edinburgh Review* and of the *Encyclopædia Britannica*. Post 8vo. cloth, 7s. 6d.

**NORTHERN CIRCUIT.** Brief Notes of Travel in Sweden,
Finland, and Russia. With a Frontispiece. Crown 8vo. cloth, 5s.

**NORTON.—The Lady of La Garaye.** By the Hon. Mrs.
NORTON, with Illustrations from Drawings by the Author. **Third
Edition.** Small 4to. cloth, 7s. 6d.

**NORWAY AND SWEDEN.—A Long Vacation Ramble in**
1856. By X and Y. Crown 8vo. cloth, 6s. 6d.

**O'BRIEN.—An Attempt to Explain and Establish the Doc-**
trine of Justification by Faith only, in Ten Sermons on the Nature and
Effects of Faith, preached in the Chapel of Trinity College, Dublin. By
JAMES THOMAS O'BRIEN, D.D. Bishop of Ossory. 8vo. cloth, 14s.

**OCCASIONAL PAPERS on UNIVERSITY and SCHOOL**
MATTERS; containing an Account of all recent University Subjects and
Changes. Three Parts, price 1s. each.

**OLIPHANT.—Agnes Hopetoun's Schools and Holidays.**
The Experiences of a Little Girl. By MRS. OLIPHANT, Author of
" Margaret Maitland." Royal 16mo. gilt leaves, 5s.

**ORWELL.—The Bishop's Walk and the Bishop's Times.**
Poems on the Days of Archbishop Leighton and the Scottish Covenant. By
ORWELL. Fcap. 8vo. cloth, 5s.

**OUR YEAR.—A Child's Book in Prose and Verse.**
By the Author of " John Halifax, Gentleman." With Numerous Illustrations by CLARENCE DOBELL. Royal 16mo. cloth, gilt leaves, 5s.

**OUT OF THE DEPTHS.—The Story of a Woman's Life.**
Crown 8vo. cloth, 10s. 6d.

**OXFORD, CAMBRIDGE, and DUBLIN MESSENGER OF**
MATHEMATICS. A Journal supported by Junior Mathematical Students,
and Conducted by a Board of Editors composed of Members of the Three
Universities. No. I. 2s. 8d.

**PARKINSON.—A Treatise on Elementary Mechanics.**
For the Use of the Junior Classes at the University, and the Higher Classes in
Schools. With a Collection of Examples. By S. PARKINSON, B.D. Fellow
and Assistant Tutor of St. John's College, Cambridge. **Second Edition.**
Crown 8vo. cloth, 9s. 8d.

**PARKINSON.—A Treatise on Optics.**
Crown 8vo. cloth, 10s. 8d,

**PARMINTER.—Materials for a Grammar of the Modern**
English Language. Designed as a Text-book of Classical Grammar for the
use of Training Colleges, and the Higher Classes of English Schools. By
GEORGE HENRY PARMINTER, of Trinity College, Cambridge; Rector
of the United Parishes of SS. John and George, Exeter. Fcap. 8vo. cloth, 5s. 8d.

**PAULI.—Pictures of England.** By Dr. REINHOLD PAULI.
Translated by E. C. OTTE. Crown 8vo. cloth, 8s. 6d.

**PEROWNE.—The Christian's Daily Life a Life of Faith.** A
Sermon preached in the Chapel of Corpus Christi College, Cambridge, on
Sunday Morning, October 21, 1860. By the Rev. EDWARD HENRY
PEROWNE, B.D. Fellow and Tutor. 8vo. sewed, 1s.

**PEROWNE.—"Al-Adjrumiieh."**
An Elementary Arabic Grammar. By J. J. S. PEROWNE, B.D. Lecturer
in Divinity in King's College, London, and Examining Chaplain to the
Lord Bishop of Norwich. 8vo. cloth 5s.

**PERRY.—Five Sermons preached before the University of**
Cambridge, in November, 1855. By CHARLES PERRY, D.D. Bishop of
Melbourne. Crown 8vo. cloth, 3*s.*

**PHEAR.—Elementary Hydrostatics.**
By J. B. Phear, M.A. Fellow of Clare College, Cambridge. **Second
Edition.** Accompanied by numerous Examples, with the Solutions.
Crown 8vo. cloth, 5*s.* 6*d.*

**PHILLIPS.—Life on the Earth: Its Origin and Succession.**
By JOHN PHILLIPS, M.A. LL.D. F.R.S. Professor of Geology in the
University of Oxford. With Illustrations. Crown 8vo. cloth, 6*s.* 6*d.*

**PHILOLOGY.—The Journal of Sacred and Classical Philology.**
Four Vols. 8vo. cloth, 12*s.* 6*d.* each.

**PLAIN RULES ON REGISTRATION OF BIRTHS AND**
DEATHS. Crown 8vo. sewed, 1*d.*; 9*d.* per dozen; 5*s.* per 100.

**PLATO.—The Republic of Plato.**
Translated into English, with Notes. By Two Fellows of Trinity College,
Cambridge (J. Ll. Davies M.A. and D. J. Vaughan, M.A.). **Second
Edition.** 8vo. cloth, 10*s.* 6*d.*

**PLATONIC DIALOGUES, THE.—For English Readers.**
By W. WHEWELL, D.D. F.R.S. Master of Trinity College, Cambridge,
Vol. I. **Second Edition,** containing **The Socratic Dialogues.**
Fcap. 8vo. cloth, 7*s.* 6*d.* Vol. II. containing **The Anti-Sophist Dia-
logues,** 6*s.* 6*d.* Vol. III. containing **The Republic.** Fcap. 8vo. cloth.
7*s.* 6*d.*

**PRATT.—Treatise on Attractions, La Place's Functions,**
and the Figure of the Earth. By J. H. PRATT, M.A. Archdeacon of
Calcutta, and Fellow of Gonville and Caius College, Cambridge. **Second
Edition.** Crown 8vo. cloth, 6*s.* 6*d.*

**PRAYERS FOR WORKING MEN OF ALL RANKS:**
Earnestly designed for Family Devotion and Private Meditation and Prayer.
Fcap. 8vo. cloth, red leaves, 2*s.* 6*d.* Common Edition, 1*s.* 9*d.*

**PRINCIPLES of ETHICS according to the NEW TESTA-**
MENT. Crown 8vo. sewed, 2*s.*

**PROCTER.—A History of the Book of Common Prayer: with**
a Rationale of its Offices. By FRANCIS PROCTER, M.A., Vicar of Witton,
Norfolk, and late Fellow of St. Catherine's College. **Fifth Edition,**
revised and enlarged. Crown 8vo. cloth, 10*s.* 6*d.*
*** This forms part of the Series of Theological Manuals.

**PUCKLE.—An Elementary Treatise on Conic Sections and**
Algebraic Geometry. With a numerous collection of Easy Examples pro-
gressively arranged, especially designed for the use of Schools and Beginners.
By G. HALE PUCKLE, M.A., Principal of Windermere College. **Second
Edition,** enlarged and improved. Crown 8vo. cloth, 7*s.* 8*d.*

**RAMSAY.—The Catechiser's Manual; or, the Church Cate-**
chism illustrated and explained, for the use of Clergymen, Schoolmasters,
and Teachers. By ARTHUR RAMSAY, M.A. of Trinity College,
Cambridge. 18mo. cloth, 3*s.* 6*d.*

**RAWLINSON.—Elementary Statics.**
By G. RAWLINSON, M.A. late Professor of the Applied Sciences in
Elphinstone College, Bombay. Edited by EDWARD STURGES, M.A.
Rector of Kencott, Oxon. Crown 8vo. cloth, 4*s.* 8*d.*

**RAYS OF SUNLIGHT FOR DARK DAYS. A Book of**
Selections for the Suffering. With a Preface by C. J. VAUGHAN, D.D.
Vicar of Doncaster and Chaplain in Ordinary to the Queen. 18mo. elegantly
printed with red lines, and bound in cloth with red leaves. **New Edition.**
3s. 6d. morocco, Old Style, 9s.

**REICHEL.—The Lord's Prayer and other Sermons.**
By C. P. REICHEL, B.D., Professor of Latin in the Queen's University;
Chaplain to his Excellency the Lord-Lieutenant of Ireland; and late Don-
nellan Lecturer in the University of Dublin. Crown 8vo. cloth, 7s. 6d.

**ROBINSON.—Missions urged upon the State, on Grounds**
both of Duty and Policy. By C. K. ROBINSON, M.A. Fellow and Assistant
Tutor of St. Catherine's College. Fcap. 8vo. cloth, 3s.

**ROBY.—Story of a Household, and Other Poems. By**
MARY K. ROBY. Fcap. 8vo. cloth, 6s.

**ROUTH.—Treatise on Dynamics of Rigid Bodies.**
With Numerous Examples. By E. J. ROUTH, M.A. Fellow and Assistant
Tutor of St. Peter's College, Cambridge. Crown 8vo. cloth, 10s. 6d.

**ROWSELL.—THE ENGLISH UNIVERSITIES AND THE**
ENGLISH POOR. Sermons Preached before the University of Cambridge.
By T. J. ROWSELL, M.A. Rector of St. Margaret's, Lothbury, late Incum-
bent of St. Peter's, Stepney. Fcap. 8vo. cloth limp, red leaves, 2s.

**ROWSELL.—Man's Labour and God's Harvest.**
Sermons preached before the University of Cambridge in Lent, 1861. Fcap.
8vo. limp cloth, red leaves, 3s.

**RUTH AND HER FRIENDS. A Story for Girls.**
With a Frontispiece. **Third Edition.** Royal 16mo. extra cloth, gilt leaves, 5s.

**SALLUST.—Sallust for Schools.**
With English Notes. **Second Edition.** By CHARLES MERIVALE,
B.D.; late Fellow and Tutor of St. John's College, Cambridge, &c., Author
of the "History of Rome," &c. Fcap. 8vo. cloth, 4s. 6d.
"THE JUGURTHA" AND "THE CATILINA" MAY BE HAD SEPARATELY, price 2s. 6d.
EACH IN CLOTH.

**SALMON. — Sermons preached in the Chapel of Trinity**
College, Dublin. By GEORGE SALMON, D.D. Fellow and Tutor. Crown
8vo. cloth, 6s.

**SANDARS.—BY THE SEA, AND OTHER POEMS.**
By EDMUND SANDARS, of Trinity Hall, Cambridge. Fcap. 8vo.
cloth, 4s. 6d.

**SCOURING OF THE WHITE HORSE; or, The Long**
Vacation Ramble of a London Clerk. By the Author of "Tom Brown's
School Days." Illustrated by DOYLE. **Eighth Thousand.** Imp. 16mo.
cloth, elegant, 8s. 6d.

**SELWYN.—The Work of Christ in the World.**
Sermons preached before the University of Cambridge. By the Right Rev.
GEORGE AUGUSTUS SELWYN, D.D. Bishop of New Zealand, formerly
Fellow of St. John's College. **Third Edition.** Crown 8vo. 2s.

**SELWYN.—A Verbal Analysis of the Holy Bible.**
Intended to facilitate the translation of the Holy Scriptures into Foreign
Languages. Compiled for the use of the Melanesian Mission. Small folio,
cloth, 14s.

**SIMEON.**—Stray Notes on Fishing and on Natural History.
By CORNWALL SIMEON. Crown 8vo. cloth, 7s. 6d.

**SLOMAN.**—Claims of Leibnitz to the Invention of the
Differential Calculus. By DR. H. SLOMAN. Royal 8vo. cloth, 8s. 6d.,

**SIMPSON.**—An Epitome of the History of the Christian
Church during the first Three Centuries and during the Reformation. With
Examination Papers. By WILLIAM SIMPSON, M.A. **Third Edition.**
Fcp. 8vo. cloth, 5s.

**SMITH.**—A Life Drama, and other Poems.
By ALEXANDER SMITH. Fcap. 8vo. cloth, 2s. 6d.

**SMITH.**—City Poems.
By ALEXANDER SMITH, Author of "A Life Drama," and other Poems.
Fcap. 8vo. cloth. 5s.

**SMITH.**—Edwin of Deira. **Second Edition.** By ALEXAN-
DER SMITH, Author of "City Poems." Fcap. 8vo. cloth, 5s.

**SMITH.**—Arithmetic and Algebra, in their Principles and
Application: with numerous systematically arranged Examples, taken from
the Cambridge Examination Papers. By BARNARD SMITH, M.A., Fellow
of St. Peter's College, Cambridge. **Eighth Edition.** Crown 8vo.
cloth, 10s. 6d.

**SMITH.**—Arithmetic for the use of Schools.
**New Edition.** Crown 8vo. cloth, 4s. 6d.

**SMITH.**—A Key to the Arithmetic for Schools.
**Second Edition.** Crown 8vo. cloth, 8s. 6d.

**SMITH.**—Exercises in Arithmetic.
By BARNARD SMITH. With Answers. Crown 8vo. limp cloth, 2s. 6d.
Or sold separately, as follows:—Part I. 1s. Part II. 1s. Answers, 6d.

**SMITH.**—Pilate's Wife's Dream, and other Poems.
By HORACE SMITH. Fcap. 8vo. cloth, 2s. 6d.

**SMITH.**—An Outline of the Theory of Conditional Sentences
in Greek and Latin. For the use of Students. By R. HORTON
SMITH, M.A. Fellow of St. John's College, Cambridge. 8vo. 2s. 6d.

**SNOWBALL.**—The Elements of Plane and Spherical
Trigonometry. By J. C. SNOWBALL, M.A. Fellow of St. John's College,
Cambridge. **Ninth Edition.** Crown 8vo. cloth, 7s. 6d.

**SNOWBALL.**—Introduction to the Elements of Plane Trigonometry for the use of Schools. **Second Edition.** 8vo. sewed, 5s.

**SNOWBALL.**—The Cambridge Course of Elementary
Mechanics and Hydrostatics. Adapted for the use of Colleges and Schools.
With numerous Examples and Problems. **Fourth Edition.** Crown 8vo.
cloth, 5s.

**SPRAY.**
Crown 8vo. boards, 3s.

**STORY.**—Memoir of the Rev. Robert Story, late Minister
of Roseneath, including Passages of Scottish Religious and Ecclesiastical
History during the Second Quarter of the Present Century. By R. H. STORY.
Crown 8vo. cloth, 7s. 6d.

**SWAINSON.—A Handbook to Butler's Analogy.**
By C. A. SWAINSON, M.A. Principal of the Theological College, and Prebendary of Chichester. Crown 8vo. sewed, 1s. 6d.

**SWAINSON.—The Creeds of the Church in their Relations**
to Holy Scripture and the Conscience of the Christian. 8vo. cloth, 9s.

**SWAINSON.—THE AUTHORITY OF THE NEW TESTA-**
MENT; The Conviction of Righteousness, and other Lectures, delivered before the University of Cambridge. 8vo. cloth, 12s.

**TAIT and STEELE.—A Treatise on Dynamics, with nume-**
rous Examples. By P. G. TAIT; Fellow of St. Peter's College, Cambridge, and Professor of Mathematics in Queen's College, Belfast, and W. J. STEELE, late Fellow of St. Peter's College. Crown 8vo. cloth, 10s. 6d.

**TEMPLE. — Sermons preached in the Chapel of Rugby**
School. In 1858, 1859, and 1860. By F. TEMPLE, D.D. Chaplain in Ordinary to her Majesty, Head Master of Rugby School, Chaplain to Earl Denbigh. 8vo. cloth, 10s. 6d.

**THEOLOGICAL Manuals.**

    **I.—History of the Church during the Middle Ages.**
By ARCHDEACON HARDWICK. With Four Maps. Crown 8vo. cloth, 10s. 6d.

    **II.— History of the Church during the Reformation.**
By ARCHDEACON HARDWICK. Crown 8vo. cloth, 10s. 8d.

    **III.—The Book of Common Prayer: Its History and**
Rationale. By FRANCIS PROCTER, M.A. **Fifth Edition.** Crown 8vo. cloth, 10s. 8d.

    **IV.—History of the Canon of the New Testament.**
By B. F. WESTCOTT, M.A. Crown 8vo. cloth, 12s.

    **V.—Introduction to the Study of the Gospels.**
By B. F. WESTCOTT, M.A. Crown 8vo. cloth, 10s. 8d.

    *** Others are in progress, and will be announced in due time.

**THRING.—A Construing Book.**
Compiled by the Rev. EDWARD THRING, M.A. Head Master of Uppingham Grammar School, late Fellow of King's College, Cambridge. Fcap. 8vo. cloth, 2s. 8d.

**THRING.—The Elements of Grammar taught in English.**
**Third Edition.** 18mo. bound in cloth, 2s.

**THRING.—The Child's Grammar.**
Being the substance of the above, with Examples for Practice. Adapted for Junior Classes. **A New Edition.** 18mo. limp cloth, 1s.

**THRING.—Sermons delivered at Uppingham School.**
By EDWARD THRING, M.A. Head Master. Crown 8vo. cloth, 5s.

**THRING.—School Songs.**
A Collection of Songs for Schools. With the Music arranged for four Voices. Edited by EDWARD THRING, M.A., Head Master of Uppingham School and H. RICCIUS. Small folio, 7s. 6d.

**THRUPP.—Antient Jerusalem: a New Investigation into the** History, Topography, and Plan of the City, Environs, and Temple. Designed principally to illustrate the records and prophecies of Scripture. With Map and Plans. By JOSEPH FRANCIS THRUPP, M.A. Vicar of Barrington, Cambridge, late Fellow of Trinity College. 8vo. cloth, 15s.

**THRUPP.—Introduction to the Study and Use of the** Psalms. By the REV. J. F. THRUPP, M.A. 2 vols. 8vo. 21s.

**THRUPP.—The Christian Inference from Leviticus xviii.** 16, sufficient ground for holding that Marriage with a Deceased Wife's Sister is unlawful. By J. F. THRUPP, M.A. 8vo. sewed, 1s.

**THRUPP.—Psalms and Hymns for Public Worship.** Selected and Edited by the REV. J. F. THRUPP, M.A. 18mo. cloth, 2s. limp cloth, 1s. 4d.

**THUCYDIDES, BOOK VI. With English Notes, and a Map.** By PERCIVAL FROST, Jun. M.A. late Fellow of St. John's College, Cambridge. 8vo. 7s. 6d.

**TOCQUEVILLE.—Memoir, Letters, and Remains of Alexis** De Tocqueville. Translated from the French by the Translator of "Napoleon's Correspondence with King Joseph." With Numerous additions, 2 vols. crown 8vo. 21s.

**TODHUNTER.—A Treatise on the Differential Calculus.** With numerous Examples. By I. TODHUNTER, M.A., Fellow and Assistant Tutor of St. John's College, Cambridge. **Third Edition.** Crown 8vo. cloth, 10s. 6d.

**TODHUNTER.—A Treatise on the Integral Calculus. Second Edition.** With numerous Examples. Crown 8vo. cloth, 10s. 6d.

**TODHUNTER. — A Treatise on Analytical Statics, with** numerous Examples. **Second Edition.** Crown 8vo. cloth, 10s. 6d.

**TODHUNTER.—A Treatise on Conic Sections, with** numerous Examples. **Third Edition.** Crown 8vo. cloth, 7s. 6d.

**TODHUNTER.—Algebra for the use of Colleges and Schools.** **Second Edition.** Crown 8vo. cloth, 7s. 6d.

**TODHUNTER. — Plane Trigonometry for Colleges and** Schools. **Second Edition.** Crown 8vo. cloth, 5s.

**TODHUNTER.—A Treatise on Spherical Trigonometry for** the Use of Colleges and Schools. Crown 8vo. cloth, 4s. 6d.

**TODHUNTER.—Critical History of the Progress of the** Calculus of Variations during the Nineteenth Century. By I. TODHUNTER, M.A. 8vo. cloth, 12s.

**TODHUNTER.—Examples of Analytical Geometry of Three** Dimensions. Crown 8vo. cloth, 4s.

**TODHUNTER.—A Treatise on the Theory of Equations.** Crown 8vo. cloth, 7s. 6d.

**TOM BROWN'S SCHOOL DAYS.** By AN OLD BOY. **Seventh Edition.** Fcap. 8vo. cloth, 5s. COPIES OF THE LARGE PAPER EDITION MAY BE HAD, PRICE 10s. 6d.

## TOM BROWN AT OXFORD.

By the Author of "Tom Brown's School Days." **Second Edition**. 3 vols. crown 8vo. £1 11s. 6d.

## TRACTS FOR PRIESTS AND PEOPLE.

By VARIOUS WRITERS.

The First Series, Crown 8vo. cloth, 8s.

The Second Series, Crown 8vo. cloth, 8s.

The whole Series of Fourteen Tracts may be had separately, price One Shilling each.

## TRENCH.—Synonyms of the New Testament.

By The Very Rev. RICHARD CHENEVIX TRENCH, D.D. Dean of Westminster. **Fourth Edition**. Fcap. 8vo. cloth, 5s.

## TRENCH.—Hulsean Lectures for 1845—46.

CONTENTS. 1.—The Fitness of Holy Scripture for unfolding the Spiritual Life of Man. 2.—Christ the Desire of all Nations; or the Unconscious Prophecies of Heathendom. **Fourth Edition**. Foolscap 8vo. cloth, 5s.

## TRENCH.—Sermons Preached before the University of Cam-

bridge. Fcap. 8vo. cloth, 2s. 6d.

## TUDOR.—The Decalogue viewed as the Christian's Law,

with Special Reference to the Questions and Wants of the Times. By the REV. RICHARD TUDOR, B.A. Curate of Helston. Crown 8vo. cloth, 10s. 6d.

## UNDERWOOD.—Short Manual of Arithmetic.

By the REV. C. W. UNDERWOOD, M A. Vice-Principal of the Liverpool Collegiate Institution. Fcap. 8vo. limp cloth, 2s. 6d.

## VACATION TOURISTS IN 1861.

Edited by F. GALTON, F.R.S. 8vo. cloth, with Maps and Illustrations.

## VAUGHAN.—Notes for Lectures on Confirmation. With

suitable Prayers. By C. J. VAUGHAN, D.D. Chaplain in Ordinary to the Queen, Vicar of Doncaster, and late Head Master of Harrow School. **Third Edition**. Limp cloth, red edges, 1s. 6d.

## VAUGHAN.—St. Paul's Epistle to the Romans.

The Greek Text with English Notes. By C. J. VAUGHAN, D.D. Second Edition. Crown 8vo. cloth, red leaves, 5s.

## VAUGHAN.—MEMORIALS OF HARROW SUNDAYS.

A Selection of Sermons preached in Harrow School Chapel. By C. J. VAUGHAN, D.D. With a View of the Interior of the Chapel. **Third Edition**. Crown 8vo. cloth, red leaves, 10s. 6d.

## VAUGHAN.—Epiphany, Lent, and Easter. A Selection of

Expository Sermons. By C. J. VAUGHAN, D.D. **Second Edition**. Crown 8vo. cloth, red leaves, 10s. 6d.

## VAUGHAN.—Revision of the Liturgy. Four Discourses.

With an Introduction. I. ABSOLUTION. II. REGENERATION. III. ATHA-NASIAN CREED. IV. BURIAL SERVICE. V. HOLY ORDERS. By C. J. VAUGHAN, D.D. **Second Edition**. Crown 8vo. cloth, red leaves, 4s. 6d.

**VAUGHAN.**—Four Sermons preached before the University
of Cambridge, May, 1861.

> No. I.—The Two Departures of Christ, and the Three Returns.
> No. II.—Suspense.
> No. III.—The Seven Spirits of God.
> No. IV.—Choice of Professions.

By CHARLES JOHN VAUGHAN, D.D. Crown 8vo. sewed, 1s. 6d.

**VAUGHAN.**—The Joy of Success corrected by the Joy of
Safety. An Ordination Sermon preached in York Cathedral. By C. J.
VAUGHAN, D.D. Chancellor of the Cathedral. Fcap. 8vo. sewed, 2d.

**VAUGHAN.**—Lessons of Life and Godliness. A Selection
of Sermons Preached in the Parish Church of Doncaster. By C. J. VAUGHAN,
Fcap. 8vo. cloth. 4s. 6d.

**VAUGHAN.**—The Mourning of the Land, and the Mourning
of its Families. A Sermon Preached in the Parish Church of Doncaster on
the Death of His Royal Highness, the Prince Consort. By C. J. VAUGHAN,
D.D. **Second Edition.** Fcap. 8vo. sewed, 2d.

**VAUGHAN.**—The Revised Code of the Committee of Council
on Education Dispassionately Considered. An Address to the Clergy of the
Deanery of Doncaster. **Third Edition.** 8vo. sewed, 1s.

**VAUGHAN.**—Sermons preached in St. John's Church
Leicester, during the years 1855 and 1856. By DAVID J. VAUGHAN, M.A.
Fellow of Trinity College, Cambridge, and Vicar of St. Martin's, Leicester.
Crown 8vo. cloth, 5s. 6d.

**VAUGHAN.**—Sermons on the Resurrection. With a Preface.
By D. J. VAUGHAN, M.A. Fcap. 8vo. cloth, 5s.

**VAUGHAN.**—Three Sermons on The Atonement. With a
Preface. By D. J. Vaughan, M.A. Limp cloth, red edges, 1s. 6d.

**VAUGHAN.**—Sermons on Sacrifice and Propitiation, preached
in St. Martin's Church, Leicester, during Lent and Easter, 1861. By D. J.
VAUGHAN, M.A. Fcap. 8vo. cloth limp, red edges, 2s. 6d.

**VOLUNTEER'S SCRAP BOOK.**
By the Author of "The Cambridge Scrap Book." Crown 4to. half-bound,
7s. 6d.

**WAGNER.**—Memoir of the Rev. George Wagner, late of St.
Stephen's, Brighton. By J. N. SIMPKINSON, M.A. Rector of Brington,
Northampton. **Third and Cheaper Edition.** Fcap. 8vo. cloth, 5s.

**WATSON AND ROUTH.**—CAMBRIDGE SENATE-HOUSE
PROBLEMS AND RIDERS. For the Year 1860. With Solutions by H.
W. WATSON, M.A. and E. J. ROUTH, M.A. Crown 8vo. cloth, 7s. 6d.

**WESTCOTT.—History of the Canon of the New Testament**
during the First Four Centuries. By BROOKE FOSS WESTCOTT, M.A.,
Assistant Master of Harrow School; late Fellow of Trinity College, Cambridge. Crown 8vo. cloth, 12s. 6d.
*** This forms part of the Series of Theological Manuals.

**WESTCOTT. — Characteristics of the Gospel Miracles.**
Sermons preached before the University of Cambridge. **With Notes.** By
B. F. WESTCOTT, M.A., Author of "History of the New Testament
Canon." Crown 8vo. cloth, 4s. 6d.

**WESTCOTT.—Introduction to the Study of the Four Gospels.** By B. F. WESTCOTT, M.A. Crown 8vo. cloth, 10s. 6d.
*** This forms part of the series of Theological Manuals.

**WHEWELL.—THE PLATONIC DIALOGUES FOR**
ENGLISH READERS. By W. WHEWELL, D.D. Vol. I. **Second
Edition,** containing "The Socratic Dialogues," fcap. 8vo. cloth, 7s. 6d.
Vol. II. containing "The Anti-Sophist Dialogues," 6s. 6d. Vol III. containing
the Republic, 7s. 6d.

**WHITMORE.—Gilbert Marlowe and Other Poems.**
With a Preface by the Author of "Tom Brown's Schooldays." Fcap. 8vo.
cloth, 3s. 6d.

**WILSON.—Memoir of George Wilson, M.D. F.R.S.E.**
Regius Professor of Technology in the University of Edinburgh. By his
Sister. 8vo. cloth, with Portrait, 14s.

**WILSON.—The Five Gateways of Knowledge.**
By GEORGE WILSON, M.D., F.R.S.E., Regius Professor of Technology in
the University of Edinburgh. **Second Edition.** Fcap. 8vo. cloth, 3s. 6d.
or in Paper Covers, 1s.

**WILSON.—The Progress of the Telegraph.**
Fcap. 8vo. 1s.

**WILSON.—A Treatise on Dynamics.**
By W. P. WILSON, M.A., Fellow of St. John's, Cambridge, and Professor of
Mathematics in the University of Melbourne. 8vo. bds. 9s. 6d.

**WITT.—The Mutual Influence of the Christian Doctrine,**
and the School of Alexandria. By J. G. WITT, Fellow of King's College,
Cambridge, and Member of the Hon. Society of Lincoln's Inn. Crown 8vo.
cloth, 2s. 6d.

**WOLFE.—ONE HUNDRED AND FIFTY ORIGINAL**
PSALM AND HYMN TUNES. For Four Voices. By ARTHUR
WOLFE, M.A., Fellow and Tutor of Clare College, Cambridge. Oblong
royal 8vo. extra cloth, gilt leaves, 10s. 6d.

**WOLFE.—Hymns For Public Worship.**
Selected and Arranged by ARTHUR WOLFE, M.A. 18mo. cloth, red
leaves, 2s. Common Paper Edition, limp cloth, 1s. or twenty-five for 1l.

**WOLFE.—Hymns For Private Use.**
Selected and Arranged by ARTHUR WOLFE, M.A. 18mo. cloth, red
leaves, 2s.

**WORKING MEN'S COLLEGE MAGAZINE.**
Monthly, 2d. Vol. I. II. and III. (1859—61), handsomely bound in cloth,
2s. 6d. each.

## WORSHIP OF GOD AND FELLOWSHIP AMONG MEN.

A Series of Sermons on Public Worship. Fcap. 8vo. cloth, 3s. 6d.
By F. D. MAURICE, M.A. T. J. ROWSELL, M.A. J. LL. DAVIES, M.A.
and D. J. VAUGHAN, M.A.

## WRATISLAW.—Middle-Class and Non-Gremial Examina-

tions. Cui Bono? By A. H. WRATISLAW, M.A. Head-Master of the
Grammar School, Bury St. Edmunds, and formerly Fellow and Tutor of
Christ's College, Cambridge. 8vo. sewed, 6d.

## WRIGHT.—The Iliad of Homer.

Translated into English Verse by J. C. WRIGHT, M.A. Translator of Dante.
Crown 8vo. Vol. 1. containing Books I.—XII., 10s. 6d.　Books I.—VI., 5s.
Books VII.—XII., 5s.

## WRIGHT.—Hellenica; or, a History of Greece in Greek,

as related by Diodorus and Thucydides, being a First Greek Reading
Book, with Explanatory Notes, Critical and Historical. By J. WRIGHT,
M.A., of Trinity College, Cambridge, and Head-Master of Sutton Coldfield
Grammar School. **Second Edition,** WITH A VOCABULARY. 12mo.
cloth, 3s. 6d.

## WRIGHT.—David, King of Israel.

Readings for the Young. With Six Illustrations after SCHNORR. Royal
16mo. extra cloth, gilt leaves, 5s.

## WRIGHT.—A Help to Latin Grammar;

or, the Form and Use of Words in Latin. With Progressive Exercises.
Crown 8vo. cloth, 4s. 6d.

## WRIGHT.—The Seven Kings of Rome:

An easy Narrative, abridged from the First Book of Livy by the omission of
difficult passages, being a First Latin Reading Book, with Grammatical
Notes. Fcap. 8vo. cloth, 3s.

## WRIGHT.—A Vocabulary and Exercises on the " Seven

Kings of Rome." Fcap. 8vo. cloth, 2s. 6d.
*₊* The Vocabulary and Exercises may also be had bound up with "The Seven
Kings of Rome." Price 5s. cloth.

## Yes and No; or Glimpses of The Great Conflict.

3 vols. crown 8vo. cloth, 1l. 11s. 6d.

## YOUNG.—On the History of Greek Literature in England.

From the Earliest Times to the End of the Reign of James the First. By
SIR GEORGE YOUNG, B.A. Scholar of Trinity College, Cambridge. Crown
8vo. boards, 2s.

---